COME SUNDOWN

COME SUNDOWN

MIKE BLAKELY

A TOM DOHERTY ASSOCIATES BOOK
NEW YORK

COME SUNDOWN

Copyright © 2006 by Mike Blakely

This book is printed on acid-free paper.

A Forge Book
Published by Tom Doherty Associates, LLC
175 Fifth Avenue
New York, NY 10010

www.tor.com

Forge® is a registered trademark of Tom Doherty Associates, LLC.

Library of Congress Cataloging-in-Publication Data

Blakely, Mike.
    Come sundown / Mike Blakely.—1st ed.
      p. cm.
    "A Tom Doherty Associates book."
    ISBN 0-312-86705-0 (acid-free paper)
    EAN 978-0-312-86705-8
    1. Comanche Indians—Fiction.   I. Title.
  PS3552.L3533C66   2006
  813'.54—dc22

                                     2005032805

First Edition: June 2006

Printed in the United States of America

0 9 8 7 6 5 4 3 2 1

COME SUNDOWN

PROLOGUE

ADOBE WALLS, TEXAS
MARCH 1927

Strike a match in a darkened room. Watch the light flare and consume the wooden stick between your fingers. Let it burn. Listen hard and you'll faintly hear that tiny blaze crackle with a youthful recklessness. Tongues of fire twist; smoke twines away in tendrils. Before the flame scorches your flesh, extinguish it—godlike—with a casual breath. Now, look closely. An ember remains in that stick-man's blackened, misshapen head. It pulses and glows and rages ever weaker to beat back the invading darkness. It is at once heroic and pathetic. And when finally it dies, that spark doesn't merely dwindle and fade. It goes out with a last sudden surge; a final hopeless stab at existence.

I have lived my life like that match. Rubbed hard against the rough essence of human brutality, I burst forth and lashed out and burned things. I left scars and corpses in my fiery wake. But one comes to regret the loss of that which he burns, and so, in time, the blistering heat of my youthful ire settled into a warmth that drew souls near where once my anger had driven them away. I became a light that guides and beckons; a willful incandescence of goodness. My occasional tantrums flared ever less frequently, and life rewarded me with a measure of steady radiance.

Still, I must have seared the fingertips of the Great Mystery, for my fire has all but gone out now, and I am that light in the head of that bent and blackened match stick. I am almost out of time, yet I refuse to go easily into the unknown.

I am a fugitive from France. I escaped long ago to a frontier that has now vanished under my very feet. I go by many names, but you can call me Plenty Man, the name given to me by my Comanche brother, Kills Something. Yes, I knew Kit Carson. I knew Peta Nocona, and his son, Quanah Parker. Various generals and governors—yes, I crossed their paths.

The battles? Valverde . . . Glorieta Pass . . . Adobe Walls . . . Horrible, bloody affairs, marked by tragic magnificence. I went and witnessed them. I often wish I had not, yet I wouldn't have refused to go, even knowing what I now know. Sometimes—on those dreadful nights when the moon is bad and the nightmares torment me—I wish that one of the tens of thousands of bullets that swarmed in those clashes would have taken my life with a quick coup de grâce. Other times, I thank the Creator that I survived to know the joys I have since known.

But I am talking in vague generalities now, and you want to hear an actual story, don't you? Come, sit under my shade tree while I fashion this rawhide into a headstall for my yearling filly. I will build it while you listen. My time grows ever shorter, and I must make things with my hands while I make talk with you, else I should lament the wasted hours along with all my other regrets.

I see there are those among you who have met me before. You have heard my tales of old Fort Adobe and the Bent brothers—Charles and William. Of Kit Carson before he ever dreamed he would make brevet brigadier. Of the last real mountain men and plainsmen—Thomas "Broken Hand" Fitzpatrick, Uncle Dick Wootton, Jim Bridger, John Hatcher . . . Good Lord, can you believe I actually knew them; rode with them; stood in their shadows? And what of the worst of the whiskey traders, Bill "Snakehead" Jackson? And of my accidental enemy, the Mescalero Apache chief Lame Deer? Do not think that I have forgotten telling some of you those stories. True tales, though they have passed through the lips of a renowned liar. I have not forgotten. My memory remains flawless. Certainly you do not expect me to repeat those things I have already told. No one wants to hear an old man's same tired stories over and over. Besides, the nature of a story, earnestly told, urges the listener to believe with the first telling, to wonder at the second, to question the third, suspect the fourth, reject the fifth, lose count after the sixth, then scoff, deride, ridicule . . .

So, for those who know me now for the first time, you must come around again some other day, and I will conjure all those memories anew.

I have many stories yet to impart, and I will begin with something new to your ears—*all* of you. I am older than almost any three of you combined. Certainly I can spin a yarn or two from my busy life that none of you has heard me tell. *"Spin a yarn."* I should not blame you all for getting up to leave this very moment. I promise from now on to avoid such cliché. Spin a yarn, indeed.

So, after William Bent and I and Kit Carson and Lucien Maxwell and Peg Leg Smith and Lucas "Goddamn" Murray and the others blew Fort Adobe to the winds, some of the ruins remained. The fort was well built, after all, of adobe bricks, the walls three feet thick at the ground. Comancheros came from New Mexico and made some repairs on the walls so that the place could once again be used as a trading post and rampart. Look yonder toward that bend in the creek. That is where the ruins of the fort stood. The ruins, after a time, came to be known as "Adobe Walls." Yes, there were two battles there, but we must all be patient, for there is much to tell. The first battle? Kit Carson's last. Some say he won. Some say he lost. Win or lose, it was his greatest fight. Kit was my friend, though I opposed him in that fight, for I had gone Comanche. He never held it against me.

But I have gotten too far ahead of myself already. Please, the second battle of Adobe Walls? That will have to wait for another telling. Get comfortable. You must want more than simply to hear an old man reminisce. You must want to understand. Relax, now. This will take a while. I have work to occupy my hands, and you have time to listen. I am ninety-nine years old. You cannot hurry me along, my friends.

I will begin with my adoptive Comanche family. Burnt Belly was my grandfather and mentor in the ways of making medicine. Kills Something was my brother. I married his sister, Hidden Water. There was a day, long ago now, when I stood over there where the Adobe Walls sheltered me from the winter wind, and learned to make arrows. I will start my tale there. Oh, this place was different then. Fresh tracks of buffalo marked the Crossing on the Canadian River. Panthers screamed in the wooded ravines. Comanche lodge poles dragged tracks where now your automobiles rut the roads. In those days they called me "Plenty Man."

ONE

The dogwood spoke to me, saying, *"Tsuh, kewesikatoo."* Instantly, I ceased to pull the hand-split stick of wood through the groove I had made in the adobe brick. I turned the straight shaft of the arrow-to-be in my hand, and listened. Again, I felt the wood speak. *"Tsuh, kewesikatoo."*

"Yes . . . Now . . . Straight."

Burnt Belly had said this would happen if I listened with a pure heart. I had heard only two words, but one of them, the Comanche *tsuh,* meant both "yes" and "now," and somehow I understood. I could hardly expect a piece of split dogwood to speak to me in complete sentences, but it had spoken, nonetheless.

I looked down the length of the shaft and found it perfectly straight as I turned it slowly between my fingers. For a moment, I regretted that I had never built a violin. There had been a time, years ago, as a boy in France, when I had yearned to hear a great spruce speak to me, saying, "My wood, well planed and smoothed by your hand, will carry a fine tone." But instead of apprenticing under the master luthiers in Italy, I had murdered my fencing instructor, stolen my music teacher's left-handed Stradivarius, and stowed away on a packet bound for America.

Not that the swordsman, Segarelli, did not deserve to die, for he had raped a girl I thought I loved. And the wretched drunk, Buhler, was never worthy of an instrument such as the Stradivarius. So I had murdered the one, and robbed the other, and fled to a new continent. Now, I was a fugitive, living among the Comanches at the Crossing of the Canadian River in the Panhandle of Texas, where no Texan dared to tread.

I felt the smoothness of the dogwood arrow shaft I had just finished straightening, smelled the aroma of the wood. Perhaps I would never build a violin, but I was making a fine hunting arrow. I had already finished making my bow of Osage orange, strung with a bowstring of buffalo sinew, split and twisted. I had collected the best turkey feathers with which to fletch the shafts of my arrows. I had fashioned razor-sharp points from hoop iron taken from an old whiskey cask. But this was the first time I had heard the voice of a dogwood arrow shaft speak, and I was moved to the point that my skin puckered with gooseflesh, and it wasn't due to the cold.

I looked toward my lodge, and saw my young wife, Hidden Water, languishing in the sunshine with her friends. Her friends worked hard on the hide of the buffalo I had shot only yesterday. They had staked it to the ground and were scraping away bits of flesh which they tossed to a pack of dogs that sat obediently nearby, keen-eyed, waiting for the next morsel. Hidden Water herself stooped over the hide and pretended to help, but she never let labor bring much perspiration to her smooth, dusky skin. In the ways of love, however, she had energy to spare, and used her beauty and wiles much to my liking. Her hair hung thick, shiny, and straight about her shoulders. She could toss that hair in the throes of lovemaking and make it whip about my neck like a horse's tail. Her hips were round and her ankles trim. Her forearms, instead of rippling with twisted muscle like most Comanche women, looked like the smooth marble limbs of sculpted Roman angels.

She tossed her black hair and looked toward me. All three women burst into laughter. They were talking about me. I had thought I might walk over to the lodge, and tell her that I had heard the dogwood speak, but I knew she wouldn't appreciate it. She would probably try to ridicule me in front of her friends, as she was wont to do, for she knew she could get away with it. I would tell her about the words of the dogwood tonight, when we were alone in the lodge.

I put the dogwood shaft away in the quiver I had made of fox fur tanned with deer brains. I chose the next shaft, and stroked it smoothly through the groove I had made in the adobe brick. This was a pleasant day and a good place to work. The sun shone bright on my shoulders, warming me against the chill of the Crazy Moon—November. What was left of the northwest corner of old Fort Adobe provided a welcome windbreak from the chill norther that had blown in two sleeps ago. I knew this particular adobe brick with the arrow-straightening groove in it as one I had molded and put in place myself. I don't know how I could remember such a thing, except to say that my memory is just perfect. I had not built Fort Adobe single-handedly, of course. William Bent and Ceran St. Vrain had hauled a whole crew of adobe masons all the way from Taos for the construction of the trading post. But, somehow, of the thousands of mud bricks, I could remember each individual brick I had made and mudded into place. A person who will listen to the soil of the earth can know it, as I knew those bricks.

Now nothing remained of the fort but the corners and the thick bases, ranging from knee high to head high. William Bent and I had destroyed the rest with a great black powder blast to keep the army from condemning it under the right of eminent domain, and quartering troops here to make war against our friends the Comanches. It had hurt, destroying the trading post I had built and loved. But it had brought me much esteem among the Comanches, for they understood that I had sought to protect them from the bluecoats. They had known, also, how much I loved that fort. Yet I had destroyed it for the good of the Comanche nation. Now, I had become one of the few white men who could live among and bring trade goods to the Comanches, and in such a way I made my living. I wore breechclout, leggings, and deerskin shirt decorated with dyed porcupine quill work. I had taken an Indian wife. I had learned to make arrows, and to hear the voice of the dogwood.

"The wood speaks to you."

I turned instantly, startled. It took me a moment to find Burnt Belly, for the sound of his voice never seemed to come from the direction of his mouth. Then I saw him sitting against the remnants of an adobe wall, the slick flesh of the lightning scar slashed across his chest shining in the sunlight. He wore only his breechclout and moccasins, for the cold did not concern Burnt Belly very much. Somehow, he had slipped inside the walls unseen to me. He had a way of appearing like that. It was said that he could make himself invisible.

"Yes," I said. "I heard it a moment ago. It said, *'Tsuh, kewesikatoo.'*"

"This I know. You heard it with your heart, Plenty Man. The same way you heard my voice just now."

I simply smiled and nodded. I could never quite determine if Burnt Belly possessed mystic powers, or was simply the best magician and ventriloquist, and the most persuasive liar, I had ever known. He was also a healer who claimed the plants spoke to him, telling him of their curative qualities. He said the lightning had instilled this power in him. One thing was certain. Burnt Belly had survived the bolt from above—the glance of the Thunderbird. Nothing else could make a scar like that.

"I have been in council with the elders," he said.

My shoulders slumped, for I could guess what this meant. I had so wanted to finish making my arrows, so that I could go buffalo hunting with a bow and quiver full of projectiles made by my own hand. "What wisdom have the spirits granted the elders?"

"The young warriors will grow restless as the winter passes. They will tire of hunting, and then they will want to raid. They will demand firewater before they take the warpath. They will trade many robes and horses for it."

I turned and halfheartedly stroked my arrow shaft through the straightening groove in the adobe. "When do they want the firewater?"

Burnt Belly chuckled. "Yesterday."

I, too, chuckled. It was my place among Shaved Head's village of the Quahadi band of the True Humans to bring firewater and other, more pragmatical trade goods. It was a role I accepted. While other bands and other tribes went to trading posts and towns to barter, the Quahadis had remained more aloof. The towns and trading posts of white men harbored evil influences and deadly diseases. I was able to live among the Comanches only because I protected them from such dangers, and brought the white man's trade to them, on their own soil. When the elders sent me for trade goods, I rode immediately, and without complaint.

Yes, I was a whiskey trader. In this I took little pride, but my mentor, William Bent, had explained it to me: "It wasn't you and me that first brung whiskey to the Indians, Mr. Greenwood. But somebody did, and now they're gonna have it one way or the other, and I'd just as soon it was you and me sellin' it to them, rather than some cutthroat. It's a necessary evil. Just mind you don't let it get more evil than necessary."

The whiskey trader Bill Snakehead Jackson had once claimed the valley of the Canadian as his own. His policy was to get the Indians so stinking drunk that he could divest them of their goods, right down to their lodges and the innocence of their daughters. By some divine stroke of luck, I had killed Snakehead in a duel four years ago. Now, the Canadian Valley was my region. I liked it that way, and so did the Comanches, not to mention their allies, the Kiowas and Kiowa Apaches. Still, I was a whiskey peddler on top of being a murderer, a thief, and a liar, and I had to live with all of that.

Worse yet, I was a genius, and I am a genius still. This is nothing to boast of, for I have, all my life, wasted my intellect. Oh, I have lived life to the bursting point, and enjoyed many selfish and thrilling adventures, but I have squandered the powers of my brain. Had I been able to avoid murder, theft, and the fugitive's lot, I might have gifted the world with a fine violin, a poem, a scientific treatise, a cure, a discovery, a symphony. As it stands, I have benefited few. I have failed in holding peace among the nations. I have created nothing that will last long after I die. Even my beloved Fort Adobe lies in ruins. I have helped to slaughter the buffalo. I have succeeded only in ransoming a few captives from the Indians, and returning them to their families. I speak thirteen languages, but in them I have nothing profound to say.

But enough of my bellyaching. You will tire of that all too soon.

"I will bridle my best pony for the long trail, and leave this camp before the sun has moved one fist across the sky," I said to Burnt Belly.

The aged shaman nodded, and rose from the ground like a much younger man. "It is the best day to go. The moon rises full tonight. I know your medicine, Plenty Man. You do not sleep when the moon stays full. You will travel far, and return in two moons, when it is good for the young warriors to ride south and raid."

"*Tsuh*," I replied. "But after the full moon I will need dogbane and moccasin flower to help me sleep at night, or I will fall into one of my trances."

"I will give you some, in trade for something I need."

"What is it you need?"

"Bring me some *good* whiskey. I know you add water to weaken the cheap whiskey you bring for the young braves. This is good. But I want some real whiskey with spirit. I do not want it to taste like the piss of a coyote, and I do not want it weakened with water. You know I never swallow the whiskey, so there is no need to weaken it. I spit it into the sacred embers of cedar, and seek visions in its flames. A small horn of fine whiskey will do."

I raised an eyebrow and grinned at the old man. "The young braves must not know that I weaken their firewater."

"I would not tell, even under the worst tortures of the most evil Pawnee squaw," he said. "Now, I want to loan you something." He approached me, an old scarred man in breechclout and moccasins. "You have been making your arrows, and I know you want to finish. That groove in the dried mud wall is a good idea, for it is made of earth, and the earth knows the language of the wood, for they have lived together since the days when animals spoke and walked about like two-leggeds. But on the trail, if you want to straighten arrows, you need a small stone with a groove. I have brought one for you to use while you are on your journey."

Here, Burnt Belly showed me both palms, empty. Now he raised his hands, clapped once, and revealed a grooved stone that had somehow appeared in his right hand. I knew a few sleight-of-hand tricks that I used to influence the Indians, but how Burnt Belly pulled off his magic, I will never know. That stone, the size of a turkey egg, appeared from nowhere.

"I will return it," I said, the astonishment plain on my face.

"I go now to prepare the dogbane and moccasin flower," he said.

Within the hour, I had caught and saddled my best trail pony—a sorrel paint stallion possessed of a smooth trot and ample endurance. His name was Major, for he had been given to me by Major James Henry Carleton for serving as his scout on a campaign against some marauding Mescalero Apaches. I had helped Major Carleton capture the camp of the renegades, and the paint horse I now rode had been the finest horse taken in the victory.

I first named the horse Major Carleton, but later began to simply call him "Major." Eventually—discovering the peculiar mischievous nature of this animal—I would come to think of him as Major-Pain-in-the-Ass. At times, however, owing to his good behavior, I would brevet him General Nuisance, but sooner or later he would always get busted back down to Major.

He was a stallion, but his demeanor was gentle, unless a mare in heat happened to be upwind. Rather than unruliness, it was his curiosity that got him into trouble. I believe that Major thought he was part human. He habitually watched what people did with their hands, then would try the same things with his mouth. He possessed incredible dexterity in his lips and teeth. He could untie himself—and other horses—and open gates, often letting stock escape.

He understood the concept of the *handle*. He could carry buckets, pump water from a well, and dump wheelbarrows. I once caught him trying to work a coffee grinder. Anything a human might pick up, Major could not wait to carry. This included sticks of wood, blankets, shovels, axes, hats, and firearms. As you might imagine, he occasionally caused some commotion around camp. However, I was always so impressed and entertained by Major's shenanigans that I could never bring myself to punish him for taking such initiative. This, of course, only served to encourage his high jinks.

As I saddled Major, he nipped at the back of my thighs to express his objection to the tightness of the cinch. Usually, I rode Indian style: bareback or with only a blanket. But when I rode for trade goods, I used my Mexican saddle. I did not want to look too Indian riding into some trading post or village. Once I explained this to Major, he heaved a huge sigh and accepted his lot.

I led a second pony—a bay—by a war bridle looped around his lower jaw. This mount I would trade for a couple of mules, which I would use to pack the whiskey kegs back to the camp on the Canadian. Before I rode west, I took a jaunt downstream, toward the camp of some Penateka Comanches who had been visiting for some time to get in on the good buffalo hunting on the ranges surrounding the Crossing.

On the way, I rode through a village of Nokoni Comanches—Chief Peta Nocona's band, which stretched almost a mile along the river bottom. Passing Peta's lodge, I saw his wife, Nadua, starting a cook fire, a number of buffalo tongues hanging nearby over a bare cottonwood branch. She glanced up at me, the blue of her eyes flashing in a way seldom seen in a camp of dark-eyed Indian women—like the tail of a deer warning her companions. At the time, I did not know the story behind this white woman living with the Comanches. Eventually, I would learn that her white name was Cynthia Ann Parker. She had been captured in a Texas raid at the age of nine. In time, Chief Peta Nocona had taken her as his wife—his only wife. She was well dressed and cared for, and seemed to go about her chores contentedly. She did not glance at me a second time as I rode by. I had been told by my Comanche friends not to try to ransom this white woman from Peta Nocona, for he loved her very much and would not part with her, so I rode on downstream to the camp of the Penatekas— the Honey-eaters from the oak-timbered hills farther down in Texas.

There was a warrior among the Penatekas who had captured a Mexican boy on a raid far to the south, across the Rio Grande. He had given the boy to his wife as a slave, and I had been told that the wife wanted to trade the boy for some goods from the old Spanish settlements. I found the lodge where the boy was kept, and saw him nearby, gathering wood. He looked to be about twelve years old. He was shirtless and shoeless in this cold, though he wore a pair of tattered cotton trousers which he had probably been wearing when captured. He had wood stacked high on his slender arm, and I saw sores on his shoulders where I feared his captors had beaten or burned him. Perhaps he had tried to run away, and had been punished. Or perhaps the woman who claimed him was just mean. These Penatekas lived closer to the Texas settlements, and were constantly harassed by settlers and the ruthless Texas Rangers. Constant warring had made them angry.

I found the woman who owned the boy. She was dressing a deerskin stretched on an upright frame made of willow branches stuck deep into the ground.

"Woman," I said, in Comanche. "Do you want to sell that captive Mexican boy?"

She glanced toward me, but not at me. "He is useful to me, but he eats much."

I resisted saying that the boy didn't seem to have eaten well in weeks. "Perhaps I could bring something from the settlements that is useful, and does not eat at all."

"I want two things."

"What things?"

"A kettle of iron. And a knife."

"That is easily done. I will take the boy with me, and bring back the kettle and the knife."

"No," she said. "I will give you the boy when you return with the things."

My pony pranced sideways, anxious to ride in the cool air. "That is no good. Then I will have that boy around my lodge when I return, and I do not want to feed him any more than you do."

"I want the kettle and the knife first," she insisted.

I shook my head. "I must take him now if you wish to trade. If I do not take him now, I must make a second trip to sell him back to the Mexicans. That is no good."

"You might take him and never return."

I drew myself upward in the saddle, as if insulted. "My word is good. Ask anyone. I will return with the things you want."

"No," she said.

I sat there on my horse for a few seconds, then reined away. I did not want to leave the boy with this woman, but I also did not intend to establish such a precedent—that I would go and fetch a ransom for a captive. I did not work that way.

"Are you going to bring the kettle and the knife?" she called after me.

I stopped and turned. "Only if I take the boy now."

"I will kill him, then. He eats too much."

"Then you will never get your kettle or your knife. Listen, woman. I have a knife here on my belt that I will give to you now. Then I will return with the kettle, and it will be a good one that is large, but not so large that you cannot pack it when your village wanders. And, as a reward for your trust, I will bring you a blanket. What color do you want?"

She looked toward the underfed boy and frowned. I removed the knife from my belt, rode back toward her, and held it out to her. She looked at the knife, snatched it from me, and drew it from its scabbard to inspect it. I could tell she was going to keep that knife.

"The color of the blanket does not matter," she said. "As long as it is not blue. That color is bad luck."

"Good," I said. As I rode toward the boy, leading the spare pony, the Penateka woman yelled in a shrill voice, ordering her captive to drop the wood he had gathered near the fire, and mount the extra horse I had with me. The boy did as he was told. I handed him the reins, and he seemed to know what to do with them. We rode back up the river, through the camps.

Arriving at my lodge, I got down.

"Wife," I said to Hidden Water. "I will ride now."

"I heard the crier," she said sarcastically. She was still kneeling on the buffalo hide with her friends, and she was bound to show off to them a little.

"Go into the lodge and fetch one of my old shirts and a pair of moccasins for this boy."

She sighed in an impudent way that might make some Comanche husbands take a stick to their wives.

"Go," I ordered. "I will bring something nice for you back from the settlements."

She looked knowingly at her friends as she rose, and they giggled. She went into the lodge. I ordered the other women to leave us. They reluctantly obeyed, and I entered the lodge, signing to the boy on the pony to stay where he was.

Hidden Water had found a shirt and a pair of moccasins for the boy, and was waiting for me inside. The boy was not that much smaller than me, for I have never weighed more than 145 pounds in my life. She tossed the things out through the lodge entrance when I entered, and told the boy to get down from the pony and put the things on. Then she pulled the bearhide cover over our lodge door.

Coming to me now in the privacy of our lodge, she said, "What will you bring me?"

"What do you want?"

"Many nice things. A blanket the color of the flanks of the forked-tail bird that darts after flying bugs. Some buttons made of the rainbow shell. Ribbons. A comb made of the shell of a tortoise. And a looking glass."

Another Comanche woman had just traded a human being to me for a kettle and a knife, and my wife wanted finery.

"A blanket that color will be hard to find," I said.

"You will do it," she replied, a coy look on her face. She took my hand and pulled me toward our couch of soft buffalo hides. She wore a streak of vermilion coloring her scalp where her hair parted, and her cheeks were also colored, subtly, as if she could possibly blush. She pulled me down onto the couch with her, and bared her legs as she loosened my breechclout.

Outside, I could hear Major pawing the ground impatiently. "I promised the elders I would ride before the sun moved one fist across the sky," I warned, my lips whispering close enough to hers that I could smell her breath, scented with mint and plums.

"This will not take long, and it will help you to remember to bring the things I want."

"*Tsuh,*" I said. "It will make my memory good."

———

When I left my lodge, I found the Mexican boy standing there, wearing the slightly oversized shirt and moccasins, holding the reins to both horses. I tossed him a blanket to wrap about his shoulders. I mounted the paint and the boy sprang onto the bay. I motioned northward, and we rode past the ruins of Fort Adobe, and up the trail that led us out of the Canadian Breaks to the vast treeless plains above the river valley. I paused at the brink to look down on the large Indian encampment. Over four hundred lodges from three bands of Comanches, harboring more than a thousand souls, dotted the valley for miles along the stream. It was a pretty sight to me, the lodges streaming smoke, their entrances all facing east, children and dogs running among women hard at work, men sitting in circles as they smoked and talked and boasted of their hunting skills and wartime exploits.

I turned away and thought about the long ride to Santa Fe. I reached into my saddlebag and pulled out some pemmican I had placed there when I saddled up. This I offered to the boy, who took it without hesitation.

"What is your name?" I asked, repeating the question in Spanish.

The boy did not answer. He chewed the pemmican, which was made of dried buffalo meat and venison, cactus tunas, walnuts, and plums, all caked together in rich buffalo tallow. We rode for a few miles, the ponies stepping into a trot in the brisk November air. The boy finished the pemmican.

"Toribio," he said.

I nodded, and smiled, and we rode another mile.

Then he asked, in Spanish, and in a very small voice, *"Cómo se llama?"*

TWO

My name? That takes some telling.

I was born with the given name Jean Guy. I will not tell my family name, for I am still a wanted murderer in my native France, at least in court or police records, if not in the memory of any living soul. After fleeing France, I chose the alias of Honoré Dumant, but the crew of the English cotton packet on which I stowed away thought I was saying Henri Dumant, so they simply called me Henry. Arriving in America, and traveling to the frontier, I was called Honoré by the French speakers who could handle it, until my friend Blue Wiggins started calling me "Ornery," which was as close as he could come to Honoré with his American accent, and even then, it sounded like "Orn'ry." About this time, Charles Bent, observing how green I was, started calling me Orn'ry Greenwood, which I accepted as a pretty good alias because it covered my French origins. Because of my youth, many of the traders I apprenticed under—including William Bent, Kit Carson, John Hatcher, and Lucas "Goddamn" Murray—called me Kid Greenwood. Once among the Comanches, my adoptive brother, Kills Something, named me "Plenty Man," saying, "Him little, but him Plenty Man." The Kiowas called me "Not-So-Big-for-One-So-Ugly," for I have never been accused of good looks. While working as a skinner for Billy Dixon on the buffalo ranges, I was heard speaking French to someone, and so it was assumed that I was French, which I am, and I was called "Frenchy," by which name I am still known to this day, as a ninety-nine-year-old genius telling you about the adventures of my wasted life.

Anyway, when the Mexican boy, Toribio, asked me my name, I gave him the Spanish version of my Comanche name, Plenty Man, saying,

"The Indians call me 'Mucho Hombre,' but you may simply call me 'Mucho.'"

On the long ride to Santa Fe, Toribio began to trust me, and told the story of his capture. It was in the Mexican province of Coahuila, on a ranch west of Monterrey, a remarkable distance south of the normal Comanche range. He was Toribio Treviño. The Penatekas had attacked his father's ranch late one evening while Toribio was carrying fodder to horses. He had been easily captured. His father had jumped onto a horse, and come to rescue him, but had been killed by a Comanche arrow. Toribio saw his father scalped as he was dragged away by his captors.

In camp that night, he was beaten with sticks, and tied in a most cruel way, his wrists and ankles bound behind his back and fastened to a tree limb above, so that he was almost suspended, facedown, with a heavy rock on his back. After a few nights of this type of indoctrination, the ill treatment simply ended, and Toribio rode with the warriors northward, as if he were one of them, though they did not feed him as well.

Arriving at the Penateka camp, he witnessed a victory dance that revolved around the scalp of his own father. He was given to the wife of the warrior who had captured him, and she beat him and burned him whenever she wanted—sometimes even when he slept. This woman had lost a brother to a raid in Mexico, and took her revenge upon this hapless Mexican boy, Toribio Treviño.

In spite of all his recent hardships, by the time we approached the ranch of Kit Carson and Lucien Maxwell, at Rayado Creek, on the Mountain Branch of the Santa Fe Trail, Toribio had become almost talkative and had put on several pounds. I had treated his cuts and burns with poultices of herbs that I had bought from Burnt Belly for such purposes, and he had healed well, for we were many days on the trail to the Beaubien-Miranda Land Grant where Kit and Lucien were building their ranch.

When we arrived, on a cold Saturday evening in late November, we found the Rayado Creek Ranch caught in the vortex of a fandango. More coal oil lanterns than I might have imagined the ranch possessed hung from beams and arbors and reatas strung from house to house, burning a liberal quantity of fuel. A bunch of Mexican laborers who rendered fine folk tunes on guitars and fiddles and squeeze boxes stood and played at the edge of a dirt dance floor that had obviously been sprinkled with water to lay the dust. Little children and grandparents and everyone in between—for the ranch was home to many families of workers—danced and whirled to the music. Fires and kettles and Dutch ovens and meat poles hung with sides of beef and deer carcasses told me and Toribio that this celebration would include an ample feast.

We studied all this from a distance of a hundred yards, as the last gray light of day slid beyond the mountains in the west. The scene invited us, for we were hungry for fresh meat and thirsty for spring water, and the activity of the fandango excited our senses so long deprived of human society. Rayado Creek gushed nearby, and a cool breeze crept down from the mountains in the west, making us yearn to warm ourselves at a fire. Lucien Maxwell's adobe ranch house, with its seven chimneys belching smoke into the darkening sky, seemed to me and Toribio as a city, so long had we been in the wilderness among nomads.

I could not help thinking how vulnerable the ranch would be to Indian attack right now, and that surprised me. Kit and Lucien were usually more careful than that. I did not see Kit anywhere in the lantern light, but I did see gangly Lucien Maxwell dancing with his wife, though he was not much of a dancer.

"Toribio," I said, "do you want to have some fun?"

He looked uncertainly at the fandango, then back at me. "Of course," he said. I'm sure he was thinking of the feast.

"We should ride into the middle of that fandango, screaming like two Comanche warriors."

"They will shoot us," he said.

"Perhaps."

The boy considered it a moment or two, then I saw him shortening his reins. "I *know* the Comanche scream," he said. I saw him smile for the first time since I had ransomed him from that Penateka squaw.

We dug in our heels and leaned forward as the well-trained Comanche ponies bolted. In seconds we were at a full gallop. Thirty yards from the lights of the fandango, I began war whooping, and Toribio joined in. We must have sounded like a hundred Comanches to the celebrants there because they scattered like quail flushed from cover. Then I saw Kit Carson stepping from Lucien's house, the muzzle of a rifle swinging around toward me, and I whipped off my hat as I entered the light.

"It's Plenty Man!" I yelled. "It's Kid Greenwood!"

Kit's shot went right through the hat I held in my hand, and I knew Kit did not often miss his target. When I reined in my pony and turned, I saw Kit Carson smiling at me.

Lucien Maxwell did not seem nearly as amused. He stalked around a corner holding an axe he had grabbed to defend his ranch. This he sank into a pine post that supported the arbor. "Antonio!" he yelled. "Where the hell are you?"

Lucien began looking about the grounds of the ranch, as one of his employees sheepishly stepped out into the light. Lucien stalked up to him and, towering over him, gave him a lecture in mixed English and Spanish:

"When I tell a man to stand guard, he had better not leave his post. *No dinero por usted esta semana, señor.* No, sir, not a *peso.* Now, you git your *cómo-se-llama* out there on guard like I told you, and don't you come back till you see the light of *mañana!*" The rancher grabbed the laborer by the collar and kicked him in the rear. This, I knew, was lenient treatment from Lucien Maxwell, who had been known to flog men for petty theft and other minor infractions.

Antonio sheepishly grabbed an old musket and trotted out into the darkness. Lucien Maxwell watched him go, then began laughing. Kit turned and waved the residents back into the light. *"Baile, baile!"* he ordered. I looked at Toribio and found him grinning. I, too, began to laugh as big Lucien Maxwell pulled me from my horse and pretended to squeeze me to death in his big arms. I could smell liquor on his breath. Two workers led our horses away as the makeshift band started playing a waltz called "El Chiquiado." It was a favorite, because to convince a señorita to dance, a young man had to compose an original verse to sing to her as everyone listened.

"You done good, Kid," said Kit Carson as he shook my hand. "Woke us up." There was no smell of drink on Kit's breath. "Sorry about the hole in your hat."

"Better there than my head."

Now Kit allowed himself to chuckle, and gave me a big Mexican *abrazo,* wrapping both arms around my shoulders and slapping my back. Kit was about my height—only five feet five or so—but he was built much stockier than me. Lucien Maxwell, on the other hand, stood over six feet tall in his boots, and towered over me and Kit.

"We figured you for dead, Greenwood." Lucien indeed looked surprised to see me. "Who's this whelp?"

"His name's Toribio Treviño. I bought him from a squaw. He comes from way down near Monterrey."

"Be darned," Kit said. "He looks hungry. *Comida?*" he asked, looking at Toribio.

"Por favor."

Kit pointed, and the boy bolted toward a big table made of hand-split pine planks. It was covered with all kinds of roasted, baked, and fried victuals.

"What are you gonna do with him?" Kit said.

"I guess I'll write and try to find his people. His mother died giving him birth, and his father was killed in the raid that got him captured, but he said he's got some great-uncles he never met."

"Well, leave him stay here till you find his folks. If that's what you want. I'll look after him. Won't be the first orphan I've taken in."

By now, the women and children were venturing out from their hiding places, and Kit's wife, Josepha, saw me. She came running toward me with a year-old child in her arms. Josepha, whom I had once saved from the same angry mob that murdered Charles Bent, the governor of New Mexico, loved me as if I were her blood brother. "Oh, *hermano,*" she said as she hugged me, tears streaming down her face. Lucien's wife, Luz, also came to embrace me, though I did not know her as well as Josepha.

"What's the cause for this fandango?" I finally asked.

"Come on, we'll show you," Lucien said.

He dragged me into his house with Kit, Josepha, and Luz close behind. Entering the first room of the adobe home, Lucien tossed his hat onto a set of deer antlers, revealing a head that had lost much hair since last I had seen him, three years before. He was only thirty-one years old, but going rather bald. He took two big steps to a handmade pine cabinet and pulled open the bottom drawer. From this, he extracted a pair of saddlebags that sagged with weight. I heard coins rattle as he dropped the saddlebags on the dirt floor packed and smoothed with ox blood. He opened the saddlebags to reveal scores of gold coins of a making I had never before seen. Lucien dipped his hand among them and let them pour between his fingers like mineral water.

"Come see, Kid."

I knelt beside Lucien and scooped up several coins. Most of them seemed handmade, for they were stamped only with crude 5s, 10s, and 20s, but I also spotted a Peruvian doubloon, an English crown, a Dutch florin, and two Spanish pesetas. I looked up at Kit and found him shaking his head with amusement, for money had never influenced him as much as it did Lucien. Josepha simply smiled and rocked the baby in her arms, and Luz tossed a stick of wood onto the fire as she hummed along with the band outside.

"Where did you get all this?" I asked. "California?"

"Exactly!" Lucien said.

"You've been prospecting?"

"Like hell I have!" He exploded in laughter as he crammed the saddlebags back into the drawer and kicked it shut. "Can you see Lucien Bonaparte Maxwell stooped over a gold pan?"

"I guess not."

"Tell him, Kit."

"Well," Kit began, "last year, me and Lucien decided we wanted to go a-trappin'. Like we did in the old days. We got together a party of eighteen men. All the old-timers. John Hatcher, Tom Fitzpatrick, Charley Autobee—you know . . . All the old survivors from the thirties, when beaver plews was worth something. Oh, we had us a time!"

"We did, Greenwood," Lucien said. "Damned if we didn't. You should have been along, and you'd have seen the last great beaver hunt. We went up the Arkansas, trapped Bayou Salado, down the South Platte, and up the North Platte. We trapped New Park and Middle Park, and just skinned us a mess of beaver."

"And sold them in California?"

Lucien laughed. "Hell, no. Tell him, Kit."

"Well," Kit said, his voice a mere whisper compared to Lucien's bellow, "the only rascal we couldn't get to go a-trappin' with us was old Dick Wootton. He said he had better things to do than trap a bunch of worthless pelts, and was going to California to make some money. You know Uncle Dick—he will find a way to turn a dollar. So, he bought nine hundred sheep here in New Mexico, and trailed them all the way to California. Went past Salt Lake."

"While we were livin' off the fat of the land and cooking beaver tail every night under the stars of the Great Shining Mountains," Lucien interjected, "old Uncle Dick was trailing a bunch of stinking wool maggots across the desert to the Pacific Ocean. We thought he was crazy. Tell the rest, Kit."

"Well, he paid four bits a head for them sheep here, and sold them at five dollars a head there."

"Sometimes five and a half!" Maxwell blurted.

I whistled as I ciphered the gross and net take instantly in my head. "So you decided to take a herd of sheep to California?"

"Now you've got us figured," Maxwell said. "Oh, God, it was miserable, proddin' them sheep along day after day, but we took five thousand head, and just made a haul. John Hatcher and Blue Wiggins went with us. We're all rich!"

"There ain't nothin' to buy between here and St. Louis, and we don't need nothin' we ain't already got," Kit said, "but we're rich, all right."

Josepha laughed.

"I've got plenty to buy," Lucien said, grabbing and hugging his wife, Luz, as she came near to him. "If I can find Guadalupe Miranda down in Mexico, I believe I can buy his half-interest in the Beaubien-Miranda Grant. I'll own it all before it's over . . ."

The Beaubien-Miranda Grant was Lucien's obsession. This former trapper, former Indian trader, former superintendent of William Bent's great fort, former hunter for the explorer John Charles Frémont—Lucien Bonaparte Maxwell was bound to be the single biggest landowner inside the territories of the United States. Eleven years before, Lucien had married Maria de la Luz Beaubien. Lucien's father-in-law, Judge Carlos Beaubien, was a Canadian who had immigrated to Taos soon after Mexican independence, and was one of the leading citizens of northern New Mexico.

Judge Beaubien and an influential native, Guadalupe Miranda, had convinced the Mexican government to grant them a huge tract of land between Taos and Bent's Fort. The Spanish government had long granted land to citizens, and the Mexican government followed the pattern, establishing a chain of land grants to the northeast of Santa Fe and Taos, designed as a buffer against American encroachment. Nobody knew yet if the U.S. government was going to honor the old Mexican and Spanish grants, but Lucien was gambling that it would, and had spent much time, money, and effort in settling his father-in-law's grant. Guadalupe Miranda had fled New Mexico during the Mexican War, and had not been heard from since. Lucien was sure that if he could locate Miranda, he could purchase his half of the grant, and become a partner with his father-in-law in a land holding that was so large that nobody really knew the extent of it, except to say that a few days would be required in riding across it.

"But I don't reckon I'll find Guadalupe Miranda riding in here tonight like you, Kid, so we might as well go on and celebrate."

"Is Blue here?" I asked. "And John Hatcher?"

"No, they stayed in Santa Fe to spend their share of the money," Kit said. "Now, come on. You're bound to be hungry as a coyote from the looks of you."

"I could eat," I said, as they dragged me back outside to join the feast and the fandango. Before the night was over, Lucien had fetched my left-handed Stradivarius, which I had left with him for safekeeping, and I was made to play along with the Mexicans under the lantern light. We played and sang until the broad eastern horizon began to turn gray.

THREE

About the time I turned twenty-two, I began drinking coffee and playing cards. This may not sound so bad, considering I was already a murderer, a thief, a liar, and a whiskey peddler, but the truth is that I used the coffee and the cards to cheat at poker. For years, I had practiced the art of prestidigitation, including many card tricks. My fingers, trained to classical music on the violin, could handle a deck of cards with equal facility. I could double-cut with one hand, deal from the bottom of the deck as smoothly as I could from the top, and palm a card while I dealt to the entire table.

The coffee? Well, I didn't drink much of it. Never liked the stuff. But a cup of black coffee can function as a mirror. I could situate that cup between me and the man I wished to cheat, and see a reflected image of every card I dealt to him in the dark, still surface of the coffee. This was a technique used by bogus fortune tellers reading tarot cards more so than by card players, so no one at the gaming tables ever realized what I was up to.

All I can say in my defense is that I only cheated one man at cards my whole life. And he deserved it. His name was Luther Sheffield, and he had, in turn, cheated my friend Blue Wiggins out of all his thousands of dollars of gold field money earned by herding sheep to California. It was my aim solely to get Blue's money back for him. That's why I started drinking coffee and playing cards.

After leaving Maxwell's ranch I had made an easy two-day ride to Santa Fe over ground I often covered in half the time when I served as a courier for the U.S. Army during the Mexican War. I rode Major and led two mules I had acquired from Lucien B. Maxwell in trade for the mount Toribio had ridden out of Comancheria. Toribio had stayed with Kit and Josepha, who frequently took in homeless waifs.

Arriving in Santa Fe, I stabled Major in a livery and went about my business of buying whiskey to trade to the Indians. Buying whiskey was perfectly legal, but selling it to the Indians was illegal, of course, so I had learned how to make my purchases quietly. I hid two kegs of cheap St. Louis rotgut in the ponderosa pine forests above the city, covering my trail to the hiding spot with the sweep of a pine branch, Indian style. I would leave them there until I was ready to pack them to Taos, where I would buy some even cheaper homemade corn liquor called "Taos Lightning."

In the meantime, I enjoyed Santa Fe's social life. I stayed at an old inn at the corner of the plaza, called simply La Fonda. I was told that it had been operating for over a hundred and fifty years. I took a room on the second floor of the adobe inn. Sleeping that far above the ground provided something of a novelty for a man who had lived for months in a Comanche buffalo-hide tipi, for a Comanche lodge embraces the very bosom of Mother Earth. The angles of the square room also troubled me at first. The Plains Indians know that a round shelter synchronizes with the roundness of all that is natural, from the circling of the seasons to the shape of the sun. The room full of square angles seemed to pull my whole body and mind out of shape at first. But the walls were adobe, and adobe is of the earth, and overhead pine *vigas* supported the ceiling, somewhat like the lodge poles in a tipi, so on my third night there, I finally got several hours of sleep.

The next day, while enjoying my lunch at La Fonda, I happened to see my friend Blue Wiggins enter and speak to the proprietor of the eatery there. I could not hear him speak, but I could tell by reading his lips and his gestures that he was offering to trade a good hunting knife for a meal. This puzzled me, for Kit and Lucien had told me that Blue had made quite a profit with them herding sheep to California. Anyway, the proprietor would have none of such a trade, so I jumped up and greeted Blue, shouting across the room.

"Hey, you old trail bum!"

"Who's that?" Blue said, for the room was dark and his eyes had not yet adjusted from the glaring sheen of the New Mexican sun.

"Your pal Orn'ry Greenwood, that's who."

A smile flashed across Blue's face, and he exploded in laughter. "Son of a bitch, if you ain't still kickin'! I heard you was scalped."

I made knowing gestures to the proprietor, and dragged Blue over to my table near the little fireplace in the wall.

"I've just come from Maxwell's ranch on the Rayado," I said. "He and Kit told me of your good fortune in California."

Blue rolled his eyes and grinned. "Maxwell offered me a job on the ranch. I wish to hell I'd have taken it now. I might still have all that money I made."

"You haven't spent it all, have you?"

"Spent it? Not much of it. *Lost* it's what I done."

The proprietor brought a mug of coffee and a few *piloncillos* of sugar.

"Where? How?" I said, before stuffing my mouth full of a delicious tortilla dipped in mole poblano sauce and *frijoles fritos*.

"At the gambling hall."

"Are you that bad a gambler?" I asked.

"No, but there's a feller over there that sure can cheat a fool like me out of a *bosal* full of gold in a hurry. His name's Luther Sheffield. Come to find out he cut his teeth gamblin' on the riverboats of the Mississippi. I don't even know how he cheated me, but he got my gold from me a lot quicker than I got it from them prospectors in California."

The proprietor brought more tortillas, scrambled eggs, onions, and beans. My temper flared like the peppers burning in my mouth to think of my friend Blue Wiggins getting fleeced by a card cheat. Blue Wiggins had once stood back to back with me, each of us with a single-shot pistol in his hand, for four hours and thirty-nine minutes, as we held off a band of hostile Comanches and Kiowas that wanted our horses and our scalps.

"Where is this gambling hall?"

"Down on Burro Alley," Blue said, scorching his fingers on the iron skillet the proprietor had left on our table. "You know it. It's the same place Doña Tules used to own."

"Used to?"

"You haven't heard she died? A year ago. This Luther Sheffield has taken her place over."

"Tell me about this gambler, Sheffield."

Blue shook his head with an embarrassed smile. "He's pretty damned slick, Orn'ry. Seems like a good sort of feller at first. Dresses like a dandy, tells a good yarn." Blue's smile slid away. "But he deals with his back to the corner, if you know what I mean. And he hired a couple of rough ol' bullwhackers to knock heads when somebody acts up in there. It ain't like it was when Doña Tules ran the place. Sheffield shot and killed some poor kid from Missouri this summer. The kid accused him of cheatin' and pulled a knife on him. That Sheffield whipped out a pocket pistol and got him right in the head."

"You know, I'm pretty good with a deck of cards," I said.

Blue laughed. "I've never even seen you deal a hand."

"I've got a fair amount of coin on me. How much did this Sheffield cheat you out of?"

"Now, Orn'ry, don't go to thinkin'. It's gone, that's all."

"How much?"

Blue's face darkened with anger and embarrassment. "Don't tell Kit."

"I wouldn't tell anybody. Just between you and me."

"Almost three thousand dollars." Blue looked down at the pine planks of the table. When his face rose again to look me in the eye, he was faking a smile. "Nothin' another drive to California won't fix."

But I knew he didn't even have enough left over to buy a cheap herd here in New Mexico. Had I not just witnessed Blue trying to trade his hunting knife for a meal? "I think I'll wander on over to that gambling hall this evening," I said.

"Now, Orn'ry, don't get riled on my account, and let that slick bastard cheat you, too."

"I don't have much to lose, anyway. Just a couple of hundred Kit loaned me until I can finish my trading at Adobe Walls." The excitement of the endeavor must have shown in my grin. "I don't mind taking a calculated risk with it. What do you say, Blue? Let's see if we can figure this gambler's game."

"How you plan on doin' that?" he said, his skepticism plain in his tone of voice.

"I don't know. We'll observe. You know what Plato said: You should learn to know evil—not from your own soul—but from long observation of the nature of evil in others."

Blue nodded as he chewed a fiery mouthful of his meal. "Who the hell is Plato?"

"The same fellow who wrote, 'Everything that deceives may also be said to enchant.' "

"You got that from one of your confounded books. Orn'ry, you're a caution."

<hr />

I asked for a pot of coffee and a pair of cups from the proprietor of La Fonda, and we went up to my room to plot our revenge on the gambler.

"We've got to act like we're strangers to each other when we go into the gambling hall," I said. "I'll go in first and ask for a cup of coffee."

"Coffee?"

"Well, I don't drink whiskey."

"I didn't know you drank coffee."

"I don't." About that time, I poured a cup of coffee from the pot I had carried up to my room. "But, watch this . . ." I got out my playing cards that I used to perform card tricks, for my entertainment, and that of others. There wasn't a table in the tiny adobe room, so we sat cross-legged on a rug on the floor. I put the cup of coffee on the rug, and showed Blue how I could see the face of each card dealt in the mirrored surface of the coffee.

Blue shook his head. "It happens too fast in a real game."

"I'll practice. I can do it."

"Even if you could see the cards that way, how could you remember them all?"

"Oh, my memory is pretty good, Blue. There are card cheats out there doing it every day. You'd be amazed at what a person can get away with."

To convince Blue, I dealt each of us a quick five-card hand, facedown, catching glimpses of his cards in the surface of the coffee as they flipped through the air toward him. Then I told him every card in his hand before he even picked them up.

When Blue looked at the cards, he nodded and grinned, seeing that I was right. "What am I supposed to do?" he asked next.

"You'll come in an hour or so after me and get into the game. Pretend you never met me before. Don't worry about winning or losing. Just keep your bets low, so you don't lose too much. Your job is to stack the deadwood."

"What's that mean?"

"When each hand is over, and you toss in your cards, facedown, stack them with the highest-ranking cards on the bottom."

"How come?"

"That way, I can gather your cards last, and your best cards will be on the bottom of the deck."

"You're gonna deal off the bottom of the deck?" he asked.

"Yep."

"Can you do that without gettin' caught?"

"That last hand I just dealt to you and me . . ."

"Yeah?"

"All off the bottom."

"Not much, hombre," he said with deep skepticism.

"I swear."

"Well, somebody's got to cut the deck. Then how do you control what's on bottom?"

"I crimp the bottom card before the cut. That way I can put the deck right back where it was before the cut, and you'd never see me do it."

"No . . ."

"I've been living in an Indian camp for the past three years," I explained. "I have an Indian wife to cook all my meals and make all my clothes. I have a lot of time to mess with. You know I don't sleep much. I practice magic tricks. The card tricks are the easiest ones."

"Son of a gun," Blue said. "This might just work."

"We're not going to get filthy rich. We're just going to win your money back."

"Agreed."

We shook hands and went on with our scheming.

That night, I polished my boots and put on my spurs. I wasn't riding anywhere, for the gambling hall was within walking distance from La Fonda, but I wanted the spurs for show. For the same reason, I donned the felt hat I had purchased the day before, and my nickel-plated Colt revolver given to me a few years earlier by General Kearny for serving as his courier through the dangers of the Mexican War.

I stepped out into the frigid evening air of a high-country winter and walked briskly to Burro Alley where several establishments of questionable repute operated around the clock. I went staightaway to the place that once belonged to Doña Tules. The moment I opened the old pine door, it was obvious that the business no longer belonged to that infamous old cigar-smoking madam. During her reign there, the place had possessed a simple honesty even if the dealers were trained to cheat for the house. A venerable warmth had resided here when Doña Tules ran the place, for everything was handmade of earth or stone or wood.

Now the place looked as gaudy as a Mississippi riverboat.

I walked in and felt the stares that shot my way as the old door hinges creaked. I jingled my spurs up to a new varnished bar that must have been hauled from Missouri on a freight wagon. I nudged aside a brass spittoon with my boot. The bartender glanced briefly at me without any hint of a greeting. He was a big bearded man with a grimy shirt under an apron that was passably clean. He was taking cigars from a box and placing them in a glass case on the bar, his thick fingers groping the stogies as clumsily as a big boar grizzly gathering bones.

"Got any coffee?" I asked.

"No," he said, without looking at me.

"Well, if you could make some, I'd be grateful."

"Do I look like a woman to you?" he growled.

"I'll pay for it, of course. I just wanted a little coffee."

"Go to hell."

"Whatever happened to Doña Tules? A fellow could get a cup of coffee in here when she owned the place."

"Well, she's dead."

"Then whom do I ask to get some coffee?"

The big man crushed a handful of cigars and charged me like a bear, his snarl revealing yellowed teeth in the middle of his beard. Only the bar between us kept him from running right over me. I took a step back to stay out of his reach.

"I told you we ain't got no goddamn coffee!" he roared.

I could feel every eye in the place on me. I glanced to my right and saw a gambler who just had to be Luther Sheffield, the new owner of the place, staring at me along with everybody else. About that time, the front door flew open, and in burst Blue Wiggins, almost an hour early, and rather drunk. With him was my old friend and mentor in the Indian trade with the Comanches, John Hatcher. If Blue was rather drunk, John Hatcher was a step ahead of him.

"By God, look, Blue!" Hatcher said in his drawl. "It's Kid Greenwood!"

Blue grimaced. "I forgot to tell you, John—"

Hatcher stormed up to me to shake my hand. "Good to see you two together again," he said. "You fellers used to be thick as fleas. Remember how you stood off them Comanches on the Cimarron? Tell it to me again, boys. But let's get some whiskey first."

"No whiskey for me," I said.

"You want some coffee?" Blue asked, rather sheepishly.

"They don't have any coffee," I said.

"Three whiskeys!" Hatcher blurted.

Blue leaned toward me to speak low. "Our plan ain't goin' so good, is it?"

I shook my head. "No, Blue, it isn't."

FOUR

The name Kid Greenwood had carried a curious reputation with it ever since my duel with Snakehead Jackson. True, I had killed Snakehead, but only because Snakehead's old Colt revolver had chain-fired and exploded in his hand, throwing off his aim. Even so, I was known as a fighter of sorts because of that damned gunfight. So, after Blue Wiggins, who was supposed to be acting as if he didn't know me, showed up with John Hatcher, who blurted out my name, revealing the obvious truth about my friendship with Blue—well, after that, everyone in Luther Sheffield's gambling hall looked at me as if I were on the verge of killing somebody just any minute. Except for the big ox behind the bar, who said, "Kid Greenwood's ass. He ain't no bigger than a cub."

Anyway, we sat down at a slender-legged parlor table that looked as out of place in the old adobe cantina as a marble sculpture on a mud fence. We talked to John Hatcher about the sheep-herding business and other adventures, until John finally got up to go relieve himself out back.

"Hell, I'm *sorry*," Blue said, reading the disgusted look on my face. "I didn't know I'd run into John. He wouldn't have it any other way. He just had to come in here. What was I supposed to do?"

"It doesn't really matter anyway, since I couldn't get a cup of coffee without killing the bartender."

"Well, the deal's off now, so let's just have us a time."

"The deal is not off," I insisted. "This is just a setback. I'll figure something out."

When John Hatcher came back to the table, he was arm in arm with a little damsel of soiled virtue who called herself Rosa. We all knew her from the days when Doña Tules had run the gambling house. She was about half Mexican, a quarter Pueblo Indian, and a quarter something else that even she wasn't sure of. She was pretty as a doll, stood five feet one, and weighed 102 pounds, all of which was rolling hell. Rosa was also crazy as a liquored Comanche. She would do about anything for a dollar, and sometimes just for the whimsical fun of it.

When Rosa recognized me, she squealed, ran to me, and plopped right down on my lap, which didn't hurt my feelings very much at all.

"Easy, there, I'm a married man," I said.

"Your wife ain't here, is she?"

"I ain't married," Blue said.

Rosa sprang from me to Blue and looked back at me with a mischievous grin that gave me an idea.

"Rosa, what would it take to get a cup of coffee in this place?" I asked.

"Come to my room. I will give you plenty of coffee and other hot things."

I smiled. "How do you like the new owner? Sheffield?"

She glanced at him across the room and made a pretty sneer in his direction. Her eyes rolled beautifully in her head. "He's all right." She shrugged.

"Well, tomorrow night, I'm going to sit at his table and play some cards, but I'll need coffee."

"You don't want to play cards with him. That's what this fool did." She wiggled on top of Blue, then abandoned him to come sit with me again. "Spend your money on me, not on cards. Both of you, I don't care. All three of you!"

"Leave me out of it," Hatcher said. "I can find my own."

"Rosa, you've got to bring me some coffee to the card table tomorrow night."

"Why do you talk only of coffee, *loco*?"

I reached into my vest pocket, fetched a five-dollar gold piece, and pressed it into Rosa's hand. "Just say you'll do it."

She opened her hand just long enough to see the coin. "This gets you coffee *and* sugar."

"Just coffee will do. The blacker, the better. Now, there's one other thing we've got to do. Go squirm around on Blue a little, will you?"

Blue grinned in appreciation as Rosa obliged, but he was getting suspicious. "What are you thinkin', Orn'ry?"

"You and I have got to get into a fight over Rosa."

"What for?" Blue said.

"No need to fight," she said. "You can share me."

"So it'll look like we're not friends anymore. For tomorrow night."

Blue let the logic sink in. "All right, as long as I get to win the fight."

"No, I've got to win."

"How come *you* get to win?"

John Hatcher threw back his whiskey and got up from the table. "I don't know what you boys are up to, but leave me out of it." He walked toward the bar.

I looked back at Blue. "She's got to be *my* girl tomorrow night. She's got to bring *me* the coffee."

Blue sighed. "I don't win the fight *or* get the girl?"

"All you get is your money back."

"Huh?" Rosa said, having lost track of the entire conversation.

Blue frowned. "All right, but I ain't gonna lose no fight easy, Orn'ry. I got a reputation to think about."

"Good. It's got to look real."

Blue wrapped his arms tighter around Rosa. "All right, well . . . Ready?"

"I'm ready," I said.

"Un momento, pendejos! Por qué quiere luchar?" Rosa rattled.

"Here goes," Blue said, and he all but mauled Rosa. He grabbed her by one of her dainty breasts, and one of her skinny thighs, and went to kiss her mouth—all so suddenly that Rosa squealed in surprise, which was my cue.

I sprang from my chair so fast that it slapped against the old dirt floor. "You're no gentleman!" I hollered as I pulled Rosa from Blue's grasp and drew my fist back to strike.

From his chair, Blue kicked me in the stomach, and sent me staggering. I charged back at him as he got up, but he spun me aside and tripped me, sending me crashing into the parlor table, which splintered into kindling. Before I could rise, Blue had me by the collar. He pulled me to my feet.

"If you're gonna win this fight, you'd better git after it," he growled in my ear.

I took Blue's advice, and elbowed him hard in the ribs. Then I spun and punched him in the mouth. Blue saw it coming, and though I only punched him hard enough to bust a lip, he threw his head upward and staggered backward as if I had knocked every tooth in his head down his throat.

Suddenly, Rosa streaked by me and sprang on top of Blue, knocking him to floor, where she proceeded to pummel him with her tiny fists. I started laughing at the sight, until the big bullwhacker-turned-bartender made his way around the end of the bar with a hickory axe handle. He roared like a bear and took a couple of swings at me with the axe handle, which I avoided with some desperate maneuvers.

I was thinking about reaching for my Colt when old John Hatcher sprang onto the bartender's back, and started gouging at his eyes and screaming like a Cheyenne warrior riding into battle. This gave me a chance to pull Rosa off Blue, who quickly kicked my feet out from under me, and resumed our fight where most fights end up, on the ground, in kicking, groveling chaos. Rosa, of course, jumped right back on top of the two of us.

I was trying to tell Blue that we'd better get out if we didn't want our skulls split with that axe handle, when I heard the pistol shot. Blue and I looked up from the floor. I pushed Rosa aside to see Luther Sheffield standing over us, a white swirl of smoke coming from the muzzle of the pocket pistol in his hand. Hatcher slid down from the shoulders of the big bartender, who dropped his axe handle, and started rubbing his injured eyes.

"Gentlemen," Sheffield said. "If I may make such a mockery of the term. Perhaps you've not been made aware of the fact that we allow no fighting in this establishment."

"No fightin'!" John Hatcher shouted. "What kind of a *cantina* don't allow fightin'?"

"This is no *cantina*," Sheffield said. "Though it may be located in the pit of this uncivilized outpost of hell itself, this is a fine gambling parlor."

As I rose from the floor, I took a good look at Luther Sheffield. In addition to the small revolver in his hand, I saw a dagger sheathed on his belt. He was no bigger than the average man, but his hazel eyes revealed his complete disregard for any amount of danger three frontier ruffians might represent. Our little disturbance had not ruffled him in the least.

"Parlor!" John Hatcher shouted. "Well, mister, I'm of a mind to clean house in your goddamn parlor. Any place with a dirt floor that calls itself a parlor ought to go on back to Ohio!"

"Now, John," I said. "Me and Blue can take our fight somewhere else. Come on, you just go with us."

I walked wide around the bartender, who was regaining his vision, and grabbed Hatcher by the elbow. "Come on, John, a man can't even get a cup of coffee here, anyway. Some parlor."

"Someone needs to pay the damages," Sheffield said.

"Damages!" Hatcher blurted.

I reached carefully into my pocket and showed Sheffield one of the gold coins I had gotten from Maxwell's ranch. I tossed it to the gambler, who showed a hint of surprise when he caught it.

"Will that cover it?" I asked. "It was just one little old *parlor* table."

"That should suffice," Sheffield said. He let the hammer down on his pistol, and slipped it into the pocket of his coat. "You gentlemen might think about minding your manners, and coming on back sometime. No reason we can't all enjoy one another's company." I knew this comment was intended mainly for me, for Sheffield wanted some of that gold I had just flashed at him.

"I'll come back with my own damn axe handle," John Hatcher said as I pulled him toward the door, taking just enough time to wink at Rosa. Blue was holding the door open for us, and we somehow got out of there without one of Sheffield's little bullets in us. We went on down the street to a place that didn't mind calling itself a *cantina* and had one grand time.

FIVE

The next night, I went back to Sheffield's gambling parlor alone. The first thing I did was to throw the bartender a five-dollar gold piece as an apology. He didn't speak, but he did put the coin in his pocket. Then I waited for Rosa to show herself, and told her to put on a pot of coffee for me. When finally I had my cup of coffee in hand, I wandered over to Sheffield's table and watched a while. He had a knack for fleecing his victims gradually, almost politely, letting them win just enough to keep them at the table. At length, a soldier lost what was left of his pay, and had to vacate his seat. It was a good seat, in that it was across the table from Sheffield, where he would be least likely to see my moves.

"Would you like to join us for a friendly hand or two?" he offered.

I shook my head. "I don't like the odds. Mathematically, I mean."

"Mathematically?"

"Blackjack favors the dealer. I prefer draw poker, provided every man at the table gets a chance to deal."

Sheffield's mouth curled as he chuckled, but his eyes did not share the mirth. "You mean, provided *you* get a chance to deal."

"No," I said.

"Then you mean provided *I* don't deal every hand."

I shrugged as I pretended to sip my coffee. "That's not at all what I said, Mr. Sheffield. I said every man at the table ought to have the chance to deal."

A couple of other soldiers who still had some pay left agreed with me.

"Let's say the winner deals," Sheffield offered. "That way, the odds will give every man an equal chance."

"Fair enough," I said.

"Deal everybody one card," a soldier said. "The high card deals first."

Sheffield shrugged as I took a seat. He dealt the two soldiers low cards. He dealt me a queen. A Missouri teamster sitting to my left got a ten. Sheffield dealt himself a king.

"A lucky beginning," he said.

It was early in the evening and the stakes stayed low. Sheffield won two hands in a row. If he cheated, I could not tell how. Then he let one of the soldiers win. The soldier slowed the game down with his clumsy dealing, but no one seemed to care. I won a hand and a small pot by pure luck of the draw and some rudimentary statistical observations. As I dealt the next hand, I used the cup of coffee to practice my trick of getting a peek at each card. The light was poor in the parlor, and the cards difficult to see, but I managed. I didn't use what I saw to cheat, and I lost the hand and the deal to the Missouri teamster beside me.

Sheffield won the deal back and began to shuffle. "Mr. Greenwood," he said. "It is Mr. Greenwood?"

"Yes. Honoré Greenwood."

"Your reputation precedes you."

"Yeah," I admitted. "Most people are disappointed when I show up after my reputation."

Sheffield began dealing. "Perhaps the story has been exaggerated, then."

"Which story?"

"The one about the duel with Snakehead Jackson."

"I don't know what all has been told," I admitted, "but I'll tell you what happened. Snakehead would have killed me if his Colt hadn't chain-fired. It exploded in his hand and made him miss. I didn't miss. I'm a pretty good shot." I looked at my poker hand, called the bet on the table, and threw two cards back.

"Still, it was a noble thing just to have the courage to meet a man for a duel of honor."

"It wasn't like that," I said. "There was no honor in it. We were on the run from a bunch of Mescalero Apaches. Snakehead's horse gave out. He wanted mine. There was no time to arrange for rules or seconds. No surgeon on hand. We just pulled our guns and shot."

Sheffield flipped a couple of cards my way. "I hear you haven't been seen in Santa Fe for some time. Speculation held that you'd been scalped."

I looked at the cards Sheffield gave me, frowned, and folded my hand. "Not as badly as I'm getting scalped here. I've been trading with the Indians, that's all. Working through William Bent's post up at Big Timbers."

Sheffield finished the deal and collected the pot. "How's business?"

I took another small sip of coffee. It tasted terrible. I had never liked the stuff. It was like drinking hot, dirty water to me. "Profitable," I said.

Sheffield was shuffling. "I've never understood. What does an Indian possibly have worth trading?"

"Most tribes trade fine furs and buffalo robes," I explained. "The Comanches, however, are rich in horses, and there's always a demand for good riding stock. Then, there's the *rescate.*"

"The what?" I saw a true glint of curiosity in Sheffield's eye as he flipped a card my way.

"Spanish for 'ransom.' "

"Ransom?"

"Captives from the settlements. Mexican and white. Mostly children. Sometimes women. I ransom them back from the Indians."

"Doesn't that just encourage them to take more captives?"

"They don't need encouragement. It's been their way since Christopher Columbus was a deckhand. They capture the children of their enemies. That's just what they do."

"Why?" Sheffield let a faint look of abomination show in his eyes.

"Perhaps to replace a dead child of their own. Perhaps as revenge for a child captured from them. Some get enslaved and beaten, some get loved and adopted."

Sheffield dealt each man his last card. "Luck of the draw," he said.

I nodded. "High stakes."

We played a few more hands, and I managed to win one. On the following hand, as I dealt, I kept close account of the cards I glimpsed in the surface of the coffee. My memory has always been perfect, and I can read from it in my mind as if reading from the page of a book, so I had no trouble remembering every man's hand. I could also guess pretty accurately which card or cards each man would want to exchange in order to improve his hand. I also saw that the bottom card on the deck was a four.

When Sheffield asked for a card, I dealt him the four from the bottom of the deck, because I knew it would be of no use for him. Getting rid of the four exposed the next card on the bottom—a nine. As I tossed cards around the table, I always dealt the bottom one as long as that card would not help the man I dealt it to—for I intended to win this hand, and retain the deal.

I had two jacks in my hand already, and as I dealt off the bottom,

COME SUNDOWN | 45

I exposed another jack, which I saved for myself. I won the hand with three jacks, as I expected. Sheffield's eyes showed no suspicion.

One of the soldiers picked up his remaining currency, and left as I shuffled the cards. Rosa brought me a new, fresh, hot cup of coffee in a porcelain cup that Sheffield must have carted from Ohio. She hung over my shoulders and kissed my face a while as I continued to shuffle, then passed the cards to the Missouri teamster to cut.

"Go on, now," I ordered, pushing Rosa away as I got ready to deal. "I'm busy."

Rosa pouted and left.

"It's plain to see who won that fistfight last night," Sheffield said.

I took the deck back after the cut and started to deal. "Well, Blue and I used to be pretty good friends, but I don't think a man should treat a woman that way. Even if she *is* a harlot."

"A what?" the teamster asked.

"A whore," the soldier explained.

"Oh."

"You're a mighty civilized man for this territory," Sheffield said to me.

"I'll take that as a compliment, coming from a son of Ohio. You are from Ohio, aren't you?"

"Born and raised. I used to ply the Ohio and the Mississippi on the riverboats. That's where I learned to play cards. A fellow who learns the rules and the odds, and exercises his memory can make a tolerable profit playing cards fair and square. I'd drift down to the Old South and fleece those rich plantation owners. I enjoyed that. No man has any business getting that rich off the sweat and blood of a slave. It isn't right."

"I'm from Mississippi," the soldier said, a slight warning in his voice.

"I'll bet you never owned a slave in your life, though, did you?"

"Nope."

Sheffield called and raised the bet of the teamster to his right. "Then I have no quarrel with you, my good fellow. You've earned your own way in this world."

The soldier called the bet. "I hope to earn a chunk more right here and now," he said, as he tossed in his raise.

"Don't misunderstand me," Sheffield said. "I wouldn't want any darkies at my card table. And you won't see any Mexicans in here, either, except for the courtesans."

"The what?" said the Missouri teamster.

"Whores!" the soldier said.

"Oh."

"Every man ought to know his place, but no man ought to be made a slave."

I called the bet on the table and tried to sort out Luther Sheffield's values. I started dealing each player his new cards. The teamster didn't have much to begin with, and I didn't help him. I knew Sheffield already had a pair of aces, so I dealt him two cards from the bottom that would not help him. This uncovered a queen that I knew would give the soldier three of a kind, so I fixed his hand to win. I did not intend to win the hand myself, because I didn't want to draw too much of Sheffield's suspicion too soon.

The betting through, each man showed his cards. I knew the soldier should win. I knew it in the core of my heart. But sometimes what you think you know just doesn't turn out to be so. Sheffield showed three aces, including the ace of diamonds that I knew damned good and well I had not dealt to him, for I had seen every card I dealt in the surface of the coffee cup. Somehow, he had stashed that ace somewhere during a previous hand, and had produced it now to complete his three-of-a-kind. I felt my own face gawking stupidly as I saw the gambler's hand, then quickly realized that I should not have been looking at his hand with such wonder had I not had any preconceived notion of what it would yield. I wondered if Sheffield was watching me. I raised my eyes to meet his, and found them piercing my stare.

Now I knew four things. One, Sheffield was cheating. Two, he knew I was cheating. Three, he knew that we both were on to each other. Four, neither one of us knew how the other was getting away with it.

I wondered what to do. Should I take a sip of coffee to bolster the illusion that it was actually there for me to drink? No, I decided. That would only draw attention to my secret, like a criminal returning to the scene of the crime. Instead, I glanced at the soldier, so that Sheffield might think I was in partnership with the man from Mississippi. In a way, I was. Though the soldier didn't know it, I had tried to fix his hand for him.

"Damn," the soldier said, seeing the three aces.

"Double damn," said the teamster.

I glanced back at Sheffield and found him still looking at me.

"I'll call your two damns and raise you a son of a bitch," I said.

Sheffield burst into laughter, and shook his head as if nothing had been learned.

The gambler won two more hands, then let the soldier win. I guess he wanted to see if the soldier was helping me cheat. Luckily a distraction walked into the parlor about that time in the form of Blue Wiggins.

"Mind if I sit in this chair," he said to the whole table.

The teamster shrugged and the soldier actually pulled the chair out for Blue. I said nothing. I looked briefly at Blue's face, and judged him to be perfectly sober, which was an improvement over the night before.

"As long as there's not going to be any trouble," Sheffield said.

"I'm here to play cards, not cause trouble."

Sheffield looked at me.

"I never start trouble," I said.

"Five-card draw," the gambler said. "Jacks or better."

Blue sat down, and Sheffield began to deal. That gambler was smooth. He won three hands in a row, then let Blue win one. Blue didn't know how to do any cheating, so it was a fair hand that the teamster won. I almost won the teamster's deal, but Sheffield showed a pair of aces. He won another four hands in a row, then dealt me a winning hand. I knew he had done it intentionally, somehow. He probably wanted to watch me and figure out my secret. I managed to deal myself a winning hand off the bottom of the deck, and won the pot. Blue threw his discarded hand down in pretend disgust.

I gathered the deadwood in, and found the ace of hearts where Blue had left it for me. This, I stashed on the bottom of the deck. By using Blue's discards, and my cup of coffee, I won four hands in a row, and began to rake in a pretty good pile of winnings. But it was too early to go for the big pot, and Blue was running low on money, so I gave him a signal we had agreed on before: I cupped my hands around the mug of coffee as if warming my fingers. This was his sign to bet high, for I was going to deal him a winning hand. I made sure I didn't deal Sheffield anything high, because I had no way of knowing what card or cards he might have slipped up his sleeve, or wherever it was that he kept them, but I knew that if he had stashed a card, it was probably going to be a big one. Blue whistled at his hand and began to bet high. He discarded two cards, and by logic I knew what they were. I dealt him three fives with an ace to boot. We both drove the betting up, and he won, which allowed him to stay in the game.

The evening wore on, and Sheffield and I managed to keep everyone in the game, though my pile and the gambler's continued to grow. We were still trying to figure each other out. Rosa brought me more coffee. I watched

Sheffield. I couldn't see how he was stashing his cards. I knew the answer was right in front of me. I had learned enough so-called magic tricks to know that his method had to be as simple as my trick of using the cup of coffee as a mirror. His hand never went near enough to his cuff to slip something up his sleeve. The only thing that seemed peculiar was his way of dragging a card all the way to the edge of the table before he picked it up to look at it.

Blue won the deal, and I took a break to go out back and relieve myself. When I came back, I had a fresh cup of hot black coffee. I sat down and played, and eventually won a hand. The timing was perfect. The betting had just about wiped out the soldier and teamster. I dealt two more hands that broke them both, and they got up from the table to retire.

"No hard feelings, gentlemen," I said, handing them each a coin. "Please have a drink on me."

Each man accepted, and walked to the bar. Now it was down to me, Sheffield, and Blue, and I had the deal. I decided it was time to make our move. I began dealing hand after winning hand to myself, and I drove up the betting even when the cards didn't call for it. I won a huge pot from Sheffield with three fives. He had three fours and an ace.

"That's a pretty tall bet for three fives," he remarked.

I smiled. "You hung right in there with three fours, yourself."

The pile of winnings began to heap up on my side of the table, and a small crowd gathered to watch the game. Twice more, I beat Sheffield, and he began to get angry. Now was the time to finish it. I gave Blue the sign, cupping my hands around the mug of coffee. By now I knew Luther Sheffield had an ace or two stashed somewhere at his disposal. If he wanted aces, I'd give him aces. I had seven cards stacked on the bottom of the deck the way I wanted them. I shuffled deep enough to keep them that way. Sheffield cut the deck, but I returned it. He watched me like a hawk, but didn't catch my sleight of hand.

From the bottom of the deck, I dealt the gambler an ace. Blue: the two of diamonds. I took something off the top for myself. It didn't matter what. Blue was going to win this hand, not me. To Sheffield, I dealt a second ace from the bottom. Blue: the three of diamonds. Again, I took my card from the top. Now, I dealt the rest of Sheffield's hand, and mine, from the top. Whenever I gave Blue a card, it came from the bottom, and he got the makings for a straight flush—the two through the six of diamonds. Now, even if Sheffield could produce four aces, Blue would win. We looked at our cards and bet, driving the wagers high.

Sheffield asked for one card, though I knew he didn't need it. I knew Blue needed nothing, but I looked at him as if I knew nothing of the kind. He just stared at his hand.

"Blue?" I said.

"Just a minute. I'm thinkin'."

I sighed.

"I'll take three cards," he said, putting three facedown on the table.

My heart pumped a load of dread into my stomach. What the hell was he doing? I had dealt him a perfect straight flush! But I knew I could say or do nothing other than pick up the deck and deal the three cards that would wreck this whole scheme for us. Slowly, I picked up the deck and, with much hidden regret, started to pull a card from the top.

"Wait," Blue said. He retrieved his three cards and rearranged them several times in his hand. "Oh, never mind, I'll just try my luck with these."

I sighed again, bigger this time, and more sincerely. I took one card for myself. My hand amounted to nothing. I didn't even have a pair. But I bet last, and when my turn came to raise, I shoved my whole pile of gold coins into the middle of the table. "This is for the whole game," I said. "No need to count. You can tell I've got more to lose than either of you. Just push in what you've got showing, and we'll call the bet even."

Blue shoved in the small pile he had left. Sheffield hesitated a few seconds, then added his stacks of gold, which amounted to just over twenty-seven hundred dollars. You may not believe that I could keep track of that, and stack the deck for two players at the same time, but I have mentioned, haven't I, that I am a genius? I'm not bragging. I should apologize rather than boast. To waste my intelligence on cheating at cards is more of a shame than an honor. But it sure was fun. I was about to outcheat a cheat.

It was up to Sheffield to show his hand first. He turned over four aces. Only two of them had come from my deck. He had pulled the other two from someplace unknown to me. "Four angels," he said, with more than a hint of arrogance in his voice. "A heavenly quartet. There's the hand to beat, boys."

I folded my hand and frowned, feigning absolute failure. "I can't do it."

Totally ignoring Blue Wiggins, Sheffield reached for the pile of winnings in the middle of the table.

"Not much, hombre," said Blue.

Sheffield froze, his hands around the pot.

Blue began showing his cards, one at a time, placing each on the table before him ceremoniously. First the two of diamonds, then the three, four, and five. Now he paused theatrically with the last card in his left hand. He raised it high over the table. I wondered what he was doing, until I saw his right hand moving toward his holstered Colt revolver. Sheffield's attention was fixed on the last card, his hands still around the pot that he already considered his. Blue had learned a thing or two from me about misdirection. He was ready to drop that card and cock his hammer.

The six of diamonds fell into place on that perfect fan of cards.

Sheffield looked at it. An enlightened glint of anger flared in his eyes, and he looked at me, instead of Blue Wiggins. He knew now that we had done this together.

"Like hell," he growled. He bolted backward and reached for his pocket pistol, but Blue had his Colt cocked and pointed in an instant.

I wheeled as I drew my revolver, jumping from my chair so quickly that I bumped the table and spilled my black coffee all over the cards. Behind me, I found the big bear of a bartender thumbing back the hammers of a double barrel he had produced from under the bar, and I let a bullet fly into the fancy mirror of the back bar behind him before he could get it aimed in my direction.

The loud report of my Colt and the shattering of the glass hushed everything in the gambling parlor. The white smoke from my pistol mingled with the gray tobacco smoke. A movement from the center of the room caught my eye, and I saw old John Hatcher appear from nowhere as he walked to the bar and took the bartender's shotgun away from him. I turned back to Luther Sheffield and saw him glaring at me. Blue's gun was only inches from his head, and Blue looked like he meant business. Now, I, too, covered the gambler with my Colt.

"The three of you," Sheffield growled. "This is robbery."

"No, this is poker," I said. "Blue won the pot. I suggest you allow him to collect."

"That hand is impossible."

"It's no more impossible than your four aces." I saw a hint of uncertainty in Sheffield's glare, so I leaned closer to him, and spoke loud enough for only him to hear. "Would you like for me to tell everyone here where you're getting those aces?"

It was a bluff. I had no idea how that slick gambler was producing those heavenly cards. But I am such a marvelous liar that I convinced Sheffield right then and there that I was on to him. It took him a few seconds, but he began to choke down his pride and anger, and regain his composure. He would need to get out of this with some dignity if he intended to keep playing cards here in his own gambling parlor. And, most important, he knew that he would never get out of this town alive if I divulged his secret methods of cheating. He had beaten too many men in the room at cards.

Slowly, Luther Sheffield's hand moved away from the pocket that held the pistol. "Gentlemen," he said, "forgive my haste. Those four aces must have charmed me right out of my senses. It's obvious that Mr. Wiggins has won the hand. And you, Messieurs Greenwood and Hatcher, may certainly feel free to escort him from this parlor as he collects his winnings and leaves. This game is now closed."

The speech made an impression on me. I had introduced myself to the gambler, but not John Hatcher or Blue. He had obviously asked about us since the brawl the night before, and knew who we were. He was warning me to get myself and my friends out of town, for he knew who we were, and how to find us.

Blue smiled as he returned his weapon to its holster. He took the coat from the back of his chair, spread it on the table and began heaping his winnings into it. He left fifty dollars in coin on the table. Having filled his coat, he gathered its edges and made it into a big sack which he lifted from the battlefield of his triumph.

"You left some," Sheffield remarked.

"For your trouble," Blue said. "And for the damages."

Sheffield tipped his hat with such poise that I had to admire him. It seemed he would survive this little setback to gamble again in Santa Fe. And he would win. And win. And keep winning until someone stuck a knife in him or shot him dead. At least, that's what I thought at the time. In reality, I could never have predicted what the future held in store for Luther Sheffield and me. Our lives would become entangled in the most peculiar ways.

Hatcher and I covered Blue's exit from the so-called parlor, and we stepped out into the cold New Mexico night. I started for my room at La Fonda, but Hatcher caught me by the sleeve.

"This way," he said. "Blue already moved your things to another room. We figured that gambler might have had you followed last night."

"Good thinking," I said.

Blue shook his makeshift sack of coins to make them jingle. He chuckled as we strode down the street.

"What are you gonna do with all that jack this time?" Hatcher said.

"I'm of a mind to make a rancher of myself. Get me some land like Maxwell and Kit done."

"Maybe you ought to take that little gal Rosa with you," Hatcher suggested. "Keep you company."

Blue shook his head. "No, John, she'll never make a rancher."

"Now, how do you know that?"

"She can't keep her calves together."

I groaned and laughed all at the same time, and we plowed ahead through the crisp mountain night.

SIX

Blue Wiggins and John Hatcher decided to take some of Blue's recovered gambling money, buy a herd of sheep, and make another drive to California. The rest of the money they buried at the hiding place where I always stashed my whiskey outside of Santa Fe. There were no banks in New Mexico back then, and there must have been millions of dollars stashed and buried here and there all over the territory. Some of it lies buried still, I'm sure.

"If we don't make it back from California," Blue said, "that gold is yours."

"I aim to come back," John Hatcher stated, as if offended.

They would spend the winter putting their herd together, and head west with the spring thaw. This, Blue hoped, would increase his holdings to the point that he could buy a sizable spread and start a cattle ranch. John Hatcher had already bought some land, but was hoping to add to his holdings. They left Santa Fe the next day, anxious to get about their venture.

I stayed, for I had other obligations. I had given Burnt Belly my word that I would return in two moons with trade goods and whiskey. I had lost only a couple of days helping Blue outcheat the cheater Luther Sheffield, so I still had plenty of time to collect my goods and get on with my own enterprises.

First, however, I had some letters of inquiry to write on behalf of Toribio Treviño, the Mexican boy I had ransomed from the Comanches. I began by writing the governor of Coahuila, since that was where Toribio had been captured, telling the governor the circumstances of Toribio's ordeal, as near as I knew them. Then I wrote to the postal authorities near Monterrey, asking them to deliver copies of the letter I had written to the governor to anyone they knew by the name of Treviño. I provided as many copies of the letter to the governor as I could make in one day, spending hours in the room John Hatcher had rented.

Finally, I ventured out to buy a meal. I remember paying for the meal, and leaving the cafe. There, my recollection ends. I woke up alone in a strange room—a small adobe room with no furniture, a washbasin on the floor. I was on a typical New Mexican mattress, covered with a worn Navaho blanket. I had been apprehensive of something like this happening, for the new moon was upon me, and the new moon always draws me irretrievably into sleep like a whirlpool drowns a bug.

This is my other curse. (The first being a genius.) I don't sleep like a normal man. During the full moon, I don't sleep at all for several days. During the quarter phases, I sleep a few hours every night, but I am tormented by nightmares and terrors that only insane men know. Then, as the new moon approaches, I am likely to fall asleep in the middle of the day. I may fall asleep walking, and continue walking, with my eyes open, yet asleep, for hours or miles. I may then wake up, exhausted instead of rested, and wonder where in the world I have wandered. The dogbane and moccasin flower Burnt Belly had taught me to use helped to make my sleep habits a little more normal, but sometimes I ran out, or got too busy to use them. And even when I used them as the old medicine man taught me, the power of the moon was still sometimes greater.

Once, while camping alone out on the plains as the new moon approached, I killed a jackrabbit to eat, and proceeded to roast it on a stick I held in my hand over a buffalo-chip fire. While monotonously turning the spit over the flames, my world went black, as if someone had blown out the flame to my brain. I woke up almost frozen to death, covered with snow, still turning that stick in my hands, though the jackrabbit had burned to a char and the fire had gone out. I had just enough presence of mind to roll myself in a buffalo robe before I plunged back into lost sleep.

So it was that I woke in Santa Fe in a strange room, thankful to be alive, but humiliated to have come to such a helpless state once again. When I wake from one of these sleeping binges, I can't just bound out of bed. First, my eyes open, but the rest of my body remains immovable, as if in the grip of rigor mortis. So I blinked my eyes for a few minutes, then began to feel some movement in my face. I was just starting to lift my head, when I heard a door open. A sudden sound can serve to charge my limbs and body with energy when waking from such a slumber, and the opening door did just that. I shot upright on the mattress and found the lovely Rosa entering the room.

"*Gracias a Dios,*" she said. "I thought you were going to die here."

"Where am I?"

"In my room. Don't worry. No one knows you are here."

I shook my head to clear my thoughts. "How long? How long have I been here?"

"Almost two days. You just walked in here. Lucky for you I was alone. You said some things, but you didn't make sense. You spoke Spanish, and English, and some other tongue I never heard at all."

"Two days?" I said. "What about . . . You know, what about your customers?"

"You have cost me a lot of money, but what could I do? You wouldn't wake up."

I sighed. It was embarrassing. "I'll make it up to you. I have money."

"I do not take charity," she said. "I always earn what I am paid." The next thing I knew Rosa was crawling into her bed with me. It took some wrestling to get out of there with my virtue intact, but I considered myself a married man, and besides, I had many things to attend to after sleeping so long.

So, as I collected my wits and my belongings, Rosa sat on the mattress and pouted. "Am I not good enough to share a bed with you?"

"I'm married."

"Most of my customers are married."

"Well, I guess I'm different."

She sniffed. "You are different, you bet. You are the differentest son of a bitch I ever met."

I paid Rosa what I would pay an innkeeper for two nights' lodging and got the hell out of there.

After posting my letters and collecting my whiskey hidden in the ponderosa pines above the city, I got out of Santa Fe and rode north into a high-country blizzard. I stopped once between Santa Fe and Taos to build a big fire so that I could warm myself. There was little risk of my fire attracting hostile Indians or outlaws. Indians always had sense enough to hole up during bad weather, and most outlaws I ever knew were fair-weather criminals. So I used the fire to warm myself and dry my snow-dampened clothes as I ate the last of my pemmican. Then I pressed on through the dark toward Taos. I knew the trails well, having ridden them all as General Kearney's top courier during the Mexican War.

At dawn on the third day of travel, I came to a place called Martin's Mill, owned by old Roy Martin. At his mill, Roy Martin spent most of his time making a corn liquor known as Taos Lightning. I bought six kegs of the stuff, packed it on my mules, and continued on toward William Bent's trading post at the Big Timbers on the Arkansas River.

It would have made sense to stay warm in Taos that night, but I rode into the mountains to spend a cold night in camp. Sometimes even a genius, by foolishness or design, must do that which makes no sense. I had once fallen in love with a Taos girl who ended up marrying somebody else. She had had no choice in the matter. Marriages were arranged among the old Mexican families in New Mexico, and men who interfered had been known to die of mysterious causes—like bullet wounds. Anyway, it was better for everyone if I stayed away from Taos. My broken heart had mended, and there was no sense in reopening the wound. I rode into the mountains.

It was cold, but the sky was spectacular. I rolled myself in a buffalo robe and watched the constellations slowly migrate westward, only the fog of my own breath standing between me and the light of stars distant beyond the comprehension of even a genius. I managed to sleep a few hours.

I rose before the first hint of dawn, and took to the trail by the time I had light enough to find my way. Major had to break through snow up to his chest crossing the divide, but he plowed on with never a touch from my spurs, blasting the air ahead of us with the warm vapor from his nostrils.

Once we crossed the divide of the Sangre de Cristos, conditions improved on the east slope. The snow was not as deep, and the late morning sun beamed down at an angle that warmed my thighs through my leather chaps. I rode on downhill until dusk and camped on a southern slope where the snow had melted and the ground had dried. I had never traveled this particular way, but I knew exactly where I was, and I knew how to get where I was going. Another two days in the saddle would fetch William Bent's new trading post.

I made a small fire, Indian style, and roasted some elk meat Roy Martin had given me. I put the fire out once I had eaten, for I didn't care to attract attention from roving hostiles, whether they be Indian, Mexican, or white. I entertained myself by practicing sleight-of-hand tricks in the dark until I got too cold. Then I rolled myself in my buffalo robe and recited Lord Tennyson until I fell asleep. I had some frightful nightmares, for I had run out of the dogbane Burnt Belly had traded to me. I was looking forward to getting back to the camps on the Canadian so I could replenish my supply.

My paint horse, Major, and my two mules were tired when I crossed the Arkansas River, but they waded into the icy waters and swam the narrow channel easily. After building a fire to dry my clothes and warm my shivering bones, I rode past the remains of Bent's Old Fort, and remembered the days I had spent there when the place had been a working trading post—the largest and grandest the West ever knew. It had stood as a great adobe castle on the plains for over fifteen years, a rendezvous for the most intrepid explorers and voyagers the frontier had ever produced, a battlement with walls so imposing that it had never been seriously threatened by any war party or army. William Bent, its builder and master, had blown it to bits to keep the government from condemning it, as he and I had destroyed Fort Adobe on the Canadian.

Downstream I rode, looking for the first of the huge cottonwoods that gave name to the place called Big Timbers—for decades a landmark on the north bank of the Arkansas. I knew from talk handed down the trail that William was building a new stone trading post at this location. About an hour before dusk I began to ride among the old cottonwoods—huge, gnarled sentinels with bark like old scabs and limbs lying around them as if the monster trees had shaken them off—huge limbs that were themselves the size of respectable trees.

Though his head hung low in fatigue, Major quickened his trot, for he knew the ancient campground and rendezvous called Big Timbers meant rest, food, and warmth for him. Major and I had ridden and camped here in the past with Comanches and Cheyennes. The sun had just disappeared, pulling with it the last of the light from the sky, when I saw the dark outline of William's new trading post. I actually heard the workers chipping stone and hammering timbers together before I saw the place. The placement of the fort was brilliant. Its back stood against a bluff, and it could be approached from only one direction, up the well-beaten trace I now rode, made wide to allow for the passage of William's huge freight wagons that came from Kansas each summer.

As I approached two large cottonwoods flanking the wagon trace, I saw two men in sombreros step into view from behind them. *"Alto!"* one ordered. Major tossed his head in the air when he saw them, for he was not yet too tired to alert me of danger.

I reined him in, and raised a hand in a friendly manner.

"*Quién es?*"

"*Me llamo Honoré Greenwood. Soy un compañero de Señor Bent.*"

"Greenwood," one of the guards repeated. He turned to the other. "*Está bien. Es el Comanchero.*"

I smiled. The guard knew who I was. "Comanchero" was a title in which I took much pride, for only few men could ride into Comancheria and ride back alive. Fewer still could turn a profit from such an enterprise. Most of them were Mexicans from the centuries-old Spanish outposts of Santa Fe, Taos, and Albuquerque. Among white men, Comancheros were few. William Bent. Uncle Dick Wootton. Ceran St. Vrain. John Fisher. Kit Carson. John Hatcher. And me, Honoré Greenwood.

One of the guards whistled a message up to the trading post through his teeth, and they let me pass. Major and the two mules trudged on up the snow-mudded trace, the stone building ahead looming ever larger. It was not one-quarter the size of William's old adobe palace, but it impressed me nonetheless—such an edifice this far beyond the frontier. The Mexican stonemasons and carpenters were finishing for the day, for their light had all but completely faded.

Just before I reached the entrance to the post, a boy darted across the road before me, then slid to a stop when he saw me coming. He hunkered behind a cottonwood stump, like a cat waiting for his prey. I grinned. He was dressed like a little Cheyenne boy, and he was carrying a practice bow with blunted arrows, with which Cheyenne boys learned to shoot. I figured him for no more than five or six years old.

Pretending I had not seen him, I rode on past the stump, though Major knew the boy was there, and he rolled a rattling warning from his nostrils as he cocked his head sideways at the hiding place. Suddenly, the boy jumped on top of the stump, causing Major to toss his tired head in alarm.

"*Ve-ho-e!*" he shouted—the Cheyenne term for "white man." With that, he let fly one of his little blunt arrows that hit me in the cheek and drew blood. It came near putting my eye out. Before I knew it, he had popped Major in the head with another arrow, causing him to rear. Had he been less fatigued, he might have thrown me clean off. Another arrow thumped me in the head behind the ear, and another hit Major's rump, making him kick and leap forward.

"Hena-ahne!" I shouted in Cheyenne. *Enough!* I wheeled Major and saw the boy standing in shock. He had not expected me to know a word of his language. He jumped from his stump and ran toward the hide lodges standing below the stone trading post, leaving his practice arrows on the field of battle.

I calmed my stock and rode on toward the stone building, rubbing my cheek and the back of my head. As I approached, I saw the familiar silhouette of William Bent walking out toward me, backlit by the flames from torches and cookfires. He carried a shotgun. He had heard the whistle from the guards below and was coming to greet the new arrival.

"Welcome," he said, cradling the double-barrel across his forearm. "What's your business?"

"Robes and ponies, mostly, William. It's Orn'ry Greenwood."

He stopped in his tracks, lowered the muzzle of the scattergun. "I might have known. Thought it was you by the cargo on your mules. But I didn't want to offend some other whiskey peddler by calling him by your name."

I laughed.

"Well, get down."

As I dismounted, William shouted orders in Spanish, and men came to take my animals to feed and shelter. I knew they would be stripped of their burdens, rubbed dry, and fed, and this made me feel good. I patted Major on the rump as a Mexican *trabajador* led him away. I followed the gesture of William's shotgun barrel and looked gratefully upon the flames that I knew would soon be warming me. We walked toward an opening in the stone wall—a portal that had not yet been framed for a wooden door. I paused before I followed William into the room, and turned to look at the post. The stone-walled buildings formed three sides of a square that backed up to the bluff to the north. The fourth side would remain open, facing the river valley to the south. It was a right smart trading post, and I admired William for its location and design. I turned back into the room and found a roaring fire awaiting me in a stone fireplace large enough to roast half a beef. I began shedding my outer garments as I walked toward the heat.

"What happened to your face?" William said. "Looks like you damn near jobbed your eye out."

I touched my wound and saw blood on my fingers. I chuckled as I threw my coat and leggings on the floor, and told William of the Indian attack

I had recently survived at the battle of the cottonwood stump. As he listened, his face darkened, and he stomped outside without a word when I finished the account. I regretted bringing it up now. I had thought he would find it amusing. I warmed myself by the fire for a few minutes, until William reappeared, dragging a boy by the arm. The boy was dressed like a Cheyenne child, but I saw the lighter skin and blue eyes of a half-breed now.

"Was this him?" William demanded.

I shrugged. "I can't be sure, William. It was almost dark. There wasn't any harm done, anyway."

He turned and towered over the child. "I'll ask you one more time, boy. Did you shoot that man in the face with your bow and arrows?"

The boy's expression showed more anger than fear. He looked me right in the eye, then smiled wickedly at the wound he had made on my cheek. *"Hehe-eh,"* he said.

William shook the boy by the arm. "In English!"

"Yes."

"Yes, *sir!*"

"Yes, sir."

With that, William whipped off his belt and struck the boy five times across his rear end. "That's for shooting arrows at your father's friend." He laid five more blows across the boy's rump, bringing tears to his eyes. "That's for lying to me about it down in the lodge. Now, get up to your room and go to bed!"

As the boy stormed out, I looked awkwardly at the floor.

"I'm sorry for the boy's behavior, Mr. Greenwood," the weary old trader said.

"No need to apologize. I thought it was funny at the time."

"Well, I don't think it's funny. You have no idea what kind of mischief that boy can get into."

"That's little Charles?" I asked, remembering the toddler I had seen last time I visited William.

"Named after my dead brother. He's got a ways to go before he makes a man like Charles, though."

"Well, he's just a boy," I said. "You should have seen me at that age. I was a holy terror." I noticed William scowling at the doorway through which little Charles had left. "Not that I could ever accomplish what your brother did."

"Not many could. You and I both know that. Little Charlie is a half-breed, anyway, and I don't see a half-breed coming to be a governor or anything like it. Folks wouldn't have it. Guess I should have thought of that before I took myself a Cheyenne wife. I've brung five half-breed children into a world that's got no use for them."

"Where are the older children?" I asked, trying to lighten the mood.

"I took them all to Westport to put them in a proper school. I thought Charles just a little too young, so I kept him back here for another year or two. I never knew how much trouble the older ones kept him out of. Now, it's just me and Yellow Woman, and she just lets him run afoul like the little half-breed that he is. I can't build this place and look after him, too. He spends all his time down in the Cheyenne camp, listening to the older boys bad-mouth the white man. He's turned into a little hellion, Mr. Greenwood."

"Oh, he'll outgrow it," I said.

"I hope to God he does. It's plain I can't beat it out of him."

The conversation lagged between us. The fire popped a small glowing ember out onto the hearth. I glanced at William's face, haggard and drawn. I had seen him look this tired just once before—after the murder of his brother, Charles, the governor of the Territory of New Mexico.

"How's trade?" I asked.

"The Indian trade has just about dried up. You're the only trader still doin' any good to speak of."

"Why build this post if the trade's dying?" I asked. "Why not turn to ranching like Kit and Lucien have done?"

"I've got my eye on a place I aim to ranch. That'll come in time. For now, this place will serve as a warehouse for the annuities the government has promised the Indians. Buffalo has gotten so scarce the Cheyennes and Arapahos are starvin' out there on the plains. Beaver Tom is gonna use this place as headquarters for his Indian agency. I've got to take care of my wife's people as long as I can, Kid. I owe them that much."

I nodded. "How about the freight business?"

"I got some pretty good government contracts to haul supplies from the states to the forts. Whatever space is left over in the wagons, I fill with my own merchandise for the stores in Santa Fe and Taos, so I do all right. If I was you, I'd worry more about myself. What do you aim to do when the Comanche trade falls through?"

The question somewhat startled me. Genius that I was, I had not admitted to myself that my commerce with the Comanches would someday come to an end. "You don't think the Comanche trade's in trouble, do you?" I asked.

William must have thought I was an idiot. "In trouble? Hell, it's doomed, Kid. You'd better start thinking about securing your own place to do a little farming and ranching when the Comanches are all killed by cholera and smallpox and bullets, or herded onto some sorry reservation. If I was you, I'd roll those whiskey barrels into the river and do what Kit and Lucien did. I'd herd some sheep to California and make enough to buy myself a spread."

"I promised Burnt Belly I'd bring the whiskey to the Crossing on the Canadian before the next moon."

"Don't you want to see California? I hear it's quite a place."

"I've got a Comanche wife waiting for me."

"Then quit her before you sire some half-breed son. What kind of a life do you think a child like that will have? Don't you understand what's happening?"

"I understand more than you think," I said. "That's why I like the Comanche trade."

"Why's that?"

"Because I *don't* understand it. Herding sheep to California—that's simple. Maybe it's a long hard trail, but it's still a simple business. That would bore the tar out of me, William. Just like every other business I know of. It's all too easy. You buy low and sell high. You cut costs, increase profits. Too easy. I wouldn't last a week. But the Comanche trade . . ." I shook my head at the elusiveness of it all. "I have no idea which way it will turn from one second to the next."

"More than likely it will involve the loss of your scalp. I can get you a piece of the Vigil–St. Vrain Land Grant, Kid. Enough to run a hundred head of cattle and some sheep to boot. I can get it for you and you can pay it off as you go."

I stared at the bare floor of the empty room. This was a prospect to ponder. I tried to envision myself farming and ranching in the foothills of the Sangre de Cristos—roping yearlings, digging irrigation ditches, following a plow, building corrals. I could see myself doing it, all right, but not here. Beautiful though this place might be—where the mountains cast the rivers out onto the plains—my soul yearned for different soil. It was the Crossing on the Canadian River that longed to nourish me in life and cradle me in death. A magical valley in the midst of the vast plains where springs issued sparkles of water and stalks of grass reached skyward in legions innumerable. Where timber twined along the rivulets and game flocked as if mesmerized. Where bluffs and breaks ducked the hard winter winds, and shady trees softened the summer glare.

"I've got my eye on another place," I admitted.

"Good for you. Where 'bouts?"

"The Crossing on the Canadian."

William did not scoff, as I had expected. Instead, he considered the prospect realistically. "Well," he said at last, "first there's the Comanche problem."

"That's not a problem to me. I'm one of them now. I speak their language. I'm beginning to understand their customs. I'm making my own bow and arrows. As long as it's Comanche soil, the Crossing is as good as mine, anyway."

"It won't be Comanche soil forever."

"Maybe the government will make it a reservation for them."

William shook his head. "That won't happen. The Crossing belongs to the state of Texas, not the federal government. The Texans hate the Comanches. They'll kill every one or drive them clean out of the state. Even if they do set up some kind of state reservation, it won't be on a piece of choice bottom land like the Crossing. When the Comanches are pushed off of it, you'll have to buy it from the state. You can't homestead it like federal land. Texas got to keep its own public land as part of the annexation agreement in forty-five. The only way to get it is to purchase it."

"Then I'd better start saving my money," I said.

"I'd tell you to buy it now, except that I know it hasn't been surveyed yet. You'll have to wait, but you're in a good position to get it, if you've got the money saved up when the Comanches are pushed off. As soon as it's surveyed, you ride to Austin and buy it. You're one of the few white men that even knows that place exists, Mr. Greenwood, and I'd just as soon see you own it as anybody. It may take five years or twenty to solve the Comanche problem, but you'd best be ready when the time comes, if you want it."

"I do," I said. I wasn't sure I wanted it that way, but some things were beyond my control. Talking with William Bent always seemed to help me find direction in my wanderings. I would possess the Crossing as a Comanche as long as I could—and help them hold it through all the diplomacy I could muster—as William had helped the Cheyennes hold on to the Arkansas Valley around Big Timbers for decades. But when the Comanches lost their hold on the Canadian, I would be prepared to buy the

Crossing where the ruins of old Fort Adobe now languished. There, I would forever welcome visitations by any of my Comanche friends who might have survived the onslaught of the white man, but I had to wonder if any of them would survive at all.

Anyway, I was thinking way too far ahead. Right now my net worth consisted of a herd of Indian ponies, eight barrels of whiskey, and a few personal effects. I was a long way from becoming a land baron.

"If it doesn't work out," William said, "I can still get you a piece of the Vigil–St. Vrain Land Grant. Me and Charles both had an interest in it, and I know Charles would approve of your taking some of his."

I nodded my gratitude. I might get scalped out there on the plains, but I would not die of starvation among my friends.

I stayed with William for two days, helping him hang the heavy wooden doors his men had built for the many rooms that faced in toward the trading post's courtyard. I was ready to get back to the Comanches with the whiskey, but knew I should rest my stock for a couple of days. Besides, I liked building things with my hands, and I felt good about spending the time with William.

On the third morning, I woke up early and donned my Indian attire—moccasins, leggings, and buckskin shirt. I parted my hair in the middle, Comanche style, and braided both sides. I stuck an eagle feather in the hair pulled tight at the back of my head, and wrapped a warm blanket about my shoulders. I packed my mules with help from the Mexican workers, and made ready to leave.

"I'll follow tomorrow with the trade wagons," William said. "I need to get away from here for a while."

"I'll tell the Comanches you're coming. They'll be honored."

"Mind what Kit and John Hatcher taught you."

"I'll be careful. I'll make cold camps all the way to the Canadian."

We shook hands and I rode, trailing my mules. As I passed through the Cheyenne village, I happened to see little Charlie Bent running among the tipis ahead of me, his bow in hand. I began to fear a re-creation of his sneak attack of three days before. But when I came near to his hiding place behind a deer hide that was stretched upright on a platform, I caught his eye, and saw no arrow aiming my way. I attributed this at first to the thrashing his father had given him for the last attack. Then it dawned on me that perhaps he was letting me pass unmolested now because I wore the dress of an Indian.

"I'll see you again, Charlie," I said, stopping Major to speak with the boy.

He did not reply.

"Stavasevo-matse," I said, repeating the farewell in Cheyenne.

"Stavasevo-matse." The boy stepped out from behind the deerskin.

"Mind your mother and father."

His boyish face looked far too serious. His reply came in Cheyenne: "I mind my mother." Then he ran away.

SEVEN

After ten days of hard travel, I neared the Crossing on the Canadian River. The only humans I had seen during the trip were the members of a distant party of mounted Indians, whom I avoided. I had spent my nights in camp those ten days fastening iron arrow points and split turkey feathers onto my dogwood shafts with sinew stripped from the backstrap of a deer I had killed on the Arkansas. Now my bow and arrows were finished, and I looked forward to showing them to Burnt Belly for his approval, for I had given them a final straightening with the grooved rock the old shaman had loaned to me.

As I approached the canyon rim that would overlook the Comanche village, I arranged the bow and new arrows in the quiver slung across my back. Major knew we were close to home, and stepped lively as we approached the Canadian breaks. I made him stop at the rim, so I could take in the view and judge the attitude of things in camp.

I looked for my own lodge first, and saw it standing where it had been when I left, two moons ago. The pole had fallen off one of the wind flaps, and I wondered why Hidden Water hadn't put it back. I was sure she hadn't done much housekeeping since I had been gone. Still, thoughts of my reunion with her had begun to stir within, and I looked forward to this night in our lodge.

Scanning the area downstream, I noticed that the Nokonis had vanished. This did not surprise me. They had come this far north to hunt buffalo and trade with the Quahadis, but I knew they would be anxious to get back to their warmer ranges away down toward the Texas settlements.

I lingered on the rim for another minute or two, looking over the beautiful Canadian River Valley that widened here at the Crossing. Again, I felt overwhelmed by a sense of belonging. This place was home—a rich basin that collected water, sunshine, and fertile silt from past floods and converted them into graze for buffalo, browse for deer, and multitudinous varieties of seeds and fruits that fed still more species of animals. Here prairies intermingled with wooded draws, creating the edges of timber that provided habitat for thousands of wild turkeys. Here the beaver dams collected running water into pools that drew flocks of migrating ducks, geese, swans, cranes, and even pelicans. Fish darted in the streams, ranging from flashy perch no larger than a child's hand to lumbering catfish the size of a grown man's leg. Here, a man with wits and ammunition, or even a wooden club and a set of snares, could eat year-round.

Every day provided a different glimpse of nature's magnificence. Bears lumbered. Coyotes skulked. Wolves prowled. Mountain lions stalked upon herds of fleet antelope. Eagles swooped and snagged fish from the river's surface. Diving hawks scattered coveys of quail. Owls flew silently along the edges of the night. And then the buffalo would come. The Crossing funneled them here, where they could migrate with ease over the mischievous Canadian. They would pour into this valley for days, converting nutritious grass into fertile dung, then they would disappear for months or even years before returning to graze on the replenished grasses.

It was ironic that I had to carry whiskey here to preserve this place as a peaceful campground. But I knew from experience that if I did not bring the liquor, and control its consumption, someone else who cared far less for the place or the souls who called it home would bring enough cursed alcohol here to destroy the entire Comanche nation. And so it fell to me— a man who had never even gotten drunk—to supply the Indians with intoxicating drink. Well, if I had to do it, I might as well do it in style.

Turning Major around to the first of my two mules, I untied my deerskin violin case from the pack saddle, and carefully pulled out the Stradivarius and its bow. I took a few moments to tune by ear, then placed the chinpiece against my jaw. I could control my mount with leg cues, in the Comanche way, so I let the reins remain draped over Major's neck, and told him to step off the rim, following the well-worn trail into the valley.

Within seconds, a young warrior guarding the ponies had spotted me, and shouted across the valley. The news traveled quickly by word of mouth through the village, and excited men and women began to step from their lodges and gravitate toward the northern side of the camp. I played an old sailing song I had learned years before, crossing the Atlantic on a square-rigger. The song was called "The Girls Around Cape Horn" and it provided just the jaunty mood I needed to announce my arrival home.

When I reached the edge of the village, warriors began to hoot their battle cries, and the whole camp came to life. I looked for Hidden Water. She usually liked to greet me when I arrived like this—the center of attention and the bringer of celebration. But as yet I could not find her in the crowd that grew around me. I played and smiled and rode at a jaunty trot, arriving in front of Chief Shaved Head's lodge, where I would unload the whiskey. I ended "The Girls Around Cape Horn" with a flourish and sprang from Major to receive the Comanche cheer of "Yee-yee-yee-yee-yee-yee-yee!" Shaved Head came out of his lodge to greet me and to see how much whiskey I had brought. He looked as though he had been napping in his tipi.

By now I expected Hidden Water to be at my side, but she had not arrived. I could sense some unspoken amusement from the crowd, but it was not considered dignified to act concerned over a missing wife, so I carried on with my chores, untying the hitches that held the whiskey kegs on the mules. I asked a few promising young braves to take hold of the kegs as I untied them so they would not drop to the ground and burst.

Still, Hidden Water had not come to me.

As I went to unpack the second mule, the old shaman, Burnt Belly, came to my side. Stepping close to me, he said in a low voice, "Do not ask about her. I will tell you in time."

I sensed he had done this to save me some kind of embarrassment. I guessed that Hidden Water had done something to shame me, so I determined to act as if I didn't even notice her absence until Burnt Belly could inform me. Still, I couldn't help but wonder: Why wasn't she here? Was she hiding? Had she left? With whom?

"*Aho,*" I said, as if Burnt Belly had merely come to greet me. "I have brought you the medicine you wanted, grandfather." I took a small flask of good store-bought whiskey from my saddlebag and handed it to the old man. He smiled and held the flask aloft for everyone to see.

"Yee-yee-yee-yee-yee-yee-yee!" sang the crowd.

"Listen," I said, raising my hands. "I have brought the white man's whiskey so that my people will celebrate my return. I will bargain with any man who wishes to have some. Bring your best ponies, and your finest robes to trade. But do not trade everything you have. In three sleeps, Owl Man will come with wagons loaded with all the things you warriors need, and all the things your women want. There will be kettles, knives, axes, and hoop iron for arrow points. There will be cloth and beads and ribbons. Blankets and shirts and coats. There will be gunpowder and salt and tobacco. Sugar and honey. Looking glasses and red ocher to paint your faces. This is the time to be happy. First, we will feast. Then you will all drink!"

The warriors rent the air with their wild screams. Chief Shaved Head took charge of the whiskey barrels, having the young warriors line them up on the ground in front of his lodge door. Now it was time for me to go to work. The warriors formed a line, starting with the most decorated men. My friend Kills Something stood fifth in this line. Though older men fell in behind him, he had earned his place as one of the elite, and would someday become a great leader if he survived another few years of raiding and fighting. All of the men in line were considered leaders of their families, and would bargain not just for themselves, but for their brothers, fathers, sons, nephews, and in-laws. The first in line, of course, was Chief Shaved Head.

Shaved Head's appearance was unusual among Comanches because he actually shaved one side of his head as instructed in a vision he had received. This produced a distinctive scalp that his enemies forever sought to separate from his skull. That scalp was likely to make a fine trophy someday for some Apache, Pawnee, Mexican, Texan, or American, for Shaved Head did not intend to die with gray hair.

I placed a large metal cup on top of one of the barrels. This would be the unit of measurement for our bargaining.

"I will have ten cups," Shaved Head said, holding up ten fingers.

My eyes widened in surprise, for though he was chief, his family was rather small, and that was a lot of whiskey for just a few people. I guessed that he was planning on sharing the whiskey with his three wives. "What will you trade?"

"Ponies."

"How many?"

"Ten cups. Ten ponies."

I smiled. Bargaining with Comanches was easy as long as you didn't get greedy with them. A white man would make a low offer and be prepared to bargain upward. This was shameful in the Comanche culture. The Comanches believed a man should flaunt his wealth. Moreover, he should exhibit his complete confidence in acquiring new wealth. Shaved Head was a proud man. He would not think of making a trifling offer in front of his whole camp.

I nodded at his bargain. "A pony for each cup is a very good offer, and more than I expected. But you are a great chief who will get more ponies on the next raid."

"If I do not, it is because I will die carrying battle to our enemies."

"I only need to know which ten ponies to take from your herd."

Shaved Head looked away from me as if to dismiss the triviality of the suggestion. "You pick. My nephew holds my herd downstream, where there is good grass. I have over three hundred horses. You may take any ten you like."

I offered my hand to seal the deal—a tradition the Comanches had learned from Europeans, and one they understood represented a covenant of personal honor.

"Wife!" Shaved Head turned toward his wife's tipi, where she stood at the opening. "Pour the water out of my best canteen—the one you made from the bladder of the buffalo I killed on the last hunt. I will fill it soon with firewater!"

The warriors sent their war cries skyward and the next man stepped up to make his bargain. Shaved Head would remember how many cups he had bargained for, and would get them later. But before the drinking started, every man would have a chance to make a whiskey deal. Then there would be a feast. Then, and only then, would the headmen bring their vessels around to the kegs to fill them. By this time, I would be camped somewhere down the valley to keep away from the drunken revelry, for a white man—even one considered an adopted member of the tribe—was a tempting target for a drunken Comanche. Hopefully Hidden Water would be in camp with me, though she still had not shown herself. I was anxious to get my whiskey trading done so Burnt Belly could tell me what had happened with her.

The next warrior was named Mexican Horse. He stepped forward and said, "Five cups."

"What will you trade?"

"Three buffalo robes, and a lodge pole for your wind flap. There is something wrong with the one that was there, for it has fallen off and no one has put it back."

The crowd murmured behind Mexican Horse, and I knew he was trying to embarrass me because my wife had not taken care of my lodge while I was gone. This, too, was the Comanche way. A weakness or shortcoming of any sort was pointed out instead of politely overlooked. Perhaps you think you've seen small towns where everyone knows everyone else's business. You should try living in a Comanche camp. Privacy is as thin as the buffalo-hide walls of the lodges. If you have a problem, you deal with it immediately or suffer the ongoing ridicule of your neighbors.

My trading career with this village would have been over had I let Mexican Horse get away with embarrassing me, so I met him head-on. "If you have something to say about my lodge, say it plainly," I insisted. "I have been away getting the trade goods the elders wanted, and I haven't been lying around camp looking up at my neighbors' wind flaps. Tell me what you mean by offering me a lodge pole."

This surprised Mexican Horse a little, but he wasn't about to back down now. "The pole for your wind flap lies on the ground because your wife has left your lodge. She went south with a warrior from the Nokonis."

This was a hell of a way to learn that my so-called wife had run off with another man, but I knew better than to let any show of emotion cross my face. "The concerns of this camp are more important than any woman who runs away from it," I announced. "First I will make the deals the elders have asked me to make for the whiskey. Then I will handle my own problems. I have no use for your lodge pole. What else do you have to offer?"

"A pony and a mule," Mexican Horse said. "You can ride the pony to the Nokonis and bring your wife back on the mule."

The people of the village burst into laughter.

"If I do not bring her back, that mule will be loaded with robes and other valuable things that are worth more than the woman. Right now I do not care if she stays with the Nokonis, as long as the man who took her pays me well for her."

Mexican Horse started to say something else, but Kills Something spoke up from behind him: "Enough about that woman." This was a remarkable thing for him to say, for Hidden Water was Kills Something's sister. "First we feast and drink. Then I will go with Plenty Man to deal with that runaway woman and see that he gets her back, or gets what he wants in trade for her."

This settled the matter for the time being, and the whiskey trading went on. As I made my deals, the women began to return to their lodges and their cook fires to prepare food for the feast.

I knew from previous experience how many cups of whiskey each barrel contained. Allowing a few cups for spillage, I sold all the liquor within a couple of hours, bartering the last cups one at a time to young warriors who had no families and just wanted to swap a hide or something for a cup of the intoxicating brew. I remembered what each man owed me. My memory has always been perfect. Besides, the Comanches were habitually honest in trade deals, and no man would attempt to cheat me. I would collect my earnings in a day or two, when the ill effects of the firewater had worn off.

By the time the whiskey was all traded, the good smells of food filled the air. Buffalo tongue and hump meat roasted on sticks suspended above the coals. Delicacies such as boiled calf stomach and broiled liver graced almost every fire. Women threw buffalo bones in the embers, then cracked them open with rocks to scrape out the melted marrow. The wives who had traded for iron skillets fried strips of venison in bear fat.

"You will come and eat at my lodge," Kills Something said. "My wife makes plenty of food."

"Gracias," I said. I walked with Kills Something to his lodge and his wife handed me a piece of rawhide to use as a plate. On this she heaped a thick stew made of buffalo meat, seasoned with wild onion, salt, peppers, and some herbs she had collected. Kills Something gave me a spoon fashioned from the horn of a buffalo. Before we ate, he offered a morsel of the food to the sky, then buried it in a small hole he gouged in the ground with a digging stick. Now that he had made offerings of thanks to Father Sun and Mother Earth, we could dig in.

I hadn't eaten much on my long ride from William's new fort, so I devoured the plate of stew and asked for more. I ate until I thought I would burst. With my hunger satisfied, all I could think of was my empty lodge and my missing wife. I felt guilty for some reason, though it was she who had run off. Certainly some of it must have been my fault. I had failed her as a husband somehow.

Perhaps my guilt stemmed from the fact that I knew I never should have taken Hidden Water as a wife in the first place. Kills Something had talked me into it. He had wanted us to be brothers-in-law so that he could assure a safe source of trade goods once he became chief. It was a marriage of commerce, not love. I admit that I had been attracted to Hidden Water from the moment I saw her. Few men would not. But did I ever love her? I had tried, but at best I could only hope that I would someday learn to love her. Now that hope was gone, and I was filled with a sense of failure that I dared not express to any of my Comanche friends. Comanches did not accept failure.

I knew what I had to do. I must follow Hidden Water. I would speak to her. If she wanted to stay with her new lover, I would have to exact some kind of payment from him, or challenge him to battle. If she wanted to come back with me, I would take her, but I doubted I could do this without fighting the warrior she had run away with. If she did come back to Shaved Head's village, I would be expected to thrash her soundly with a stick in front of the entire village to punish her for her disrespect. Some warriors might even insist that I cut off the end of her nose. None of this appealed to me.

Kills Something must have known what was on my mind. "My sister brings shame to our village," he said. "I wanted to go after her when she left, but Shaved Head and Burnt Belly agreed that you should be the one to go."

"It is my problem."

"She is my sister. I will go with you. Sleep this night, then we will go."

I nodded, then rose and walked away. The feasting was about over. The drinking would soon start. I didn't like watching an Indian camp in the throes of drunkeness, for fights would break out and blood would spill. Some men would abuse their women. The usual Comanche dignity would transmogrify into something bizarre and ugly. And this was my fault, for I had brought the whiskey. Yet the elders had asked for it, and had I not brought it, some other whiskey trader would have brought four times the amount of alcohol, and totally impoverished the village.

I avoided my empty lodge and went to catch a fresh horse, leaving Major to rest and graze in the valley. I rode downstream, out of earshot of the drunken debauchery that was about to erupt in camp. I would roll myself in a buffalo robe and catch a few hours of long-overdue sleep. I welcomed the prospect. It was better than worrying about my runaway wife.

EIGHT

I woke to the crisp winter smells of fresh air and forest mulch. I heard wind whispering through bare branches. For January, the morning felt warm. I opened my eyes. The valley seemed peaceful. Then I remembered Hidden Water and wished I could go back to sleep.

I rose, gathered my weapons, and rolled my robe. When I arrived at the village, I found a boy tending my herd of horses near the camp. This herd did not include all the ponies I had acquired in trade for whiskey, for I had yet to choose them. I reasoned that Kills Something had told this boy to gather my ponies so that I could pick the ones I wanted to ride south-ward. I also found a large pile of well-tanned buffalo hides stacked near my lodge, in addition to a few other things I had traded for, including a new pair of mocassins, a deerskin shirt, and the raw hide of an elk that was good for patching things.

Kills Something was waiting at my lodge, his pony staked beside him. He rose to his feet when he saw me. *"Tsuh?"* he said. The word meant "yes," but here he was asking me if I was ready.

"I must move these hides and other things into my lodge before we leave."

"I will tell my wife and her sisters to do it. Catch your horse."

"I need to eat."

"I have food for two days packed in a bag."

I sighed, and looked around the beautiful valley. I kicked off my old, worn mocassins and tried on the new ones I had traded for a cup of whiskey. They fit perfectly. I took off the soiled deerskin shirt I had been wearing for days and days, and put on the new, soft, golden one with remarkably long fringes on the sleeves. This had cost me two cups of whiskey. I took my war bridle and went to choose a horse from my herd. I also picked a couple of extra mounts so I would be assured a fresh horse every day on the trip.

In less than two hours after my waking, I was mounted and crossing the Canadian River to begin my search for my runaway wife. I had my brother-in-law and friend, Kills Something, by my side and I knew he would ride through hell with me before he would desert me. Now that I was riding, moving, and taking action, the task did not seem so ominous.

Worry is the greatest natural waste of time known to humankind. If a problem can be solved by taking action, then there is no need to worry. If a problem cannot be solved, then all the worry in the world will not help. Perhaps you know this from your own life, your own experiences. Think back to the things that have worried you in the past. Did the worry help? No. Did you take action and solve the problem? Good. Did you find the problem hopelessly unsolvable? That's too bad, but your worrying did not accomplish anything.

Simplistic? Yes. I admit that I was still wasting my time with worry as I rode south with Kills Something. I'm as human as you. But at least I was looking my reason for worry right in its ugly face and saying to it, figuratively if not out loud, "I am coming to do battle with you."

The Nokonis ranged south of the Quahadis, about five days' ride for Comanche horsemen, who could easily cover thirty miles in a day. We expected to find them along the Wichita River. As we rode, a thought began to creep into my mind. I actually wanted to get rid of Hidden Water. I realized that I was not in love with Hidden Water and never would be. I just wanted out of my Comanche marriage. The question was how to make that happen while still retaining my prestige as an Indian trader and an adopted Quahadi Comanche. I reasoned that my best bet would be to ride into that Nokoni camp all full of indignation, and demand payment for my stolen bride. If my bravado worked, I would ride away with my spoils and go on about my business as a wilderness Indian trader.

The variable that concerned me was the unknown nature of Hidden Water's new husband. How fierce of a warrior was he? Hopefully, he would have enough sand in his craw to insist on keeping his new prize so that I wouldn't have to take her back. But would he pay me for her with horses and hides, or would he want to fight? If he intended to make a show of killing me to win Hidden Water and bolster his own reputation, then I was in trouble. I would either get wounded or killed in the duel, or I would kill or wound Hidden Water's new husband, perhaps angering the Nokonis while winning back a woman I didn't even want. This was going to be tricky.

Kills Something and I rode southward until we happened upon a pair of Nokoni Comanche travelers riding north to our camp to trade for whiskey. They had four extra horses with them, for which I traded four cups of whiskey, which was about all I had left. I told them the whiskey was in the lodge with the fallen wind flap back at the Quahadi camp. They insisted that I take possession of my horses then and there, lest any of them go lame, run off, get stolen, or die, thus depriving them of a cup. They told us where to find the camp we sought, and ensured us that the beautiful Hidden Water was there.

We followed their directions and found Hidden Water's new village camped at the confluence of the North Wichita and the South Wichita. Over a hundred lodges stood among the river bottom timber, and meat was hung everywhere on curing racks. Hides of deer and buffalo were plentiful, and the Nokonis seemed busy and happy. I remember thinking that it was a shame that I couldn't just leave them alone. However, I knew I had better put on my fighting face and prepare to bluff Hidden Water's new husband out of a few mounts or something, however ridiculous that seemed—trading a wife for horses.

We rode into this camp a little after noon, and I began to shout.

"Aho!" I said. "Listen! I am looking for a woman that ran away from me. She is called Hidden Water. I am Plenty Man, of the Quahadis! Tell the man who stole my wife that he must come here and face me now!"

We had ridden right into the camp with our herd of spare horses, and couldn't have caused more of a stir had we thrown a rock into a hornet's nest. Boys and girls began running everywhere to spread the news of our arrival, while men and women began to gather around us, anxious to witness what would happen between me and Hidden Water's new husband.

I continued to talk loud and posture about on my mount for what seemed like a very long time. Finally, I sensed the approach of my rival. The crowd of Nokonis parted and he walked into the circle of people surrounding me and Kills Something, and the horses we had brought with us. He carried a shield and a lance. He was big for a Comanche, and that made him easily bigger than me. I figured he was about my age, but he had seen more battle than me and had the scars and the glare in his eyes to prove it.

Rarely had I seen a more athletic Comanche fighting man. One look told me that this warrior feared nothing, least of all me.

"I am Plenty Man, of the Quahadis," I said, my voice cracking. "You have taken my wife. Who are you?"

"I am called Bear Tooth," he said, without raising his voice. "Who rides with you?"

"My brother-in-law." I glanced at Kills Something and saw him glaring. I wished I could have looked as formidable.

Bear Tooth tossed his head like a horse. "What do you want here?"

I knew what I was supposed to say. I wanted payment for my stolen bride, or I wanted battle. But I just could not get my mouth to speak it. "I have ridden a long way," I said, stalling. "I will not leave here until I am satisfied."

Bear Tooth tucked his lance under his arm, angling the point toward me with menace. "What do you want?" he repeated.

"I want . . . I will tell you what I want . . ." About this time, I knew my plan to try bluffing Bear Tooth out of some payment for Hidden Water was probably about to get me lanced to death, so I acted on a sudden and desperate whim. "I want to give you these horses!" I announced, gesturing toward the six spare mounts in my remuda.

"Horses?" he growled.

"Yes, take these horses, my friend. I want you to have them. You have made me very happy!"

The people began to murmur around us, and I glanced at Kills Something to see the confused glare he shot toward me.

"You came to fight for the woman, *tsuh*?"

"Fight?" I threw my head back in maniacal laughter. "Who would fight for a woman that lazy? I came to *thank* you. That woman is so worthless that she does not know how to drive a stake pin by herself. Her hand does not fit the strap of a water bag. She cannot start a fire without stealing an ember from her neighbors!"

An old woman began to laugh. "It is true!" she said. "That is the laziest girl I ever saw. She will not carry more than four sticks of wood in her arms."

Voices rose around us as the people chuckled, or questioned one another in confusion.

This only seemed to annoy Bear Tooth. "Enough talk," he said. "You have come a long way. You must want a fight."

"I will fight the man who tries to make me take that lazy woman back."

"She is not lazy when I tell her what to do!" he answered, jabbing his lance toward me.

"That is the same thing I thought at first, but give her time. She will get plenty lazy."

"She already is!" the old woman yelled. "Those Quahadi girls are the laziest I have ever seen."

"Don't judge our Quahadi women by Hidden Water's laziness," I said. "We have others who make good wives."

"Wait!" Bear Tooth said, shaking his shield. "Did you come to fight for the woman, or to demand a price for her?"

I sighed and rolled my eyes at the aggravation of having to explain it all again. "I came to give you a gift of thanks for taking her away. I have brought you these horses."

Now Bear Tooth's own people began to laugh at him. Some of his fellow warriors jeered. One said, "Take the horses, brother, your woman needs them to carry her wood." Another said, "Tell Plenty Man six horses is not enough to make up for your taking such a lazy woman."

"I have my *own* horses!" Bear Tooth said.

"You shall have more!" I said.

About this time, I noticed that Chief Peta Nocona had pushed through the crowd of people to listen to the confrontation.

"It is *you* who should want to take horses from *me*," Bear Tooth said. "Are you not ashamed that your woman has run away with me?"

"Ashamed?" I laughed straight up at the sky. "I am only ashamed that I did not get rid of her sooner. Please, take the horses, my friend."

"No, *you* will take horses from *me*. The woman is not lazy, and you will either take six horses, or we will fight!"

"Six horses?" I said. "No, I could not. I came here to give *you* horses. But I can see you are a proud warrior and able to get your own horses, so take only four horses from me, my friend, because I respect your pride."

"I will not take any horses from you. You will take eight from me, for the woman is a good woman, and the most beautiful woman in this camp."

"A hot meal is a beautiful thing, too," I said, "but you will not being seeing much of that. She doesn't know how to cook!"

The old Nokoni woman howled with laughter, and many of the others joined her.

"You will take the eight horses, or feel the point of my lance," Bear Tooth said.

"I can see you are a warrior with much medicine, so I will keep all but three of my own horses, even though I brought them all to you to show my thanks. But I could not take eight horses for the woman. That would make my heart feel bad."

"I do not care how your heart feels. You will take eight horses, or you will fight."

"Such a woman does not call for a fight, my friend. You will see soon enough that I speak the truth. So, please take just two horses from me. This does not begin to show my thanks to you."

Now Hidden Water herself arrived. I spotted her near the old woman who had spoken so harshly of her. She did not seem the least bit ashamed to show herself in front of me. In fact, she seemed amused by the confrontation, though she hadn't yet heard Bear Tooth and me arguing over who was going to pay whom. I must admit that her beauty made my breath catch in my throat, but she had caused me a lot of trouble by running off with Bear Tooth, and I felt no desire for her.

"I will not take horses from you," Bear Tooth said, flabbergasted at my whole attitude. "I do not need your thanks for anything. You should be demanding horses of me. You should have the courage to challenge me to a fight!"

"My courage and my medicine are strong," I said. "Especially since I got rid of that lazy woman. That is why I want to thank you with a gift of horses. Please take at least one!"

Now Hidden Water caught on to my ploy, and I saw the fury consume her lovely face. "You skunk!" she shouted at me.

"You see how disrespectful she is!" I laughed. "I am so happy she is no longer my wife."

Hidden Water stalked across the circle of people to confront Bear Tooth. "Tell him he must demand payment for me. Many horses! Or he must fight!"

"Silence, woman," Bear Tooth said, shoving her aside. "I have already told him."

The old crone laughed so hard that her knees buckled, and she patted the ground in appreciation of the whole ridiculous scene.

"You may refuse the gift I have brought for you," I said. "That is your choice. But that woman will suck the *puha* out of you like a calf sucking a cow. So I will keep my horses, but I cannot accept any of yours, because you will need them when your powers start to weaken."

"My powers are plenty strong!" Bear Tooth declared.

"I see that, but you have not been with her very long. You will need all the wealth you can get hold of when things start to go bad."

Hidden Water gasped at my gall. "I would kill him for saying such a thing about me!"

"Woman, shut your mouth!" Bear Tooth growled.

Hidden Water implored Kills Something now. "Brother," she said, "tell my husband that I never made Plenty Man's power go bad."

Kills Something would not even look at her. "I am not your brother."

Now Chief Peta Nocona stepped forward, into the circle made by his people. "A strong warrior," he said, "proves his faith in his own *puha* by giving away all his horses. Plenty Man comes here and offers all these horses to a man who has taken his wife. That is the strangest thing I have ever seen, but I see that Plenty Man's powers are great because of it. He shows Bear Tooth that he is not injured by having a woman taken away from him—especially one that would run away willingly. If Bear Tooth believes in his own powers, he will give *all* of his horses to Plenty Man to prove it. Then we will see if this woman truly has the bad power to weaken a warrior's medicine."

"As Peta Nocona says," Bear Tooth announced, "you will take *all* of my horses. I have twenty-two. *And* I will give away everything I own in a big give-away dance tonight. Everything but my sacred weapons."

"Everything!" Hidden Water screamed with great indignation. "No, you will not!"

"Everything! My lodge, my robes, even the mocassins on my feet! Even those on my wife's feet! You will see that my medicine is good, and we will work to get new things. I will hunt buffalo, and my wife will tan the hides and make a new lodge."

"But I have a lodge! Almost the biggest in camp!"

"No longer! Plenty Man, any boy in camp will show you which horses are mine. You will take them with you when you go away. I have spoken!"

Before I could respond, Bear Tooth wheeled away and stormed off through the crowd of people, with Hidden Water jabbering at his heels.

Peta Nocona looked at me and smiled slightly. "There is going to be a dance and a feast tonight. You should stay and enjoy the hospitality of my people."

"We will," I promised.

The old Nokoni lady was still laughing as the crowd of people began to disperse, for all were now excited about preparing for the give-away dance. Kills Something rode up next to me. "You have strange medicine, brother."

"It is stranger to no one than it is to me," I admitted.

———

We made camp on the outskirts of the village, and rested a while. Then I strolled among the Nokoni lodges to look for captives I might ransom. The only white person I saw was Peta Nocona's wife, Nadua, whom I had last seen in the camp at the Crossing on the Canadian. As I saw Nadua preparing buffalo meat for the feast, I approached her casually, and spoke to her.

"Do you know who I am?" I asked.

She glanced at me and nodded, then went on about her work.

"I have been told that there is something I should not speak to you about."

She stopped her work and stood to face me, though she would not look at my face. "I have a child. My son, Quanah." She pointed to a boy of about five years of age attempting to climb onto a gentle old horse near the lodge. "Do not speak of taking me away. My husband would be angry. I must stay with my child."

"That is good. If you choose to stay with the True Humans, that is up to you. But if you wish, I can take a message to your old people, so they will know you are well."

"No," she said. "They must not know anything of me. They will try to come and get me. Please do not tell them where I am."

"Do not be afraid," I said. "I will say nothing unless you want me to."

She looked about nervously. "Go away, so I can work."

"*Tsuh, tsuh.* I am going to speak to your son, but I only want to encourage him about riding horses."

Nadua nodded as if to give me permission. I think she just wanted to be done with me. It was clear that I made her very nervous.

I walked toward the horse that Nadua's son, Quanah, was trying to mount. The old horse had a rawhide thong tied into its mane. The thong dangled just low enough for the boy to grab. He was supposed to be able to climb up that thong and mount the horse, but he was young for this maneuver, and having trouble. He had a quiver full of practice arrows on his back and a little bow over his shoulder, and these impeded him when he tried to climb onto the horse.

"Do you need help?" I asked.

He turned, looked up at me, and smiled, but said, "No."

Looking around, he spied a log on the ground from a tree that had been blown over in a storm. He led his old nag up next to this, climbed up on the log, grabbed the rawhide thong—higher up this time—and succeeded in clawing his way high enough to throw his leg over the pony's back. Pulling himself upright, he looked back at me, smiled again, and said, "You see, I do not need your help."

"I see that. Show me how you will hunt the buffalo on that horse."

Quanah lifted the bow over his head and pulled an arrow from his quiver. He goaded the old horse to a trot as he did this, and without touching the reins of his war bridle made the horse stop and turn using only his feet and legs to signal the mount. Now he notched the arrow onto the string and came trotting back toward me. The log became his buffalo, and he sent an arrow thumping into its flank. The wood was rotten enough that the blunt arrow stuck. This was impressive enough, but within two seconds, that little Comanche rider had another arrow notched, and as he trotted by the log a second time, he sent another arrow into the log only a finger's width from the first.

"Yee-yee-yee-yee-yee!" I yelled. I glanced back at Nadua, and saw that she was smiling at her son's accomplishment.

Little Quanah, which meant "the Fragrant One," held his bow above his head in triumph and urged the old mount into a slow lope. He rode in a circle around his imaginary kill and grinned at me as he passed. Suddenly, the old horse stumbled, and fell to both knees, pitching Quanah forward. He grabbed the mane, breaking his fall, but he hit the ground hard anyway, and one end of his bow jabbed him in the thigh, scratching a red streak across his flesh. Worse still, the old horse stepped on the boy's shoulder as it struggled to regain its footing. The hoof luckily slid off him before the animal put its full weight on that leg, but it still scraped Quanah's shoulder badly.

The white man in me wanted to run and pick the boy up, but I held myself back. This was a Comanche camp, and everything about the Comanche way prepared a True Human—man, woman, or child—to accept pain and go on without complaint. Several older boys who had seen Quanah fall gathered around to laugh at him, but he ignored them. I knew his scrapes and bruises had to hurt, but the little warrior did not even touch them. He just picked up his bow and his spilled arrows and went to catch his horse.

Angrily, he grabbed the reins of the war bridle, but he did not jerk them, nor did he strike the old mount. Instead, he pulled the pony's head down to his level and gave it a good long lecture about watching where it was going and keeping its four feet under it, lest he should have his mother cook it for the give-away dance that was going to happen that very evening. That settled, Quanah led his pony back over to the log and remounted.

As he rode away to some other adventure, I looked toward his mother. She watched him disappear behind the lodges, no emotion showing in her face. I had to wonder if she remembered being coddled as a child after some accident; if she recalled her white parents comforting her after a fall, or calming her fears after a nightmare. Her blue eyes darted toward me for a second, then she stooped back to her work with the buffalo meat.

After leaving this camp, I would not see Nadua, or Quanah, for seven years. And oh, how things would change.

NINE

Seven years flew, like seven good friends ridden down the trail, never to return. Seven winters, as the Indians would say, each colder than the last. Seven times the earth circled the sun, spinning as it circled, its own moon whirling about it in turn. And me, in the middle, wasting seven years of my life among the Indians.

I don't mean to suggest that nothing happened to me in seven years. Plenty happened. I rode, traded, ransomed captives. I sold the horses and robes I acquired and spent money on jags with my friends. Some of the money I buried for later use, or deposited in banks that were beginning to show up in the Texas and Colorado settlements.

I scouted for Kit Carson on some of his punitive expeditions against renegade Jicarillas. Otherwise, I tried to keep peace among the Indians, as did Kit and William Bent. But the whites were coming in increasing numbers, making peace difficult to achieve. Settlers pressed onto the fringes of the rich Comanche ranges. Prospectors found gold in Colorado, stirring the Cheyennes to warfare. Hunters shot buffalo by the hundreds and thousands, driving the nations of the plains to acts of utter desperation.

That is all I will say about those seven years, for you want to know about the battles at Adobe Walls. About Kit and Quanah. I must include William Bent, too, for in those days, the societies of seven nations revolved around the wisdom and diplomacy of this gifted Indian trader of the plains and mountains. I will hold to my narrative of those events, and not bore you with every little thing that happened to me, personally, during those years. Suffice it to say that I fairly wallowed in the revelries and agonies of life.

In September of 1860, I completed a successful summer trading expedition among the Comanches and Kiowas here at the Crossing on the Canadian

River. I took a large herd of horses to William Bent's trading post at Big Timbers. My Comanche friends, Kills Something, Fears-the-Ground, and Loud
Shouter rode with me to help herd the horses and to hold council with
the Cheyennes. When we arrived at William's substantial stone trading post,
we found that he had turned it over to the U.S. Army. An officer there told
me that William had established a new trading post and ranch at the mouth of
the Purgatoire River, where it emptied into the Arkansas River, a day's ride
above Big Timbers. The place was called Bent's Stockade.

So we camped at William's former trading post, which the army was
now calling Fort Fauntleroy. I stayed up most of the night, keeping the
horses bunched. Kills Something relieved me before dawn, and I caught a
few hours of sleep. The next day we rode up the Arkansas, letting the
horses graze as we trailed them, for I wanted them to arrive in good shape.
In the late afternoon, we spotted a small gathering of Cheyenne tipis across
the Arkansas, near the left bank of the mouth of the Purgatory. On the opposite bank of the Purgatory's mouth, we found William's Mexican workers busily clearing fields and building rail fences. We saw the defensive
stockade surrounding the ranch buildings and pens—a great circular wall
made of vertical timbers set side by side, sharpened to points at the top.
Effective, but not nearly as impressive as the towering adobe walls of
Bent's Old Fort had once been, or even the stone-walled trading post at
Big Timbers, now housing Fort Fauntleroy.

As we swam our horses over the Arkansas, I heard a bell ring three
times from the stockade, and assumed it sounded to announce our arrival.
We landed just upstream of the Arkansas's confluence with the Purgatory
and rode toward the stockade. Riding around the curved north wall of the
stockade, I gathered that William had had his laborers dig a huge circular
trench, into which the butt ends of the timbers had been set upright and
lashed together with rawhide. The result was a battlement too high to
breach and too thick for a bullet to penetrate. Each log tip had been sawn
to a point, probably by two men laboring over a double-ended logging
saw. My only concern was that it might be set afire, especially in years to
come as the green timbers cured.

Coming through the gate, I saw William letting down the rails to a large
log corral. I recognized Kit Carson standing there with him in a plain store-
bought suit. A third man was there, and I recognized him as William's son-
in-law, Tom Boggs, who had been gone several years to California. Tom
and I had both served as couriers for the U.S. Army during the Mexican

War, and I had bought my first horse from him, years before. I herded the ponies between a large cabin, which I assumed was William's, and a bell standing on a post—the one that had tolled three times to announce our approach across the river. With the help of my Comanche friends, I worried the horses into the corral, then got down to shake hands and slap shoulders with the men I had not seen in too long.

"Mr. Greenwood," William said, "I thought you would never more be seen among civilized men. Where have you been?"

"Out yonder," I said, gesturing toward the wild Comanche range.

"There's a lot of yonder out there," Kit said.

"Less than last year."

"That's true." Kit gave me a big Mexican-style *abrazo,* almost squeezing the wind from my lungs in his crushing embrace.

"You back for good?" I asked Tom Boggs.

"For good or bad, I'm back," Tom said. The years in California seemed to have treated him well, for he looked lean and strong, his face bronzed by the outdoor elements. I had always admired Tom for his good looks, common sense, and rock-solid character.

"How's Rumalda?"

"She's fine, Orn'ry, and she'll be glad to see you alive. We'll ride up to my cabin later and surprise her."

About this time, two young men rode in through the stockade gate from the field the Mexicans were clearing. They dismounted and approached. I didn't recognize either, but the younger of the two looked Indian, though he wore white man's clothing. The older was clearly of Anglo stock.

"Mr. Greenwood," William said, "you remember my eldest son, Robert. He's nineteen now. Just back from St. Louis."

"Yes, good to see you again," I said, shaking Robert's hand. "You've grown so much I didn't recognize you. Last time I saw you, you were no more than twelve."

"Likewise, good to see you, Mr. Greenwood." He spoke perfect English, but his face looked very Cheyenne, for his mother was the daughter of a chief. "I remember you well from when I was a boy."

"You remember Robert's elder sister, Mary, don't you?" William said.

"Of course." I glanced around, but did not see a woman present.

"Well, she married a danged old saloonkeeper in Missouri."

"Is that so?"

The American man beside Robert Bent began to chuckle, and held his hand out to shake mine. "I'm R. M. Moore," he said. "I was that danged old saloonkeeper. Now I'm not sure what I am, other than a greenhorn out West."

I shook his hand. "Perhaps you're an empire builder, like your father-in-law."

"Maybe a stockade builder at best."

My Comanche friends had been standing by patiently, so I introduced them. They shook hands with the newcomers and the white men they already knew and respected, then mounted and rode toward the village of tipis downstream to meet or get reacquainted with the Cheyennes camped there. The rest of us sat on the ground, Indian style, and shared intelligence from our far-flung travels. Tom told about California. Kit told about the Jicarilla and Ute troubles. William groused about the gold fever to the north and the Cheyennes' retaliatory raids on wagon trains and settlers. I related what I knew about the Texans' encroachments on Comancheria, and the battles spawned because of it. Robert Bent and R. M. Moore told us of news from the east—particularly the rumors of impending warfare between the Northern and Southern states.

When I asked William why he had abandoned his stone trading post, he said, "The new Indian agent showed up with a wagonload of annuities owed to the Cheyennes. Damned fool. It was months late, half what they were promised, and he wanted to store it all in my commissary. I told him he could build his own commissary, that I was a private trader and didn't feel obligated to store the government's property. I was afraid the Cheyennes would attack my post to get the things they were owed, and I didn't intend to get caught in the middle of that. We stayed up all night augerin' about it, and I finally just decided to turn the whole damn place over to the government. The agent promised rent, but I've yet to see it."

When I asked Kit about Lucien Maxwell, he said, "Aw, Kid, you ought to see the place on the Cimarron. Lucien took and built him a gristmill thirty foot tall, of stone. He got claim to the whole Beaubien-Miranda Grant, by act of Congress. He figures he owns more than a million acres of land. All I know is that it takes more than two days to ride acrost it."

"That's what brought me and Rumalda back from California," Tom said. "She owns about two thousand acres of the Vigil-St. Vrain Land Grant, and we're confident Congress will recognize it, too, even though it's even bigger than Maxwell's grant. We're squattin' on Rumalda's land right here and now, as a matter of fact. This is the parcel she got—the northeast corner of the grant. Ceran St. Vrain is Rumalda's godfather, and he saw to it she got a share of the grant."

The talk of land turned to talk of family, so I asked Robert Bent how his two younger brothers were doing in school. "I remember how Charles ambushed me with his practice arrows when he was no more than six," I said. "He almost unhorsed me."

Robert chuckled, but his face showed that he missed his younger brother, and worried about him. "He hasn't changed a whole lot. Charles stays in trouble all the time in school. He'll fight any bully that calls him 'half-breed' and makes them call him 'Cheyenne' before he'll let them up off the ground. He just wants to come back to the plains. He doesn't have much use for school."

"He better find a use for it," William growled.

"And George?" I asked.

"George gets along fine until Charles drags him into some kind of trouble. You'd think it would be George keeping Charles *out* of trouble, since he's older, but he lets Charles talk him into the damnedest schemes."

"You mind your language, son," William warned.

"Sorry," Robert said, looking at the ground. "Anyway, all George can talk about these days is the war fever. He wants to join the South and fight. I kept telling him to stay out of it, but he's got his mind set on going off to fight. I think a lot of it is Charles egging him on, even though Charles is only thirteen, and too young to take up a rifle if the fightin' does start."

We sat on the ground for hours and talked. Most of the men gravitated to the corral fence where they could lean against the rails as their legs stretched out across the dirt, or crossed Indian style. I ended up using the bell post as my backrest. I looked up to study it once. It was a large bell— like one that would grace the belfry of a church—with two trunnions resting in an iron cradle upon which it could swing, pendulumlike. An iron arm jutted from one side of the bell, and from the end of the arm dangled a rope, which was now swaying gently in the breeze. It was a nice, big bell for such a far-flung frontier settlement, and the post made a fine backrest as I talked with my friends and new acquaintances.

When dusk approached, we decided to ride to Tom Boggs's cabin, a couple of miles up the Purgatory, to surprise his wife, Rumalda, who was a friend of mine from the old days in Taos. Tom and Rumalda and the other newcomers had built cabins upstream at a place they were calling Boggsville, in honor of Tom.

Tom had chosen a fine piece of property for his fledgling settlement. The ground was almost level, sloping just slightly toward the bed of the Purgatory, which flowed a mere arrow shot away. Old cottonwoods shaded the ground he had staked out. As we rode through a scattering herd of sheep, I saw smoke issuing from the cabins that stood in rows along what might someday be streets. As we rode into Boggsville, I smelled food, and my hunger started to gnaw at me, so I asked Tom Boggs, "What's on the menu tonight, Tom?"

"The *menu*?" he replied. "Antelope, cantaloupe, and shit. But we're out of antelope and cantaloupe."

All the men roared with laughter at my expense, but I didn't even care. It felt good to be back among these friends.

After a couple of days of feasting and yarning and overseeing the ranch work, Kit announced that he was riding west to do some elk hunting in the San Juan Mountains he knew so well as an old trapper and trader. William and Tom and their partners were too busy building their new enterprises, but I relished the idea of taking the trail with Kit. We loaded one mule with provisions and equipment, and led two others on which to pack elk meat.

On a clear day, a rider who stood in the stirrups of a tall horse, and rode just a little west of Boggsville, could see the Spanish Peaks, ninety miles away. It was wide-open country, still green in September, blazing hot at noon, and cool enough for a blanket at night. It was peppered with antelope and sometimes trodden under by buffalo; blustery, usually dusty, but sometimes boggy; consistent in its constant production of surprises.

Riding west through this country, Kit and I had plenty of time to talk. Kit had been Indian agent for the Jicarilla Apaches and the Utes for several years, so much of our conversation revolved around them. "The white men ain't gonna quit comin'," he said. "They'll take over this whole country and there ain't nothin' nobody can do to stop it, so the only hope for the Indians is to take up farmin' and ranchin' and live in houses. Some of them are startin' to see it that way, but others get riled and want to fight if you even mention it. Those damn prospectors keep pressin' onto land the government set aside for the Indians. It's the yaller metal, Kid. Makes them fools crazy. Now, it's the buffalo hunters, too. They're killin' 'em for hides alone and leavin' the meat to spoil. If that won't rile an Indian, I don't know what would. Hell, it riles me. But I've tolt the Indians, Kid, it's like trying to hold back a great storm cloud. I've tolt 'em that when they murder white people, I will respond with force, and by God, I've done it. You know. You've rid with me a time or two. It's unpleasant business, damned unpleasant, but I don't know any other way short of all-out war, and it may come to that anyway."

These problems clearly troubled Kit. He felt caught in the middle, for he was as much an Indian at heart as he was white. Though he could neither read nor write, he could speak seven Indian languages, and he understood the Indian mind. On the trail, he lived like an Indian, for he had learned from them long ago. He was universally respected among the tribes of the plains and mountains, even when he rode against them with army troops to punish some killing or raid. The Indians called him "Little Chief " and told many stories about his bravery. I had heard these tales among Kiowas, Comanches, Cheyennes, Arapahos, and Utes.

Kit's job as Indian agent was tough, and took him away from his family often. But after he had vented his frustrations to me on the trail, he seemed to feel better, and let the matter drop. From then on, we talked about game sign, though there was less of it than in years past to talk about. I asked Kit about the old days trapping beaver in the mountains, and he told me many a rollicking story of his exploits.

Toward the end of our second day of travel, we rode around a bend and spotted a large buck drinking from a beaver pond. The moment we came into view, he threw his head up, looked at us for one second, then turned to run into the nearby pines. The sight reminded me of the opening lines to *The Lady of the Lake,* so I began to recite:

> *The stag at eve had drunk his fill,*
> *Where danced the moon on Monan's rill,*
> *And deep his midnight lair had made*
> *In lone Glenartney's hazel shade.*

Kit looked at me and his mouth dropped open. "That's a purty batch of words. Did you just make that up?"

I laughed. "Not me, Kit. That's Sir Walter Scott."

"Say some more of it."

So I continued to recite from memory as we rode to some camp-ground Kit knew of up the trail. He made me stop often and repeat certain lines, and he seemed quite enthralled with the epic poem that began with a stag hunt and led the listener through battles and desperate romance. I continued to recite the poem to Kit that night in camp as he lay back against his saddle and smoked his old clay pipe. The mood of *The Lady of the Lake,* though set long ago and far away, suited the tone of affairs on the plains, with some factions spoiling for war, and others trying hero-ically to avoid it.

Kit stopped me and repeated certain lines he particularly liked:

> *Now man to man and steel to steel*
> *A Chieftain's vengeance thou shalt feel*

Then . . .

> *. . . my pass, in danger tried*
> *Hangs in my belt and by my side*

And, later . . .

> *Slight cause will then suffice to guide*
> *A Knight's free footsteps far and wide*
> *A falcon flown, a greyhound strayed,*
> *The merry glance of mountain maid;*
> *Or, if a path be dangerous known,*
> *The danger's self is lure alone.*

TEN

We had a fine hunt. We were far enough into the mountains that few prospectors had passed through the country, so game was plentiful. I shot a young bull elk and a cow. Kit shot a cow and a big mature bull. Four shots were enough. We did not intend to draw attention to ourselves with gratuitous gunfire. Though we were in Ute country, and Kit was on good terms with the Utes, you never knew in those days when a roving band of angry Pawnees or Blackfeet or Apaches might be prowling, looking for the game we were harvesting, or scalps from foolish white hunters.

We spent a day skinning elk and quartering meat, hanging the quarters high in ponderosa pines several hundred yards from our camp. There were grizzlies in those mountains, and Kit insisted we avoid them at all cost. He had seen friends mauled, and had, himself, had narrow escapes from huge bears.

The next morning, we went to pack the elk meat on our mules, and found that a grizzly had indeed tried to claw our meat down from the trees where we had hung the quarters. Almost all the bark had been stripped from the tree where the meat hung. Judging from the size of the scrape marks on the tree trunks, the bear was a huge one. The smell of the big grizzly terrified the mules and horses, and they pranced constantly as we tried to pack the meat, and flinched at every little flutter of leaves in the forest. Kit and I kept our rifles within reach as we packed the mules, and watched constantly over our shoulders.

I was scared. The forest was thick around us, and even a big bear might sneak quite near without our seeing him. I knew that one or two rifle balls might fail to stop a charging grizzly. Still, there was no leaving our elk meat behind. It took us hours, but we got it all packed on the mules and left that place, to everyone's relief, without ever actually seeing the bear that had terrified us so. I have always wondered if he saw us.

We rode east with our little pack string, retracing our path through the San Juans. The trail often led above the timberline, and the views of craggy peaks jutting above the clouds awed me. I was happy to share the company of an experienced mountain voyageur, and wondered if I could find my way out of this maze of valleys and ridges should something happen to Kit.

I was riding Major, my veteran paint stallion. He was now twelve years old, which was rather aged for a frontier mount, yet I had spared Major many a hard mile by using other horses for punishing rides whenever I could. In those days, I rarely traveled without a spare mount or two. So Major was still plenty sound for his age, and possessed the experience and good judgment few other horses could equal. On top of all that, he was a handsome paint, flashy and well muscled, and many a rider had envied my ownership of him over the years.

Kit decided to take us back toward William Bent's ranch on a new trail that would swing down to the San Luis Valley. As Indian agent, he wanted to check on some Utes he thought would be camping there.

"It's a good trail," Kit claimed. "I've traveled it before. Twice't."

∼∼∼∼∼

The trail *was* a good one, at first. It wound gracefully among evergreens and bluffs, just a few hundred feet below the timberline. Then, we rounded a mountain bend and found that an avalanche had torn down the steep slope ahead of us and carried away boulders, trees, and soil, leaving only a shifting mass of scree underfoot where once a level trail had stood. As avalanches rate, this had been a rather minor one—only about a hundred yards in width. Still, that would be one hundred yards of unstable footing underneath our animals, with a steep slope below strewn with slick plates of rock that dropped at a sheer angle five hundred feet to a beaver pond below that looked no bigger than my thumbnail held at arm's length.

"Well," Kit said, looking up and down the path of the avalanche. "Let me test it."

He dismounted and went ahead on foot, checking each step, catlike, before placing his full weight on the shifting rocks. He continued like this, step by step, sometimes moving rocks ahead of him by hand, until he reached the other side of the avalanche, where the trail became solid again.

Now he turned around and came back the same way he had gone, again testing each step before he committed his full weight to the slope. Halfway across, I saw him stop, stand erect, and turn his back to the slope. He stood there half a minute in the middle of that avalanche's path, staring out at the valleys, cliffs, waterfalls, and timbered mountainsides below. Finally, he resumed his cautious return to my side of the avalanche and set foot on firm ground.

"The only other way is to go back where the griz was this mornin' and try to find another pass from there."

"That's a long way back," I said, remembering my fear of the unseen bear.

"Yep."

"It's only a hundred yards or so across," I observed.

He nodded. "Lead your horse. If the critters slip, don't try to help 'em, Kid. Look out for yourself."

I dismounted and swallowed hard. I tried to remind myself that this was the nature of life in the wilderness and if I wasn't up to crossing an occasional landslide, I should stay in town with the white women.

"You ready?"

"Yes, sir."

" 'If a path be dangerous known,' " he said, quoting Sir Walter Scott. " 'The danger's self is lure alone.' " He grinned at me, then turned away and started across, leading his horse. He went faster this time, knowing his pony might lose patience and panic if he progressed too slowly. I followed, leading Major. Behind me came the mules, whom I trusted to follow even though I had untied the lead ropes lest one of them slip.

Kit came to the place halfway across where he had stopped to gaze out over the valley. He took a step. His horse followed, and the rock that had supported Kit slipped away under the weight of the horse. The mount panicked, scrambling for footing, and I remember thinking that I wished we had ridden mules instead of horses. Kit's poor terrified horse clawed his own footing right out from under him. Kit tried to help the horse briefly by pulling the reins, but the cause was lost and Kit reluctantly cast the reins aside as the horse's hind legs slipped out from under him.

I could only watch. I dared not even move. I will never forget what happened next. I can see it as clearly now as when it occurred. The falling horse clawed for purchase with his front hooves and tore the shifting rocks right out from under Kit's boot. But Kit was wise to the dangers of the mountains and the evils of bad trails, and he threw himself back onto the slope spread-eagled, catching himself with his hands. Kit's right leg stuck out into thin air, for the mountain slope had disappeared under that leg. And at that moment his doomed horse made a desperate lunge with his head and neck and slung the long leather reins whiplike toward Kit. One of the reins lashed out at Kit's ankle, and like an impossible tendril of some killer vine, it wrapped around Kit's boot and spur twice, snugged somehow under its own tautness, and entangled man with horse.

Nine hundred pounds of horseflesh now plummeted down the slide and Kit, like a calf at the end of a vaquero's reata, shot down the slope behind the struggling horse. I watched in horror, my feet fused in place on the shaky slope. Kit kicked at the tangled rein, but it remained fast. He reached for the rein to free himself, but the horse flipped, throwing his head and yanking Kit down the landslide. The horse rolled again, right over Kit, and the gnashing sounds of sliding rock coupled with the grunts of the poor falling beast almost drove me to helpless insanity, for I could do nothing but watch.

Now, miraculously, Kit kicked free from the tangled rein. Here the avalanche's path angled just enough to the right around a point that I thought Kit might land on the point instead of continuing his slide hundreds of feet below. I prayed he would make that point, my whole body wound as tight as steel cables.

The horse slammed against a boulder at the very edge of the rock slide a hundred feet below me, and Kit hit the same rock face just feet away from his mount. He landed on his head and his left shoulder, and came to a sudden stop that made me think of an egg dropped on the floor. The rocks that had been loosened continued to slide away downhill for several seconds, then everything became still and quiet except for the groans of the dying horse.

"Kit!" I yelled, as Major tossed his head behind me.

Slowly, I saw Kit roll onto his back. He lifted one arm and motioned for me to continue my crossing. I was astounded that he was alive, much less conscious.

Now I looked at the path that had evaporated before me. I had to cross. There was no going back. I turned straight up the mountainside to get above the place where Kit's horse had fallen and pawed away the footing. Major followed, dipping his head low to look at the shaky ground ahead of him, and snorting at the rocks as if to warn them. The mules followed Major, seemingly as unconcerned as mountain goats. We climbed above the place where Kit's horse had destroyed what little integrity the slope held. I now turned back toward the far side of the rockslide, hoping the footing would bear our weight.

I angled slightly downhill now, heading for the place where the trail resumed. I could see it clearly, but I dared not rush toward it. I tested every step, and the animals stayed right behind me. Ten steps from good soil, a mass of loosened scree shifted under me and my horse, and we slipped a foot downward in a sudden plunge, then somehow found tenuous footing as the rocks we had loosened slid and skipped down the precarious slope. When I finally reached solid ground, I nearly dropped to my knees to kiss the earth, but there was no time for such foolishness, for Kit needed my help.

Leaving the beasts on the trail, I climbed downhill to the place where Kit had landed. I found him sitting up against a rock, rubbing his left shoulder. His face looked as stoic as ever, but I could see pain in his gathered brow. The dead horse lay beside him, its neck broken.

"How bad are you hurt?" I asked.

"I'll live."

"Can you walk?"

"I 'magine I can, here directly. It's my chest that hurts. And my shoulder. I landed on my shoulder."

"Is it broken?"

"I didn't hear nothin' crack, other than my skull slammin' agin' that there boulder."

"If you hadn't hit that boulder, you'd still be falling."

"I ain't complainin'." Kit reached up to me with his right hand. "Easy," he said.

Gently, I helped him to his feet. He winced, but made no whimper. In fact, to my surprise, I heard Kit chuckle. I feared for a moment that he had lapsed into delirium.

"One time, Kid, right after Peg Leg Smith cut his own leg off to keep the gangrene from a bullet wound from killin' him, his friends was haulin' him home on a litter slung between two mules. That was the only way they could think to get him out of there with one leg cut off at the knee. Well, that litter busted on a steep trail, and Peg Leg fell about as far as I did, I guess. Maybe fu'ther. Landed in a stream and laid there cussin' in the cold water. Couldn't get out. He didn't know how to get around yet, one-legged. His friends made their way to him and stood around laughin' at him a while, then finally pulled him out. They tell me he cussed all the way back to Taos."

I smiled at Kit, amazed that he had felt compelled to tell me a story just now, but I guess he was trying to make a point. "Do you want me to try to get your saddle off that horse?"

"Naw, Kid, the tree's probably busted. My rifle slid on down the mountain, so it's lost, too. Just get the bridle and the canteen, if you would."

I salvaged what I could from Kit's saddle and we climbed back up to the animals I had left on the trail. I insisted that Kit ride Major while I hiked ahead on foot with my rifle.

Kit was in pain, and couldn't move his left arm or shoulder for days. He would always claim that he merely "sprained" his shoulder in that fall, but I think he cracked a bone or two, and suffered some internal bruising or bleeding. In fact, he never fully recovered from the accident. It changed his posture a little—not so much that you'd notice unless you knew him well. And though he had many a fight and a hard ride still ahead of him, that little fall in the San Juans would come back to haunt Kit in the final days.

ELEVEN

While Kit convalesced from his accident, I stayed around William's stockade and helped him build fences of split pine rails lashed together with rawhide. We also surveyed the course of an irrigation ditch using a transit William had hauled west. The ditch would catch water from the Purgatoire and cast it out on a gently sloping field of about 230 acres. The Mexican laborers were busy clearing this field of rocks, which they used to build a rock fence around the field itself.

At night, I would entertain the Americans, the Mexicans, and the Indians with my violin, which I had previously left with William for safekeeping. I carried it now in a fringed and beaded deerskin case that a Comanche woman had made for me in trade for a hatchet. Between the classical concertos and the folk songs, I managed to find something everyone could appreciate, and when things got particularly dull, I could always fiddle behind my back, behind my head, or between my legs. Herr Buhler, my old violin instructor at the Saint-Cyr School for Boys in Paris, would have gone mad had he ever seen me playing between my legs on the left-handed Stradivarius that I had stolen from him. But I imagined that he had probably drunk himself to death by now anyway.

It felt good to play again. I hadn't made music in a while, and was rusty, though no one noticed but me. After a few nights of playing, the fluid strokes and sharp staccatos came back to me, though my fingertips hurt from lack of conditioning. One night, we even had a square dance, with Tom Boggs calling.

Freight wagons would come through on this, the mountain branch of the Santa Fe Trail, so we enjoyed newspapers and other things from back East. A few Americans decided to stay at Boggsville to tend flocks or herd cattle or clear fields for William. With every new arrival came more talk of the political excitement involving slavery and states' rights. At William's stockade, we had heard rumors that certain Southern states had entertained debates on the subject of secession in their houses of congress— this in response to a growing abolitionist sentiment in the North. The abolitionists believed the federal government should abolish slavery, while the Southern states maintained that the constitutional provision for states' rights, particularly in the Tenth Amendment, gave the states the authority to decide whether or not to allow slavery. There was talk in the North of ratifying another amendment to the Constitution—one that would outlaw slavery. Most agreed that the slave states would secede should such an amendment pass, or even come before Congress.

On the plains and in the mountains, we knew this business was serious and dangerous. Men of both loyalties—North and South—now lived out West, including enough zealous abolitionists and secessionists to foment considerable violence. Opinions differed as to just how serious the trouble might get.

"If South Carolina secedes," Tom Boggs said one night, "hell, the army and the navy will just march right in there and blow hell out of the place. How does one state expect to stand up against the whole federal government?"

But William grunted and shook his head. "I don't know. Could be they'll all secede at the same time, or one after another. The Union Army isn't big enough to stop them from Virginia all the way to Texas."

"But the South couldn't win a war like that," said R. M. Moore. "The North has all the manufacturing plants."

"The only thing the rich men in the South think they can't do," William said, "is let their slaves get taken away from them. They know that would crush their economy. They may be gentlemen of honor and intelligence, but they have acquired their wealth on the backs of people that are whipped like dogs, and they are not about to give up that wealth and go out in their own fields to pick their own cotton. They are just arrogant enough to drag the whole republic into a bloody war so that they can go on trading people like animals and living high on the hog because of it."

This surprised me somewhat, coming from William, for he had owned a slave himself in the past, a manservant named Dick Green who had worked at Bent's Old Fort as a blacksmith. However, I had known Dick Green, and knew that William treated him like any other man. Dick had ridden and fought alongside white men, Mexicans, and Indians, and had drawn wages like anyone else at Bent's Old Fort. I could see now that William might have bought this man to thwart the institution of slavery rather than perpetuate it.

"If it comes to war," I said, posing a question for discussion, "how will it affect us out here in the territories?"

William puffed on his pipe for a few seconds. "Colorado and New Mexico territories are mostly Union in sympathy. I don't think there will be much trouble this far west."

"Maybe not," Kit Carson said. "Except for the gold. Takes money to make war. The South could go after the Colorado gold fields. Maybe even California."

"You think so?" Tom Boggs said.

"Like William said, they're arrogant. They think they can do whatever they take a mind to do. Especially the Texans."

"The worst trouble will come from the Indians," William added. "We saw it during the Mexican War. When civilized men go to fightin' one another, the Indians always sieze the opportunity to make raids and take back land they've lost. Can you imagine what a time the Comanches will have in Texas if the Texans secede and go to fightin' the Union? I wouldn't want to be a farmer on the fringes of Comanche territory right now."

And so the speculation rambled, day after day, night after night, no one really knowing what to expect. And so it goes on, year after year, war after war. We could never have understood at that time that the War Between the States would last so long, or that the frontier would pass so quickly. The Comanches who laughed at me as I sawed my fiddle in contorted poses could scarcely have grasped how quickly everything they knew and loved would vanish in flame and dust.

———

I've mentioned the big bell at William's stockade, mounted on the top of an eight-foot pole set in the ground. I asked William about it one day. "Come from a school that burnt down in Missouri. I hauled it out here."

The bell had three purposes, William said. If visitors were seen approaching the stockade, the bell was rung three times to alert everyone of a new arrival. I remembered having heard this bell sound thrice the first time I, myself, approached the stockade.

"Of course, you know by now that I use it to call the horses," William continued. Every day, before hay or grain was fed to riding stock in the corrals, the bell was sounded five times. This trained the horses to expect feed at the sound of the bell. Often, riding stock was turned out to graze around the stockade. If William wanted the horses back inside the corrals in a hurry, all he had to do was ring that bell, and the horses would come running for their feed. The signal for feeding time was five rings, as opposed to the signal for approaching riders—three rings. This number made no difference to the horses, of course, only to the men. The horses would come running at the mere sound of the bell, no matter how many times it tolled.

"There's one more use for that bell," William said. "We haven't had to use it yet, but you ought to know. The guards are trained to ring hell out of that bell in case we're ever attacked. So if you ever hear three bells, you know somebody friendly's a-comin'. You hear five, you know the stable hands are feedin'. But if you hear more than that, grab your guns, Mr. Greenwood, and take your place on the wall."

One night I decided to sleep under the stars inside the protective walls of the stockade. I preferred this to sleeping inside as long as the weather was neither too wet nor too cold. I found a place where the stockade wall blocked the cold north wind, and rolled myself into a buffalo robe. I kept a pistol under my rolled jacket, which I used for a pillow, and I placed a rifle at my feet. This way, whether I had time to roll to my feet or not, I would have a weapon at my disposal.

I spent most of the night reciting poems to myself, and thinking about the problems of the plains and the rest of the world. Finally, toward dawn, I fell asleep and began to dream of Mescalero Apaches crawling over the stockade walls to kill me, accompanied by ogres and carnivorous creatures of the most terrifying ilk. I remained thus tormented by the machinations of my own twisted mind until the bell began to ring. The first few tones frightened away my nightmarish attackers just before they scalped me alive.

Then my eyes opened, and I saw the pewter cast of a not-quite-dawn hanging heavy in the sky. The bell had rung four times. Now five . . . A pause. Then it rang again. And again! I reached under my coat and took my pistol in hand, glancing both ways along the pointed tops of the stockade timbers. I saw no attackers coming over the wall just yet. My mind was still trying to sort nightmares from reality.

The bell rang on, so I fought the buffalo robe until I kicked it aside, letting the cold air hit my body. I rolled to my feet, and thought about picking up my rifle. Instead, I decided to jump up on a large oaken barrel so

I could look over the stockade walls. I had slept in my clothes and boots, so I sprang immediately onto the cask, put there for that purpose, and risked a peek over the wall. In the dim light, I could see no attackers, but that bell was still clanging away—and in a most irregular cadence, as if the guard ringing the bell was quite agitated—or even wounded.

I jumped down from the keg and scooped up my rifle as I sprinted around stacks of wood, around a smokehouse, and past a hand-dug well. I darted among other outbuildings as I ran toward William's cabin at the center of the stockade. No shots yet fired, I thought. But over the sounds of my own footsteps and my own heavy breathing, I heard hoofbeats, voices shouting, and doors flying open as men woke and came alive to answer the call of the bell.

The attack was coming from the east, I surmised. From the timber along the river. But who? Pawnees? Apaches? Blackfeet? Outlaws? Texas warmongers? As I came around a dormant freight wagon, a horse lunged at me, shoving me down behind a wagon wheel, and scaring the liver out of me. I looked for a rider, but there was none. Were the attackers inside the walls already? Stealing horses? How had this mount escaped the corrals? Rolling out from under the wagon, I regained my feet and finally sprinted around the toolshed—the last obstacle between me and the bell.

I found a dozen men standing around with guns in their hands, shaking their heads as horses milled everywhere in confusion. And at the bell? Major. My horse. He held the rope to the bell between his teeth, and he was pulling down with his powerful neck, swinging the bell so hard that it almost flipped over in its cradle every time he yanked the rope. The relieved men began to chuckle, and they all looked at me as I slid to a stop upon the field of battle, for they all knew I owned that horse. Major saw me, too, and he finally turned the rope loose and looked at me as if to say, "Where the hell have you been?"

William was standing at his open cabin door, his shotgun in one hand. He scowled at me, though I could tell he was holding back a grin. "Mr. Greenwood!" he shouted. "Your goddamn horse is hungry!"

The men burst into laughter at my expense. As they jeered me, I saw Major's lips groping comically again for the knot at the end of the rope. He managed to get in two more rings before I got to him, took the rope away from him, and pushed him toward the corrals. "Come on, Major," I groaned, heading for the feed troughs. I knew I would have to pour some grain to get the horses all back into the corrals. Major followed, truly believing he had just ordered up his own breakfast. Now I saw where Major Pain-in-the-Ass had used his teeth to slide the poles aside at the corral openings, dropping one end of each pole so he and the other horses could step out of the corral enclosure. All this in order to get at that confounded bell.

As I trudged toward the corn crib, Major shoving me between the shoulder blades from behind, I heard William shout, "Who's trainin' who?"

The laughter roared. It got worse. Within minutes, a relief party from Boggsville had arrived, for the bell could be heard even that far away. So I had to hear it from Tom Boggs and his men, as well. William put me to work gathering eggs and firewood for his wife, Yellow Woman, so she could cook a hearty breakfast for everyone who had responded to Major's false alarm. I didn't hear the end of it for years.

Winter came to William's stockade, and with the frost and snow came my plans to ride back into Comancheria to begin the winter trading. Kills Something, Loud Shouter, and Fears-the-Ground were eager to go home. They would be returning to their camps and families with much to show. On their fleet Comanche ponies, they had won many a horse race against the Cheyennes and had gifts of deerskin and metal to show for it. The Cheyenne women produced some of the finest quill work and bead work on the plains, and the Comanche women coveted their wares. Also, I had paid my Comanche friends well with gunpowder, lead, bullet molds, hoop iron for making arrowheads, and fancy silver conchos pounded from Mexican coins. These they wore in their hair, around their necks, and upon their deerskin shirts as we rode away from Boggsville and Bent's Stockade.

"Get us some horses," William had told me. "More than usual."

The reason went unspoken, for it was unspeakable. War devoured horseflesh as surely as human flesh. By this order, I knew William believed that war would begin soon. And so I rode again as a pawn on mankind's chessboard, a mere cog in the great machine of humanity. I flatter myself to think that had I lived an honest life I might have used my God-given gifts of intelligence to deter wars, rather than feed them with the meat and bones of horses. But, alas, a fugitive lives a wasted life.

TWELVE

No one covers ground a-horseback like a Comanche. We covered more than forty miles a day on our return to the Crossing on the Canadian River. Our ponies, lightly encumbered with pad saddles and war bridles, carried us on all day at a long trot or a slow canter. Kills Something was the largest man among us, and he could not have weighed over 155 pounds. The spare horses carried the pack saddles loaded with things like blankets, metal pots, and gunpowder, but we had enough spare mounts to distribute the weight among three pack saddles. The Comanches, incidentally, were the only Plains Indians I ever saw to adapt the white man's way of using pack animals. Other tribes used only the travois. Anyway, we got back to the site of old Fort Adobe in a mere five days. Had we not been encumbered by the pack animals, we could have made the trip in three and a half days.

Our return caused much celebration. Little Bluff's band of Kiowas were in camp with old Shaved Head's Comanches, and the Kiowas had attacked a wagon train on the Santa Fe Trail and had killed and scalped a white man, and had gotten away with five mules and two horses, with only one Kiowa warrior slightly wounded by a bullet through the flesh of his arm. This warrior's arm was swollen to the size of a cantaloupe, but he danced the scalp dance that night with the rest of the men and women, circling the scalp on the pole.

"Does that wound hurt?" I asked him.

"The bone is not broken," he replied.

I found the Kiowa chief, Little Bluff, and he greeted me like a brother, for I had not seen him in over a year.

"Why did your hunting party attack the white men's wagons?" I asked the Kiowa leader.

"They behave like fools in our country."

"What do you mean?"

"They were killing buffalo and only taking the tongues and the humps, leaving the rest to rot. I tried to make talk with them, to tell them we would hunt and trade meat to them. I rode toward them alone, with a white flag, but they shot at me. I heard the bullet cut the grass just in front of my pony. They were foolish. They did not keep guards around their camp. They were easy to attack in the morning while they were hitching the animals to the wagons. We could have killed more of them, but it was only a warning."

"The soldiers may come to punish your people if you continue to attack the wagons," I said.

Little Bluff laughed. "Who will lead them here? You? No one else knows the way."

"I will never lead your enemies to you. But there are others who know the way."

"Who?"

"Some of the Apaches and Pueblos are serving as scouts to the army."

Little Bluff tossed the idea aside with a wave of his hand. "If the bluecoats come in numbers too great to fight, we will move south into the country where only Kiowas and Comanches know how to find water. The soldiers will be easy to kill when their ponies die of thirst."

My talk was meant to warn Little Bluff away from attacking too many wagons on the trail, but he seemed to have a logical answer to all of my arguments. After all, this was his country by birth, blood, and sacrifice. The United States may have included this wild region on its paper maps, but the hooves of Kiowa and Comanche ponies on this soil meant more than all the treaties in government archives and all the deeds in all the courthouses of the so-called civilized world. Just as the Kiowas and Comanches had invaded this country to take it from the Apaches and Tonkawas, so were the Americans and Texans now invading it to take it from the Kiowas and Comanches. It was the old story of human arrogance, one nation against another, one civilization crushing the last, in turn to be crushed by the next. There was little I could do about it other than watch.

We stayed in camp at the Crossing for several days, resting and feasting on venison, black bear, and antelope. Yet the buffalo were nowhere to be seen here this year, and the people began to feel anxious about starving through the winter if we could not kill some buffalo and dry some meat.

Then came word from the south. Peta Nocona's band of Comanches had made a sweeping raid on the Texas settlements and had come away with many horses and several scalps. Then, retreating into Comancheria, the raiding party had found large herds of buffalo. Now a camp had been established on the Pease River, where women and Mexican slaves pounded and dried meat that would last through the winter.

When this news came, the elders called for a council in the lodge of Chief Shaved Head. Any council caused excitement among the people of a camp, and this one was no different. It began with a gathering outside of Shaved Head's lodge. His lodge was made of seventeen buffalo hides—the largest I ever saw. Old Shaved Head entered the lodge first, followed by my friend Kills Something, for Kills Something had risen to a rank almost equal to that of Shaved Head.

After Shaved Head and Kills Something entered the lodge, other elders filed into the tipi, including the mystic, Burnt Belly. They circled around the inside of the walls until they came to the entry, then they continued to circle in ever smaller rings, making room for another row of warriors against the tipi walls as they continued to spiral inward. In this way the lodge gradually began to fill with warriors in descending authority. The warriors knew where they stood in rank to one another, so the highest-ranking men entered first, and when the lodge got full, the youngest warriors just had to listen from outside. I knew my place, as well. I was not Comanche by blood, but I had taken Apache scalps and defended Comanche camps, so I stepped in line behind the warriors who had earned more coups and war honors than I had.

My battle honors put me about halfway between the fire in the center of the lodge, and the portal through which we all had entered. Once inside, we all sat down and waited as Shaved Head lit his pipe. He drew some smoke from the pipe, and when he exhaled the smoke he patted it on his chest as he chanted a prayer to the spirits. The smoke would carry what he felt in his heart up through the vent hole at the peak of the tipi, and into the Shadow Land where the spirits dwelt. He then passed the pipe to Kills Something, who did the same, passing the pipe among the inner circle of elders so that all the wisest men of the band might let their hearts be known to the spirits.

When the elders had smoked, Shaved Head began to speak. He was old, but his voice was strong and certain.

"The Great Circle goes around and around, like the ring of warriors who have entered this council lodge. It goes around and the True Humans go with it, for this is the way of the Great Creator and the spirits who guide us. The Circle comes now to the Beaver Moon. Winter comes soon after. It is time to hunt buffalo so our women can make meat to feed our children.

"Now, the spirits do not send the herds to this camp. The Great Mystery always tries the skill of the True Humans, and we must always use the wisdom of our hearts to survive because the spirits like to see us struggle, and that is good, because it makes us strong. We must find meat. My heart tells me we must leave this camp to find it.

"You have heard the criers in the village. Chief Peta Nocona of the Nokonis has found large herds of buffalo to the south. Even now his women and his slaves butcher the carcasses and make meat. The ravens gather over their camp. Peta Nocona has sent riders to tell us this. The riders say that his hunters have been wise and careful. They have hunted the small herds among the hills and have used the power of the wind so that the big herds have not been frightened away. Peta Nocona's riders invite our hunters to go south and hunt the buffalo in their country, and have a feast, and let our young warriors find brides among his people. His warriors have taken scalps from *tejanos* and they wish to hold a great scalp dance.

"The spirits tell my heart that this is good. This camp is old. The grass is gone. The wood is gone. The deer and antelope and bear have fed us, but we must have buffalo meat for the winter. To the south we will find great herds. I have seen this in visions. We will find timber and honey, and tall grass for our ponies. We will find women for our young men, and nuts from the pecan trees to make pemmican. It is time to move our village. I have spoken."

The men in the lodge remained quiet while Kills Something prepared to speak, for it was his place to talk next. He waited for some time, then looked at old Burnt Belly and said, "Grandfather, do you have something to tell the council?"

"*Tsuh,*" said the old man. From his cross-legged sitting position he suddenly rose to his feet as if lifted by strong arms from above—a strange thing to witness from a man apparently so old and feeble. This seemingly effortless ascension startled everyone who saw it and charged the air in the lodge with mystical anticipation.

"For three moons now I have seen visions," Burnt Belly began. "Listen, my brothers, these are powerful things. When the spirits give the True Humans great power, it shines and dazzles us, and makes us smile, and gives us courage. But we must remember that the great shining visions of power come fastened to dark dangers, as night fastens itself to day. The darkness holds power equal to the brightness. The brightness leads us to glory, the darkness to destruction. I will tell you of my visions now, but you must remember that we ride forever in twilight, and if we lose our direction, we will turn into the darkness rather than the light.

"In my visions, I have seen a good time that begins with a great hunt. We will have much meat and we will dance with brothers of other bands of the True Humans. This time of feasting and celebration gives us power from the Shadow Land, strength for our bodies and our horses, and courage to protect our country.

"Then, the vision changes . . ." When he said this, Burnt Belly spread his arms and tilted his face upward and threw his voice so that the words seemed to come down from the smoke hole instead of up from his mouth. The men in the lodge shifted nervously when this happened, for ventriloquism and prestidigitation always shook the Comanche mind.

"The spirits have shown me a great war—white man against white man. The soldiers will go away to fight other white soldiers. The *tejanos* will go away to war. No palefaces will remain on our borders but women and children. In my visions, I have seen our warriors raiding the places where the white men have built their square lodges of trees that once held turkeys and black bear. We will take back the camps that the white men have spoiled along the streams. The water will run clear again, and the grass will grow tall where the iron tools have torn up the earth. We will capture the white children left behind to teach them the Good Way, and make the white women good with the seed of our bravest warriors, and take scalps from any white people who try to keep our country from us longer!

"This I have seen in visions of bright splendor, sent to me by the spirits. But beware, my brothers. Remember the darkness. You must pray and seek wisdom before you act upon my visions. You must hold council and search the hearts of your elders. Greed for land and white women and battle honors will destroy the bravest warrior. You must remember the whole good of the True Humans in everything you do in this time—this coming time of victory upon victory, this good time of dancing and feasting, this gift of many seasons. I have spoken."

Burnt Belly sank back to his place on the ground, and now Kills Something took his turn to speak. "In three sleeps, I will ride south with a scouting party to find the buffalo near Peta Nocona's village. If the elders decide to pursue the visions of Burnt Belly, then the whole village will follow my scouting party. By the time the village arrives, my party will have scouted two sleeps in every direction for enemies, and we will have made the first buffalo kills. Then the whole village of the great chief Shaved Head will enjoy the hunt. Even the youngest warriors will make their first kills.

"I will take only twelve riders with me on my scout. The others must guard the village as it moves. I will accept some warriors who have taken scalps and made many buffalo kills. I will take others who are young and inexperienced, but show great promise. Many of our best warriors must remain behind to guard the village as it moves.

"I believe in the visions of Burnt Belly, and I believe in the wisdom of our elders. The great time of victory upon victory will begin soon. I have spoken."

Kills Something sat down to let the next highest-ranking warrior speak. So the council continued, each man giving his opinion, each agreeing with Shaved Head and Kills Something, each placing the greatest faith in Burnt Belly's visions. When every man had had his say, the council was adjourned and the warriors all filed out of the lodge. Kills Something found himself besieged by warriors volunteering to ride with his advance party of scouts. Most of them he refused, telling them that they must stay with the main village to protect the women and children should enemies attack. He did allow eight young warriors to join the party, one only twelve years old. The older scouts would be Loud Shouter, Fears-the-Ground, Kills Something himself, and me. The four of us had ridden far and traveled well together.

That night, I went back to my tipi and pulled the bearskin over the entrance. I tied a rope to a lodge pole above me and sat on the ground with my legs crossed. Using the rope to help pull myself up, I rose from the ground as I had seen Burnt Belly do in council. I did this one hundred times. If I practiced this exercise enough, I reasoned, I would strengthen the necessary muscles and be able to rise straight up from the ground without the help of the rope. Showmanship and oratory skills went a long way in a Comanche council.

THIRTEEN

Our trip to the Nokoni camps was one of the finest I ever took anywhere. The weather remained crisp and sunny, warming slightly as we rode south. The time had come for the deer to rut, and everywhere we saw large bucks with sprawling antlers—sometimes emerging right in front of us, oblivious to everything but their own lust as they followed the scent trails of estrus does; sometimes barreling at astonishing speeds after comely females; sometimes battling each other in vicious squabbles that could be heard a mile away as their antlers crashed together.

A Comanche scouting party could easily cover forty miles a day in those times. Furthermore, fifty miles was not out of the question, but there was no need for us to ride that furiously as we searched south for Peta Nocona's village. So it occurred that on our fourth day of riding, we struck the North Pease River and found a trail leading west.

We got down from our horses to talk about this trail leading west up the right bank of the North Pease—except for Fears-the-Ground, who almost never got off his horse.

"Indian ponies," Kills Something said. "No metal moccasins."

"No pony-drags," I observed.

"True. Maybe a war party. Maybe scouts."

"What nation?" I asked.

"I will ride upstream to look for signs of our people," said Fears-the-Ground.

"And I will ride downstream," I said.

Kills Something gave a sign, and I leapt back onto my pony. I took off at a trot downstream as Fears-the-Ground turned upstream, and the rest of the party led their mounts down to the water to drink and rest. As I rode

along the riverbank, I kept a close eye on the trail, hoping to find a Comanche trail sign. The Comanches had devised many such signs. Sometimes grass was bundled and tied. Sometimes tree trunks were blazed with
a hatchet. Sticks might be found protruding from the soil. Rocks might be
piled in coded fashion. So I rode, keeping my eyes trained on the ground
and the trees and brush near the trail. I knew I might have to ride for hours
before finding a sign, so I settled onto my Comanche pad saddle for a long
jaunt.

I already knew a few things about this trail. There were some fifty to
sixty warrior-hunters in the party. The lack of pony-drags told me there
were probably no women or children riders. Because I didn't see many individual sets of tracks coming or going, it seemed these riders were at
ease, confident, and unconcerned about enemy movements around them.
Otherwise, they would have been sending out many scouts. The trail
seemed to be only a couple of days old, judging by the freshness of the
dung piles, and by the way the stalks of grass had begun to rise back toward the sky from where the hooves had stomped them down.

I rode for over two hours, then finally found what I was looking for. A
gathering of small white stones caught my eye a few steps to the left of
the trail. The stones had been set down in the shape of the first quarter of
the moon. It was as if this message had been left especially for me, for my
life revolved around moon phases. The sign meant that the party had passed
this spot at the time of the first quarter of the moon, which had risen three
nights before. To the east of the image of the moon, two sticks jutted from
the ground, one slightly taller than the other. This meant that the party had
been two days on the trail from the old camp. To the west of the image of
the moon, a line of pebbles indicated the party's direction of travel—the
very direction from which I had ridden.

Now I had a good idea of what was going on. We had heard that Peta
Nocona's band had set up a large camp on the Pease River, and had killed
plenty of buffalo nearby. The warriors had left the women behind to butcher
the kill and dry the meat, and had ridden west to establish a new camp. From
reports we had received from outriders, I knew that Peta's camp was several
weeks old. It had been established as a main supply camp for Peta's raids on
the Texas settlements. I knew that Peta's village could not muster more than
about a hundred warriors, so it seemed that virtually all the men had ridden
west to find the new camp. This had to mean that scouts had ridden far and
wide and had found no signs of enemies within a hundred or more miles in

every direction. Otherwise, the men would never have left their women and children unprotected at the village.

Once I deduced all this, I turned my pony upstream and struck a canter. My mount was a young sorrel mare, gifted with endurance and hard, tough feet. I returned to Kills Something's party in half the time it had taken me to trot downstream. Kills-Something looked with approval at the sweat covering my horse, and asked what I had learned. Fears-the-Ground had not yet returned, so I reported what I knew.

"Good," Kills Something said. "Now, from this place, we will follow the trail, the way Fears-the-Ground has ridden. Once we have found the Nokonis, we will send riders back to our main village to guide them to the new place."

Three days later, we found Peta's main camp on the upper Double Mountain Fork of the Brazos River. This was one of the largest Comanche camps I ever saw. It seemed that Peta had invited Comanches of many bands to gather with him here, hunt buffalo, and talk of war with the Texans. Tipis flanked the river on both sides for almost four miles. The little river provided a good stream of fresh water, owing to good autumn rains on the Llano Estacado, yet was narrow and shallow enough to cross with ease. Just upstream of the camp, the jagged canyon walls of the Caprock rose, forming numerous draws and side canyons where deer and bear might hide, adding to the plentitude of buffalo in the area.

We had seen the smoke from the cook fires hanging in the sky for half a day before actually seeing the camp, so we knew we would find a large one. Even this could not have prepared us for the sight. The moment I saw the camp over the brink of the river valley, I whistled low through my teeth. "That is a large camp," I said.

"Many lodges," Loud Shouter said. "Too many to count."

"I hope each lodge has at least one pretty girl in it," said one of the young scouts.

"You will have to use the breeze and stalk them like deer," replied his friend, just downwind from him, "for your scent will spook them an arrow shot away."

The warriors all laughed at the young suitor, and Kills Something suggested that we visit a creek that issued into the river downstream of the lodges, to bathe before entering the great camp. This was done, and then we went to meet the people of Peta Nocona's camp.

When we approached, we encountered a sentinel some distance from camp. Seeing us, he leapt on his horse and prepared to ride back to camp to spread the alarm if necessary. By now twilight had fallen, and we might have been a dozen Texans in the fading light, so the sentinel was cautious.

The Comanches and their allies had a sign that they would give in those days to indicate from a distance that they were friendly, for often parties were spotted from such a distance that they could not he identified. Kills Something ordered us to line up abreast so that we could give this sentinel the sign. The twelve of us brought our horses into an even row. Kills Something then rode ahead of us about twenty steps. Here he stopped, then turned to the right, again about twenty steps. He stopped, then returned to the line the same way he had ridden out, following the right angle.

The sentinel now made the same maneuver in response, and we all knew that we could enter the camp. This simple sign could be seen at a great distance and saved the Indians many an anxious moment as unidentified strangers approached encampments. When used from a great distance, the maneuvers were executed on a grander scale, so that they might be seen and understood from miles away. If the U.S. Army or the Texas Rangers had ever figured out this signal, they might have charged many an ill-prepared camp and committed even more outrages than they ultimately did.

We were only about five hundred yards from the sentinel when he responded to our sign, so we struck a canter and rode to the edge of camp with our sentinel acting as our escort. The sights, sounds, and smells of the village greeted us as we began to pass among the hide lodges. We were hungry, and the aroma of roasting buffalo hump filled the air. Having just bathed in chilly waters, we all longed to warm ourselves at one of the many fires we passed as we rode at a walk through the camp. Laughing children darted all around us, running foot races and shooting blunt arrows. Young girls ceased their gossiping to turn and judge the young riders in our band.

By now it had dawned on me why Kills Something had chosen the young scouts for this expedition. Among the twelve of us were eight youths who would probably be looking for wives soon. Kills Something had brought these young men along on the advance party to give them first crack at all the marriageable girls gathered here. They would probably never again find this many young women to choose from in one place.

I could see the looks of excitement on the faces of these warriors as we passed the crowds of comely Comanche girls.

It was customary for an arriving party of visitors to seek out the chief of a village, so our escort took us to Peta Nocona's lodge—a large tipi overlooking the prettiest part of the river valley. We found him outside of this lodge, preparing to put on an elaborately decorated headdress made of buffalo horns and the shaggy hide from the head of a big bull. In addition to the headdress, he had donned finely beaded deerskin leggings, and had painted his face in preparation for a dance. When he saw us coming, he put the headdress aside for the moment, and came to greet us.

We all swung down from our horses when we greeted Peta. Instead of shaking hands with each of us, he raised his palm in friendship to us all, and said, *"Aho."*

We repeated the greeting, and Kills Something alone stepped forward to shake Peta's hand. "We have decided to join your great camp-together," he said. "This is our scouting party. The rest of the village will follow."

"Tsuh," said Peta with a smile. "This is good. Our camp gets larger and stronger. The buffalo are plentiful near here. We will hunt by day and dance by night. All the chiefs of all the bands will meet in council and we will seek the wisdom of the spirits. My heart tells me that this is the beginning of a good time for the True Human Beings."

"We will camp tonight," Kills Something said. "Tomorrow, we will send scouts running back to our main village to guide them quickly to this place. Our people long to feast and dance with your people, and all the other bands gathered here. If you wish, I will send one of my scouts to your camp on the river where your women and slaves are making meat."

"Tsah," Peta said. "My warriors are ready to hunt, so it is good that one of your scouts will ride to my old camp and bring along the women and children. They have been too long in that place, and it is time that they join us. My wife, Nadua, is there, and I want her here in my lodge. Yes, send one of your scouts. That is good."

"Tsah," Kills Something replied.

Peta turned to a boy sitting on the ground near the fire, gnawing on a rib bone. "My son," he said. "Run through the whole village. Tell everyone that the scouts from Shaved Head's band of the Quahadi have come to camp with us. Tell everyone in this camp that they must not refuse these scouts anything they wish to have. They will have food to eat, robes to sleep in, lodges to shelter them, supplies and weapons of any kind that they will need to ride again tomorrow and bring still more True Humans to this great gathering in this sacred place. Now, go!"

The boy threw his rib bone to a nearby dog and sprang to his feet. At this moment, I recognized the boy as Quanah, the son of Peta and his captive white wife, Nadua, who was known as Cynthia Ann Parker in the Texas settlements. In an instant, young Quanah was running up the river, weaving among the tipis, repeating Peta's orders to the camp. It impressed me that Peta would trust the duties of village crier to a son only twelve winters old, and that young Quanah took on the responsibility with such alacrity.

The people in Peta's camp knew more about hospitality than any people I ever met. They sought us out, bringing robes, roasted buffalo meat, curdled buffalo milk mixed with blood, pemmican for our ride the next day, rawhide bowls filled with buffalo stew seasoned with wild onions, and buffalo horn spoons with which to eat it. They brought gunpowder, lead for bullets, blankets, hand mirrors for signaling one another from a distance, flints for making fire, and more tobacco and coffee than we could use in a week. They offered us fresh horses to ride the next day. They vacated two lodges so that we could all sleep comfortably. We wanted for nothing.

After we feasted, we watched the mounted procession leading up to the great scalp dance. It started with Peta himself riding a horse through the camp, his buffalo headdress on his head, his recently taken scalps tied to his tomahawk. There were hundreds of dancers following Peta, and they all dressed up as animals, wearing headdresses made of cranes, eagles, antelopes, deer, bear, mountain lions, and wolves. The riders arrived and dismounted at a large dance ground that had been left open among the lodges. Drums began to beat, and the warriors began to dance in their elaborate costumes.

One visiting chief named Tasacowadi wore an incredible headdress and cape made from the hide of a huge spotted jaguar that he must have killed far to the south in Mexico. Tasacowadi meant "great spotted cat" and I could see that the killing of this cat must have granted powerful medicine to the slayer for him to take his name from the cat he had killed. Tasacowadi and all the other dancers did their best to imitate the sounds of the animals they were portraying by roaring, squawking, screaming, howling, and growling while they danced. Other dancers sang a rhythmic series of syllables that had no meaning, as white people will sing "fa-la-la-la" and "fiddle-dee-dee." At one point in the song, however, everyone, including the spectators, would scream the most bloodthirsty war cries they could muster. I can't remember a more entertaining spectacle.

The dance went on and on, but we were tired and had to ride hard the next day, so one by one our scouts retired to the lodges that had been provided for us. Kills Something and I stayed up latest. The phase of the moon was such that I knew I wouldn't sleep more than a couple of hours, though I had chewed my dogbane root and drunk my tea of moccasin flower. As the hundreds of dancers continued singing and shuffling across the dance ground, Kills Something said that he would spread his robes and sleep, and that I should try to do the same.

"Yes, I will," I promised. "Even if I cannot sleep, I will rest my body so that we can ride tomorrow."

"When the sun rises," Kills Something said, "I will lead two of the scouts back to our main village. The rest, I will send in different directions. We must scout the country for our enemies. Once our village has arrived here, our people will be safe. Until then, we must stay alert."

"Yes. It is good to be cautious. Peta has made a great raid on the Texans, and they may be looking for revenge."

"That is true. Here is what I want you to do, my brother. I want you to ride to Peta's old camp, where his women and children and slaves are still pounding and drying meat. Make them travel quickly to this new place. Like you, I fear that Peta has grown careless and has not scouted enough. He has left his women behind unprotected for too many days."

"I agree. It is not possible to be too careful."

Now Kills Something sighed and looked up at me. "My brother, I send you to Peta's meat camp for a reason. Once, you followed my sister when she ran away with another warrior. We have not spoken of this since, for I told you then that I would no longer claim her as my sister if she would run away from my brother-in-law like that. But time goes around in a great circle, and seasons follow seasons. My heart was once hard and cold to think of my sister, but now it has warmed. Still, I will not claim her, and I do not wish to speak to her. But I ask you, my brother, to see that she is well. I could not do this myself without going back on my word, and I cannot ask another warrior. That is the only reason I ask you, though it is much to ask, for you were the one most wounded by her leaving."

I looked at Kills Something, and clasped his hand in mine. Smiling, I said, "Nothing my brother asks is too great."

FOURTEEN

The next morning, I borrowed a lean bald-face gelding from one of Peta's warriors and struck out to the northeast to follow the trail back to Peta's old meat camp. Kills Something and the others loped off to fulfill their own duties, scouting the area, and bringing our main village to this great camp-together that Peta had organized. My borrowed bald-face horse could cover some ground. He possessed a long-reaching trot as smooth as a boat skimming the surface of still water. This made for easy riding and for three days and nights I did nothing but ride by the light of the sun and the light of the moon. We rested only between sundown and moonrise, when I would nap, and hobble my pony to graze or sleep as he saw fit.

I knew I was getting near when I saw the ravens and vultures circling in the sky in the distance ahead. I had just pulled the reins of my war bridle to stop the bald-face gelding on a high point of land along the Pease River so I could get a feeling for the lay of the land. I was no more than twenty minutes from the camp, it seemed, judging from the carrion eaters that dotted the sky ahead.

Over my left shoulder to the northwest, I had been watching the approach of a blue norther. It looked like a big, windy one. A wall of clouds the color of a bad bruise boiled with menace and stretched for hundreds of miles away to the northeast and southwest. Below the blue clouds I saw a layer of dark brown dust that the winds had torn from the earth. It seemed from the dust that the norther was going to blow in dry. The clouds were now looming almost over me, and I knew any minute the wave of frigid air would tear at my Comanche braids and chill me to the marrow. The weather had been so mild when I left Peta's big camp-together that I had carried only one blanket with me with which to stay warm. I was glad to be near the meat camp now, where I knew I could borrow a buffalo robe.

Already, my pony was snorting in anticipation of the cold northern air, and trying to prance right out from under me, so I made him charge down the high hill into the river valley where we might find some protection from the winds. Within minutes, an icy blast roared through the treetops, tearing away the last of the autumn leaves and sending them fluttering around me. When the wall of winter wind hit me, the temperature plummeted so quickly that I felt as if I had jumped into a pool of snowmelt. My pony ramped and kicked one hind leg out, accompanied by a resounding fart, as a greeting to the northern invader. A smattering of rain and sleet began to pepper me, but only for a mile or so, failing to totally soak me. Then, the dust cloud roared overhead, and grit began to collect in my eyes, nose, and mouth. I glanced up once to see a brown swirl cupping its dirty hand over me as a wave curls onto the beach.

To my relief, the dust soon began to dissipate, leaving only cold wind and occasional barrages of sleet to accost me. Even this did not concern me much, for I knew the camp was near, with plenty of meat and tipis for shelter. I had slept on the ground and eaten next to nothing for three days.

The ravens had been blown into the next river valley by the blue norther, but I knew instinctively where the camp lay. I came to the base of a high bluff between me and the camp and decided to ride up onto it so I could make my presence known and give signs of friendship before I blundered into the village.

I climbed to the top of the bluff overlooking the camp and drew rein. The cold had apparently driven many mothers inside the lodges to bundle up their children, for I saw only a few women tending the strips of meat that hung on racks and cured in the smoke over fires. Several adopted Mexican captives were in view. To my right, the wall of brown dust was blowing away. To my left, the cloudy sky promised much cold and little sunshine. The camp lay in front of and below me, but no one had yet noticed my presence on the bluff above them. I looked across the string of forty-seven lodges strung out along the narrow river. A woman emerged from her tipi now, wrapped in a red trade blanket. Dogs trotted through camp, in search of scraps. Wisps of smoke twisted away from the cook fires and smoke holes on the brisk north wind.

Now a sudden motion caught my attention on the far side of the camp and my eyes quickly pulled that way. For a moment or two, I could identify only an unknown object moving fast through the trees toward the camp. Then I made out the shape of a horse and rider in the lead, followed by more movement behind. The faint sound of hooves reached my ears. More riders charged through the cover of trees, then more. The leader broke into the open as a Comanche woman turned to look at him, caught completely by surprise. The lead horseman's wide hat brim flapped in the wind and a puff of white smoke seemed to appear from his outstretched arm. I heard the pistol report and saw the woman fall backward, holding her face with her hands. Already the rider was charging past her and the sickening wave of panic swarmed from my head, into my chest and guts.

These riders had come under cover of the dust storm. These Texans, these soldiers, these attackers numbering in the dozens, the scores. They rushed into the lower end of the camp, revolvers blazing away at the fleeing forms of women, children, and Mexican slaves.

"No!" I shouted, feeling my eyes widen in terror. The next thing I knew, my gelding was charging down the bluff into the middle of a mounting massacre. I rode into the upper end of camp shouting, "Run! Run! The Texans have come! They are killing us!"

Mothers with wild eyes of fear threw back the hides covering their doorways and bolted, carrying their babies, dragging their older children, dodging any way they could in the confusion. Bullets popped against the hide lodges, adding to the chaotic din of gunfire, hoofbeats, and screaming women.

The riders kept coming, fifty, sixty, seventy, one hundred strong. There were some uniformed soldiers among them, but most wore civilian clothes and big hats. They bristled with pistol barrels and sawed-off shotguns.

I continued riding right into the teeth of the attack, not knowing what I would do, other than scream at the women to run. I pulled my revolver from the waist of my breechclout, realizing that I looked as Indian as any Comanche on the range, and I saw the leader of the charge riding right toward me. I fired a shot past his head, intentionally missing him, hoping to simply halt the charge without killing a fellow white man in the battle that had sucked me in. He tried to shoot back, but found his revolver spent, so he tucked it into a saddle holster and took hold of a short-barreled twelve-gauge shotgun tied to his saddle horn with a thong. Other attackers passed the leader as he slowed down and straggled to get his shotgun free.

The attack was about to engulf me, and I knew I had to put up some kind of a front.

Reaching deep into my stomach and chest for the wildest battle cry I could conjure, I felt my bald-face mount spring under me, right into the maw of the fray. I fired my five remaining shots over the heads of the white men, and this little bit of resistance stalled their attack and gave some of the fleeing women and children a chance to escape. I shoved my pistol back into my waistband, and reached for my bow in the quiver. I rode behind a tipi to string the bow. Four bullets tore through the buffalo hide of the lodge and sang past my ears.

A Comanche bow does not string easily, but such was my strength in this moment of terror that I had no trouble bending the bow to loop the end of the bowstring over the end. I knew I had to do some fancy riding now, for the hardest-looking group of white men I had ever seen had roared past me, leaving dead and wounded women behind as they looked for more victims.

Again, I screamed with all the rage of the grizzly and all the anguish of the mountain lion, and charged through the attackers. I notched one of my hunting arrows—I owned no war points. This I sent slamming into the thigh of a blue-coated soldier. I saw gun barrels angle my way, so I threw myself to the right side of my pony and flung another arrow over his withers as I charged crosswise through the column of attackers. Again, the white men scattered, and I wondered how fiercely they would have fought had Peta's most scalp-decorated warriors risen to face them about now.

I felt the impact of the bullet hit my horse's neck. He stumbled, and I dropped to the ground, knowing the gelding was about to fall or roll on me. As the heavy thud of the poor dead horse shook the ground, I sprang to my feet to find a soldier charging me with a cavalry saber. I dodged the blade and jabbed the soldier's horse in the flank with the arrow I had just drawn from my quiver, causing the mount to squeal and charge out of control. I ran now with bullets humming and horses pounding their hooves all around me. I jumped behind a meat rack and drew my bow, loosing an arrow that flew through the high crown of some cowboy's hat without touching his scalp.

I noticed another cowboy charging my way, seemingly unaware of me, for he was looking everywhere in the confusion for someone to shoot at. So I grabbed a stick of firewood about four feet long and as big around as my arm, and rose from nowhere as he trotted by. He was looking the wrong way. One step and I was within reach. The hackberry branch hit him square in the face and knocked him from his mount. Luckily for me, the cowboy held one rein as he fell, keeping his horse from running off. I grabbed the rein, kicked the hapless young attacker in the other side of his face, and found myself mounted on the captured horse in an instant.

By now the main charge had passed me by and I knew that I could do nothing but pick up a straggling Comanche or two and try to carry them to safety. I saw the occasional arrow fly through the sky and knew that at least a few adopted Mexicans or enraged women had tried to put up some kind of a fight. I angled across the camp, and saw a mounted man in a hat chasing a woman who fled on foot. I knew her at a glance, even from behind. It was Hidden Water, sister of my friend Kills Something—Hidden Water, my former Comanche squaw-wife.

As I gave chase, the man fired, his bullet hitting Hidden Water in the calf, and throwing her to the ground. As she crawled desperately away, I let another war cry sing from my throat and notched another arrow. The white man looked back at me briefly, fired an errant shot at Hidden Water as she scrambled across the ground, and then turned tail to join the safety of the main party.

"Plenty Man!" she screamed as I rode up to her. "Please help me!"

"Get up!" I ordered. I held my hand out to her and cocked my foot in the way Comanches had of helping a second rider mount behind.

Hidden Water winced as she rose on her one sound leg. Blood streamed from the wounded right leg. My captured ranch horse was either scared to death of Indians or blood, for he wanted nothing to do with the wounded woman, but I yanked reins and kicked flanks and made the horse approach her, for she could not walk on the leg. Never the toughest Comanche woman, Hidden Water nevertheless grabbed my hand with desperate strength and hopped on her good leg so that she could step on my upwardly cocked foot to swing her wounded leg over the horse. I could tell by her gasp of pain that the leg hurt terribly, but she managed to get mounted behind me. I glanced down at her wounded leg, and it looked straight, so if the bone was at all touched by the bullet, at least it seemed that it hadn't been completely shattered.

The only option I had now was to run, and this horse I had captured was inclined to oblige. He wanted out of that camp as badly as Hidden Water and I. I charged up the river valley, looking for others I might help in some way, but mainly looking for an escape route. The attackers were all ahead of me now, having left behind several dead and wounded women and children, and a few adopted Mexican captives who had put up a fight.

As we galloped onward, a woman stepped from her hiding place in the brush ahead and waved me down. As I slowed and approached, she dragged a startled three-year-old from the brush pile and held him up to me.

"Take my son," she begged.

Again, I had to urge the terrified horse closer to the woman, but I got near enough to grab the child by an arm and pull him to the saddle in front of me. "Hide!" I ordered. "When they are gone, go upstream, and I will bring help back." I left the mother behind and galloped onward again, finding a steep draw up the bluff to the left that I thought I could negotiate.

Just as I started up the draw, I heard hoofbeats and shouting across the river. I turned and saw a Comanche woman running on a horse, with a child in her lap. A second glance told me this was Nadua, Peta Nocona's wife, for I saw streaks of blond in her greased hair, and caught a glimpse of the terror in her blue eyes.

Two men chased Nadua. One wore the uniform of a lieutenant in the U.S. Army. He aimed a revolver at the fleeing woman and surely would have shot her in the back, or tried, had not the other man intervened.

"Wait!" the man in cowboy garb shouted. "She's white!"

So instead of killing Cynthia Ann Parker outright, the men overtook her and caught the reins of her horse to drag her back to their version of civilization, and the family she scarcely remembered, to kill her slowly with white women's clothing, greasy food, and curious stares. As I left the scene, I heard Nadua wailing in terror and sorrow, screaming as she clutched her child, shrilling the piteous lament of a girl once captured from the Parker family—a good Baptist family that had moved too far into Comanche country—shrieking the first verse of a long death song sung by a good Comanche wife and mother who had lingered one day too many at an old meat camp. It was the most tragic song I ever heard sung by man, woman, child, or beast.

With my heart sinking into my guts, I turned away and urged the captured mount up the draw. Once he got started, I looped the reins over the saddle horn and began to reload my revolver while the cow horse climbed. From the rim of the river valley, I saw women and children darting among the bushes, and I shouted instructions to them in Comanche to hide and then move upstream when it was safe. A few shots were still echoing from the valley below, and I could only imagine the soldiers and rangers and cowboys were finishing off wounded women and children.

My mount sprang easily into a lope when I touched my heels to his flanks and we began to make our escape. Then I heard a war cry down in the valley and rode to the brink of the bluff to peer cautiously over it. I saw an Indianized Mexican named José, mounted and fleeing from the white man who had led the attack earlier. I knew José from my earlier visit to Peta's camp. He had completely adopted Comanche ways, and looked Indian from his deerskin leggings to his braided black hair. Behind him, he carried a young Comanche girl and seemed about to make good on his escape into the timber when the white man giving chase loosed a lucky pistol shot that hit the girl in the back, mortally wounding her. As she fell from the pony, her death grip dragged José to the ground with her. He sprang instantly, drew his bow, and sent an arrow into the hip of the white man's horse, which began to buck. Even as he tried to regain control of the horse, the white man continued to fire, and one of his shots happened to hit José in the elbow, spinning him to the ground as it shattered the limb.

The ranger got his wounded horse under control and sent two more deliberate shots into José's body, but the Mexican would not easily die. He crawled up under a small juniper tree and began singing his death song. The ranger, and a Mexican vaquero who had ridden to the ranger's aid, looked down on the wailing José for a few seconds, then the white man gave the order. The vaquero killed José with a load of buckshot. As I backed away from the bluff, I saw the two attackers picking up José's shield, quiver, and bow. Hidden Water and I, with the wide-eyed Comanche child, picked our way carefully upstream.

Years later, I would piece together various intelligence concerning this massacre. The leader of the attack was a captain of the Texas Rangers called Sul Ross. A tough man with some experience as an Indian fighter, and a natural leader, Ross had been given orders by Governor Sam Houston to retaliate against Peta Nocona's band for the raids of last fall. Houston was unusually friendly toward Indians, having lived among the Cherokee, so this was a rare order no doubt precipitated by political pressure and the severity of the recent Comanche raids.

Armed with his gubernatorial orders, Sul Ross had recruited forty rangers, and seventy civilians—mostly cowboys—and had also secured an accompaniment of twenty soldiers from the Second Cavalry at Camp Cooper. On top of this, he contracted two Tonkawa scouts to guide the punitive company into Comanche country. The two Tonkawas succeeded in finding Peta's vulnerable meat camp, a feat that probably would have eluded the white men.

After the fight, Sul Ross would claim that the man he had killed—the Mexican named José—was actually Peta Nocona, the great chief. Largely on the basis of this claim, and the fact that his outfit had recaptured Cynthia Ann Parker after almost a quarter century with the Comanches, Sul Ross would become governor of Texas, and later president of Texas Agricultural and Mechanical University. His very name would become legend in Texas. Because Peta typically stayed deep in Comanche country and was rarely seen, Ross's claim would not be disputed for decades.

A few years after the Pease River massacre, while returning a ransomed white girl to Fort Griffin in Texas, I ran across one of the Tonkawa scouts who had led Ross to the meat camp massacre—the Battle of Pease River, as the Texans gloriously referred to it. The scout, in broken English, told me his story as he gestured with a bottle of whiskey in his hand:

"Me tell Ross big camp ahead. Many warriors. Me lie, lie, lie. Want rangers kill Comanche squaws. Me hate Comanches. Big dust come up, cold wind. Dust hide soldiers; hide rangers, hide cowboys. Comanches no fight much—boys and squaws. Ross kill Mexican Joe. Him think he kill chief." Here, the Tonkawa had laughed. "Him no see different—slave; chief."

The Tonkawas had long since been pushed out of their country, caught between Comanches and white settlers. They had sided with the whites, for the Comanches had victimized them for generations. The Tonkawa scouts had led Sul Ross to a Comanche camp they knew was inhabited mostly by women and children, but had told the ranger leader he would be encountering Peta's best warriors. This invalid intelligence had brought the blood of the white avengers to a fighting boil, and they had charged the camp intent on killing Comanches that had recently killed their own countrymen—their own kin in some cases.

I believe Sul Ross was an honest man and that he truly believed he had killed Peta Nocona. He was naïve to believe his Tonkawa scouts, but perhaps to assuage his own conscience, he could believe nothing else, even to his death. He had to tell himself and his people that he had met at least one warrior on the battlefield, for he and his men had slaughtered dozens of unarmed women and children. This atrocious act of war, however, met with little disapproval on the Texas frontier, where Peta Nocona's warriors had so recently raided, burned houses, stolen horses, killed men, scalped and raped women, and carried away children.

The Comanches believed that the spirits wanted them here on this good measure of Mother Earth. The whites believed God Himself had led them to the salvation of the selfsame country to wrest it from waste and make it good with fences, crops, and domesticated cattle.

Violence begets violence. It was the Indian way from the time when animals spoke and walked about like two-leggeds. It was the way of common white-skinned people from before the days of barbarians and feudal marauders. The Comanches had taken this land by brutal force from the Tonkawas and Apaches, and now the whites were taking it from the Comanches with equal brutality and force, and superior weaponry and supplies.

War breeds as much cowardice as courage. I had the ability to move among the civilizations of both red and white men. I saw cruelty among them both. I also saw mercy and honor. The variations rested not so much with the cultures as with individuals. Among these individuals were men like Charles Goodnight, the cowboy who had spared the life of Nadua—Cynthia Ann Parker—and had recaptured her from the Pease River camp. Later, Goodnight would become a cattleman renowned among cattle kings. He would feed starving Comanches with his own cattle and raise buffalo on his ranch for reservation Indians to hunt as in days of yore. Perhaps he did these things to make amends for his part in the Pease River massacre. Only Goodnight could say, and he did not speak as much about the incident as Sul Ross did.

I would gather all this later. At the time, all I could do was ride westward with a wounded former wife and a rescued child. The captured horse did not possess the smooth trot of the slain Indian pony that had carried me to this awful place. He pounded our bones with every step. As we jolted onward, Hidden Water buried her face between my shoulder blades and, in her pain, wrapped her arms tightly around my waist and began to wail a soul-shattering song of mourning. It was cold, and we had no blankets. The child in front of me wept tears that spattered on the saddle horn, but even at his tender age, he knew a warrior did not cry aloud.

FIFTEEN

Seven bedraggled riders struggled toward Peta's new camp on five horses. There were three women, two children, an adopted Mexican captive, and me. After riding almost all day, we stopped to tend wounds. Hidden Water's was the worst. We packed the wound with grass and bound it with deerhide cut from the end of my loinskin. We had no lodge poles with which to make a travois, so Hidden Water had to ride behind me and suffer the jolting trot of the ranch horse I had captured. We journeyed on in mourning and misery. We took five days covering the ground that I had ridden in three on the bald-face pony.

When we reached Peta's new camp, Hidden Water's leg was swollen to twice its normal size. Her husband, Bear Tooth, was summoned and came to carry her away to a medicine man. He did not thank me for rescuing her.

Our arrival threw the big camp-together into turmoil. Peta came, and I had to tell him that his wife, Nadua, had been captured. "They saw her eyes, and did not kill her. She is yet alive."

"And my daughter?" Peta asked.

"Nadua carried her at the time. Your daughter was captured, too, but she is unharmed."

"You are white!" said an old man. He had a tomahawk in his hand which he raised above his head as if he would strike me with it. "You led the *tejanos* there."

"No!" said a woman who had escaped on a horse with her child. "Plenty Man fought them. He was alone, but he rode into the middle of the bluecoats and *tejanos*. His battle cry scattered them, and gave some of us a chance to get away. They would have killed me and my son if Plenty Man had not been there. They might have killed us all."

"He took no scalps," the old man said.

"He counted one coup and captured a horse," my defender replied.

"My daughter was in that camp!" the old man shrieked.

"Then you should pray she lives," I said, my impatience certainly coming through in my tone of voice. "We must send riders back to help the others who are wandering here on foot. Some will be wounded, I am sure. Some may not be far from the place of all the killing."

"Plenty Man speaks wisely," Peta said. His face drawn with grief over the news of his wife and daughter, he nevertheless set about the business of leading his people. "I will send a rescue party for the survivors, and a burial party for the dead. I will ride there myself. Perhaps I can overtake the *tejanos* and get my wife back. Plenty Man, you will stay in my lodge while I am gone. You must rest there. You look almost dead. No one will bother you in my lodge."

Peta turned away to organize his rescue party, and I went to his lodge where I would be safe. I had expected that some of the more excitable relatives might blame me for the raid. I was white, like the attackers. Those who were missing wives and daughters and sisters would want some white man to pay. As I entered Peta's lodge, I saw Kills Something running toward me. He had brought the main village to the great camp-together the day before.

"My brother," he said. "I have heard the story."

"I am tired," I said.

"Go in the lodge and sleep. I will guard the door. No one will bother you. Sleep as long as you want."

I nodded my gratitude, and that is the last thing I remember clearly for a while. I must have collapsed onto one of Peta's comfortable buffalo robe beds. I fell into a fitful sleep and dreamed some horrible dreams. Wave upon wave of angry Texas Rangers and blue-coated soldiers attacked me. Their bullets sang all around me. When I turned to run, I would find the old Comanche man with the tomahawk raised over his head. The attackers just kept coming and killing. I would run to protect some child or woman, but the white men would cut them down before I could get there.

These dreams seemed to last a long time, then my sleep became a black void. In this blackness all I could hear was the wailing of women in Peta's camp. Even in the dark recesses of my sleep, I reasoned that the survivors had told of those they knew were dead, and the relatives of the slain women and children were mourning, slashing themselves with knives, keening their songs of anguish. I slept with this song of misery in my head for a long, long time.

___

When I woke, my eyes opened, but my body would not move. I saw young Quanah sitting cross-legged on a robe, looking at me. This was, after all, his lodge, too. My ways of sleep, as I have mentioned, are so peculiar that I sometimes cannot move when I wake. My eyes will open, but my body will not move until I hear some sound. So I just lay there on my robe, staring at Quanah, who was staring at me, until I spooked him.

"Are you dead?" he finally asked.

These words, ironically, jolted life into my body. I blinked my eyes until my face would move, then my head and neck and shoulders, then the rest of my body. I rolled onto my back and looked up at the smoke hole. "No, I am not dead," I responded.

Quanah went to the door flap and pulled it aside. "He is awake," the boy said.

I saw Loud Shouter stick his head into the lodge. "You have slept through almost three suns," he said, as if in reproach for my laziness.

"That must be why I have to piss so badly," I muttered.

"Hurry," Quanah said. "I want to hear how my mother was captured." He said this in such a serious, stoic manner that I was compelled to follow the orders of a mere boy.

"I will tell you if you will find me something to eat," I said. "We had little to eat on the ride back from that terrible place, and now I have slept so long that I am about to starve."

"I will bring you some food," Quanah said, and he bolted outside.

I took care of my business and found Quanah and Loud Shouter waiting with a bowl of stew that had been cooking a long time and was filled with tender morsels of hump meat and tongue, flavored with tallow, salt, and wild onions. It was delicious. I told young Quanah what I had witnessed concerning the capture of his mother, and he thanked me for the intelligence. In that boy, I saw a wisdom, and a toughness of character, and a leadership quality seldom found among humans of any society. His eyes, though sad to think of his lost mother, were bright and thoughtful. He was smart, and he knew already how to ask his own questions and gather first-hand intelligence. He sought the truth, and remained unmoved by rumor and unbridled emotion. Unlike some others in camp, he refused to blame me for the disaster of the massacre merely on account of my whiteness. He was, after all, half white himself, and must have experienced occasional social ostracism because of it, even though his father was a chief. All this, I believe, went toward building young Quanah's fiber as a future leader of the Comanche Nation. And oh, how vigorously he would lead . . .

For a while, we feared Hidden Water would die. Her leg became seriously swollen with infection. She lapsed into delirium and mumbled strange things. Kills Something advised her husband, Bear Tooth, to take her to our medicine man, old Burnt Belly, who went out into the woods and prairies to listen to the plants talk. Then he made a poultice of something he would not reveal, and burned cedar, and made lengthy incantations over the patient. There were no amputations among the Comanches. The leg would either heal, or it would kill Hidden Water. But Burnt Belly's treatment worked, and Hidden Water's leg began to return to its normal size. When she woke, she asked if she would have a scar.

"You will have a great one," Burnt Belly said.

Hidden Water wept for hours. She was very vain. After she recovered, she would go to great pains to conceal her scar. She would wear leggings long after the cold moons had passed, and tailor her summer dresses longer than she did in the days when she reveled in showing off her shapely legs. She never thanked me for getting her out of that camp. She did not like to speak of the incident at all.

Bear Tooth, however, did thank me for saving his wife after she recovered from the wound. He was quite devoted to her. Though she was never the best Comanche wife when it came to cooking and housekeeping, she made up for her shortcomings between the buffalo robes at night. Bear Tooth loved her enough to give me seven horses as a reward for bringing her home. I always suspected, however, that he did this under pressure from Peta himself.

After Peta returned from the rescue-and-burial detail, the great camp sank into howls and shrieks of mourning that lasted through the two coldest moons of the winter. When the mourning finally dwindled to a merciful end, the Comanches at the great camp-together began to speak of revenge on the Texans. The chiefs of the various bands held many a council of war in Peta's lodge. This went on night after night for yet another moon. War chiefs and peace chiefs alike were unanimously in favor of attacking white settlements, but the questions of how, when, and where stirred much debate. Some wanted to attack in mass, as the Comanches had done in 1840, when over a thousand warriors rode all the way to the coast of Texas and sacked the town of Linnville, driving the citizens right into the very surf.

"I remember that raid," old Burnt Belly said to the younger chiefs when his time came to speak in council. "It was twenty winters ago. The glory of the raid was great in the beginning. We took scalps in three of the *tejano* towns and stole so many horses that they raised a great dust cloud in the sky. I had much fun taking things from the trading lodges near the beach while the frightened palefaces watched from wooden canoes in the big water. I got ribbons to tie in my horse's tail, and a good black hat shaped like the kettle my wife cooks with. And I got a cloth coat that I wore through the winter, and a thing on a stick that would spread out in a circle and make a shade from the sun, but when I made it spread out, it frightened my horse, so I threw it down."

Burnt Belly pantomimed his reminiscences, making the chiefs and leading warriors in the council lodge laugh in appreciation. "But," the shaman reminded them, "though that was a glorious raid at first, you must remember that all the medicine went bad. Someone must have killed a coyote or a skunk, or spoken to an owl, because as we were taking all our scalps and captive women and stolen horses back to our own country, the *tejanos* attacked us and ruined our raid. Our large war party was too easy to find. The *tejanos* killed many of our warriors. It is not the way of the True Humans to attack in great numbers, as the white people fight. The good way is to strike in small war parties, attack quickly, surprising our enemies, and ride hard to get away from the *tejanos* who will surely follow."

Burnt Belly's warnings convinced the war chiefs, and they began to talk of ending the great camp-together so that the various bands could spread out along the frontier and attack isolated ranches and small communities of whites. Once the questions of how and where were settled, the only remaining decision involved when. Burnt Belly settled this issue, as well.

One night in council, after all the war chiefs had given their opinions on when the attacks should begin, they finally turned to Burnt Belly and asked his advice.

"The time to raid begins now," he said. "Do not hurry about it, but prepare well, for you will have plenty of time to make your raids. Season upon season. Victory upon victory."

"How do you know this, old man?" asked Tasacowadi.

"Last night, in my lodge, I had a vision. I saw a great battle in a strange place, far away, with big guns that shook the earth like thunder. I watched the battle as it was happening. It was at a place by the big water. There were no True Humans or other redmen in the battle. Only whites."

"What does it mean, *kunoo*?" asked Kills Something, using the respectful term meaning "grandfather."

"It means the war between the whites has begun. The *tejanos* and their allies are on one side. The bluecoat soldiers are on the other. Now, the bluecoats will leave our country and go away to fight, and no longer will they protect the houses of the *tejanos* where we will raid. Now, even the rangers will go away to this great war. Only a few of them will stay behind to guard against our attacks, and we will sweep over them like a great stampede of buffalo."

"Are you sure, old man?" Peta asked.

"I have seen this vision, given to me by the spirits. I watched the first great battle between the whites. Now, they will fight and kill each other like crazy men. I hope they all kill each other to the last soldier, then we can have our country to ourselves again. I do not know if they will, but I know this: the more they fight each other, the more land we will take back from those whites who invade it and chop down trees and tear up the earth and block up streams and frighten away game with their noise. The great war has begun, my sons. Now the time to raid begins."

I had been in camp with Comanches for months by this time, and hadn't heard any news from the outside world, so I could not appreciate the scope of Burnt Belly's vision at the time. But I made a mental note of the date, employing the unerring calendar that forever worked clocklike in my head. The date of Burnt Belly's vision was April 12, 1861.

The day after Burnt Belly's vision, the great camp-together began to break up. Women took lodges down and Burnt Belly came to me and told me that it was time for me to bring trade wagons to the Big Crossing on the Canadian River again, for Kills Something's warriors wanted to resupply before taking the warpath against the whites, and they had plenty of horses and buffalo robes with which to barter. It had been decided that the Stag Moon, July, would signal the beginning of the Comanche raids on the Texas frontier. So I bid farewell to my Comanche friends and struck out with my own herd of horses to William Bent's Stockade at the mouth of the Purgatory River.

My trip was relatively uneventful, except that I was chased by a hunting party of Mescalero Apaches, my bitter enemies, and had to leave a dozen horses behind for them to capture before I finally outdistanced them. I still got to William's stockade with twenty horses, so the trip was not a total loss. Anyway, a trader who had well-nigh gone Indian did not have that much use for money in those days. I could live off the fat of the land. Hell, I could live off the gristle of the land if pressed hard enough.

The farms and fields of William Bent and Tom Boggs were beginning to take shape. When I arrived, in early May, I found their fields dotted with sheep and cattle, and rowed with corn.

I told William that the Comanches would be waiting to trade hundreds of horses to us at the Crossing by June. This is what he had sent me to arrange, and he was pleased that I had succeeded. He offered to buy the small herd of horses I had brought with me, but urged me to sit and talk with him for a while before we got down to business. We pulled two chairs out of his cabin so we could sit in the sunshine and smell the cool high plains breeze as we talked. Along with his chair, William carried a newspaper, folded and tucked under his arm.

"Things must be going smoothly enough," I mentioned. "I've been out of touch, but I haven't heard of any Cheyenne troubles."

William frowned. "There's trouble coming, I fear. I've resigned as Indian agent for the Cheyennes."

"Why?"

"You know I've seen the need for some time now for a treaty. One that would secure a permanent homeland for the Cheyennes on paper, recognized by Congress. I knew the Cheyennes would have to give up some of their old haunts, but I wanted to get financial compensation for them when they did give it up."

"I remember you planning for it over a year ago."

"Well, the Indian Bureau finally sent a delegation out here to hold a council with the Cheyennes and Arapahos. Typical government fiasco. I didn't even get word they were coming till they were almost here. They didn't give me any time to send word out to the Indians so I could plan a council. So when the delegation got here, only a few Arapahos happened to be at the fort, and no Cheyennes at all. But at least I got a look at the treaty they had drafted. That's what convinced me I needed to resign as Indian agent."

"I gather the conditions weren't favorable."

"Favorable to the politicians, maybe. They wanted to force both tribes onto a reservation between the Arkansas and Sand Creek that was no bigger than Maxwell's Ranch. Well, Maxwell may be a big man, but he's just one man. And they wanted to push two nations onto a reservation the size of one white man's ranch?"

"What about the remuneration?"

William rolled his eyes at the sky. "Ha! They offered four hundred fifty thousand dollars, payable over fifteen years. You're good at numbers. Figure it out."

"Thirty thousand a year, and the two tribes have to split it."

"Exactly. Fifteen thousand dollars a year for each tribe. Hardly fair pay for a territory the size of a European country. And they were supposed to use the money to buy everything they needed to start farms. Now, you tell me—what the hell does a free Plains Indian know about starting a farm?"

"Jack," I answered.

"I couldn't put my name on that treaty, Mr. Greenwood, so I resigned."

"So, that ended it? With the treaty and the reservation, I mean?"

"Hell, no. The bureau convinced Albert Boone to take over as agent. I guess they figured the Indians would respect the grandson of a great frontiersman like Daniel Boone. Albert managed to round up a few Arapaho and Cheyenne chiefs at Fort Wise, lavished a wagon full of presents on them, and convinced them to put their X marks on a treaty they didn't even understand. The bulk of the Cheyennes and Arapahos didn't even know it was going on."

"Same old story," I said.

"Unfortunately." He swatted at a fly with the newspaper he had carried out of the cabin. "I should have done something about it. Maybe I shouldn't have resigned, after all. I don't know. Anyway, the government recognizes the treaty, but the Indians don't, of course. It's gonna lead to trouble sooner or later."

I nodded. "Don't blame yourself, Colonel Bent. There are forces out there beyond our control. We do our best. I don't know what to do for the Comanches and Kiowas half the time. I try to advise them, but I'm just one voice."

Of course, William was anxious for news from Comancheria, so I told him what I knew. You may have wondered about this. I gathered a lot of information among the Comanches in those days—information that could have saved the lives of white people, if taken seriously. You may ask yourself what you would have done in my place. Would you have sent word to the Texas settlements that they would soon be under attack by vengeful bands of Comanches? Would that not endanger your Comanche friends?

With matters of this nature, I always sought William Bent's wisdom. For more than three decades, he had urged peace among the plains tribes where others had fomented warfare. He knew what to do and how to look at the problems on a grander scale. So many free traders, like me, came to him with news gathered from the scattered bands of the roaming nations that he possessed a greater intelligence than anyone alive concerning Indian affairs on the Great Plains and in the Rocky Mountains. He knew the attitudes among the various tribes, the movements of war parties, the epidemics of diseases in various Indian camps, the locations of buffalo herds, the wealth of each village in robes and horses. His mind held a social, military, political, economic, and demographic map of the nations that constantly changed and evolved season upon season, moon upon moon. Hell, he knew what most of the influential chiefs had for breakfast. So it was natural that I would take my concerns about the coming Comanche raids to William.

As I moved my chair over a little, keeping the shadow of the cabin from chilling me, I said, "The Comanches will begin raiding the Texas farms and towns in July. I've heard them make their plans in council. Should we warn somebody?"

William rolled the newspaper in his hand and thumped it against his other palm in an absentminded gesture of frustration. "It won't do a damn bit of good. Nobody knows where the Comanches are going to strike. There's not enough of them to raid the whole frontier, so they'll just pick at it here and there. We can warn the Texans, and maybe they'll post lookouts for a while, but then they'll get complacent after a week or so, and all our warnings will be forgotten. Anyway, if they didn't want to get raided, they shouldn't have moved into Comanche country with their guns cocked and their surveying instruments over their shoulders."

"Still," I said, "shouldn't we at least attempt to warn them? To protect ourselves, if nothing else."

William rubbed his brow. He must have been weary of worrying himself over Indian affairs. "You're right, of course. We ought to be able to tell 'em we told 'em when the scalps start to peel. It's our duty to report these things, even if nobody takes heed. I'll write a letter to the governor in Austin, if I still remember how to write. I haven't dipped into my inkwell for months. If I write the Texas governor, maybe he'll get the newspapers to print up some warnings."

"I've heard that Governor Houston is sensitive to Indian affairs."

William looked at me with a wry twist to his mouth. "Governor Houston's been kicked out of office, Kid."

This news astounded me, for Sam Houston was among the greatest of Texas heroes. As a general, he had won independence for the Republic of Texas from Mexico, twenty-five years ago. He had served as president of the republic, U.S. senator from the state of Texas, and most recently, governor. "What could Houston possibly have done to get kicked out?" I asked.

"He refused to take the Confederate oath."

My mind did everything it could to reject the obvious. "You mean Texas seceded?"

William reached for the newspaper under his arm. "You probably don't even know that Lincoln won the election last fall, do you? Then it started with South Carolina, back in December. After that, it was Mississippi, Alabama, Georgia . . . One secession after another. I forget what order they all came in. Anyway, the army will need plenty of horses."

All I could say was, "You don't mean . . ."

William tossed the newspaper onto my lap. It was a copy of the *St. Louis Democrat,* only four weeks old. It must have just arrived at William's stockade on one of the Santa Fe Trail freight wagons he contracted to haul goods for the army forts out West. The front-page headlines read:

WAR! WAR! WAR!
FORD SUMTER CAPTURED!
Details of the Artillery Battle
Major Anderson Surrenders to General Beauregard

As I scanned the highly inflamed account, I could not help noticing the date of the attack: April 12, 1861.

SIXTEEN

A remarkable thing happened to me out West as the Civil War was beginning to rage in the East—a thing I thought would never happen to me again. I fell in love. It wasn't like the time I fell for Gabriella Badillo in Taos, when her beauty instantly overwhelmed me and sent me spinning into terrific cartwheels of elation like a bird shot from the sky. I had become too cynical for that. No pretty face could warm the cockles of my heart with a smile or a glance—I wasn't even sure my heart had cockles anymore. No, this time the feeling overtook me by degrees, one word, one laugh, one touch at a time.

The woman I fell in love with caught my eye at first sight, but her real beauty would take its time revealing itself to the depths of my heart. It began when I rode up the Purgatory from William's stockade to visit my old friend Tom Boggs, at Boggsville. Tom and Rumalda, and their growing brood of children, were still herding sheep and cattle, tending gardens, and still planning to dam the Purgatory and scratch out a canal.

Boggsville, tiny and remote as the place might be, always afforded a certain charm to a rider approaching from the vast plains that surrounded it. Perched on a parcel of fine, level ground near the Purgatory yet beyond the reach of flood waters, shaded by the boughs of ancient cottonwoods, it was the kind of place an Indian would choose to make a camp, a soldier would occupy as a supply depot, or a trapper-trader would envision as a site for rendezvous. Tom Boggs was part Indian by nature, though not by blood; part soldier by necessity of the times; and part trapper-trader by experience. Thus it was logical that he had chosen this spot to settle.

The log cabins Tom had built here only added to the wild, rustic allure of the place. The day I rode up from William's stockade to visit the denizens of Boggsville, I found three Cheyenne tipis standing between the log cabins and the Purgatory, and they, too, pleased my senses. As I rode my Comanche mount into the settlement, two young Cheyenne women happened to be walking up to the cabins from the tipis. I spotted Tom Boggs sitting on his east-facing front porch, his hands busy with some task. My horse snorted, and Tom looked my way.

I arrived at the porch about the same time as the two Cheyenne women. One of them wore a yellow blanket, probably of Navaho making, for it was a fine one, worn casually over one shoulder. This woman glanced toward me without meeting my eyes, in the Indian way. Her face was pretty—bronzed and broad and strong—yet delicate by Cheyenne standards, a people renowned for their physical good looks. The woman with her looked like an elder sister.

I got down from my horse as Tom Boggs smiled at me and stepped down from the porch. In his left hand he held a horsehair headstall he had been building. His right hand came forward to shake mine.

"Well, I'll be doggone," he said. "Look what the wind blew out of Comancheria."

I shook Tom's hand, then turned to tip my hat to the Cheyenne women. The one with the yellow blanket tipped her head forward in an almost imperceptible nod, still refusing to meet my eyes with hers. And that, for the time being, was that. As I have said, the years, and my experiences, had tempered my vulnerabilities to the charms of pretty faces.

"I fear the wind will be blowing hot down there when I return," I said to Tom.

"Then don't go back."

"I must, and you know it."

He grinned ever larger as he finally got through shaking my hand. "I guess so." He turned to the visiting Cheyenne women, and spoke to them in Spanish, saying, *"La mujer de la casa está lista. Momento, por favor."* He stepped up on the porch and cracked the front door, saying, *"Rumalda, querida, tenemos visitantes. Y una sorpresa."*

The lady of the house was ready, he had said to the women outside. And to Rumalda, inside the house, he had said, Dear, we have visitors. And a surprise.

Within seconds, Rumalda came to the door and gasped with appropriate delight when she saw me. She jumped off the porch and embraced me, seemingly amused by my embarrassment.

"It is so good to see you again, Rumalda," I said.

"My dear Honoré," she said apologetically, "I have promised to trade some things with my Cheyenne friends."

"We will visit later," I replied. "I'll be around for several days before heading back to trade with the Comanches."

Tom slapped me on the shoulder and said, "Come on, let's go look at the cows."

Well, I had seen cows before, but the prospect of a ride with an old friend on this fine day suited me, and we spent hours seeking the high rolls in the plains to count heads on cattle. We found the cattle thriving on the rich prairie grasses, and only once did we ride into a flurry of black vulture wings to inspect the carcass of a calf that had fallen victim to wolves.

"We lose a third of our calf crop to wolves," Tom said. "Seems these ol' cows can fight 'em off most times, but the calves don't have a prayer if they get caught away from their mama. Any wolf you see, Orn'ry, I want you to kill it, you hear?"

"I hear you. How's the market for cattle? Is it worth the trouble?"

"It is now that the war has started. We're filling army beef contracts in three territories. We've trailed cows as far north as Fort Laramie. That's to say nothing of the beef we send to the Indian agencies."

"Speaking of Indians," I said, rather casually. "Who are the women camped at Boggsville?"

"Daughters of Lone Bear. The oldest one, called Amache, is married to John Prowers."

"I remember John—from Bent's Old Fort. He still trading?"

"That he is. Left his wife and her sister here for safekeeping so he could make the rounds among some Utes."

"What's the sister's name?"

Tom chuckled. "They call her Appears-with-the-West-Wind. I can't pronounce it in Cheyenne."

"Nomeme-ehne," I said.

"That sounds about right. I'll tell you something else about those gals. They're smart as a whip. They speak about a dozen languages between them, and they act like they can't speak English, but they sure understand it. They'll talk to you in Spanish, but not in English. West Wind—the one you fancy with the yellow blanket—she can cipher numbers, too. Does it all in her head. She can multiply and divide, count money—American or Mexican— and even figure percentages and exchange rates, all in her head."

"How do you know that?"

"John Prowers told me. Says sometimes he takes the sisters around to the trading houses and camps and to the Indian agency, and West Wind helps him make his negotiations and divvy up goods and things. Says she never makes a mistake."

"Are you sure she hasn't been to school somewhere?"

"No, she can't read or write."

This I found interesting. I had known many an Indian among the various tribes to possess intelligence beyond the common white man, but few so readily grasped things to which their cultures had never been introduced—like percentages. Almost all Indians could count into the hundreds and thousands. They could leave painted representations of numbers in the form of pictographs. The Indians also used common sense division and multiplication.

But seldom had I heard of an uneducated Indian who could figure percentages and count money. Especially a woman, for women were expected to keep their minds on their work and their children, and they had plenty of both to tend. This West Wind, the pretty and unassuming Cheyenne girl with the yellow blanket, was becoming more and more interesting to me. I understood a mind that needed no prodding to cipher. My mind forever whirred with numbers and fractions, angles and degrees, equations and co-efficients. Was West Wind a genius like me? Imagine two souls such as ours meeting way out here in one of the last wild places. What were the odds?

Of course, I was letting my hopes get too far ahead of probabilities, but some things did supersede mathematical chances.

Luckily, about that time, something occurred to take my mind off the intriguing West Wind. We trotted over a rise in the prairie and spotted a lone wolf skulking along about three hundred yards ahead. Instantly, the wolf tucked his tail and ran for his life. Without a word, Tom Boggs spurred his cow pony to a gallop. As he charged ahead of me, he took his reata down from his saddle strings and built a loop. Tom had lived for years in California and had learned to whirl a rawhide noose from the old rancheros. His cow pony was trained to chase whatever fled, be it bovine, equine, bruin, or canine, and a run of almost two miles got us close enough for Tom to throw a loop at that terrified lobo. With no timber in sight, the wolf had nowhere to brush up.

By the time the rawhide passed over his nose, Tom was already jerking the slack with one hand and his reins with the other. The pony slid to a stop on his haunches, the rawhide tightened, and the wolf somersaulted at the end of the rope. The poor fear-stricken canine jumped up in an instant and ran, half-blinded by shock, right under Tom's horse, who started bucking as the reata sang about his ankles. I drew my pistol, paced the doomed wolf with the muzzle, and sent a bullet through his brain, for I was a good pistol shot, even when shooting from the saddle at a moving target. The wolf's body folded and rolled and he lay there limp, the only movement about him being the wind making his fur wiggle.

Tom's horse only bucked harder when I fired, but Tom seemed un-flustered. Even with his pony crow-hopping and switching ends, Tom had kept an eye on the wolf and my marksmanship, and now, as he forked his spry mount and pulled at the bridle reins, he sang out, "Good shot, Orn'ry!" A moment later, he yelled, "Yee-ha!" and soon had his wild cow pony checked.

The wolf? We left him to the vultures, of course. It was probably one of the wolves that had been preying upon Tom's calves. Maybe not. Those were the days when a man was honor bound to kill a wolf on sight. The days when men were not afraid to ride green horses that were not afraid to run wild carnivores. How could I have known then that in years to come, I would sit outdoors at night and almost weep for want of hearing the lonely howl of a wolf?

SEVENTEEN

I had decided to call her "Westerly." It meant the same as West Wind, so it translated just as well from the Cheyenne Nomeme-ehne—Appears-with-the-West-Wind. Westerly. I liked the ring of it, and hoped she might also. So, the next morning, while going to catch a pony that had wandered a short way away in his hobbles, I passed near the Cheyenne tipis and saw her carrying wood up from the timber along the Purgatory.

"Good morning, Westerly," I said.

She stopped, and almost looked into my eyes. She answered in Spanish, saying, "That is not how I am called in English."

"It means the same."

She shifted the load of sticks and limbs in her arms. "How do you say it?"

"Westerly."

She made a pretty little smirk with her mouth, and lifted her eyebrows. "I like it better," she said, still refusing to speak to me in English. Then she went on her way with her heavy burden of fuel.

I caught my pony and spent the day riding wild horses that I was grooming for the saddle horse trade, knowing they might end up on some bloody battlefield under uniformed cavalry soldiers.

At dinner that day, Tom told me of his plans to lay out a large central plaza in Boggsville. The log cabins were temporary, he said, and he intended to build a new adobe home for his family, and a large adobe trading house, both of which would face the plaza. He wanted Boggsville on the map someday as a real community, with a market, a school, an inn, a cafe, and a church. He asked me to help him plot the plaza and survey the lots surrounding it.

I thought about it all afternoon while working with my horses. I calculated the angles at which the sun would cross the sky during various times
of the year, so that the placement of the plaza might take full advantage of
the sunshine during the winter and the shade trees during the summer.
I decided that the town's eatery should situate on the southwest corner of
the plaza so that the prevailing chinook winds would carry the inviting
aroma of cooking food across the village square. The winds would also
carry dust from the approaching wagon road and odors from the community refuse heap away from town if both were located south of the settlement. I envisioned rows of cottonwoods lining both sides of the road to
town to greet the weary eyes of sojourners with a cultivated suggestion of
the island of civilization lying just ahead at Boggsville.

So that evening, while Tom was away checking on one of his sheep
camps, I located the southwest corner of the proposed plaza, and began
making the calculations necessary to plot the town square and all the lots
around it. As I drove an iron stake pin into the ground as a corner marker,
I sensed someone approaching behind me, and turned to find Westerly just
a few steps away.

"I wish to ask you something," she said in Spanish.

"Of course," I replied.

"I want to know if you can teach me something."

"What would you like to learn?" I rose and faced her, the lowering sun
shining on her pretty face under the limbs of the big cottonwoods.

"I want to know how the shapes speak in silence."

"What shapes?"

"The shapes on the paper."

"You want to read?"

She nodded. "And write."

"I will do my best to teach you."

"When?"

"Tomorrow morning. We will start at dawn. There, on the porch of the
Boggs house."

She smiled as if she were embarrassed and excited all at once. I suppose she may have thought I'd refuse her. It had taken some courage to
make the request.

"Thank you." She turned away.

Before she could get too far away, I said, "Why do you want to learn to
read?"

She stopped, and turned sideways to me, but did not face me. "It is good magic."

"That is true. But why me?" I asked.

"The people who know you say you are clever. I can see for myself that you are kind and patient."

"I will try not to disappoint you."

She smiled again, and went away.

The full moon was approaching in two days, so sleep was out of the question, and all I could do all night was worry about my newfound role as abecedarian. How was I going to teach this young Cheyenne woman to read and write? I realized to my own shame that I had never taught anyone much of anything, save the Indians I had learned to drink whiskey. I had met a lot of Indian women over the years, but none had moved my heart the way Westerly was beginning to do—not even Hidden Water, my former Comanche wife. If I should fail in teaching her to read, I would surely fail with her in every other way. Something in the core of my heart told me I had better take my role as her tutor seriously.

When we met in the morning, I gave Westerly a piece of paper upon which I had written the twenty-eight alphabetical characters used in the Spanish language. I had decided to teach her to read in Spanish, since English was fraught with so many illogical inconsistencies in spelling and phonetics. In Spanish, each character generally made one and only one sound, which greatly simplified the teacher's job. I wrote down only the lower-case characters. We would talk about capitals and other complications later.

Westerly looked at the letters for a while, then looked back up at me and shrugged in disappointment. "I do not hear them speak."

"You will. Each of these shapes makes its own sound. Each one can only make one sound. To speak, two or three or more of the shapes must work together."

She looked again, and cocked her head a little to one side. "I still do not hear."

"The magic will come to you in time. First, you must learn the sound that each shape makes."

"I do not understand how these shapes on the paper make sounds."

"The shapes are called letters," I explained. "It is easy to learn the sound that each letter makes."

"How am I to learn, if I cannot hear them?"

I looked out toward the Purgatory, and saw the sky-colored plumage of a migrating mountain bluebird streak by. "That bird," I said, pointing. "Do you know it?"

"Yes," she replied, quickly catching sight of the bird as it swooped up to a cottonwood limb. She seemed a little irritated that I was bird-watching instead of teaching her to read.

"Did you hear it make a sound?"

"No."

"But you know the sound it makes."

"Yes."

"That is the way with the letters. Each makes a sound. When you see the letter, your heart will think of the sound it makes. The sounds of the letters, together in little groups, like flocks of different birds, make the words that we speak."

"Different birds do not flock together."

"Yes, all right, the letters are not *exactly* like birds. They will flock together in many different ways."

"But I still do not know what sounds the letters make. I cannot hear them."

"You will not hear them until someone shows you the magic. That is why I am here. With my own voice, I will teach you the sounds the letters make."

She seemed very puzzled. "You make bird noises?"

I laughed. "No. The letters make different kinds of noises. Not exactly like bird sounds."

Again, she looked at the letters on the paper. "There are so many."

"Not at all. There are more different kinds of birds in the sky than there are letters on this page. You must know one hundred different birds, and the sounds they make. Yes? You will learn the sounds the letters make, for you are smart. When your eye sees the letter, it will tell your ear what sound the letter makes. Your heart may hear these sounds in silence, or it may tell your mouth to speak them."

Now Westerly was getting impatient. She pointed to the first letter, *a*. "What sound does this one make?"

I made the sound of the Spanish letter *a*. She repeated it. She pointed to the letter *b*. I made its sound. We move on to *c*. We made our way through the entire alphabet during the next hour, repeating the sounds until I could point at each letter, and Westerly could make the sound it represented. She learned quickly and had no trouble memorizing.

"I do not think these letters make sounds at all," she said finally. "You have tricked me. I am the one making the sounds."

"It seems that way at first. But soon, the magic will come to you, if you continue to study and learn. In time, you will be able to open a book, and though your *eyes* see the letters making words, your *ears* will hear. Not so much the ears on the side of your head, but the ears in your heart."

I saw a twinkle of intrigue in Westerly's eyes. "What is the next thing to learn?"

"I will show you how to put the letters together now to make a word."

And thus my tutelage of Westerly began. I could only guess and hope where it might lead. With every word I taught her, I came a little closer to falling in love with her, though I tried to steel myself against the very real possibility that she wanted nothing more from me than reading and writing lessons. For a long time, it was difficult to tell. She was, after all, a Cheyenne woman, and women of that nation prided themselves on propriety and chastity. Flirtation was not regarded as a virtue among the Cheyenne. But eventually, I would discover a true friend, a passionate lover, and an intellectual confidante. For the first time in my life, I would begin to see myself growing old and gray with a woman I loved.

EIGHTEEN

By June 1861, William Bent and I had made our plans to trade with the Comanches at the ruins of Fort Adobe. I was ready to go. Boggsville was a fine place, but it was named for Tom Boggs, not me. The Crossing on the Canadian was my home place, and it was calling to me, beckoning me even into the midst of the coming fray between the North and the South, between the Comanches and the Texans.

I would go first with a mule train of whiskey. After the drunken revelry, William would send the wagons laden with trade goods. I had requested that John Prowers drive the wagons. William and everyone else certainly knew why. If John drove the wagons, he would bring his wife, Amache, who would surely bring along her sister, Westerly. Our frequent lessons had attracted much attention and caused some speculation. We no longer sat across from each other at the little table on the porch. We sat side by side.

"I know what kind of lessons you've a mind to teach her," Tom Boggs said to me one day, a ribald grin on his face.

"It's all been very proper," I insisted.

"Maybe so. But you ain't foolin' anybody."

I had to put up with a lot of that sort of teasing. Only William kept quiet on the matter of my relationship with Westerly. Oddly quiet.

Anyway, Westerly was learning rapidly. She was spelling almost flawlessly, writing full sentences, and learning the usage of such things as upper-case letters, punctuation, and paragraphs. She had absorbed the nuances of sentence structure, conjugations, transitive and intransitive verbs, direct and indirect objects. Her Spanish vocabulary was flourishing. Her mind was like a whirlpool, and she devoured information, put it to instant use, and then immediately sought further knowledge. Her confidence in her own intelligence had soared. She arrived early for our lessons. I engaged in some self-flattery regarding my skills as an educator, but I knew in truth that my student was simply too percipient not to grasp anything explained to her in a rational, logical manner. Her acuity, in fact, constantly challenged my ability to teach at an ever higher plane and a rapidly accelerating pace.

Neither of us wanted the literacy lessons to end, so I had concocted a way to carry on my relationship with Westerly by including her in the trip to the Canadian. William had agreed, but I could tell something was bothering him about the entire situation. I sensed a buried undercurrent of disapproval when it came to my interest in Westerly.

———

Kit Carson came to visit William's stockade before I left for the Canadian with my whiskey. I was delighted to see the old voyageur, as was everyone on the Purgatory. William and I, and Tom Boggs, gathered with Kit under a brush arbor at William's stockade where we could sit at a table carried from William's house, and play Kit's favorite card game, seven-up, which was also called by the name "old sledge."

Kit had aged noticeably since I last saw him. It seemed the miles and the years had finally begun to take their toll on his rawhide constitution. He carried himself stiffly, and I knew that the shoulder he had injured in that bad fall in the mountains the year before still galled him with pain. He was too tough to wince, but I could see his eyes flare with pain at times when he dealt the cards.

"You come lookin' for Utes, Kit?" William asked as we played cards. "I can tell you where all the bands are."

"I'd be obliged," Kit replied. "Got news for 'em. I ain't their agent no more. Bill Arny's taken over, and the agency has moved to Maxwell's Ranch to get away from the Taos lightnin' stills."

William fanned his cards in front of his face. "Did you resign or did you smart off to your government boss and get fired?"

I, too, was curious to know why Kit had quit as agent. Probably to accept a commission in the army. But *which* army? His family ties were Southern, but his loyalties had remained with the Union since the Mexican War. He had ridden with Kearny and Frémont and many a lesser known officer.

"I got offered another government job. A tougher one, but one I thought needed doin'." Kit threw a trump card to win a trick. "I'm raisin' a volunteer company."

We sat in silence for a while, throwing cards for the next point, until William broke through the tension with characteristic candor. "Well, which side, damn it?"

Kit grinned at the intrigue he had generated with his arrival. "Y'all know I'm Southern by birth. My brothers have gone seccesh. My whole family, far as I know. Some of you boys may lean South yourself. Every man's got to make a choice, seems to me. I don't hold nobody's choice agin' 'em." He dropped his last card faceup on the pile, a jack of clubs, the trump suit, winning the trick. "But I'm loyal to the Union. I've been named lieutenant colonel of the First New Mexico Volunteer Infantry. Anybody wants to fight for the Union can ride south with me."

"This is Colorado Territory now," William said, quite curtly. He seemed irritated—either at the card game or at the news Kit had brought. "The Colorado volunteers are already forming up in Denver."

"I've wandered a bit off my range as far as recruitin' goes," Kit admitted. "But I'm honor bound to see that the Utes are taken care of as best I can. And I figured I'd come see my friends and tell 'em which way I aimed to lean."

"I'm leanin' right down the middle," Tom Boggs said. "Unless the Texans fight their way into Colorado. Then I guess I'll have to join up and fight for the Union."

"I'm too old to muster," said William, which was interesting because he was the same age as Kit and we all knew it. "But I'm sure worried about my boys in St. Louis. I hope they don't get hotheaded and join the Confederates." He helped gather the cards and pushed them toward me, as it was my turn to deal. "You know I'm loyal to the Union, Kit. Me and Mr. Greenwood have already started figurin' on how to get horses from the Comanches to sell to the Union Cavalry."

I took up the cards, cut them one-handed, and commenced some fancy shuffling tricks, drawing a suspicious glance from Tom Boggs, with whom I had never played cards. "How many frontier officers have gone South?" I asked in a quiet voice, only now feeling the onslaught of war creeping onto the plains.

Kit rubbed his left shoulder irritably as he watched me deal. "Everybody you might expect. Colonel Fauntleroy, General Twiggs. Colonel Albert Sidney Johnston left the Pacific and went to Texas. Alex Jackson resigned as

secretary of state of New Mexico and went with Colonel Loring to Texas.
Captain Crittenden left Fort Stanton. Major Sibley left his two companies
at Fort Union and rode for Texas."

"Sibley?" William asked. "The Walking Whiskey Keg? Did he take
his tent with him?"

We all chuckled. Major Henry Hopkins Sibley, a renowned drunk, had
invented a military tent that resembled a tipi, and had convinced the U.S.
Army to manufacture thousands of them. The irony now was that the Union
would use Sibley's own tent against his Confederacy, for he hailed from
Louisiana.

"Who does that leave that's loyal?" Tom asked.

Kit studied the six cards I had dealt him, and glanced at the trump card
I turned up. "Me, Ceran, Captain Pfeiffer, Major Morrison, Colonel Sumner, and a few in California. And the old guard in New Mexico is loyal to
the Union—the Vigils, Pinos, the Chaves boys, the Valdezes, the Chacons,
the Bacas, the Archiletas—they've all volunteered for the First and been
made captains and lieutenants."

William shook his head and frowned. "What do you reckon will happen, Kit?"

"There are loyal spies in Texas. We're already hearing from them in
coded letters. The best guess right now is that Sibley, or Johnston, or
somebody who knows the lay of the land, will lead the Texas volunteers
up to El Paso del Norte and march north to take New Mexico. If 'n we
don't whup 'em there, they'll march for the gold in Colorado. That's the
best bet. They may even have their eyes on California."

A sickly silence hung over the card table like the dried sage and brush
from the arbor overhead. Through it all, we played our cards without com-
menting on them, each man knowing the rules of engagement well enough.

"Brother against brother, friend against friend," William said. "I don't
much care for the prospect of it at all."

There was more silence as the cards turned, then Kit looked at me.
"I'd heard that Kid Greenwood had come here to visit a spell. That's really
what brung me here."

I looked at Kit in astonishment, and felt the eyes of every man at the
table on me. "Huh?" I said, in all my luminosity. "I mean, *sir?*"

"I'll need a courier and a scout. You and Tom were the two hardest
riders in the West during the war with Mexico. Tom's got a family to look
after now, but you're still bachin'."

"But what about the Comanches? The horses? We've made our plans to trade."

"Nobody can handle the Comanche trade but Mr. Greenwood," William said, quite sternly. "I need him."

"You've got time to make some big horse trades. I can get word to you through William. When I need you, I'll send for you."

I threw in my last card and sat there, speechless.

"You don't have to answer right now," Kit said. "Go see your Co-manches. Do your job. Then come join me if your guts tell you to. Like I said, I don't hold any man's choice agin' him." Kit turned his last card up on the table, again winning the trick, and this time securing enough points for the game. "Seven-up!" he sang, and leaned back in his chair to gloat over his victory. Colonel Carson knew how to play a winning hand.

<hr>

Later that evening, Kit and William came to my room in William's stockade. I had just finished a tutoring session with Westerly and I felt all aglow, for she had touched my wrist during our lesson. This was the first time we had actually touched. Kit and William, by contrast, wore rather droll expressions.

"Mr. Greenwood, I'll get to the point," William said. "It's about that young squaw."

"Westerly?"

"Yes." He sat in the only chair in the tiny adobe room, and Kit leaned against the door frame, smoking his clay pipe. "It's your business, and none of mine, but I urge you to think things through. Kit agrees."

"I had me an Arapaho wife once," Kit said. "Name of Grass Singing. Pretty name, pretty gal. She gave me my daughter, Adalaide."

"I know all that, Kit. What's it got to do with me?"

"Everybody knows you're sweet on that Cheyenne girl. But think about it, Mr. Greenwood. Think down the trail a piece."

"William, you've had a Cheyenne wife as long as I've known you," I said.

"That's how come me to butt my nose in your business. Once was the day when every white man out here had him a squaw wife. Now things have changed. I've got five half-breed children who don't know if they're white or Indian, and don't fit in anywhere they go."

"I'm just teaching her to read. We're making words and sentences, not half-breed babies."

"Be honest with yourself, Mr. Greenwood. She's a fetching young gal, and you'd share a blanket with her tonight if you could."

"William, with all due respect—"

Kit raised a hand as a peace offering. "Kid, you're a grown man, and you're gonna do what you want to do. Me and William just wanted you to know what you're up against. Poor Adalaide, back in St. Louis. When she was goin' to school, the other rotten little kids made sport of her terrible. It ain't easy for a half-breed child in the white man's world. And I'll tell you something else. Proper women in polite society will scorn a squaw wife, and her squaw man, too. It happened to me when I had me that Arapaho wife. I like to never lived it down. It embarrassed me fierce to admit to a real lady that I'd laid in a lodge with a squaw. I'm surprised sometimes that Josepha would have me at all, knowing I'd once been a squaw man, and her from a good family."

"I don't have much to do with polite society," I argued.

"You will," William said. "It's comin'. In your lifetime, you'll see schools and churches on these plains. Your wilderness won't last forever."

I sat in silence for a moment. Had I not respected William Bent and Kit Carson with every fiber of my heart and mind, I might have been angry. I knew they were only trying to spare me some pain they had themselves lived through. "I've had a Comanche wife before."

"Didn't work out, did it?"

"No. But this is different. I don't know that I'll marry Westerly, or if she'd even have me, but if I do, I'll make sure it's right. I'll think through everything you've said. I'll give you my word on that. But I make my own way and make up my own mind. You gentlemen know that."

William nodded. "I've said my piece. I won't bring it up again."

"If we didn't give a damn for you we never would have brought it up in the first place," Kit said, a kind smile on his leathery face.

"I know that, Kit."

William rose from the chair. "Listen, Kid, it's been a long time since I heard you saw that fiddle. Why don't you play a song or two for me and ol' Kit. We'll roll up the rugs and get the gals to dance with us."

With my mind whirling around the warnings of my frontier mentors, and my heart aching for another moment with Westerly, I was hardly in the mood to entertain. But music was scarce out there in the wilderness, and the bearer of it carried with him a responsibility to share it for the public good. I pulled myself up off my pallet, got my left-handed Stradivarius out of its deerskin case, and began tuning up. At least no one would talk at me while I played, and I could think. And perhaps some of my angst would vent from my soul through the music, like steam from a pressure valve. Then there was one further thought. Perhaps Westerly would come around and hear me play. She probably did not even know that I possessed the gift of music. I craved her attention.

"It'll do me good to play a few," I said.

William smiled—a rare expression for his face these days—and left to make arrangements for my impromptu concert. Kit remained behind, watching William go. Finally, he turned back to me and said, almost in a whisper, "Kid. There's somethin' else . . . Somethin' I wanna . . ."

"What is it?" I replied, sensing the gravity in his tone.

"That girl. That Cheyenne girl . . ."

"Yes?"

"You been teachin' her to read and write?"

"Yes, sir."

"Kid, you know I . . . Well, they mean to make me a lieutenant colonel."

"I know that, Kit, you told me."

"Well, the hell of it is, I cain't even *spell* 'lieutenant colonel.' I cain't spell much of nothin' at all. My name's about it, and a few leetle-bitty words. I know I'm just a volunteer, but those boys in the regular army . . . You ever heard of an officer who couldn't read or write his own orders?"

"You'll have an adjutant for that. A scribe."

"I know that, but . . . An officer ought to be able to read his own."

I had never seen such fear in Kit's eyes. "Don't worry," I said. "We'll start tomorrow evening."

The worry melted from his brow and poured into his smile. "You reckon you can open an ol' rusty trap like mine?" he asked, tapping his temple with his trigger finger.

I tucked my fiddle under my arm. "Colonel Carson, by end of this war, I'll have you reading and writing like a West Point graduate."

NINETEEN

I slept only about an hour after the last dancer tired and drifted away to bed. When I awoke before dawn, I knew I would sleep no more that night. Too many uncertainties about the future writhed in my brain. Surely you have lain in your own bed and pondered and worried and fretted over the vagaries of human existence yourself. Silence and darkness can sometimes amplify the disquietudes of love, money, pride, fear, heartaches and ailments, angers and regrets, until a body attempting to lie in repose will twist and sweat as if undergoing calisthenics. You have experienced this as well as I—that is certain—but though you know now that you are not alone in this, that does you little good when you are the one tossing sleeplessly. Now you know how I felt when I awoke early that morning, worried with war, romance, and my doubts over my own personal value to humankind.

I will tell you this: there is no sense in lying about in your own self-pity and wallowing in your own bed of anxiety. Get up! Wash the dishes. Organize the clutter. Fold the linens. Sweep the floor. Write a letter. Stack the wood. Light a fire and look around. You'll find what needs doing.

Me? Luckily, I had horses to ride, so I rose from my pallet and pulled on my clothes. It was still dark, but I lit a candle, made my breakfast, and gathered my tack.

Of the twenty horses I had brought from Comanche country, only two had been ridden when acquired from the Indians, and even they were green. In order to get top dollar for these mounts, I had spent many a long day training them at William's stockade. Actually, the money meant less to me than the pride I took in training a horse that would neither fear nor hate a man, but would partner up with a rider and carry him with willingness and dignity. Initially, I had broken them the Indian way, riding them in deep water, mud, or sand. This tired the horses quickly, and I could work several horses in a day if I stayed at it hard enough.

Once each horse had been saddled three times and ridden the Indian way, I had started taking them on longer rides on solid ground. Each needed many a mile, so I could ride only two or three a day. My job was to make each horse responsive and obedient to the bit and the reins, and to pressure from my knees, heels, voice, and even the slightest variation in posture in the saddle.

To accomplish this, I had to repeat the commands and cues scores of times—turning, stopping, changing from walk to trot to canter—always with consistency. And I had to outlast the animal's resistance to my control, for most horses would test my ability to dominate them. A green horse with only its fourth or fifth saddle on might kick, paw, or rear even before the rider mounted. After I got aboard, the horse might buck, ramp, or bolt recklessly away—anything to get rid of me. I found all of this highly invigorating.

That morning, after my breakfast of leftover cornbread and beans heated over the coals of last night's fire—I decided to take on the least willing of the mounts I had been training, and confront her problems. She was a black-and-white pinto filly—not too pretty, but built for long rides. She was a true Indian pony of mustang blood, not some long yearling stolen from a Mexican ranch. Her head, which was too large for her body, sported a moose nose and eyes that walled white with suspicion and fear. Her neck tied in too high at the withers, and her tail set too low to suit me, but she was sound and could be made to ride.

It took some time to get the filly caught, bridled, and saddled, but finally I was ready to go.

I mounted, pulled her head to the right, touched her with my spurs, and got her to walk. Immediately, she tried to put her head down and buck, but I yanked her head back up and pulled her hard to the right to turn her in a tight circle. This was a method I had seen good trainers use among the Comanches and the Mexicans. A rider could usually exert his control over a pugnacious mount by pulling the animal's head around and making it turn in a small circle. This almost always daunted the animal and taught respect for the hard metal bit in its mouth.

Within a few minutes, I had the pinto filly trotting and cantering around the pen fairly well, though she constantly lurched and shied at nothing, and forever tested and protested. Whenever her protests became too disrespectful,

I would muscle her head around this way or that, cut her in a small circle, and reassert my impression of control over her. Now she needed about two hours of hard riding at a steady trot and canter. I got down to open the gate and begin that very endeavor.

I had been so focused on this filly that I had lost track of almost everything else around me. So it was that I was quite surprised to look into the adjoining pen of horses to find Westerly throwing a saddle on one of the better horses in the bunch—a four-year-old bay gelding with a Mexican brand. This four-year-old was smart and agreeable and had been among the easiest to train. Westerly had chosen well, though I could not quite fathom why she was saddling one of my horses.

"What are you doing?" I asked, a smirk on my face.

"You have too many horses to ride. I want to help."

"You don't have to. I will manage."

"I want to. You have helped me learn. I want to do something in return."

I smiled. The prospect of riding with Westerly was even more appealing than the thought of riding alone. "It is going to be a hard ride. These ponies need lessons."

"I will help you teach them, as you have taught me. I can ride as hard as you."

I opened the gate and got on the filly. It would be well to make the horses ride together for a change, I thought. Westerly was opening her own gate and leading her bay gelding out. The bay had learned well, and did not protest much when she mounted. He hadn't bucked since the first time I saddled him. I nodded the crown of my hat toward the west, and we took off at a trot.

For three hours we rode the plains around Boggsville and William's stockade, trotting, loping, galloping; turning and stopping; crossing trickles of water and fallen logs in the Purgatory bottoms; introducing the horses to new experiences. For three hours we did not speak. We simply rode. Sometimes side by side. Sometimes one ahead of the other. For three hours we communicated with our smiles and our eyes. My filly jumped a jackrabbit once and almost bucked me off. Westerly laughed, then covered her mouth at my mock glare. On we rode, until our green mounts were lathered with sweat and holding their heads low in fatigue.

"I'm getting hungry," I said.

Westerly smiled. "We can take these horses back and saddle two fresh ones. Then we can ride them to my lodge and tie them to the trees there. My sister and I will make some food. My sister's husband killed a stray buffalo yesterday. After we eat, we can ride the two fresh horses as we have ridden these this morning."

"I would like that," I said.

We rode on for another half-mile, both of us feeling comfortable in our silence.

"I am happy," Westerly said then. "I am happy that my sister and I will go with you to trade with the Comanches."

I nodded. "Yes. I am happy about that, too." We rode until William's stockade came into view over the ridge. "Your father, Chief Lone Bear," I said, leaving the comment half finished.

"Yes?"

"Where does he camp?" This was practically a wedding proposal, and we both knew it. If Westerly wanted to share a lodge with me, she would tell me where to find her father.

"Big Timbers," she said, her eyes cast down toward the mane of the horse she rode. She glanced toward me, and smiled. "He goes there to collect the treaty gifts from the fort."

I nodded. "I will go see him."

By the time we rode into the stockade, we were both quite flushed. William happened to step from his house as we rode by to turn the tired horses into the corral. He watched us pass for a few seconds, then put his hands on his hips and shook his head. I could only shrug at him and smile.

⚊⚊⚊⚊⚊

A few days later, I took seven green-broke horses to Chief Lone Bear and told him I wanted to marry his daughter. I told him that I could speak Cheyenne, that I could hunt and ride and fight, and that I would always see that Westerly and her family were taken care of. After he looked me and the seven horses over, he agreed.

I kept the bay gelding Westerly liked, to give to her as a wedding gift. For my own mount, I kept that hardheaded pinto filly. I don't know why. She didn't like me very much.

William chided me when I returned to the stockade. "You could've got top dollar for those horses from the army," he said. "Now all you've got for all your work is a wife and a bunch of in-laws."

Kit Carson was there, too, laughing and shaking his head stiffly. "You can't talk no sense into him, William. Just look at his face. That young man's love-struck."

The ceremony was simple. Westerly's sister and the other women of Boggsville carried the bride to me on a blanket whose edges they all held. They eased her down to the ground in front of the porch to the Boggs cabin, where I was staying at the time. I came out of the cabin and Westerly rose to her feet to meet me at the bottom of the porch steps. John Prowers draped the blanket upon which Westerly had arrived around both our shoulders at once, and we went away to a lodge my new Cheyenne wife had raised up the Purgatory.

She was nervous that night. Cheyenne women prided themselves on remaining chaste until marriage. Westerly had rarely touched a man before, much less felt her bare breasts pressed against a man's chest as they pressed hot against mine. I treated her with all the patience and gentleness I had, and introduced her to many new pleasures I'm sure she never knew existed.

Later, in the faint moonlight that filtered in through the smoke hole of the tipi, she lay on her side, her body warm against mine, and for the first time stared long into my eyes, a faint, bewitching smile curling the very corners of her mouth as her fingers explored scars she found on my body.

TWENTY

Burnt Belly let his open palm brush across the stalks of the cattails at the edge of Adobe Creek. "Ah," he said. "Here is one." He stooped and pulled the stalk from the creek bed, finding the root swollen with starch, ready for crushing into a fine white flour. He handed it to me to rinse. "Now, *you* touch the plants, and find another good one," he said.

I tried to listen, but the stalks were not talking to me. Finally, I chose one at random, hoping for a lucky pick. "This one," I said, wrapping my hand around the stalk. I pulled it, finding the rootstock conspicuously thin.

Burnt Belly laughed at me. "That one is not ready yet. You do not know how to listen."

"I'm trying to listen, but I hear nothing."

"Stop trying," he replied. He tilted his head up the creek bank, urging me to follow him. He led me to a Yucca plant perched at the edge of the cutbank, its roots holding the soil together. "What do you feel from this plant?"

I wrapped my palm around one of the many bayonetlike daggers that protruded from the center of the plant. I shook my head, unable to feel it say anything to me. "I know that the fibers can be stripped and twisted into a strong cord. I know that the young bloom is good to eat in the spring. The new seed pods can be boiled and eaten."

"You have seen the women use the plant in these ways. You are not feeling anything."

"You told me to stop trying."

"Do not *try*. Just listen."

I must have been trying, because I didn't hear a thing from that blasted plant.

Burnt Belly frowned. With his first two gnarled fingers, he gently touched one of the daggers, stroking it, feeling the point. "The roots. She tells me the roots can be made into a tea that will ease pains in the joints of old people like me. You do not *hear* that?"

"Maybe I did not touch it in the right place."

"It does not matter where you touch it! Come. Try this one."

The old shaman led me to a weed growing up from a place where the creek bank had washed out. The weed stood three feet high. It had coarse stems and rough, misshapen leaves. I detected a slight acrid scent when I got close to the plant. Weary of my failures as a shaman, I absently reached out and touched the weed at the base of one of those flowers, and when I did, I felt a sudden pang that made me draw my hand back.

"Tell me," Burnt Belly said. "Quickly."

"She is dangerous."

"Yes! Poisonous. Almost any part of this plant can kill you. It has been used to murder people. Now you hear, but you are only listening for danger. Listen for the good things, as well."

"I will try," I said.

"Do not try! Do. Know in your heart that you can hear the voices of the living things."

I turned to the nearest plant—a willow tree. I already knew that the willow had many uses to the Indians. Like the yucca, a cord could be twisted and woven from strips of bark; children made whistles from tubes of bark carefully slipped off a stem; the inner bark was dried and ground into a flour; crushed roots were soaked in water and grease by vain warriors to prevent dandruff; tender willow leaves were used as a poultice on wounds and cuts. And as I placed my palm gently around a branch and let my thumb fall seductively into a fork of the branch, I faintly heard the willow speaking to my heart, trying to heal me and all of humanity with ancient medicine. It was confusing, for the willow seemed to have much medicine to offer. The voice of the tree buzzed like a beehive and mumbled like a friend trying to speak to me through a roaring wind. I could not quite make out what she was trying to say. Then, a word or two came clear, but not so much a spoken word as an unpainted portrait of an idea.

My root, steeped in water, renders a cure for internal bleeding, and choking in the throat. My bark, made into a tea, relieves pain that comes with urination.

I wondered in amazement if I had really heard this, or if my mind had just concocted something out of desperation. I turned to the medicine man to tell him what I had heard, but I could tell by the pleased look on his face that he already knew. Just then, a boy's voice shouted from the village strung out along three miles of Bent's Creek, Adobe Creek, and the Canadian River. The boy was the camp crier, sent to spread the news of some important event. We were near enough to hear the boy shouting, but too far to understand his words.

"We must go back to the lodges," Burnt Belly said. "Something is happening."

Westerly and I had been in camp with Kills Something's band of Quahadi Comanche for five months now. The trade for horses had proven highly profitable, for the Comanches were raiding a frontier the Confederacy could not protect, driving away thousands of fine mounts. Westerly and I would gather the horses here, and wait for the next trade caravan from William's stockade to bring things the Indians wanted in trade for the horses. In this way, horses from Confederate Texas became Union remounts.

Westerly and I lived in a cozy tipi that we had raised near Kills Something's lodge. We were completely satisfied with working the horses by day, reading to each other by firelight, and making love in our lodge after dark. She had become the perfect mate, partner, and lover, and I could only congratulate myself for having the good sense to take her for my wife, against the advice of my mentors in the Indian trade. I fell more in love with her every day.

In my spare time, I had begun to take some lessons from Burnt Belly on medicinal uses for plants, but the studies were difficult because the old man wouldn't just teach me. He said the plants themselves would teach me, and constantly urged me to seek some kind of mystic level of wisdom I scarcely knew how to achieve. It seemed that I had discovered something important with the willow tree just now, only to be interrupted by the boy shouting in the village.

The old man and I walked out of the woods to the prairie that served as our campground, and saw what had caused the commotion. John Prowers had arrived with another string of trade wagons from William's stockade. Three canvas-covered Studebaker prairie schooners were sliding and crunching their way down into the Canadian Breaks a mile to the north, followed by a larger Conestoga pulled by six fine mules. Burnt Belly stopped and squinted at the sight, as I went over to Westerly who was waiting for me at our lodge door, a beautiful smile on her face. Her sister was coming, and we would enjoy brisk bouts of commerce for the next several days. I came to her and took her by the hand.

"I know you have missed your sister."

"Yes, I have," she admitted. She gently squeezed my hand and gave me a beautiful smile. Then she turned her eyes to the wagons that came lumbering toward camp behind teams of tired mules.

The appearance of the wagons and the announcement of the camp crier had stirred the peaceful village of hide lodges into an anthill of activity. Women dropped their chores and grabbed their children to greet the wagons. Old men who had been napping or making weapons emerged from their lodges. Warriors working with horses, and boys tending herds, galloped to the north to salute the trade wagons and all the good things they carried.

"Look!" Burnt Belly said, from where he had stopped to watch the arrival. "That boy rides with the speed of an antelope!"

I followed the medicine man's eyes to find the horse that streaked fastest across the grassy prairie toward the wagons. For a moment, the rider and mount disappeared behind the ruins of old Fort Adobe, then reappeared on the other side, seeming to have gained even more speed. The pony was a shiny black with a flowing tail and a mane that must have brushed the boy's face in the wind. Even at this distance of a half-mile or more, I knew the rider was Quanah, the Fragrant One, son of the great Chief Peta Nocona and the white woman, Cynthia Ann Parker.

Quanah was fourteen now, and on the verge of manhood by Comanche standards. His first raid would soon come, and by the looks of the way he rode, he was ready. Mind you, I myself could ride in those days. I could hold my own against most of the warriors in races and feats of equestrian skill, for I had trained with them as an adopted member of Kills Something's band. So for a rider to fill me with awe was rare. Quanah, even as a boy, was such a rider.

As he charged toward the wagons, he threw himself first to one side of the horse, then the other. He whirled and sat the thundering black steed backward, his arms raised, his voice yelling, "Yee-yee-yee-yee!" loud enough to be heard all over the valley. He faced forward again and circled the first wagon at a speed that seemed impossible for a horse making such a tight circle. The antics of the horse and rider enlivened the mule teams, increasing the grind and rattle of the big wagons. They trundled to the north edge of camp and drew to a stop, with Quanah and other boys circling on fleet ponies.

Westerly ran to meet her sister, and I walked to the lead wagon, driven by John Prowers.

"How'do, Greenwood?"

"Fine, John. You?"

"Got here with my hair." John watched Quanah ride away with the speed of a hawk. "Who is that kid on that black pony?"

"Chief Peta Nocona's son. His name's Quanah."

"The one that's half white?"

"That's him."

"Some rider. Even for a Comanche." John climbed down from the wagon, clearly relieved to have his feet on solid ground. He pushed at the small of his back. "How's the mood here?"

"Good. The whiskey's all gone. I don't expect any trouble. How are things back at William's stockade?"

John frowned. "The wagons came from St. Louis. Word has it that William's boys, George and Charles, have joined the Confederacy."

"Charles?" I said, remembering the little boy who had once ambushed me with a toy arrow. "He can't be more than fourteen."

"Lied about his age."

"Good Lord," I muttered.

"Yeah, William's worried plumb silly. I've got a letter for you." He reached into a vest pocket and produced an envelope folded twice to fit into the pocket. "I was told to protect this with my life, and burn it if I couldn't get it to you on time."

I unfolded the letter and saw Kit Carson's name on it. Back at Boggsville, I had begun to teach Kit to read and write, but I didn't recognize the handwriting on the envelope as his. He had apparently gotten some soldier or clerk to pen this letter for him. I tore open the envelope and read the missive. It was rather formal, as I might have expected, having been dictated to a scribe. The gist of it was that Kit was practically begging me to join him with the New Mexico volunteers as a scout, scribe, and courier.

The great Kit Carson was calling me to arms. What man could refuse such a charge? My eyes stared at the page I had already read. I felt filled with everything from pride to sorrow. I looked up, straight into Westerly's eyes, though she stood some distance away at the next wagon with her sister.

The smile melted from her face, and sadness filled her eyes. She sighed and forced herself to smile at me as if to say she understood. Then her eyes looked downward as she pretended to listen to some story Amache was telling, though the joy of her sister's arrival had drained from her heart.

The irony scalded. The very paper upon which the letter had been written seemed to strike my fingertips with lightning that jolted my soul like the bolt that had scarred Burnt Belly years ago. These consonants and vowels, verbs and nouns, sentences and paragraphs, the very things that had brought Westerly and me together, were now calling me away to war in a letter from an illiterate man.

TWENTY-ONE

October 20, 1861

Lt. Col. Christopher Carson
First New Mexico Volunteers
Fort Union, Territory of New Mexico

To: Mr. H. Greenwood, esq.

Dear Mr. Greenwood,

Duty calls. Our honor and courage, our love of country, and our loyalty to the flag beckon us into the fray. A glorious struggle lies before us.

Our distant sources in Texas inform us that the erstwhile Maj. H. H. Sibley, United States Army, now commissioned Brigadier General H. H. Sibley by the Army of the Confederate States of America, is raising, equipping, and drilling an army in San Antonio, Texas. The purpose and aim of this army, according to our intelligence, is to invade New Mexico and Colorado, secure the gold and silver fields for Confederate exploitation, and conquer California, providing the secessionist government with the California gold fields and western ports.

In advance of Sibley's Brigade, Rebel Col. J. R. Baylor has already invaded the Mesilla Valley from the south and taken Fort Fillmore. It is possible that the Mexican states of Chihuahua and Sonora may be persuaded to join the Confederacy.

The war has come to our country, Mr. Greenwood. Liberty is at stake. The secessionists must not achieve their goal of conquering the southwest. I call upon your devotion to freedom and your duty to your government. I need the services of a scout and courier. There are few here that know the country like you, Mr. Greenwood, and none that I trust more.

I urge you to ride immediately for Fort Craig, where our army will soon amass to repulse the invaders from Texas. I appeal to you as my friend. I need your help. Please come.

Yours truly,
Lt. Col. Christopher Carson
First New Mexico Volunteers

P.S., I am blessed once again. Charles Carson was born to me and Josepha just days ago in Taos.

That letter from Kit worked a curiously profound effect on me. He was calling me to defend a country I did not even claim. I still thought of myself as a fugitive from France; a man with no country, other than my adopted Comancheria. True, I had served the U.S. Army as a spy, scout, and courier in the Mexican War. True, I had ties to New Mexico, which had remained loyal to the Union, and, yes, she was being invaded by an enemy. Still, I did not consider myself a legal citizen and would never have thought of voting.

I did not go once again to war in pursuit of some lofty ideal or glorious call to sacrifice. I went because Kit Carson was my friend and he had called for my help. Time was, I had called for Kit's aid, and he had come. The moment to settle up had arrived. Kit must have known this when he dictated the letter. Why else would he appeal to my friendship, then add that personal postscript about his new son. He may as well have written, *You must come help me protect my wife and children from the invaders.*

My honeymoon was over. I left the trading at Adobe Walls to John Prowers. Westerly would return to Boggsville with Amache and John. Westerly understood. A Cheyenne woman took pride in a husband who rode away to seek honors in battle. Our last night together was at once sad and wonderful. She drifted away in my arms, but I could not sleep. I held her, and thought about the beautiful warmth of her body. In the middle of the night she rolled away from me. I touched her hair so as not to wake her, and took my leave. In the moonlight that poured in through the vent hole of the lodge, I wrote a love letter to her in Spanish, saying I would miss her, but that I would think of her every day while I was away, and then return to her embrace as soon as I could.

I cinched my Mexican saddle on a good horse and rode for Fort Craig.

TWENTY-TWO

CHRISTMAS DAY, 1861

I caught up to Kit in Albuquerque, New Mexico, awaiting orders for his volunteers to march south to repel the Texans. A soldier pointed out his adobe house to me, and I rode wearily after the grueling miles from Adobe Walls to meet with my old friend. Approaching his house, I saw Kit burst out through the front door with a Navaho blanket over his shoulders. A bunch of children came clambering after him, tugging at his sleeves and coattails, giggling and squealing with joy. There were seven of them. Four were his own, and the other three were either playmates of the Carson children, or orphans Kit and Josepha had adopted. They ranged in age from ten to two. Josepha came outside after them, holding her baby in her arms, her face beaming with joy at having Kit home for a while. Some eighteen years younger than Kit, Josepha still appeared the radiant young Spanish beauty who had stood loyally by her husband for over a decade and a half.

I reined in my pony to watch, as Kit took the blanket from his shoulders and spread it on the dusty ground. Now he made his children line up along one edge of the blanket and stand at attention like soldiers. Kit lay down on the blanket, his children staring down at him, anxious and excited. *"Listo . . ."* he said, telling them to get ready in Spanish. "Go!"

The children pounced on their father like vultures on a corpse and began rifling through the pockets of his coat and his trousers, as Josepha laughed and Kit groaned in fake agony. The children mined all manner of Christmas candy, trinkets, and toys from Kit's pockets, giggling with delight as they found their surprises. Finally, they withdrew from the field of conquest, comparing their winnings—except for five-year-old Christopher, who straddled Kit's torso as if he were a horse, and tasted a peppermint candy cane.

Kit sat up and hugged the little boy, smiling even as he winced against the pain in his troublesome left shoulder. The boy ran away to play with his siblings, and Kit laboriously rose from the blanket, rubbing the shoulder that galled him so these days. He happened to look my way about that time, and his eyes grew large with surprise as he recognized me astride my mount.

"Chepita!" he said to his wife, for that is what he always called her. He pointed at me. *"Mira!"*

Josepha gasped with joy and handed the baby to Kit. She ran from the front door to greet me, wrapping the rebozo tighter around her shoulders against the December chill. I dismounted and led my horse toward her. We were like brother and sister, and her embrace melted the miles of cold camps lingering in my bones.

Josepha led me by the hand toward the house. Kit had his eldest son, William, take my horse away. Putting their arms around my shoulders, one to each side, the couple beamed at me and led me to the door, the younger children trailing behind. "Kid, there will be no talk of war today," Colonel Carson ordered. "This is Christmas. You'll feast with us and rest your carcass."

They began lavishing me with a variety of leftover victuals, and we talked about friends, but as promised, we made no mention of war. After young William Carson came back from caring for my horse, Kit whispered something to him and sent him outside again on some mission. It was an hour or so later that the boy showed up, and with him two familiar faces entered the little adobe serving as the Carsons' temporary home. The first face belonged to my old friend Blue Wiggins. The second I scarcely recognized, for the boyish visage of Toribio Trevino—the former captive whom I had ransomed from the Comanches years before—had grown into young manhood.

"*Hola, Mucho,*" he said. Short for my Comanche name, Mucho Hombre—Plenty Man. There were more handshakes and *abrazos* among us than we could notch on a tally stick, and we spent the rest of the day telling one another of our travels and exploits. Blue had been back to California several times and had given up gambling. He had bought some land and was trying to make a living farming and raising stock. Toribio's people had never been located in Mexico, so he had continued to live on Lucien

Maxwell's ranch and had become a skilled vaquero in recent years. Both Blue and Toribio had joined Kit's company of New Mexico Volunteers. I told of my wanderings among the Indians, but we still refrained from war talk at Kit's insistence.

"There's another old acquaintance of ours among the volunteers," Blue said.

"Who's that?" I asked.

"That gambler. Luther Sheffield. He's with Pino's company—the Second New Mexico."

My mouth dropped. "Does he remember you?"

"I'll say he does. Pulled a gun on me the instant he saw me."

Kit chuckled. "You boys should know better than to make enemies of gamblers and the like. There's nothin' like a good game of seven-up with your friends, but you all should know to stay out of them gamblin' dens."

"Yes, sir," I said to Kit, then turned back to Blue. "How did you keep from getting shot?"

"I was with a bunch of our boys, and when Sheffield pulled the pistol, they jumped on him and took it away from him. He was pretty riled. Said he'd kill me sure before it was all over."

"I don't guess he'll be too happy to see me, either, will he?"

"Your name came up. John Hatcher's, too. Luther's got a good memory."

"Where is John Hatcher these days?"

"He tried to make a farm out of some land out on the Rayado. Got a corn crop in, but a grizzly bear come through in the night and ate just about his whole field. Stomped down what he didn't eat. So John built him a platform out in the cornfield and slept up there every night till that griz come back. Shot him dead. Big ol' boar. After that, John took bear huntin' fever and went on the warpath for griz. Claimed he'd rid the whole territory of 'em."

I could just see old John Hatcher out there in the mountains, checking tracks and claw marks on the aspens. It was well in my heart that he had not ended a farmer.

The next day, Kit, Blue, and I took a stroll down to the camps to look over the Union troops. Colonel Carson, of course, was immensely popular among the soldiers of the First New Mexico Volunteers, which he commanded, and they virtually mobbed him as he made his unannounced inspection of the camp. Blue and I finally had to break away and continue our observations on our own.

Blue and I had always had a knack for getting ourselves into trouble when together, and we wandered into the camp of the Second New Mexico Volunteers. Both of us knew very well that Luther Sheffield had been elected a lieutenant in this regiment, and that we were quite likely to run into him, and we did.

We saw him carrying an armful of clothing to the laundry tubs situated downhill from camp.

"I'll be damn," Blue said. "There's Luther."

"Looks like he's unarmed."

"Not likely."

"He sure has changed," I said. "He doesn't look like much of a dandy gambler now."

"I think he's seen some hard times. I heard he lost that gaming parlor of his in Santa Fe a long time ago."

"Let's go talk to him," I suggested.

"Huh?"

"Maybe we can smooth things over."

Blue shrugged, and went along. "Not likely."

We approached Luther Sheffield as he sorted his clothing on a rude wooden table next to a collection of leaky wooden washtubs, and a metal caldron suspended over a bank of coals.

"Hello, Lieutenant Sheffield," I said, still ten steps away.

Sheffield looked quickly my way, hawklike and suspicious. The years had drawn his facial features tight around his cheeks and jaw. The elegant gambler I had outsmarted years ago was gone. The hands that had once expertly palmed cards now fumbled with soiled uniforms. I saw the gleam of recognition flare in his eyes, and he reached for the pocket of his trousers, where he probably still carried that little revolver. I was wearing my Colt in a holster, and that alone stopped Lieutenant Luther Sheffield from pulling his gun on me, for he knew I would get to mine first.

"Just like you two bastards to gang up on me again."

"We don't want no trouble."

"That's what you said the night you ruined me."

"Who ruined who first?" Blue said.

"Nobody made you sit down at my table."

"Nobody turned me away when I came to win my money back."

"That was a long time ago," I said. "In games of chance somebody has to win, and somebody has to lose. That's been years ago, and we're on the same side now."

"You're not on my side, Greenwood. You ruined me. My luck went bad the night you walked out of my gambling parlor. You leave a trail of that goddamn Indian medicine everywhere you go. I couldn't win enough in poker to keep my head out of water after you left. You busted me back to a whiskey peddler and a pimp."

"I didn't do any such thing, Luther. I helped a friend win some money back. I used the same kind of tricks you used."

A tiny, shriveled old woman was walking up behind Sheffield, lugging two buckets of water. She had a hand-rolled corn-husk cigarette jutting from her mouth. The water buckets looked as though they weighed more than she did, and I felt sorry for her, but I couldn't help her and keep an eye on Luther all at once.

"You don't know a goddamn thing about my tricks, and you never will, you amateur. No professional would ever enter a colleague's own gambling den and fleece him with the kind of rude cheating you used. There's a code among professionals, and you broke it."

"I'm not a professional gambler," I said.

"You're a dead man, is what you are."

"Now, hold on—" Blue said.

I silenced Blue with a wave of my hand. I knew I was in no danger from Sheffield at the moment, but the rage was building in his eyes and I could tell he meant to kill me at his first opportunity.

The old laundry wench had come up to the tubs with her buckets of water. Her hair, streaked gray and black, was hanging in her face. She poured the water from the buckets into the caldron, and stooped to throw another stick or two of wood on the fire under the caldron. From the glance I risked at her, she struck me as witchlike.

"Cup of black coffee," Sheffield said, shaking his head. "What a low grade of trickery. When that little whore who helped you fessed up about that coffee she kept bringing you, I gave her a beating she'd never forget. And every blow had your conscience on it, Greenwood."

Now the old hag at the laundry fire paused in her toil, whipped her hair out of her face, and looked at me and Blue with beady black eyes. I scarcely recognized her.

"Isn't that right, Rosa, *my love*?" Luther Sheffield gestured toward her as if he were an actor in a play.

I could not believe it was her. The young Latin sprite I had once known had aged three years for every one. She took the half-smoked cigarette from her wrinkled lips and gave me a sad little smile, then shot a glare at Sheffield.

"I am too busy for your *shit*," she said.

"Busy, busy, busy," Sheffield said in a singsong voice. "Washing all day, whoring all night. You made her a slut and me a pimp, Greenwood. I'm not proud of it, but how else is a man supposed to make a living when his gambling luck's been tainted? At least a pimp can get elected lieutenant in the volunteers."

Rosa refused to take another look at any of us. I felt sick to my stomach, and I could see the same look of self-disgust on Blue's face when I glanced at him. I wanted to argue with Sheffield. I wanted to convince him that he had chosen his own path in life and that he had no right to blame me for his misfortune. The truth was that I would have to convince myself, first. In the end, all Blue and I could do was to back away until we were out of range of the pocket revolver we suspected Luther Sheffield carried in his pants.

"You'd better watch your back in the heat of battle!" was the last thing Sheffield shouted as we turned away from the pimp and the whore we had created.

⸻※⸻

Three days later, Kit sent me south with dispatches for Colonel Canby, at Fort Craig. Canby sent me farther south to look for the Confederates, who were supposed to be marching from San Antonio by way of El Paso del Norte. All this involved days of hard riding, which led me to the Confederates in camp at Fort Bliss. I knew better than to get captured by Confederate scouts, so I watched from safe distances, covering my tracks and sneaking around at night, Indian style, when I moved. I estimated the strength of the Confederate brigade at two thousand, five hundred men. With optics supplied by Colonel Canby, I spotted General Sibley, himself, and his second in command, Colonel Thomas Green.

The most peculiar discovery I made was a company of lancers. Yes, lancers! The lances seemed to be all of sixteen feet long, each with a fluttering red pennant, triangular in shape, and a steel blade that glinted in the sunshine. Each steel blade seemed a foot long. There were fifty-two of these Confederate lancers attached to the Fifth Texas Cavalry.

Certainly, I thought, this was all for show. All students of military history knew that lances wielded by charging British horsemen had helped break the Sikhs at Aliwal in the Punjab in 1846. The charge had been glorious, but costly, the lancers suffering forty percent casualties. Certainly General Sibley knew that galloping lancers would be mowed down like wheat by well-trained Union riflemen.

Anyway, with the information I had gathered, I slipped away to the north and rode hard back to Fort Craig.

TWENTY-THREE

I woke from a sleep of two and a half days, finding myself in the bunk I had been given in Kit's room of the officers' quarters. I stared for a while at the writing table across the room, where Kit and I feverishly studied letters in our spare time. I rose finally, pulled on boots, walked groggily to the latrine and back, and tried to enjoy a cold breakfast consisting of jerked meat, hardtack, and water. Afterward, I strolled to the western extremities of the fort to check on the progress on the earthen breastworks Colonel Canby had ordered built to reinforce our defenses. The wind was out of the south today so the dust raised from all the digging drifted mostly away from the interior of the fort.

Fort Craig sprawled across the flats near the west bank of the Rio Grande, at the northern end of the famous Jornada del Muerto—a one-hundred-mile shortcut devoid of water. If not for the excitement of impending war about the fort, this place would have had nothing more to offer than sagebrush, dust, and coyote tracks. A lonely place—dry, stark, and foreboding—it was nonetheless striking. The river could not be seen down in its channel from the fort, but its presence comforted everyone in this parched valley.

Across the river valley, the bank rose abruptly into a bluff that discouraged attack from the east. To the west, foothills of the San Mateo Mountains loomed, pinching the roads and trails together here between river and mountain, making this a logical site for a fort established originally to guard the

Chihuahua Road, long known as the Camino Real. In the distant south, the bare rock pinnacles of the Organ Mountains scratched at the horizon.

I climbed to the top of the newly made bulwark at the western edge of the fort to find hundreds of regular soldiers and volunteers busily picking and shoveling at a dry moat being dug around the perimeter. Mule teams pulling larger shovellike contraptions gouged and scraped and carried tons of gravel and dirt to where it was most needed as the soldiers heaped and shaped it into an earthen bastion, several feet high.

Before this war, the grounds around Fort Craig had remained as the Great Mystery had created them, and an entire enemy battalion could have simply charged across level ground among the adobe barracks and magazines and commissaries. The earthen breastworks being hastily thrown up would vastly improve the defenses of the fort and complicate any enemy attack. Colonel Canby had designed them well, beginning by ordering his soldiers to set a solid row of cottonwood pickets vertically in a narrow trench. The tops of the pickets stood about waist-high to a man. Then a moat was dug in front of this row of pickets, and the dirt and rock dug up from the moat was heaped behind the pickets, sloping sharply upward from the upper stubs of the cottonwoods. An attacker would have to cross the moat, climb onto the top of the row of cottonwood pickets, then scramble up the steep earthen embankment made of loose gravel. This would prove especially difficult with rifles and cannon raining lead and canister among the attackers. Colonel Canby had ordered his men to stay off this rampart once built, lest it should crumble.

I looked with approval upon the preparations, and thought Canby wise to have ordered the improvements. Hunger still gnawed at my stomach after my tidy little breakfast, so I walked over toward the sutler's store, hoping to find a tin of smoked salmon or oysters to top off my meal. As I came around the magazine, I noticed six soldiers laughing as they worked on some project near the carpenter and blacksmith shops. Veering that way to investigate, I saw that two of the men were using black paint to stain a large, straight cottonwood trunk that had been carved into the shape of a twenty-four-pound howitzer. Three others were patching an old cannon carriage that would, I presumed, carry the fake gun to the bastions in view of the approaching army of Texans. The sixth soldier was actually taking the time with a mallet and chisel to chip away at the muzzle of the wooden replica, making it just deep enough to cast a shadow and complete the deception.

"This will hardly win you boys a job at the armory," I commented as I walked by.

They looked up at me and grinned.

"Beats the hell out of shoveling that dirt wall out there," one replied.

I bought my tin of smoked salmon from the sutler, but before I could open it, I heard a cheer go up among the soldiers outside, and heard the bugler signaling "assembly" followed by "boots and saddle." I rushed outside to find infantrymen running back into the fort with their shovels and picks as cavalry soldiers rushed for the corrals. I grabbed a passing private by the sleeve and asked what the commotion was about.

"The Texans are coming to fight!" he said, pointing to the south. He seemed quite elated at the prospect of a battle.

I rushed around the corner of the sutler's store, ran past the entrance to the stables, and climbed up on the earthen breastworks at the south end of the fort. This part of the bastion had been completed first, as the Texans were expected to attack from this direction. When I reached the top of the bastion, I found Colonel Canby peering southward through his field glasses, an unlit cigar in his mouth. He was a big man—tall and of ample girth—but healthy and able to lead. I had seen him often with a cigar in his mouth, but had never seen him smoke one. I had, however, seen him light a pipe. He was clean shaven, with a full head of black hair that he never seemed to comb. At forty-four years of age, he was only a year younger than his opponent, the Confederate General H. H. Sibley, who was leading the Texas brigade to challenge Fort Canby. Sibley, known as "the Walking Whiskey Keg," was the inventor of the the Sibley tent.

Canby gazed out across the desert to the south, as did the officers with him—his second in command, Colonel Benjamin Roberts, volunteer commander Colonel Kit Carson, and the commanders of the artillery companies, Captain Alexander McRae and Captain Robert H. Hall.

Canby slid a glance toward me as I came to Kit's side. He had an arrogant way about him, but commanded respect. "To your guns, gentlemen," he said, and the two artillery captains went separate ways, Captain Hall to his two big twenty-four-pounders to the west, and Captain McRae to his battery of twelve-pounders on the bastion to the east of us. "Don't fire the Mormon guns!" Canby ordered, causing the excited young captains to laugh as they trotted to their positions.

The "Mormon guns" were the wooden dummies the soldiers had been building. They gave the impression that Fort Canby had twice the firepower it really had, for I could see several of the wooden replicas jutting toward the enemy.

As the artillery officers left the embankment, Captain Paddy Graydon, a fellow scout, joined the officers. "Hey, Greenwood," he said.

"Paddy," I replied.

"Well, lookee there," Paddy said, peering south at the line of Texans that had drawn up in battle formation, just out of range of the cannon. Though they were almost a mile away, I could make out a vast commotion along their line of men as they thrust their arms into the air, waved their flags and guidons, and jeered us on to fight.

Meanwhile, Canby's cavalry and infantry filed out in a long line of battle beginning at the fort, and stretching east. And here things stood, the two armies taunting each other like schoolboys wanting to fight, yet afraid of getting hurt.

Canby lowered his field glasses from his eyes. "I wish I could have seen the look on Sibley's face the moment he laid eyes on our new battlements."

Colonel Roberts chuckled. "I searched all over New Mexico for a Sibley tent we could set up as a target for artillery practice," he said. "Wouldn't that taunt hell out of the old rascal?"

"Mr. Greenwood, do you recognize their regiments?" He held the glasses toward me, but I did not take them.

"Yes, sir. That's Sutton's Seventh Texas Cavalry on their right. The Fifth Texas in the middle, afoot, under Green. And the Fourth Texas under Scurry on their left, with Teel's light battery on the flank." I had done quite a little bit of scouting and observing since reporting to Fort Craig.

Canby grunted as if impressed. "Do you agree, Captain Graydon?"

"Yes, sir."

"What do you think they'll do, Ben?" Canby asked his second in command.

Colonel Ben Roberts had commanded Fort Canby for a time, and knew the surrounding terrain well. "They won't make a frontal attack on the fort unless they're more foolhardy than we think. According to Greenwood and Graydon they're armed mostly with shotguns and revolvers, with one company of lancers and only one equipped with rifles. Our rifles would mow them down before they could get in close to the fort. No, they'll try to draw us out for a battle on the open field. All this is just for show."

As Roberts spoke, a company of infantrymen trotted into position behind us, protected by the breastworks.

Canby turned to them and bellowed, "Come on up here and let them see you, boys!"

The company captains ordered the men forward and a long line of rifle-wielding Federals joined the officers on the top of the bulwark. One of the privates raised his rifle and gave a yell, and the whole line of Federals joined in. When the yell died down, we could faintly hear the southern breeze carrying the Rebel yells of the Texans to us from a mile away.

Canby chuckled a little. "Where will they attempt to draw us out, Ben?"

"I believe they'll cross the river and pass behind the mesa, then try to recross above us at the Valverde Ford. Their spy company has reconnoitered the field there. Graydon's boys have seen their tracks."

"Kit?"

"I think Ben's right. I wouldn't attack this fort, would you?"

"Can we hold them at Valverde Ford?"

"We can and we must," said Ben Roberts. "But we must secure the bosque where the cottonwoods will give us cover. We cannot let them get into position ahead of us. More important, we must hold this fort, with its supplies. The Texans are just about destitute after that long march from San Antonio, and we must die before we resupply them."

Canby lifted the glasses back up to his eyes. "Our spy companies are watching them closely. We'll know when they move. Between Graydon and Greenwood they haven't made a move yet we didn't know about." He lowered the glasses and looked at Paddy and me. "I want you two back out there. You're to be my eyes and ears. I must know the moment the enemy attempts to flank our fort and move north. There's a supply train on its way here now from Albuquerque. Seventy wagons. If those supplies fall into the hands of the Confederates, we have failed miserably."

"Exactly," said Ben Roberts. "Our boys will fight them if we must, but, most important, we must deny the enemy our supplies. Frankly, that's more important than killing them. Without stores, they are finished."

I grumbled and kicked at the gravel of the bulwark.

"Do you have something to add, Mr. Greenwood?"

"I agree with Colonel Roberts. No army can last without supplies. But these Texans will last longer than you'd expect. They already have. They've marched hundreds of miles on half-rations, covered in vermin, debilitated by disease and Apache raids, and they've come with lances, shotguns, and pistols, yet look at them begging a fight even now. Their clothes are threadbare.

They're making shoes of rawhide. They're freezing and hungry and a quarter of them are sick, and they haven't taken one step backward. If they successfully maneuver around Fort Craig, they will march all the way to Santa Fe, supplies or not."

Roberts snorted. "Not likely."

Kit warned me with a glance.

"No disrespect intended, sir. That's my opinion based on what I've observed. I've gathered that Sibley himself is drunk and ill, but their men look up to Colonel Green. There's no quit in them."

Canby turned to Colonel Carson. "Kit?"

Kit shrugged. "God only knows what a Texian can't do. The thing we've gotta ask ourselves is, what is our duty? What is right? I believe it is our duty to turn back this invasion of Rebels on American soil. If we fail at that—and we may fail, boys, because those are some two thousand fightin' Texians out there—if we fail at turnin' 'em back, we've got to die holdin' our supplies. That is, I believe, our duty."

Canby nodded. "Then that shall be our plan of battle. Repel them if we can, without undue losses in wounded and dead. If we fail at repelling them, we must fall back and hold the fort at any cost. Any cost whatever."

Colonel Roberts nodded grimly, and we watched the troops taunt one another for two glorious hours.

TWENTY-FOUR

I spent the next three days in the saddle, flanking the enemy troops, and reporting back to Colonel Canby on their movements. I rode only the fastest mounts from the fort's string of cavalry ponies. Should I get captured by the Confederates they would surely hang me for spying. After their big show at the fort, the Rebels had withdrawn to the south, then crossed the river and ascended the bluff to the east of the fort. They camped beyond range of our big twenty-four-pounders, but we all knew they would not remain in camp long. Their provisions were running low. The Texans had to make a move and get on with their invasion. When they made that move, it was likely to be swift and violent.

Colonel Canby took his cavalry and Captain McCrae's artillery across the river to attack the Texas camp, but Sibley had chosen the campsite well, in a mesquite grove on high ground. As Canby ordered skirmishers within rifle range of the Texas camp, the Texans answered with well-directed artillery fire, scattering a company of New Mexico volunteers under Miguel Pino. With darkness coming on, Canby decided to withdraw, but he wisely sent a company of regular infantrymen to hold the bluff that overlooked Fort Craig from the east to prevent the Texans from using that vantage to shell the fort.

That night, I stood on the battlements of Fort Craig and looked east. I could see the campfires of the Federal troops that held the bluff, and far beyond them, on that high mesquite grove, I watched the fires of the Texans' camp twinkle. The night was so still that I could hear voices from across the river. As I stood there watching, thinking about Westerly and my Comanche friends, worrying about war tearing the whole world apart, I heard someone walking up the gravelly breastworks behind me. Turning,

I saw Captain Paddy Graydon climbing up to join me. Paddy and his volunteer spy company had been almost as successful as I had at following enemy movements and gathering information.

"Kit told me I'd find you here," he said. "Are you up for some entertainment?"

"My violin's at William Bent's Stockade," I said.

He laughed. "That's not what I had in mind. The quartermaster has given me two old broke-down mules, but I think they've got one last run left in them."

"And?"

"McCrae gave me four boxes of howitzer shells that were damaged when a caisson rolled down an arroyo."

"Two mules and four boxes of shells," I said, trying to piece his plan together.

"The boys have fitted the shells with fuses and they're loading them on the mules. If we get close enough to Sibley's camp, we can light those fuses and run those mules in among the Texans. What do you say?"

I began laughing. "Well, Paddy, that's quite a plan, but I've come up with one of my own, and we just might be able to put the two together."

"What have you been scheming?"

"I feel like a Comanche tonight. I thought I'd sneak into their camp Indian style and run off as many horses as I could. Their mounts have got to be thirsty, and it shouldn't take much to get them running for the river. Your mule attack should provide just the diversion."

"Then you'd better get goin'. The boys are cinching the panniers on the mules right now."

The post sutler was still in his store, selling vastly overpriced shots of bad, watered-down whiskey to the few soldiers who happened to have money. Most of the soldiers hadn't been paid in months. I bought a hunk of beef tallow from the sutler and wrapped it in a piece of cloth. Nobody asked me what I wanted with the tallow, and for that I was grateful. They probably assumed I was going to fry something.

I saddled an old cavalry mount that I knew to have an independent nature—one that didn't seem to have much of a need to consort with other horses. This animal would keep quiet, I reasoned, if he caught scent of strange horses on the wind. I rode out of Fort Craig, crossed the river, picked my way up a steep arroyo, and hailed the sentries surrounding the camp that held the bluff. I received permission to enter the camp and spoke to a lieutenant, telling him of Graydon's plan, and my own. When the horses came stampeding to the river I didn't want these soldiers thinking they were under attack. They would help me gather the horses at the river and herd them into the corrals of the fort.

Now I rode toward the Texans' camp, but before I got close, I pulled my horse up in the desert and unsaddled him, leaving the saddle under one of the taller mesquite trees so that I could find it later. I also removed the headstall and bridle bit and replaced them with a simple Comanche war bridle which consisted of a rawhide cord looped about the mount's lower jaw.

The night was cold, of course, but I stripped naked and put on my Comanche breechclout and moccasins. I took the beef tallow from the cloth and rubbed the greasy substance all over my exposed skin, and even into my hair. Finding a patch of loose dirt, I lay down in it and rolled like a dog wallowing on a carcass, covering myself with dirt that stuck to the tallow. Now I could lie on the desert ground and disappear like a lizard. This was a trick I had learned from the Comanches, perhaps the best and proudest horse thieves the world ever knew.

I mounted my horse bareback and rode Comanche style well around Sibley's camp. The cold desert air crept into my skin like ice, but I remembered my Comanche training and took it with pride. The warmth of the horse felt good between my thighs. I knew from spying on the Texans earlier that day where they held their herds of loose horses, and how far out their sentries were stationed. I decided to raid the herd of the Seventh Texas Cavalry because they were camped farthest south and most vulnerable. I rode as close to the camp as I dared, holding to low ground where my silhouette would not stand out against the sky. Finally, I dismounted, hobbled my horse, and took the war bridle from his lower jaw. I crept ahead on foot.

The fires of the Confederate encampment flickered in tiny sparks. They had probably burned up just about all the wood in the area. I slunk forward in a crouch, pausing often to watch and listen, knowing I could not pause long, for Paddy Graydon's two shell-laden mules were bound to be storming into the Texas brigade any minute.

I could hear the horses snorting now, and milling about. The restlessness of the herd pleased me, because I knew now that the animals were indeed thirsty and already thinking of making their own break for the river. As I crept nearer to the remuda, I suddenly heard something thump in the dark to my right, and saw the outline of a sentry strolling my way, stumbling as he tripped over a rock in the darkness. I melted into the ground. Precious little moonlight filtered through the clouds, but a man could see the dark growth of brush standing out against the tawny soil of the desert floor. I had become part of that soil.

This sentry trudged toward me, making his rounds. He would have been easy prey for Mescalero Apaches, had they chosen this night to raid the Texas camp for horses. He came closer and closer to me, and I began to get nervous. I feared he would trip over me and find me out. I didn't want to have to draw my knife and kill him, but this was war, and I would do it if I had to. Three steps away, he veered just enough to keep from tripping over me, but he stepped on the last two fingers of my right hand—and stood there! Thankfully, he faced toward the horses and away from me, so he didn't see me. I feared he would take a step backward and trip over my head. My heart pounded into the desert and I was sure he would hear it because the sound of the blood pulsing in my ears almost deafened me.

I could feel this sentry shiver through the worn soles of his boots. Now, suddenly, I understood why he had stopped here. The man was urinating on a cactus not four feet from my head. I felt a droplet or two splatter the tallow-caked dirt that covered my outstretched arms. Finally, the sentry finished his ill-timed business and trudged on around the horse herd he was guarding. That man would never know how close he came to getting knifed that night in the desert, for I had not signed on to the spy service to be trampled and pissed on.

When the sentry faded into the dark, I crept forward more quickly, knowing I was inside the perimeters of the camp now. A horse sensed my approach and flinched, his four hooves pounding once in unison on the ground. He lowered his head and let a low rolling snort rattle from his nose. I crouched and made a soft grunting sound the Comanches used to charm horses, hoping to make friends with some mount I could catch and ride out of here.

The horse stalked downwind of me and flinched again when he smelled me. I'm sure the scent of the tallow must have confused him. I grunted again and moved just enough for him to see me, hoping I would not send him running prematurely. The horse raised his head and warned his equine companions again with that rattle. Some of the other horses began to investigate my presence, and one calmer fellow approached cautiously, his head low, his breath blasting the ground. I kept grunting, and he came closer.

"Hey, Billie!" The voice came from behind me, some distance away. "What are them horses snortin' at over there?"

"Hell, I don't know. Some booger they made up, I reckon." This had to be the voice of the sentry who had stepped on me. He was closer than the other voice.

"Well, why don't you walk over there and calm 'em down? We can't have 'em stampedin' the whole remuda."

I grunted and reached for the horse. The old mount saw my hand and stretched his neck to get a smell of me.

"Why don't you walk over there and calm 'em down your own damn self?"

"Why don't I walk over there and bust you upside the head?"

The horse sniffed my finger. I moved my hand, and he let me stroke his muzzle.

"I'd save myself the walk, if'n I was you."

I rose slowly, grunting to charm the horse. Though his herd mates backed away and made more snorts, he stood still and let me stroke his jaw and neck. That Comanche horse grunt, if you knew how to use it, could sure charm the fear out of a well-chosen four-legged.

"You meet me over there where them horses is about to booger, and after we get 'em calmed down we'll see if we can't find us a way to settle whether or not I ought to whip your ass."

I had the rawhide cord around the horse's neck now, and was slipping the loop of the war bridle between his teeth to tighten it around his lower jaw.

"I'll settle the question for you, by God."

I stroked the horse on the withers as the two sentries walked toward me. I grunted at that horse and petted him and he stood there and those sentries got closer and closer. I already had the reins gathered in my left hand, along with a handful of mane. I knew I had better mount and spook the herd toward the river, and hope I did not get shot in the process. Then, a rumble of hooves came from a mile away on the other side of camp, and the sentries stopped twenty steps from me.

"What's that?" said Billie.

"Hell, I don't know."

In the distance, through the high, dry desert air, I could hear men hollering at the tops of their lungs, and could only surmise that Paddy Graydon's boys were spooking the mules into the Sibley brigade. All the horses around me had their heads high in the air, and one let out a whinny so close and loud that it hurt my ears.

"We're under attack!" Billie said.

The rumble of the hooves seemed to fade a little, and then a far-off blast shook the cold air—a peculiar blast, unlike any artillery shot ever heard—the blast of a bunch of howitzer shells chain-firing a hapless mule into the Shadow Land. Horses and sentries flinched, and I swung up behind the withers of my captured mount and dug in my heels. I just flat-out *screamed*—releasing all my spring-loaded tension in one madcap Comanche battle cry. Instantly, I was galloping all along the fringes of the remuda, spooking the horses toward the river. The second mule exploded in the distance, and one of the sentries took a shot at me, shouting something about Indians. I don't know how close he came to hitting me, but I was clinging to the off-side of my horse like a Comanche raider, so the Texan had little chance of killing me anyway.

The herd was in an all-out stampede for the river, a hundred horses strong, and the Texas camps were in chaos. I rode behind the remuda and screamed once more, then curled back to the place where I had left my horse from Fort Craig. I jumped off and removed his hobbles so he could follow back to the fort, then I rode like a racehorse jockey through the cold dark night, thundering with pure, unbridled exhilaration across the rough desert ground. I could not wait to get back to the fort and write of my exploits in a lengthy letter to Westerly. She was going to be so proud. A hundred horses!

TWENTY-FIVE

When I caught up to the confiscated horses, the Union soldiers were holding them at the river, letting them drink. By this time, I had gathered my saddle, bridle, and my clothes, my intention being to wash the dust and dirt from my skin before dressing. I announced my presence before I rode in among the Union soldiers, for I did not want them mistaking me for an Indian or a Confederate soldier. Only a couple of them got a good look at me in the dark as I rode upstream. Some private, who was closest to me, said, "What in the hell happened to you?"

I simply answered, "I went Indian a little while."

I rode to the river above the herd, where the water would run clearer. I waded into the shallow stream, and with a chunk of lye soap I had brought with me in my saddlebags, I began to scrub the dirt and tallow from my body and my hair. This was a slow process, and the night was cold, and the water was colder. But I had seen Comanches lower their children into holes stomped through the ice of mountain streams to steel them to a lifetime of harsh winters. I knew I was tough enough to take it if they were.

Still, it felt good to get into my clothes and coat and hat and gloves, and better yet to get in front of a fireplace in Kit's quarters at the fort. Before long, Paddy Graydon came knocking on the door, anxious to debrief after our joint missions. I told him of my successes as he and Kit laughed about the Texas sentry standing on my fingers while he relieved himself. I asked Paddy how his boys had fared, and he shook his head rather sheepishly.

"Everything was going so well," he began. "We found where the Fourth Texas was holding their mounts. We got close, up the head of an arroyo, without being spotted by their guards. We lit the fuses on those shells, and spooked those old mules out of that arroyo and got them running at a gallop toward the camp. We were downwind, so I figured those mules would smell the Confederate herd. We'd stumbled onto a pretty good gap between the sentries, and there was nobody there to even shoot at us. So we ran those mules as close as we dared, then pulled rein and turned tail.

"I was already cackling to myself. I just knew those old mules would lope right through their camp and explode all over those Texans on their way to join the remuda of the Fourth. But when I looked back, I swear, the damned old beasts had decided they didn't want to secede after all, and they were following us back to the fort! I told you those mules had one more good run in them, and I was right because they were *gainin'* on us! Those burning fuses just seemed to get closer and closer in the dark. We had to do some tall ridin' to stay out of range of the explosion, and I'm sure we came closer to killing ourselves than we did any of the enemy."

I sat on the hearth and laughed until my stomach hurt, and that felt good. "Well, it was the perfect diversion for me," I finally said, trying to ease Paddy's embarrassment.

"I reckon, but it just goes to show you, a man cannot trust a mule to follow orders," he mumbled.

I got a few hours of sleep that night under warm blankets, but I was awake well before daylight, so I took a hot bath to wash away the remnants of the greasy tallow still clinging to my skin and hair. Then I dressed for battle, ate some breakfast, and went out into the dark to saddle a horse. I rode my mount out of the corral and up onto the earthen bastion to the east, where I remained a short while, preparing myself in the Comanche way to get wounded or killed, giving it all over to the spirits to decide so that I wouldn't have to worry about it. The charcoal sky hung cold and cloudy, but the desert can charm a soul in any kind of weather, especially from the back of a good pony. Looking over the faintly lit valley that lay between the two armies was like watching a mountain lion sleep at my feet. It was beautiful and peaceful, but I knew when it awoke, it might rip me to shreds or snap off a leg in a moment of fury. Today I would see what war between white men was all about.

I left the fort and rode across the river to spy on the Texans from the vantage points that by now were well-known to me. Even before first light, I could tell by the sounds in the distance that the Rebels were on the move. I rode farther east to get a closer look, and at daybreak almost ran smack into a column of Texans heading for Fort Craig under Lieutenant Colonel John S. Sutton. I managed to dodge behind an outcropping of black lava stone without being seen. I regarded the movements for a moment or two, and thought about galloping back to the fort to report to Colonel Canby that the fort would soon be under attack. But something about this movement seemed less than threatening. The men, all mounted, rode ahead at a disinterested trot, slumped in their saddles. Their morale did not indicate that they were riding into battle. Their shotguns hung by leather straps from their saddle horns, and those who owned revolvers had them tucked away inside their tattered coats. How in the hell were men wielding shotguns and revolvers going to attack a fort bristling with cannon and rifles?

I watched as Sutton angled his column toward high ground that would be in clear view of the fort. He *wanted* Colonel Canby to see him. This was no attacking column. This was only a feint. Now I had a decision to make. I could ride hard back to the fort and report to Canby what I knew, but Canby would soon see the enemy anyway. Colonel Canby was well versed in the bloody art of war, and would suspect a ruse. I chose to let him figure this much out himself.

From the informal conference on the bulwarks four days earlier, I knew that Canby and Roberts expected the Texans to attempt to take the Valverde Ford. I deemed it my responsibility, at this time, to find out if Rebel General Sibley indeed had this goal in mind.

I dropped into an arroyo and rode north up the river valley. When I came to the pass between the Mesa de la Contadera and the bluffs to the east, I hesitated. The promontory, called Black Mesa by the white men, was part of the system of high bluffs to the east that had been separated by eons of erosion—like a peninsula that had become an island. The pass between the mesa and the bluffs was narrow with steep sides, and would provide me with little opportunity for escape should I encounter the enemy. However, it led to the Valverde Ford, so I decided to take it, and I did so at a reckless gallop over gullies and around fallen boulders.

I plunged ahead, knowing I had to gather some kind of useful intelligence within the next few minutes to be of any service to my superiors. When I came out of the pass, where the valley opened up ahead of me, I came across a trail so fresh that the horse turds were still steaming. I turned left and followed. Pursuing the trail over a nearby sand hill, I drew rein on the brink and saw what I had been seeking ahead of me. A company of mounted Texans proceeded toward the river. These men carried rifles with the stocks on their hips, as if they had come prepared to fight at any moment. Because only one unit of Texans possessed long firearms, I identified the advance party as Major Charles Pyron's Company B, Second Texas Mounted Rifles. By the brief glance I took at this enemy column, and the sign I saw on the ground, I estimated the number of men at 180.

Still undetected, I turned back down the sand hill and spurred my mount back through the Black Mesa pass. I galloped as hard as I could to the river and picked my way across, letting my pony find footing in the silt and quicksand. Then I ran hard for Fort Craig. I found Colonel Canby on the front porch of the commander's quarters, peering through his field glasses with a fresh cigar jutting from his stubbled face. Kit and Governor Henry Connelly stood at his side. Canby was watching the men under Sutton make their feint across the river, in clear view on the high bluffs.

I sprang from my winded pony and joined the men on the porch.

"Report," Canby said, without even lowering the optics from his eyes.

"That's a battalion under Colonel Sutton. They've got Teel's battery with them. But it's only a ruse."

"How do you know?" He still hadn't taken the glasses from his eyes.

"I rode around Black Mesa and found a hundred and eighty Texans on their way to the Valverde Ford."

Finally, Canby turned to glance at me, then squinted toward Black Mesa. "I've already anticipated that maneuver. Did they see you?"

"No, sir."

"How fast were they traveling?"

"At a fast trot, with their rifle butts on their hips."

"Who was in command?"

"Major Charles Pyron."

"You saw him?"

"No, sir."

"Then how do you know he was in command?"

"It was his Company B, Second Texas Mounted Rifles. The only Texans who have rifles."

"Yes, I know. Very well. I've already sent Colonel Roberts to the ford on this side of the river. Ride to him quickly and tell him what you've told me. Tell him to hasten to the ford, cross the river, and secure the cottonwood bosque. Then you ride back to me, and be quick about it. Now!"

As I leapt from the porch, the thought struck me that Canby was wielding a bit more arrogance today than usual, perhaps because he knew a battle was at hand. Perhaps because the governor of the territory was standing at his shoulder.

I swung into the saddle without putting a foot to a stirrup, and pushed my mount to a gallop. Within a few minutes, I had overtaken the back of Roberts's column and stormed past them to deliver Canby's message. Roberts smiled and had a sergeant bellow the order for his entire force to strike a canter toward the river. I turned back toward the fort. Before I got very far away, however, I heard the distant crackle of rifle fire behind me. I passed two more companies of Union cavalry riding to reinforce the Valverde Ford, and felt the excitement of the whole dangerous enterprise charging me with energy. My mount felt it, too, and charged forward faster.

Canby and Kit were in conversation on the porch of the commander's quarters when I ran up the steps.

"My boys have drilled, but they ain't been shot at," Kit was saying. "Give us some high ground and let them see the battle from a distance for a spell to get their heads set on what has to be done. Then, when the time comes, throw us in there and let us do our share of fightin'. I don't want them scatterin' with the shock of the first shell that falls."

Canby nodded vacantly. He seemed to have too much on his mind to contribute much to the talk, but he knew Kit was no coward. "Take your company and anchor my far left flank without crossing the river. Hold the Albuquerque Road. Graydon's spies report some Texans may have crossed upstream to attack our left flank, so stay ready. Your men can watch the battle from there and gather their wits. But I *will* throw you into it when I need you."

I then reported to Colonel Canby that I had heard the first shots of the battle in the bosque.

"So it begins," Canby said.

"Come on, Kid," Colonel Carson said to me.

The First New Mexico was already mounted outside the bastions and waiting for Kit to lead them.

"I'll need a fresh horse," I said.

"Get it and catch up."

I picked another mount from the Fort Craig stables and rode back toward the ford once again, overtaking Kit about halfway to the battlefield. Sporadic firing crackled ever louder as we rode nearer, and the men began getting excited. When we rode up to within view of the ford, I found the valley a chaotic swarm of men moving around afoot and mounted, scrambling for positions as bullets flew. Texans were pouring down from the bluffs to reinforce their advance guard. Several hundred yards away, I could see them stretching their lines out to their right, using an old channel of the Rio Grande to their advantage for cover. Meanwhile, Roberts's men correspondingly spread their lines to the Union left while captains and lieutenants shouted orders and messengers rode every which way in confusion.

From high ground, our unit caught glimpses of the savage battle raging in the cottonwood bosque across the river and to the right. It seemed that the Union cavalry unit under Major Duncan had run into fierce resistance from Pyron's Texas Rifles, who also wanted the cover of the timber. I saw Colonel Roberts himself charging toward the bosque, haranguing his troops to fight like hell and drive the Texans out of the trees. With Roberts urging the men on, the Union infantry and some of Duncan's dismounted cavalrymen managed to push the Texans back to the far side of the bosque.

This done, Colonel Roberts came charging back to his command post on our side of the river, his big mount crossing the ford in huge lunges through the water. I saw the fury on Roberts's face as he met Kit at the overlook.

"Why in God's name can't men follow orders!" he bellowed. "I *told* Duncan to take the timber, and he stretched his lines to the left. Where is my artillery, Kit? Have you seen my guns?"

"They're a-comin', Ben. They're a-comin'."

"What are your orders?"

"I'm holding the Albuquerque Road on the far left flank for now."

"If you encounter any Rebs on the left, send Greenwood immediately to tell me about it."

Kit nodded and led his regiment into position. When we arrived on the road at a narrow place between the bluffs and the river, Kit ordered two companies to dismount, find cover, and guard the road to the north while the rest of us sat on our horses and watched the battle take shape down at the ford. It was almost ten o'clock in the morning when the artillery pieces under captains McRae and Hall rattled into place on our extreme right flank. Within minutes, the gunners had unhitched their mule teams and unlimbered their guns, and were lobbing shells over the heads of the Union soldiers and into the Texans who were still holding the far fringes of the bosque.

From the safety of our high ground on the wagon road, we watched as Rebel artillery came trundling down from the far bluffs across the valley, the guns hastily taking up positions at intervals all along the Confederate line, the heaviest collections of guns situated on the flanks. In response, Colonel Roberts also spread his artillery out along our front line. And now the roar of shot, shell, and canister came from both sides of the Valverde Ford as metal ripped apart the timber and the earth, and occasionally a man or horse. Smoke gathered down in the Rio Grande breaks, but our Union gunners soon began to get the better of the artillery battle. Captains Hall and McRae had twenty-four-pound howitzers and twelve-pound napoleons in their batteries, while the Texans had only twelve-pound mountain howitzers and six-pound napoleons.

I knew there had to be dead and wounded on both sides down in the bosque where the worst close-range clash had occurred. Beyond that, both forces seemed to have stayed out of the range of small arms fire from one another. But the artillery continued to ravage both lines. Guns roared and shells sang through the air. Grapeshot and canister whistled. The sand ridges behind which the Texans took refuge exploded with well-placed Union fire. I began to see the pitiful sight of wounded horses limping and floundering about, and reasoned that some men were probably in the same awful fix.

Captain McRae unleashed the devastation of his big guns on the part of the bosque still held by Pyron's hard-fighting advance guard of Texans. Pyron had refused to withdraw even after repeated Union charges through the cottonwoods. Now, I watched in sheer astonishment as the trees used by Pyron's men for cover shattered under fire of shell and shot and flew limb from limb through the air.

"I don't reckon those boys will hold that bosque much longer now," Blue Wiggins said, walking his horse up next to mine.

"No," I agreed. "But look at the middle of their line." I stood high in my stirrups, as if that would help me see better. "Captain Teel is getting his guns into position." It was like watching a bloody chess game; I'm a very good chess player, and suddenly I saw the next several moves coming together, and knew I had to do something. "Kit!" I yelled.

Kit spurred his horse to me. "What is it?"

"Teel's guns. He's going to hit McRae hard and I don't think McRae can see him from where he is."

Kit had probably never played chess in his life, but I had seen him run a game of checkers in less than a minute. He didn't take long in reading what would happen if McRae's guns fell. "Ride, Kid! Tell McRae. Hurry!"

When I spurred, my horse took off so fast that I almost went right over the cantle of the cavalry saddle. McRae's battery was at the opposite end of the Union line, and I knew I didn't have much time to cover the distance. I have made many a hard ride in my time, and felt many a joyful gallop pull at my hat brim. But that ride—with smoke stinging my eyes and nose; with cannon fire pounding my eardrums; with the tide of a battle carried on the hooves of my mount—that ride will forever last in the fiber of my heart and brain and soul.

As I dashed toward McRae's battery I could tell that he had not turned a single gun in preparation to return the fire that Teel was about to drop on him. Looking left as I charged desperately on, I could see that Teel had cleverly sneaked his artillery in place unseen by trundling down the bed of the old river channel. He had pulled two pieces out of the riverbed, but still had them hidden behind a high sand hill from McRae's vantage point. His twelve-pound mountain howitzers could lob shells over those sand hills at a high trajectory and drop them right into McRae's lap. I watched those guns disappear behind the sand hills as I galloped to McRae, and so I knew that McRae could have no inkling of what was about to happen. Moreover, I knew that I was riding directly into the path of Teel's fire. I spotted a lone mesquite on the ridge behind Teel that I would use as a mark to remember his position. I judged the distance between McRae and Teel at eight hundred twenty yards.

When I came within shouting distance, I screamed McRae's name. His ears must have been ringing from the heavy fire, for he failed to hear me until I was right on his shoulder. He looked up and saw the glare in my eyes and gave me his undivided attention.

"Teel is in place where you can't see him." I pointed generally toward the lone mesquite on the distant bluff behind Teel. "You have ten seconds to turn that twelve-pounder."

"Action left, boys!" McRae shouted as he rushed for the gun, leaning his own shoulder to the trail spike to swing the cannon left. He looked back at me as the men toiled with worm, sponge, shot, and ramrod. "Where, Greenwood?"

"He's below that lone mesquite on the bluff." I will always admire Captain Trevanion T. Teel of Light Company B, Sibley's brigade, for what happened next. His first shot hit almost dead on target. I remember flying through the air. I remember heat, and a familiar taste in my mouth. I remember landing on my back on something very hard and feeling the pain of having all the wind knocked out of my lungs. I could neither hear nor see anything for an undetermined amount of time. Vacantly, I thought I was probably dying.

When finally I sucked a ragged breath in, I heard the screams of men and began to see a peculiar kind of light. I blinked and blinked and finally I saw the gray winter sky. I sat up and looked down. I found myself sitting on a case of howitzer shells, covered with blood. I felt the horror of knowing I could not survive long if all that blood was mine. I lifted both hands in front of my face to see it they were still attached. They were. I moved my feet to see if my legs still worked. They did. With terrible anticipation, I touched my face, expecting that maybe half of it was gone, but I found all my flesh in place. My hat was gone, but my skull and scalp were still on.

I sucked in another painful breath and saw what remained of my horse lying thirty feet away. The blood I wore was horse blood. Teel's first shot had exploded right in front of me and ground that poor mount to stew meat in a single blast. But the body of the poor beast had protected me.

I slid off the ammunition chest, collapsing at the wheel of the limber, still in somewhat of a daze as my vision and my hearing came back to me. I spat out the taste of horse blood.

Suddenly, I found Captain Alexander McRae in my face, shaking my shoulders. "Range? Range!"

"Eight hundred twenty yards," I muttered, barely able to hear my own voice above the ringing in my ears.

We heard the whine of Teel's second shot, and McRae tackled me and shoved me under the limber carriage as the shell exploded a little long this time, blowing a hole in the side of the canyon breaks behind us.

"Range, eight hundred twenty!" McRae shouted back at his gunners before dragging me out from under the limber and lifting me to my feet. "Do you *know* artillery?" he asked.

"I've read the manuals."

McRae turned and watched a cannoneer remove the ramrod from the breech of the howitzer. "Ready!" the gunner ordered. "Fire!" The man at the right wheel yanked the lanyard attached to the primer tube in the vent hole and the big gun belched and leapt backward, smoke and fire spewing large from the muzzle and narrow from the vent hole.

"Turn that napoleon!" McRae ordered. His composure astounded me as he looked at me. "Find a point where you can see both Teel and me," he ordered. "Do you know the signals?"

I nodded. I really had read the manuals.

"You'll have to direct my fire. I can't see the son of a bitch!"

"My horse is dead."

"Then *run!*" he ordered, shoving me back the way I had ridden in.

Genius that I am, this had not occurred to me, but now I set to at the fastest sprint I could muster. Having just caught my breath in the first place, the run up the valley slope almost killed me, but I arrived at a point of observation in time to see McRae's second shot from the napoleon gun. It hit a bit short, but served its purpose as it blasted away much of the sand hill that was concealing Teel's battery. Teel sent a third round slamming into McRae's position, and I saw one of the gunners fly through the air and I knew he was dead before he hit the ground. It reminded me pitifully of a cottontail carcass being tossed about by a playful dog.

McRae was furious, and I could hear him shouting and driving his men faster as his artillery muzzles began to roar his epithets across the valley to his enemy, Teel. He'd fire, and look up at me, and I'd signal him with my arms, telling him how to correct his aim. His third shot actually hit a Texas artillery piece, and crippled Teel's ability to fight back. When McRae had three guns trained on Teel, he sent a soldier to relieve me of signal duty, and I was free to get back to the First New Mexico Volunteers.

I looked around for a horse, but all I could find was a huge mule. I could tell from the rigging he wore that he had torn away from an ambulance or a supply wagon. He was spooked, and I was able to catch him only because he dragged a long rein that he kept stepping on. He didn't want to have much to do with me, caked as I was with horse blood and dirt. I caught the dragging rein and calmed the mule a little by making Comanche horse grunts at him. I drew my knife and cut away the busted leather rigging. I cut the reins down to about eight feet and led the mule up next to a boulder to facilitate my mounting him. All this while shot and shell and grape whistled and boomed and pounded.

When I rode back to the left flank, the boys looked at me in astonishment. Several of their mounts shied. Blue urged his horse near and said, "Where in the hell did you get so bloody?"

"A shell landed under me. This is horse blood, not mine."

"Well, go wash it off," Kit ordered. "You're spookin' the men *and* the horses. And get yourself another mount from one of the boys afoot. You might just as well paint a bull's-eye on yourself up there on that beast."

"Yes, sir."

As I rode the mule down the slope to the river, I heard Kit say, "You done good. Teel pulled back to the old river channel."

I lay down in the cold river and let the gore wash away from me and my clothing. Refreshed by the frigid bath, I rode back up the slope and traded the giant mule for a good-looking horse tied at the picket line. One of the volunteers guarding the road shouted at me in Spanish, saying to get away from his horse. I shouted back that I had orders from Colonel Kit Carson to pick a fast horse, and if he didn't like it, he could take it up with Kit. The volunteer cussed me soundly in Spanish, but I took the horse.

TWENTY-SIX

I spent the next hour carrying dispatches from one officer to the next as the battle continued. My horse exhausted, I returned to the fort to report to Colonel Canby, and to pick fresh mounts. I found him on his front porch, buttoning an overcoat. The governor was still at his side, but had pulled a chair out on the porch to listen to the distant cannon fire.

I jumped from my saddle, stood to horse, and saluted. "Colonel Carson scouted the road to the north and found no sign of the Texans trying to flank us on the left," I said. "Pino's Second New Mexico Volunteers are on their way to take Kit's position now."

"Where's Kit going?"

"Colonel Roberts has just ordered him to the front line to take command of Duncan's men. Most of them are Mexican, and Kit speaks Spanish well. Duncan doesn't. That's why he's had trouble advancing."

"Very well," Canby said as he buttoned his overcoat. "Kit should be an inspiration on the front. Tell Colonel Roberts that I am on my way to assume command."

I rode hard, made my report to Colonel Roberts, and watched the progress down below for a minute while my saddle pony blew. The men in the middle of the Union line, with their rifles outreaching the scatter guns and revolvers of the Texans, had pushed the Texas middle back from sand hill to sand hill, and forced the Rebels almost all the way to their last line of defense—the old dry river channel. Here, eventually, the Texans would either die in a horrible slaughter or strike out like two thousand diamondbacks in a rattler's den. There would be no retreat.

"Have you caught a glimpse of General Sibley all day?" Colonel Roberts asked me, speaking loudly above the continual rumble of the cannon.

"No, sir. I think he's commanding from the rear. I've seen many a courier ride up the trail to the bluffs."

Roberts turned his field glasses to the right to watch a skirmish between some Union snipers on the top of Mesa de la Contadera, and some shotgun-wielding Texans sent to force the snipers off the high ground.

Roberts chuckled. "If Tom Green takes command, we will have a proper scrape on our hands."

"Yes, sir, I agree."

"Carry on, Greenwood. Tell Kit his boys had better be ready for it."

"Yes, sir."

I loped back to the far Union left. The first thing I did when I returned to my unit was to replace the horse I had taken and set that big mule free. The man whose mount I had commandeered smiled and saluted me with relief. What fool would want to ride into battle with his head and shoulders sticking up above everything else in the entire command?

Finally, I rejoined Kit and Blue as they sat their saddles and watched the battle below. I reported to Kit, and he nodded his agreement to the orders to the front. His face showed neither fear nor foreboding.

"We'll watch here a spell, yet," he said. "When we see Pino coming to relieve us, I'll give the order. I don't want the boys thinking about it too long."

Looking beyond the middle ground between the two armies, I sensed the Confederates preparing to make a move in the deadly chess game below. I saw couriers scrambling everywhere behind the Texas lines. It seemed the entire Texas brigade was in confusion. Then I saw a particular rider, and pointed him out to Kit. "Look, there's Colonel Green himself. Look at him ride!"

"He's taken command, then," Kit said. "Somethin' *will* happen."

We watched Colonel Thomas Green, the old veteran of San Jacinto and Monterrey, as he galloped his steed behind the sand hills almost a mile away, often in the line of Union rifle fire.

"My God," Blue said. "What are they aimin' to do?"

He pointed, and I saw the red pennants rise aflutter in the air as steel points poked skyward on long wooden poles. Captain Willis L. Lang's Company of Confederate Lancers was poised to attack.

"You don't reckon they'll really charge with them spears?" Blue wondered.

"Maybe it's just a diversion," I commented. "Surely they won't charge rifles with lances."

The moment the words left my mouth, a yell rose from Lang's gallant horsemen, and they charged over the sand, among the scattered cottonwoods, their pennons wiggling like little red minnows in a sea of smoke. They angled to the Confederate right, gaining speed.

"They're gonna strike the Pikes Peakers!" Blue said. "The boys from Colorado!"

"Probably think they won't fight because they're not in regular uniform," Kit said. "That's a mistake. Those boys from the mountains are tough."

Not only were the Colorado volunteers tough, but they had drilled enough to know how to meet a cavalry charge. They formed a skirmish line in two ranks as the lancers charged on through lead and smoke, half of the Pikes Peakers taking a knee while the others stood behind the kneeling men and waited, their rifles ready. I could only imagine how fearsome those galloping lancers looked to the Colorado volunteers—and how ominous that line of armed infantry must have looked to Lang's charging company.

In the middle of that raging battle, a hush fell over the valley. Cannon and rifle fire ceased as every soldier in the battle turned to watch the spectacle of fifty primitive weapons riding down upon the muzzles of a hundred rifles. I've seen my share of charges and attacks and counterattacks. This one beat anything I had ever imagined for sheer bravery and disregard for danger. Those horsemen wielding the ancient weapons would neither slow nor falter. If anything, they charged ever harder at the Coloradans.

I held my breath. Blue groaned.

Under his breath, Kit said, "Hold your fire, boys," as if the Colorado volunteers might hear him.

The gap between the two forces closed and the valley got so quiet that I thought I could hear the flapping of the pennons. The lancers fanned out and their steel blades began to dip. A ragged line of smoky white muzzle blasts appeared; horses fell as if tripped, and men tumbled from the charging mounts. The sound of the rifles hit us like a drumroll as lances jabbed sand and snapped. Yet the surviving lancers charged on—horse-borne pikes into Pikes Peakers.

The second rifle volley hit men and horses almost point-blank and the clash became a close-quarters bloodbath. The Coloradans used their bayonets while the Texans—many of them wounded—drew revolvers. The lances were scattered like splinters. Only one had drawn blood, plunged into the thigh of a Colorado scout—an old mountain voyageur called

"Cheyenne Dutch." Captain Lang himself was wounded too badly to fight, as was his second in command, Lieutenant Demetrius M. Bass.

Half of Lang's company of lancers were already killed or disabled by wounds. None had managed to stay in the saddle and most of the horses were dead. The lancers who survived fought afoot now, blasting at bayonet points with their Colts. The Texans who had carried two pistols in their belts stood a chance of fighting their way out of the ranks of the Coloradans. Others drew their bowie knives and hacked away in desperation.

Somehow, the surviving lancers regrouped and fell back together, dragging some of their dead and wounded. The Coloradans pursued them, some having found the time to reload. It was the saddest, most spectacular charge I could envision and it made my blood boil with rage that General Sibley, the drunken tent inventor, would send men to their deaths in such a foolish way.

As the few surviving dismounted lancers fought their way back, they were joined by reinforcements from the old river channel—comrades who had watched their courageous charge and now came to cover their retreat with shotguns and pistols. The pursuit of the Colorado volunteers faltered, and at that moment, Captain Trevanion T. Teel loosed a round of cannon fire from one of his field guns. Captain Teel, who had already blown a good horse right out from under me, exhibited his artillery skills again as a round of canister cut through the Pikes Peakers and shattered their counterattack.

The tide changed once again, and the chess pieces shifted. The right Texas flank, inspired by the gallantry of the lancers, and now encouraged by the artillery support, advanced at a determined trot and drove the Coloradans back toward the river. Teel kept his fire directed ahead of the advance and our Union left crumbled just across the river from our position.

"Where the hell is Pino?" Kit muttered. He wanted us in on the fighting now, but he could not move until Pino came to take our position.

As the Union left reeled backward, the Union right advanced, aided by blazing artillery of Hall's battery. The beleaguered Texans who had held the fringes of the bosque for hours, turning back charge upon charge, could now hold out no longer, and I could see them even across the mile of smoke, pouring out of the timber and falling back to the old river channel. It was as if two separate battles were going on within this one battle. The Rebel right was gaining ground, as was the Union right. The entire line of battle shifted counterclockwise from a hawk's-eye view.

And here, things sulled as dozens of wounded men pumped their last pints of blood into Rio Grande Valley sand. The occasional artillery blast tested one line or the other, and a few sporadic rifle shots cracked, but the battle had fallen into a lull by unarranged mutual consent. Men were exhausted. Ammunition was scarce along both fronts. Supply wagons with reloads, food, water, and medical supplies began to advance from the fort on our side, and from the Texas supply train across the valley.

We had some time to rest and consider what we had seen. We ate some hardtack and jerked beef and washed it down with water from our canteens. No one in the First New Mexico Volunteers seemed too hungry. The hardest part was yet to come, and we knew that. We dreaded that. Yet we ached to get on with it and get it done. Nothing was worse than sitting here waiting.

TWENTY-SEVEN

"Look," Blue said. "That looks like Pino's boys coming down the road."

"That's them," I agreed. "They're escorting the rest of McRae's battery."

Kit nodded. "Prepare to mount!" he shouted, his old warrior's voice booming with extraordinary resolve. Captains and lieutenants passed the order on down the line until every last man had heard. "Mount!" Kit ordered. "Form fours!" he shouted.

Within seconds the First New Mexico Volunteers were mounted and filing into their familiar positions by squadron and platoon. As they moved into place, the men were quiet, except for the rattle of their equipment and the hoofbeats of their mounts. Kit rode to the center of the right flank of his regiment.

"Listen, boys," Kit said in a voice loud enough to carry to the farthest man. *"Oigan, hombres."* He would give the whole speech alternately in Spanish and English.

"You've seen what can happen down there. Now, them Pikes Peak boys looked brave and fought hard. They remembered their drillin', and stood their ground. They did good. You'll do good, too. Listen to your orders and do what you're told. I know you'll be brave and do your part. It's time for us to ride down there and win this battle for our country, and for the notion that men ought to be free. That's what we're fittin' fer. Don't forget that. These Rebels—well, they're *tejanos*. You all know that they've wanted to get their hands on New Mexico ever since Sam Houston won at San Jacinto. They've sent expeditions here to conquer us before, and failed. They've attacked our trade wagons to Missouri. They've sent agents to build Texas counties out of our pueblos and our valleys. Now, they've sent a whole army, but we won't let 'em take our country. No, sir! Our side is in the right, and we have no choice but to fight them that's in the wrong and come invadin' our country. Now, check your weapons and get ready. I'd sooner die than give up a single pumpkin patch to them no-'count Texians!"

A Mexican soldier let loose a *grito*—half shout, half scream; a yell that expressed both joy and sorrow—and a host of others released their anticipation with battle cries lost in the smoky valley air.

"Move 'em out, Blue."

"Squadrons—trot! *March!*" Blue said, and we all began our movement toward the front.

We stayed on the main road until we came face-to-face with Miguel Pino's volunteers. Kit and Pino exchanged salutes, and Kit led his men down off the road, toward the Valverde Ford—a remote river crossing out here in the wilderness, now the unlikely object of such violence and bloodshed.

We passed field hospitals where men groaned and screamed in pain. Others sat with bloody, bandaged stumps where arms and legs had once grown, blank expressions on their faces. We passed soldiers smoking pipes, or eating hardtack and beans. Some laughed at jokes; others pointed to places along the front and recounted the battle so far. We came to the river and crossed the ford handily. It was a good, solid crossing, used for centuries. A shell sang through the air and exploded fifty yards to our right. Horses ramped and bolted, but the men held them in check and regrouped, with the exception of one volunteer who rode his bucking mount for almost a full minute as the boys cheered him on. Finally, the bronc stumbled and the rider jumped off, but a comrade dashed forward and caught the horse by a rein. The gamely rider remounted, and now the pony seemed to have bucked himself out, and resolved himself to the fate of a war pony. We rode on toward the front.

There was something of a gap between Captain Selden's hard-bitten fighters, who had steadily advanced and Duncan's men, who had held their ground but failed to move. That gap was ours to fill.

"Kid, see if you can round up Selden and Duncan so we can have a parley."

I rode among the ranks shouting for the unit commanders until I found Selden on the left, and Duncan on the right. They met Kit at the head of his column. The uniforms of both men were covered in dirt. Selden's right cheek was black with powder.

"Gentlemen," Kit said, "Colonel Roberts has ordered me to move my boys in between your two commands. Captain Duncan, I've been ordered to take command of your unit as well as mine, only because I talk some Spanish, and I know a lot of your boys don't speak English. When it starts, I'll give my orders in English and Spanish. My scout, here, Mr. Greenwood, speaks a tolerable good Spanish hisself. He'll pass my orders to your Mexican volunteers, Captain Duncan, so place those boys on your left, if you would, so they'll be closer to Mr. Greenwood."

"Kid," Colonel Carson said to me, "you'll be busy riding between me and Duncan with orders and communications. I'll use Blue as my courier between me and Captain Selden.

"That about does it, unless you gentlemen have somethin' to throw in."

"It's an honor to have you alongside us," Selden said. "And we need your fresh troops. My boys have maneuvered since last night, and have fought hard. They're about done in, but they've got one more good scrape in 'em."

"That's all we'll need." Kit said.

"Do I have the authority to give orders to my own men?" Duncan said.

"Sure you do, as long as they don't go against the grain of what I've ordered. I'll be gittin' my orders from Colonels Canby and Roberts, but I'll also have the authority to give good commonsense orders of my own. I'd expect no less of you."

"Then I may use your scout, Mr. Greenwood, to translate my orders to my Mexican troops as he moves between us?"

"I'm sure Mr. Greenwood will cooperate."

I nodded. "With pleasure," I said.

Duncan breathed a sigh of relief and nodded back. It was plain he had been frustrated all day long by his language difficulties.

"Now, gentlemen," Kit said, his voice striking a hard and certain timbre I had scarcely ever heard him use. "We've got to hold the middle of this here line together. *We must not fail.* We've got the satisfaction of knowing we are on the right side of this fight, and the honor of knowing our nation will stay free because of our sacrifice, should any of us fall in battle. You can tell your boys to fight like hell. We are here to do our duty, and we are *right.*"

That simple speech from Kit Carson visibly moved the two captains. It was not so much the words he chose as the determination in his voice and the conviction in those battle-hardened eyes. Duncan and Selden saluted Kit and rode back to their units to move into their positions.

As Kit gave orders to throw his men into battle formation by companies, a cheer rose from the west, and we turned to see Colonel Canby riding down from Fort Craig, following the escort for the third section of
McRae's gun battery.

"Are they cheering Canby or the guns?" Blue asked.

I chuckled.

"I'm plumb happy to see 'em both," Kit remarked. "Kid, let's me and
you ride up there and parley with the colonel."

We loped across the ford and joined Colonels Canby and Roberts on
the eastern riverbank. The unlit cigar still jutted from Canby's mouth. Dust
and powder burns covered Roberts's uniform, for he had made several hard
charges across the river to bark orders at subordinates. A few other officers
joined the commander there as Roberts pointed out the positioning of the
troops.

"We've taken the bosque . . ." Roberts was saying as we rode up. "Finally. Wasn't easy, and there have been casualties." He pointed to the
northeast. "I know we've disabled at least one of their howitzers, but that
goddamn Teel is still pounding away at us. He keeps moving around in the
riverbed where we can't see him to shell him back."

Canby grunted, whether in approval or amusement, I could not tell.
"How do you see it, Kit?"

Kit turned his weathered face to glance across the battlefield. "Ben's
got 'em backed up as far as they can back up. They've got to fight now.
They can't get out of this valley quick enough to retreat. But that
riverbed's a strong position for 'em, Ed. Real strong."

"Can we take it with a direct bayonet charge?" Canby asked.

"It wouldn't be advisable," Roberts said.

"Kit?"

"They'd lay us low. Most of 'em are carrying twice-barreled scatterguns loaded with buckshot. Then there's some with Colts. Those sand hills
and that old riverbed are like breastworks. If we charged 'em head-on,
they'd cut our infantry down at close range."

Colonel Edward R. S. Canby looked over the battlefield and terrain
for a few seconds, and shifted the cigar in his mouth. A few flakes of snow
fell on his hat brim and shoulders, and melted.

"What if we flank them? Get our rifles and artillery into that old
riverbed where we can enfilade their position beyond the range of their
short arms? What then?"

"Makes sense," Roberts said. "Their lack of rifles is their weakness. We should take advantage of it."

"We'll push them right up that old river channel and beat the hell out of them," Kit added, a determined grin curling one side of his mouth.

By now, Captains McRae and Hall had joined us, having left their batteries of big guns to get in on the battle plans.

"Which flank is their weakest?" Canby asked.

Roberts pointed southeastward. "Their left. We've engaged them for seven hours now. Our artillery has pounded away at them, and our infantry has driven them back out of the cover of the bosque. They've got to be tired."

"Do you agree, Kit?"

"Yep. Their right flank is feelin' cocky about now. They pushed our left back after that charge by their lancers."

"So we agree that their left is weak," Canby said. "Here's what we'll do. Captain McRae, you're to move your entire battery to our left flank. You will serve as our pivot point. I urge you to make good use of those guns when we attack. Weaken their position ahead of our attack. Stay ahead of our charge. I don't want you firing on our own men. Understood?"

"Yes, sir," McRae said with a nod and a confident smile.

"Captain Hall, your battery will anchor our right flank and support our attack in the same way. However, you must be prepared to move forward as our flanking maneuver succeeds. I want your guns on the rim of that old riverbed at the earliest opportunity. You'll fire over our infantry and weaken the enemy in advance of our charge. You must remain mobile."

"I understand, sir."

Now I could see that Colonel Canby had some grasp of the vast human chessboard before him, though he had remained back at the fort all morning. "With our left flank as our anchor, gentlemen, we will attack with our right. Captain Duncan will lead, followed by Carson and Selden in a sweeping maneuver. Dismount your men and move forward as skirmishers. We will swing our right flank and force them northward up the old river channel. Captain Lord's cavalry will remain mounted and support the entire right flank as a reserve unit. Is there anything else?"

"I'm concerned about cover for McRae's battery," Colonel Roberts said. "As we sweep them up the old riverbed, we'll drive them en masse right into our left flank. They'll attempt to capture the battery."

Canby sank his teeth into his cigar. "I'll order Hubbell's and Mortimore's volunteers in place to guard McRae's battery, and reinforce them with Plympton's regulars. Mr. Greenwood, you'll carry orders to Colonel Miguel Pino and his volunteers and assign them the duty of serving as reserves. Should the enemy threaten McRae's battery, Pino is to leave his post on the wagon road and hasten across the river to defend the guns. When you've delivered those orders, get back to the front with Kit."

"Yes, sir," I said with a nod.

"Get back to your troops, gentlemen, and listen for the bugle."

I reined my pony away from the officers to deliver the orders to Colonel Pino. My heart pounded and my stomach twitched. I had prepared myself for battle in the Comanche way—giving my fate over to the Great Mystery—yet this war council I had become a part of now swept me up into a torrent of anticipation, energy, and fear. I did not fear for myself, for I was insignificant. But there were thousands of human souls in this valley caught in the unavoidable vortex of impending bloodshed. I hated playing a part in that, for men were going to have their bodies ripped limb from limb in very short order, like those cottonwood trees pounded by the cannonade down in the bosque, their branches hurtling through the air. I dreaded it. Yet I knew my part in what I believed to be right. Men should not build their fortunes on the backs of other human beings. That was what this war was about, even here, in the remote valleys of New Mexico, far from the nearest working slave plantation. The Texans had come here as if on some gallant quest to hold on to their way of life. But there was nothing noble about working a fellow human into an early grave through a life devoid of dignity. I knew slavery was wrong, among any people. Here was my chance to do something about it, bloody as it might become. I was ready.

When I galloped to Miguel Pino's position, where Kit and Blue and I had watched the battle all day, I found Lieutenant Luther Sheffield standing in my way on the road, a government rifle in his hands. I put my own hand on the butt of my Colt to check his move. He didn't point the rifle at me, but he cocked it.

"Damn it, Lieutenant, I have orders from Colonel Canby to deliver to Colonel Pino. There's no time for our personal quarrel here and now."

"Give me the orders. I'll deliver them."

"I can't do that. My instructions are to deliver the orders myself."

"You're awful goddamn full of shit. You're nothing but a messenger boy."

"Are you going to let me pass or not?"

Sheffield sneered. He truly hated me. "I'm gonna let a bullet pass through your guts. You better pray I don't get within a hundred yards of you down there on that battlefield when the shit starts."

With that threat, he uncocked the rifle and stepped aside. I rode on by, but kept an eye on Sheffield, and an ear tuned to the sound of that rifle cocking again. I found Colonel Pino and delivered my orders. On my way back down the road, I didn't see Sheffield and could only imagine that he was lying in ambush behind some boulder. I rode fast, and got back to Kit's First New Mexico Volunteers on the front.

When I arrived, the men were dismounting, every fourth man taking his mount and three spare horses to the rear of the company. I found Blue Wiggins as he handed his reins to Toribio Trevino, who was not happy about being ordered back from the front line.

"Mucho," he complained as I rode up. "Why must I hold the horses?"

"Because you're ordered to. Don't worry, you'll probably still get shot at anyway."

"I want to make the attack."

"Maybe you will. There's no way to tell how this is going to turn out. You just be ready to do your duty."

He sighed and frowned. "Yes, sir," he groaned.

"Kit's over yonder," Blue said, pointing.

I saw Colonel Carson afoot in the middle of his line of troops, rubbing his left shoulder. We rode to him—I on his right, Blue on his left. Snow fell in larger flakes now and the air grew damper and colder. Blue and I dismounted and stood to horse.

And we waited. A few minutes seemed like half a day. As we stood in excruciating anticipation, I saw Lieutenant Colonel John S. Sutton's battalion from the Seventh Texas Cavalry come trailing down from the Confederate supply train on the bluffs.

"Wish we'd have attacked before Sutton got in," Kit said, loud enough only for me and Blue to hear.

"What do you think Green will do, Kit?"

"Ain't no tellin'. What do *you* think?"

"He knows he's got to attack well before dark. I'd say within the next twenty minutes."

"Yep. But where will he attack?"

"Our left flank. He'll go after McRae's battery."

"He might. He might go after both batteries. Attack both our flanks."

"I don't think he'll get Hall's battery on our side. We've got the bosque as cover, and Duncan's men seem ready for one last fight. I know we're ready. It's McRae's battery on the left that worries me. Did you notice, just after the Rebel lancers charged, that the whole line of battle shifted? Their right flank gained ground, but so did ours."

"I seen it."

"If that happens again, they'll push our left flank back into the river, with no cover."

"I know. But you've got to understand, Kid. Colonel Canby's got to do more than fight this battle. He's got to protect the fort and all the supplies there. He's got to consider the possibility that he might lose this battle when the big charge comes. He's doing the right thing. By attacking with our right flank, he's pushing the enemy away from the fort. If we do get whipped, and have to retreat, at least we'll fall back between the enemy and our fort where we can defend the supplies and ammunition."

I suddenly felt stupid for not considering what might happen beyond Valverde Ford. I had gotten so caught up in the chess match that I had failed to look at the larger picture. Kit was right. Canby was right. Perhaps I was a genius, but I had little experience in tactics of large-scale battles, and how those battles fit into the bigger picture of the war. These men were leaders. I was a pawn. I would always remember that, and try to know my place thereafter.

Kit looked at me and read the expression on my face. "That left side worries me, too, Kid. But our job is the right side, and we'll do our duty."

"Yes, sir."

He sighed and rubbed his shoulder. "Remember when I fell off that mountain?" He smiled up at me.

"I still have nightmares about it, and I wasn't even the one who fell."

"This shoulder always tells me when a cold, snowy night is comin' on. It's right handy knowin' sometimes. Like one of them gypsies lookin' into that glass ball."

I chuckled. "You're a tough old hunk of rawhide, Kit."

"Too old for this." He drew in a rasping breath and looked up and down our line of volunteers. "I've passed through this place from time to time for thirty-five years and nothin' real good ever happened here. Nothin' real bad, either, I reckon. Not as bad as today. But I never really liked this place after forty-six. Left a bad taste in my mouth."

"What happened in forty-six?"

Kit caught himself rubbing his old injured shoulder absentmindedly, and made himself quit. "You remember those days. You was runnin' dispatches for General Kearny here in New Mexico. I was with Frémont in California. Well, after we seized California for the states, Frémont and Commodore Stockton sent me east with dispatches for Washington, D.C. I had Lucien and about a dozen other men with me. I was real happy about ridin' back East, because I aimed to stop over in Taos and stay with Josepha a few days. We'd hadn't been married but about a year and most of that time we'd been apart because of the war and all.

"Well, we passed through here with no trouble; then we ran into General Kearny just south of Socorro, headin' for California." Kit chuckled. "He wasn't too happy that Frémont had beat him to claiming California. Anyway, Kearny had ol' Broken Hand Tom Fitzpatrick with him as a guide, but Tom had never been over the Gila Trail to California, so Kearny ordered me to turn around and guide him back to California and let Broken Hand carry the dispatches to Washington. Well, I didn't like the sound of that at all, and I told Kearny my orders were to carry those dispatches all the way to Washington myself. Of course, the real thing was that I wanted to see Josepha. There I was, just eight days away from my Chepita, and Kearny's orderin' me back to California."

A shell exploded into a sandbank just a hundred yards ahead of us and sent shrapnel and dirt and driftwood flying every which way. One of Selden's men got hit in the face with something, and his comrades rushed to him to inspect his wound.

"That Captain Teel is homing in on us," Kit said. "We'd better attack pretty soon, or he'll tear us asunder like a grizzly bear." He cupped his hands around his mouth and shouted, "Lay low, boys! Hunker down until we hear the order to charge!" He watched as the men lay down on the ground, some of them using tree limbs and driftwood as breastworks. Kit and I, however, remained on our feet.

"So, what did you do back in forty-six?"

"Didn't have much choice. I turned around and went back down the same trail I'd rid up. First night's camp was right here at this ford." He turned and pointed to the west bank of the river. "Right about up there where Hall's battery was a while ago, on that flat ground. I was so down, Kid, I couldn't hardly stand it, and I told Lucien that I was gonna desert and ride to see my wife. He talked me out of it. Said they'd know just where to find me, and probably drag me out of Josepha's bed and shoot me in the yard. Funny, ain't it? It's usually me talkin' Lucien out of some hot-headed foolishness, but it was him cooled me off that time. He made me write a letter to Josepha right then and there. Well, it was him that wrote it, but I told him what to say, and he flowered it all up. Best we could do."

"A place like this remembers things like that for you—good or bad. It all comes back to you when you set foot on familiar ground."

Kit grunted. "Maybe you got somethin' there. I sure do miss my wife right now, just like I did in forty-six. That woman has put up with a lot of nonsense married to me all these years. I wonder what she's doin' right now. And the children."

"I know what you mean. I worry about Westerly."

Kit put his hand on my shoulder and shook me like an eagle snatching a fawn up from the ground. "I regret stickin' my nose in your business about that Cheyenne girl," he said. "I'm glad you did what you knew was right, and didn't listen to me. You and Westerly make a fine couple. And don't you worry, we'll see our families again when we get this done."

I smiled and nodded. We stood there in silence for a long minute as the artillery rumbled and random rifle shots cracked. Finally, Kit looked back toward Canby's command post, which had crossed the river to our side, and said, "Come on, Colonel, let's *get it done*."

A few seconds later, as if by Kit's command, Hall's twenty-four-pounder roared, and a bugle signaled our advance.

"Jump up, boys!" Kit yelled. "Go steady, and don't get ahead of the men on our right."

I exchanged looks with Kit briefly, mounted, and rode to my right to translate the orders to the Mexican troops in Duncan's outfit, riding behind the ranks as I shouted. We picked our way through the light timber of the cottonwood bosque that had been blasted for hours, stepping over branches and avoiding an occasional corpse. We saw a few forward skirmishers among the Texans withdraw to better cover as they saw us advance.

"Hold your fire!" Kit insisted.

We had walked steadily ahead for about two hundred yards, when a distant cheer rose up from the Texas ranks, and five companies of Confederate cavalry appeared over the brink of the old riverbed, four hundred yards away to our left, charging directly toward us.

"They're coming for Hall's battery, boys," Kit said. "Be damned if we'll let them have it. Steady, now, hold your fire!"

Looking back through the cottonwoods, I saw a courier riding at a full gallop toward McRae's battery, and I knew Canby must be sending the order to fire among the Texas cavalry charge. The minute that rider would take getting to the battery would seem like a week at hard labor. Two hundred screaming Texas horsemen galloping headlong toward us as we stood there waiting did little to bolster our morale.

"Company, halt!" Kit yelled. "Prepare to fire by ranks!"

I rode right and repeated Kit's order in Spanish to Duncan's Mexican troops, my voice cracking as I yelled. Our pivoting maneuver had stopped as we fell into a defensive mode, waiting to greet the Confederate cavalry charge. I could feel the ground rumbling as it came on.

"Steady," Kit ordered. "Hold your fire, boys . . ."

Now a round from Teel's battery whistled overhead and exploded in a whir of canister behind Duncan's troops. I saw three men fall, wounded or dead. As cavalry, infantry, and artillery fire closed together like gnashing teeth, I felt the dreadful thrill of war charging my limbs with energy just waiting to erupt. It seemed Colonel Green of the Texas brigade had chosen to focus his attack on Kit's command—on *me*. The thick of the struggle was about to close down on us like a bear trap.

"Hold your fire!" Kit repeated. "Form up, boys! Take aim. Wait . . . Wait . . ."

The Texas cavalry was coming at Selden's men to our left, but angling toward our regiment of volunteers. They seemed to be somewhat uncertain as to the exact location of Hall's battery, if indeed that was their goal, for the cannon were partially concealed by the timber of the bosque, and hard to locate at a full gallop. Another shot from Teel tore through the branches of the cottonwoods to our right.

"Wait . . ." Kit said. "Pick yourself a target, boys . . ."

I could see the faces of the Texans now. I could see unshorn locks streaming out from under their dirty hats. I could hear their horses snort as they leapt sand hills and came on. I could see fists gripping pistols pointed skyward. The moment those pistols began to angle down toward our boys, Kit gave the order.

"Ready . . . Aim . . . Fire!" he yelled, in the same calm, commanding tone of voice he had used dozens of times on the training fields.

The first volley sent horses and riders tumbling, and the charge veered more to our right. I drew my pistol and found a human target. My pony was prancing and the Texans were riding by fast, but I was an instinctive pistol shot, and I killed a man I never met, and whose identity I never knew, with a bullet that tore into his heart and sent him sprawling—a man who probably believed he was fighting for his homeland, the great state of Texas.

Now a shell from McRae's six-pounder landed on the other side of the charging Texans, upending a horse and rider in a spew of blood and body parts, driving the startled horses of the Texans even closer to our rifle range.

Our second rank of riflemen had stepped forward, and knelt to aim.

"Fire!" Kit yelled again, and the devastating barrage turned the charging Rebel cavalry into a stampeding retreat. Now Duncan's waiting rifles opened up and his men further scattered the attackers, killing and wounding several of the Rebels, destroying the Texas cavalry assault aimed at Hall's battery.

"Reload and move forward!" Kit yelled. "Steady, boys. Steady!"

Our sweeping maneuver resumed, slowed only a few minutes by the cavalry assault we had turned and now pursued. I was almost disappointed that the Rebel charge had been so easily repulsed, and I began to wonder what in the hell Colonel Green was thinking over there, across the lines. I felt an urge to press forward and finish this battle. We had our wing on the move, just as Canby had planned, and I wanted to beat the Rebels now and end it.

But at this moment a huge roar of voices rose from our left—like no shout I ever heard—and fifteen hundred Texans leapt up from the old river channel, six hundred yards away. Hall was moving his battery and could not respond, but McRae was ready and fired a twelve-pounder into the Rebel line. I saw a strange thing happen to the Texas charge when the big gun roared. It disappeared. The attackers dropped as if every last one of them had fallen into a hole. After the shell exploded, they leapt back to their feet and came on again.

I could see Canby's battle plan crumbling. Our right flank was still strong and still sweeping the Texans around to our left, but our left flank was about to face a hellish firestorm of buckshot and pistol slugs. The Texas cavalry charge that had felt so desperate at the moment now seemed to have been nothing more than a dangerous feint by the Confederates. They had drawn us in pursuit to our right—perhaps farther than Canby had intended—away from the real battle that was about to transpire at McRae's battery of big guns.

We swept around to the left as ordered, and now I found myself on the rim of the old river channel, but most of the Texans had cleared out and moved away from our advance. Hall had his battery on the brink of the riverbed, as ordered, but found no one upon whom to fire. Outmaneuvered, we continued our pivoting movement, finding resistance only from a few Texans holed up in the rocks, some of them too badly wounded by earlier fighting to get in on the massive charge to the left, but still alive enough to shoot and reload.

Amid the roar of cannon and musketry, I rode to the rim of a sand hill and watched the line of Texans sweep onward toward our left flank. Every time McRae's guns flashed, the Rebels would instantly fall facedown until the artillery shells exploded, then they would leap again and continue their charge. I could do nothing but watch. My orders were to stay with Kit's unit, and in fact I was out of position now. I should have been down in the old river channel, passing on orders in Spanish to Duncan's Mexican troops, but there was little to pass along down there, and I was mesmerized by the spectacle of warfare—drawn to it in a worrisome way. I wanted in on it. It made me feel sickeningly denied. I wanted to ride into the maw of it. I feared this feeling, the way a man afraid of high places fears he might leap from one.

I watched the cannon fire, the Texans drop, and spring again to their feet, the charge closing on the waiting Union rifles. I kept one eye on my unit down in the old river channel, but could not tear my attention away from the imminent bloodbath far to my left.

And then the clash came at McRae's battery. The Union gunners fought valiantly and stood their ground as the Pikes Peakers kept up a steady fire. Twice, they drove back charges by the Texans, supported by some companies of the New Mexico volunteers who had come forward to support the artillery. But finally the defenders around McRae's battery began to fall to the increasing blasts of shotguns ripping buckshot into them at close range. The startled New Mexico volunteers behind McRae's battery fell back and ran into Plympton's regulars behind them. Even some of these regulars broke ranks and retreated, leaving McRae and his gunners to die. Only McRae's men and a few volunteers from Colorado—the Pikes Peakers who had decimated the charge of the lancers—stayed to meet the final wave of Texans wielding scatterguns, Colts, and bowie knives.

I watched from that sand ridge as slug after slug staggered Captain McRae himself. Yet he remained on his feet and his revolver continued to spew white smoke at enemy targets. At last, he was leaning on the wheel of a howitzer carriage when a young Texas Rebel ran by, pausing just long enough to blast the courageous artillery captain with buckshot.

And all I could do was watch in horror. I saw our cause at Valverde on the verge of collapse. I saw Colonel Canby's horse fall under him as he ran among the panicked troops, trying to restore order. A soldier brought him another horse, but the time wasted only made things worse. Volunteers and regulars alike retreated en masse to the river, and the Texans pursued. The Confederates were turning McRae's cannon now—turning the captured Union guns on the Union soldiers themselves.

I felt useless. I looked down into the old riverbed to my right and saw the line of soldiers continuing on their successful sweep of the right flank, but I knew we were too far out of position to help in the real battle at the other flank. As I watched helplessly, bullets occasionally thudded into the sand around me from snipers who lobbed errant pistol shots at me beyond effective range. I spotted Kit, still leading his men as ordered, advancing rapidly up the dry river channel. Yet his success on this flank was not enough to save the entire battle. I knew then that we should have forsaken that old channel like the Rio Grande herself had done long ago.

At last I saw a courier riding furiously toward me and a wild-eyed private stopped at my side in a spray of sand and asked for Colonel Carson.

"Down there," I said, pointing. "Are we being called back?"

The courier nodded and galloped on toward Kit.

I did not wait for the rest of my unit. I rode immediately toward the melee at the ford. As I galloped I saw Captain Richard S. Lord's reserve cavalry charging toward the McRae battery in an attempt to recapture it. I rode to join the charge. A grass fire made my mount balk, but I spurred and whipped that terrified beast on through the smoke and flames and crackling stalks of grass. Across the river, I could see Miguel Pino's volunteers, the officers trying to get the soldiers to cross in support of the cavalry charge, the soldiers reluctant to wade into the battle just as so many other terrified volunteers were scrambling the other way across the river in retreat.

As I galloped on, my horse seemingly anxious now to join the mounts of the cavalry charge, I closed in on the flanks of Lord's riders. One of them saw me coming, and, mistaking me for a Texan, took a shot at me with a revolver, but missed. I shouted my identity and joined the cavalry charge, my own revolver at my shoulder, five shots left in its chambers.

We charged on toward the artillery, but the front lines of the battle had become blurred, as Texans swarmed into retreating Union soldiers and overran them. We began to ride within range of the Rebels' shotguns and pistols, but we were riding among our own men, as well, and the confusion kept me from finding a clear target. As I was on the right side of the cavalry charge, there were more enemy soldiers and I began to choose targets, looking for the Texans who might be leveling a shotgun barrel on me and my fellow riders.

I saw a bloody Confederate soldier drop to his knees, seriously wounded, and let both barrels of his scattergun go before he fell facedown. He was out of deadly range, and so the buckshot from his muzzles scattered, one ball wounding my horse in the rump and causing him to ramp and crow-hop in abject terror. I found myself pulling leather as others charged by me, and managed to get my pony under control, but he favored his right hip, and could not keep up.

As I fell back among the ranks on my wounded mount, shotgun and pistol and rifle fire began to pour into Lord's cavalry from every direction. We had ridden right into a crossfire from ally and enemy alike, still short of recapturing McRae's battery. The leading horses ahead of me began to drop, and I knew that our charge would fail. The vortex of this melee had sucked me in, and I heard lead hum past my head from every angle. Lord's cavalry was about to suffer decimating losses for naught and my brain swam with fury and desperation.

My mount, however, seemed to have gotten over the initial shock and pain of his minor hip wound, and I knew I must use what he had left, or die here in a hail of bullets. Something snapped and I went Comanche. My very thoughts started speaking the Comanche language. I saw a circle— the powerful symbol of Comanche existence in all its completeness. The enemy was too great to circle, so I decided to build a ring of hope around my own.

I loosed a Comanche yell that came as much from the Shadow Land as it did from my own throat, then I dropped to the left side of my horse, leaving my right leg thrown over the cantle of my saddle. I held reins and mane in my right hand, while my left hand held my revolver under the neck of my horse. Around the fringes of Lord's men I rode, taking my first shot to the east, hitting a Texan in the shoulder and staggering him back, spoiling his aim at me.

I screamed again and continued northward, my pony instinctively making the curve of the circle for me, unwilling to leave the rest of the cavalry herd. When my pistol pointed north, I saw a lieutenant shouting orders no one heeded. Just as I fired at him my pony jumped a cottonwood limb, throwing off my aim, and my bullet merely grazed the lieutenant's thigh. I got a good look at this enemy officer's face.

My right leg over the saddle was getting tired from holding my weight, but tired meant nothing in Comanche. My mount charged on around the cavalry herd, and men seemed to stop and stare. My circle seemed to gather Lord's men closer, and they began to cover my circling maneuver with a determined fire.

I circled to the west, where enemy soldiers were mixed with Union boys, some in hand-to-hand struggles with bayonets and knives. I chose a wild-eyed Texan as my target on the west and shot him through the midsection as he prepared to club a wounded Union regular with his spent shotgun.

And on around to the south I charged, finding the enemy soldiers drawing back from Lord's men. I pulled myself back into the saddle and sent my southerly shot skyward, having fired now to each sacred point of the horizon. With a final Comanche yell, I returned to the point where my circle had started, completing the protective spirit-shield I had cast around the cavalry. A bugle sounded retreat far across the river, and Captain Lord gave the order to withdraw. We rode out of that maelstrom of bullets as we had ridden in, pausing only to pick up unhorsed riders. After I made my circle, not a single man reported being struck by a bullet, and many a cavalryman would later credit my circling maneuver as our salvation.

As we followed the bugled order to retreat, we could still hear the screams of men up the river, where the bloody Texans had begun to massacre the fleeing Union troops as they floundered across the river. Reaching the Rio Grande downstream of the massacre, I found the sandy water streaked with red. Kit arrived, having remounted his men and reluctantly followed the order to retreat. We crossed the river here in safety, away from the horde of Texans who had attacked and overwhelmed our left flank, and captured McRae's battery. I began to feel the sickening feeling intensify in my stomach. I decided to ride upstream to see if I could reload and cover the retreat of some of our boys.

Without asking permission of anyone, I turned upstream, and found a relatively safe place behind a row of willows to reload. As snow fell on my sleeves, and stuck there, my trembling fingers fumbled with powder flask, ball, and percussion cap. The sky seemed to have darkened quickly in the last few moments, and I knew nightfall was upon us. The cold and snow would spell misery for the wounded men tonight.

After reloading, I continued upstream, still listening to shotgun blasts and the screams and pleading of shattered men. Coming around a bend in the river, I saw a Union soldier kneeling and taking aim through the willows. He fired at a Texan across the river, the soldier dropping and groveling on the ground after the shot. Now I recognized this Union sniper as Luther Sheffield.

"Hey!" I shouted.

Sheffield's head turned, his crazed eyes locking in on mine. "Now I'm going to kill you," he said, as he bit the paper end off a load of powder and poured it down the muzzle of his Sharps carbine.

"Not today," I replied. I drew my pistol and showed it to him, but it seemed to make no difference to him.

"Right now." He pushed a patched ball into the muzzle and drew his ramrod from the holder under the barrel.

"I will not simply sit here and let you kill me."

He glanced up at me, no semblance of human reason left in his eyes. He pulled the ramrod from the barrel, and I charged him. He was trying to cock the Sharps when my boot kicked him in the chest, the weight and power of the horse behind me. Sheffield rolled down the rocky riverbank, losing his hold on the rifle. I rode in between him and the firearm and swooped low to pluck the gun from the ground, Indian style. I heaved it over the willows and into the river.

Sheffield struggled to his feet. "Goddamn you, you little son of a bitch!" He pulled a dagger from his belt and ran at me. I avoided him easily on the horse, but he kept coming, crazed by battle and hatred. He chased me until he was almost exhausted, so I jumped down from my mount to face him and put an end to this ridiculous conflict.

He came at me with the knife and I leveled my pistol on him. I suppose I should have shot him right then, but for some reason, I could not. Instead, I grabbed his wrist as he made his thrust at me, and clubbed him smartly over the head four times until he dropped to his knees, then fell facedown, unconscious. I kicked the knife away, picked it up, and threw it in the river.

I stood there, breathing hard, looking down on Lieutenant Luther Sheffield's battered and bleeding head. A cheer rose from across the river, as if an audience had seen me defeat my demented nemesis. I looked around until I found my horse standing a short distance away, hip-cocked. Wearily, I trudged toward him and realized that the gunshots had ceased. When I reached my mount, and looked downstream, I saw a white flag of surrender waving on the road to Fort Craig. Now I understood the cheer of the Texans. The battle was over, and Canby had admitted defeat. Yet there was strategy in his surrender. Now, the Union troops could fall back and hold the fort and its supplies—the truly important mission.

I holstered my sidearm and mounted. My mount's wounded hip had become sore, and he limped so on the way back to Kit's unit that I finally just got down and led him. When I reached the First New Mexico Volunteers, I found Blue Wiggins and asked him what our orders were.

"We're to pick up the wounded men and make fires to keep them warm until the surgeons can work on them. We're to pick up the dead, too. Both sides. It don't matter now."

So I recrossed the Rio Grande with Blue, wading knee deep across the Valverde Ford. We turned upstream, where the worst fighting had occurred. Suddenly, a young Confederate soldier appeared on top of a little sand hill. "Hey, you boys!" he said. "Come help me."

He disappeared behind the sand hill, and Blue and I followed, peeking over the hill cautiously. We saw the Texan cradling a regular Union soldier in his arms. "I knifed him just before I seen the white flag," he said. "I wish to God now I hadn't done it."

The Union soldier was conscious, but staring in shock as blood from a belly wound darkened his shirt.

"What'll we do with him?" The Texan's youthful voice was frantic. "Where's the doctors?"

"Let's carry him over toward the timber where we can start a fire to keep him warm," I said.

Blue and the Texan grabbed the wounded soldier's arms, and I hooked my elbows under his knees as if he were a wheelbarrow. His face made grimaces as we moved him, but he did not speak or cry out. We had to carry him over two hundred yards until we found some men stoking a fire with a few other wounded soldiers already stretched out on the sand nearby. The man we were carrying died before we laid him down. I watched his head fall slowly back, and felt the life go right out of him.

"Now you'll be fine," the young Texan said to the dead man. "You just wait and see."

Blue and I looked at each other and walked away to find another body. As darkness fell over the valley and cold sank in, we wandered the battleground and picked up casualties, occasionally helping other soldiers—Union and Confederate—as they carried wounded to the fires. Dead men could simply be dragged. The work did not take as long as I had expected, for there were several hundred men doing exactly what Blue and I were doing. There were about two hundred dead on both sides, and about two hundred fifty wounded, total. The majority of the dead and wounded were Union men, but not by a great margin. Both sides had suffered terrible losses.

When finally we could find no more casualties, Blue and I decided to walk to the nearest fire to warm ourselves before we figured out what to do next. I was tired and hungry and thirsty. My body ached all over, and I began to feel a rare need to sleep. We joined a dozen men grouped around a fire, avoiding eye contact with the Texans. There were soldiers from both sides around that fire and they were talking about the charge of the lancers.

"I will never forget such a sight," one of the Texans said. I glanced up and recognized his face—it was the lieutenant I had shot in the leg while riding a circle around the Union cavalry, my bullet's path through his limb amounting to little more than a flesh wound. "There should be an epic poem penned about it," the lieutenant continued, "more famous and recited more often than 'The Charge of the Light Brigade.'"

"Those men died heroically," I replied, feeling my fatigue sink in. "Such valor is unforgettable."

The lieutenant looked at me. "Perhaps we should all introduce ourselves," he suggested. "I am Lieutenant Joseph Sayers."

I nodded. "Honoré Greenwood." And the rest of the men gave their names. I would never forget the lieutenant's.

Years later, Joseph Sayers would run for governor of Texas and win as a former Civil War hero. He would serve at the turn of the century, about ten years after the governorship of Sul Ross, whom I had also shot at, and winged ever so slightly, at the Pease River massacre of Peta Nocona's meat camp peopled mostly by women and children. This would make me the only man I know of in Texas history to have wounded two governors-to-be on the field of battle. The Lone Star State is lucky that I am not a perfect marksman, for both men proved to be adequate leaders.

TWENTY-EIGHT

I slept but a few hours after returning to the fort. Gunfire woke me early in the morning—the first of many salutes—followed by a mournful rendition of taps which would play again and again that day. After breakfast, I grabbed a shovel and started digging graves with a hundred other soldiers. Entranced in the routine of the chore, and thinking of the battle the day before, I almost missed Luther Sheffield sneaking up on me.

I looked up barely in time to see the shovel he wielded swinging toward my head. I reacted just quickly enough with my own shovel to deflect the blow, but it knocked me into the grave I had been digging. As I looked up at Sheffield's crazed grin and maniacal eyes, he raised his shovel once again to bash in my skull. I was helpless, hemmed in by the sides of the shallow grave. Just as he prepared to kill me, a soldier shoved him aside, and others pounced on him and took his weapon away. I crawled out of my grave. Sheffield was dragged away to the guardhouse and locked up. He was eventually court-martialed and busted down to corporal, but he remained in the service.

Anyway, after I crawled out of the grave that Sheffield almost forced me to adopt as my own, Kit found me and ordered me to ride back to the battleground and keep an eye on the Texans. So I rode up onto Mesa de la Contadera and watched the enemy pass the day digging their own graves. They didn't leave Valverde until the following day, crossing the ford they had won, and moving north with their wounded. They made no attempt to take Fort Craig. We would learn soon enough through dispatches that the enemy had established a hospital at Socorro, left a small guard there, and moved north on Albuquerque. Later, I would hear the stories of how many a mortally wounded Rebel breathed his last in that hospital. It was there that Captain Willis L. Lang, severely wounded while leading the charge of the Texas lancers, put his own pistol to his head and by his own hand ended his suffering and his life. His second in command, Lieutenant Demetrius M. Bass, also died there from his seven wounds. So much for the glory of that charge.

The Texans beat us at Valverde, but they didn't win much. They had failed to capture any provisions, and in fact had lost food and supplies due to the persistence of Colonel Miguel Pino and his Second New Mexico Volunteers, who had harassed the Texas supply train for hours and destroyed one of their wagons. Ironically, Colonel Canby blamed Pino and his volunteers for the loss on the battlefield.

Well, a commander has to blame somebody to keep his military career intact after a defeat, but it wasn't fair for Canby to put the onus on Pino. In his official report, Canby said that Pino's men had failed to cross the river to support McRae's artillery when the massive Texas charge came. The truth is that by the time they got the order to move forward, a river crossing would have been suicidal. Canby also blamed the volunteers under Hubbell and Mortimore for breaking and running in the face of the Texas charge. Well, they did break and run after repulsing the Texans three times and then getting overrun with buckshot and pistol slugs and suffering the heaviest casualties of any unit on the Union side of the battle. Hell, I'd have broke and run at that point, wouldn't you?

Many a Federal soldier who fought that battle has said to me over the years since that if Colonel Ben Roberts had been left in command on the battlefield, the Union would have won. When Canby finally came down from the fort, he made rash moves, placed our artillery in vulnerable places, and failed to respect the leadership of the Rebels' Colonel Tom Green and the tenacity of the Texans themselves.

By the by, Colonel Green's tactic of ordering his charging Texans to hit the dirt when they saw the flash of cannon fire was a stroke of genius. Many a Rebel saved his own hide by taking a dive before the artillery shells burst among the lines.

In my opinion, as I look back, Canby's pivoting maneuver took those of us on the Union right too far out of action to be of much use in repulsing the Texas charge. Then, when we were ready to move left to recapture McRae's battery, we were ordered instead to retreat. Also, Canby had three horses shot out from under him while the Texans were charging. He was in the thick of it, and you have to give him credit for that, but he couldn't get his orders to his subordinates in time when the charge came. Seven hundred Texans charged seven hundred yards in seven minutes. It happened just that fast and Canby failed to, or was unable to, react. So he made scapegoats of the New Mexico volunteers. Except for Kit's regiment. Oh, he spoke highly of Kit and the First New Mexico Volunteers.

Colonel Carson became the new temporary commander of Fort Craig as Canby took to the trail of the Texans. I stayed at the fort with Kit for a time. We were entrusted with protecting the supplies and ammunition there, and also saddled with the responsibility of turning back any Confederate reinforcements that might come up from El Paso. Kit kept mounted patrols constantly afield, but we encountered no threat from the enemy.

Dispatches from the north kept us loosely informed on the progress of the Texans, and they did indeed make progress. They sacked villages along the Rio Grande and marched unopposed into Albuquerque, then Santa Fe, raising their Rebel flag over the old Spanish Palace of the Governors. Kit had sent Josepha and his children back to their home in Taos, so they were safe for the time being, but he worried. The news from the north was often conflicting, and our information incomplete, so I volunteered to carry dispatches and gather intelligence, and to return to Fort Craig when I could. I looked over Kit's shoulder and instructed him on spelling and grammar as he penned several letters to his fellow officers. Then he sent me on my way with the correspondences.

I rode northeast, avoiding Albuquerque by riding to the east of the Manzanos and the Sandias until I came to Galisteo, a village about twenty miles south of Santa Fe. As far as I knew, the Rebels were still in Santa Fe, so I avoided the old city and took a road I knew well from my days as a courier during the Mexican War. The road led from Galisteo northeastward over Glorieta Mesa, joining the Santa Fe Trail at the east end of Glorieta Pass. Glorieta Pass—the gateway to the West in New Mexico—was of huge strategic import, so I thought I should ride there to see which army might have possession of it, before I went on up the Santa Fe Trail to Fort Union to deliver my dispatches.

The Galisteo Road was a rough cart path that ran over Glorieta Mesa. Along this road, I found no sign of the passing of either army. But I decided to ride down some woodchoppers' trails I knew of to reconnoiter the west end of Glorieta Canyon. There was a place there called Johnson's Ranch, which I knew I could spy upon by looking down from the bluffs of Glorieta Mesa. I dismounted a mile from Johnson's Ranch, and sneaked forward on foot.

Keeping a close watch for sentries, I sneaked up to the edge of the mesa and looked down on Johnson's Ranch. There, I saw some eighty wagons—the supply train of the Texas invaders. These were more wagons than the Rebels had had at Valverde, and I reasoned that they had commandeered equipment and supplies on their march up the Rio Grande, though the Union troops had tried to destroy everything they left behind in their retreat to Fort Union.

I saw a single six-pound cannon on a little knoll opposite the canyon entrance from me. This, and about two hundred guards, judging from the number of cook fires I counted, were all that had remained to guard the supply train. I had to reason that the rest of the Texans had entered the canyon—a narrow, nine-mile defile that led up to and over Glorieta Pass, and down to the east entrance of the strategic canyon.

Having reconnoitered Johnson's Ranch, I sneaked back to my mount and hastened on to the east entrance of the canyon. There was a place there, at the end of the Galisteo Road, called Kozlowski's Stage Stop. I was anxious to see which army held it, so I trotted on up the Galisteo Road, watching far ahead for sentries, until I came to the bluffs overlooking the Santa Fe Trail where it entered the east end of the canyon. Peering cautiously over the brink, I found the advance guard of the Federal Army of the Department of New Mexico at Kozlowski's Stage Stop. I knew the geography of the area. The Union Army would have to hold this position at the east end of the canyon of Glorieta Pass to prevent the Texans from attacking Fort Union and perhaps pressing on to Colorado.

Now I had a grasp of the situation. The Rebel Army had left Santa Fe, heading for Fort Union, and the advance Federal troops, mostly Colorado volunteers, had intercepted and blocked them at Glorieta Pass. The bending canyon through which the Santa Fe Trail led here was nine miles long. The Texans were somewhere in that canyon, prepared to press eastward and capture Glorieta Pass as they had taken Valverde Ford.

I hailed a sentry and identified myself. As he led me to the commander of Union resistance, this sentry told me that sporadic fighting had been going on for a couple of days, the two armies alternately pushing each other up and down the strategic canyon.

I was introduced to the Union commander at Kozlowski's Stage Stop, Colonel John Slough, of the First Colorado Volunteers, recently arrived from Denver. We shook hands, and I delivered my dispatches from Kit. Slough turned them over to a courier of his own who would take them on to Fort Union. This suited me, as I was tired of riding, and sensed that something of significance would take place here at Glorieta Pass, and I didn't want to miss it.

Colonel Slough and I talked a while about enemy movements. He struck me as a man of intelligence and good qualities. He was direct and confident, appeared temperate and healthy, his thoughtful eyes set close under a handsome brow, his full black beard parting into two long branches. I liked him automatically, for he made me feel free to speak and express my opinions. He was a lawyer from Denver, who now found himself in charge of the Federal resistance at Glorieta Pass. With his command of thirteen hundred soldiers, he seemed to have the east end of the strategic canyon pass well guarded. As we stood conversing between some adobe buildings and a row of cottonwoods, we heard occasional sniper fire up in the canyon.

"Those Texans keep testing our front," he said, looking up the old trade road that led from Missouri to Santa Fe. It snaked gracefully along the canyon floor, bluffs pinching it in on either side. "I'm afraid they're spoiling for a fight."

"What will you do?"

He smiled. "Spoil 'em. They've pushed us back this far with some hard fighting, but tomorrow we're going in to retake the canyon. We must. We've lost five good men, and I won't let their lives go for naught. If we hold this pass, we hold Colorado."

Just then I heard the footsteps—*felt* them, in fact—of someone marching up behind Colonel Slough and me. I turned to behold a bear of a man descending upon us, his whole body and every movement bespeaking impatience, resolve, and more than a touch of arrogance. The man had a chest a barrel maker would admire, and arms that strained at the seams of his sleeves. His anvil of a chin sported a good crop of whiskers.

"Colonel Slough," he said, making a salute that could have cracked a skull had someone gotten in the way of it. The earth ceased to shake as he came to a stop beside us.

"Major Chivington," Slough said, returning the salute.

In spite of the polite formalities, I could feel some tension between these two leaders of the Colorado volunteers.

"I've an idea," Chivington announced, glancing suspiciously at me.

"This is Mr. Greenwood, chief scout for Kit Carson's regiment," Slough explained.

Chivington looked me over, apparently finding me trustworthy, for he continued. "You intend to engage the enemy on the morrow, do you not?" His voice carried like that of a trained actor.

"I do."

"My scouts tell me that Sibley's supply train has come up from Santa Fe and is encamped at the other end of Glorieta Pass, at a place called Johnson's Ranch."

"Mr. Greenwood, here, has just told me the same story," Slough said.

Chivington looked down on me, standing a foot taller. "You saw them with your own eyes?"

"Yes, sir. Not three hours ago. There are eighty supply wagons guarded by two hundred men and a single cannon."

The major turned back to the colonel. "Give me four hundred men, and I'll cross that mesa." He pointed up the steep road that had delivered me hither. "We'll take their supply train by surprise from the rear. If we destroy Sibley's supplies, he's finished."

Slough looked skeptically up at the piñon-studded mesa. "That road leads to Galisteo, Major."

"There must be a way to cut across to Johnson's Ranch."

"I know the way," I said.

Chivington swiveled his gaze around on me like two bayonets. "How do you know so much?"

"I carried dispatches for General Kearny in the war with Mexico. Sometimes Glorieta Pass was occupied by enemy guards, so I'd go over Glorieta Mesa. There are some old woodcutter's trails that lead from Johnson's Ranch to the Galisteo Road. If you cut straight over the mesa, due west, it's only about seven miles from here."

"You'll go as my guide," Chivington said to me. He turned to Slough. "Colonel?"

"Mr. Greenwood has orders to return to Fort Craig with my dispatches," Slough said, pausing to look back up at the mesa. He smiled, and it seemed to me that he liked the idea of getting the hulking Major Chivington out of his way for a while. "But I see no harm in his leading you over the mesa to harass the enemy rear on his way back to his regiment. Meanwhile, I'll attack the Texans' front in the canyon."

Major John Chivington grinned with anticipation. "I'll take Colonel Chaves's New Mexicans as mounted guards, and pick some boys from the First Colorado to make the attack."

"Report to me with a detailed plan when you've made your preparations."

Chivington grabbed me by the sleeve and dragged me away with him as if I were his kid brother. We spent the next hour or so talking about the logistics of crossing over seven miles of rough mountain road with four hundred soldiers. Then Chivington commenced to talk about himself, and I learned more about him than I cared to know.

A native of Ohio, he had been born to the plow and the lumberjack trade. As a young man, he had heard "the call of the Lord," as he put it.

"I cussed a preacher at a log-rollin', and later felt so bad about it that I knew I had to repent my ways."

He decided to become a preacher himself. Though not well educated, he caught up, and completed all the studies necessary to become ordained in the Methodist church, all the while supporting a bride at the carpentry trade.

Assigned a church in Missouri before the war, he told me, he fell into disfavor with some Southern-thinking members of the congregation by preaching abolition from the pulpit. When some malcontents brought tar and feathers to the church one Sunday, Pastor Chivington ascended the pulpit with two Colt revolvers.

"Do you know how much tar it takes to cover a two-hundred-sixty-pound servant of the Lord? Well, they didn't have enough tar, and they didn't have enough sand in their craws to use what tar they had."

He had been known since as the "Fighting Parson," an appellation he now seemed determined to live up to. Reassigned by the church to Denver, Chivington had cleaned house with an axe handle when he found a saloonkeeper had moved into what once had been the Methodist chapel.

"I told him he'd better clear out or I'd use his head for a mop and his butt for a bootjack. You don't go turning the house of the Lord into the devil's parlor. Do you drink, Mr. Greenwood?"

"No, sir."

"Good. Our Colorado volunteers are mostly miners, and they *will* drink. A lot of Irishmen. Only thing worse than a drunken Irishman is a drunken Indian." He began to chuckle. "But of course, 'drunken Indian' is redundant, isn't it?"

"You've never seen a sober Indian?"

"Not in Denver. Anyway, a heathen is still a heathen, drunk or sober. I don't know how progressive you people are down here in New Mexico, but

Colorado Territory is ready for statehood—just as soon as we rid ourselves of secessionists and savages, and I mean to do both. Why, if it wasn't for the First Colorado Volunteers, the Texans would already have stormed Fort Union!"

Then Major Chivington commenced to brag about how his men had been the first to engage the Texans in Apache Canyon; how they had surprised some thirty members of the Rebel advance guard and captured them without firing a shot; how they had scaled the slopes on either side of the canyon and fired on the main body of Texans, driving the Rebels back over Glorieta Pass toward Santa Fe.

I remember thinking that Chivington was already practicing his campaign speech. As soon as I could excuse myself, I took my leave and went to find the regimental blacksmith. After some hard bargaining, he let me have an old rat-tail file that I thought I might find a use for on the morrow.

⟪⟫

The next morning found us riding up the Galisteo Road to the top of Glorieta Mesa. The major and I led the way on horseback, followed by a mounted company of New Mexico volunteers under Lieutenant Colonel Manuel Chavez. Behind the New Mexicans came four hundred Colorado infantrymen. The old cart path to Galisteo was steep and rough in places, but easily traversable by hardened dragoons and foot soldiers.

After a march of three miles, I cantered on ahead with the mounted New Mexicans. It was Colonel Chacon's job to scout southward on the Galisteo Road with his cavalry to make sure no Rebels were coming up from the southwest. When the road turned sharply away from Glorieta Canyon, I stayed behind and let Chacon's men ride on. This point along the Galisteo Road was about two miles from Johnson's Ranch through the ponderosa and piñon pines, so I waited here for the foot soldiers to catch up. While I waited, I took all my dispatches from my pockets and hid them under a rock. Should I get killed or captured in the coming attack on the supply train, I did not intend to let my correspondences fall into enemy hands.

When Major Chivington arrived, I showed him the trail, and he gave orders for the men to fix bayonets and proceed forward silently. The major dismounted and followed me through the woods toward the enemy. Chivington was almost twice my size, and I had to stop often to wait for his bulk to catch up. He lumbered like a grizzly where I bounded like a mountain goat. Four hundred infantrymen trailed behind. The scrub oak thickets and pine forests proved somewhat difficult for a large body of men to traverse, but we plunged ahead with all possible haste down the narrow trails used for generations by woodcutters.

In the distance, we could hear artillery, and knew that Colonel Slough had entered the east end of the canyon to engage the Texans head-on. Colonel William Scurry had been in command of the Texas advance for days, and I knew from Valverde how hard he and his men could fight.

Major Chivington was huffing like a locomotive by the time I led him to the bluffs overlooking the Texas supply train. He looked distastefully down at the rugged slopes below, and waved his second in command forward—a regular army officer named Captain Lewis.

"Lewis," the major whispered, between gasps for breath. "Lead the men down that ravine to the right. Keep them quiet. Remember the element of surprise."

"Major, with your permission," I said, "I'll take a platoon and disable that six-pounder across the way." I showed him the file I had acquired from the blacksmith.

Chivington liked the idea. "Very well," he said. "Godspeed, gentlemen."

Captain Lewis motioned for our troops to follow us down the ravine.

"He's not going down there with us, is he?" Lewis said, a smirk on his face.

"Apparently not."

When we had climbed down to the mouth of the ravine, still undetected by the enemy, I picked twenty-four soldiers as my platoon—rough-looking boys from the Colorado mines. I divided them into two ranks and told them how we would attack the artillery position. The rest of the men would storm the wagons, driving the Texas guard to the west, and setting the wagons afire as they gained ground.

Lewis cocked his revolver and glared back at the men. "Do your duty, soldiers!" he said, right out loud. He turned toward the enemy and yelled, "Charge!" running toward the wagon train. A battle cry rose from the ravine as men poured into the open, quickly rushing among the buildings of Johnson's Ranch, and into the array of wagons. Captain Lewis fired the first shot.

I led my platoon at a sprint around the right of the wagons, watching surprised Texans jump and run before us, most of them unarmed. My own revolver was in my hand, cocked, but I didn't intend to fire it frivolously. Shouts and gunshots began to fill the air, and I could see the gunners on the knoll wheeling the cannon. They fired a shell toward the ravine from which the Union men were still pouring, but it sailed high and exploded harmlessly against a bluff.

As the gunners began to reload their piece, my platoon charged their position. Only three riflemen were there, protecting the artillerymen, and my force vastly outnumbered them. They were surprised and rattled, and their rifle fire missed us as we charged up the slope toward them. The six-pounder barked again, harming no one, and the riflemen around the cannon fumbled to reload their weapons.

I stopped and raised my Colt, though yet out of pistol range. "First rank, prepare to fire," I ordered. I waited for their rifles to rise, then said, "Fire!" I added a pistol shot to the barrage. One Texan answered with a double load of buckshot that tore through our line like a swarm of hornets, one piece of shot ticking my ear. Looking back, I saw all my boys still standing.

"Reload!" I ordered. While the first rank tore paper cartridges with their teeth and groped for ramrods, I said, "Second rank, prepare to fire. Fire!"

Another dozen rifle balls peppered the gunners. "Second rank, reload. First rank . . ." I waited for the last couple of men to replace their ramrods. "Charge!" I led the way, firing my revolver deliberately and sparingly. The Texans looked down at our charging bayonets and quickly abandoned their cannon, scrambling out of sight down the other side of the hill. My platoon raised a cheer as we captured the artillery piece. Sporadic firing continued among the wagons below us, and smoke began to billow from burning canvas and lumber. I saw one soldier using a shovel to toss live coals from a campfire into a wagon. A group of four men pushed an already burning wagon into another to catch it, too, on fire.

The excitement of our charge and the success of our attack began to stir me. My heart pounded and I realized that I was gasping for breath. We had completely routed our enemy, but I reminded myself to remain cautious. Then I looked across the canyon and saw Major Chivington standing alone on the opposite bluff, his hands on his hips as he watched his men swarm through the Texas camp.

"That's quite a pulpit he's got there, ain't it," one of the men said, sneering through his words.

"Hey, look here!" said another. "There's blood!"

"I knew I hit one of 'em!" boasted still another.

"You didn't hit nothin'. That was my man."

"The hell it was!"

"Hey, let's turn the cannon on the bastards!" another soldier suggested, watching the Texas gunners run for their comrades, who had been driven to the far end of the supply train.

"No!" I replied. "Our orders are to disable the piece. First rank, form a defensive line between us and the wagons. They may try to reclaim this piece." The second rank was just now coming up the hill, having reloaded. "Disable that cannon!" I said to them.

The men looked at me, then at one another. "How's a feller do that, exactly?" one of them asked.

I shook my head and ordered the second rank to take a knee behind the first rank, in case the Texans should indeed try to recapture their artillery. I found an axe that the Rebels had used to chop open crates of shot and shell. Using the axe, I drove the tail of the regimental blacksmith's rat-tail file into the vent hole of the captured six-pounder. I drove it in as far as it would go, and then beat on the side of the file until it broke off, leaving the tail wedged in the vent hole. This would prevent the enemy from inserting any more friction tubes into the vent hole to fire the cannon.

I looked down at the wagon train now, and found almost the entire supply camp in flames. I decided to double-spike the cannon for good measure. "Grab the ramrod!" I said to the soldier nearest to me. I found a metal fuse gouge on the ground and picked it up. Next, I grabbed a six-pound cast-iron cannonball from an ammunition crate. I jammed the shot and the fuse gouge into the muzzle of the piece together, and pounded them in as far as I could with the back of the axe head.

"Stick that ramrod in there," I ordered one man. I turned to the next nearest man. "Grab that mallet, and beat the shot in there as deep as you can."

This was familiar work for men accustomed to hard rock mining with handheld drills and ten-pound sledgehammers. The soldiers gleefully drove the jammed shot irretrievably into the barrel of the gun tube. When this was done, I ordered my squadron to descend the hill and help set the supply train ablaze. They went at the new task with alacrity. About that time, one of the wagons exploded, apparently laden with ammunition. I saw one of the Union soldiers being dragged away, and hoped he was just injured and not dead. It turned out he was merely stunned, and was our only casualty.

Soon Captain Lewis had completed firing the last of the wagons, and ordered a retreat up the ravine, to commence our return to camp, seven miles away. We all got out of the canyon safely and met Colonel Chacon's men back on the Galisteo Road. From there, we could look to the north with pride and see the smoke billowing from the burning wagons.

"You've won a bold victory here today!" Chivington said, addressing his men in a booming sermonic tone. "By risking your lives to destroy the supply train of the secessionists, you've won the West for the Union!"

A cheer rose from the men, who had indeed fought well and struck decisively, surprising and defeating the enemy without even drawing much blood. As the men laughed and talked over their victory, the big major turned to me and said, "We'll march immediately back to Kozlowski's Stage Stop. Colonel Slough may need reinforcements."

"I'll be heading back to Fort Craig," I said. "I have dispatches to carry."

Chivington snorted at me. "Lost your stomach for fighting?"

I raised an eyebrow and drew my head back in disbelief. "Have you forgotten who stormed the artillery while you watched from the bluff?"

Chivington brushed my comment aside. "This was a mere skirmish here today. Why risk your tactical leader in such a small scrape? I'm destined for the glory of a greater battlefield. Someday you will see. However, I'll mention you favorably in my report."

"Don't bother, Major. I'm not in this for the accolades."

"Very well. You may have to slip past some of the enemy down the trail. Take care of those dispatches."

"I know my orders."

With that, I parted ways with Major John M. Chivington, but not for long. At least, not long enough to suit me.

When I arrived back at Fort Craig, I told Kit the good news of the destruction of the entire Confederate supply train up at Glorieta Pass. Soon, dispatches arrived informing us that the Texans were moving south. Colonel Slough had been hit hard at the opposite end of Glorieta Pass, but had held. With their supplies completely destroyed, the Texans had no choice but to retreat.

At Fort Craig, we prepared for a possible attack, should General Sibley attempt to capture our supplies to replace the loss of his own. Instead, he bypassed Fort Craig, taking a hard road through the San Mateo Mountains to the west. The Rebels retreated on back to Texas, demoralized, beaten, and starved. And so ended the grand Confederate scheme to conquer the West.

Kit came to me in the officers' quarters one morning while I was reading a letter for the hundredth time—a letter from Westerly that had somehow found its way to me.

"Kid, we've got new orders," he said, with a smile spreading over his face.

"We do?"

"Colonel Canby's taking command of Craig again, and we're to ride to Albuquerque to form a new regiment. The First New Mexico Cavalry."

"Who the hell are we going to fight?"

"We'll worry about that when the time comes. First, we're riding to Albuquerque to have us a victory fiesta for ridding the territory of those blasted Texians!"

Tenderly, I folded the letter in my hand. Any hope of reuniting with Westerly melted like a snowbank under the hot desert sun. Though we had turned back the Confederate invasion, the Union Army was not yet done with Kit Carson, or me.

TWENTY-NINE

We arrived in Albuquerque to a hero's welcome. The citizens of the town came out in droves to welcome the volunteers who had fought the bloody Texans. Most of the the First New Mexico Volunteers had transferred into our newly formed First New Mexico Cavalry, but Kit would do some additional recruiting while we were here, and there was no better way to get that done than to throw a big fiesta.

Before we turned in that first night in Albuquerque, Kit put on his spectacles and had me help him pen an order. The directive ordered Captain Raphael Chacon's Company E out on a lengthy scout down the Pecos to watch for Confederate movements and Indian troubles. They were to ride that very night.

"Luther Sheffield's in that company, isn't he?" I said.

"Is he?" Kit said with a grin.

"You don't have to protect me from Luther."

"Wouldn't think of it. A moonlight drill is good for the boys, that's all. Just help me finish the dispatch, Kid. That's an order."

Early the next morning, Kit and I began making plans for our feast, securing a beef and a couple of goats to butcher, along with a whole flock of chickens. I sent some trustworthy young soldiers abroad with silver to purchase large quantities of raw ingredients such as eggs, corn, cheese, flour, lard, beans, tomatoes, onions, peppers, spices, and herbs. While the men of the First slaughtered and butchered the livestock, the women from the nearby neighborhood made tamales, tortillas, frijoles, mole poblano sauce, *pico de gallo,* and many other tasty things. Kit gave Toribio the task of cleaning the guts from the slaughtered animals to use as casings for the spicy chorizo sausage the Mexicans so loved. Soon, the smell of large quantities of cooking food began to serve as an open invitation to the fiesta for the entire neighborhood.

Kit's friends ranged from American soldiers to Mexican merchants to Ute Indian scouts to Comancheros, to local elected officials, so the fiesta grew that first day to the point that it spilled beyond his neighborhood and out into the street, meandering like a lava flow past the army camp of the newly formed First New Mexico Cavalry, and down toward the open flood plain of the Rio Grande on the western edges of town. Here was ample room for all the horse- and gun-related events apropos to a proper frontier celebration. By the middle of the day, more cook fires were burning and additional goats and sheep and pigs and chickens were being brought to slaughter.

That afternoon, Kit came to me as I roasted half a calf on a spit over a bank of coals. He had two saddle blankets and two bridles over his right arm. "Catch us a couple of ponies, Kid. We'd best ride around and say howdy so's everybody knows it's our fiesta."

I understood his point. As long as everyone knew this was Kit's celebration, there would probably be no trouble. The fact that it was my party, too, didn't count for as much, but it didn't hurt, as I had earned about thirty-eight percent of the reputation Kit commanded. I was honored to ride along. I turned the roasting of the calf over to my helpers and fetched two ponies from the corrals behind Kit's adobe house.

We rode around the entire periphery of the gathering of celebrants, all the way to the river and back. Then we rode right through the middle, taking care not to kick dust into anyone's cook fire. The ride took almost two hours, as everyone wanted to thank Kit for the grand feast and fiesta. All the while, he subtly recruited dozens of young men into the ranks of the First New Mexico Cavalry, making comments like, "Wul, the heros of the territory ought to have a right proper fiesta! The boys of the First fit the Rebels! Choused 'em all the way back to Texas! Any man who rides with the First deserves all the glory, by God!"

Oh, we feasted! Of course we disdained the use of silverware and dishes, wrapping any morsel that would fit into a tortilla, or just grabbing a piece of meat or a tamale with our bare hands. The old frontiersmen would cut a piece of beef from a carcass roasting over a fire, holding one end in a bandana to keep from burning their fingers. They'd grab the other end in their teeth and stretch the portion of meat between teeth and bandana, then use their knives to carve off a bite, their whiskers brushing the blade.

Horse races enlivened the crowd about once per hour, and the free exchange of many ponies and much money hinged on the outcome of each race. Later, we held target-shooting contests at the riverbank. I won every shooting match I entered, only because Kit's eyesight had deteriorated somewhat with the years, while mine remained perfect.

That night, music and dancing took place by the light of twenty-three coal oil lanterns gathered from God-knows-where and hung from ropes strung on a circle of poles hastily set not so deep in the river-bottom silt. Several large canvas wagon sheets spread inside the circle served as a dance floor. When the weight of the ropes and lanterns began to pull the poles inward, threatening a collapse upon the illuminated dancers, some commonsense engineers (some of whom were drunk) went to bolstering the poles with props that jutted into the dancing area, or guy ropes that stretched outward and led to stakes driven into the sands.

Of course, it was inevitable that someone would trip over a prop or guy rope, and it seems several someones did, with a simultaneity that tested one's belief in sheer coincidence. I was playing with the loose-limbed orchestra at the time. It happened on the violin section's finger-plucking part of "Jesusita in Chihuahua," which must have been the signal. Three dancing couples inside the ring, and two men pretending to be drunker than they were outside the ring, all tripped over props and ropes with such precision that the entire framework of poles and ropes collapsed inward on the dancers. Someone kicked one of the lanterns, spilling kerosene and igniting the canvas dance floor. What followed was accompanied by screaming and laughing and scrambling every which way, during the course of which more lanterns broke and flames spread.

No one got seriously injured, and I quickly reorganized the orchestra and called for a soothing moonlit rendition of a Mexican love song I had recently learned called "Al Corre y Corre." The erstwhile dance floor turned into a bonfire that warmed against the chill of the high-desert night as everyone gathered around, some arm in arm, singing,

> *Ven, ven, joven querida*
> *Aquí a las flores*

A mis amores
Hacerme feliz

I played until the rims of the Manzanos and Sandias began to show against a slate sky, then I went back to Kit's house for an hour or two of sleep.

THIRTY

Days of recruiting, drilling, scouting, and waiting for orders turned into weeks then months. My frustration began to build, for I knew that I could have ridden to Boggsville and back three times to see Westerly. Yet Kit insisted we remain ready to ride at any moment, should the Confederates attempt another attack. And reports of Indian troubles began to increase, the redmen having taken advantage of the army's preoccupation with the Rebels.

Finally, Kit came to me one day with a piece of paper rolled in his hand. He handed it to me, and I read it. Since I possess the innate and irritating ability to remember such minutiae, I will tell you that the missive represented, in writing, Special Order Number 176 from the Department of New Mexico, Assistant Adjutant General's Office, Santa Fe, dated September 27, 1862. In so much military mumbo jumbo, the First New Mexico Volunteer Cavalry had received orders from Brigadier General James Henry Carleton to reoccupy Fort Stanton, which had been abandoned since the start of the war.

Since that time, the Mescalero Apaches had been raiding Mexican villages along the Pecos, and attacking freight wagons on the old Chihuahua Trail. They had killed sheep herders and prospectors, stolen hundreds of horses from ranches, carried children away from villages. This while the army had been busy dealing with the threat from the Texans. Now, Kit was ordered to reoccupy Fort Stanton, in the heart of Mescalero country, in order to deal with the Apache menace.

I forced a smile and handed the dispatch back to Kit. "When do we go?"

"We ride at dawn." Kit looked weary. He took a deep, labored breath and tried to shrug the persistent ache from his left shoulder. Weary or not, he was ready to lead. For some disturbing reason, I wasn't so sure I was ready to follow.

Something nagged at me even as I made my preparations to ride ahead of the First New Mexico Cavalry and scout the way to Fort Stanton. Some voice, with which old Burnt Belly could have had a conversation, tried to speak to me, warn me, protect me. But I was no mystic; at least not of Burnt Belly's caliber. I could tell only from the *tone* of the barely heard whisper—the mumble that made me strain so to hear it—that grave danger lay before me.

The next day, on the trail, the chant I could not quite attend mumbled as if waiting just beyond the next rise. But scouting ahead of the regiment over the next rise, I felt no closer to it. It continued to bother me, like an invisible mosquito hovering about my ear. And all along the trail to Stanton, day after day and night after night, it hummed like a distant blooming tree swarmed by honeybees. Yet, in dreams, I could not find the tree. Not that I dreamed much, for I could not sleep. On rare occasions, when I did sink into a few minutes of slumber, an unintelligible whisper, so real that I felt breath in my ear, would make me bolt from my bed, gasping for air and reaching for weapons.

When we reached Fort Stanton, the voices that had attempted to warn me ceased. This was even worse than not having been able to understand them as they haunted me day and night. Now they were just gone, and I knew I had missed whatever wisdom they had offered. I still was not sleeping well, and I felt a certain dread about having ridden into the lair of my enemies, the Mescalero Apaches.

I know I have mentioned it before, but let me refresh your memory. My very first year on the frontier, while standing night guard over some horses at a camp in the Sangre de Cristos, I shot a wolf that I feared would kill a little watchdog I had back then named Jibber. Well, it turned out not to be a wolf at all, but a Mescalero brave dressed in the hide of a wolf to fool me and my camp mates. He had surely come for horses or scalps, and I had unknowingly prevented his raid. This warrior I had accidentally killed was the son of the Mescalero chief Lame Deer, who had sworn to avenge his son's death to his dying day.

Years later, I had successfully rescued a captured child from Lame Deer's winter village in the Guadalupe Mountains, earning more hatred from the chief, and therefore the entire Mescalero tribe. All this meant that I traveled through Mescalero country at great peril. My scalp was worth more than a hundred horses to them. The chance to slowly torture me to death was a thing all Mescalero braves dreamt of. Foolishness, loyalty to Kit, and the fear of cowardice were the only things that had brought me here in the first place. I was absolutely out of my mind to be taking up arms against the Mescaleros.

The day we arrived at Fort Stanton, Paddy Graydon, Kit, and I took a stroll around the grounds to assess damage to the post's buildings and try to decide where to start repairs. The Union forces had attempted to fire the post when they retreated in the face of the Confederate invasion from Texas the year before. A lucky rainstorm had quenched the fires before they could do extensive damage to the stone and timber buildings, but Indians and area settlers had carried off much of the lumber to burn or build things.

Paddy Graydon saw this as an opportunity. Paddy, you will recall, was the mastermind who had tried to stampede the mules loaded with howitzer shells into the camp of the Texans before the battle of Valverde. Paddy had a mind for such schemes. He was known as an energetic thinker, a brave man, and a congenial fellow, and now served as captain of H Company, First New Mexico Cavalry. He was trying to convince Kit that the three of us should become silent partners in a timbering firm that would sell lumber to the army in order to make the repairs on Fort Stanton.

"You think that's legal?" Kit asked.

Paddy avoided the question. "Look at all the money Lucien Maxwell has made contracting to the army while you and me have been out here getting shot at."

"That's Lucien. He's a private citizen. We're soldiers."

Paddy waved the suggestion off. "We're volunteers. Somebody's gonna get the contract. Might as well be us."

Kit scuffed at the dirt with the toe of his boot. "I think we can do the timbering on our own. No need to contract anybody. It'll save the government some money and give the boys something to do."

Paddy sighed and turned to the north as he heard the clop of hooves coming at a trot. A young soldier, covered in dust, his horse lathered with sweat, stopped several steps away and dismounted, pulling an envelope from inside his cavalry tunic as he approached on foot.

"Colonel Carson," the young soldier said with a salute, "General Carleton sends his warmest regards." He handed the sealed envelope to Kit.

"Thank you, son," Kit said, taking the envelope. "Tie your horse and get some grub. I'll have somebody see to your mount for you."

"Yes, sir." The private dismissed himself with a salute and turned to drape his bridle reins over a hitching rail in front of the ruins of the officers' quarters.

"Report after you've et," Kit added. "I want to know what you saw between Santa Fe and here."

"Yes, sir." The courier turned and walked toward the supply wagons.

"I don't have my spectacles on me, Kid," said Colonel Carson, as he handed the letter to me. He sometimes used this as an excuse when his mind was just too weary to work at his newly acquired reading skills. I opened the dispatch and began to read: " 'By command of Brigadier General Carleton . . . so on . . . October twelfth . . .'"

"The twelfth?" Paddy said. "That boy made pretty good time."

Kit lifted his chin. "Go on, Kid."

I slogged through the preliminary niceties and got to the meat of the missive. Kit was being ordered, as we suspected, to engage the Mescalero Apaches in combat in order to put an end to raids, killings, and kidnappings. But the orders went beyond anything we had expected, to the point that my voice darkened and my brow gathered with disbelief as I read:

> All Indian men of the Mescalero tribe are to be killed whenever and wherever you can find them. The women and children will not be harmed, but you will take them prisoners, and feed them at Fort Stanton until you receive other instructions about them. If the Indians send in a flag and desire to treat for peace, say to the bearer that when the people of New Mexico were attacked by the Texans, the Mescalero broke their treaty of peace, and murdered innocent people, and ran off their stock; that now our hands are untied, and you have been sent to punish them for their treachery and their crimes; that you have no power to make peace; that you are there to kill them wherever you can find them; that if they beg for peace, their chiefs and twenty of their principal men must come to Santa Fe to have a talk here; but tell them fairly and frankly that you will keep after their people and slay them until you receive orders to desist from these headquarters; that this making of treaties

for them to break whenever they have an interest in breaking them will not be done any more; that that time has passed by; that we have no faith in their promises; that we believe if we kill some of their men in fair, open war, they will be apt to remember that it will be better for them to remain at peace than to be at war. I trust that this severity, in the long run, will be the most humane course that could be pursued toward the Indians.

The Indians are to be soundly whipped, without parleys or councils except as above.

I looked up at my friends, my mouth hanging open at the severity of our orders.

"About time we cleared these savages out of this country," Paddy said, rubbing his hands together eagerly.

"The most humane course?" I said, looking at Kit.

Kit shrugged. "You know General Carleton don't believe much in smokin' with Indians."

"But these orders don't make sense in the field. On one hand, we're to shoot any warrior we see on sight. On the other hand we're to tell them under flag of truce that their flag of truce means nothing. Then what? Shoot them down the moment they drop their flag?"

"Exactly," Paddy said. "And if they can, they'll kill us on sight, so we can't go soft on them."

"You ought to know," Kit reminded me. "These Mescaleros have had a bounty on your scalp for well onto twenty year."

I folded the orders and handed them back to Kit. "But are you sure this is right?" It was the question Kit always asked himself and others. "Is it *right*?"

"I've thought on it, Kid. I've known General Carleton for years and I've fought bad Indians with him." He slapped the orders against his open palm. "Yes, it's right. It's hard, but it's right. I feel for the poor ignorant critters, Kid, I really do. But there won't be nothin' left of 'em if we don't tame 'em. The white man will kill every last one of 'em if they don't civilize. And they won't civilize easy. We've got to make 'em do it by force. That's the only way they understand. All we can do is take the fight out of 'em and try to get 'em a good piece of land to call their own. General Carleton is right. This is the only way."

Paddy slapped me on the shoulder. "He said not to harm women and children. That's honorable, Greenwood. You've spent too much time among the heathens. You better whiten up, now." He chuckled. "Just think of the country that will open up. Anyway, seems like you'd rest easy with the Mescaleros whipped. Take that bounty off your head."

I clenched my jaw tight. They were right about one thing. This was going to happen the way General Carleton wanted it to happen whether we brought it about or not. But Paddy and Kit did not know how my mind worked. I was looking back into history, five thousand years, then reflecting the past into the future. What I saw was the fall of the Mescalero nation, sure enough. The U.S. Army was too powerful not to succeed. But it would not end there. Another raiding tribe would come next. Perhaps the Arapahos or the Navahos. Perhaps my wife's own people, the Cheyennes. Then another would fall, and another. The Utes, the Pawnees, the Shoshones, the Crees, the Blackee, the Crows, the Sioux.

And then, finally, my own adopted people, the Comanches, and their allies, the Kiowas. Swept from my valley on the Canadian where the rain pelted the ruins of old Fort Adobe, where the buffalo crossed the river, where the black bear lumbered, and the deer nervously browsed. Pushed onto some uninhabitable reservation to starve in humiliation, drown in white man's drink, and die of civilized diseases.

What Paddy and Kit could never grasp was the fact that I possessed the benefit—or perhaps, here, the curse—of a broad historical view and an appreciation for philosophical thought. I knew from my historical analyses, and from my mystic explorations with old Burnt Belly, that time did not simply stretch out and away in one direction on a straight line like an infinite bow string. Instead, time was a place where a rolling wheel touched a vast plain. It was a great hoop forever trundling forward on a limitless surface. It was even, perhaps, a collection of hoops and wheels of different and constantly changing sizes rolling along together, sometimes side by side, sometimes one within the other. The part of each wheel that touched the surface of time would leave its mark, then roll up and away. But that nick in the wheel would come around to rut the shifting steppes of time again, though the circle might grow to such a size that a thousand years would pass, or shrink so suddenly that its stamp would touch again tomorrow. And who is to say that one of the ever-revolving hoops might not rise above the plain and float, spinning, for a generation; or that one wheel might not careen away in a great circle above the plain to come crashing violently down again in a year, or a season, or a lifetime.

What happens happens again. Joy begets joy. Anger breeds anger. Evil whirls into darkness. Light spirals into goodness. I could see it coming now, all too clearly. The Indians and their way of life would vanish before my eyes, within my lifetime. And I would do my part to bring it about. No man could remain neutral. A great sadness descended upon me, like a suffocating blanket soaked in blood. I feared that by taking up arms in subduing the Mescaleros I would set in motion the machine that would eventually destroy my own Comanche family, and Westerly's people, the Cheyennes, and all the other free plains tribes. Perhaps this was what the voices had tried to tell me on the way to Stanton.

"You all right?" Paddy said, grabbing my shoulder. "You look pale, Greenwood."

I turned and walked away, taking the young courier's horse by the reins to find the poor beast some grass.

What was left of Fort Stanton lay on a level sward along the south bank of the Bonita River. *Bonita,* Spanish for "pretty," fit the little stream well. Timbered with cottonwoods and willows, it twined in gentle curves across the high prairie, its waters cool and clear. The grounds of Fort Stanton afforded a fine view of Sierra Blanca to the southwest, looming at an altitude of twelve thousand feet. To the northeast, the Capitan Mountains rose, their piñon-covered shoulders climbing to ten thousand feet. Low hills surrounded the fort nearby.

One evening, not long after we arrived, a man named Charlie Beach rode into the camp we had established just downstream of the fort. I had met Charlie before, and we had always gotten along fine. We both traded among the Indians. Charlie with the Mescaleros, I with the Comanches and Kiowas. It seemed that Charlie had gotten afoul of the Comanches sometime long ago, the same way I had gotten crossways with the Mescaleros. So we didn't compete for trade and we stayed out of each other's territory simply because we had grown accustomed to having hair on our heads and wanted to keep it there. We both belonged to the fraternity of Indian traders, and as such felt a common bond. We weren't friends, really, for I hardly knew Charlie, but we understood each other's lingo. However, I was often suspicious of his motives, for he didn't have many good things to say about the Mescaleros, the very people who kept him in business.

"Bunch of *tiswin*-slurpin' savages," Charlie said that night over a plate of beans he shoveled into his mouth with a piece of hardtack. We were sitting outside of Kit's tent, prodding Charlie for information.

"What's that *tiswin*?" Paddy asked.

"The foulest drink ever concocted," Charlie said. "Them squaws take maize kernels and let 'em sprout, then they chew 'em up and spit 'em into a pot. They ferment it in there and it turns into *tiswin*."

"Good God," Paddy replied, a disgusted frown on his face. "They drink squaw spit?"

"It's nasty stuff, but they're pretty nasty critters."

"Whereabouts have you seen them camped lately?" Kit asked.

"I left Manuelito's camp way down in the Guadalupes, but their harvesttime is about done, so they'll break camp to go huntin'."

"Where do you reckon they'll hunt?"

"Like as not the Sacramentos for elk and such. Unless they take a mind to hunt up some poor Mexican's sheep herd."

Kit questioned Charlie for quite some time on the location of other camps, the strength of the tribe as a whole, and information on which Mescaleros had done the most raiding. There was a chief named El Listo, or the Ready, whose warriors Charlie claimed had been most active on the warpath, but he said Chiefs Manuelito and Long Joe had also led raids.

"How many braves you reckon they could muster if they all got together?" Kit asked.

Charlie snorted. "There ain't more than five or six hundred Mescaleros left—men, women, and children. I bet they couldn't muster three hundred armed bucks. Besides, they're scattered and don't usually come all together."

"Too bad," Paddy said. "We'd have an easier time of it striking them all at once and just mopping up the whole country of them."

"That ain't gonna happen," Charlie replied. "You'll have to hunt 'em down like coyotes." Charlie finished his beans and dropped his tin plate into a tub of water for someone else to wash. "You got a place where I can spread my bedroll?"

Paddy jumped to his feet before Kit or I could speak. "Come on, Char-lie," he said. "I'll show you where to settle in."

As they walked away, Kit stood and pressed his hands against the small of his back as if it ached. "*Buenas noches.* Kid. I'm about tuckered."

I nodded at Kit as he ducked into his tent. By the firelight, I saw Paddy glance back toward the tent, then he leaned closer to Charlie Beach as they walked away. Paddy said something that made Charlie look at him with some surprise, then they faded into the darkness.

THIRTY-ONE

The nights grew cool at Fort Stanton, but the days remained mild as autumn approached. I kept myself busy scouting with various companies of Kit's command, or helping with the repairs to the post's many buildings. I personally supervised the cutting of timbers and the fashioning of them into a flagpole that we set deep into the earth in the middle of the parade ground. Gradually, Fort Stanton began to once again function as an operating frontier military post.

The task of feeding the regiment required constant attention. Supply wagons came and went, but many of the volunteers also hunted and fished in their off-duty time to help feed themselves and their comrades. I enjoyed the solitude of hunting, though I had to remain extremely watchful in Mescalero country. One afternoon I returned to the fort with a bull elk skinned, quartered, and packed on a mule. The bull was a big one, with six points on each of his sprawling antlers. While the boys were congratulating me, I happened to notice Charlie Beach's horse tied at the officers' quarters across the parade grounds. I hadn't seen Charlie since his earlier visit, but I recognized his horse and saddle. The horse had lost at least a hundred pounds, so I figured that Charlie must have been doing some hard riding of late.

"I'd give a month's pay for one of those tenderloins," a private from C Company said.

"What pay?" replied his sergeant. "We ain't seen pay since we left Albuquerque."

"Well, if I had it, I'd give it up for some of that elk."

"Tell you what, boys," I said. "I'm going to take the backstraps to the officers' quarters. You boys can have the rest if you'll stake the hide out to dry for me and take care of my animals."

The dozen men around me approved immediately and began untying the quartered meat, the hide, and the antlers.

"What about the horns?" one man asked.

"Hang them up on the sutler's store," I suggested.

I grabbed the two heavy backstraps that I had separated from the carcass before quartering it, and lugged them toward the officers' quarters. I opened the door to find Kit, Paddy Graydon, and Charlie Beach bent over a map hand-drawn on a piece of parchment. Captains Abreu, Sena y Baca, Eaton, Chacon, and Bergman were also there, some smoking pipes or sipping whiskey. They all looked over the map with varying degrees of interest, until I walked in with enough meat to feed them all.

"Meat!" Paddy said. "Good for you, Greenwood."

"*Chihuahua!*" Captain Sena y Baca grinned with expectation of a good meal. "*Dos grandes pedazos de carne!*"

Charlie Beach looked up with his finger still on the map, and his eyes grew as big around as duck eggs. It seemed he hadn't seen that much meat in years.

"We'll fry a mess of that up directly," Kit said. "Take a look at this here first, Kid."

I dropped the heavy load of fileted backstrap on the corner of the rough-hewn dining table and joined the officers to observe the map.

"Charlie spotted a war party on the move," Paddy announced. "Says we can probably cut them off in a day or two."

"Whose band is it?" I asked.

"Looks like old Manuelito himself. And Long Joe was with him."

"What made you think it was a war party?"

"Well, I didn't get too close," Charlie said. "But I seen feathers in their horses' tails, and some of the bucks was wearin' paint, I think."

"It doesn't matter anyway," Paddy said. "We have orders to kill them wherever we can find them."

Kit tapped the place on the map where the party was supposedly heading, east of Dog Canyon on the south flanks of the Sacramentos. "It's your time to go out," he said to Paddy. "Get your company in the saddle as soon as you can and start tonight. You should cut their trail by sundown, day after tomorrow, if you ride hard."

"Yes, sir," Paddy said, his enthusiasm for the enterprise evident in his voice.

I thought it coincidental that Charlie Beach had brought this information around just as Paddy's company was due to ride out on the next scouting expedition. "Colonel Carson," I said—I always called him Colonel Carson around the other officers out of respect—"I'd like to request permission to ride with Paddy's company."

Paddy and Charlie exchanged glances.

Kit smirked. "Paddy?"

Paddy shrugged. "You're welcome to ride with me anytime, Greenwood. You know that."

"What about all this meat you kilt?" Kit asked.

I smiled at him. "I'm sure you gentlemen will enjoy it."

"I'll chop the wood," Charlie said, eyeballing the raw meat and licking his lips. "I haven't et good in days."

The map Charlie Beach had drawn showed a trail that led along the southern flanks of the Sacramento Mountains. I had never been on the trail and that was one of my reasons for wanting to ride with Paddy—to see some new country. In those days I would ride at the drop of a hat. Pardon the cliché. I'd ride *before* the hat dropped. Hell, I'd ride if there wasn't a hat within two hundred miles, and sometimes there wasn't.

According to Charlie, the Mescaleros under Manuelito were heading for the Chihuahua Trail to raid whatever trade wagons they could find, and attack any unprotected village they could along the way. This all seemed plausible if indeed the Indians were wearing war paint, as they had been for months.

I rode a good young buckskin gelding on this scout. He wasn't well trained yet, but he had bottom, as the old-timers used to say—meaning he could reach deep and run fast for a long time when hard-pressed. As for weaponry, I carried my Henry repeater in a saddle scabbard, and my Colt revolver in a holster on my hip. I also slung my bow case and quiver across my back. In desperate situations, a scout sometimes had to kill silently to protect his company. I also carried a sharp knife on my belt, and—for this particular ride—my old cavalry saber. I fairly bristled with arms.

After two days of scouting ahead, I let the company catch up to me to hold council with Paddy.

"How far you reckon that trail is now?" Paddy asked. "The one where Charlie says we should find the Indians."

"Can't be more than five miles ahead." I gnawed off a bite of salt pork and reached for my canteen.

"I'm going to let the boys rest an hour. You ride ahead and find that trail. If you see Indian sign on it, trail them until you can figure how long since they passed. If you don't see sign, turn east and try to find them coming."

I nodded and turned for my mount.

Think about your image of the flamboyant frontiersman of the Old Southwest. Does his saddle glisten with silver conchos? Do his bridle bits jingle in tune with his spurs? Does his steed prance, stamping hooves and tossing its head? Do his nickel-plated six-guns glint in the sunlight? Does his brightly colored scarf play upon the wind? If such represents your image of the quintessential trailblazer, I'm afraid I would have seriously disappointed you. On scouts into enemy country, I was the plainest plainsman you've ever seen. I was downright drab. Everything I wore blended in with things already there. Even my horse matched the color of dirt. My guns were shinier on the inside than they were without.

I hit the trail we sought, and saw no sign of an Indian party having crossed. Obliterating the tracks I had made near the path, I kept my distance from the well-used Indian trail and turned east to look for the war party. According to Charlie Beach, it would number thirty riders or more. A party that size would be easy to spot from a distance, so I had no need of getting closer. My main concern was watching for *their* scouts, and spotting them before they spotted me.

I had the advantage of knowing they were coming. They, on the other hand, knew nothing of my presence. That's the main reason I saw the advance rider before he saw me. I ducked behind a sand hill and let him pass. I had no idea how far ahead of the main party he rode. After he had passed on to the west, I continued east.

Within ten minutes, I could see dust hanging in the air, and knew the main party was near. I peered over a rise, nothing more than the top of my head showing. As it came into view, I saw that the party numbered thirty-eight. Six of the horses pulled travois. Nine women carried babies on cradle boards, and others rode herd over older children. A few elders brought up the rear. I counted fourteen warriors, ranging in age from about fifteen to about forty-five. A chief rode point on a tall claybank horse—a mighty fine looking animal. I assumed this was Manuelito himself, the recognized head chief of the entire Mescalero Nation. None of the riders seemed to be wearing war paint, but from this distance it was hard to tell. I saw no feathers in the tails of their horses. This, to me, looked like a village on the move, or a hunting party heading for the mountains, not a raiding party.

Even so, I felt as if I were staring into the maw of a yawning lion. If old Manuelito were to discover such an enemy to his people as me, my life would not equal the worth of a farthing.

As soon as I could do so without being seen, I turned north and rode hard enough to make good time, but not so hard that I kicked up dust that could be seen by the Indians. The afternoon had grown old, and I knew Paddy's company would have no chance to intercept Manuelito before nightfall, but perhaps he could make up some time during the night and strike the trail ahead of the Mescaleros after dawn. Then what? Did Paddy intend to do battle with a hunting party? Our orders from General Carleton were clear: kill Mescalero warriors wherever we could find them. Take women and children prisoner. Give no quarter, make no talks of peace. Paddy had been anxious to engage the Indians in battle. A clash seemed sure to happen in the morning.

I met Paddy's oncoming party half an hour before sundown and held a council with him, telling him what I had seen.

"Can we get ahead of them, and surprise them on the trail in the morning?"

"Yes. They'll be in camp by now."

Paddy nodded and glanced at the sky to judge what light we had left. "I'm going to order the column to leave the trail and head across the country to the southwest. We'll ride until it's too dark to see. Then we'll wait for the moon to rise and mount up again."

"What if it's just a hunting party or a village on the move?"

"We have our orders," he said.

"What if they sign for a talk?"

"Not likely they will, but if they do, we'll talk. All I can do is tell them what the general said. If they don't agree to send their headmen to Santa Fe, there will have to be a fight. No way around it."

I sighed. Wrong or right, our orders were clear.

"Are you with me, Greenwood?"

"Of course. I wouldn't have come along if I wasn't."

Paddy turned in his saddle. "Squad, forward!" he shouted, echoed by his sergeant. "March!"

The grinding of hooves against rock and dirt cut the serenity of the desert evening, and equipage began to rattle and jingle. We angled off the trail and followed the next order to canter as we weaved our way among thorny bushes and cacti. I glanced back and saw the four columns break and re-form, the horses shying from and leaping over spiny thickets. The mounted squadron numbered forty-two men armed with carbines, most of which were Sharps single-shot, breech loaders. A good many of the volunteer soldiers also carried revolvers of various makes. Against such firepower, Manuelito's warriors would not have much of a chance should a battle commence. As we rode, I judged the caliber of the men as well as their arms. They were tough soldiers. Most of Paddy's company had been in the volunteer service for over a year now. Many had seen bloody action at Valverde with me and Kit. By now they were trail-hardened and wilderness-trained.

In those days, young men of ambition courted dangerous service in the Indian wars. They sensed the frontier would not last forever. Each looked ahead to the days when he would charm a desirable lass with his Indian-fighter reputation, when he would stand upon a stump in some new town and recount his exploits against the red-skinned enemy as he sought votes for mayor or sheriff or senator; when he would stroke his gray chin and tell his grandchildren about taking an arrow or a scalp. These men were ready to kill some Mescaleros. As their scout, I knew I had better get ready to do the same.

THIRTY-TWO

My blanket felt good against the cold October air that seared my nostrils and lungs. I had slept an hour and nineteen minutes before waking, knowing I would not go back to sleep. Paddy would rouse us all soon, I knew, and the day—likely a bloody one—would commence. But for now, I was content to hold my body heat under the plain gray woolen blanket of Navaho make, to watch the shoulders of the Sacramentos don the first hint of daybreak, and to listen.

A pack of coyotes jabbered up some lonely canyon, perhaps celebrating a kill. They were cautioned by the deep-throated howl of a Mexican wolf, closer to our camp. The morning was still, and a man could hear things a long way away. The shrill whistle of a bull elk in rut filtered down the mountain slopes, through the alligator juniper and piñon pine, coming to my ears as a whisper I knew no other man heard. They called it bugling. To me, it had always sounded more like someone learning to play a woodwind.

A common yellowthroat fluttered noisily onto the thin, thorny branch of a catclaw acacia, known as *uña de gato* to the Mexicans. The cocky little warbler with the black eye mask of a bandit cheeped out *"witchity-witchity"* as he rode the limber bouncing branch of the catclaw only an arm's length from my motionless body. I blinked, and the yellowthroat fluttered away.

We had reached this place in the night, finding the old Indian trail by moonlight. Paddy had ordered us to unsaddle and dismount. We needed as much rest as we could steal. While the soldiers had spread their blankets and staked their horses, and the guards had taken their unenviable posts, I had stood in the moonlight, my hands raised to the Great Mystery. I had chanted under my breath. The spirits had spoken to me, assuring me that the Mescaleros were the enemy of the True Humans: the Comanches. They had challenged me to be brave in battle, to seek danger, and win honors. This I knew the spirits demanded, my Comanche brothers expected, my white comrades relied upon, and even my wife understood. I was ready for battle.

Now I lay at the western edge of camp, my back to the troops. The canyons of the Sacramento Mountains soared above the cacti and thorn bushes, their pine-studded rims catching sunlight now. The aromas of leather and horse sweat filled my nostrils from the saddle I used as a pillow. My guns lay under my blanket at my feet, Indian style. Most of the soldiers had retired with their revolvers and carbines beside their heads, thinking that made them handy. But the Indians knew that a predawn attack would likely cause a man to cast off his blankets and spring to his feet, leaving his weapons within reach only if they had rested at his heels as he slept. And I, though white as snow by blood, had absorbed the ways of Indians into my flesh. I lay with my weapons at my feet.

The call to rise came not from a bugle-blowing reveille, but from sergeants walking quietly among the troops, nudging them sternly with the toes of their boots. I was on my feet with my horse saddled by the time the sergeant had reached my edge of camp. I took the time to urinate on a cholla cactus, wondering if the plant would appreciate the moisture or not. I tried to listen for the voice of the plant, but my mind was elsewhere. I mounted and rode to the first ridge to the east. I found a place where I could peek over the ridge and watch the trail to the east, the top of my head barely visible between bushes to anyone approaching from that direction. Only now did I take a drink from my canteen and fish around in my saddle pocket for a hard piece of jerked beef.

As I watched the trail and waited, I also took note of Captain Paddy Graydon's preparations for battle. He had his men form up in a single rank crossing the trail. The men stood four feet apart, facing east, each holding the reins to his mount. The ends of the line curved slightly forward, creating the beginning of a semicircle. Paddy started at the northern end and rode along this line, instructing or motivating his troops. I wished I could hear him, but I could not.

We waited longer than I had expected, but two advance scouts from Manuelito's party of Mescaleros finally came into view on the next ridge, about a half-mile apart, one on either side of the trail. I signaled to Captain

Graydon, who ordered his troops to mount. I watched nervously as the scout on my side of the trail approached my ridge. Paddy already had his men moving forward, but the brave was going to discover me before the soldiers could come up to help. I drew my Comanche bow from the bow case, hooked a leg around it to bend it, and fixed the buffalo sinew bow string tightly in place. I took a dogwood arrow from my quiver and notched it on the string. The scout was going to cross the ridge just thirty paces to my left. An easy shot. I knew I had to kill him to prevent him from riding back to the main war party to alert them.

The warrior was cautious as he approached the ridge. He craned his neck to see over it, into the next draw. The moment his eyes turned toward me, I said, "Huh!" loud enough to startle him. I drew my bow. He had the chance to surrender, but I knew he would not, and I had orders to kill any Mescalero warrior on sight. The Apache reacted quickly and bravely, yanking a factory-made trade hatchet from his waistband. He drew it back to throw it, but my arrow sped true and pierced his chest. He rolled backward from his pony without a sound and lay motionless on the ground.

To my astonishment, the soldiers down the slope behind me raised a cheer. Angered, I wheeled my horse to the right and saw the other advance scout alarmed by what he had heard. He had not seen me kill his compatriot. Paddy was chiding the troops for making so much noise. I dropped lower behind the ridge that separated me and the other scout, and rode hard to the south. The curious brave urged his pony far enough forward that he could peer over the ridge, and he saw me, saw the array of soldiers, saw his friend's riderless pony. Outnumbered and alone, he wheeled to the east.

My Comanche war yell burst from my lungs and my horse lunged his head and neck harder in pursuit. Now my choice of pony made me proud, for that buckskin tore dirt from the desert and crashed recklessly through thorns to catch the fleeing rider. I dropped the reins across his neck and drew another arrow from my quiver. Before the rider could reach the next ridge, I had pulled within range. I sent my arrow flying with all the force of the bow combined with the charging pony. It sailed a little higher than I had intended and hit the warrior where his right arm joined his shoulder, knocking him forward. He tried valiantly to hold on, but his pony shied left to avoid a cactus patch and the warrior fell hard to the ground.

I charged on. The Mescalero rose, drew a knife with his left hand, and turned to face me, his right arm dripping with blood and hanging uselessly at his side. The arrow was sticking through his shoulder, but he didn't have time to break it off. I wished for a Comanche shield as I closed on him, but all I could do was ride down on my enemy and kick him in the chest to knock him down. He struck with his knife and the razor-sharp blade pierced my left calf so deep that I felt the steel briefly scrape my bone. Pain shot up my leg and forced a yell of agony from my throat.

All the hundreds of races and riding contests I had run with my Comanche friends remembered themselves to me. With reins and leg pressure I sat the buckskin instantly on his haunches and wheeled him all in a second. One more leap put me back over my enemy. I dove from the saddle onto the warrior's chest, this time pinning his good arm. I drew my own knife as he struggled under me. I avoided looking into his eyes, and plunged my blade between his ribs. He lurched, and I withdrew my blade to stab again.

The cheer rose again from the ridge behind me, and again Paddy barked at the troops for breaking the silence. My heart pounded so that I could barely breathe. I knew what a Comanche warrior would do now. I made a quick, brutal slash across the forehead of the dead Mescalero. I grabbed his long hair, spun my body to sit on the ground above his head, placed both feet on his shoulders and pulled hard. I had to take a wrap with the warrior's locks around my palm, for his hair was dressed with bear grease and slipped in my grasp. I was charged with strength by combat and pain from my leg wound, and the scalp peeled away from the skull easily, with the same sickening sound a snakeskin makes coming away from the writhing body of a headless rattler. I cut the scalp away from the dead man's skull.

I stuffed the horrible trophy in my saddlebag without looking back at my victim. I sheathed my knife, mounted, and rode at a canter to the other Mescalero's body. Some soldiers had gathered around to inspect the trappings of the dead brave. "Step back," I ordered, knowing I had to finish this quickly. They watched, stunned, as I scalped the corpse the same way I had the other.

"Goddamn!" one soldier said, as I mounted. I rode away to the place where I had prayed and chanted the night before, trying to calm myself. My lungs and chest hurt from the sheer exertion of battle. I didn't have much in my stomach, but what I had there wanted out. The blood of my enemies covered my hands, and my own blood dripped at a troubling tempo from my left stirrup. I felt a scowl on my face, and I shook my head to rid myself of it.

Paddy came loping to me. "You all right, Greenwood?"

"My leg's wounded. Pretty bad, I think."

"Get down. Let's see."

I dismounted and sat on the ground. Paddy unceremoniously sliced open the leg of my trousers.

"Those are good buckskins," I complained.

"Better to cut it open now. Leg's gonna swell anyway."

"I'll doctor it. It won't swell."

"Right," he said, the skepticism thick in his tone of voice. "I forgot you were part medicine man. Well, you can patch your pants good as new later." He whistled through his teeth as he pulled back the bloody buckskin.

"How bad is it?"

"You were lucky. It's a hell of a gash, but you won't bleed to death. Must have missed the big veins. Hope you don't get the gangrene."

"I can make a poultice."

Paddy grunted. "Out of what?"

"Cedar. Alder. Maybe some milkweed."

"Well, there's cedar everywhere, but I don't know where you'll find that other."

"I can hear some up that draw," I said.

"*Hear* it?"

"Burnt Belly taught me. The plants speak if you listen."

Paddy Graydon's brow gathered as he regarded me with concern. "You're teched, Greenwood. You're talkin' loco."

"Just find me something I can use for bandages," I said. "I'll do the rest."

I found an alder bush in a dry streambed, as I expected. I hadn't really heard it speak. I just figured I was likely to find some there. Maybe I *had* heard it. *Quién sabe?* Anyway, I peeled some of the inner bark of the alder bush and laid it over the opening of my knife wound. Paddy came with some strips of fairly clean white cloth he had found somewhere and helped me bind the wound.

"We'd best hurry," he said. "The main party can't be far away now."

"Yeah."

"That was a hell of a thing to watch, Greenwood, you killing those two scouts without a gunshot. Now we can surprise Manuelito when he comes over the ridge. The boys are all fired up to fight after watching you."

"Wasn't much else I could do."

"There's many a man couldn't have done it at all. What is that name the Comanches call you?"

"Plenty Man."

He nodded as he made a knot in the bandage to finish it. He had done a nice, neat job of wrapping my aching leg. "Well, I don't have much use for a Comanche, but I'll agree with them on one thing. For a little cuss, you're plenty man."

I sighed. I felt weary. "Well, it's not over. The real fight's yet to come."

He pulled my blood-crusted buckskins over the wound and helped me to my feet. "Yeah, I know. I can't hardly wait."

I mounted on the right, Indian style, so I wouldn't have to use my wounded leg to step up. Paddy and I rode to the ridge to wait for the Indians. He had his men poised just behind the ridge where I had killed the first Mescalero scout. I peeked over the ridge and saw three soldiers on foot using mesquite branches to obliterate the tracks I had made chasing down the second scout. They had already covered up the blood and any other signs of the struggle. They finished their task hastily, and rejoined the rest of the party behind the protective ridge. Now only Paddy and I remained far enough forward to peer over the ridge. My leg began to ache, and I felt ill, but I tried to emulate a good Comancbe warrior and embrace the pain. We didn't have to wait long. Within ten minutes, Manuelito himself came over the ridge, riding his fine tall claybank, probably stolen from some white man's ranch.

Paddy held his palms toward his soldiers as if to say, "Get ready, boys, but wait . . ." Manuelito came on down the opposing slope, his best warriors behind him. They could not see us, for Paddy and I barely peeked over our ridge, and even then the tops of our heads were obscured by brush. A cavalry horse snorted behind me, but apparently the Mescaleros did not hear it over the noises of their own party on the move. Now the younger braves were coming over the ridge across the draw from us, followed by women and children. The first woman to ride down sat on a huge red mule pulling a travois. This, I assumed, was Manuelito's wife, as she led all the other women.

"That lanky buck behind Manuelito's got to be Long Joe," Paddy whispered.

I nodded.

Paddy's palm was still turned to the troops. He waited until Manuelito had reached the bottom of the draw and the whole party was within view on the slope facing us, all of them between two hundred and three hundred yards distant. They made easy targets for good marksmen. My heart began to sink with dread. I knew our orders all too well. I expected Paddy to order a charge at any second, but instead he motioned to his men with his fingertips, as if to say, "Step forward, boys."

I was dumbfounded at this order. The entire company moved ahead at a walk. He was going to show himself to the enemy, spoiling the element of surprise.

"Paddy!" I hissed, between my teeth.

He silenced me with a fierce glance, placing his trigger finger to his lips.

The line of troops stepped to the ridge, each man turning his mount a little to the right, as if preparing to fire his carbine. Manuelito pulled the reins of his war bridle when he saw us deployed before him. I expected him to turn tail and flee, his warriors guarding the retreat of the women and children. To my surprise, he did not. He simply raised his hand to stop the advance of his party. The Mescaleros all sat proudly but calmly on their mounts. The terror I had expected to see among them failed to materialize, and I was confused by their nonchalance. Manuelito lowered his hand, then raised it again, this time in a sign of greeting.

"Ready!" Paddy yelled.

Carbines rose for action all along the line.

"Paddy," I said. "Manuelito wants to talk."

It was José Largo—Long Joe as the Americans called him—who understood first. He wheeled his mount and tried to warn the party. Manuelito sat his claybank with his hand raised in peace.

"Fire!" Paddy shouted.

Gunfire rumbled like a bad drumroll. A line of white smoke balls blossomed as bullets hummed across the draw. Manuelito took a rifle ball in the stomach and crumpled, his palm still open and empty. José Largo pitched forward from the impact of the shot that hit him between the shoulder blades. Three other Mescaleros jerked unnaturally in their saddles and fell. One of them was a woman. I will never forget the horrible image of all that human flesh and horse flesh and the surrounding earth taking the impact of invisible missiles. It was like firing both barrels of a scattergun into the surface of a calm pool.

The Indians fled in terror now, some of them obviously wounded, judging by the way they swayed on their mounts.

"Charge!" Paddy screamed.

I glanced at him and saw a terrifically maniacal look in his eye as he leapt forward on his mount. The men, drilled in his kind of volley and charge, slipped the barrels of their carbines into the leather rings fixed to their saddles, drew revolvers, and charged, each trying his best to catch up to Captain Paddy Graydon.

I loped along to the rear, having lost my stomach for the fight. I rode by the body of Manuelito, reposed in an uncomfortable position on the ground. He had signed for a parley and had been answered with lead. Something, I now realized, was wrong with this whole encounter. The Mescaleros had not been prepared for trouble. The two scouts I had slain earlier had died too easily. My stomach twisted with nausea and guilt. What *was* this? I couldn't explain what had just transpired in this lonely draw, but I knew one thing for sure. This was not honorable warfare from any fighting man's point of view—white or Indian. I had just witnessed a massacre.

I came to the Indian woman who had been shot from her horse as she fled. As she lay on her back, eyes closed, I saw her chest lurch in a gasp for breath. Jumping from my mount, I approached her, noting the blood-stained ground beneath her body and the bloody tear in the front of her dress where a bullet had left her body. I could hear pistol shots in the distance.

"Puedo ayudarle," I said in Spanish. "I can help you."

She lay with one arm pinned behind her back, as if she had fallen on it. But as I approached to look at her wound, her eyes flew open and the hand lashed out from under her, grasping a knife that almost cut my throat before I could leap back.

"Please," I continued, in Spanish. "I want to help you."

She spat on me, and winced in anguish from the pain that the exertion of spitting had caused her.

"Drop the knife. Please. I want to save your life."

She glared at me with all the hatred and anger a small Mescalero woman could possibly contain. "You are *him,* aren't you?" she hissed.

"Whom?"

"The one who killed Lame Deer's son. The trader who lives with the Snake People."

"I am called Plenty Man among the Comanches. Yes, I trade with them. The killing of Lame Deer's son was an accident, a long time ago."

She shook her head. "Now you have done this. You are with the other one."

"The other?"

"The other trader. *Beach.* You are with him in this." She was weakening. Her elbow slipped out from under her and she fell back on her shoulder blades, but she still watched me and she still held the knife.

"What of the trader—Beach. What did he tell you?"

"You *know.*"

"I do not. I was told by Carson—Little Chief—to seek battle with your warriors. My own Comanche spirit-protectors instructed me to go to battle and fight. That is all I know of this."

"You lie."

"I did not fire into your people. The soldiers did. You must tell me what you know."

She looked at me with confusion. "Manuelito wanted peace. This he told Beach. Beach said we must ride to Santa Fe to talk with the big soldier chief. Beach said he would help."

"Help how?"

"He would send soldiers. *Friendly* soldiers."

I looked at her with astonishment. "An *escort?*"

She grimaced and nodded. "To Santa Fe."

Now my head spun in realization of how stupidly I had been used by Beach and Graydon. A cold shame gripped my heart and my stomach to think of the cowardly way I had ambushed two unsuspecting scouts seeking an escort; how I had stood and done nothing as forty-two soldiers poured lead into a peace party.

"I must save your life," I said. "Please, let me. You must tell what you know to Little Chief and to the big soldier chief in Santa Fe."

"*You* tell them. I am ready to die."

The guns had faded now in the distance. I knew she was right. I had to tell Kit and General Carleton about this. The woman's head fell back on the sand and her grip slackened around the knife. Quickly, I grabbed the weapon and used its razor-sharp edge to cut open the front of her blouse. The wound was bad. The bullet seemed to have passed through her stomach and intestines, and perhaps through her liver, as well. Blood oozed up from the bullet wound in swells. I cut away a corner of a blanket she had been wearing about her shoulders and pressed it as hard as I dared on the wound, trying to stem the blood flow. I covered her with the rest of the blanket as I did this, trying to keep her warm. But there was no saving her. Her body began to tremble and breath rattled in and out through her throat. Her breathing stopped first, but her heart beat for a minute or two after that. Mercifully, it ended at last. I closed her eyelids and covered her face.

I checked the bodies of the slain men. All were dead. I laid them on their backs and crossed their arms over their chests. I covered them with blankets, as well.

By now, the soldiers were returning, driving captured horses and mules before them. There were sixteen mounts in all. The tall claybank of Manuelito and the big red mule ridden by his wife were among them, the travois having been cut away from the mule. Some of the soldiers brandished scalps. One in particular rode to me and said, "Lookee, here, Greenwood. I got me one, too!"

I simply looked away with disgust and guilt.

Paddy rode up. "What happened to you?" he asked.

"I tried to save that woman."

He nodded, a bit of concern in his eyes. "Too bad about her. Stray bullet. I told the boys before the fight to avoid that." Now he pointed with pride over the ridge. "You missed it. We killed five more warriors in the chase. Wounded some others. Got some good horses."

"No prisoners, Paddy?"

He glanced at me and shook his head. "They ran like skeered rats. There was no catchin' 'em with anything but bullets."

"Any of our boys killed?"

"No casualties. Excepting your knife wound."

I sighed. "I'd just as soon bury the dead Indians and get the hell out of here."

"*Bury* 'em? Their people will just come dig them up."

I knew he was right about this, so I let the argument go.

"What's got into you?" Paddy said.

"I just didn't like the way it happened. They didn't have a chance."

"Given a chance, they would have killed some good boys." He paused. "That squaw say anything, Greenwood?"

"Yeah. She wondered if I was *him*."

"Him? Who?"

"Never mind. It happened a long time ago."

Just then I noticed a soldier pulling the blanket off the body of Manuelito. He drew his knife and grabbed the dead chief's hair.

"Hey!" I yelled.

The soldier looked at me, confused.

"No! You didn't earn that!"

The soldier looked at me, then at Paddy, then back at me. "Well, you took a scalp. Hell, you took two!"

"I shouldn't have. It wasn't right."

"No scalping," Paddy said. "That's an order. There's no time. You men have performed well, and now it's time to ride hard back toward Stanton. You've all earned some rest and some hot grub."

This seemed to satisfy the men, and we all began to prepare to leave the scene of the slaughter. I rode to the place where the bodies of the two dead scouts had been hidden after I killed them—behind some bushes down the draw. I got down and removed the scalps from my saddlebags. It was too late, and it didn't make up for anything that had happened, but I gave those gory trophies back to the Mescalero warriors, tucking them into their shirts so they would find them there in the Shadow Land and put them back on their poor, naked skulls.

THIRTY·THREE

The trail back to Fort Stanton was bad. I was hungry. I couldn't sleep much, for I had run out of the roots of moccasin flower and dogbane. When I did doze, I witnessed night terrors such as I hadn't experienced since I was a lad in France. I would lie down and stare at the stars, and constellations would come to life as grizzlies or rattlesnakes or mountains lions gnashing at me with fang and claw from the heavens. I would suffer all this with my eyes open, yet I could not move. And I could *hear* the beasts as well. Their growls and hisses drowned out all other strains until I would suddenly scream, so that I could move, and I would find myself at the edge of camp, among the normal nighttime sounds. The soldiers surely thought I had gone mad. Even when I did indeed truly fall into slumber with my eyes closed for even a few minutes, I would have nightmares of dead Indians walking about in search of their scalps, and I would cry in my sleep out of shame and guilt.

During the day, I began to have unreasonable fears about being murdered on the trail. I kept forgetting that Luther Sheffield was in another unit of the volunteers. I would ride for hours with my hand on the butt of my revolver, watching for him to leap up from behind some bush to shoot me. Then I would remember that he belonged to E Company, and was probably back at Fort Stanton peeling potatoes. In these lucid moments, I would tend to my leg wound, which throbbed and ached fiercely. I would limp about collecting medicinal plants along the way, and replacing the bandages. I would cock my head, trying to listen to the voices of the herbs, like a bird listening for a worm crawling through the dirt. The soldiers avoided me, for I'm sure my behavior bespoke insanity.

Then it was Captain Paddy Graydon whom I fancied my assassin.

Paddy knew that I knew about his conspiracy with Charlie Beach to lure the Mescaleros into what they thought was a friendly escort. Paddy would surely attempt to kill me before we reached Stanton, to prevent me from telling Kit. I was convinced of this. I would ride within sight of him all day long to watch for his move. Then, at night, I would sneak away into the dark to make my bed, so he couldn't find me and murder me in my sleep, should I happen to chance upon a moment of sleep.

Apparently, I rode all the last day of the return to the fort in the grip of one of my peculiar trances, for I don't remember a thing about that day. Had anyone wanted to murder me, that would have been the time. All I know is that I awoke in my bunk in Fort Stanton. As chief scout for the regiment, I had my own room. It was small, but comfortable. When I woke, I was lying on my side. I saw a fire that someone—probably Kit; maybe I, myself—had kept going in the fireplace. My eyes could blink, but I could not move the rest of my body. I looked around the room as much as possible by moving my eyeballs.

There was a big bucket filled with ashes where a man could attend to his bodily functions without going outside in the cold night, for the ashes would smother all odors. My clothes were hung neatly on pegs on the wall. The lid of my writing desk was open, as if I had endeavored to pen a letter to someone. The stool that went with the desk, however, was upside down, and my hat was hung on one of the upturned legs. This was the kind of foolishness I engaged in when in my trances. The deerskin was pulled over the window, but the light of day peeked in around the edges. I blinked and blinked until I could move my eyebrows, then twitch my face. I turned my head on my neck and the mobility slowly came back to the rest of my body.

I sat up on my bunk and rubbed my face. I could hear men chopping wood outside. I saw a small pile of jerky on the mantel, and a canteen hung on a peg below. I got up, found my knife and carved away a few chunks of jerky. I ate as I thought. I drank some water. I made use of the bucket full of ashes. I knew, in my instinctive way, that I had slept for two days, and that it was now ten forty-four in the morning. One thing had come clear to me in my sleep. I could no longer serve Kit as chief scout for his regiment. I could not lead Indians to slaughter and extermination— not even enemy Indians like the Mescaleros. I would have to tell Kit about Charlie Beach and Paddy Graydon, and I would have to resign my post as chief scout. Neither one would be easy.

Then, a happy thought occurred to me. I could find Westerly at Boggs-ville and make the winter trading run to Comanche country. I could camp again near the ruins of old Fort Adobe, where the army dared not venture. I could snuggle with my wife through the long winter nights in our hide lodge. I could hunt buffalo with my brother, Kills Something, and my Kiowa friend, Little Bluff. I could seek the spiritual wisdom of good old Burnt Belly. It would be hard telling Kit what I had to tell him, but then everything would get better.

—⁓⁓⁓—

I ate the rest of the jerky, cleaned myself up with water from the wash-basin, put on laundered clothes, gathered my resolve, and stepped outside. I looked across the parade grounds to the commander's quarters and saw one of Kit's favorite ponies tied to the hitching rail. Kit always saddled a horse first thing in the morning and kept it handy, just in case he might need to mount and ride at a moment's notice. I knew he was in his quarters, so I cut across the parade grounds to speak with him.

I passed a couple of soldiers who touched their hat brims in respect or awe or fear of me—I could not tell which. Just as I stepped up on the gallery of the commander's quarters, a motion to my left caught my eye. I glanced, then stopped to take a better look. About eighty yards away from me, I saw the Mescalero trader Charlie Beach leaving the grounds of Fort Stanton. There was no mistake about it. He rode the late Manuelito's clay-bank horse, and trailed the big red mule on a lead rope. These were the two finest animals taken from the Mescaleros during the chase that followed the massacre. My audience with Kit suddenly seemed a far less ominous task.

Kit looked up from his desk when I knocked on his door. Since he had endeavored to become a man of letters, he had taken to wearing spectacles with little round lenses, which he had bought at a trading house in Santa Fe. He smiled and waved me into his office with a piece of paper he held in his hand.

"Come in here, Kid, I need you. What in the hell does this say?"

I took the single sheaf of paper from his hand and glanced over the handwriting on it. "A Corporal Evans is requesting that you approve his purchase of a bottle of whiskey from the sutler's store. For medicinal pur-poses."

Kit rolled his eyes to the ceiling. Then he began to chuckle. "These boys! A week ago, some private from Company A came with a written re-quest to buy some molasses to cure his cold. Molasses is skeerce, so I have to approve the purchase. It said 'molasses,' Kid, and I'm sure of it. I read it hard enough to see the *m* and the *o* of '*mo*lasses'."

I shrugged. "Molasses can soothe a cough."

"But since then, three other boys have come in here tellin' me they needed to buy molasses, too. They had the written orders from the sutler, and hell, I just took 'em at their word and signed off on it without the trou-ble of readin' every order. They all sneezed and coughed a little. Come to find out, only the first order really said 'molasses,' and the other three said 'whiskey'!" He laughed out loud and slapped his knee. "The sutler men-tioned it to me, and I went back to dig out the orders. These boys will test a man at every bend in the trail, Kid!"

"I guess they will," I said. "Sometimes it isn't so funny, though."

The smile melted from Kit's face, and he took the glasses off. "Sit down, Kid. Tell me what happened out there."

"You've got Paddy's report?"

He eased into his chair behind his desk. "I want to know what *really* happened."

I told the whole story to Kit. How I had too easily killed two scouts, how Manuelito had signed for a parley, how the dying Mescalero woman had told of an escort, and how I had just seen Charlie Beach ride out with the two finest animals captured from Manuelito's herd.

Kit frowned as he placed his chin on his interlaced fingers. "Paddy said you might have some wild things to say. He said you'd gone plumb crazy after the fight. Said you'd scream in the night and ride all day like a dead man in the saddle."

"I can't deny that. I had one of my spells. But I was all right until after the fight, and I know what I saw and heard. You can get on your horse right now and overtake Charlie Beach and see what he's riding."

Kit raised his hand to settle me down. "I saw him saddle the claybank this morning. I believe you, Kid. The question is, what's the right thing to do about it? A thing like this, you've got to have enough evidence to make a charge. More evidence than just a yaller hoss and red mule."

I nodded. "The word of one screaming crazy man doesn't count for a whole lot, does it?"

He scoffed. "I know your ways, Kid. You can't help that." He stood and walked to the window, an aging legend in a uniform that was using him up like fuel in a flickering lantern. I wished Kit had never allowed himself to get caught up in the workings of the military machine. I imagined him briefly in some beaver camp or trading post, wearing his drab civilian garb, telling stories by the fireside, laughing with his friends. I sat silently for a while, wondering how I would begin to tell him that I had to resign as chief scout of the regiment. I had decided to start by saying, *Kit, I've come to a difficult decision,* when he turned to me and looked me right in the eye.

"Kid," he said. "You need to get shed of this place."

"Sir?"

"Don't take it personal, now. I'll miss you. You know the country better than most. Some parts you know better than me. But you're in danger here. It was one thing when it was just that crazy son of a bitch Luther Sheffield wantin' to kill you. I could handle that. But now, I don't know who might be after your scalp. I don't know how rotten this whole thing with Charlie Beach is."

"You want me to clear out?"

"For your own good, Kid. But that's not all. I want you to ride to Santa Fe and give a written report to General Carleton about what you saw and heard on this affair with Paddy and Charlie Beach. And there's one other thing."

"Something else?"

He opened a desk drawer and pulled out three sheaves of parchment. "I got this letter from William Bent. I picked through it, word by word, like you've been tryin' to teach me. I think I get the gist of it."

"And?"

"It looks like young Charles and George Bent have run off with the Indians. William wants you to go find them, and bring them back to Boggsville. I think you ought to go."

The wind fell out of the speech I had prepared, but the relief was welcome. I pretended to think it over for a while, and replied, "Whatever you say, Kit."

"Good. I'll have some dispatches for you to carry to General Carleton, but if anybody asks you where you're going, tell them I've sent you to Albuquerque for supplies."

I got up. "I'll be ready in an hour."

Kit came around the desk to walk me to the door. He put his hand on my shoulder. "I will look into the affair with Charlie Beach, Kid. I prom-

ise you that. If what that squaw told you is right, it was a bad piece of soldier work, and I won't stand still for it."

I shook his hand and thanked him. An hour later, I was on my way
north.

━━━➤➤➤➤━━━

I handed my report to General James Henry Carleton in person at his office in Santa Fe. Unvarnished fact made up the whole of the document.
I included neither speculation nor analysis. I would let the general draw
his own conclusions. He took the report, and the other dispatches from Kit,
and tossed them on his desk. Then he asked me a lot of questions about
conditions at Fort Stanton. I answered all his queries, but when he asked
about the episode with Manuelito, I simply said, "It's in my report, sir."

"You were there?"

"Yes, sir, as scout for the company."

"That was some stroke of warfare, killing two enemy chiefs and nine
warriors in one battle."

"Eight warriors and one woman."

Carleton looked at me with surprise. His only view of the fight had
come from Paddy Graydon's pen.

"It's in my report," I repeated.

He seemed puzzled, yet intrigued.

I did not know General Carleton well, though I had known him a long
time. Years ago, he had given me my favorite pony—the paint horse
named Major. He was a small yet impressive man with a big cavalry mus-
tache. I considered him smart and energetic. He was unwavering in his
harsh stance against the Indians. He struck me as the quintessential soldier, and I respected him, though I disagreed with his severe tactics. He
was also very persuasive, for he talked me into serving as his courier for a
couple of weeks before I rode on to Boggsville. I missed Westerly fiercely,
but I agreed to carry dispatches for a while, partly because I wanted to see
what would become of the Graydon-Beach affair.

As Carleton's courier, I made several hard rides to places like Fort
Union, Albuquerque, and even as far as Fort Craig. Returning from Craig,
I heard the news that Captain McCleave had ridden out of Fort Stanton
with his company and encountered several hundred Mescaleros camped at
Dog Canyon, on the southwest slopes of the Sacramentos. McCleave and
his troops had whipped a hundred or more warriors in a fair fight, and

driven them out of the canyon. As a result of this fight, and the ambush on Manuelito's band, the surviving Mescalero chiefs went to Fort Stanton to turn themselves in to Kit. Kit told them they had to ride to Santa Fe to parley with the "Big Captain." So Head Chief Gian-nah-tah and four other leading chiefs rode to Santa Fe with a military escort to talk to General Carleton. I was there at the meeting. I heard Gian-nah-tah speak.

His name, in English, meant "The One Who Is Always Ready" or simply "The Ready." The Mexicans had always known him as "El Listo." He spoke in anger to General Carleton and the other officers and Indian agents and members of the territorial government who gathered at the Palace of the Governors to hear him talk. A translator—a Mexican man who had lived among the Mescaleros as a captive boy—converted the speech to English for the military council.

The Ready told of the harsh conditions his people had to suffer. Constant encroachment of whites onto their lands, game depleted and scattered by market hunters and soldiers. Of course they had raided ranches and villages. The ranches and villages had invaded a country the Mescaleros had held for generations.

Then came the matter of the ambush on Manuelito's and Long Joe's people. Here, the ire of The Ready showed in his flashing eyes and pointed gestures. "The trader, Beach, lied to those people. They were told they would find friendly soldiers waiting for them. The soldier captain they met on the trail was promised as an escort to Santa Fe. But they were killed by soldiers who are too cowardly to fight warriors with honor and must trick them with false promises."

Then he looked at me, and pointed, with all the hatred a man could possibly harbor in his soul. "You were there. You did not stop the massacre. It was a trick, and a lie. It has been told that you did not fire into those people, but you did not stop the soldiers!"

General Carleton turned and looked over his shoulder briefly, to see who The Ready was pointing to, then turned back to listen. I sank down in my chair like a craven murderer.

The Ready continued: "And now Beach owns horses that belonged to those people killed by your soldiers. How can proud warriors fight against soldiers who lie and trick us? You are stronger than we are. We have fought you so long as we had rifles and powder, but your weapons are better than ours. Give us like weapons and turn us loose, and we will fight you again! But we are worn out now. We have no more heart. We have no provisions, no means to live. Your troops are everywhere. Our springs and water holes are watched by your young men. You have driven us from our last and best stronghold, and we have no more heart. Do with us as may seem good to you, but do not forget we are men and braves."

And so The Ready had his say. It didn't count for much. By this time, General Carleton and a board of officers had already established a new fort at a lonely place called the Bosque Redondo on the Pecos. The new post was named Fort Sumner. Even before The Ready's speech, it had been decided that the Mescaleros would be sent there and made to farm. The experiment would prove disastrous, for most soldiers knew less about farming than Apaches.

And Charlie Beach? General Carleton took another look at my report after The Ready's talk. He had Beach arrested and thrown out of the Territory of New Mexico. All the animals taken by Paddy Graydon's soldiers—including the claybank and the big red mule—were returned to the survivors of the ambush. A small consolation for women and children who were still mourning the loss of murdered warriors.

Nothing could be proved against Paddy Graydon. He admitted that perhaps he had used poor judgment in giving the horse and the mule to Charlie Beach, but said at the time that he thought it an appropriate reward to an informant who had advised him on the whereabouts of the enemy. He would always claim that Manuelito's band was a war party. He had General Carleton's orders to kill Mescalero braves "whenever and wherever you can find them" in his defense. And—though Paddy would claim I had lost my mind shortly after the episode with Manuelito—he would always sing my praises as a fighting man for the way I had dispatched the two advance scouts. I am sorry to say that the unfair conflict became a part of my reputation as some kind of killer-hero. Ironic that such a tribute to my bravery was in fact one of the events in my life that made me feel the most cowardly. I would lie awake many a night wondering what would have happened had those two scouts actually been expecting an enemy war party instead of an escort.

THIRTY-FOUR

Finally, I relieved myself from General Carleton's service, and rode north for a long-overdue reunion with my wife. I put some tracks behind me on the last day of my ride to Boggsville. I wanted so badly to see Westerly. When I crossed that last divide between Boggsville and everything south, the sun was just setting beyond the Rockies, whose peaks loomed far to my left. My reins were swinging in a steady pendulum rhythm. My tired horse lifted his head as he came over the rise and saw the trees and lodges, the houses and smoke trails. He seemed to know we would end our journey here.

Two Cheyenne lodges stood in the usual place, between the town and the Purgatory River. I angled toward them. Out came Westerly and her sister, one from each lodge, having felt my hoofbeats through the ground. John Prowers stepped out behind his wife. When they recognized me, Westerly left the lodges and walked to meet me. Then she ran, wanting to put some distance between us and the others.

Before I reached her, I reined in my horse, swung my leg over the pommel, and dropped from the saddle, landing flatfooted. In seconds she was there, her embrace virtually clashing with mine. The horse circled at the end of his reins, stepping between us and the lodges, as if he wanted to provide us with the privacy we desired.

She kissed me, somewhat out of breath, cupping her hand around the back of my neck to pull my mouth hard against hers. Her lips and tongue and hands shot excitement and desire through my body. She broke away, panting.

"I have missed you, husband."

"Oh, I have missed you, Westerly. For four hundred and thirty-two nights my heart has howled in my chest, like a coyote."

She smiled. "When you are away, my heart sinks like the moon setting behind western clouds. But now you are here, and my moon is rising."

I glanced over the seat of my saddle. "I should greet them at the lodges, I suppose."

"No. They can wait. I want to be alone with you." She looked up. "The sky is happy. You have your blankets. Let us sleep on the open ground to-night."

I smiled. I was famished, but my lust for my wife and her body and her lovemaking skills outshone all other hungers. I mounted and cocked my foot so she could step on it like a stirrup and swing onto the saddle skirt behind me. My mount let out a huge sigh. As I turned I saw Westerly's sister making protests. John Prowers stood with his hands on his hips in the twilight. He looked to be chuckling.

We rode a short distance, just over the ridge to the south. I unsaddled and let the pony go. Westerly spread the blankets. The thatch on the ground was thick, like a corn-husk mattress. She pulled off my boots, laughing as she fell backward on the ground with the second boot. I helped her back to her feet and we undressed standing up, watching each other. The horse rolled, and we both paused to watch.

"If he rolls all the way over, he's worth ten dollars," I said.

She had heard this droll axiom among white horse traders. "And if he rolls all the way back, he is worth twenty."

The horse indeed made himself worth twenty dollars as he tried to rub the lingering impression of the saddle from his back. Then he struggled to his feet and walked toward the river for a drink, snatching stalks of grass as he left us there alone.

Naked, we lay down on the blankets and her body fell against mine like a breeze that touches a still pool of water and enlivens the surface. Electricity raced from every place her cool little hands touched me. We kissed and groped each other everywhere. She seemed to have thought about what I would like, what would surprise me, what would make me gasp with pleasure, what would make me moan. There is nothing like love on a Navaho blanket spread on the thick grass of the high plains on a spring night. There is nothing akin to the embrace of a woman who has lost all of her inhibitions for you and you alone, and revels in watching you ache for more of her pleasures. No love surpasses the love of a man for a woman when she pleases him with such physical ecstasy and yet also fills his heart with yearning for her voice, her glances, her smile, her very presence.

We made love every which way we could think of, sometimes sleeping for an hour and waking to renewed passion. We rolled off the blankets and onto the grass more than once. She challenged me, wordlessly, to try anything I wanted, rewarding me for new experiences. At last we had to quit, collapsing in fatigue, pulling blankets over us against the chill night air.

I slept hard until the morning sunlight and the birdsong woke me. Westerly was gone. So were my clothes. I'm sure she thought this was very funny. Not too much later, she returned with breakfast in iron pots and pans which she carried in a big round basket covered with a newly tanned golden deerskin.

"And my clothes?" I said.

She giggled. "You don't need clothes to eat your breakfast."

"Westerly . . ."

"Eat your breakfast. If you are good, I will bring your clothes back."

I sat and ate with the blanket wrapped around my waist. Her smile was devious. She had brought thin antelope steaks fried in lard, scrambled eggs, biscuits with butter and honey, cow's milk, and coffee. Westerly loved coffee, though she knew I didn't drink it. She had gone to a lot of trouble to cook all this and carry it to me. I ate everything she gave me, and finally she retrieved my clothes, which she had hidden not far down the trail.

Dressed again, full and happy, I lay back on the blanket, using my saddle as a backrest. "Did you see my horse?"

She nodded. "He stands near the corral, where the other horses are penned."

"The town has grown."

She nodded. "A little. Mary and her husband moved from the stockade and built a new house there. John and Amache are building a log house, too. Tom and Rumalda are building a trading house. Sometimes the wagons come here on the way to Santa Fe and there are many good things from Missouri, if you have money to buy the things."

"Maybe you and I should build a house here," I suggested.

The shocked expression on her face made me realize what I had said. I was a drifter and an Indian trader. Westerly had grown up wandering with her Cheyenne villages in a buffalo-hide lodge.

"A house?" she said.

"If you want one. We wouldn't have to stay in it all the time."

"Could I keep a lodge, too?"

"Of course. We could still keep moving to trade with the tribes. But a house would be warm and comfortable in the winter. You could be close to your sister and friends here."

"I would like that. Of course, I want to ride with you, when you go trading."

"Of course. I have silver and gold coins cached in a dozen places in the mountains. Kit and Josepha keep some money for me in Taos, and Lucien Maxwell holds a large sum for me at his ranch. We could buy a parcel of land from Tom and Rumalda, and purchase many of those fine things from Missouri."

"We could live here when we want, and wander when we want."

"Yes." I felt a strange, wonderful sensation, making plans with my wife. "We will camp in the mountains when the summer heat comes here on the plains."

"Yes, and camp with your Comanche family when the buffalo hunts begin."

"We will trade for many horses."

"I will help you herd them back to the corrals here for the winter."

"And in spring, we will break horses, and sell them to the army. And to the settlers."

"Even if we spend all of your gold and silver, we can hunt and fish and be happy. And perhaps we will make babies."

I grinned. "Surely we will."

"But I hope not too soon. I will use some stone seed. I want a few seasons with just you and me, my husband. I am in no hurry for children. But someday . . ."

"Yes, someday." I returned her smile and reveled in the glow that shone all about her, the sparkle in her eyes, the beautiful curves of her cheeks and graceful jaw. Her lips were wet and full, her hair undulating on the cool prairie breeze. Then her eyes turned on me and pierced my heart and soul. A Cheyenne woman—even were she your wife—did not often look directly into your eyes. Her face became expressionless.

"Tell me about the battles," she said.

"You've heard?"

She shook her head. "No. I felt it. I saw things in a dream. Tell me, my husband."

I took a long drink from my canteen and proceeded to tell about Valverde and Glorieta Pass. I told it as a warrior should. I recounted my exploits, and those of my friends, Kit and Blue Wiggins, and the others.

Then came the story of the Mescalero massacre. Westerly realized my shame at having been used in the Graydon-Beach conspiracy.

"The dishonor is theirs, not yours, my husband. You could not have known the hearts of those men were bad."

I shook my head. "I was a fool. I saw Charlie Beach and Paddy Graydon together more than once before the ambush. I should have known."

She caressed my face. "No. They might have been talking about anything. You were betrayed by someone you trusted. A fellow warrior you had fought with before. There is no shame in this for you, and even the spirits of your enemies know what is true."

I sighed and sank deeper into her healing embrace. "Well, it won't happen again. I've resigned as scout for the army."

"I am happy that you have now broken with the soldiers. The war between the white nations has made them all crazy for killing, and they have turned their thirst for blood on the Indians. The white fathers in the East have forgotten about the treaties they signed. Of course, some Indians will retaliate and this just makes things worse. It is happening everywhere, not just with the Mescaleros. I fear it is just the beginning."

"Yes," I said. "I am afraid, too. And in the midst of my fear over it, I had a vision."

"Tell me."

"It was odd. A number of hoops were rolling across an endless plain. But not *just* rolling. Whirling at different speeds. Sometimes floating. Sometimes one within the other. And they changed in size, sometimes gradually, sometimes all at once."

"What color were the hoops?"

"Different colors. Some had angrily colored spots on them, like red and black, and when those spots touched the plains, the grass would burst into flame. Some were colored like the sky and the spring leaves, and they could put out the fires on the plain where they touched."

"What does it mean?"

"I cannot say for sure, but I have been thinking about it. I think the plains are all of creation, and the blades of grass are people—different kinds of grasses for different nations of people."

"And the hoops?"

"The hoops pick up and carry things that happen between peoples."

"Hmmm," she said, a wonderful moan of understanding. "What happens does not just go away. It comes back around on the hoop and touches the people again—touches all of creation."

"You understand."

"I understand the vision," she said, "but not what it tells us to do. One hoop, rolling steadily along, would be simple, yes? But many hoops? Different sizes and colors, always changing? It is complicated." She shifted her body so she could lean against me.

"Yes." I snuggled into our new position, my body molding to hers. "It is complicated."

"What happens between you and me, my husband, always makes a beautiful color where the hoop touches. May it come around often."

I had no words to answer her, and needed none.

———

We did finally walk back to the lodges along the Purgatoire. John Prowers was sharpening an axe with a file. He looked at us and said, "You two appear rather flushed." He grinned. "I heard the strangest howling of coyotes last night. Or maybe wolves. No, it was more like a barking of a prairie dog, or the yelps of a couple of mating porcupines."

"All right, John," I said, blushing.

He laughed and shook my hand. "Good to see you back among us, brother."

———

I made the rounds in Boggsville that morning, then, after lunch, Westerly and I rode the short distance down the Purgatory to its mouth on the Arkansas to visit William at his stockade. The stockade seemed sadly quiet as we rode nearer. I remembered days at Bent's Old Fort where, even in the dead of winter, all kinds of industry and amusement continuously ground out a daily routine. Now the fur trade was long gone, and the Indian trade had dwindled to a few buffalo robes and ponies. Still, William hung on here at the stockade. I saw smoke trailing away on the north wind, and a tattered American flag flapping at the top of a tall lodge pole.

Westerly and I found the gates open to the east and rode in. I heard the familiar sounds of a hammer beating an iron horseshoe on an anvil. "Hello, Colonel Bent!" I shouted as we drew rein and waited at the gate. A Mexican laborer with a hammer in his hand looked around a corner of the stables about the same time William stepped out of the door in his shirt-sleeves, a shotgun leading his way. When he recognized us, he broke the double-barrel open and smiled.

"Come in here, Mr. Greenwood! Bring your wife and light for a spell."

We tied our ponies and gladly entered the warmth of William's cabin. Westerly and William's wife, Yellow Woman, were fast friends, and quickly withdrew to their own end of the cabin as they carried on in their native Cheyenne tongue. As I watched them walk away, arm in arm, I thought it odd that Westerly, though younger, had retained more of the traditional ways than Yellow Woman. The elder woman had been married to William so long that she dressed mostly like a white woman, except for her moccasins and leggings.

William lit his pipe and poured himself a fresh cup from the pot on the woodstove. We talked for a long while about mutual friends and happenings all across the frontier and in the East, with the war. Finally, William began to broach the subject of his sons, Charles and George.

"You got my letter," he said.

"Yes, sir. At Fort Stanton."

"In times of peace, I wouldn't let it worry me—the boys going into camp with their Cheyenne kin."

"Has there been fighting between the Indians and soldiers?"

"Just a skirmish or two, so far. But I've lived away out here for a long time, Mr. Greenwood. I can scent trouble like a trail hound."

"What do you smell on the wind?"

"The Confederates have sent agents out among the southern plains tribes. All of them. The Comanches, Kiowas, Apaches, Cheyennes, and Arapahos. They're trying to recruit the Indians to their side."

"*White* agents?" I asked.

"No, they didn't have the *cojones* for that. They sent white agents to the territory first, to persuade the civilized tribes. The Cherokees, Choctaws, Creeks, Tonkawas, and some others have gone over to the Confederacy. The agents who went to talk to the plains tribes were mostly Cherokee and Choctaw."

"Are the plains tribes going over to the Confederacy?"

"Oh, hell, no. They want no part of it. You know, a lot of rich Choctaws and Cherokees in the territory have big plantations and African slaves. That's why they've gone secesh. They want to hold on to their slaves. But the plains people have got all they want as long as there's still buffalo to hunt. They don't want to have any truck with the Rebels whatsoever."

"Then why should you worry about trouble?"

"Because word is already out in Denver that Confederate agents have visited Indian camps on the plains. That's all some hotheads need to convince themselves that the Indians have turned Rebel." He puffed hard on his pipe, clearly excited and uneasy about the prospects.

"Why don't we ride to Denver and tell them the truth?"

William blew an angry cloud of smoke out of the side of his mouth. "I've written letter after letter to the governor, telling him the Indians want no part of the war and ought to be left alone to hunt. But these politicians have got their own schemes in mind. They *want* an Indian war."

"Why in God's name would they want that?"

"The regular troops have all gone east to fight. It's a volunteer army out here, and they all want Indian-fighter reputations. They want to force the Indians off the land so they can settle it up with white farmers who will vote for them for killin' off heathen redmen. It's politics of the worst kind, Mr. Greenwood."

"You're afraid George and Charles will get caught up in it."

"Yes. I'm afraid in general that the whole Cheyenne nation will be wiped out by zealots. I'm afraid my wife's people will be slaughtered in ambushes and massacres. But I'm particularly concerned about my boys. They both fought for a time with the Confederates back East. They've already absorbed an ill view of a Union uniform."

I nodded. "If fighting breaks out, they'll side with their Cheyenne kin." I was thinking of my adoptive Comanche relatives, and knew I would also help them defend their rights to their own hunting grounds if soldiers should attack. For the Bent boys, the bond was even stronger. Half their blood was Cheyenne.

William leaned toward me, his chair squeaking. "Can you find them, Mr. Greenwood? Can you bring my boys home?"

I sighed and rubbed my chin. "I have no doubt that I can find them. Convincing them to come home is a different matter."

"Of course, I'll pay you, and I'll outfit you with whatever you need. Will you try?"

"Of course I'll try. The pay doesn't matter. I'll do my level best. I'll take Westerly with me. We've already talked about it. She's handy on the trail and she'll help me move more easily among the Cheyenne."

"Yes, that's good. You know I'd go myself, if I could. But I'm getting old, and I'm needed here to keep things calm."

"I understand. I'm glad you called on me. I'll handle it as best I can."

With that, our business was over, and William seemed somewhat relieved. I knew the feeling, and I'm sure you do, as well. When a problem festers in your mind, it can rob you of sleep, haunt your every waking hour, distract you from your business. It perches on your shoulders like a corpulent vulture, its dull, troublesome plumage looming dark over your head. But, having taken the first step toward solving your problem, do you not feel as if a burden has flown from your shoulders? Even though your problem may remain unsolved, you have sent it off to soar elsewhere for a while, for you have begun to rid yourself of it. Do not let the talons of trouble cling long to your flesh, my friends. Take action, like William Bent. Perhaps he could not solve all the problems of the plains, but he was never one to stand long at a buzzard roost.

At twilight that day, a large village of Cheyennes rode to the stockade to camp. They seemed excited, and in good spirits. We soon found out why. They held a scalp dance that night. Westerly and I went to the camp to observe. I saw the scalp on a pole. I suppose it could have been a Pawnee or Ute scalp, but it looked more like the locks of some unlucky white plainsman.

In the morning, I went with William to question the camp chief, Long Chin, about the scalp. The chief and William had been friends for a long time, and in fact, Long Chin was William's brother-in-law—the brother of both William's first, Owl Woman, and his current wife, Yellow Woman. After the death of Owl Woman, William had married her sister, Yellow Woman, for that was the Indian way.

When William asked about the scalp, Chief Long Chin readily admitted that it had been taken from a white man.

"Why was this man killed?"

"He was killing buffalo."

"Perhaps he was hungry," William argued.

"He only took the hides. Maybe a tongue or a hump sometimes. It is happening more. They are killing and skinning, leaving the meat to rot."

"You should have come to me."

"You were not near. It was far out on the plains. I sent some warriors to ask this man why he left so much meat go to waste. When he saw my warriors coming, he shot one of them and wounded him. Before he could load that big rifle again, my warriors rode him down and killed him."

William shook his head. "This is not good. If word of this gets to the soldiers, they will want to punish you."

The chief bristled. "This man shot first at my warriors. He was hunting on our land, wasting meat in the winter when we need it most. He was the one who should have been punished, and he was. Now, since the white hunters have scattered the herds, we have come here for rations and gifts. If white hunters are going to ruin our hunting, the white government must provide us with rations."

"Long Chin, we have been friends and brothers for many years. You know I will not let your people go hungry before I have given you my last scrap of food from my own meat pole. You will have your rations, and your gifts, as well. But you must promise to stay away from the white hunters. Let me handle them."

Chief Long Chin made no such promises, for he was a member of the elite Dog Soldier society, and would not avoid a conflict with an enemy. He only said, "I will send the headman of every family to your stockade to get the rations."

As we rode back to the stockade, William looked at me and said, "This is a risky proposition, Mr. Greenwood. It looks as though I'm rewarding him for killing a white man. But I know Long Chin, and he tells the truth. These hide hunters are getting bolder."

"When did this start? Why?"

William smirked. "In Europe, they've finally discovered what we've known for decades—that buffalo leather is superior to cowhide. They're making belts out of it in Europe to run big machines in the factories. To make things worse, the Queen of England has ordered that all of her harness leather for her stables must be made only of buffalo hide imported from America. Now every snob in England wants to hold tanned buffalo-hide reins in his lily-white palms. It's become quite a fad. Like beaver hats in the old days."

"There was a time when I thought the buffalo herds would be safe forever. I never thought of men killing them for hides alone."

"It surprised me, too, the first time I saw it. A dozen carcasses lying on the plains, skinned. Too much meat for even the buzzards and crows to eat, gone to waste."

"No wonder the Indians are angry."

"I'd say they're justified in being riled." He looked over his shoulder at the Indian camp. "Can you help me dole out rations this afternoon?"

"Of course," I answered, though I didn't look forward to handing out canned, pickled, and smoked foods to proud Cheyennes who would rather kill their own fresh meat on the free and open plains.

THIRTY-FIVE

The next day, Westerly and I crossed the Arkansas and rode generally northwest. We led a pack mule that carried provisions and some trade items like knives, hatchets, mirrors, trade cloth, and beads. Westerly knew the winter camps. We checked first along upper Horse Creek, above the place where it disappeared into the sand. We found the remnants of a camp: small rings of blackened stones that had enclosed cook fires; larger rings of stones that had weighted down the bottoms of tipi covers to keep the cold northers out. The grass around this camp was all but gone.

The trail was too old to follow, save for the cropped ends of grass stalks where ponies had grazed as they moved along. We found another abandoned camp on upper Rush Creek, and another on the headwaters of the Republican River. The camp on the Republican included buffalo bones, so we knew the People had enjoyed a successful hunt.

"I believe we will find some hunters on Surprise Creek," Westerly said.

"I haven't heard of that creek. Why is it called Surprise?"

She smiled knowingly. "You will just have to wait and see."

The creek did surprise me. Instead of running along a low wrinkle in the plains, it meandered across a prairie that looked positively level. We rode up to within twenty paces of it before I even noticed it. "This must be Surprise Creek," I said.

Westerly laughed, her eyes twinkling.

We found tracks running downstream and followed them until dark. We camped that night on the plains, rolled together in blankets, on top of a sheet of oiled canvas that we could also fold over us in case of rain, snow, or bitter cold. Wolves and coyotes howled around us. The sky was so big here on the open plains that we seemed to look downhill at the stars on the horizon. The vast grasslands sure seemed peaceful for such troubled times.

The next day we found a small group of young hunters. They had succeeded in killing three buffalos. These warriors had heard that George Bent was camped with Chief Sand Hill's band of Cheyennes over on the Smoky Hill, so Westerly and I left them with some knives and hatchets as gifts for their hospitality, and turned southward. Four days brought us to the Smoky Hill River. We found a large camp of Cheyennes under Chief Sand Hill and some Arapahos under Chief Left Hand camped at the confluence of Ladder Creek and the north fork of the Smoky Hill. George had gone off with some Dog Soldiers to raid the Pawnees, so Westerly and I made camp and waited.

Three days later, George returned, and to my delight, he had Charles with him, having found Charles at another Cheyenne camp on the south fork of the Solomon. George seemed happy to see me, but Charles remained aloof. I let them rest up from their raid into Pawnee country—though they had returned with neither scalps nor stolen horses—and waited until the next day to begin persuading them to return to William's stockade.

I went to George's lodge about midday and said, in Cheyenne, "May I come in?"

"Who is it?" Charles said from inside.

"It is Plenty Man."

There was a pause, then George's voice said, in English, "Sure, come on in, Orn'ry."

I slipped quickly between the bison-hide lodge covering and the bearskin door flap, trying not to let the precious warmth slip from the lodge. "I brought some chips," I said, laying an armload of dried buffalo chips on the ground beside the small fire in the middle of the lodge. There was little timber left at this camp.

"Good," George said. "Are you hungry?"

As my eyes adjusted to the dim light, I saw Charles lounging on a mattress of buffalo robes as George watched a hunk of hump meat roast over the fire. Charles did not get up to greet me, but George stood, shook my hand, and offered to share the hump roast with me.

"No, thanks," I said. "Westerly just cooked some stew for me. It was good. An antelope I shot two days ago with wild onions and greens and some potatoes and carrots I carried from your father's stockade."

George nodded. "How is Father?"

"Very well. But worried."

Charles snorted. "Worried? About what?"

"You know your father. He takes a lot of responsibility upon himself. He's concerned that the war fever will infect the plains. In fact, it seems that it's already happening."

George nodded. "It is happening. Every village has a story about how some hunting party or camp's been attacked without warning by soldiers. Unprovoked."

"It's not an especially good time to be traveling with Indians on the plains."

"You know what I think is behind it?" George said. "Colonel Chivington is commanding the Colorado volunteers now. I think he's afraid he'll be ordered east to fight the Confederates in Kansas. I think he'd rather battle bows and arrows than Rebel guns."

"The son of a bitch is a coward," Charles said bitterly.

George glanced at his younger brother. "Chivington doesn't give the Cheyennes much credit as fighters. The tribe has been at peace for so long."

"Thanks to your father," I added.

"Partly. But Chivington's convinced that we can't fight. He has no idea what kind of a hornet's nest he's about to stir up."

"He's gonna wish to God Almighty he *had* gone east to fight Rebels after he tangles with us!" Charles's eyes glinted with malice, as a short burst of laughter rasped from his throat.

I couldn't help noticing that George and Charles had spoken in terms of "we" and "us," as if they were wholeheartedly Cheyenne though they were only half-blood, and had lived east of the plains for ten years attending school.

"You know, if you boys would come back to your father's stockade, maybe we could make a difference. Your father's been writing letters to Governor Evans, but he's not being taken seriously. Maybe if we all got together and rode to Denver, we could tell the governor what's really going on out here and avoid a war."

George seemed to give the thought some credit, but Charles just hissed and rolled his eyes.

"I'm not going back to that stinking stockade to shovel shit for an old man who never wanted me around anyway. I'm a Cheyenne warrior. It's time to lay in meat and hides for the winter. Time to make weapons for the spring raids."

I knew better than to push the issue at that point. "Speaking of laying in meat," I suggested, "do you think Chief Sand Hill would let us go out on a buffalo hunt together? Westerly and I cut the path of a large herd two days' ride northwest of here, and the herd looked to be drifting south and angling this way."

George's eyebrows rose, and Charles sat up eagerly on his couch of buffalo robes.

"Well, you boys are probably tired right now. Tell me tomorrow if you want me to take you to the buffalo."

With that, I rose and stepped out of the lodge, into the cold wind.

—⁓⁓⁓—

Early the next morning, George and Charles came to my lodge and asked me to speak to Chief Sand Hill with them.

"Don't let on it's a big herd," Charles said. "We don't want every damn buck in camp coming with us."

I grinned at Charles. "You reckon a real Cheyenne warrior would want to ride with a paleface like me and a couple of half-bloods anyway?"

George chuckled.

"Who are you calling half-blood?" Charles said, though he knew very well what he was.

Chief Sand Hill gave his permission for our hunt, but warned us not to frighten the herd away if it was a large one. We were to hunt the stragglers and kill only as much meat as we could carry. Our real mission was to scout the size of the herd and report back to camp. We were also to look for prospective new campgrounds, with plenty of grass, water, and fuel. We took the rest of the day preparing for our ride, planning to leave before dawn.

That evening, the camp crier ran through the village, announcing the arrival of some Sioux warriors. It didn't take long for the news to get around that the Sioux men had brought a war pipe with them, and wanted the Cheyennes to smoke and commit to open warfare with soldiers. The Sioux had been having trouble with soldiers and settlers from Minnesota to the Black Hills, and they were seeking allies for an all-out uprising. Chief Sand Hill announced a council in his lodge for that night.

Being a visiting white man, I didn't rank high enough to get into the lodge, but I stood outside and strained to hear the talks going on inside. I stood beside another white man—a greasy loafer who went only by the name of Carter. He claimed to be a trader, but I knew or had heard of every trader between the Rio Grande and the Missouri and this man was no trader. He was one of those shiftless frontier wretches who had some-how learned to cadge his existence off Indian generosity—a white beggar among redmen. He had married a Cheyenne woman from a large family so that he could bum food and other goods off his many in-laws.

"What are they saying?" Carter asked me, as I strained to listen through the doubled winter hides of the big lodge.

"You don't speak Cheyenne?"

"Of course I do, but I'm hard of hearing."

I tried to close my nostrils against his unpleasant odor, for he stood up-wind of me. "The Dog Soldiers want to smoke the war pipe and go with the Sioux to fight white soldiers. But Chief Sand Hill and the elders are against it. That's Sand Hill speaking now. He says he's been east to the cities of the whites. He's met the Great Father. He says there are more white people than there are grains of sand in the Smoky Hill River. He says we must do all we can to avoid war with the white soldiers."

"We?" Carter asked. "You gone Injun, squaw man?"

"I'm just repeating what he said. I'm adopted Comanche, not Cheyenne."

Carter looked at me with disbelief. "Well, I've heard all I need to hear."

<hr />

Early the next morning, as George and Charles and I were preparing for our hunt, the Sioux warriors left, and half a dozen Cheyenne Dog Soldiers went with them. The Dog Soldier society consisted of veteran Cheyenne warriors who endeavored to seek danger in battle. They were skilled at war-fare, reckless, and unbelievably courageous. Though Cheyenne, the Dog Soldiers commonly rode and camped with the Sioux in those days. I don't know when it started, or why, but the Sioux welcomed and respected them. So when six Dog Soldiers rode away to the north with the Sioux warriors, I didn't think much of it.

We took six horses—three to ride and three to pull our camp equipage and hopefully return dragging meat. George and I exchanged much con-versation on our way west. He asked about Kit and many other mutual friends. Charles, on the other hand, didn't want to talk about a white man at all. Most of his conversation was in broken Cheyenne, which I guess he thought I couldn't understand, for sometimes he talked about me in rather unflattering terms.

Finally, I cut my pony in front of his and said, "If you have something to say about me, say it to my face, like a man. I understand Cheyenne better than you do. My wife is Cheyenne. You're speaking a mongrel mixture of Cheyenne and Arapaho."

Charles's face turned crimson with embarrassment and rage, and he kicked his horse to gallop on ahead of us.

"He is very angry," George said.

"At whom?"

George shrugged. "At our father, for sending us away to school. At every kid who ever called him half-breed. At the white folks back in Westport who wouldn't let us in their stores or houses. At the Union soldiers for shooting at him. And especially at himself for being half white."

"All the same things could be said of you. Why aren't you angry?"

George rode along for a few seconds, then looked at me, and smiled. "Who says I'm not?"

We found the buffalo the next day. The herd seemed to have fragmented, for there were only a couple of hundred big woolly beasts in the bunch we found. We stayed downwind and sneaked up on a dozen stragglers, riding within shooting range with buffalo robes over our backs to fool the beasts into thinking we were their brothers. Once within range, we slipped from our horses and each of us killed a bison with our rifles. George and I killed cows, and Charles shot a yearling bull. That was all the meat we could carry back to camp on our travois, so we spent the rest of the day skinning and butchering. To skin each carcass, we tied one horse to the horns and one to the hide and had them pull in opposite directions as we helped cut the skin free from the meat with our knives. We stayed busy until dark, then enjoyed a feast of buffalo tongue and hump ribs.

"We may be cooking this little bull with his own dung," Charles mused, for our only fuel was buffalo chips.

"The odds against that are quite magnitudinous, but anything is possible."

"The odds can kiss my rosy red ass," Charles replied.

"You really *have* gone Indian if even your ass is red."

George burst into laughter, which very soon infected me with its contagious nature. Charles tried to be angry, but soon the laughter got even to him and he begrudged himself to chuckle and shake his head.

The following morning, as we rode into a perfect crimson fireball of a rising sun, pulling our meat-laden pole drags behind us, I asked the boys whether they would like to ride with me and Westerly back to William's stockade, and perhaps even go trading with us among the Comanches.

"I don't know why I'd go back to that goddamn stockade," Charles said. "The old man never has anything good to say to me."

Later, Charles's pony pulled a little ahead of me and George. The elder brother leaned toward me and said, "I'm going to visit Father in a month or so. I'll try to bring Charles with me, but he's got a mind of his own, you know. It wouldn't hurt if you'd talk to Father and tell him to ease up on Charles a little."

I thought about this as my eyes habitually scanned the far horizons for trouble. "The idea of my lending advice and counsel to the wisest man I've ever known makes me very uncomfortable."

"You're no idiot yourself. You can find a way to say it without really saying it. And William Bent is not perfect. He's made mistakes like everybody else."

"He thought he was doing the right thing sending you boys east for schooling."

"He sent Charles too young. It was me and Mary and Robert ended up raising him, and we didn't know anything about raising a brat kid. We were brat kids ourselves. The whole business has made him mean. He drew blood in the Confederate Army. He told me he killed a Yankee or two, and I believe him. He wants more killing now, and I'm afraid he'll find it."

"He wants to kill white men, doesn't he?"

George nodded. "He hates being half white. He'd kill it inside himself if he could." George twisted in the saddle to check the load behind him on the pole drag, and to glance across the horizon for trouble. When he turned back to the rising sun, he said, "The Cheyennes don't call him a half-breed."

⁕⁂⁕

George did return to William's stockade for a time, but Charles did not come with him. The younger brother had absorbed a passion for the unbridled life of a rising Cheyenne warrior. George soon went to rejoin the Cheyennes, as well. In the years that followed, William would always give me credit for saving his relationship with George. Still, I always felt that I had failed him for not reuniting him permanently with both sons.

And remember the wretched squaw man, Carter? The man who claimed he was hard of hearing because he couldn't speak Cheyenne, though he was married to one? Well, Carter, I would learn in later years, rode to Denver and managed to obtain an audience with Governor Evans. He told the governor that the Cheyennes and the Sioux had smoked the war pipe together out on the Smoky Hill River and that both tribes were going to unite for a war on whites come spring. For this colossal lie, Governor Evans granted Carter the rank of lieutenant in the Colorado volunteers.

THIRTY-SIX

Home collects your powers while you wander, and holds them for you until you return. *Home* goes with you when you drift away again. *Home* returns to you in your dreams far afield. *Home* gives you life, but *home* wants your corpse when your life has flickered and died.

A true Comanche could call several places home. All over the plains and mountains and woodlands, mystic locales called to the True Humans, the *Noomah,* the Comanches. A single warrior could seek medicine in many far-scattered points on the sacred Mother Earth. This was one of the disturbing realizations that made me know I was not a true Comanche. I called only one place home—the place where I now spend my last days, awaiting my ultimate end. This crossing on the Canadian. This canyon basin along this bend in the river. This prairie guarded by bluffs, tickled by spring-fed creeks, dappled by timber, gouged by the talons of the thunderbird, smothered by the blankets of blizzards, seared by the wrath of a vengeful Father Sun, drenched by impossible deluges, galled by falling fists of ice, and goaded to whistling madness through the teeth of the wildest storm. This is the only place that charges me with medicine, heals me, holds me, and needs me almost as much as I need to call her home. Without this hallowed mother soil to catch my tears, and these brotherly bluffs to echo my crazed screams of anguish, I would surely have gone mad long ago.

You have come to hear things about Kit Carson and young Quanah Parker. Things worth my telling. I apologize for my digressions, but there is so much to tell. Too much, in fact. Most of it will be lost; that which has happened. Lost forever. I was lucky to have seen it, I suppose, though its memory has become my lament. You want to know about the battle? Yes, the battle is coming. Yes, I was there when Kit died. I will tell about that, too. The sun has raged across the sky like a flaming chariot and I have reduced winters to minutes, moons to moments. I will render the rest in good time. I will take up the story right here. Yes, home.

I awoke in my lodge to the smell of tallow cooking in an iron skillet. I had slept hard for many hours—an uncommon but welcome thing for me. Though my eyes opened, the sleep demons still had hold of my body and for a time I could only blink and glance about. The sky through the smoke hole above me was the color of a great blue heron. Dawn was coming, and Westerly was preparing breakfast. I smelled bone marrow and cornmeal now, in addition to the tallow, and I heard the pleasant sizzle of the corn cakes on the skillet. My face was cool, but my body warm under the heavy buffalo robe. I could feel the warmth of the place to my left where Westerly had lain not long ago. She had risen to add sticks to the small fire so she could cook our morning meal.

Unable to move, I nonetheless rested easy. My lodge was secure and I felt happy, though I needed to go outside into the cold and relieve myself. Soon enough. For now I lay there and blinked up at the inside cone of my lodge. The lower ends of the lodge poles were covered over by hides hung inside, providing a second wall of protection from the cold. With the tiny cook fire going, my home was cozy. I raised my eyebrows and got the rest of my face to move. Now the demons lost their hold and I felt movement twitching down through my torso and into my limbs.

I rolled to my side. Westerly glanced at me and smiled. I smiled back at her and admired her graceful movements by flickering firelight.

"The skillet is good," she said. "I like using it."

"You are quite progressive for an uncivilized squaw."

She knew I was joking, but she threw a stick at me in retaliation. "It remembers the flavor of things," she said.

"The more you use it, the more seasoned it becomes."

She nodded. "I suppose you heathen palefaces have come up with a few good ideas."

I lobbed the stick back at her. She smiled, quite proud of herself for the jibe, and continued her cooking.

Boldly now, I threw the warm covers aside and summoned my adopted Comanche vigor to face the cold. Wrapping only a blanket around my naked body, I slipped through the smallest opening I could make between the buffalo hide and the bearskin door covering. My bare foot landed in snow that came to my ankle. I took but a few steps from the lodge and let go a steaming stream as I looked around at the dark blue lines of the horizon. The fragrance of wood smoke tinged the frigid air. A vagrant flake of snow landed on my face. I heard muffled laughter from a nearby lodge. An owl hooted, and another answered. My feet were aching by the time I turned back to the lodge, and I thought about the vulnerability of naked humans in such a wild land.

I stepped back into the welcome warmth of the lodge and got dressed in breechclout, leggings, moccasins, and buckskin shirt as Westerly finished cooking. She had honey to pour on the corn cakes and cold spring water to wash it all down. After breakfast we sat and talked about how long our meat supply would last, about our neighbors, about the weather and grass for the horses, about the dreams we had dreamt last night, and what they might mean.

In the middle of our conversation, we were startled by a voice that sounded as if it came from someone sitting right between us: "I am coming in, Plenty Man."

I recognized it as Burnt Belly's voice and rose to greet him as he stepped in from outside. He had a finely tanned buffalo robe pulled over his head and around his shoulders. For his conjures and cures, Burnt Belly had earned many fine things.

"*Aho,*" I said. "Sit here, grandfather." I offered him the buffalo hide couch with the back rest.

"I will," he replied. "But only for a moment, to warm my old bones."

"We have corn cakes and honey."

"Had I known you were coming, I would have cooked more," Westerly added.

Burnt Belly brushed the offer away. "My third wife—the one who is young, but not so pretty—is a very good cook. She does almost nothing all day but tend the fire and prepare food, so I always have plenty to eat. Look . . ." He let his buffalo robe fall open. He was shirtless underneath, for he liked to show off the scar of the lightning bolt that had charged him with strange powers many years ago. It angled across his shoulder and chest, and broadened over a belly that indeed revealed a degree of prosperity. He held the paunch proudly in both hands and smiled at us across the fire.

I laughed and said, "My heart is glad that you have come to visit this morning, grandfather."

Burnt Belly put his hands together in front of him as if cupping something between them and said, "I have brought some things you will be needing."

When he opened his hands, a bundle of deerskin appeared, though it was too large to have been concealed by his hands just moments before. I was fairly adept at sleight-of-hand tricks myself, but was frequently amazed by the skills of old Burnt Belly.

"Thank you," I said, rising to take the bundle from the old shaman.

"I discovered a surplus of dogbane and moccasin flower, and I thought of you."

It was unusual for Burnt Belly to bring my cures to me without my asking for them, so I was a bit confused. Quite the haggler, the old man never gave his treatments away except to those afflicted with absolute poverty. I was considered quite wealthy in this village, so the offering from the old man surprised me. I could only assume that he wanted something of me.

"My supply has been dwindling rapidly," I said. "I thank you for bringing these things to me."

"Do the nightmares still visit you?"

"Only when I am away and run out of the cures."

"You will never be completely cured. You must always keep a supply of your herbs and roots on hand. You had better start taking time to collect them yourself. Do you think I will live forever?"

I smiled. "No, but I think you may outlive me. Only the Great Mystery knows."

He scoffed knowingly. "The Great Mystery tells those of us who listen. The time will come when you must seek your own herbs."

"I have begun to collect some for myself, and my wife is learning to help me."

"That is good," he said. "Very well, I must be going now. There is a child across the village with a case of colic. I have been summoned." He rose with much greater agility than one would expect of a white-haired old man, wrapped his robe about his shoulders, and stepped toward the door. He paused before he stepped out.

"Is there anything else you wanted to say, grandfather?" I asked.

He turned and smiled. "I had a strange vision. You must make new arrows. *Sacred* arrows."

"War points?"

"No. Hunting arrows."

"Why, grandfather?"

He shrugged his shoulders. "I do not know. The vision was like a blizzard. I could not see much. Only you, shooting an arrow from the back of a fast buffalo horse." He looked at the skillet next to the fire. "Perhaps I *will* have a taste of one of your corn cakes."

Westerly darted to the skillet and scooped up a cake to give to the old man.

"A person should never pass up a chance to eat or sleep. Remember this when you are tired and starving."

I nodded and smiled as the shaman stepped out.

After a few moments, Westerly whispered, "His voice came into our lodge when he was still outside." Her eyes were wide with wonder.

"He has the power to make his voice speak wherever he wants it to speak."

"And the bundle in his hands," she hissed in a whisper. "Where did it . . . How?"

"He has the power of the Thunderbird in his blood. You saw the scar."

"It is a wonder it did not kill him."

"It is a wonder. He is a man of great powers and wisdom. His advice should always be heeded."

"Yes. I think you should fashion new arrows, as Burnt Belly says."

"I was thinking more of the other advice. Never miss a chance to eat or sleep. We should share another corn cake and take a siesta."

Westerly smiled. "I know the kind of siesta you like." One eyebrow lifted seductively.

I shrugged innocently. "It is the advice of the medicine man."

She scolded me with her expression, yet nonetheless took a bite from the delicacy she had prepared and handed the rest to me. As she licked her lips, she loosened her deerskin shirt and pulled it over her head. Laying it neatly aside, she wriggled out of her finely tanned skirt and slid under the buffalo robes, the nipples of her firm breasts pointing through the cool air to the narrowing peak of the lodge. Once under the covers, she removed her breechclout and tossed it aside. I did not take long in joining her, naked, under the warmth of the buffalo robes.

I spent some of the happiest days of my life in the summer of the year the white men numbered 1863. On the Kiowa calendar, this time was called the "Summer of No-Arm's River Sun Dance." Yes, the Kiowas had a calendar. And they still maintain it, I assure you. I became well acquainted with the Kiowa calendar in 1863, for Kill Something's band of Comanches decided to join Little Bluff's Kiowa band to travel, hunt, camp, and raid together. I spent hour upon hour with old Little Bluff himself, studying the symbols on the calendar.

The Kiowa calendar was actually a history that recorded past events through symbols. The seasons got their names on the Kiowa calendar through remarkable events. Take, for example, the case of the "Summer of No-Arm's River Sun Dance" in 1863. That summer, a large bunch of Kiowas gathered on Walnut Creek, a tributary that joined the Arkansas River on the south bank of the Great Bend. A white man named William Allison kept a trading store nearby. The Kiowas called him "No-Arm." He actually had one arm, but the other had been shot off in a gunfight with his stepfather, whom he had killed in the same violent affair. In the Indian way of thinking, if a man had no arm where once an arm had grown, then he should be called "No-Arm" even though he still had his other arm. The Summer of No-Arm's River Sun Dance was named for the large Kiowa Sun Dance that occurred near No-Arm's trading post that summer.

Some of Little Bluff's warriors rode to Kansas for the gathering and came back to tell us all about it. But Westerly and I were content to stay in the Comanche camps that summer, moving with the Indians, making trades for horses and captives. There were plenty of both that summer. The Comanches and Kiowas were raiding extensively along the Texas frontier and on into Mexico.

That summer, in fact, some of Little Bluff's warriors rode south to Mexico and stayed gone so long that we began to fear their entire party had been wiped out. When they finally returned safely, laden with spoils, they told stories of riding far, far to the south where they found strange forests. In these forests, fantastically colored birds flew and little people with long tails swung through the treetops. Those Kiowas could ride.

The ransom trade kept me very busy that summer. I did not always bother with the captives who were well treated by their captors. But occasionally some squaw would see fit to torment a captive child in retaliation for a husband or brother lost on a raid. The unfortunate child was usually starved, beaten, and made to work every waking hour. Sometimes a captive boy would be pitted repeatedly against Indian boys in wrestling matches or fights in which sticks were used as weapons. These could be very cruel affairs, and I always tried to intervene. I would first attempt to trade for the captive. If successful, I had to decide whether or not to try to return the child to his home, or find a suitable adoptive family among the Indians. It was not possible to return every captive. There were just too many that summer.

If a trade for the captive was refused, I would attempt to get the camp to ostracize the aggressor until the beatings and cruelty ended. On a few occasions, I actually had to take abused children from their tormentors, at peril of my life. But when things cooled down, I always gave a couple of horses or something of equal value to the former owner of the captive to smooth things over.

Also, that year, I spent much time learning from the conjurer Burnt Belly. I think my reputation as Burnt Belly's protégé helped me in the ransom trade, as well. The Indians were terrified of hexes and many of them worried that I or my mentor would put a curse on them should they cross me in a trade for a captive. In reality, I never knew Burnt Belly to even consider cursing another human. His medicine was all about healing.

The old shaman drew extensive maps, showing me the locations of springs and rivers of medicinal waters, and detailing the types of maladies each water source might cure. The maps also showed the locations and ranges of herbs and other curative plants. He lectured on the power of smoke as a carrier of prayers to the Great Mystery, and used it to bless the new sacred hunting arrows he had instructed me to make. He taught me chants and drumbeats known to cure ailments, aid in meditations, and induce visions. I would observe for hours as Burnt Belly chanted, prayed, smoked, spat whiskey on coals, and fell into the deepest trances. I'm not sure I understood all I learned, but in regard to the medicinal qualities of plants, I excelled.

I learned to hear the voices of plants that summer better than I might ever have imagined. They would speak to me in whispers, shouts, or songs. Once, years later, while riding far to the north to ransom a captive for a wealthy ranching family, I camped high in the mountains in a grove of spruce trees. I happened to put my hand upon an ancient spruce that played a song for me with the voice of a violin. It almost broke my heart. I could have been a master luthier. This tree *wanted* to make music.

If Burnt Belly had become my mentor, I, in turn, became the mentor of young Quanah, the son of Peta Nocona. Quanah would ride with me to the Texas settlements to return captives. He seemed very curious about the whites, perhaps because he was half white himself. With Quanah along, I would usually bring captives to the German-settled town of Fredericksburg because this was the only town on the Texas frontier that had struck a viable treaty with the Comanches. The Germans had convinced the Indians that they were a different tribe, with a different language, and were not Texans. This treaty was never broken by either the Comanches or the German settlers, so Fredericksburg became a trade center for the True Humans. The Germans there would make sure that any captive I delivered would be returned to his or her home. They would also collect my ransom fee for me and hold it until I could return.

Quanah was fascinated by the whites and their strange ways. In days to come, he would rise to the status of a great war chief who valiantly fought white encroachment. Still later, he would negotiate treaties with the whites to save the Comanches from annihilation. I flatter myself to think that Quanah learned at least some of his diplomatic skills from me.

Anyway, while not ransoming captives, trading for horses, studying the Kiowa calendar, or learning from Burnt Belly, I spent my time with Westerly. She loved written language, so we spent much time writing with anything we could find. We made quill pens from wild turkey feathers, ink from berries. We wrote on deer hides, scraps of parchment, canvas, or anything else we could find. We would have entire lessons drawn with sticks in smoothed sand.

Writing supplies were hard to come by, but reading material was plentiful in camp that summer. The warriors were raiding the settlements so much that they frequently came back with newspapers and books. The Indians particularly liked books for several reasons. First of all, there were often woodcuts or line drawings in the books of the day. The Indians found these illustrations hilarious, for they usually depicted white people. Secondly, the Indians held a certain reverence for books as mystical objects. They realized that books held ideas and information that only one familiar with their magic could retrieve. But, mostly, the Indians valued paper for starting fires, and a bound book provided an easy, compact vehicle for carrying this kindling. Westerly and I would often trade a horse for a new volume in English or Spanish, for the book could take us to places no horse could go.

I devoured Indian life in the camps that summer, and into the fall of 1863, and the following winter. I knew that war was raging back East. I knew that Kit Carson had begun a campaign of attrition against the

Navahos to the west. I knew that the Cheyennes and Arapahos were growing more and more frustrated with white attacks to the north. But in Comancheria life was good. We camped beyond the reach of Texans who attempted to follow Comanche raiding parties, and lived unmolested out on the wild plains.

In November, Satank's band of Kiowas joined Little Bluff's and Shaved Head's people, and we had a grand camp-together in the pecan groves of the San Saba River, near the ruins of a presidio that had been vacated by Spanish soldiers a hundred years before. Here, the women gathered and shelled a crop of pecans that beat anything even the oldest elders could remember. While the nuts were being gathered and cracked, it was decided in council that scouts should ride out in every direction looking for buffalo. My brother, Kills Something, came to me after the council and asked if I would ride with him to look for the herds. I agreed to do just that, of course.

"My brother," Kills Something said, after we made our plans to leave. "For riding with me on this search, I am going to give two very good horses to you."

I knew I would insult him should I refuse, so I said, "Then I will ride even harder in search of the buffalo, so that the glory of finding a great herd will belong to my brother and me."

"I staked the two horses near your lodge. The sorrel is named Tu Hud. The bay is called Castchorn."

I knew by this that the horses must be fine ones, so I went to see them. The sorrel named Tu Hud, which meant "All Horse," was huge for an Indian pony, standing over fifteen hands. He was light reddish with a long flaxen mane and tail. The bay pony had a black mane and tail and a star on his face. He stood about fourteen hands, which was plenty of horse for a scrawny rider like me. His name, Castchorn, meant "Buffalo Getter." Both were excellent animals, and I was proud to own them.

The night before we left, Kills Something and I sent prayers up to the spirits to grant us the power of finding buffalo. The Indians were quite competitive in this business of scouting for herds. The bringer of meat was a hero second only to the slayer of enemies. Everyone wanted to locate the biggest concentration of buffalo, so we prepared to ride hard and cover much country. Kills Something and I vowed to ride all the way to Adobe Walls and back if we had to. We had both had fleeting dream-visions of buffalo coming down from the north.

And, of course, I remembered Burnt Belly's vision of me shooting sacred arrows. I had made four such arrows, which I carried in my quiver now, awaiting the chance to use them. Burnt Belly had personally blessed them with smoke and much chanting.

The next morning, I mounted Tu Hud. Kills Something and I struck out to the north, covering ground like few of history's horsemen could imagine. Tu Hud indeed proved to be "all horse." We rode north until we crossed the Colorado River. We then rode upstream, almost due north at that point, until we hit the old trail angling over toward the Double Mountain Fork of the Brazos River. We continued north, crossing the Salt Fork of the Brazos, and intending to head up the two forks of the Wichita and the three forks of the Pease River. We would split up during the day, in order to scout twice the country, then we'd rendezvous at prearranged camps come sundown. In those days, a man could see signs of buffalo a long way off, so we would put as much as twenty miles of space between us during the day.

Let me tell you, I did some tall riding. The air was cool and Tu Hud willing. I was lean and light, carrying nothing with me but my bow and arrows, a small stash of pemmican, a bundle of my medicinal roots, and a knife. The big sorrel ran as if he carried no burden whatsoever. I would pick a spot on the ridge before me and dash toward it at a trot, a lope, or even a gallop. Arriving at the ridge, I would stop to observe the country, and let my pony blow, then I would take off for the next ridge.

We encountered obstacles to negotiate, but that made the riding more of a challenge to horse and horseman. We might come to a thicket and have to pick our way through it, jumping dead timbers and ducking low limbs. We might come to a cutbank that ran for miles along a creek, but Tu Hud and I would jump off a bluff the height of a tipi, as long as a goodly pool of water waited to catch us. We might ascend a slope only to find a vast rimrock, taller than horse and rider, barring our way for miles on either side, but that sure-footed sorrel could find footholds a mountain goat would envy. *That* was the best riding I ever did—blazing my own path across a trackless wilderness, determined to meet my Comanche brother before sundown every night.

On the seventh morning of our search, I woke before dawn, feeling a strange voice speaking to me from the earth. As Kills Something and I found our horses in the dark, I said, "Do you hear it?"

"Yes," he said.

"Can it be?"

"I pray that it can be, but I have never heard it—felt it—like this."

We both heard it, though neither of us could explain it. If we strained to hear, we heard nothing out of the ordinary. But when we stopped trying, we sensed it—absorbed it. It was as if thunder were rolling somewhere so far away that we could not detect it, yet somehow we knew about it anyway.

We rode with the first birdsong. Before Father Sun even peeked over the horizon, we found ourselves approaching the divide between the south fork and the middle fork of the Pease.

"Now I see it, as well," Kills Something said. "Yet I don't see it at all."

"Yes, in the sky."

"That color. Have you ever seen that color at dawn?"

"Never."

We exchanged glances and urged our ponies to a run up the gentle slope of the divide. Then we approached the high ridge of land, and the country before us seemed poised to rise into view. Now the sound we could hear but not hear earlier hit us full in our faces like the crash of surf on a beach when you come over the last dune. Just then, Father Sun shot the day's first glance over the skyline, painting the dust-laden air the shade of autumn maple leaves. Another step brought into view the high ground ahead, and the sight of it bewildered the eye. It writhed with dark ripples, like mice scurrying about under a single buffalo robe.

But this was God's own buffalo robe, made of living bison. It shrouded His hills and valleys as far as the eye could penetrate through the haze of red morning dust that hung over it. It began just below us, at the headwaters of the middle fork of the Pease, and grew thicker with every wave of land until it disappeared in the haze. It was as if Mother Earth were too bashful to let Father Sun gaze upon her nakedness, and had pulled a living buffalo robe over her bare flesh to conceal her beauty.

"How can we explain it to the elders?" Kills Something said, his face blank and staring in wonder at the impossible herd.

"We must admit to them that we cannot explain it, and yet we must try."

"Let us look upon it for a while. This may be the greatest herd we will ever see."

I watched and tried to gather it in for a spell. Suddenly I realized how still my mount stood. Tu Hud didn't even seem to be breathing. He had never seen anything like this, either. The eyes of riders and horses alike stared in absolute wonder, trying to fathom how so many huge beasts could possibly come together in one place.

Of course, we had to turn our backs on the spectacle soon enough. The hard ride that had taken us seven days from the San Saba only took five days returning, for we held to the trails and rode for all the glory we knew we would win at camp. Our horses must have run off a hundred pounds each on that trek, earning a long rest and much grass.

THIRTY-SEVEN

The report we gave in camp called for a great council outside of Little Bluff's lodge. Some scoffed at our claims, but Kills Something and I stood firm in our insistence that the herd was truly historic. It took us hours to convince the whole village to move that far north, but no other scouts had found large amounts of game, so eventually the elders recommended the move. Shaved Head, Little Bluff, and Satank gave the order.

By the middle of the next day, most of the village was on the trail, with Kills Something and me scouting ahead. This village did not move nearly as fast as we had on our search, of course, and my Comanche brother began to worry.

"We will take at least ten sleeps reaching the buffalo," he complained as we waited on a ridge for the camp to catch up.

I shrugged. "Maybe nine if the herd continues to move toward us."

"That is still a long time. What if the herd scatters?"

"Even one half of one half of one half of that herd would satisfy this village."

"What if the herd stops and turns back? Buffalo do strange things."

"You worry too much, my brother. Your medicine is strong. We have both had visions of buffalo, yes?"

"That is true," he conceded.

"I know why you worry."

"Do you?"

"Yes. You know it is time to take your place as chief of the band. Shaved Head is old now. He thinks more like a peace chief than a war chief. That is good, for he has gained much wisdom and gives good counsel. But every band of True Humans needs a fearless war chief. You have already proven your courage in many battles, but if you deliver meat, the people will see you as a leader who can provide food as well as lead a war party. A great hunt will make you *Chief* Kills Something."

He could not hold back a brief smile. "You see many things others miss, brother. Yes, I am worried about the great herd we saw. Anything could happen." He gestured to the sky. "The Thunderbird could light the grass with his hot glare and fan it to a firestorm with his wings. The whole herd might stampede all the way to Osage country."

I chuckled. "There is no need to worry. A hard winter always brings the herds south, and this will be a very cold one."

"How do you know?"

"The thick winter coats started early on the horses. The cranes were almost as early as the teal as they flew south. And what of the big crop of pecans? The leaves dropping early from the cottonwoods? Other plants have told me in voices that only Burnt Belly and I can hear."

"You are spending too much time with that old man. You must be careful. The people fear a conjurer."

"Not one who conjures meat."

Kills Something laughed. "True."

"Everything will be good. Do not lose faith in your medicine, brother."

He nodded. "You are right. It is up to the spirits. I can only pray and lead. I will not worry about it more."

Eight days later, scouting ahead, Kills Something and I encountered the great herd, still en masse. We rode back and ordered an immediate return to the last creek crossed. It held but little water, but would have to suffice as a campsite. The lodges were raised by sundown and preparations under way for a morning hunt.

Now Kills Something's leadership abilities began to show. He boldly took over the organization of the hunt, not even bothering to ask the permission of the three chiefs. From each band, he chose six leading men, including the three chiefs and himself. "You will each choose ten hunters," he said to these men. This would put eighteen parties of ten organized hunters in the field—180 hunters. "Satank's band will be in the west, Shaved Head in the center, and Little Bluff in the east. Keep three arrow shots between each party of ten. My brother, Plenty Man, will give the first signal with his gun. When you hear the shot, each party will charge into the great herd and cut out a part of it—maybe one hundred animals. You will kill until your arrows are all spent."

Chief Satank was skeptical, for no one but Kills Something and I had yet seen the herd. "Eighteen different hunting parties? This herd cannot be so large," the Kiowa chief complained.

"You will see in the morning," Kills Something insisted. "*Fifty* hunting parties could make meat from this herd. But we can raise only eighteen."

"What about the younger warriors?" little Bluff asked.

"They will be allowed to ride in after the headmen. Plenty Man will give a second signal with his gun. The young hunters may go after the main herd, or chase buffalo that escape the hunting parties of ten men. Everyone will have a chance to make a kill."

I realized that Kills Something had reserved a place of honor for me in the organization of the hunt. It would be my responsibility to judge when the young hunters could make their charge.

"Who will serve as Watchers?" Little Bluff asked.

Kills Something thought about this for a moment, for it was important. The Watchers were chosen from one of the warrior societies to police the hunt. It was their job to prevent anxious young hunters from sneaking away to get their kills in early, which could scatter the herd and ruin the great hunt for everyone. After due consideration, Kills Something gestured to Little Bluff and Satank. "The Horse Headdresses will serve as Watchers over the Kiowa bands." He turned to Shaved Head. "Uncle, I believe the Little Horses should be Watchers over the *Noomah* hunters."

"That is a good choice," Shaved Head replied. "They are young men and will remember when they, too, as boys, wanted to sneak away early."

"Yes, and the boys will listen to them," Little Bluff agreed, "for they are just a little older than boys themselves."

"What will the punishment be for anyone sneaking away to hunt before the signal?" said Satank.

"The Watchers may destroy all the weapons and take all the horses of anyone who attempts to hunt early," decreed Kills Something.

"And if someone should make an early kill? What will be done with the meat?"

"What do you suggest?"

Shaved Head tossed his one braid over his shoulder. "There is much excitement about this great herd you have found. Some boys might risk their weapons and horses if they think they can get meat. So I believe a kill made early should be destroyed. The hide should be slashed and the *kwitapu* from the guts should be rubbed on the meat to make it spoil."

Little Bluff chuckled. "With my hunters, I will see that the *kwitapu* is rubbed on the hunter, as well as the meat. *That* should take away the desire for any boy to make an early kill."

"Agreed," Kills Something said, chuckling at the prospect. "Send the criers for your villages to my lodge and I will tell them what to say to the people."

Shaved Head made no complaints about Kills Something usurping his authority. It was as if the old chief had grown weary of leading, and looked forward now to the less rigorous role of peace chief. He knew Kills Something was ready to take command.

The chiefs and the hunt leaders all went their own ways, but Kills Something held me back. "These hunters will be so far scattered that the ones to the far west and east will not hear your gun."

"I thought of that," I said.

"Do you know what to do?"

"I will find some young men who have guns. We will sit our horses all along the line, just far enough apart that we can each hear the next man's gunshot. I will fire first, and the man to either side will fire next, and so on, all the way down the line."

Kills Something nodded. "Choose *Noomah* boys in the middle and Kiowa boys on either end. After they fire the second signal, they will want to hunt with their brothers."

"Yes, of course."

"Now, listen, my brother, you must choose the moment well for the second shot. If you signal too soon, the younger hunters will ride in and scatter the small herds that the older and better hunters have cut out. If you wait too long, the stragglers that escape the older hunters will run away too fast to catch. And also, the boys will get restless and charge before the signal is given. Then we will have trouble with the Watchers."

"I will look over the hunt from high ground," I promised, "with an eagle's eye, and the hunger of a wolf."

~~~~~~

The hunters assembled in parties well before dawn and left for their positions to the east and west. At first light, I found myself waiting near the brink of a ridge. The main herd began on the other side of the ridge, and Kills Something had ordered no man to across that high point of land before the signal shot. He sat his pony beside me, waiting.

"I had a very strange dream about you last night," he said.

"About me?"

"You were lost in a snowstorm. Everything was white, and you were in it. But you did not complain. You had no warm clothes, yet you did not even shiver. You were happy in that blizzard, brother."

"What does it mean?"

"Only the spirits know." He judged the far hills, coming into view now out of darkness. "It is time."

"I agree."

"I will ride ahead and make the sign."

Kills Something loped his mount up to the top of the ridge. Behind him, the organized parties of ten waited to charge. Next, the Watchers of the Little Horses brotherhood spread in a line, each within sight of the next, policing the front. And behind them waited the younger hunters who would make the second charge.

Finally, with gray light bathing the landscape, Kills Something waved his bow at me. I pointed my rifle skyward and fired, the charge kicking hard at my outstretched arm. Immediately, I saw the white smoke from the next riflemen in line, then heard the reports from their weapons. The veteran hunters charged forward in their parties of ten. Some of them yelped a brief note of joy before they thundered over the ridge.

The Watchers and the rest of the young hunters moved forward to the top of the ridge to look beyond and witness the hunt from high ground. When I reached the brink of the divide, the buffalo were already stampeding in terror. The beasts were so taken by surprise that they fled in every direction, some coming straight toward us. From my vantage point, I could see three of the parties of ten at work. Kills Something's band was in front of me, Shaved Head's to the right, and Fears-the-Ground's to the left. As Kills Something was closer, I watched him and his nine men with most interest.

As the buffalo dispersed, Kills Something took advantage of the distance between beasts. He charged right in among the terrorized bison, his riders following him, and began to cut off about eighty animals. Riding like a leaf in a windstorm, he passed lumbering beasts and began to make a circle around the herd he had cut off. A cow came near him, so he shot her through the ribs and charged on.

I glanced left and right. Fears-the-Ground's party was on the verge of circling a small herd as well, but Shaved Head's men seemed to have let their intended prey break back into the main herd, which was now rumbling the very earth under us so hard that we could feel it even through the legs of our mounts. The ponies became nervous and began to prance. A few crazed bison charged past the Watchers, and the nearest of the young hunters gave chase. The stray buffalos had charged into these youths, so I saw no harm in the boys pursuing them, but it only made the rest of the young men more anxious and the Watchers were shaking their lances at the youths, trying to hold them back. Soon, it would be like trying to hold back a blue norther, but I waited as many more moments as I dared, though I raised my rifle as a hopeful sign to the young hunters.

I watched Kills Something lead his hunters around the bunch of animals they had separated. The moment I saw him making the final curve that would encircle the small herd, I let my rifle speak. An excited battle cry sounded all along the line, and all the remaining hunters charged, including the Watchers. Some of the young men had trouble with their horses, for few ponies had ever ridden into such a melee of hooves, hides, and horns.

I, myself, sheathed my rifle and pulled my bow from my quiver. Quickly, I strung the bow, then reached over my shoulder for an arrow. By now every hunter had ridden into the herd, save a few who had fallen from bucking horses. But I was riding Castchorn—Buffalo Getter. Kills Something told me that the good bay pony had been caught wild running with some buffalo, and he held no fear of the herd. He bolted into the midst of the chaos, huffing great blasts of hot breath into the cold air.

The nearest beasts were scattering with unexpected speed, and I knew I would have to ride into the escaping main herd to find a decent number of animals to bag. My bay seemed to sense my plan, and ran straight ahead at a full gallop while the thunder of hooves shook the ground and the sky from every quarter. The dust began to thicken and sting my eyes, but I charged on until I had passed every other hunter, and began to catch up to the slower buffalo.

The air became almost as black as the herd with dust kicked up by ten thousand hooves. I soon realized that I was running to no avail, for I had not come within range of a target. I endeavored to pick a single animal out of that mass of meat and run that beast down. I found what looked like a two-year-old cow, with a fine hide and a fat-layered carcass. She would make good meat and bear a fine robe. I urged my bay onto her right flank, came within range, drew my bow, and let the arrow fly. It disappeared into her side, though she seemed unaware. As I drew another arrow over my shoulder, however, I saw her cough a breath of red froth into the dust, and stumble, finally tripping and rolling tail over horns. Castchorn dodged her as he raced on into the herd.

In that mad gallop, I trusted my horse to find footing and concentrated on my arrow, trying repeatedly to notch it on the bow string as the bay lurched under me. I happened to have chosen one of my new sacred arrows from the quiver. Finally, I got the arrow in place and looked up for my next victim. I blinked the gumming dust away from my eyes and realized that I had become surrounded by stampeding buffalo. I looked left for a target, but something made me glance right. I could not even say what it had been—a flash of something. But it was gone now, in the dust. Just as I looked away, I glimpsed it again. Something pale in that cloud of dark dust. Again, it vanished, so I eased the bay to the right to get a closer look.

I had begun to question my eyesight, when I saw it again—this time for sure. A white animal ran with the buffalo. I remembered a hunter along the line to my right who rode a white horse. Had he fallen? Should I try to catch his horse for him? I angled quickly in front of a young bull to get a closer look, when the view came clear. The white beast was a buffalo. An albino bison.

My heart leapt. I had heard the stories. They were rare. They were sacred. The hides were more valuable than their weight in gold to collectors in the east and in Europe. To the Indians, the beast represented great medicine. The robe could lend power and protection. A single white robe was worth sixty normal ones, or fifteen horses loaded with guns, blankets, and food. A desire seized me to bag that beast for personal glory and big Comanche medicine for my adopted people.

I angled in for the kill, but several beasts ran between me and the albino. My bay mount, Buffalo Getter, was still game, but breathing hard from the run. I had to drop back a little to get behind a cow, then I urged the bay back up to speed. At this rate, I wasn't sure I could close on the sacred bison before my pony gave out. I was gaining ground, but not fast enough. I knew my range with the bow and arrow. At this distance a rib could stop my razor-sharp iron tip. I thought briefly of my rifle, but a kill with a bullet would not rate like one with a sacred arrow, and my bow was ready to draw. Three beasts between me and the albino. Now two, but the bay was winded. I had one chance left. I sucked dust into my lungs and released a battle cry that rent the air like a bugle note.

When the bay heard me, he snorted, lowered his lunging head, and somehow summoned another morsel of speed. I passed one of the lumbering obstacles, then the next, seconds narrowing on my chance to make that rarest of kills. Now! Yes, I could do it. The shot would be to my right, which was not natural, but my Comanche riding and shooting drills had schooled me in every conceivable shot. I twisted to the right and drew my bow, holding it almost horizontal, with the butt of the arrow shaft at my belt—a shot from the hip. There was no aiming this missile. I had to *feel* the way home for that arrow. I had mere moments to shoot. I felt the rhythm of the horse and watched the same motion in the white buffalo.

Then the air fell silent. Everything vanished in that cloud but the albino. The gait of my pony and the tempo of the buffalo's hooves meshed as if orchestrated. The arrow connected before I even let it fly.

The din of stampeding tons burst into my skull again as the mass of white fur fell rolling behind me. I could not safely stop, but I pulled the bay back to a slower canter, then to a lope, letting the straggling buffalo thunder past us. The bay heaved for wind as he slowed to a trot, the bison now spreading out around me. Still, I had to trot another half-mile to safely emerge from the tail end of that monumental stampede.

I walked my mount back, letting him cool gradually as he caught his breath. I felt an unerring sense of direction leading me to that sacred kill, and I saw it a quarter-mile away through the settling dust. She lay there at rest; a mound of coarse, snowy fleece. She seemed out of place in the earthy world of soil and grit kicked into billowing clouds and hanging over her still like a death shroud.

I began to get very excited. The kill filled me with pride such as I had never felt. I was one of a mere handful of hunters, Indian or white, who had even seen a white buffalo, let alone bagged one with a perfect arrow shot. In seasons to come, I would collect all the information I could on white buffalo, written and oral. By estimating the size of the great herds and figuring the frequency of sightings of white bison, I was able to calculate the odds of occurrence of the white phase among normal buffalo. Generally, I discovered, fewer than four white buffalo were even sighted per decade. Kills were even less frequent. One hide dealer in Westport, Kansas, after twenty years of buying and selling bison hides, told me that he had bought only five white ones. My calculations held that a white buffalo was one in seven and a half million.

But that day, as I rode up to the carcass that from a distance looked like a great cache of pearls and ivory, I could think only of the spiritual power inherent in that uncommonly creamy coat. *This* was the reason

Burnt Belly had urged me to make sacred arrows. Had he known? Could he foresee my future? I could not think of it right now, because I was simply overwhelmed by accomplishment.

I rode up to the carcass, which lay tail toward me. Though the coat was discolored with brown dust, I could easily see its pure milky beauty awaiting its cleansing. I wanted to get down and touch that sacred beast but I knew I should ride around her to make sure she had indeed given up the ghost. So I circled to look at the eyes, and to make sure they were open in death. I gasped, as if encountering a freak of nature in a circus sideshow. The horns and nose of the beast were pink. And the eyes—indeed open in the death stare—were pink, as well. I might have expected this, but the discovery startled me nonetheless. This was a true albino, not just a light color phase sometimes seen—a cream or cinnamon variety. I didn't have to be a thunderstruck shaman to sense the sanctity in this rare gift from the spirits.

For a moment I didn't know what to do next. I longed to tell Kills Something, Burnt Belly, and especially Westerly, but I did not yet care to leave my prize unattended on the plains. Would wolves come and violate that perfect white hide? No, I would leave my hunting shirt on the carcass so the scent would frighten away the carnivores. Would someone else try to claim my kill? No, my sacred arrow with my own personal identifying markings was even now imbedded in the body cavity of the beast. I got down, crouched to touch the woolly white head, then stood to offer my thanks to the skies. I took off my deerskin shirt and draped it respectfully over the horns and eyes of the head. She was, I reckoned, a two- or three-year-old cow. Such a prize could not survive to grow much older with every hunter on the plains after her hide.

Finally, I mounted and rode back to the south where most of the other kills had been made. Before I crossed over the nearest hill, I turned and looked back at the white carcass on the ground, as if to make sure I had not dreamed the whole episode. Then, I urged Castchorn to an easy lope and rode in all my bare-chested glory back toward the rest of the hunters.

I passed a young hunter who was proudly removing a hunk of liver from his kill. He looked at me, his mouth bloody. "You have many arrows left in your quiver," he said, taunting me in cocksure Comanche style.

I noticed his own quiver was empty, as if he thought this were a contest to see who could shoot the most arrows. "I shot only twice," I admitted, "but both shots killed."

"Ha! I killed three!"

"It is too bad that you have no wife to skin and butcher for you."

He frowned and threw his chest forward. "It is too bad that you have no shirt!"

Whatever that was supposed to mean, I let it go. When I approached the place where my hunt had begun, I noticed some commotion going on to the east where Shaved Head's party of ten had charged the herd. I saw Burnt Belly riding that way with Kills Something, so I urged my horse into a lope and caught up with them.

"What is the trouble?" I asked.

Kills Something's face showed his worry. "A buffalo charged Shaved Head and knocked him from his horse. Some of the buffalo stampeded over him. They say his leg is broken."

Burnt Belly said nothing, but I fell in with the two of them and went to see about Shaved Head. He lay on the ground, propped up on his elbows. His face showed no pain, but his right leg was clearly misshapen. Burnt Belly swooped gracefully down from his mount, and crouched over Shaved Head's leg. He prodded and felt for a few moments.

"This is not bad. It will heal. The bone is not even sticking out. The buffalo who stepped on you must have known you were a chief." Burnt Belly looked up toward me and Kills Something. "These young men will help me get him back to the camp. You two have bigger things to do than worry over a chief who cannot even walk."

It was true that Kills Something, as hunt leader, and de facto chief in Shaved Head's place, would have many problems to deal with now in the aftermath of the hunt. He turned his horse and looked out over the dead carcasses strewn across the hunting ground as we rode away at a trot. "The hunt has been good, but now there is much to be done."

"Yes, brother. Listen, I must tell you what happened to me."

"You can tell your hunting stories later," he said curtly.

"No, I must tell you now. You need to know what I have done."

He read my tone of voice, and turned his attention away from his duties to me. "What has happened? Something bad?"

"No. Something good. Something better than good."

"Tell me. I have no time for mysteries."

"I killed two buffalo. The second one was special."

His jaw muscles tensed with impatience, and his brow furrowed. "What is special about killing a buffalo?"

"This was no ordinary buffalo. This one was *white*."

His eyes glanced all over me and my horse, as if trying to decide if I were playing a trick on him, or if I had simply gone mad. "White? What do you mean?" he demanded.

"The robe. White as the whitest blizzard. White as a lone cloud in the summer sky. White as the froth on a mountain river or the bloom of a yucca."

He looked at me in disbelief for a moment or two, then I saw the realization spread across his face. He took in a deep breath and leaned toward me to put his hand on my shoulder. "Where is your shirt?"

"I left it on the white buffalo, to ward off wolves."

He tried to remain the stoic leader, for we both knew he would become chief of the band with Shaved Head nursing a broken leg, but Kills Something could not hold back a slight smile. "Get your wife and go take care of that kill," he ordered. "Be very careful with the hide. Say the proper prayers."

"I will."

"Have you told anyone else?"

"No. The white buffalo is beyond the rest of the kills. There will be no one in sight."

"Good. Tell no one, and do not bring the hide into camp until sundown. Everyone must make meat now, but if they hear of your kill, they will all abandon their duties to go see it."

I did as Kills Something ordered. I got Westerly, who was ready to go to work. I also got another shirt, for my skin looked like gooseflesh in the cold air. I did not tell Westerly about the white buffalo, as I wanted to surprise her. When she saw it, she almost wept. She was so moved that she could not speak. Her people, the Cheyennes, venerated the white bison as highly as any nation on the plains. We offered prayers of thanks to the spirits in both Cheyenne and Comanche, then meticulously went about our task of separating the sacred hide from the rare beast.

By sundown, Kills Something had told Burnt Belly about my kill, and the old shaman had made medicine and consulted the spirits. When Westerly and I came into camp at dusk and unveiled the white robe, Burnt Belly was already prepared. Criers scurried through the camp and crowds gathered to see the holy pelt. When the gathering reached its zenith, Burnt Belly called for silence and told what must be done with the hide.

The wives of the warriors of the Big Horses Brotherhood would make a special lodge for the white robe, where it would forevermore reside. Westerly, as wife of the man who had killed the sacred beast, would choose three women to help her cure the hide. The three women would come from the three villages of Indians camped here together—two Kiowas and one Comanche. Organizing this project came as quite an honor for Westerly, for she was Cheyenne by blood, but she was my wife, and I was a full member of the tribe, especially now. She was quite pleased, as was almost everyone in the big camp-together. Feasting and dancing followed Burnt Belly's announcement, and few went to sleep before dawn.

The days that followed brought all manner of problems to bear upon Kills Something. First, there were several disputes concerning who had killed which buffalo. Though the arrow markings should have prevented this, some buffalo survived a first arrow, only to be killed by a second arrow shot by a different hunter, and this almost always led to each hunter claiming the kill. Witnesses had to be called to testify, and Kills Something had to decide the conflicts as quickly and fairly as he could, calling upon the wisdom of elders to help in making his decisions.

One hunter had made four clean kills, then shot a fifth animal that had already been wounded by a younger warrior who had only managed to shoot the one beast. When Kills Something heard this case, he became furious at the more successful hunter, saying, "Would you let a brother go hungry while you already have four buffalos killed? You must not believe strongly in your medicine if you must hoard meat that way! The shot this young man made would have killed the buffalo, and you had no reason to add your arrow to his! If you have any faith in your spirit-powers, you will hold a great giveaway feast and prove it! Now, go!"

In addition to the disputes, there were a few cases involving impatient hunters who had sneaked past the Watchers and started killing before the signals had been given. Again, witnesses had to be consulted, and alibis corroborated. A couple of the accused Kiowa hunters were found guilty, and the Horse Headdresses indeed took all their weapons and horses from them, and destroyed the meat and hides they had bagged. One of these young hunters from Little Bluff's band was held down to have buffalo *kwitapu* rubbed over him as well as his kill, as Little Bluff had warned.

Then there was the problem of water. The small creek along which we camped soon became fouled by people, animals, and the business of butchering. Kills Something ordered the camp to move west to the stream called Running Water where it issued from the canyons of the Caprock Escarpment. The little river was known to have plenty of clear water. The march was to be made in haste, so meat would not spoil. There were nearer rivers to the north, but the elders knew their waters would have been muddied by the stampeding of the great herd.

So it was that on the Running Water, Westerly tanned the sacred hide while I was made to tell the story again and again of how I had made the kill. Great quantities of meat were consumed, sun-dried, smoked, even salted by those who had traded for salt. The pecans gathered on the San Saba were added to dried meat, pounded thin, encased in cleansed intestines, and flavored with wild fruits. There was wood and grass on the Running Water in quantities sufficient to last through the process of preserving all the meat taken in the hunt. When that wood and grass gave out, Kills Something ordered the move to the Crossing on the Canadian River, our favorite winter campground, there in the shadows of old Fort Adobe. Satank and his people went elsewhere, but Little Bluff's people followed Kills Something to Adobe Walls. There we camped in peace into the winter, living the good life for a while.

It was simply understood now that Kills Something was our war chief, while the venerable old warrior Shaved Head nursed his broken leg and graciously accepted his new role as peace chief. And I, an adopted Comanche, white by blood, had become a hero to Kills Something's band. I can say without boasting that in the entire band, only three men were more respected than me. They were Kills Something, Shaved Head, and Burnt Belly—the war chief, the peace chief, and the medicine man. I was the trader, the apprentice conjurer, the translator, and the slayer of the fabled white buffalo, whose robe would surely protect us all from destruction. Life was good that winter, and I did my best to enjoy it and pretend that it would last.

Yet, my heart knew better. Wandering Indians and Comanchero traders from New Mexico brought disturbing news from the world outside of Comancheria. Trouble continued in the East with the war raging, Yankees and Rebels both trying to sway the Indians to their bloody causes. Trouble raged in the West, where Colonel Kit Carson's forces had invaded the very heart of Navaho country, striking where no soldiers had ever ridden before. I knew the hoops of time would roll and whir and come crashing to earth again, and I feared they would in time come violently trundling down the Canadian River Valley to my very home.

THIRTY-EIGHT

Methodically, with the meticulous care of an apothecary, I spread the circle of doeskin before me across the blanket upon which I sat cross-legged. Upon this doeskin I placed a bundle of cranesbill geraniums that Burnt Belly had uprooted and washed several moons before. The aroma of smoke filled the lodge, for the old healer had just lifted a red-hot stone from the fire with a chokecherry fork and placed a few dried fir needles upon it. As my mentor had instructed, I dissected the stalky little flower, making separate piles for roots, stems, and leaves.

Burnt Belly was chanting under his breath, producing a low hum that was not unpleasant to listen to. Suddenly, his chant ended, and he reached for the small jug of trade whiskey I had brought to him. He pulled the stopper and tipped the mouth of the jug up to his lips. I did not see him swallow, but he held the whiskey in his mouth until he replaced the stopper and put the jug aside. Then, he leaned forward and spat the whiskey out on the fire, making it flare and sizzle. He laughed a raspy old chuckle, obviously pleased with the way the whiskey fueled the flame.

"That is good." He went back to his work with some other herb he was preparing for his practice. "That cranesbill is very useful," he said, gesturing to the plant I held in my hand. "Every warrior should carry the powdered root on raids. It stops bleeding. So, you will grind that root in the stone bowl when you get it all taken apart."

"What about the other parts of the plant?" I asked. "How should I prepare them?"

"Let the leaves remain whole. They can be eaten to stop bleeding inside or to stop loose bowels. Or they can be made into a hot poultice for rashes or other skin problems. They can be boiled to a potion that will wash out evil of the mouth, or the eyes. My sits-beside wife puts a bit of the leaf in my parfleche bags to keep meat fresh."

"Where are your wives today?" I asked, looking around the lodge. It was one of the most spacious tipis in the camp and it seemed especially large when the women were absent.

"They have gone to the lodge for unclean women."

"All four of them?"

"*Tsah.* Women are very strange creatures. You know, of course, that they have an unclean time of bleeding with every moon, and they must go to the lodge for unclean women until that time is over."

"Yes, so their unclean time does not spoil the good things the spirits have given us."

"True. But I would make a wager that you did not know this: when women live in a lodge together—even if they all have the unclean time at different phases of the moon when they start the living together—after a few moons, they will all begin to have the unclean time *at the same time!* They claim that they do not have any control over this, but I am not so sure."

I smiled. "Do you think they intend to do it?"

"I suspect that this is so. This way, all four of my wives get to go away to the lodge for unclean women together and leave me here to take care of myself."

"But how can they make the unclean time change?"

"They are all *witches,*" he said, glaring at me. Then he burst into laughter and shook his head. "Perhaps not. But I do know that while they should be chanting and praying to cleanse themselves out there in that lodge, they are instead making jokes and telling stories and laughing. I have heard them from far away, cackling like a bunch of grackles. I can hear things from farther away than anyone else because of the Thunderbird power."

I reached for the stone metate and the pestle that went with it—things I had brought to Burnt Belly from New Mexico. I began grinding the roots of the cranesbill geraniums into a powder. "Does the power of the Thunderbird also show you how to make your voice sound as if it is coming from a place other than your mouth?"

Burnt Belly glanced up at me briefly, as if to warn me. "I learned that from the thunder."

"How?"

"What do you hear when you listen to thunder?"

I shrugged. "A rumble. Sometimes a loud blast."

"You are not really listening. There are voices in the thunder. Perhaps a person must be struck by lightning to hear the voices. I would not recommend that you try that."

"What do the voices say?"

"Many things. But your question was about the way my voice speaks where I want it to. The voices in the thunder taught me this. You can learn it, too."

I looked up from my herbalist's chores. "How?"

"A noise is not just a noise. A sound is like a person with a false heart. It behaves one way in one place, and another way in different surroundings. I can cast my voice off a stone bluff, but not off the moist dirt at my feet. The stone bluff listens and repeats what it has heard immediately, like a gossiping woman. Mother Earth is wiser. She just listens. Hard things make sounds echo. If they are far away the echo comes after my voice. If they are close, there is still an echo, but it comes almost at the same time as my voice. So, listen to the objects around you. Touch them. If they are solid and slick, they will throw your voice for you. It takes practice and much thought, but you can learn it. Like most magic, there is really no secret to it at all"

"I win practice it."

"Do not dwell on it. It is just a trick."

I worked with the mortar and pestle until I felt a pang of hunger. "We should go to my lodge so my wife can cook some fresh meat for us," I suggested. "I killed a fat squirrel yesterday, and a rabbit the day before. She will make a stew for us."

"Good," he replied. "Your wife is a good wife. I think she is afraid of me."

"Only a little. She likes you, grandfather."

"I like her, too. She is Cheyenne, and that is good. The Cheyennes are good people, and their women are pretty. When I was a boy, we were at war with the Cheyennes. It is better now that we are allies. Come, we will see how a Cheyenne woman makes stew."

Burnt Belly dropped his herbs, rose, and drew his favorite buffalo robe around his shoulders for the short walk to my lodge. When we got there, he held me back and pointed to the smoke hole of my tipi. "Those lodge poles are hard and polished. They will cast your words down into the lodge if you will your voice to go there."

I tried to somehow focus my voice in one direction, saying, "Your husband is home with Grandfather Burnt Belly."

No one responded.

"Westerly!" I said, louder. "I am home." There was no answer. "She is not here."

We stepped inside and found the fire burned down to a few coals. I saw a sheet of paper at my feet and picked it up to read Westerly's handwriting on it. I had to laugh.

"What does it say?" the shaman asked.

"It says, 'Husband . . . I have gone to the lodge for unclean women.' "

Burnt Belly grinned and said, "Witches! Now we must do our own cooking."

He took the note from me and looked at it as I threw some small sticks on the coals. He smelled it, and held it to his ear for some time.

"I hear voices in thunder," he said. "But you . . . You hear voices from a thing that makes no noise at all." He shook the missive at me. "*This* is magic."

After a time, Peta Nocona's village came to camp near Adobe Walls, bringing young Quanah. They located some distance down the river so as not to crowd our horse herd with their own, for grass was growing scarce. I rode to their village one day and found Peta Nocona himself making arrow points from a barrel hoop with a file. I noticed an open gash on his upper arm. An arrow wound, he said, received in a fight with some Utes in the mountains.

"You should go see Burnt Belly about that," I suggested.

"I make my own medicine," he said. Peta—once a powerful force among the Nokoni Comanches—had grown sullen since his wife, Nadua, had been recaptured by whites at the battle of Pease River and forced to adopt her old identity of Cynthia Ann Parker. He never again attacked a Texas settlement, and seemed to have lost his interest in leading his people. He had not taken a wife to replace Nadua.

I left Peta and sought out Quanah. As soon as he saw me, he said, "I have heard a story that you killed a white buffalo, uncle." He used the term of respect when he addressed me now, though I was not really his uncle.

"It is true."

He smiled, his eyes glinting with anticipation. "You must tell me."

So I repeated, once again, the tale of my famous hunt to my young friend who called me "uncle." Life was good that winter. Very good for a while. But very good things, like very bad things, never last very long.

THIRTY-NINE

The Moon of Hunger rose on a bleak and leafless world. Ice and snow invaded the Crossing on the Canadian, draping the old Adobe Walls with a lacework of white. It seemed everything living and edible had gone into hibernation on another continent. Since the big hunt where I bagged the white buffalo, the great herds had drifted on and splintered into many far-ranging bunches of skittish animals. Spring seemed years away, and the last morsels of dried meat and pemmican had disappeared. The hunters could not even locate a stray antelope or deer. This was called "the Time When Babies Cry for Food."

We killed and butchered the poorest horses first. No one wanted to even think of eating the better horses, and we hoped it would not come to that. Horses would be needed to move when the weather broke. Some wealthy families owned many surplus horses, but most claimed no more than half a dozen mounts. A Comanche without a horse was something less than a True Human. Still, it was better to be poor and afoot than dead of starvation, so the promising yearlings began to fall to the arrow and the knife. Only the finest horses were kept alive on cottonwood bark that the young boys had to strip from the trees in the bitter cold.

A council was called in the cruel clutches of a blizzard. The people were restless and angry. News from the north had filtered down. It was said that the raiding Cheyennes and Arapahos had been given gifts by Owl Man—William Bent—to settle them down. Little Bluff, the old Kiowa chief closely allied with our band of Comanches for so many years, stood and spoke at this council, his voice stern, his hands translating his Kiowa words to sign talk.

"For many moons we have raided the *tejanos* and left the Americans alone. Our hunters have watched the wagons go by on the trails to the north of here, and have not bothered them. Our scouts have seen the tracks left by bluecoats, but have not followed them to hunt scalps or count coups. Now, while we starve, the Cheyennes and Arapahos are getting gifts and rations of beef from the Americans because they *have* attacked white wagons and killed white herders. It is time to end the starvation of our people and do what the nations to the north do to get beef. It is time to make war on the whites. Not just the *tejanos. All* whites!"

The younger warriors spoke in time, most of them agreeing with Little Bluff. When my chance came to speak, I rose, and defended my mentor, William Bent. "Who has seen Owl Man give rations to Cheyennes who have been raiding?" No one spoke or raised a hand. "I have seen him provide food many times for his people. He is adopted Cheyenne. But would he give his people food and gifts as a reward for raiding? I know Owl Man, and I know that he would not. Two winters ago, Owl Man gave rations to a band of Cheyennes who had had a fight with a white hunter who killed buffalo only for the hides. It was proven that the white hunter shot at the Cheyennes first, wounding one of them, and so they were only protecting themselves. This hunter was killed in the fight. These Cheyennes were given food because they were hungry and they had come to the Cheyenne agency to ask Owl Man for rations. They were not given food for being bad. I was there with Owl Man when this thing happened. I know what I am talking about. The story has been told too many times by those who were not there, and the truth has been told right out of it. It is not a good idea to attack the wagons or villages of the Americans. To do so would not bring us rations of beef. It would bring war parties of bluecoats to our country in numbers never seen before. When this blizzard breaks, we must move to better hunting grounds or raid for more horses and cattle in Texas. We must not take handouts from Americans. War with them is not the best way. I have spoken."

My opinion was not popular with everyone. Some young warriors, when they had their turn to speak, reminded the council that my blood was white, and that my wife was Cheyenne. But old Shaved Head, speaking now as a peace chief, rose to my defense, scolding the young warriors for criticizing me.

"Plenty Man is my grandson. He is pure *Noomah.* Many times his counsel has saved us from trouble with whites. He moves among the whites as easily as he moves among True Humans, but his heart is always *Noomah.* His bravery shall not be questioned, nor should his wisdom. He has said many times that if war comes with bluecoats or *tejanos,* he will protect his Comanche family. If we raid American wagons, it will not fill our stomachs with food. The spirits test us every winter, during the Hunger Moon, and this winter is no different. Listen to Plenty Man. He is the slayer of the white buffalo whose robe even now protects our village and will bring meat to those who have faith in spirit medicine. We must hunt and raid to the south, and leave the Americans alone. I have spoken."

At this point, Quanah rose from the outer ring of young men. "I am riding tomorrow," he said. Every face in the big lodge turned to look at the brash young warrior who had been mourning his father's death for almost two moons, for the wound Peta had received in the fight with Utes had festered and killed him. "I will raid far to the south. There will be many horses and cattle. We will find game. I have sent prayers to the Great Mystery on the smoke of green cedar. I have had a vision. I do not fear this blizzard. My spirit powers will find shelter for all who follow me. Anyone brave enough to ride with me tomorrow will share in the take and go hungry no more. I have spoken."

Now Chief Little Bluff rose again, chuckling at Quanah's swagger. "The young men are brave and reckless. I am old, and careful. I would rather die in battle than freeze to death with an empty stomach. So I will starve through this blizzard in this camp, but when the snows have ended, I will starve no more. I will lead all who wish to teach the Americans a lesson. For many years I have tried to get along with white men. It is like trying to reason with the snowflakes in that blizzard out there. But no more. No longer will they scatter our game and cross our country without paying. Now is the time, while they are at war with one another in the east. Now is the time to strike and take our country back! I have spoken."

After the council, a few restless young Comanche men agreed to brave the blizzard and go south with Quanah, while most of the Kiowa warriors embraced Little Bluff's philosophy. The people of Kills Something's band were divided. Some vowed to follow Little Bluff. Others leaned toward the advice of Shaved Head and me. One thing seemed clear to me. Trouble was as sure to come as the changing of the moons. War fever had infected even our remote outpost on the Canadian.

The blizzard and the starvation did end, of course. A large herd of buffalo was located by scouts and Kills Something's people moved way out onto the Llano Estacado to hunt and feast. Westerly and I went along and enjoyed the new season of prosperity. Men went down to the Texas settlements, and even into Mexico, and returned with horses and captives. Quanah's party, though only five strong, enjoyed tremendous success, helping to build Quanah's reputation. As spring came on, the people broke into smaller camps and scattered across the plains all along the great escarpment known as the Caprock—a continuous uplift stretching hundreds of miles and sculpted by eons of erosion into innumerable canyons. They knew that if they were attacked here by Texans, they could ascend the escarpment and flee onto the vast high plains where the Texans still feared to ride.

The spring and summer was a good one for Kills Something's people, though I knew Little Bluff and his Kiowa and Comanche followers were stirring up trouble to the north, raiding wagon trains on the Santa Fe Trail, attacking camps and ranches, and even riding into lonely New Mexican villages to kill and steal. I feared this would bring retribution down on all of us. Through Comanche travelers, we also heard of soldiers attacking Cheyenne, Arapaho, and Sioux camps for reasons no one could explain. We even heard that the old Cheyenne chief Lean Bear, a longtime friend of whites, had been murdered by soldiers without warning or reason. In retaliation, some Cheyenne warriors—especially the Dog Soldiers—had raided ranches and stagecoach stations, killing and taking captives and loot. All this worried Westerly, for most of her family still lived out on the plains with the roving Cheyennes.

When the grass got high enough to provide ample graze, Westerly and I gathered a large herd of horses we had acquired in trade, and rode back to Adobe Walls to rendezvous with John Prowers and his wife, Amache, who was, of course, Westerly's sister. Kills Something sent four young men to escort us and help us with the horses. We found John and Amache already in camp, waiting for us. They had raised a fine Cheyenne lodge just outside of Adobe Walls. Inside the walls, John had constructed a makeshift corral for his horses, and a fortification of sorts, should some hostile party attack, be it Pawnee, Apache, or a renegade band of Rebel deserters.

Westerly immediately went off with her sister, whom she had not seen in months. John and I had the chance to converse in the shade of a brush arbor he had raised inside the adobe walls, for the spring days had begun to get very warm around high noon, and the shade was welcome. He had built the arbor in a place where the southern breeze could snake through the ruins of Fort Adobe, making the place quite comfortable. I sat on a small keg of black powder, leaned against the adobe wall, and whittled on a set of bois d'arc stake pins I was making to keep the best of the horses safe from theft during our coming trip to William's stockade. John lounged across the ground in the shade of the arbor. He always seemed most comfortable sprawled out on the earth herself.

"Nobody thought Kit could do it," he was saying. "Everybody thought the Navahos were untouchable up in those canyons. Kit came at them from the west—out of a new fort they built in Arizona country, called Fort Canby, after you-know-who. Kit had orders to kill any braves he found on sight—like you and him did with the Mescaleros."

I winced a little at the memory, but John did not notice.

"A lot of the same men you fought with at Valverde are still with ol' Kit. They were all eager to see Canyon de Chelly and, by God, they did. They rode into that canyon and took to huntin' Indians. Killed a few. Captured some women and children. A couple of squaws were killed, I think, by accident or something. But the main thing was, Kit found their crops. He had his boys chop down three thousand peach trees up in one of those side canyons. Three thousand! And they had squash, and pumpkins, and beans. There was a cornfield in there that Kit told me took three hundred men all day to destroy."

"You've talked to Kit yourself?" I set aside a finished stake pin, and picked up another bois d'arc stob to whittle on.

John nodded. "Saw him in Santa Fe last February. He told me all about it. Said destroying those crops hit the Navahos harder than a thousand bullets could have hit 'em. But that was only the start. The Navahos fought back. They attacked supply trains and killed or wounded some teamsters and enlisted men on escort duty. They even ran off a herd of mules from Fort Canby, right under Kit's nose. That got General Carleton plenty mad back in Santa Fe, and he sent orders to Kit to stop coddling the Navahos and go into Canyon de Chelly and roust 'em."

"I've heard some fantastic tales about that canyon."

"Kit said it beats just about all he's ever seen. The walls go up a thousand or fifteen hundred feet. There's water in hidden places up the side canyons. Said there's regular stone houses two and three stories high built into the cliffs. Some places the main canyon's miles wide, but there's other places in the side canyons where a man has to turn sideways to slip through. The Navahos would shoot down from those cliffs and roll boulders down, too. In fifty-eight, Colonel Miles scouted the entrance and said no command should ever enter it. But Kit had orders to do just that."

"I don't guess General Carleton cared to lead the campaign himself."

John chuckled. "No, he left it to Kit. But you know how cautious Kit is. He thought it out and planned. He waited till it snowed, knowing the Indians would be near starving by then. He set up a supply camp at the west canyon entrance and sent out parties to explore, kill warriors, capture women and children, and destroy any more food they could find."

"Ruthless business," I grumbled. I didn't like the sound of it at all. Kit destroying crops? Starving Navaho children in the middle of winter? This was the man who always asked what was *right*.

"Kit said it was the only way to stop the Navaho raids." John sat up suddenly, and drew two ragged lines, roughly parallel, in the loose dirt—a crude map of Canyon de Chelly. With his trigger finger, he made a point at the west end. "After Kit set up his camp at the west entrance to the canyon, here, he sent Captain Pfeiffer way around to the east entrance of the canyon." He scraped a half-circle in the dirt that went far to the south and entered the east opening between the lines. "Pfeiffer fought his way through first—east to west—and turned up at Kit's supply camp with prisoners and a few scalps. Well, that ended the mystery as to whether or not a company of soldiers could make it through the canyon. Took all the fight out of the Indians, and Kit's boys started to mop up. Next thing you know, Navahos were coming into Fort Canby to surrender by the hundreds. There was more than three thousand of 'em before it was all over." He dusted his hands and lay back down on the ground, propped up on one elbow.

"What did they do with all those prisoners?"

"They marched 'em to the Bosque Redondo, where the Mescaleros were being held."

"That's a long march."

"It was bad, too. The army hadn't planned rations for that many prisoners. A lot of those Navahos took sick and died—old folks; children. And more died when they got to the Bosque. Some kind of fever. They were supposed to be growing their own food there, but worms and grasshoppers had eaten all the crops and Indians starved by the scores. That wasn't Kit's fault. He was just following orders and the army didn't provide him with the food he was supposed to have for those poor savages."

I shook my head. The fact that I had resigned as Kit's scout for his Indian wars was but little comfort when I thought of Navaho children dying
far from their canyon homes in a desolate prison camp. "I've caught wind
of trouble in Cheyenne and Arapaho country, too. What have you heard?"

Now John's mood darkened, for this business struck closer to his
home in Boggsville. "The army ordered troops to go out on the plains, find
some Indians, and attack them. Nobody really knows why. Rumors of
raids, I guess. I heard old Chief Lean Bear rode out to parley with Lieutenant Eayre and was fired upon not twenty paces from the troops. He died
wearing the peace medal President Lincoln had given him in Washington."

I remembered that chilling day in New Mexico, when Paddy Graydon
fired on Manuelito's people, and my knife blade got stuck suddenly in the
stake pin I whittled.

"They say Lieutenant Eayre's detachment would have been clean
wiped out if old Chief Black Kettle hadn't prevented the warriors from
slaughtering them. Eayre only had about a hundred men, and there were
five or six hundred Cheyenne and Arapaho warriors camped nearby that
Eayre didn't know about. William went out there and calmed things down.
His boy George was there, too."

"And Charles?"

"Charles didn't show himself. He's out there running wild somewhere. Did you hear about Satank?"

"Nothing since he left our camp after the big buffalo hunt last fall."

"A couple of months ago, he rode up to Fort Larned to talk to the officers. Some excitable young sentry pulled a gun on him, and Satank shot an
arrow through the boy before he could even fire. Killed him. The bugler
started blowing, so Satank's people ran off the horse herd so the soldiers
couldn't follow."

"Oh, no. Now Satank's a marked man, and he sometimes camps with
us."

"It gets worse," John said. "The army's building a new fort on the
Canadian at the mouth of the Conchas."

"That's on the old Comanche Trail to the Llano Estacado."

"That's no accident. The rumor is that General Carleton is going to
send Kit out here to punish the Kiowas and Comanches for raiding."

I tipped my head back and laughed.

"What's funny about that?"

"Carleton thinks he can send a single regiment out here to do battle with the Kiowas *and* the Comanches? That's funny, John. But it won't be funny if it actually happens."

"Well, Kit rounded up more than three thousand Navahos in the last campaign, didn't he? And with just a few hundred soldiers."

"The Kiowas and Comanches don't have any peach orchards to chop down. They don't live in little stone houses up in some canyon. The army will be lucky to even find any Kiowas or Comanches to do battle with, and if they do, they better be ready for an entirely different kind of campaign."

"You know Kit," John said. "He's savvy to the ways of these wild Indians."

"If I know Kit the way I think I do, he'll have the good sense to resign if he's ordered into Comancheria."

John seemed confused by my stance on this subject. "I thought you and Kit were pals."

I whittled a couple of strokes on the stake pin. "Kit taught me to always ask myself one question. *Is this right?* And it's not right for the army to charge in here and punish a bunch of Indians when they don't know if they're guilty of raiding or not."

"They *have* been raidin', Orn'ry. You know that."

"Some of them have. But you can't blame the whole tribe for the actions of a few young hotheads out to make names for themselves."

"Well, the chiefs have got to start controlling their hotheads, or there's gonna be a war."

"Somebody needs to tell them that."

"Why don't you?"

"Believe me, I have, John, but these Indians know I'm not the Big Captain. If General Carleton wants to avoid an Indian war the likes of which the army has never seen, he better have some respect for the Comanche and Kiowa leadership, show his face, and have some talks."

"General Carleton doesn't have much use for smokin' the peace pipe with Indians."

"No, he'd rather send a regiment out here to force them out of their own country and onto some death trap of a prison camp. And *that's not right.* Not only that, it's not possible. You're talking about battling the best light cavalry the world has ever seen on their own ground, and their tactics are like no cavalry maneuvers ever taught at West Point. Don't forget where you are, John. This is Comanche country, paid for in blood generations before we were born. They'll defend it as sure as you'd defend your country if somebody invaded it. What if I moved into your neighborhood and spread a bunch of damned diseases among your children and then scattered your game off until you were starving, then sent soldiers in to attack you?"

John stood, dusted himself off, and walked to the edge of the adobe walls, obviously agitated. He looked out at the Cheyenne tipi his wife had raised. We both heard the laughter of Westerly and Amache coming from inside. He shook his head and turned back to me. "You're my brother-in-law, Orn'ry, and to me that means as much as you being a blood brother. I guess we've married ourselves into a mess with our squaw wives, but they're Cheyenne, not Comanche. Not Kiowa."

"I was adopted Comanche before I ever met you, John. Before I ever met Westerly. Anyway, if the army goes after the Comanches and Kiowas, who do you think will be next?"

John nodded and looked at the ground. He knew I was referring to the Cheyenne and Arapaho problem. "I hope it doesn't come to that."

"There are men out here on the frontier who would rather make their reputations skirmishing with Indians than marching straight into battalions of Rebels. But they don't know what they're getting into. They don't have the proper respect for the Plains Indians as fighters. Kit's successes are deceptive. The Mescaleros were small in number. The Navahos were dependent on their crops. These roaming plains tribes will prove far more difficult to conquer. It can't be done in one winter's time. It would take years. Maybe decades."

"What if Kit *does* come, Orn'ry? What are you going to do?"

I tossed aside the stake I had whittled on a bit too much. "I don't know."

"You know he'll want you to guide—scout for him."

"I've thought of that."

"What if he asks you?"

I picked up another bois d'arc stick, my sharp blade slicing through the bark to the bright orange-yellow heartwood. "I'll guide a peace delegation out here to negotiate a treaty. But I won't lead armed troops to attack my own people."

John looked at the toe of his boot. He did not reply. He stood there in the sun for a moment, then kicked at a piece of an old adobe brick and returned to the shade of the brush arbor. His body folded like a marionette whose strings had been cut, and then stretched out once again across the ground. He pulled his hat over his eyes. For a long while he said nothing. I thought he had gone to sleep to the rhythm of my knife blade on the wooden stake pin I was fashioning.

"You'll never guess what I went and did," he said, pulling his hat aside to grin at me.

"You didn't soil your britches, did you?"

He laughed hard. "No, I bought a hundred head of cows at Westport and drove them all the way across the plains to Boggsville. Cost me near every spare dollar I had. They fared the winter better than the sheep. Coyotes caught a couple of cows down when they were calving and killed 'em. Lost a calf to a wolf, and one to a lion, but I still came out with a decent calf crop."

"Sounds like a risky investment."

"It is. But that high plains prairie grass sure puts the weight on them beeves come springtime. If we come out of all this Indian trouble, Orn'ry, I might just make a rancher. I'm going to buy another fifty or so cows when we sell the horses."

"Are you looking for investors?"

"You want in?"

"Sure. I haven't got much use for cash money. I'll throw in with you."

John smiled and lay back with his fingers intertwined behind his head.

"You'll never guess what *I* went and did," I said.

"What?"

"Have you ever seen a white buffalo?"

John scoffed. "That's a tall tale. I don't think they even exist."

I laughed, and peeled away another curl of wood with my blade. "Have I got a story to tell you . . ."

FORTY

I rode my old paint stallion, Major, into the herd of Missouri shorthorn cows and their half-grown calves. John Prowers had herded the shorthorns from Missouri. The cows made way for Major, allowing me to push through the herd with my lariat ready in my right hand. I was looking for late calves that had been born after the spring roundup and had not yet been maimed with John Prowers's brand and ear mark.

Looking over the backs of the cows, I finally spotted the last of the unmarked calves—his long, notchless ears betraying him. I slipped into position, my loop hanging from my palm. The calf was not even aware of me yet, so I was able to approach his right flank. The cows parted, and I whistled to spook the target to my right. His ears swiveled. He saw me, and trotted away. My loop whirled twice—vertically to my side, rather than horizontally overhead as when roping a beef by the head. The rawhide noose flipped under the calf's belly, and stood on edge in front of his hind legs for a second. Before the stiff rawhide loop could collapse, the calf stepped into it and I jerked slack. Taking two wraps on the saddle horn, I reined Major away quickly to tighten the loop on the calf's hind ankles before he could kick it loose. I dragged him away by the heels, scared and bawling.

I rode between Westerly and Amache to get to the branding fire. They, along with Rumalda Boggs, William Bent, William's daughter, Mary, and her husband, R. M. Moore, had been holding the herd loosely bunched so I could heel-rope the "slicks" as Tom Boggs called the unmarked calves. We had gathered this herd on the south bank of the Arkansas, across from the site of Bent's Old Fort—Fort William, as the trappers sometimes called it. As my pony dragged the calf from the herd to the fire, I could look across the river and gaze upon the place where once great adobe walls had towered, like those of a castle. It was all gone now, but my memory could still see it. Just below our herd was the river ford where an Apache arrow had once hissed through the air and imbedded itself in my shoulder blade. The scar itched as I remembered.

When I approached the fire, John Prowers grabbed the tail of the calf, and Charlie Rict grabbed the rope leading to my saddle horn. By pulling in opposite directions, they flipped the two-hundred-pound victim onto his right side. Charlie Rict knelt on the frightened calf's neck and shoulder and pulled up on the left foreleg to hold the beast flat. At the same time, John sat on the ground behind the calf, forced the right hind leg forward with his boot and pulled the other hind leg back with his hands, tossing my loop aside as he did so.

With the squirming bull calf constrained, Robert Bent applied the hot iron on the shoulder, pulling the brand away as the calf thrashed in pain, so the mark wouldn't smear, then reapplying the glowing brand. The odor of burning hair and flesh assaulted my nostrils the way the poor beast's bellowing belabored my ears, but this was business and the calf had to be claimed. Now Tom Boggs moved in with a sharp knife to crop the left ear and notch the right, carelessly tossing the pieces he had cut away to be scavenged by coyotes later. Next, he moved toward the testicles with the bloody blade.

"Don't cut this one," John said. "I'm keeping him." John nodded at Charlie Rict and they both released the calf at the same time. As John turned loose the calf's hind legs, the two-hundred-pound bull thanked him by kicking him hard in the chest as he sprang from the ground. Tom Boggs laughed—he could tell that John had not been seriously injured. I chuckled along as I coiled my reata.

"You little son of a bitch!" John yelled as he stood, rubbing his chest. "After all I've done for you!"

"Could have been worse," Tom said. "Could have been your teeth."

"Could have been worse for him. Could have been his balls." He looked into his shirt where the hooves had skinned him. "We need to go down to Maxwell's Ranch and steal us some Mexicans for this kind of work."

"We've got Orn'ry, there. He ropes as good as any Mexican Maxwell's got."

"He don't count. He's usually out there skinning white buffalos and such. We need some *permanent* Mexicans around here. And something other than these shorthorns for them to gather."

"They look good," Tom said. "They've fared better than I ever thought an American beef would."

John shook his head. "When the war's over, I'm gonna find me some Kurries."

"Some what?" Robert Bent said.

"Kurry cattle, from Ireland," I explained.

John gestured at me. "Maybe some Black Angus from Scotland." I had suggested the possibility of importing breeds that thrived in the Highlands of the British Isles, hoping their characteristics might prove equally well suited to life on the high plains. My brother-in-law liked the idea.

"I'm betting the Herefords will do as well as any," I said.

"Well, we'll see in good time."

The men kicked some dirt onto the coals of the branding fire and got mounted. We had been out three days, gathering these cattle and camping on the plains at night. I had spared Major any of the hard chasing and had only used him to rope and drag calves. He was fourteen years old now, still sound, and vastly experienced in many types of human enterprises. He really seemed to enjoy this business of herding cattle, and would watch a herd as if eager for some half-wild brute to just try breaking free.

By whistling and shouting, we started our branded cattle moving lazily toward William's stockade, but they seemed in no hurry to get there, and daylight would not wait on our arrival. Once there, we would pen the herd and rest easy for a night. Tomorrow we would sort the cattle, turning the keepers loose on the open range, and herding the market beeves to Fort Lyon. There, the army would buy most of them to feed to soldiers, and the Indian agency would purchase the rest to issue as rations to friendly Indians.

So with three days' worth of dirt and sweat clinging to us, we pushed the cattle homeward, content with our success. I was wishing the beeves would move along a little faster when I heard John Prowers shout back at me from the front of the herd: "Orn'ry, ride that paint up here and give 'em something to look at."

Major had a wide white butt that would attract the attention of the dumb beasts, give them something on which to focus, and encourage them to follow. As the sun sank behind us and my stomach started to growl, I loped forward along the left flank of the herd.

It was then that I happened to spot a large group of riders on a ridge ahead and to the left of us. I slowed to a walk as I caught up to Westerly, who had been tending the flank in front of me. "Do you see them?" I asked.

"Yes, I just noticed them."

"Can you tell who they might be?"

"Indians wouldn't show themselves out in the open that way."

"They must be white."

"Soldiers?"

"That would be my guess. I'm going to ask John if he wants me to ride ahead to see about them."

"Be careful."

I smiled and loped Major forward to lead the herd and to talk with John. I pointed out the riders. He hadn't seen them yet, for he had been concentrating on getting the herd to follow him. We contemplated who the horsemen might be for a while. We decided to continue on our way, which would take us about a mile to the south of the party on the hill. At twenty-six, John was ten years younger than me, but these were mostly his cattle, so I considered him in charge of this operation. Besides, he had years of experience on the frontier working for William Bent, and typically made good decisions.

We rode for almost half an hour, the herd assuming a proper pace, when we noticed some riders coming at us at a canter from the larger party. As they neared, I noticed that the leader of the party rode head and shoulders above his companions—a big man on a huge horse. The glint of metal on his blue tunic identified him as an officer of the U.S. Army. The party rode toward a point in front of our herd, as if they meant to halt our progress.

"You want me to ride out and meet them, John?"

"Let's both go." He signaled for William and R. M. to take our places on the point. The two of us loped to meet the approaching men. As we came nearer, I recognized the army officer.

"That's John Chivington."

My brother-in-law answered with a groan.

John M. Chivington, the Fighting Parson, the self-proclaimed hero of Glorieta Pass, had gone on to achieve the rank of colonel, and now commanded the Colorado volunteers. I knew all this from newspapers and word of mouth. His arrogance and ambition, I had been told, had grown beyond his elevation in rank.

We watched as the party of eleven riders slowed, engulfed by the dust they had kicked up. I knew these men were probably from the Third Colorado Cavalry—the "Hundred-Dazers" as they were called, for most had recently signed on for one-hundred-day enlistments, as if the Indian problem could be solved in a single season. They looked as tough as any bunch of men I had ever seen—most were out-of-work miners and bullwhackers and such. Not one wore a uniform. They dressed in store-bought or handmade garb ranging from buckskins to broadcloth. None had been shaved or shorn in weeks. Their weaponry were plentiful and plainly displayed.

John raised his hand as a greeting.

"Halt there!" Chivington shouted, though we had already stopped to wait for him.

"Hello, Colonel Chivington," John said.

"Do I know you?" His soldiers made a half-circle around us.

"We met just the once, down at William Bent's Stockade."

"Can't say as I remember." The booming projection of his voice strained my ear. He looked at me. "But I remember you, all right," he said, smiling uncomfortably. Chivington had done some boasting about Glorieta Pass, but he never voluntarily admitted that he had fought the whole battle from the safety of the bluff overlooking the Texas supply camp. He knew that I knew. "Mr. Green?"

"Greenwood."

"Of course. I see you made it safely off Glorieta Mesa."

"Yes, sir."

"What are you men doing out here?"

John glanced at me and answered by jutting his thumb behind him toward the herd.

"I can see cattle. Where are you going with them?"

"Bent's Stockade."

"Why?"

John sighed. He clearly did not like being interrogated. "I have a contract to supply beef to Fort Lyon."

The colonel leaned back in his saddle and smiled. "Well, praise the Lord. That's mighty fine. You boys seen any Indians?"

We shook our heads.

"Indian sign?"

"Nope," John said.

"You'd better watch your scalps out here."

"We're on good terms with the Indians."

Chivington chuckled, and few of his men joined him. "The only Indian on good terms with me is one with a bullet through his skull. Why aren't you men riding with us? Are you Rebel sympathizers as well as Indian lovers?"

"I haven't seen any Rebels around here to sympathize with," John replied.

"No, because me and my boys from the First turned them back at Glorieta Pass." Chivington offered an obligatory gesture in my direction, as if swatting a fly away. "Greenwood, here, helped."

All this time, the herd had been coming up behind us, and now Chivington got a closer look at our wrangling crew. "What in the name of . . . Those are Indians!"

"That's my wife," John said, his voice a plain warning. He pointed toward Amache.

I pointed toward Westerly. "And mine."

Chivington grunted and spat on the ground. "Squaw men. Apparently you haven't heard."

"Heard what?" John demanded.

"By order of Governor Evans and General Blunt all Indians who don't want to be considered hostile—and as such treated as enemies—must report to the Sand Creek reservation."

"I'll take that under advisement," John said.

"I highly recommend that you do more than take it under advisement. If you are found harboring hostiles, you'll be arrested."

"What authority do you have to arrest me for living in my own house with my own wife?"

Chivington tapped the eagle insignia on his shoulder. "This authority. If your wife is Indian, she must report to the reservation."

Now John was getting angry. He had lived on these ranges much longer than the colonel and didn't appreciate being bossed around in his own home country. "That's a load of shit, Colonel. My wife lives with me, and you will pay hell arresting me for that. I'll have a letter to the governor penned before my lamp goes out tonight, and we will just see about your authority."

"Easy, John," I said under my breath. I looked back toward the herd and saw William Bent trotting toward us. This gave me some relief, for no one was more highly respected than William in the whole Arkansas River Valley, and he had a knack for calming tense situations.

"Yes, you'd better listen to your friend and go easy, Mr. Powers."

"That's *Prowers*."

"I don't care what your name is."

Before John could reply, William Bent rode within earshot and said, "Hello, Colonel. Is there any trouble?"

Chivington recognized William and seemed to cough up a great deal of the sand he had had in his craw. "There will be, if these squaw men don't send their Indian wives to the reservation. Governor Evans ordered it."

William looked over the faces of the cavalry men with his calm gray eyes. "Well, now, Colonel, my wife is Cheyenne, too, you know." He chuckled a little. "I guess you could say I'm an old Indian fighter—my wife's an old Indian."

The Hundred-Dazers laughed.

"But she's no threat to anybody other than me. Same can be said of these boys' wives. I promise you we'll take their war axes away from them and give them washboards."

Again, the volunteers chuckled.

Chivington mustered his gall. "Rules are rules. Next time we pass by your stockade, all the Indians had better have reported to the reservation given to them in the treaty of 1861. I'd escort them there now, but I've got worse hostiles to hunt."

William did not flinch. "I'll take it up with Major Anthony at the fort when we deliver the cattle."

Again, Chivington tapped his shoulder. "I outrank Major Anthony."

"You've got fancier jewelry on your shoulder—I'll grant you that—but Major Anthony is regular army. I'm sure he'll grant exceptions to the rules."

"I wouldn't chance it, but it's up to you. We can deal with it next time we meet. For now I'm ordering you to send all Indians on your property to the reservation. I don't care who they're married to or by what kind of heathen ceremony."

William shrugged—a marvelously insolent gesture of complete unconcern.

"Now, since those are army beeves, I'll take one for my boys."

"The hell you will," John said. "It doesn't work that way. I supply the fort. The fort supplies you."

"I'm cutting out the middle man." He grinned and turned to the man at his right. "Sergeant, pick a fat one."

The un-uniformed sergeant smiled and spurred his mount, but John cut him off. "You don't pick them, I do!" he said. "These cattle are private property. I pick the ones I choose to sell to the army and it damned sure won't be the fattest. I'm trying to build a herd here."

"There's a war on," Chivington said, his sanctimonious voice a condemnation. "Soldiers must eat." He gestured to his sergeant again, but William joined John in blocking the way.

"Hold on, now!" William shouted. "We can work this out! Colonel, I know you need meat for your men, but Mr. Prowers needs compensation for his investment. He's gone to a great deal of trouble and expense to establish this herd here so that the army can feed its troops. Now, if you'll produce a voucher, I'm sure we can cut out one of the market steers for you. There's one that's been limping along behind and slowing us down anyway, John. I'll see to it that Colonel Chivington's voucher is honored at Fort Lyon if you and Mr. Greenwood will go cut that steer from the herd."

John sighed, but offered no complaint.

Chivington frowned. "Sergeant, ride back and tell the lieutenant to write me out a voucher for one beef."

William looked at me and John. "Well, go on," he ordered, glancing toward the sun, "the day's wasting."

By the time we got the steer away from the rest of the herd, William had the voucher in his hand and the conflict seemed to have been resolved. Then Chivington led his men in a cavalry charge on that lame steer and began shooting at it just as they passed by the left flank of our herd. The shorthorns bolted and broke past the flank riders on the right. They ran for almost four miles before we could overtake them and turn the miniature stampede. I have never in my life heard such cussing as when John Prowers expressed his opinion of the infuriating Colonel Chivington through the settling dust of the Colorado high plains.

FORTY-ONE

The letter arrived at Boggsville on September 3, 1864. My heart plunged as if into a cavern when I touched it—even before I saw the handwriting on the sealed envelope. You must remember that Burnt Belly had taught me to hear the voices of living things, and the paper in my hand had once been part of a tree, with perhaps some wool or cotton fibers added to it—all materials from plants or animals that even through the transmogrification of the pulp mill could still communicate feeling to me. This missive portended ominous doings.

I took the letter from the army private who had delivered it from Fort Lyon, and turned it over to see Kit's handwriting. I had to smile a little, even through my dread of what intelligence Kit's hand might impart. He had learned his letters with remarkable fluidity for one who had started so late in life to read and write. I leaned on the handle of the hoe I had been using to weed my vegetable garden against the almost-varmint-proof, rawhide-and-picket fence I had built around the garden patch, and took the envelope in both hands.

"There's lunch up at the trading post," I said to the courier, pointing the way for him. He smiled and rode toward the towering cottonwoods of Boggsville.

I tore open the wax-sealed envelope and removed a single sheaf of parchment—Kit's personal stationery as opposed to government stock. The letter written upon it was also in Kit's own hand, lending the impression that this was a plea too personal to communicate through an adjutant.

Fort Sumner, N. Mex. Awgus 22, 1864

Honoré Greenwood, Esq.

Mr. Greenwood:

Things are not awl good here. The crops did not make on ac-count of worms and bugs. Awl the fire wood has got burnt and the Indians dig roots to cook weevily korn. They dont cook it good enuff and it makes them sik as dawgs. But thare are other matters for me to attin to now and ergently I ask yore help.

About Awgus 10, some Comanchies attackt lower Cimarron Springs, kilt five white men and run off oxin from a waggen train. Gen. Carleton has got awl het up about it and wants the Indians punisht. I fear a campane aginst the Comanchies is upon us. I will need yore advise and assistans. Will you come to Santa Fe upon gitting this letter?

I remane, your faithful frend and companyon,
Col. C. Carson, 1st N.M. Vols.

P S I am awful sorry for my bad spellin

A moment of panic overwhelmed me and I wondered why I had not faced up to this impending reality before now. The news of the Cimarron Springs killings had reached Boggsville nineteen days ago, giving me plenty of time to react. Yet I had failed to do anything about it. I should have prepared. I should not have been hoeing a goddamn fenced-in garden where a letter from Kit might find me. I should have been so deep inside the middle of Comancheria, or so far out on the plains among Westerly's people, that no written plea could ever have fallen under my gaze. The paper crumpled in my grasp and I flung my hoe violently into the ripening stalks of corn. I should have been . . . What? Hiding from the inevitable?

Now my knees buckled and I sat on the ground, leaning against the pitiful modicum of protection the tightly woven picket fence afforded a garden that was sure to be decimated by raccoons and black bears on one of those nights when the guard dogs fell into insensible sleep. That garden didn't belong here any more than I did. I cradled my head in my hands and fought back the urge to weep. I would not take up a campaign against my own adopted people. Yet I could not bear to think of deafening my ears to the pleas of one of the finest friends and bravest men I would ever know.

I heard an armload of firewood rattle on the pile and looked up through the open gap in the garden fence to see Westerly near our lodge. She felt me watching, and her eyes swept her surroundings until she spotted me through the gap I had left open. Though I tried to pull myself to my feet in time, she knew something was wrong at a glance. I believe she even knew *what* was wrong. She stood there for a while, staring sadly at me. Then she smiled, and strolled toward me.

I met her at the gap and handed her the letter from Kit. Her brow furrowed a little, and she blinked and even smiled at the attempts at spelling. Westerly herself had become nearly flawless at spelling and grammar in Spanish and English, and daily harangued me to teach her more French. She finished the letter and looked up at me.

"He should spend more time learning to spell and less time listening to General Carleton," she said. She giggled at this, trying to prevent my mood from plunging into depths of hopelessness as it was wont to do.

"What am I to tell him?" I asked, unable to join her in her amusement.

She took my arm and led me out of the garden. "You will know. Your heart is good and it will always guide you if you listen to it." She stopped suddenly, and turned toward me. "Perhaps you should talk to Owl Man."

A bright spot appeared in my vision of a future that had gone dark the moment I touched that letter. I nodded. Yes, William. William Bent. Owl Man, the wise one. Perhaps William would know what to do.

~~~~~~~~

William and I sat at his desk at the cabin inside Bent's Stockade. He had lighted a lantern and now pulled on a pair of spectacles. He read the letter. He sat back and frowned as he pulled off the spectacles, his droll and weathered face revealing decades of struggle and toil. Then, out of nowhere, he laughed and shook his head. "I can't believe you've actually taught that old voyageur how to read and write at his age—*our* age."

"You're only fifty-five," I said. "Born the same year as Kit, right?"

"Sure, but we started grousin' about gettin' old twenty years ago. I never dreamed Kit would learn his letters back then. Not that he's learned it all, judging by this letter, but no more than I put pen to paper these days, I doubt I could beat him in a spelling bee."

"He could have dictated it to his adjutant," I remarked.

William grew pensive and folded the letter. "No, he could not have, Mr.

Greenwood. Not *this* letter. He's convinced himself that he needs you bad, and that puts quite a burden on your shoulders, doesn't it?"

I nodded.

He handed the letter back to me. "We might have seen this coming."

"I thought the same thing."

"You might have gone into hiding, but that would not have suited you long." He put an elbow on his writing desk and lowered his brow into his hand. He rubbed his temples, then slowly lifted his face, letting that roughened palm stroke his deeply etched visage until his chin came to rest on his knuckles. "He left you some room to maneuver."

"Sir?"

William pointed at the letter. "Kit's always been a man to think and choose his words carefully. The letter says he *fears* a campaign against the Comanches may be coming. That means it's not what he wants. And he asks only for your advice and assistance. He's not ordering you to take to the trail as his scout, and I don't think he ever would, though he might ask you to, if it came to that."

"I couldn't do that."

"I know you couldn't. Kit suspects it, too, and he wouldn't fault you for refusing, but you'd better be prepared for him to ask you."

I shuffled my feet and shifted in my chair. "So you think I should go to Santa Fe and meet with him?"

He glared at me. "What else? You have no choice. You're in the middle of this."

I sighed and rolled my eyes. "How the hell did I let that happen?"

William looked at me, bewildered. He scoffed. "You found a home out there on the Canadian. I don't even know why you're here now. Avoiding your responsibility to your home place, maybe—I don't know. You're so clearly suited to that place, and it to you . . . You don't *see* that, Mr. Greenwood? After all these years?"

I felt quite ashamed, sitting there under the glare of a better man—a man I should have been trying to emulate all along, instead of getting embroiled in wars between white men or planting my garden in the wrong place. This was William's range, and he had served it as steward and sage for well onto forty years, keeping what peace he could in troubled times, fighting with his wits—and with his weapons when diplomacy failed. I might have been trying to accomplish the same on the Crossing of the

Canadian where the adobe walls built by my own hand slowly crumbled into ruin. I was *already* in hiding—avoiding my responsibility to my Comanche brothers and sisters. I should have been hoofing the trails from Adobe Walls to Santa Fe for months, desperately seeking a solution to the conflict that now seemed too near to stop.

I mustered some gall and looked up at William. "What could I possibly accomplish in Santa Fe now?"

"You could try to stop the campaign."

"I've met with General Carleton before. He doesn't believe in smoking the pipe with Indians."

"I said you could *try*. You've got to do something. You've been sent here."

I narrowed my eyes, trying to figure what he meant. "Sir?"

"I never quite understood why you came to the frontier from wherever you came from, Mr. Greenwood, but it's never been my place to ask. You could have accomplished anything you wanted back in some civilized country. You're a man of intelligence and learning. You're honest and you want to do what's right. You could have gone anywhere and done anything, but you ended up here. I bet you don't even know why. Something, somewhere, lured you to this place—or more exactly to that place you love out there on the wild Canadian. You may never know why, but you're supposed to be here. You've got the brains and the heart and the will to serve your home place and your people, so *use* them."

I sighed deeply and felt a great power engulf me, as if I had been sucked up into a thundercloud to absorb all the energies of its winds and lightning bolts. For too many years, I had merely played at solving the problems of Comancheria. I had occasionally voiced my opinion in the council lodge. I had casually met with military and government officials on behalf of the Comanches, but only at my convenience. Never had I committed to apply all my energies and talents to the cause of avoiding a Comanche war and securing a permanently recognized nation for my adopted people. I had failed miserably, and had perhaps waited too long to accomplish anything now, but I knew I must try anyway. The power of the mystic Thunderbird beat heavily in my chest.

FORTY-TWO

I made Santa Fe in four and a half days. That amounts to about sixty miles a day on horseback over mountains and rough country. That sounds incredible even to the best cowboys today, but I had honed my riding skills among Comanches, and I knew where to find fresh horses along the way at the ranches of friends.

I carried with me all the cash I had on hand at Boggsville—some three hundred dollars. In addition to that, I dug up a cache of four hundred thirty-five dollars in gold coin that I had buried some years before above Taos after returning from a successful mule-trading venture to Missouri. I also counted on later gathering over two thousand dollars that I had been keeping at Maxwell's Ranch for over a decade. I was prepared to spend all of my money now, in the form of bribes or gifts—whatever it took to avoid a campaign against the Comanches the likes of which had defeated the Mescaleros and the Navahos and sent them to the squalor and hellish internment of Fort Sumner and the Bosque Redondo.

Arriving at Santa Fe, I took a room at La Fonda, shaved, and had a bath. That very afternoon, just before the shops closed, I bought some attire befitting a frontier diplomat, and went to bed, having slept very little on the trail. I didn't sleep much that night, either, but three hours a night is typical for me when the moon is waning, and I felt refreshed the next day.

I began gathering information. I spoke with Comancheros who had recently been out among the Comanches and Kiowas and I learned the locations and attitudes of as many bands of Indians as I could. I spoke with friends of mine who were officers in the volunteer army and tried to judge the overall attitude of the military toward a Comanche/Kiowa campaign. I found out that General Carleton intended to recruit Mescalero Apaches and Navahos to act as guides and scouts for the coming campaign. That failing, he intended to recruit Ute warriors. This I had expected. Kit had employed Utes to defeat the Navahos, and General Carleton believed in constantly pitting Indian tribes against one another to prevent them from uniting for an all-out war on whites.

While learning what I could about the attitude of the army, I also evaluated the military's ability to mount a campaign out on the distant plains. I collected intelligence about available stockpiles of weapons and ammunition and supplies that would be needed to support a regiment moving against the Indians. I looked over the condition of riding stock and wagons, and judged the morale of the volunteer troops themselves. I felt like a spy again—like when I went to San Antonio to observe and infiltrate the Confederate Army. Only this time I was spying on the U.S. Army for the benefit of the Comanche/Kiowa alliance. I was a turncoat, and that amused me greatly.

My third day in Santa Fe, I happened to run into the Indian agent for the Comanches, Martin Stocker. His agency headquartered at Maxwell's Ranch, but he had come to town to meet with General Carleton to discuss the Comanche situation. Stocker was a middle-aged man who had spent much of his life in government service. He spoke some Spanish, but no Comanche. Nevertheless, he was a good man and was serious about his job as Comanche Indian agent. We had met before at Maxwell's Ranch, but Stocker didn't even recognize me shaven, and in store-bought clothes. When he remembered who I was, he asked me to join him for lunch. We went to a place the Mexicans frequented so we would not be bothered by eavesdroppers.

"Did his highness, the general, summon you to town for a royal audience, as well?" he asked, just before shoveling a large portion of enchiladas into his mouth.

I smirked at his sarcasm. "No, Kit asked me to come."

He nodded as he chewed and swallowed. "So Kit's going to be sent out to round up the Comanches like he did the Mescaleros and the Navahos."

"I don't know that for sure, but it seems possible, unless the campaign can be avoided."

He gestured at me with his fork. "Listen, Mr. Greenwood, I'll do all I can to keep this campaign from happening. I could use your help. The better course of action would be to send a peace delegation into Comancheria."

"I agree," I said, savoring the taste of a beefsteak that had been pounded thin, grilled, and covered with a fiery sauce made of tomatoes, onions, and hot peppers. "If you can convince General Carleton of that, I will volunteer to guide the delegation onto the plains."

He grunted his approval as his eyes watered. Sweat was dotting his forehead. The ability to enjoy real Mexican food took some time to acquire for most Anglos. Stocker was no native here, but he was trying to adapt. He swallowed, bolted a glass of water, and took a huge bite from a tortilla, knowing the tortilla would cool his burning mouth more so than the water. "It's more likely," he finally said, "that they'll ask you to guide a war party."

"That I cannot do."

He looked at my face for a long moment, as if to judge my sincerity. Then he grunted and risked another fiery mouthful. Stocker asked me a lot of questions about the Comanches I had lived with. I avoided answering in too much detail and claimed that I had not been among the Indians very long, and not very recently, either. I considered Stocker an ally in my campaign to avoid a campaign, but I still did not want to give him too much specific information that he might eventually pass on to military authorities. I think he sensed my reluctance to cooperate fully, for he gave me a strange look, grinned, and ceased his interrogation. "Perhaps it is better that I don't know everything about my charges at this point," he said.

I shrugged.

"There's going to be a meeting with General Carleton tomorrow morning at headquarters. I would like for you to come. I need some support for the cause of peace."

I nodded. "I will be there. That's why I came to town."

Colonel Christopher Carson arrived in town that afternoon, having come down from Taos where he had spent a few days with his family. Kit never attempted to make anything of an entrance wherever he went, but the town was buzzing with the news of his arrival by the time Martin Stocker and I stepped out onto the street from inside the cafe. I walked to the plaza that stood south of the main entrance to the old Palace of the Governors, where General Carleton made his headquarters. I knew Kit would be quartering there. I sat on the dirt of the plaza grounds, leaning against a tree for almost two hours, just watching, gathering my thoughts and my resolve, and enjoying the beautiful September afternoon.

Finally, I saw Kit step through the adobe portal of the palace. The military authorities had attempted to Americanize the look of the centuries-old Palace of the Governors by tacking up a long porch roof along the entire front of the building. There Kit stood under that shingled awning. He was looking old. His grizzled face seemed drawn, his eyes sunken. He carried his left shoulder slightly forward because of that fall in the mountains, four years ago. He stood with his feet set wide apart, still standing firm. His pale eyes darted attentively here and there about the plaza, and he seemed to be searching for something—maybe my arrival, I thought, flattering myself. He had taken to growing his hair long. Though thinning with age, it brushed his shoulders in a rare display of flamboyance that in reality was probably nothing more than an aversion to sitting still in a barber's chair and being lauded for his conquests and begged for stories of the Indian wars. His eyes were just about to locate me when someone recognized him and grabbed his hand to shake it. The next thing I knew, there were three or four, then half a dozen, then ten men and boys gathered around the great Kit Carson, slapping his back and shaking his hand. He bore it as long as he could, then begged his leave and slipped back into the sanctuary of the palace.

I reported to Military Headquarters of the Department of New Mexico early the next morning. I found Kit standing in the courtyard of the palace with a cup of coffee in his hand, talking to General James Henry Carleton himself. The two men had campaigned against Indians together when Kit scouted for the then-Major Carleton in the First Dragoons. Carleton was fifty years old now, Kit fifty-five. They were both small of stature, but tough as tempered steel. They were brothers in the Masonic Lodge.

Other than that, Kit and Carleton seemed to have little in common. Kit was frontier born and raised, schooled in the wilderness. Carleton was from Maine, raised a Christian and a gentleman, educated in classrooms and taught to excel at everything he took on. Carleton had proven himself a valiant soldier at Buena Vista in the Mexican War, and in numerous campaigns against the Indians. He was tough and relentless. He believed God had sent him to the frontier to tame the heathen Red Man.

Kit saw me and came to shake my hand, then wrapped his arms around me in a back-slapping *abrazo*. "I scarcely recognized you in store-bought clothes," he said. "How's that little squaw wife of yours?"

We talked and laughed together until the general stepped nearly between us as if annoyed at being ignored. "What brings *you* here, Mr. Greenwood?"

"Kit wrote, requesting I come."

The general's eyes darted between Kit and me. "How did you know to be here this morning? You've obviously just now seen Kit for the first time in a great while. I just scheduled this meeting yesterday."

"I had lunch with Martin Stocker yesterday. He told me about the meeting."

"Did he?"

"Yes, sir."

"Kid Greenwood knows the Comanches, Jim. He's traded with them for years, and has lived in their camps. That's why I asked him to come."

The general nodded. "I'm aware of all that. Very well, you may stay, Greenwood." He pulled a watch from his pocket and frowned at it. About that time, Martin Stocker walked briskly into the courtyard. "Mr. Stocker, you are almost late," Carleton scolded. "Come into my office, gentlemen."

We filed into a cool adobe room where we found a table spread with woefully incomplete maps of Comancheria. We pulled up chairs and sat down as the general offered coffee, which all of us declined. Carleton lit a coal-oil lamp, then sat.

"You know why you're here," he began. "The time has come for our government to deal with the Comanche and Kiowa problem. The Kiowas have been making raids on the Santa Fe Trail for months. Now, it seems, their allies, the Comanches, have joined in the mischief with that raid down at Cimarron Springs."

"Begging your pardon, General," said Agent Stocker, "but I have had no confirmation that those Indians were positively identified as Comanche."

"They wore buffalo horn headdresses and carried long lances. And the riding skills were those of Comanches. They used their horses as shields at a full gallop. That's Comanche."

"Assuming the reports are accurate," Stocker said, "the raid amounts to a crime against the citizenry, not an act of war. There is no evidence to suggest that the entire Comanche nation has become hostile."

Carleton snorted. "Comanche is synonymous with hostile. Literally. What does 'Comanche' mean, Kit?"

"It's Ute for 'our enemies,' " Kit replied.

"There you have it," Carleton said.

"The ancient enemies of the Utes do not necessarily have to become the enemies of the American people."

"They have attacked an American settlement and killed American citizens."

"Not as a nation. Those were the actions of a few renegades who should be hunted down and brought to justice."

"That is exactly what I mean to do," the general announced. "They will be hunted down. They and any Indian who harbors them must be taught a lesson."

Stocker's face was turning red. "General, there is no reason to go to war with the Comanches. The best course of action would be to send a peace delegation into Comanche country and treat with them. They should be required to give up their captives and turn over the renegades who have engaged in raids. Then they should be provided with presents and rations, and shown the road to peace."

"Presents!" Carleton roared.

"Yes. Just as William Bent has been authorized to grant presents and rations to the Cheyennes and the Arapahos."

"William Bent does not operate under the jurisdiction of the Department of New Mexico. If he did, he would not be giving *presents* to the Indians."

"Mr. Greenwood has offered to guide a peace delegation out onto the plains," Stocker said.

The general glared at me. "Is that so, Mr. Greenwood?"

"If you will allow me an observation," I answered. "I have spent some time in Comanche camps, trading for horses and buffalo robes. They do not want war with Americans. They are too busy raiding Texas to give a hoot about New Mexico. Since the war began they have reclaimed hundreds of miles of the frontier in Texas. As such, they are fierce enemies of the Confederacy, and therefore allies to America. I agree with Agent Stocker. The American government should seek a treaty with them and keep them pitted against the Texans."

General Carleton stood silent for a moment, actually considering my point. "That is an argument worthy of consideration," he said. "However, I believe the war against the Confederacy will soon be over. The Rebels cannot hold out much longer. Texas will soon fall under the Stars and Stripes again. When that happens, we will again inherit the war against the

Comanches. To treat with them now only to turn on them then would not be honorable. The only course is to mount a punitive campaign against them. We have proven this course of action against the Mescalero Apaches and against the Navahos. Both tribes have been subdued, and reports of their murders and rapes and thefts have virtually vanished. *That* is the way to achieve peace with the Indians. Whip them soundly and start them on the road to Christianity and civilization. And *that* is what I intend to do." He pounded his fist on the table with each "that," leaving no room for negotiation.

"Sir," I said, "with all due respect for the military leadership you and Colonel Carson have proven to possess, the Comanches will not be defeated as easily as the Navahos and the Mescaleros."

Carleton smiled. "Now we're getting down to some important business. Explain your statement."

"The Comanches don't grow crops. They don't have vast orchards or pumpkin fields for Kit's troops to destroy. You might surprise them and run them out of one of their camps and capture and burn their lodges and all their accoutrements only to learn that they have made new lodges and weapons within a matter of days. Their country is vast and uncharted. Their commissary is the buffalo and the deer, and they know where to find the herds and how to subsist on rabbits and rats on the way to the herds. Their tactics of evasion and escape are unparalleled. And all this is to say nothing of their fighting skills, which are unconventional and extraordinary."

"I admire your respect for the enemy, Mr. Greenwood. But they can be routed. The Texans proved that at the battle of Pease River."

"The Texans are braggarts. That was not a battle. It was a massacre of women and children and Mexican slaves. There were no warriors present in that camp."

"You're mistaken. I've read the reports. Chief Peta Nocona was killed."

"I am *not* mistaken, sir. I was in that camp. I witnessed the slaughter. The man Sul Ross claimed was Peta Nocona was actually Peta's Mexican slave—a captive. Peta Nocona died less than a year ago, of an infected wound received in a fight against Utes."

The general looked at me as if I had lost my mind. "Even assuming you are correct, it changes nothing. The Comanches are raiding with the Kiowas and they must be punished. I will not entertain fanciful notions that they are somehow invulnerable to attack. If they prove more difficult to subdue than other tribes, so be it. Colonel Carson knows the Comanches every bit as well as you do, Mr. Greenwood, and he will adjust his tactics and keep after the scoundrels until victory is achieved and the Comanche menace has been removed. *That* is what we are here to discuss."

Agent Stocker turned to Kit. "Colonel Carson, certainly you must see the benefits of attempting a lasting peace with the Indians."

Kit drew a deep breath and thought about the question as he absent-mindedly curled the corner of one of the maps on the table. "I feel for the poor devils, Martin, I really do. But they savvy just two things. Friend and enemy. A friend is somebody stronger than they are. An enemy is weaker. If we want to be friends with them, we have to show them our strength. That's their way. The elders in the Ute tribe tell me that only a few generations back the Comanches moved down here from up north and just flat kicked hell out of the Apaches to take the plains. That's what they do and that's all they understand. They will hate our guts if we just sit on our asses and let them raid our towns and ranches. They will respect us if we take the fight into their own country."

"Where is the authority for such action?" Stocker demanded. "There is no proof that the Comanches want war with us. Only a few of them have been accused of raiding. Does this warrant a campaign of attrition against them?"

"Mr. Stocker," said the general, "I appreciate your commitment to your duty as agent to these savages, but believe me, I *have* the authority to order a campaign. Your suggestion that not all the Indians are guilty is a point worth considering, however. So I will allow someone familiar with the Comanches to go along with the troops to identify the friendlies and try to keep them out of the fighting." He looked at me when he said this.

"I've offered to guide a peace delegation into Comanche country," I replied. "For now, that service is all I am willing to commit to."

"Suit yourself, Mr. Greenwood. You are not the only scout available to this department. At this meeting, however, you may prove of some service by identifying known campgrounds of the enemy and informing Colonel Carson and myself of the strength of the enemy warriors, their weaponry, supplies, et cetera."

Martin Stocker stood up suddenly, his chair scooting across the floor behind him. "Gentlemen, I must respectfully excuse myself from further involvement in this affair. This meeting has evolved into a council of war. I will not stand by and watch plans being made to attack and kill the very people whose welfare I am charged to protect. You should know, General, that I will protest this campaign in a letter to my superiors at the Bureau of Indian Affairs, and to President Lincoln himself."

Calmly, Carleton looked up from his maps. "I would expect no less of you, Martin. Thank you for coming."

When Stocker stormed out, I considered following him. But I was not as reputable as he. I was sneaky. I wanted to investigate General Carleton's plan and determine what he had in mind in the way of a campaign against the Comanches. In making this decision, I indeed became a spy again. I was collecting intelligence that I hoped would benefit an enemy of the United States of America. Oddly enough, I felt no guilt in this act of treason toward the United States. In fact, when I thought about my Comanche brothers, I liked being the scoundrel that I was. My disloyalty to Kit, on the other hand, gave me no small amount of shame. He may have been the only man alive who could have talked General Carleton out of the campaign, but he was convinced that the Indians had to be warred into peace.

Carleton began asking me numerous questions about the Comanches and their haunts. Some of them I answered honestly, knowing that one band's location months ago would prove useless intelligence now anyway. When asked about their favorite campgrounds, I was evasive, except when I knew that Kit knew the answer as well as I. I didn't want Kit to catch me lying for the sake of the Comanches. But in spite of what Carleton believed, Kit Carson did not know the Comanches the way I did. He knew the Utes, the Navahos, the Mescaleros, the Arapahos, and the Cheyennes *better* than I did. But not the Comanches. So I could get away with spreading a modicum of false information without Kit or Carleton knowing.

When asked about Comanche strength and supplies, I erred on the side of weakness. I didn't want to paint the Indians as too powerful, for fear Carleton would order even more recruits and arms to go out against them. What I did find out in this meeting was pretty much what I had already suspected anyway. Carleton would commit some three hundred cavalry and infantry troops to the campaign, plus another hundred Ute scouts, if they could be recruited. Fort Bascom, the new post on the Comanche Trail, would serve as the jumping-off point for the campaign. Preparations should begin immediately and the campaign launched as soon as possible before winter came on.

When the meeting was over, Kit and I walked down the street to a cafe. Kit knew the owner, and asked for a table in the back, where no one would recognize him. We ordered a couple of steaks and talked about friends and family all through our meal, without mentioning a word about the meeting in the general's war room. Finally, though, as Kit pulled his napkin from the front of his shirt and threw it on the table, his face turned grim and he looked me right in the eye.

"You know what I need," he said, as a statement more than as a question.

"You need intelligence."

He nodded. "I need to know where they're at, and what their strength is."

I sighed and put my silverware down, my appetite suddenly gone. "I'm going out there, Kit, but not necessarily as your spy. I believe this campaign against the Comanches is wrong. I'm going to try to do something about it."

"What can you do, now, Kid?"

"I've got to try something. Anything. Those are my people. They trust me. Maybe I can try to get the major chiefs together and ride in for peace talks."

Kit shook his head. "There's no time. You know the bands are scattered from hell to breakfast. Anyway, even if you could talk the chiefs into begging peace, which I doubt, General Carleton has already sent orders to Fort Bascom to turn all flags of truce away. He will not treat with the Indians, Kid."

"I can't just let this happen. And you don't have to, either. You could resign your commission. Look at you, Kit, they're using you up like an old horse that ought to be out to stud."

Kit chuckled. "There's more life left in me than you think, Kid. And I need the salary to support Josefa and the children. Anyway, I've never resigned from anything in my life. It is my duty to follow orders."

"You weren't always a soldier."

"No, but it suits me. I believe my men need to be led, and I believe the Indians have got to be whupped into accepting civilization. Otherwise, we'll have to kill 'em all before it's over. With your help, we could whup 'em quick and save more of 'em in the long run."

I stared at my plate and searched my heart. "You're not going to whip the Comanches, Kit. I don't care if you muster a thousand men. You'll lead them all to slaughter on the plains. I don't want to see your last campaign end in a horrific defeat."

Kit smiled. "Those Comanches have sure got you hornswoggled. I know it won't be easy. That's why I need your help. But it can be done. The Comanches will not hold the southern plains forever."

"I can't help you this time, Kit. My heart's not in it." I felt crushed to admit this, yet the honesty in my words bathed my soul with relief of the burden.

Kit leaned forward, his elbows on the table. "Listen, Kid, you're going out there anyway. Just keep your eyes and ears open. You'll know when I'm coming, so ride out and meet me for a parley. You can tell me whatever you want to, or tell me nothing at all. Just meet me halfway and talk. Can you just promise me that much?"

I thought for a while as Kit's eyes searched mine. "If I hear you're coming, I'll ride out and talk. But it will only be to try one last time to talk you out of this campaign."

We left it at that, and said our farewells. I retired to my room and began writing letters to the commissioner of Indian Affairs, to senators, to the secretary of war, the secretary of state, and to President Lincoln himself, begging them all to call off the campaign. I knew the odds were against me. Most if not all of my letters would probably fall into rubbish bins or fireplaces. Even should one get read, and answered, the reply would probably come too late to make a difference.

After posting my letters, I made immediate preparations to ride into Comancheria. I had heard the government viewpoint. It was time to seek the wisdom of Burnt Belly and test my brotherhood with Kills Something. I felt as if the fate of the entire world rested on my shoulders. In reality, looking back, I was nothing more than a pawn in a trifling struggle that would scarcely warrant a paragraph in the book of world history. But it was my paragraph to write, and I was prepared to fill my inkwell with blood.

FORTY-THREE

Burnt Belly sat cross-legged before the fire in his lodge. It was a small prayer fire, for the weather was pleasant, and the heat of fires not needed. The bottom of the buffalo-hide lodge cover was rolled up two fists above the ground to draw the temperate air in as the warmth of the fire sought escape through the smoke hole. The old shaman pulled a mouthful of whiskey from the small jug I had brought him. He took a healthy pinch of black powder from the buckskin pouch. All at once, he spat the whiskey and threw the black powder into the fire, causing the little blaze to flare. Now he resumed a chant that meant nothing in the Comanche tongue, but as far as I knew might very well have been the language of the spirits. This had been going on since dawn, and the sun was now plunging toward the western horizon. All day, I had listened to the chants, fed the fire for Burnt Belly, smelled the smudges of cedar and fir whose smoke carried prayers up to the Great Mystery.

Suddenly the chant ended. "They are coming," Burnt Belly said. "In two moons."

I had not even told him about the campaign yet—only that I needed to seek his wisdom and advice. It is possible that Comanche and Kiowa scouts had been keeping an eye on the construction of Fort Bascom, and had simply surmised that the attack was imminent. It was possible that Burnt Belly had reasoned that the soldiers must strike before winter fairly set in. Or it is possible that the spirits told him the future. With Burnt Belly, one never knew.

"Yes," I said. "Three hundred bluecoats and a hundred Utes."

"Fools," he said. "Let them come."

"Would it not be better to ask for peace?"

"What peace? The same peace that the Mescaleros and Navahos got at that slave camp on the Bitter Water?"

"A different peace. One that allows us to stay in our own country with honor."

"The blades of our lances will win that peace. I have had visions. Our time to show our strength draws near to an end. The great war between the whites is almost over. The *tejanos* and the bluecoats will soon be one people again. Before that time comes, we must take everything we can and drive every hostile white man from our country. Then, the battle will become one to hold what we have won. The bluecoats and the *tejanos* do not respect an enemy who wants peace. They understand only the arrow and the bullet and the knife. Let them come into our own country, and we will teach them respect."

This echo of Kit's observation almost amused me. "Little Chief will lead them. He has defeated the Mescaleros and the Navahos."

Burnt Belly scoffed. "They are weak. Both people are our enemies. We might have defeated them ourselves, generations ago, but we have let them survive so that we may raid their fields and herds. Little Chief will find one of our horseback soldiers worth ten of their warriors."

"I tried to tell them not to come. I did not say too much, but I tried to tell them they could not defeat the Comanche and Kiowa alliance. They would not listen. They are too full of arrogance and pride."

"Little Chief is your friend," he said.

"Yes, but my loyalty lies with my brother, Kills Something, and the Comanche people."

"You speak the truth. Your heart is Comanche, but it runs with the blood of a white man. You want to fulfill your promise to fight against the whites who will invade us, but now you see that you must do battle with your own warrior-brother, Little Chief."

"It troubles me, but I have spoken in council, and I must defend my people if the bluecoats come, no matter who leads them."

"So be it. Little Chief is a great warrior. He will fight hard and he will expect no less of you—even as his enemy. The Great War between the whites has turned friend against friend and brother against brother. Each man must answer to the call of his own heart. Do not let it trouble you. It is the way of a warrior."

"You have answered my two questions. The one about peace, and the one about my friend Little Chief, who now is destined to become my enemy. Now I must decide how to prepare my people for the attack."

Burnt Belly took another pull from the jug and cast the whiskey and powder into the fire once more. He looked at me, smiling. "That time was just for fun." He reached his hand toward me. "Help me up, nephew. I have been sitting here too long and I am old and stiff."

I went to help him, but before I could take his hand, he rose magically, with a strength and balance a man of his years should not have possessed.

I smiled. "You are as tricky as our ancestor Brother Coyote."

"The trickster loves his life, even knowing his enemies lie waiting to take it from him at every turn in the trail. Do not let these times weigh so heavily on your heart, nephew. These troubles are not of your making. You have been guided here by spirit powers beyond your understanding to protect your people. You must do your duty, but do not suffer it too deeply. Good times follow bad. Our warriors live to fight and die for their home. That is the way to the rewards of the Shadow Land. Come."

He beckoned me to step outside and I beheld a striking sunset blazing almost bloodred through the dust of some distant buffalo herd. A flock of a dozen mourning doves rocketed overhead, streaking at enviable speeds toward a favorite watering place. The voices of children at play bubbled up from the camp situated all along the Concho River. A drumming of hooves drew my attention across the stream, where two young warriors ran neck and neck on the racecourse. The aroma of cooking food made me hungry.

"The spirits have granted us a great day to be together once again," he said. "Tomorrow we will call for a council of war. Kills Something will have two moons to prepare the warriors. You, nephew, must make many hard rides to gather supplies—powder and lead, knives and iron for arrow points. You must trade for these things a little at a time in many different places, so the whites will not know you are supplying our people. Then we will move our village to a place of strength. Where do you suggest?"

My answer came quickly. "At the Adobe Walls."

He nodded. "Yes, the Crossing. That is the place I was thinking of, too. But all *that* will begin tomorrow. For now, we will go see what my third wife has cooked for our evening meal in her lodge. People laugh at me because I married her and she is not very pretty. But she makes me very happy when she cooks, and I already have two pretty wives. Come, I am as hungry as a coyote named No-Leg."

The council was held the next day, and as Burnt Belly and I recommended to the elders, it was decided that the village would move to Adobe Walls after the warriors had been drilled and I had gathered the supplies. I would use pack mules to transport the wartime provender. Six warriors were assigned to me to help me with the pack mules. Two of them were my old friends of the warpath, Loud Shouter and Fears-the-Ground, who were now respected raid leaders and wealthy horse owners with two wives each and several children.

The only other warrior of any standing to accompany me was young Quanah, son of the great chief Peta Nocona, whose name would never again be spoken among the Comanches, for Comanches did not speak the names of their dead for fear of being haunted by specters from the Shadow Land.

The other three mule tenders were young warriors who did not relish the idea of being assigned to a mere supply run. Their names were Blackbird, Turtle, and Tobacco Boy. The day we left the Concho, these three boys rode with scowls on their faces, tugging angrily at the lead ropes of their mules, for we passed by their young friends outside of camp, going through all the fantastic battle drills the Comanches had developed to prepare for war. As their friends held wild races and rough contests designed to hone hand-to-hand fighting skills and rescue abilities, they could only mope and lead their mules, tied head to tail behind them.

As we left Kills Something's village, however, I explained to them, mostly in sign language, how important and dangerous our mission was. We would have to ride to the fringes of enemy territory near the Texas settlements, and would be in constant danger of being discovered. If found and attacked, we would have to fight our way back toward Comancheria and use our most sophisticated tactics of evasion to get our war supplies back to Kills Something's camp. This element of danger seemed to cheer the boys up and we got along better for the next few days. Each of my six men tended three mules, giving us eighteen beasts to load with ammunition and other necessities.

We went to Fredericksburg first, for it was the supply point nearest to the Concho River. I have told you about Fredericksburg before. Unlike the residents of any other town anywhere in Texas, the German immigrants of Fredericksburg were on good terms with the Comanches. So Loud Shouter rode to town with me. We claimed to be going into business together hunting buffalo for hides and meat. This was old news in Fredericksburg, for the town had forged a treaty with the Comanches saying the Indians would supply the settlers with wild game if the whites would refrain from hunting. In return, the German immigrants supplied the Comanches with domestic crops and manufactured supplies. We had no trouble purchasing a muleload of black powder, lead, bullet molds, and a pair of rifles.

Next, I left my Comanche helpers in a supply camp just upstream of the so-called Marble Falls on the Colorado River. The falls were of limestone, not marble, but misnomers were common on the frontier. From the supply camp, I rode alone to Austin, the capital of the Confederate State of Texas. Suspicions here were much more intense than in the remote village of Fredericksburg. Still, claiming to be a buffalo hunter and a trapper, I managed to purchase a muleload of supplies. When asked why I wasn't attached to some Confederate unit, I claimed that I had already served with the volunteers at the battle of Valverde, and had been mustered out. This was true, even though the volunteers I served with were Union.

From Austin, it was on to Salado. I moved very quickly from town to town, keeping my Comanche helpers out of sight in camps to the west. This business of supplying guns and ammunition to Comanches and Kiowas was highly illegal and could have gotten me hanged—probably by a lynch mob—had I been discovered. Therefore, I made my supply sweep across the settlements hastily, lest news of my last purchase should reach the next town before my arrival. As long as I got back into Comancheria before anyone realized I had made multiple purchases of ammunition and guns, I figured I could get away with my crimes against Texas.

I was the first of a new breed of Comanchero. Allow me to explain what I mean by that. The original Comancheros came out of New Mexico in the 1700s, rode eastward into Comancheria and traded Spanish goods to the Comanches in exchange for hides, meat, and slaves captured from other tribes. In those days, the Spaniards considered the Comanches an unconquerable enemy nation of savage heathens. The Comancheros held the respect of the Spanish people for their bravery and ability to function beyond the Comanche frontier. They were flamboyant plains traders who captured the imagination of every adventurous boy and every dark-eyed señorita.

By the time of the War Between the States, however, the word *"Comanchero"* had taken on a sinister ring to Americans. The Anglos of that time did not consider Comancheria unconquerable. By unspoken policy of the American mind, the Comanches were an enemy who would eventually be removed from the land. The Comanchero, therefore, was a traitor and a criminal. This new breed of Comanchero was what I had become. Hell, I think I invented it, to tell you the truth. But I did not consider my actions wrong. The land simply belonged to the Comanches, paid for in blood. They should have been left alone to live in it as they saw fit.

But history teaches that all the should-have-beens in the world cannot prevent a civilization from being overrun by an aggressive, numerically superior, more technologically advanced nation. The Comanches had overrun the Apaches and Tonkawas a hundred fifty years before, and now they were being overrun themselves. It's easier to see all that now, many years later. At the time, however, all I felt in my heart was the "now" of the situation. The Comanches were good people—no less perfect than any other civilization. They had won this land, and served it well as stewards. They deserved to hold it, and I was on their side, no matter how hopeless their cause.

You ask: *Good people? What about the atrocities?* Yes, some warriors participated in horrors of mutilation and torture. Rape was ceremonial, and believed to make the enemy woman *good* with Comanche seed. But these acts of terror occurred less commonly than you might think, for the history of the Comanche wars was written by whites—wartime propaganda. And the atrocities were most often in response to some white outrage. Women and children massacred, whole villages intentionally infected with smallpox and other virulent diseases, warriors ambushed and slaughtered under white flags of truce.

I feel no shame in admitting my loyalty to the Comanches. Their way was as good as any other civilization's. Better in many respects.

Anyway, after making a small purchase of supplies at Salado, I moved on to Gatesville, Waco, Meridian, and Fort Worth. Some of these towns boasted a precarious telegraph service by this time, fed by gossamer wires tacked to trees more often than actual poles. So, to distract attention from my stockpiling of powder and lead, and to keep the news of my shopping spree from spreading, I had the Comanche boys who rode with me cut the telegraph lines outside of each town the night before I was scheduled to make my next purchase.

I had to explain to the young warriors how the talking wire carried the white man's messages by magical means. They didn't want to believe me at first, but I convinced them finally and they agreed that the wire should be cut to aggravate the whites. To cut the wire, a couple of them would find a secluded spot along the line a good safe distance out of town. A warrior would stand on the back of a well-trained pony with a pair of nippers—supplied by me, of course—whereupon he would reach high and cut the wire.

In some places, however, the wire was too high to reach even standing on the back of a horse, so one warrior would throw his lariat over the wire, then feed the tail end of the rope through the honda to make a loop around the wire. By tying the end of his lariat to the tail of his horse, the warrior could pull the telegraph wire downward and sideways, low enough so that his partner could cut it. Simply cutting the wire would never suffice, however. A lengthy section had to be taken out of it and hidden to keep it from being too quickly repaired.

From stories I gathered later, these assaults on the telegraph wires were blamed on everyone from Union spies to cattle rustlers. No one ever dreamed that the Indians understood the significance of the early telegraph lines, so they were not even considered as the culprits. I had the Comanche boys use shod horses borrowed from nearby ranches to make the tracks along the telegraph lines look like those of white men. The boys would return the horses before dawn, so the ranchers would not come looking for stolen stock and discover our mobile supply camp. It wasn't easy for me to convince a young Comanche to return a fine horse he had stolen, but Loud Shouter and Fears-the-Ground helped me maintain discipline in this matter, and the element of danger in taking and returning the mounts began to appeal to the boys.

I also ordered my men to build their fires like a white man would. Indians put one end of a stick or log in a fire so that it burns off and can then be pushed in to burn more. White men typically lay the middle of a stick over the fire so that both ends must then be pushed in, which is only half as efficient as the Indian method. Frontiersmen knew the difference and could tell by the remnants of a burned-out fire which method had been used, so I had my Indians use the white man's method in order to take the onus for our shenanigans off the Indians.

In spite of all my precautions, I ran into some serious trouble outside of Jacksboro. Since the beginning of the Civil War, the Comanches had raided Jacksboro so often that the population had plummeted from about 1,600 to fewer than 700 souls. Since most the able-bodied fighting men were away at war, the town had been left vulnerable. This only seemed to serve Jacksboro right. Before the war, a local newspaper called *The White-*

man had devoted itself to printing the policies of Indian removal from the surrounding area, and regularly published rabid editorials attacking the Indians. Now the red men were the ones removing the whites. The surviving settlers there had become quite vigilant in the face of frequent raids.

Because of all this, I made a rather small purchase of ammunition, along with an Enfield rifle, some camp supplies, and a farrier's file. It was the latter that excited the local gossip after I left, for it was known that Indians often converted files to lance blades by firing them red-hot, beating their edges thin, and honing them to razor sharpness. After I left town, a half-dozen citizens, perhaps better described as vigilantes, tracked me down and overtook me. I could have quit my pack mule and fled on Tu Hud, one of the fine ponies that Kills Something had given me, but I risked talking my way out of the situation, so that I could save the supplies on the mule.

After the men from Jacksboro surrounded me, their leader said, "We'd like a word with you, sir." He was older than the others, with gray beard stubble on his face. Like the rest, he seemed to come from rough stock. They all wore drab work clothes and rode well-worn saddles. I could not help noticing that a couple of them carried lariat ropes.

"What's this about?" I replied, affecting a Southern drawl.

"What is your name?"

"John Palmer." Yet another alias.

"And your business?"

"I'm a hunter and a trapper."

"What about that file you purchased in town?"

I shrugged. "I like to keep my pony's feet in good shape." One of the men rode around my outfit, apparently looking for brands on my horse and mule.

"Where are you from, Mr. Palmer?"

"From South Carolina, originally, but I've been driftin' west since I was a kid."

Another man spoke up: "Are you kin to Elijah Palmer over to Denton?"

I shook my head. "I ain't kin to nobody, sir. I'm the bastard son of a barmaid. That's why I come to the frontier."

The leader of the band raised his chin at me. "A man favoring your description purchased some powder and lead and a steel hatchet and some other things in Fort Worth recently. We know this is true from a reputable source."

"Wasn't me," I said. "I ain't been to Fort Worth." The worry was sinking to the pit of my stomach, but I held on to my lying skills and refused to blink.

"Sounded like your description."

"Well, I guess I ain't the only ugly bastard in Texas buying powder and lead. I got all I need here on this mule."

"Why would a man need a whole muleload of powder and lead?"

"I aim to go out among the buffalo with a hunting party of Indians."

Just the word "Indians" made eyebrows rise. "*Which* Indians?" the leader demanded.

"Some Kickapoos up in the territory. Got to have enough powder and lead to take some hides *and* defend ourselves from them goddamn scalpin' Comanches out there on the buffalo range." The men now had me completely surrounded, and I was ready to draw a knife or a pistol and go down fighting rather than be lynched.

"How old are you, Mr. Palmer?" the vigilante leader asked. It may have been an absentminded gesture, but he fingered the coil of a lariat tied to his saddle as he said this.

"Thirty-eight, near as I can figure."

"An able-bodied man like you ought to be serving in the war."

"I served in Sibley's brigade. I fought at Valverde and was captured at Glorieta Pass."

They asked me a lot of questions about the campaign, all of which I managed to answer convincingly, for I had seen much of it with my own eyes.

"What happened to you after you was captured?" one of the men demanded.

"The Yankees gave me amnesty so long as I swore not to rejoin my unit."

"No shame in breaking a promise to a Yankee, now, is there?"

"I'm loyal to Texas," I said.

"Sounds like you're loyal to yourself more than anything."

I could feel the tension still building among these men, and I detected a murderous blaze burning ever brighter in their eyes. It was a look I had seen before in the eyes of cowardly bullies who had convinced themselves that they had the right to murder anyone who disagreed with their beliefs. I knew I had to break that gang mentality, so I addressed the leader of the bunch. "May I have a word with you privately, sir?"

This surprised the head man, but intrigued him, as well. He liked being singled out as the leader of the gang of thugs. After thinking a few seconds, he said, "Boys, wait for me in the shade yonder. Not too far off, now." The other men groused, but did as they were told. When they had pulled away, their captain said, "Don't try anything funny."

"Of course not. I simply need to confide in you. What I'm about to tell you cannot be repeated. Not even to your men."

The man squinted. "All right."

"I'm operating under direct orders from President Jefferson Davis himself. I was recruited because of my knowledge of the frontier and the Indians. I've worked as an Indian trader for twenty years."

"What kind of orders do you have from Jeff Davis?" he said, rather incredulously.

"I'm to organize a battalion of civilized Indians—Kickapoos, Shawnees, Cherokees, and Choctaws—and harass the Union troops in New Mexico and Colorado."

"Let me *see* those orders," he said.

"They don't issue written orders for this kind of campaign, sir. But they did supply me with some of this." I reached toward my saddlebag.

"Easy," he said.

I moved slowly and produced a bundle of gold U.S. coins tied up in a rag. I handed it to the vigilante leader, keeping it low, so the others could not see it. "Untie that and have a look."

He did so, revealing ten twenty-dollar gold pieces. "What's this?"

"A reward for your loyalty to the Confederacy. Drop the coins into your boot top and hand the rag back to me, down low so your boys can't see it. You can tell them you checked my orders and handed them back to me. Don't ride back to town too fast, or your boot may jingle." I smiled.

He grinned back at me with one side of his mouth and began letting the coins fall into his boot top where he had tucked his trousers inside the leather. He handed the white rag back to me, as if to return my papers, and I replaced it in my saddlebag.

"In case you're wondering," I said, "that's the last of my money. If I had more, I'd give it to you. I won't need money where I'm going now."

"I'm satisfied," he replied. "We should shake hands now and go our own ways."

I nodded and offered my hand. As he shook my right hand, I sat ready to draw my knife from my left hip, but he didn't try anything. I waited for him to turn away first. When he did, I reined west at a walk, angling away so I could glance over my shoulder and watch the actions of the men. When I gained a line of timber, I passed out of sight of them and urged my mount and the pack mule in tow to a trot. When I knew I was out of earshot, I struck a gallop.

My young Comanche helpers were only a few miles away, and I reached them in less than an hour. "We must go," I told them. "Now!"

They gathered the mules and packed them hastily while I rode to a high point and watched my backtrail. I never saw anyone following, but I decided to take no chances. When the boys finished packing the mules, they signaled, and I rode back to the supply camp. "Now we must all take different paths," I ordered. "We may be followed. Ride hard. Three sleeps upstream there is a camp where a creek runs into the river. There is a big prairie dog town there—the first one you will come to up the river. Do you all know the place?"

They all signed yes.

"That is where we will meet in three sleeps. Now, go, and ride fast."

The boys scattered, and I went back to my high vantage point to watch for hours, but no one ever followed. Still, it was a good idea to have sent the young warriors ahead on different paths. I was not trailing any mules, so I knew I could make better time than the boys. The moon rose full that night, and I couldn't sleep anyway, so I just rode all night, Tu Hud having grazed and rested while I had watched the backtrail to Jacksboro for hours.

FORTY-FOUR

We rendezvoused at the prairie dog town camp and rode west with our ammunition and provender. Our path took us up the left bank of the river the white men called the South Wichita. Grass and game abounded, so men and beasts ate well as we traveled. The new moon came on, so Fears-the-Ground and Loud Shouter found a secure camp and posted sentinels for a couple of days, knowing my powers often went bad during the dark phase of the moon. But Burnt Belly had sent plenty of dogbane and moccasin flower root with me, so I did not fall into any strange trances or suffer night terrors. I did, however, sleep a day and a half straight through without waking.

Thus refreshed, I started us west again and we reached the head of the river eleven days after the last quarter of the moon. I mention the last quarter because we found a trail at the head of the South Wichita made by our people—Kills Something's village moving north, toward Adobe Walls—and on that trail we found an arrangement of small white stones in the shape of the waning quarter-moon. This was a message from Kills Something, telling us when he had passed this place, so we knew that he had been here eleven days ago.

Only two days later, however, we rode into a camp Kills Something had established on the headwaters of the North Pease to wait for us and our supplies. The commotion we created riding into camp with eighteen mules laden with guns, powder, lead, iron, steel, and various provisions, can only be described as unbridled elation driven by uninhibited abandon. The most joyous singing and dancing began as we rode in among the lodges, and we were literally pulled from our mounts and paraded through the entire camp. The boys who had complained upon leaving the Concho that they were missing the martial exercises now felt quite proud of their enormously successful supply run to the Texas settlements.

A feast began to shape up and a dance area was cleared in the center of the village. All the warrior societies put on their fancy headdresses of bison horn, deer antler, and the heads of every imaginable creature from cranes to wolves to bears to jaguars to lions to foxes to antelope. Women who weren't cooking danced while the warriors got ready, then the sun set and feasting and dancing began in earnest.

My party of young warriors was seated in the middle of all this, and we were not allowed to get up for anything, except for relieving ourselves in the shadows. All night the people brought us food and drink, blankets to keep us warm, buffalo robe couches upon which to lounge, and tobacco for the boys' pipes. I even pretended to smoke a little of this tobacco myself, which caused great joy, for I was known as one who normally abstained from such. At daylight we were finally allowed to retire. I was shown to one of Burnt Belly's wives' tipis that she had vacated for me, and there I finally enjoyed some peace and quiet. I stayed there relaxing the better part of the day and even slept an hour or so.

That night I was summoned to a council in Kills Something's new eighteen-skin tipi, one of the biggest bison-hide lodges I ever saw. I was third in line behind the war chief, Kills Something, and the peace chief, Burnt Belly, as we entered. This was a high honor to enter the lodge third and to sit in the middle of the circle as the rest of the warriors spiraled in around us.

After the usual preliminaries of lighting and passing the village's medicine pipe, Kills Something rose and said, "Everyone knows that my brother, Plenty Man, has returned from Tejas with so many good things that all the unmarried girls in the village want to be his second wife. We must all remember how he got these things. My brother has traded for many seasons and has taken our horses to sell for the paper and the metal that the white men hold more valuable than anything. This paper and this shiny metal belonged to Plenty Man, not to any of us. And my brother has taken all of this paper and all of this metal and he has traded it for guns, and bullets, and powder, and all the other things we need to defend our country. But these things do not belong to us. They belong to Plenty Man. He could have traded his paper and his shiny metal for anything— horses or whisky or land that the white men hold, or food or jewelry or wagons or even boats that the white men take on the water. But instead he brought all these good things here. And now, if you warriors want to have some of these things to fight with, I think you must trade with Plenty Man, for he has used all of his wealth to get them. We will hear what he has to say. He will tell us of his trip to the towns of the *tejanos,* then I think he will say what each of you must give in trade for the weapons you want. I have spoken."

Kills Something sat down and I looked at Burnt Belly, for he had the right to speak next. He said, "I want to say only that I am ready to hear Plenty Man speak. I have spoken."

So I rose and began to tell the tale of my recent supply run up the frontier. There were some runny parts, like when young Blackbird swatted young Turtle's horse on the rump while Turtle was standing on the horse's back trying to cut a telegraph wire and Turtle fell into a thorn bush. I spoke at length and told about each town I entered and each ranch we passed, because this was all very interesting intelligence to any Comanche warrior who might be planning a raid.

I had practiced this speech for hours in my mind, straddling my horse day after day on our return from Texas, and I took my own sweet time telling the saga. Finally I got around to answering Kills Something's question about how much a warrior might have to trade to get ahold of some fighting supplies. "Now you know that six young men went with me to the Texas towns. All these young warriors were brave. So each one of them will keep a new rifle and enough powder and lead for the winter, and enough iron to make twenty new arrows each, for they have earned it.

"But now there is the question of what to do with all the rest of the supplies. I have learned much from my Comanche brothers, uncles, and grandfathers. I know that the white men are fools to hold their paper and metal money so precious. So the loss of this money means nothing to me. I have also learned from my Comanche family that the greatest way to power and strong medicine is to give up all wealth in a give-away dance so that a man can prove that he believes his medicine is strong and that he trusts that his spirit-protectors will help him get the things he needs again to be a warrior. Therefore I have decided that tonight I will have a great give-away dance. All the things my nephews and I brought back on the mules will be given away to any warrior who needs them to fight and hold our country. This will make me happy. It is good. I have spoken."

That night, in that camp, I became a bigger hero than Ulysses S. Grant and Robert E. Lee rolled together. I played my violin for hours as drums beat and joyful people danced. Children played while puppies chased them around the lodges. My three youngest warrior-helpers—Blackbird, Turtle, and Tobacco Boy—slipped away, one by one, with young women, and I know that all three of them found their first brides that night. Elders sat and smiled and chanted, remembering all the good old days of the past. The first quarter of the moon sailed over the camp like a beacon of good fortune. The True Human Beings were ready to meet the invaders we all knew were coming.

On our way north to Adobe Walls, we met Little Bluff's band of Kiowas, and they agreed to join us. We reached Adobe Walls on the tenth day of November, 1864. The summer had been generous with rainfall, and tall grass grew for miles up and down the Canadian River bottoms. Kills Something went into camp downstream of the old ruins of Fort Adobe while Little Bluff encamped a few miles upstream of us. I knew it was time for me to keep my promise to Kit to ride up the Canadian and have one more talk with him before this insanity began. I took Tu Hud and left Adobe Walls.

My third day on the trail, I found Colonel Kit Carson's column on the warpath, already about halfway between Fort Bascom and Adobe Walls. He was closer than I had expected he would be, and I chided myself for underestimating the great Kit Carson. Organizing an invasion force the likes of which he now led required an indomitable spirit, especially considering the endless string of military orders that had to be satisfied. Kit must have worked incredibly hard and slept very little getting ready for this campaign.

I spotted Kit's advance Ute scouts first, and decided I would retreat for the time being and cover my tracks rather than announce my presence to the Utes. They might have known who I was and might have caused me trouble, for I was a fast friend of their sworn enemies, the Comanches. I therefore withdrew back down the river until the advance Ute scouts went into camp that night.

After dark, I put on my white man's clothing and saddled All Horse to ride far around to the rear of the invading column. There, I dismounted, and had little trouble leading my horse past the sentinels, using some cedar brush for cover. Once inside Kit's camp, I boldly and rather arrogantly rode right up to the supply wagon and announced my presence to some soldiers gathered around a small fire there.

"I'm Honoré Greenwood," I declared, "and I'm here to see Kit Carson." My eyes were adjusting to the flicker of the campfire when a reply came:

"You've gotten careless, Greenwood."

I recognized the voice as that of Luther Sheffield. My eyes must have widened with some alarm.

"Relax," Luther said, standing, his palms open to view. "I'm not even carrying a gun."

I remained motionless in the saddle. Sheffield had changed so much since the last time I saw him at Valverde that I hadn't even recognized him when I rode up. He had gained weight and appeared hale and sober. His face, once sunken and sickly, had fleshed out again. Though it had been many years since Blue Wiggins and I had conspired to cheat Sheffield out of the winnings that the gambler had dishonestly taken from Blue, I saw a hint of that old parlor owner's dash finally lighting his eyes up again.

"Who the hell is this guy?" one of the soldiers said.

"He's a Comanchero and a card cheat, but other than that he ain't so bad."

I noticed the stripes on Luther's uniform. "I didn't recognize you, Sergeant Sheffield."

"No matter. Why don't you tie that pony and I'll walk you over to Kit's tent."

I dismounted and dropped the reins. All Horse didn't need to be tied. "I'd be obliged."

Sheffield turned and led the way. I caught up to him and walked by his side as we passed among the soldiers, lounging and talking low near their fires.

"A lot has changed since Valverde," the old gambler said. "I got rid of that whore Rosa. She was as bad for me as I was bad for her. Last I heard, she was running a laundry in Santa Fe, making an honest livelihood."

"That's good to know," I said.

"I gave up the bottle after I got busted down to corporal. It was either that or drink myself to death, so I kicked it. I stopped taking the laudanum and all the other shit I was killing myself with, too."

"You look a hell of a lot healthier for it."

"The army's been good for me. The discipline, and the camaraderie of the men. I've found out I can lead these boys, Greenwood. I earned these stripes in the Navaho campaign."

I didn't know how to reply, so I just walked along with him until I saw the tent we were approaching. Sheffield stopped short of the place and turned to me. "I owe you," he said. "You could have killed me at Valverde, the day I tried to murder you. Or you could have caused me a lot of trouble over the affair. I could have been shot by a firing squad if you'd have pushed the matter."

"I suppose so," I said.

"Anyway, I'd like to let bygones be bygones."

I thought about that for a second, then simply held my open palm out between us. Luther Sheffield—the man who once wanted nothing more than to see me dead—shook my hand like a gentleman.

"I'll tell Kit you're here." He turned away and walked to the tent. He spoke with someone at the tent flap for a moment, then returned to me. "Kit's asleep. His adjutant wouldn't let me wake him. He said to report at dawn."

I nodded. "Very well."

Sheffield smiled. "Your old friend Blue Wiggins is in camp. Do you want to go hunt him up?"

"Do you get along with Blue all right?" I asked, with some skepticism.

Luther chuckled. "Like I said, a lot has changed."

"Yes, I'd like to see Blue. Haven't seen him since I left Fort Canby."

We found Blue Wiggins camped with his mess mates and had a boisterous reunion. Also in Blue's "mess"—as the smallest grouping of soldiers was termed by the ever-so-eloquent U.S. Army, I found Toribio Trevino. When he saw me, he came forward and gave me a tremendous *abrazo*. "*Hola,* Mucho," he said.

I was well pleased with how tall and strong Toribio had grown. We sat and talked and gnawed hardtack for quite some time. I asked Toribio if he had had any luck contacting any of his surviving relatives down near Monterrey, Mexico, where he had been captured as a boy by Comanches.

"No, Mucho," he said. "I have written letters, but I get no answers. I don't remember enough to know where to send the letters. The names of my relatives were lost to my memory while I was a captive. There are a lot of Trevinos in Mexico. But I am planning to go down there. I didn't want to for a long time. That's the place where the Indians caught me. I saw my father killed and scalped there. I didn't want to go back. But now I am thinking I must go down there after this campaign, when I am mustered out of the volunteers. I still have some revenge to take on the Comanches for the way they took me from my family and the cruel way they treated me. After I get my satisfaction in battle, I can go home and see if I have any family left down there."

The men sat quietly and listened to Toribio make this speech. His voice was so sure and strong that I almost could not believe he was the same timid captive I had ransomed years ago.

"This man is Mucho Hombre," he finally said, pointing to me. "He rescued me from those savages. They would have tortured me slowly to death if he had not paid my ransom and returned me to civilization. I owe him my life."

All this praise was embarrassing to me, but I took it with as much grace as I could muster. "I didn't do much," I admitted. "Just got you out of there. Kit and Lucien Maxwell are the ones that gave you a home and made you the man you are today." In reality, I felt that I had virtually abandoned Toribio after I ransomed him. I had turned him over to better men than me to see after his upbringing. Kit Carson was the real influence on Toribio.

"Well, I owe a lot to old Mucho here, myself," Luther Sheffield said. "It all started back in fifty. Or maybe it was fifty-one."

Blue Wiggins began to chuckle. "It was fifty."

"So it was. I was a no-'count gambler up in Santa Fe at the time . . ." And so Luther began telling the story of how Blue and I had gotten crossways with him over a poker game. It was an odd surprise to be able to listen to the story now and not worry about Luther pulling a gun or a knife on me.

Most men don't change all that much during the course of a lifetime. Most are shaped by the time they reach manhood, like pieces of hot iron forged and hammered, then cooled and hardened into what they are. Occasionally, though, you meet a man with the ability to reshape himself, to step back into the fire made white-hot by the breath of the bellows and bend himself into a new kind of tool. Luther Sheffield had become such a man. Smart, confident, and adventurous since boyhood, he had let his talents lead him onto the dark path of gambling, whoring, and drinking. His vices had whittled away at him until he was almost nothing. At some point, though, he had taken a frightful look into the mirror and made a tough but final decision.

Now Luther was back. He was more a man than he had ever been. I am proud to tell you that he would never slide back into his old ways, either. He did not last as long as me, but that is probably for the best. Living to the age of ninety-nine is not all one would crack it up to be, as they say. I always wondered how one would "crack" something "up" to "be" anything in the first place, but let us not stray onto that point.

No, Luther died at the age of fifty-nine while serving as town marshal in Trinidad, Colorado. I was his deputy at the time. We were attempting to arrest a gang of three drunken cowboys who were shooting out the gas streetlights in town. Luther ordered them to disarm, but they began shooting at us, so we returned their fire. Luther killed one and wounded another before one of them shot him through the heart. I finished off the wounded cowboy and killed the third without getting a nick. But Luther lay dead, taken so quickly that the shot could not possibly have hurt.

It was a tough blow to lose my friend that way at the time, but now I can't help thinking that that bullet through the heart spared him from suffering the ravages that time takes on a human body. I have watched decades carve my face and twist my frame while Luther rides a flawless shadow horse beyond the Great Divide. Sometimes, on those frightfully lonely nights before the moon rises dark, when I hear the demons clawing at the cracks of my shanty to get at me with their merciless talons—sometimes I can't help wishing I had taken Luther's bullet that day in Trinidad, and that he had gone unscathed.

FORTY-FIVE

Orion went to bed with his sword on, lying down ever so slowly on the western horizon, his head to the north. When he slipped beyond the skyline, Kit stepped from the tent. I startled him a little at first glance, for I stood very close to the tent flap. Then he recognized me in the pastel glow of the coming day and smiled.

"Kid," he said, taking my hand. "You showed up after all."

"I promised I would."

"Yes, you did. I should never have doubted." He looked toward the commissary wagon. "Coffee!" he ordered.

"Yes, sir," came the reply as a cook, lying under the wagon, kicked off a blanket and crawled out of bed. "Give me five minutes, Colonel Carson."

Kit tilted his head toward something to his right. "Come with me. I want to take a look at something."

We began walking, Kit moving stiffly, for the night had been cold and his body had ridden more hard miles than all the men in his cavalry combined. We passed by something I had failed to see last night in the dark. A battery of two twelve-pound howitzers stood against the stark light of the eastern sky.

"Have you been out there among them?" Kit asked.

"Some," I said. "I passed through. I went down to Texas for a while."

"See any big camps?"

I shook my head, because I knew he was judging my face out of the corner of his eye. "They're all out moving around in small bands, following the buffalo."

"Maybe that's better," he said. "I know we can whip a bunch of them at even odds."

"You want my advice?" I said.

"I'll sure listen to it."

I walked eight slow steps without speaking, then said, "I know you've got to go hunting Comanches and Kiowas, because you've already come this far. But just because you're hunting them, doesn't mean you have to find any."

Kit chuckled. "You know that would never float. My men want a fight. I've got Ute scouts who can read a trail better than you and me together. Everybody would know if I went dodgin' instead of houndin'."

"You could lose every last man, Kit. You've only got fourteen officers, three hundred twenty-one men, and seventy-five Ute Indian scouts."

He stopped and glared. "How do you know that?"

I frowned at him. "You know me. My mind can't help but count everything my eyes see. You had a thousand men against the Navahos, and they were easier prey up in that canyon. Their fortress became their own trap. You won't trap the Comanches or Kiowas. They'll scatter in a dozen directions unless they've got you outnumbered, then they'll ride circles around you and pick your men off one by one until you're all dead."

Kit shrugged and motioned me onward with a nod. "Like as not, I guess. No man lives forever. But I aim to give it my best and punish those devils for the raids and murders. I've asked myself time and time again if this is right, and I know it is, Kid. It may not be purdy, and it may not be fair. But it's right. Those poor savages have got to be whupped into takin' the white man's road. If they don't, not a one of them will be left alive."

He stopped on a little rise and looked down into the Canadian River Valley. "There it is," he said.

I looked, but didn't see anything other than the river and some crooked arroyos. "What?"

"The place I wanted you to see."

"Why?"

He pointed. "See those flats down there by the water, just upstream of that draw? That's where it happened."

"What happened, Kit? What are you talking about?"

"The murder of Mrs. White. Fifteen years ago. She was traveling with a caravan on the trail to Santa Fe when her fool husband decided to go on ahead with his carriage, since it traveled faster. Some Apaches attacked them in camp. Killed Mr. White and four other men, and carried away Mrs. White. When word finally got back down the trail, Major Grier went out to track 'em, and I signed on as scout, hoping to rescue Mrs. White. By that time the trail was hard to follow. It was a week old, and covered by some snow and by buffalo herds crossin' over it. And you know how them Apaches can doctor a trail when they know they're gonna be followed."

Kit smiled, though his eyes remained sad. "But that Mrs. White. She was helping me. At every camp, she'd leave a little bitty piece of cloth off'n her dress. Maybe just a thread or two sometimes, so's the Indians wouldn't see it. Still, even with her help, it took me twelve days to catch up to her. By then, she'd been a captive almost three weeks."

He paused and looked down at the flats below, yet his eyes were really looking *back* fifteen years. He sniffed some good, cold air and blinked once, slowly. "That twelfth day, I seen a blue norther comin' and knew if we didn't find them Apaches come sundown, we'd lose Mrs. White. The blizzard would cover their trail for good. So we whipped it up as best we could. Then we rode up over this rise, right here. I was out ahead of Major Grier, and I spotted the Indian camp down there on those flats. He rode up beside me, and I said, 'Major, we must charge that camp *now*!'

"Well, Kid, there was another scout in the party name of Leroux, and he didn't know coons from ringtail cats. He said we ought to wait a minute and reconnoiter. Major Grier was a good officer, but he was green and he didn't know which of us to listen to. I told him, 'They've already spotted us, Major, order the goddamn attack *now*!' and you know I don't use such language lightly. He was drawing breath to say something, and I think he was gonna make the order, and I believe we still could have saved that poor Mrs. White. But just then a bullet struck the major in the chest and he fell off'n his horse and landed right where you stand—right under your feet. The bullet come a long way from down in that camp and maybe didn't have too much powder behind it. It just bounced off the major, but it stunned him bad and knocked his wind out.

"The soldiers wouldn't charge on my order and I couldn't take the camp alone. By that time the Indians were scramblin', taking what they could to run. When I finally got the major mounted and the order given, it was too late. We charged, but the Indians had already carried Mrs. White outside of camp and shot an arrow through her heart."

Kit bowed his head and pinched the bridge of his nose. "That poor woman was starved and beaten by them savages. And mistreated in every way. You know what a savage will do to an enemy woman. And yet she'd left those signs along the trail, still hopeful until the moment that arrow pierced her heart."

"Sounds like plain bad luck," I said. "That other scout and the bullet causing the hesitation. Wasn't your fault. Like you said, you couldn't take the camp alone."

"That ain't what bothered me worst. There was somethin' else."

"What?" I asked, trying to imagine what else could have gone wrong.

"After we buried Mrs. White we went back to the camp to burn it. One of the soldiers found a book. I couldn't read it, of course, so the major showed it to me with a big ol' grin on his face, and read some of it to me out loud. It was what you call a novel. A storybook. And that there storybook writer who writ it had made me the hero in it. *Me.* Kit Carson. Oh, you should have heard tell of the way I could slaughter redskins in there. I could follow a cold trail by the dark of the moon. There was not a thing in the world I could not do. I was some hero in that there novel, Kid."

"Where'd they find the book, exactly?" I asked.

Kit looked me in the eye, knowing I already understood him. "In one of the lodges. The signs were plain that it was the lodge they kept Mrs. White in. That book was hers. She'd been readin' about me. She must have prayed I'd come rescue her. She might even have seen me mounted right here when we hesitated and got her kilt instead of rescued. That haunted me a long time, Kid. The more I thought about it, the more I fretted over her disappointment in me when that arrow flew and I didn't come to save her.

"The trip back to Rayado was bad. The norther hit and it was the worst blizzard I ever saw. One of the dragoons froze to death in his sleep and other boys lost fingers and toes. It was miserable. But my misery was all in my heart. Colder than that blue norther. I have never in my life failed so bad. I just kept thinking about what might have happened if we'd charged that camp at first sight and saved that poor woman. If I could have been the Kit Carson she'd read about instead of just the fool I am. Time has eased it some, but I still regret it to this day. Especially here, looking down on where it happened."

"What happened to the book?" I asked, not really sure that it mattered.

"It's at Maxwell's Ranch. I go look at it now and then to remind myself of the two things Mrs. White taught me. Never give up hope, and don't hesitate when you know you're right. She did her part. She didn't give up. I failed. I hesitated. For her sake, I will never let it happen again." He turned back toward the wagons and campfires, turning his back on fifteen years of regret. "Renegades have got to be punished, Kid. Swift and sure."

The bugle sounded reveille back at the camp and Kit nodded toward the cook's wagon. "I bet my coffee's ready. Come on."

We walked back to the camp in silence. I felt gloomy, and had begun to think that maybe I should not have come at all, though I was only keeping my word to Kit. I glanced over toward All Horse. After my arrival last night, one of the soldiers had unsaddled him and tied him to a stake pin driven into the ground. He recognized me as we walked nearby, and gave a low nicker, perhaps complaining about the stake rope.

We got to the cook fire and Kit took his tin cup of hot black coffee from the cook. He seemed to have forgotten all about Mrs. White, for he slurped the coffee with pleasure, and smiled. "Kid, my plan is to march upstream to Adobe Walls. We'll leave our wagons there and go north with pack mules. I've heard tell that the Indians are camped on Paladora Creek. I need to know what you know about the enemy out there. You could save lives."

Though Kit's intelligence about Paladora Creek was highly flawed, his plan of storing supplies at Adobe Walls was going to lead him right to the Comanches and Kiowas by pure luck. In an instant I knew that I bad to bluff my way through this interview with Kit and escape back downstream to warn Kills Something and Little Bluff of the coming attack. "I haven't heard of any big camps on Paladora Creek. Other than that, I don't know what to tell you, Kit."

"You mean you *won't* tell me."

"I didn't say that."

"You've got to know something that would help. My Ute spies reported to me last night. They've backtrailed you coming up the Canadian River Valley. I know you've been out there with the enemy, Kid. I only want to know what I've got ahead of me. I've got a lot of good boys to take care of here."

I had never dreamed that I would be interrogated by my friend this way, and I felt suddenly foolish and naïve. Kit was going to do his duty, and not even my friendship with him would interfere. His was a singleness of mind a man had to admire even if it violated the trust between us. I had underestimated him once again.

"I have nothing to tell you, Colonel."

Kit smiled. "Thought you might say that." He put his coffee cup on the wheel of the cook wagon. "Well, I can't let you go back out there."

"What do you mean?"

"You know too much, Kid. I'll have to send you back to Fort Bascom and keep you under guard until this business is done."

My mood darkened and my anger boiled up like a thunderhead. "You told me to come in for a talk, Kit, and I did. You said I could tell you all I wanted to or I could tell you nothing at all. Those were your words."

"I didn't make any promises about what would happen after that. I'm not a fool, Kid. I know what you're gonna do. You're gonna go back out there and warn your Comanche brothers that I'm comin', and I can't have that. You've counted heads. You know our strength."

"I'm a free trader, not your spy. Did you think I was going to lead you right to the Indians so you could slaughter them? This smacks of the Charlie Beach and Paddy Graydon affair."

Now it was Kit's anger that flared. He pointed his finger at me in a warning. "You've got no call to associate me with that business. This is nothing like that. I haven't offered to pay you for setting up an ambush like those two scoundrels. I haven't offered you anything at all. Your loyalty to the government is in question, Mr. Greenwood, so I'm placing you under guard and taking you out of the way. Now, I'll have your weapons, please."

I took a step backward and swelled up like a mustang stud about to battle a rival. "The hell you will. Not without a fight. I am loyal to what is right, not to a white man's government. And you have no authority to arrest me."

"I'm not arresting you. I'm detaining you. I'll have your weapons now. We have no time for foolishness."

I stood there defiantly, my every muscle wound tighter than a steel spring. I shook my head. "No, sir, you will *not* have my weapons."

"Then we'll have to take them from you by force."

Kit looked away from me toward the nearest mess of soldiers and I chose that moment to bolt like a rabbit toward All Horse. I sprinted with every morsel of energy I had. Kit began to shout orders to the astonished men to stop me. All Horse saw me coming and threw his head up in alarm, but did not pull against the stake rope. I drew my knife as I ran and made one slash at the rope about eight feet from the leather U.S. Army halter some soldier had put on All Horse. With my next bound I was on Tu Hud's back and we instantly thundered north toward the Canadian breaks. At one leap we were at full gallop, using all the Comanche horse-and-rider skills we had learned together through days and days of training.

"Get him!" Kit was screaming. "Get that man!"

A soldier angled in to my right to grab my leg, but I nudged All Horse in the right flank and he darted away so quickly that the solder fell flat on his face as he made his dive and grabbed thin air. Another couple of soldiers rushed for my halter, bravely stepping in front of the galloping steed. I grabbed mane, tucked my legs under the curve of my mount's ribs, and made a kissing sound that was All Horse's command to jump. He slowed his gallop just enough to gather himself and made an enormous leap right over the heads of the two stunned soldiers, who fell back in fear of the hooves that flew inches from their faces.

The silence of the leap ended with the drum of hooves falling heavily on the desert, and I knew we could make our escape if we could just get by the sentinels. The arms were stacked and I had made my break so quickly that no one had had a chance to grab a rifle and take aim. I looked over my shoulder and saw Kit Carson sprinting toward me, shouting something I could not make out over the rumble of hooves and All Horse's snorting for air. But the men nearer to me began to pass the shouted order out to the sentinels, each man in sequence cupping his hands around his mouth to yell at the next. Finally the order came to the men nearest to me and even though I raced ever farther away from them, I heard one shout in a high, boyish voice:

"Shoot the horse! Shoot the horse!"

No! Not Tu Hud! Not All Horse! No, please, God, no . . .

A sentinel rose from a rock he had been sitting on not thirty paces away. I had failed to see him sitting with his back turned to a cholla cactus, which had concealed him. He heard the order and began to shoulder his rifle. He looked young, tired, and scared. I angled away, toward the head of a draw I hoped would conceal me if I could reach it. Over my shoulder, I glared at him and pointed, saying, "No, by God! Do not shoot my—"

The white smoke spewed from the muzzle and Tu Hud squealed in frightful agony. He was all horse to the end, trying for the draw, but his knees buckled and he fell hard on his nose, spilling me over his head. Dirt hit me in the face and broke my nose, but all I could hear were the horrible sounds of All Horse grunting and thrashing on the ground in pain. I sprang to my feet and turned in panic to see him cough a spray of blood into the air. I ran to him, but his eyes rolled and he could only beat his head against the ground. My teeth gritted and my eyes filled with tears as I drew my revolver. I walked around him as he thrashed piteously on the ground. I aimed instinctively, waiting until the great head rested for a moment on the dirt. I shot Tu Hud behind the ear, ending his pain.

The sentinel was reloading, looking fearfully at me as I walked away from the carcass of as fine a horse as a man would ever care to straddle. My revolver remained in my hand and blood from my broken nose ran down my face. My thumb clicked the hammer back as more soldiers came sprinting toward me on foot. Behind them, some cavalrymen had mounted and were coming to surround me. Kit was running behind the first row of soldiers and I recognized some friends—Toribio, Blue Wiggins, and Luther Sheffield—coming to keep me from being killed.

"Drop it, Kid!" Colonel Carson was shouting. "Drop the gun!" Soldiers came and made a half-circle around me, their rifles shouldered and aimed in front of wild eyes. My revolver still pointed downward. One upward flick of the barrel would create an instant firing squad. My anger was so intense that I almost did not care. I shook with rage. My ire blasted blood from my nostrils. I have been known to go *berserk* in battle—like the legendary Viking warriors who gave rise to the word—the berserkers who would fight as if possessed by demons and kill and maim with unnatural strength, scarcely to remember their deeds later. I was on the verge of going berserk right there and then and it scared the hell out of me, on top of the wrath that fueled it.

"Drop it now!" Kit ordered.

I stood in defiance of the order.

"Come on, Mucho," said Toribio. "You can't win against so many. Don't be loco."

I barely heard all these words through the roar of the fury inside my skull. I had just enough sense left to let the hammer down easily on the revolver. It seemed like someone else doing it, as if I floated above my body, watching it happen.

"Good," Kit said, his voice like an echo in a cave. "Now drop it."

The rumble around me reached a plateau that was almost calming. It was the moment that makes the back of your neck crawl before the lightning bolt strikes. The crouch of the cat before the leap. Instead of dropping the revolver, I flipped it in my hand, making a club of the walnut grip.

"If you want my weapons, you come take them like a *man*!" I said, my voice building to a shout. I yanked my knife from the scabbard and flipped it all the way around in my palm, the blade ending up pointing downward the way it had come out of the sheath. I did not intend to cut anyone, but they didn't know that, and the knife would keep them back for a while. "You murdering sons of bitches!" I yelled. "You horse-killing bastards! Goddamn every one of you to hell! You come take my weapons like men!" I was screaming with such maniacal ire that I could feel the words tear my throat.

A moment passed and Kit said, "Take his weapons."

No man moved.

"I am ordering you men to take his weapons from him now, goddamn it!" And he did not use such language lightly.

A brave but foolish private made a dash at me and grabbed at my knife hand. I easily avoided him and clubbed him to the ground. Another couple of men rushed me, but I whirled and hacked with my blade, hitting one in the nose with my pistol grip and kicking the other in the testicles.

"Oh, hell," Kit growled, and he stalked toward me, one hand in a fist. I was so mad that I didn't care if it was Kit Carson, I was going to crack his head open like any other man. Something passed before me like the shadow of a vulture and I felt a noose tighten around my chest. It was my own rope, taken from my saddle back in camp. I was pulled backward as Kit rushed me. He grabbed the wrist of my knife hand with a bone-crushing grip and with his other fist he thumped me on my broken nose. With both hands now, Kit twisted my knife out of my grasp and I fell back roaring and thrashing. I got in a kick at Kit's bad shoulder, but the rope pulled me far enough away that the force was taken out of the blow.

Soldiers jumped on my arms and legs. One lost his balance in the fracas and fell close enough for me to clench his ear between my teeth. He screamed as a fist pounded my eye, but I tore at that ear until blood spurted and a piece of it came off in my mouth, which I spat at the bastard who was pounding my face with his fist. More blows hit me all over, and Kit yelled, "Enough, boys!" but some youth had already begun to strike with his rifle butt. The last thing I remembered was a racking blow to my head above the right temple, then all was lost.

FORTY-SIX

I dreamed that I could fly, so I went to visit my wife. Yes, I could fly in this dream, but I was wounded somehow and my head ached and now and then a drop of blood would fall from my face like a colorful tear and spiral away under me toward the earth. Flying was painful and difficult, but I wanted to see Westerly, so I flew north across country I knew well, until I saw the towering cottonwoods of Boggsville looming beside the Purgatoire.

And I saw Westerly by the river, looking south, just standing there, staring, her hands embracing her belly where our baby grew ever larger inside her. She looked so sad and lonely that shame filled me for ever having left her. I swooped over and around her, but she did not see me. Finally, a drop of blood fell from my battered face and spattered on her hand like a red raindrop. She looked at it, then looked up, fearfully, dreadfully. I tried to speak to her, but couldn't, and her mouth gaped and her eyes bulged and she screamed in terror at whatever shape she saw in me.

A gust of wind caught me and carried me away from her as she fell onto the grass and tried to hide from the horror of *me*. The wind carried me west, along the Arkansas, where I saw something spread upon the plains, lifting a cloud of dust like a herd of buffalo. But this was no herd. It writhed like a bed of dark maggots on a carcass, and as I got closer, I saw column upon column of cavalry soldiers, and then I could hear them, their horses' hooves stomping in rhythm like the chug of a huge steam engine about to explode with excess pressure. The soldiers rode the trail that came out of the mountains and led to Boggsville and William's stockade. They were marching step by step closer to my Indian wife, and I could not stop them, for I was just a bird caught in a gale that carried me high up into a storm cloud where hailstones pelted my face and lightning threatened to rake my flesh.

I woke with a gasp and found myself horizontal on the ground, shivering. A fire burned before me, but I was too far away from it to feel much warmth. A flake of snow fell on the side of my face, melted, and ran tickling across my nose. Two soldiers sat across the fire, closer to its warmth. I squinted to bring them in view, and felt dried blood crack on my cheek. My head felt as if it had a large rock on it, and my stomach roiled with nausea. When I tried to move, I found my hands restrained behind my back and felt the cold steel of shackles. With some effort, I sat up, and found the soldiers staring at me. One was white, the other Mexican. Neither looked happy.

"It's about time," the white soldier said.

I looked at my surroundings and found myself in the place where Kit and his men had camped, but all the troops were gone now, save these two. I chose to speak in Spanish, saying, "Looks like you boys will be left out of the fight."

The Mexican soldier answered in his native tongue: *"No mierda, genio."* No shit, genius.

"What did he say?" the white man asked.

"He said you were the ugliest damn gringo he ever saw in his life."

The white man frowned at me and said, "He ain't as dumb as he looks, is he?" He looked suspiciously at his Mexican comrade. "What did you say back to him?"

"I said, 'No shit, genius.' "

The white man chuckled, then glared at me. "You speak English from now on, you hear? If you don't, I'll take and tap you on the skull where that rifle butt hit you."

I struggled to my knees and crawled closer to the fire to warm myself. "I need water."

The Mexican took my canteen and held it to my mouth so I could drink.

"Let's get his sorry ass in a saddle and get the hell out of this godforsaken place."

There were three horses saddled, one with my rig, the others with army tack.

"What are your orders?" I asked, as I struggled to my feet.

"We're taking you back to Santa Fe to have you hung as a spy," the white soldier said. He stared at me with a poker face for a couple of seconds, then doubled over with laughter, slapping his knee. "You ought to have seen the look on your own face just now. No, we're to take you back to Fort Bascom and hold you for a few days then turn you loose."

I looked at the Mexican for confirmation, and he nodded, his eyes revealing his disdain for this whole business. I asked for my gloves, hoping they would unshackle me, but they put the gloves on for me behind my back. We went to mount and I told them I should have the shackles in front so I could rein my mount.

"Shut up and put your foot in the stirrup," the soldier ordered. "You ain't gonna be reinin' no horse nowhere for a few days."

So I had to mount with my hands shackled behind me. I had not intended to make a break for it should they have removed the cuffs. I only wanted to get them back on, one click looser over my gloves, so that I could later slip out of them. But the two men were taking no chances with me, having seen my most violent behavior only a few hours earlier. We rode off to the west at a walk. My head pounded, and I felt close to vomiting any second, though my stomach held no food. My one goal now was to escape and ride back to Adobe Walls to warn the Comanches and Kiowas camped there that soldiers were coming. I knew I probably wasn't going to accomplish this today, however, so I decided to strike up a conversation.

"I don't remember you boys from Valverde."

"You wouldn't remember me unless you'd have found me behind the tree I's usin' for cover. I wasn't about to let no Texan get a shot at my sorry ass."

"I joined the army for the Navaho war," the Mexican said. "They killed my mother and father years ago."

I asked about the Navaho campaign and got the two men telling stories and pretty soon we were just like old friends, except that I had to wear handcuffs behind my back. Still, I had befriended my captors, who really had nothing personal against me. Sam, the white soldier, who was from Kentucky, seemed pleased to be relieved of duty in the Comanche campaign and claimed he had had some pretty bad dreams about what was going to happen to him out there if he went. "I haven't lost no Comanches, so I don't see the point in huntin' any."

Francisco said he wasn't afraid of Comanches, but he had signed on to fight Navahos and would just as soon go back to his farm on the Rio Grande now that the Navahos were all rounded up at the Bosque Redondo. Everyone suspected that Kit's regiment was going to disband after the Comanche campaign, and the two men were eager to get back to their civilian lives.

We stopped that night where the invading force had made camp two nights before on its way east. My escorts finally unlocked my cuffs so I could accomplish some necessities which they didn't care to help me with, but they kept me guarded at gunpoint the whole time. When they went to lock the shackles again, I held my hands in front of me, but that wouldn't do for Sam. He insisted I keep my hands behind my back. And he gave his weapons to Francisco while he locked me up, so I couldn't grab them away from him.

"Put the irons on over the gloves, if you would," I said. "They're cutting into my flesh around my wrists."

Sam checked, and sure enough found the raw marks I had purposely made in my skin to trick him into putting the cuffs over my gloves, thus making them one click looser. I could have slipped those cuffs off that night and made a run for it, but my body was exhausted and I needed a day or two more to get over the beating the soldiers had given me. I also needed to eat, and regain my strength. So I spent three days riding west with Sam and Francisco, slowing our progress as much as I could so I would not get too far away from Adobe Walls. I regaled my captors with my finest stories of my exploits on the frontier, and they came to like and respect me.

There comes a time in the night when men and even dogs fall into a state of sleep so deep that nothing short of a touch or a loudly spoken word will wake them. And though I am usually immune to the mystic powers of this time, and though it varies from one night to another, I always know instinctively when the time comes, for my cerebrum and viscera operate in accord with the moon, the planets, the tilt of the earth on its axis, the fires of the sun.

So it was that on the third night—at 2:38 in the morning—I slipped my gloves off in the dark. Then using the grease from a piece of salt pork, I oiled my wrists and the shackles decorating them. Years of using my hands to accomplish card tricks and other illusions allowed me to make the span of my knuckles almost as small as my wrist, so by relaxing one hand and methodically working the circle of steel past my knuckles, I was able to slip the cuff off in less than a minute. The second hand proved even easier, as I could now hold my arms in front of me. I left the cuffs on the ground as a symbol of my freedom and rose silently to my feet.

I took all the food and water in camp, leaving Sam and Francisco their weapons with which to protect themselves. I would have taken a weapon, but the soldiers had wisely fallen asleep with their guns in their hands, or under their heads. They were only a day's walk from Fort Bascom. I left the saddles on the ground and, taking one saddle blanket to ride Indian-style, I led the horses away from camp. I tied the tail of one horse to the head of a second with a lead rope. I would lead two spare horses and ride the third.

I threw my saddle blanket on my mount and tied a rope loosely around the girth of the gelding, and over the top of the blanket, making a Co-manche loop. For hard riding in rough country, a rider could slip his bent knees under that rope, between the rope and the horse, the thickness of the rider's thigh tightening the rope. The rope would then hold the rider firmly to the horse, yet the rider could easily come loose by straightening his knee. Why no other nation of equestrians in the history of horsemanship had come up with this simple means of riding is a mystery. I suppose the spirits saw fit to give it only to the True Humans.

~~~~~~

Let me try to describe to you a long, desperate ride beginning in the mid-dle of the night, when the moon has moved on and the sun has yet to breathe light across the cheek of the face of Mother Earth. You begin this way: You choose a star in the east that comes and goes between the inky masses of clouds—clouds that are visible not because you can see them, but only because they blot out the specks of light in the sky as they float ominously overhead.

You choose your star and trust your horse. You wonder how your horse can see anything in this blackness. Then you wonder if he *can* see, or if he can somehow divine his way over the rough terrain in total darkness. As you ride ahead at a trot, leading your spare mounts, you scan the horizon—a place where the stars end and black nothingness begins—straining for a glimpse of a starlit silhouette: a mesquite limb that might rake you from the saddle, or a landmark that might help you know your place.

You ride on, trusting your horse and your luck. You follow that star, ever rising. You ride an hour on faith alone. Two hours. Then, in a blink, you notice that pale hint of a glow in the east, and hope rises like your star. You ride on, humming tunes to the steady rhythm of the horse beneath you, and your way grows ever brighter.

Now the sun appears, molten red, over the rim of the world, and you nudge your tired horse to a lope. You relax a little, for you can at least look for trouble now, and the faster gait is smoother on this pony. But you worry still, for your haste prevents you from watching properly for danger, and you have four sleeps of travel yet before you.

You ride into the morning. You switch horses and stand with your own feet upon the ground for a precious few minutes before mounting again to ride on. You're tired already, but your ordeal has only begun. You reach into the pits of your resolve, summon your Comanche stamina, and go to save your people. The sun blinds you, then warms you, then casts your shadow before you, and you see your shape in silhouette on the ground, so you sit taller astride your loping pony and play the part of the hero you hope you will live to become.

Another night. A few hours of sleep between the setting of the moon and the rising of the sun. Another mount, another day. Your stomach is empty, your canteen dry. No food, brackish water. Exhaustion. Antelope dash across the trail in front of you, and you wish you could ride at such speed. You cut the trail of the legions that grind along ahead of you and you remember the peril to come. They are riding with cannon down upon your village at the Crossing. You shake the doubts away and grit your teeth, feeling like rawhide and sinew a-horseback, and you ride. And ride. Ride . . . A spring of sweet water. A piece of hardtack discarded by some bluecoat. A jackrabbit bolts from right underfoot, but you have no weapon with which to bag him, no means of making fire, no time to roast even a morsel of meat.

A siesta in a patch of good grass for your ponies. Astraddle again, riding. Gaunt now, like your poor stolen nags. You accept the stiffness turned to aching throbs all up and down your frame. It hurts to crane your neck to see the beauty of the sunset behind you. The moon, the dark, the sunrise. You hate riding. You never want to ride again. You'd rather cross the ocean on a yardarm than ride one more step. But you kick at the ribs between your heels and read the sign left plainly by wagons replete with provender.

A flock of cranes circles overhead, fluting a pretty symphony—a musical warning of the norther that has pushed them toward warmer waters. And the blue cloud descends from the frozen reaches of the North Pole. Snow falls on your miserable beasts and makes you shiver in great convulsions. You must hide overnight in a cave you carve out of a cutbank on the north side of a creek. You rise at dawn, stiff and weak. You ride through drifts and thank the spirits for sending just one night of snow.

You ride, and you take heart, for you are closing ground. The sign becomes fresher upon the new-fallen snow. Your ride is almost over. You welcome even the prospect of chaos on the battlefield over this damned riding. You know where you are. Just miles from the Crossing. The old Adobe Walls stand waiting. Your people do not know the danger that descends the valley. You turn loose the two poorest mounts and make one last push. It is time. The sun crouches behind the horizon ahead of you, poised to rise on what could be your day of glory, your day of great failure, or your last day on Earth.

FORTY-SEVEN

Before dawn, I came upon the supply train, the wagons having been left in the rear under guard. I had expected this. Darkness prevented me from actually seeing the wagons, but my mount, fatigued as he was, lifted his head and perked his ears at something down the trail, so I drew rein to listen. I heard two sentries in conversation. In that frosty, rarefied atmosphere, a spoken word could travel a long way. As I had not heard human voices in days, these knifed through the natural sounds of the valley like an alarm. Kit would have been furious had he known his sentries were conversing in anything more than a whisper.

Having first heard the voices, I waited to listen for more. I heard a mule stamp a foot. I heard a loose corner of canvas flapping against the side boards of a wagon in the brisk north breeze. The wind shifted on an errant gust and I caught the faint odors of gun oil, manure, and salt pork. This was when I surmised that I had ridden upon the supply wagons and that Kit's main attacking force had ridden on ahead. I reined my mount away before he could nicker to the mules at the camp.

I avoided the supply wagons, riding up a steep ravine on my jaded mount to the rims of the Canadian canyon. On the bluff tops, I found the riding somewhat easier than in the canyon. Here, the ground was more level and the vegetation widely spaced. And I would have the advantage of being able to look down into the valley from high vantage points when dawn came. I struck a lope and rode wide around the heads of the arroyos, holding to flatter ground.

When dawn finally bathed the valley with enough light to make visible the scene below, I rode to a point of land overlooking the bottomlands and, concealing myself behind a juniper bush, I took a peek. In the distance, less than three miles away, I saw the smoke trails of a sizable Indian village. Faintly, I could make out the shapes of ivory-colored tipis, which color told me that this was a Kiowa village. Just my side of the village, I spotted a herd of horses, and knew that some young men or boys would be guarding them through the night.

Now, just below me, I witnessed the movements of Colonel Christopher Carson's column of cavalry, infantry, and artillery, with his Ute scouts making up the vanguard. I knew he could not see the Indian village from his position down in the canyon, for his line of sight was interrupted by a bend in the valley, and by clumps of cottonwoods and other timber. But soon, Kit's Utes would discover the Kiowa herd and the pony guards, and the action would commence.

Now I looked far down the valley, past the Kiowa village, to the timber of what I knew was Bent Creek. Beyond that creek stood Adobe Walls, for I knew exactly where I was. Beyond Adobe Walls, Adobe Creek wound through the prairies. And beyond that, fully six miles away, I could see the smoke cloud of a larger Indian village where I had last left Kills Something and his allied bands. For a brief moment, I considered riding to my old-friend-turned-enemy, Kit Carson, to warn him of the superior force he was about to blunder into. I could not, of course.

I turned away from the bluff and braced for the last leg of my ride. In my exhaustion and excitement, something odd took place. A feeling of calm came over me, and I felt my weight lift, aiding my pony in his last punishing run. I felt as if in a dream, and Vivaldi's *Four Seasons* began to play in my head, as clearly as if an entire orchestra had crowded into my skull. I rode effortlessly through Concerto no. 1 in E Major: Spring. *Der Frühling; allegro.* Trancelike, I flew along the bluffs, outdistancing the soldiers below, soaring along like an eagle toward the Kiowas to warn them of their danger.

As I galloped, I made suppositions. The village I had seen was Little Bluff's, which would make it some 170 lodges strong, each lodge housing one or two warriors. Fewer than three hundred unprepared Kiowa warriors could not hold off a surprise attack by over three hundred soldiers with Ute scouts advancing and cannon trailing. So, I decided my job was to dash into the village and urge a hasty retreat downstream, where the Comanches were in camp beyond Adobe Walls.

As I sailed along the bluffs in the light of dawn, I heard shots, and knew Kit's Utes had engaged the Kiowa sentries guarding the horse herd. At that moment, I plunged down an arroyo and hastened to the camp of hide lodges. I began to yell, "Yee-yee-yee-yee!" like a Comanche warrior as I charged into the village. Warriors were stepping out of their lodges with weaponry, for some had been awakened by the smattering of gunfire. I galloped straight to the large lodge of old Chief Little Bluff and found him flinging the bearskin covering of his doorway aside as he squinted against the light and leapt out into it.

"The bluecoats are here!" I said, in the Kiowa tongue. "They are more than three hundred, with Ute scouts in the lead. You must retreat, Uncle. We will join with the Comanches, and then turn to attack!"

A young warrior from a lodge nearby pointed at me and said, "He has led the bluecoats to our camp! Plenty Man has led the enemy to attack us!"

"Silence, you young fool!" the old chief snapped. "Look! His pony is almost dead. He has ridden to warn us. Look closer. See the cuts and bruises on his face! They have tortured him. Plenty Man has escaped the enemy to warn us. Do you not remember the weapons he brought to us? The white buffalo he killed to protect us? Now, we must do as he says. Send your families downriver to the Comanches. We will hold the village until our women and children have escaped. Hurry! Everyone!"

I dismounted, throwing my leg over my poor, stolen horse; leaving him there panting, his head low. I moved with the rest of the warriors toward the upper end of camp, though I had no weapon with which to meet the Utes. I picked up a stick of hackberry from a woodpile and advanced, shouting into the lodges I passed, urging the men to fight and the women to retreat with their children.

Chaos engulfed the little village as the Kiowas and their Kiowa-Apache friends emerged from their lodges to the prospect of violent death. I saw a woman running with a child—but she was running along with the warriors, into the fray. "Mother!" I shouted, catching her by the arm. "The warriors are running to meet the enemy. You must run the *other* way!" I pointed eastward. Wild-eyed, she did not seem to want to believe me, until she noticed another mother dragging a child by the arm, while carrying an infant on her back, and she followed them toward the Comanche village downstream.

Riderless horses began to stampede into the village, having escaped the Ute scouts who had captured most of the herd. I wished for a lariat, for I could have lassoed one that came nearby. A few sentries who had been guarding the herd came sprinting wild-eyed into camp, shouting their warnings. Behind them rode the first of the Ute invaders, having taken the time to change their pad saddles to stolen horses. One rode up behind a fleeing Kiowa sentry, whom he shot in the back of the head with a pistol. After that shot, the firing became general between Utes and Kiowas, and absolute chaos ensued, with bullets and arrows flying in every direction, men shouting, women screaming, and horses galloping everywhere in terror.

I remained in the calm of my trance, with Vivaldi's own orchestra playing in my head. *Largo e pianissimo sempre.* I had accomplished my mission. I had warned the Indians. I marched into the thick of the skirmish with my chunk of firewood in my hand. A mounted Ute warrior spotted me and, considering me easy prey, angled toward me, drawing a bow. I have never been more certain of my impending death. I simply knew I would be killed.

Then a bullet hit that warrior in the back and spilled him from his mount before he could loose his arrow. I found out later that the Kiowa warrior Stumbling Bear had saved my life by killing the Ute warrior about to ride me down. Remarkably, the dead warrior's horse ran straight to me, and I caught the reins of the war bridle. A moment later that horse threw his head in front of my face and took a bullet that would have blown the orchestra right out of my skull. Sprayed in hot blood from the horse, I found myself knocked backward, during which time I saw an arrow pass by me and I heard it pop through the whitened buffalo hide of a Kiowa lodge. Another Ute warrior rushed past me but only glanced at me. Seeing me painted in horse blood, he must have thought me dead or mortally wounded.

Regaining my senses, I realized that I had avoided two arrows and a bullet meant for me. It was as if angels were brushing me aside, out of the paths of the deadly projectiles, and I felt that I must have some reason for living, so I sprang from the ground and ran ghoulishly, blood drenched, back through the village so that I might in some way aid in the retreat. As I sprinted, I spotted a Spencer repeating carbine someone had dropped on the ground. It was a Kiowa or Ute weapon, decorated with brass tacks hammered into the stock, with a feather tied to the barrel by a horsehair, to aid in judging windage. I grabbed it up, and as I ran through the gunfire, the shouts of battle, and the rumble of hooves, I checked the breech and found one live round in the chamber. This rifle also had a seven-shot tabular magazine in the rifle stock, but I had no time to determine how many rounds it held.

Sunlight glinted in my eye, the great orb having ascended the canyon bluffs. I caught the putrid smell of offal, and glanced to see a battle-gutted horse thrashing piteously on the ground. I wished that I could use my one sure bullet to end its misery, but I dared not.

I ran past the Kiowa lodges and into the Kiowa-Apache part of camp. There, I saw the old Apache chief Iron Shirt standing at his lodge door, chanting a death song. He was wearing the ancient Spanish coat of mail that had given him his name years before. "Grandfather, you must retreat with the rest of us!" I shouted. He did not even look at me. He kept his eyes fixed on the invaders advancing lodge by lodge toward him, and I knew he had chosen to stand and die.

I left Iron Shirt's lodge, and came upon a young warrior who could not have been more than thirteen, trying to string his bow to meet the enemy. "Run, boy!" I ordered. "String your bow later!" But just then an arrow struck him in the hip, knocking him from his feet. As he tried to drag himself to safety, I ran to him, broke the arrow shaft off, and threw him on my back to carry him away. I retreated until my leg muscles and lungs burned, carrying the boy with me, until White Bear rode past me on a fine horse that he must have had staked overnight in the village.

"I will carry the boy," White Bear said, with amazing calm. He was a young man, but experienced in warfare, and years later would become known as a terror to Texas settlers, who knew him as Satanta. I helped White Bear lift the wounded boy up onto the horse.

"I will come back for you, Plenty Man," he promised.

"Do not worry about me," I replied. "My spirit powers are strong today."

He smiled and carried the boy away at a gallop.

I had to stop to catch some wind, so I turned back toward the attackers and found a Ute brave galloping my way with a cavalry revolver lowering to fire at me. I raised my carbine to my shoulder and fired, hitting the Ute man in the Adam's apple, and almost tearing his head completely off. I ran to capture the weapon he had dropped, though bullets and arrows hissed through the air all around me. I even took the time to touch the dead man with my rifle barrel so that I could claim the coup later in council, should I survive.

A bugle sounded advance not far up the canyon—the first bugle call of the day—and I knew the cavalry would soon be following the Ute scouts rank by rank. I backed away from the attack, trying all at once to watch for enemies amid screams and shouts and gunshots and hoofbeats while checking my captured weapons. I found the magazine of the Spencer car-bine empty. The cylinder of the Remington percussion-cap revolver held four loads. I sensed that most of the women and children had escaped the village by now and that the Ute charge had been almost halted by a stub-born Kiowa resistance. Still, I caught my first glimpse of blue-coated cav-alry coming up behind the Utes, and I knew it was time to draw back if I wanted to survive long enough to help protect the Kiowas in their retreat.

Though still panting from having carried the wounded boy on my back, each breath fogging the cold air, I turned and ran to the last row of lodges on the east end of camp. Here I found a few veteran warriors making a last stand to allow their families to reach the timber of Bent Creek to the east. The woods and brush would conceal them as they made their way to the Comanche camps. So I turned to face the attackers, joining the Kiowa and Kiowa-Apache defenders. The feeling of calm that had borne me this far still survived through the battle, and the string section of Vivaldi's orches-tra tripped every so lightly through the end of the first concerto of the *Four Seasons. Danza pastorale: Allegro.*

Along this line of warriors I found Stumbling Bear, Lean Bear, and Chief Little Bluff. Soon, White Bear came riding back to the line, having taken the wounded boy to safety. These men, and some younger braves, held the edge of camp and kept a steady stream of bullets and arrows fly-ing westward toward the attackers. They used their own lodges as their breastworks, for in the winter the tipis were double-walled and stuffed with grass for insulation against the bitter cold. Few rifle bullets could pass through four layers of buffalo hide, avoid lodge poles, and still hit a target with killing force. Yet the Utes continued to advance lodge by lodge, and more bluecoats began to appear through the gun smoke be-tween the lodges.

Little Bluff looked over his shoulder at the families fleeing across the open prairie behind us. "Tomorrow we will teach our women to run faster!" he shouted, pausing to draw his bow and shoot an arrow that un-horsed a Ute warrior at a remarkable distance. "But today we must make one charge on the enemy so our children and women can reach that tim-ber. I will be the first to count coup on that enemy warrior I just shot, and you younger men will not beat me to that honor."

The firing along our line ceased as each man prepared to charge the enemy in a counterattack. The resident orchestra in my head had lapsed into Concerto Number Two—Summer. The minor-chord renderings of the phantom players suited the mood of impending combat. *Der Sommer. Allegro non molto.* Lean Bear began singing his war song of the Sentinel Horses warrior society. Somehow, it blended with and became part of the orchestra in my fatigued mind.

White Bear took up Little Bluff's challenge to race for the coup honors, as he loosed a Kiowa war cry and sprinted forward. Like hounds on a trail, the rest of us sprinted forward, a step behind White Bear. I felt the surge of energy battle can generate and ran forward with the Kiowas, shooting my revolver into the front line of the attackers as I screamed. My hair felt as if it were standing on end, and my heart beat like a drum at a scalp dance. I raced forward until a Ute warrior appeared through the smoke, and I fired at him as he shot at me with an arrow. My bullet hit him in the chest, killing him, as his arrow nicked my ear, loosing a trickle of blood that joined the horse blood already crusting upon my skin in the dry autumn air.

I fired my Remington revolver three more times, its eruptions joining the general gunfire and war cries of our desperate little counterattack. A couple of Utes were killed in this maneuver, several wounded, and the rest frightened into a momentary retreat as they stampeded back into the leading line of cavalry soldiers marching methodically through the camp that the Utes had already cleared for them. I saw Stumbling Bear pursue these fleeing Utes all the way to the front line of the cavalry, where he shot and killed a bluecoat—the first of Kit's volunteers to fall in the battle.

Now, Stumbling Bear turned back toward the cover of some lodges, and the rest of us fell back with him. The advance of Utes and cavalry had sulled, and we left their front line in confusion as we retreated clean out of the camp and over the prairie the women and children had already crossed. As we ran, I heard the bugle order a halt, and I knew we would not be pursued immediately. This relieved me, for many of us were on foot, and could have been ridden down by the attacking horsemen. But for now, the soldiers were content with having captured the Kiowa village.

I felt stronger than I might have expected, trotting through the tall grass to Bent's Creek, carrying the Spencer carbine and the Remington revolver. I had ammunition for neither, but knew I would find it in Kills Something's camp, for I had led the supply run for such materiel myself. Once we reached the timber, we began to find the wretched refugees war always produces. Old men and women sat among the trees, panting and staring, too exhausted to go on just now. Wounded women and children gazed about in shock, and warriors—some just boys in their first fight—bled from all manner of horrible wounds.

Little Bluff walked up to a young man named Two Birds, who had been wounded in the belly from an arrow that had passed all the way through him. The chief began to laugh and point at the warrior where he lay. "Look what has happened to Two Birds!" the old chief shouted. "He has become a woman! Get up, if you want to be a man again, and go to the next camp!" To my surprise, young Two Birds stood and lifted his chin in defiance of the pain, though his face quivered in agony. He turned and began stumbling eastward.

Others could not be rallied by insults. Those who could ride were put up on horses, behind or before riders. Those who could not even stand were placed on blankets. I grabbed the corner of a blanket bearing a young woman who had been shot through the leg by a rifle ball, her leg shattered. How she had gotten this far, I never knew—perhaps on some rescuer's back. Three other men took up the other corners of the blanket and we started eastward across the prairie of Adobe Walls.

I looked to the north and saw the old ruins rising on the familiar ground. Memories came avalanching down on me. I remembered placing many of those adobe bricks myself, years ago. I recalled the days and nights spent inside and outside of those walls with friends—white, brown, and red. Whatever it was that I had tried to accomplish by building that adobe fort here had failed. In the confusion of the day, I felt that all the suffering and dying surrounding me now was my own damned fault.

And still, Vivaldi played in my head. *Adagio—Presto.*

FORTY-EIGHT

Help came from the Comanche camp before we reached Adobe Creek. Kills Something's people, having heard the shooting, had sent riders to the bluffs above to observe. These riders, upon seeing the Kiowas running from their camp, knew a serious attack had occurred, and now sent ponies pulling pole drags to bear the wounded Kiowas and Kiowa-Apaches to the safety of the large Comanche encampment. I happened to see Fears-the-Ground riding one such pony, and summoned him to take the woman with the broken leg.

"Is all that blood yours?" he asked, staring at the dried black stains all over me.

"Only a little. The rest is the blood of my enemies." This was a lie, of course, for most of the blood had come from an unfortunate horse. But I wasn't opposed to telling a lie to boost my warrior's reputation.

Fears-the-Ground's smile came and passed quickly. "The crier said soldiers are attacking."

"Yes," I replied. "They have taken the Kiowa camp."

"How many?"

"Not enough to defeat us if we gather our warriors quickly to face them."

He nodded and turned his mount back toward camp, bearing the wounded woman across the prairie on the travois. I ran afoot to the village and went straight to Kills Something's lodge. There, my adopted brother was busy gathering reports from the riders who had ascended to different high places to view the action upstream. When he saw me, his eyes widened in surprise and he summoned me forward.

"My brother," he said. "What has happened to you?"

"I was captured and beaten by the bluecoats, but I told them nothing." I paused to gasp for breath. "I escaped and rode ahead of the soldiers to warn Little Bluff's camp. Only a few Kiowa warriors were killed, and some people wounded. The bluecoats have not had enough. They will try to attack your camp next, my brother."

"How many bluecoats?"

"Only three hundred, and seventy-five Utes." I did not mention the supply train, miles upstream. Secretly, I wanted Kit to have an escape route if he proved wise enough to take it. Had I mentioned the supply train, Kills Something would have sent a party to slaughter the guard there, capture Kit's provender, and cut off his retreat. Kills Something's village and the others downstream numbered over one thousand lodges, and I knew we could mount almost three thousand warriors, including the Kiowas and Kiowa-Apaches who had already been run out of their village, and a band of Arapahos who had taken refuge here to escape the troubles in Colorado. Kit would be lucky to get out at all, but I wanted to leave him some kind of hope. In spite of everything that had happened, I still held his friendship dear.

Kills Something nodded and thought for a moment, as the leaders of the warrior societies waited for his decisions. "We have no time for a council of war," he said, "but we have time to put on our paint and headdresses and catch our best war ponies. Crier, tell the first-year men of the Little Horses society to join the Kiowas and go to meet the enemy. They must go afoot, hiding in the grass or the timber along the creek. They must shoot well and hold the soldiers back until the rest of us can get mounted. Then we will teach these bluecoats not to invade our country. Go!"

The warriors dispersed with a general battle cry that echoed off the bluffs in the cold morning air.

Kills Something looked at me, and summoned me closer with a gesture of his chin. "What else must I know, my brother?"

"Their leader is Little Chief."

He frowned a little, then let his expression turn to an anxious grin. I supposed this was either because he admired my loyalty to him over Kit, or because he wanted to face the great white warrior Little Chief in battle. Perhaps a bit of both.

"What else? Horses? Guns?"

"Half the bluecoats are mounted. They will come first. Then the foot soldiers. They are all well armed with rifles."

"Our warriors are also well armed. And our horses rested. Theirs will be tired."

"Yes, but the Utes have already captured the best Kiowa ponies. And my brother, you must listen. They have big guns coming up from behind. The thunder guns that roll on wheels like a wagon. The guns that shoot twice." The Indians referred to the howitzers this way because the cannon would shoot the shell, then the shell would explode on impact—shooting *twice*.

"How many thunder guns?"

I held up two fingers. "The big guns make much noise and they shoot far, but they are slow to load and to turn and to aim. Against good Comanche riders, they will do little harm. We must tell our warriors to ride hard and keep moving. Any one bunch of braves that gathers in a group will become a target."

He put his hand on my shoulder and shook me, as if gauging my resolve. "You look like an antelope that has been run by coyotes, then ripped apart by their teeth."

"I am not wounded. The blood is not mine. I have time to bathe in the creek and put on my war paint. Then I will be good again."

Three miles away, the clarion note of the U.S. Army bugle signaled the advance and I knew Kit's forces would move forward to take Adobe Walls. There would be little resistance from the Comanche snipers, who would let them have the ruins of the fort. But they must hold Adobe Creek at all cost. "They are coming now," I said.

Little Bluff nodded, a grim visage shadowing his face like a war cloud. His wife stepped from the lodge with his shield, and handed it to him, followed by his quiver and bow case, which he strapped on his back. Lastly, she gave him a Henry repeating rifle and a cartridge belt laden with ammunition. He looked up at the cloudless sky. "It is a good day for a battle."

I left Kills Something and went to my lodge to gather my weapons, my Comanche clothing, some pemmican, and a pouch of black war paint made from animal lard and charcoal. Leaving my lodge, I headed toward my favorite bathing pool on Adobe Creek. I began at a trot, but then felt so utterly exhausted that I had to slow to a walk. I began to doubt my ability to participate in the coming battle. This filled me with shame, and I knew I had to summon new energy.

Reaching the pool, I stripped myself of my white man's clothing and stood in the cool November air. I raised my eyes to the heavens and lifted my palms to the sky. I knew the spirits would disapprove should I pray on my knees like a white man. The Great Mystery scorned a man who would grovel and kneel. I was exhausted, but I could still stand. I prayed to the spirits of the winds, the storms, and the flaming stars to lend me strength for one more day. I began to yearn for the cold embrace of the clear waters, and the next thing I knew, I was falling into the pool, though I didn't recall making the decision to dive in.

The water hit me like a cymbal crash, though I knew Vivaldi had written none into his piece. Spirits had slipped into the orchestra. *Presto. Allegro.* And the composition lapsed into "Autumn." *Der Herbst.* Concerto no. 3 in F Major. I remained submerged until my lungs burned, then I surfaced like an otter, shaking the water from my hair as I felt the energy seep back into my pores. I rubbed the blood from my skin, then clawed my way out of the pool. I stood in the sunshine to put on my moccasins and breechclout.

Many sounds accompanied the orchestra between my ears. From the Comanche camp came shouts and hoofbeats, from the Kiowa camp came the distant victory cries of the Ute scouts and the soldiers. Occasional gunshots and bugle signals punctuated the general din as enemies took potshots at one another across the Adobe Walls prairie. When my face had dried, I opened my paint pouch and colored the left half of my face black. This was my own design; a reflection of my "moon medicine." It represented the half-moon—the phase that granted me my greatest powers. Next, I donned my weapons—bow and arrow, and a revolver with a cartridge belt—and picked up my war bridle.

I walked quickly to the horse herd, which had been moved closer to camp so that the warriors could choose their mounts. Well over one thousand animals milled about as Comanche men looked for favored war ponies. I caught the first horse that would let me within reach, looped my war bridle around his lower jaw, and sprang onto his back. From the back of this horse I was able to move through the herd until I spotted Castchorn. When I rode to his side and spoke to him, he made no objection to my slipping off the pony I had caught, and onto his back. Once mounted on Buffalo Getter, I felt ready to ride to the battle front. Mounting this good horse only made me remember how the soldiers had killed All Horse, and I became angry and eager for vengeance.

I rode westward at a trot and slipped through the timber of Adobe Creek until I could see the ruins of the old fort through the branches. At first glimpse, I saw a number of U.S. cavalry horses corralled within

Adobe Walls. The cavalrymen had dismounted and scattered, lying in the tall grass. Thus deployed as skirmishers, they were firing randomly at distant enemy figures—Kiowas and Comanches who were also creeping about in the grass, they, too, seeking clear shots at the foe. Just outside Adobe Walls, I recognized an officer looking through a telescope. It was Major McCleave of the First California Cavalry. I did not know him well, but I had met him once in Santa Fe.

Now, from my left, I heard a war whoop and saw some fifty Comanches riding hard toward the walls, making a charge on Major McCleave's position. He began shouting orders, urging his men to reload and hold their fire until the Indians came within range. The major tucked his telescope under his belt and drew his revolver. The Comanches thundered forward, scattering as they flew. Riding nearer, each warrior slipped to the right side of his mount, clinging to his galloping steed with a left leg thrown over the rump and a right arm thrust through a loop under the pony's neck. As though this were not a difficult enough feat of horsemanship, each warrior armed with bow and arrows drew his bowstring from this precarious position. The riders with rifles and revolvers had an easier time of cocking their weapons in preparation to shoot.

McCleave shouted the order to fire just as arrows began to fly. One Indian pony fell, shot through with a rifle ball. The rider rolled through the grass, but sprang instantly to run to safety. Two Comanches peeled quickly back to their unhorsed comrade and, riding one to either side, grabbed him by the arms as he ran and lifted him to the back of one of the rescuers' ponies. Bullets cut the grass all around the three escaping men, but failed to connect. The charge thus thwarted by the soldiers, the Indians galloped away to regroup in the timber. It seemed to me that the soldiers had failed to account for the speed at which the Indians rode, and had missed all but one horse. As far as I could tell, the Indian arrows had also failed to draw enemy blood. But this was only the first charge.

A far-off bugle call drew my attention toward the west, and I noticed a number of soldiers galloping from the Kiowa village toward Adobe Walls to reinforce Major McCleave. I watched them approach until I recognized Colonel Kit Carson himself leading the reinforcements. Far behind Kit's column, I saw the two gun carriages of the howitzer battery, and all the ammunition-laden mules and soldiers attached thereto.

Those mountain howitzers did not include caissons and limber carriages like most artillery. All the ammunition was carried on pack mules,

402 | MIKE BLAKELY

and the gun carriages themselves could be dismantled and packed on a mule in minutes should trails too rough for wheels be encountered. Perhaps Kit should have ordered his howitzers broken down for this run, because the two cannon had come upon an obstacle in the form of a little ravine that knifed across the prairie. Though not very deep, the cutbanks of the ravine seemed specially designed by Mother Earth to obstruct the progress of axled wheels. A travois, I mused, would have had no trouble scooting up the bank, though I didn't suppose a howitzer would have proven of much service from a pony drag. The ill-designed carriage wheels under the howitzers spanned a narrow breadth, and they tended to fall over sideways quite easily. I watched with some amusement as mules strained against their harnesses and men afoot struggled to turn spoked wheels up the vertical dirt bank.

Another Comanche battle cry rose from the timber, and a second charge sped toward the Adobe Walls, timed to beat Kit's reinforcements there. Castchorn and I could wait no longer. I wanted to get a closer look at the action, so I added my war whoop to the effort and sprang forward from the timber. I galloped past a couple of Kiowas still hidden in the grass and rode to a spot on the prairie where I knew I would join the charge from the left. I drew my revolver and felt Castchorn reach top speed, my hair whipping in the air, still wet from my bath in the creek. As the Comanche assault neared, I turned to my right, joining the other riders, falling into place third in line. The riders slipped to the sides of their mounts, and I did the same as white puffs of rifle smoke began to appear. I heard a bullet sizzle through blades of grass under my head and I cocked my revolver. I didn't intend to shoot any of the soldiers, some of whom I had served with at Valverde and Fort Stanton, but I rode close enough to fire a shot into Adobe Walls, just for the fun of seeing the dirt rain down on Major McCleave.

Suddenly, the horse in front of me took a bullet and stumbled, spilling the rider. I raised myself upright on Castchorn and angled him toward the fallen rider. The warrior was shaken, trying to rise from his knees. He was facing me, so he saw me coming, and raised his right hand. I tucked my pistol under my belt and grabbed my mount's mane with my left hand, extending my right hand downward. Castchorn and I had practiced this rescue maneuver hundreds of times, and he knew to ride close to the man, to change the lead of his gait so that he could push off with his front right foot when the extra weight pulled him right, and to time the meeting so that his feet were planted when I pulled the man aboard. Bullets hissed around us as our hands met and I leaned hard to the left as the warrior did his best to leap upward. Then the warrior was astraddle behind me as if by magic, and I had scarcely slowed from a full gallop. The men at Adobe Walls actually cheered me for the rescue as I bore my fellow attacker out of rifle range to the timber along Adobe Creek.

Castchorn exhaled great blasts of air from his nostrils as the warrior slipped down to his feet.

"You are Plenty Man?" he said.

"*Huh,*" I answered. I saw that he was younger than me, but had a battle scar above one eye.

"I will tell the story of how you came to help me in the council lodge when my turn comes to speak."

"You mean if you survive the day," I answered, smiling.

"Yes. I am going back to the herd for another pony. I *will* charge the bluecoats again."

"What is your name?"

"Battle Axe." He pulled a shined and sharpened hatchet from his breechclout belt. "The one I carry is the one that struck me here." He pointed to his scar, then touched a scalp he wore on his belt. "The scalp I carry is from the Pawnee warrior who owned the axe before me."

"May your spirit-protectors watch you closely the rest of the day, brother."

"And yours," he said, turning away to trot back toward the village and the herd.

I reined in Buffalo Getter upstream, letting him blow as we walked through the relative safety of the timber. To my left I could hear and catch glimpses of another desperate charge on the soldiers, but the answering gunfire doubled that of the last charge, and I knew the company of cavalry Kit had led to Adobe Walls had arrived and joined the action. I was anxious to make another charge, for the exhilaration of galloping through the enemy gunfire had electrified me with dangerously addictive thrills. But before I charged the soldiers again, I felt compelled to get a closer peek at the workings of Kit's command inside old Adobe Walls.

FORTY-NINE

I knew every bend in the creek and every rise in the prairie floor of this sheltered canyon. I knew it almost right down to every tree and rock and weed. I could drift like a wildcat along the fringes of the battle scene, undetected. Indeed, in my peculiar heightened state of alertness brought on by the odd combination of fatigue and excitement, I felt as if I had shifted my very being into the form of a specter. All the things Burnt Belly had tried to teach me about the spirit world became lucid. Castchorn and I could blend our colors with those of the natural world around us. From the corner of your eye, you might catch a glimpse of us moving, but when you looked right at us, we would vanish, like a spotted trout in a clear stream. I had become invisible.

I rode up Adobe Creek to a point where a slight rise in the prairie concealed the dash that I made to the west, where I gained the base of the bluffs. Here, enough brush grew to hide my approach as long as I rode with my head pressed down against my buckskin's neck. Springs at the base of the bluffs fed grass and bushes that stood tall enough to obliterate my outline. The blades of grass and seed heads waved in the breeze, gathering my horse and me, passing us along unseen, blade by blade. We assumed the colors of dried bluestem, naked branches, and rocky dirt slopes. I felt that not even a wary deer would have noticed us.

I rode around the bend of the bluff to the timber and underbrush of Bent's Creek. Here, I dismounted and tied Buffalo Getter. I slipped silently down the stream on foot to the place where the timber came closest to Adobe Walls. I peeked just far enough through the trees to get a glimpse. All around the ruins of the old fort, soldiers swarmed as the dismounted cavalry continued to hold off charges by the Indians. The mounted assaults by Comanche riders had become larger and bolder, and had begun to claim casualties among the bluecoats. Soldiers were carrying or dragging a few wounded comrades to a makeshift hospital the surgeon had established in the southeast corner of the old fort, where the walls provided protection. The horses were crowded against the north wall where they, too, were shielded from Indian gunshots.

I eased to the edge of the timber to take a broader view of the prairie, and I spotted Kit and some of his officers on the small hill that rose like a buffalo hump in the prairie about a hundred yards north of the ruins. This hill was only about thirty feet higher than the rest of the prairie, but the elevation provided a fine view of the field. I had often stood or sat upon that hill myself, in times of peace, looking over the beauty of the remote canyon. Now, I dropped to the ground and crawled through the grass, wanting a still closer look at what had become Kit's headquarters on the little knoll.

As I inched along, I heard the rattle of gun carriages and, within seconds, the artillery teams were galloping by me to join Kit on the knoll. The gun carriages passed so near that the ground shook under me; behind them came the panting gunners running along on foot. Still, I felt no fear of being seen, for I had become a spirit stalker. Crawling close enough to hear voices, I stopped to raise my head higher so I could peek through the tops of the stalks. I saw Lieutenant Pettis marching up the slope from his guns, where he had dismounted.

"Lieutenant Pettis reporting for duty, sir," he said.

"Pettis," Kit said, pointing to the timber along Adobe Creek, where another Indian charge was taking shape. "Throw a few shell into that crowd over there."

"Yes, sir!"

Pettis trotted back down the slope to his battery at the base of the knoll and began shouting orders: "Unhitch those guns! Action right!" He waited impatiently for the artillerymen to unhitch and turn the mountain howitzers. "Load with shell. Load!"

While this went on, I rose just a bit higher to see the Comanche front. At least a hundred warriors had gathered for a charge, but the arrival of the artillery seemed to have made them uneasy. They milled about along Adobe Creek, waiting for some warrior to lead the charge. Beyond the creek, in the direction of the Comanche village, I caught glimpses of a great number of horsemen gathering, and I could even hear the shouts of the chiefs haranguing the warriors for the coming battle. I knew there were at least twelve hundred fighting men mounted on fine war ponies, and I knew that Kit knew it, too, for he could see the village of almost four hundred lodges in view through the bare branches of the timber.

Kit's Ute scouts had now ridden up from the captured Kiowa camp and had gathered between Adobe Walls and the Comanche front and were taunting the Comanches. At this moment, the skirmishers on both sides stopped firing for a few seconds, and Lieutenant Pettis's voice bellowed: "Number one! Fire!"

The blast lifted the muzzle of the howitzer and pitched it backward on its battered carriage wheels. Before the shot had landed, Pettis ordered, "Number two! Fire!"

The first shell exploded just short of the Indians along the creek, and the second ripped through the branches over their heads.

"Reload!"

Some of the war ponies bolted in fear of the blasts, and the rest of the Indians just sat their mounts in utter awe of the thunder guns. The shouting of the chiefs from the timber had hushed, and even the Ute scouts seemed shocked into silence.

"Number one, fire! Number two, fire!"

When the fourth shot cratered the prairie just two horse lengths in front of the Indians, the Comanche front crumbled and commenced a wild retreat through the timber, back toward Kills Something's village.

I heard Kit chuckle. "Well done, Pettis! They won't charge us for a spell now. Reposition your guns up here on this rise and stay ready." He grabbed Major McCleave by the arm and started down the hill toward Adobe Walls. "Bill, post your skirmishers around those howitzers. We must protect them guns at all cost."

"Yes, sir."

"And have every fourth man unsaddle and water the horses, then stake them yonder to graze." He pointed to the tall grass that hid me between the ruins and the creek.

"Yes, sir."

"The boys can rest a while and eat breakfast. Directly, we'll have us a council of war in the old fort. Pettis," he shouted over his shoulder, "you'll join us when your guns are in place."

"Yes, sir!"

I shrank back into the grass and crawled carefully toward the ruins. By the time I got close enough to hear, the horses had been led out of the walls and taken past me to the creek. The surgeon and a few wounded men remained inside the walls, where they had been joined by Kit, Pettis, Mc-Cleave; Captains Birney, Witham, Fritz and Deus; and Lieutenants Taylor, Heath, and Edmiston.

"We can take that village," Captain Birney insisted, as I crawled within earshot of the council of war, listening to the talk come over a low spot in the crumbling adobe walls. "With Pettis's support, we can capture the entire valley."

"I agree," Lieutenant Edmiston said. "My boys didn't march all the way from California to turn back at the decisive moment."

The other officers chimed in until everyone was talking at once, and Kit had to quiet them like a father taking control of his children. "Easy, boys. Let's think this out. I can see a camp of four hundred lodges from here, and it disappears around the bend. Who knows how big that camp is. But there are at least a thousand warriors waiting in that village, plus three hundred or so we drove out of the Kiowa camp. We're outnumbered at least four to one, and they're well mounted. I know you boys want that camp downstream, but maybe the best thing to do is to fall back to the Kiowa camp and burn it, then decide if we should fight our way on down the river. We'll know by then if our guns can hold back their charges. Pettis is good with his guns, but you boys have not even begun to see a real Comanche charge. And don't forget about our supply wagons. We must protect our rear, boys."

"But we've demoralized them, sir," Pettis complained. "Now is the time to strike."

"You've stunned 'em, Pettis. Maybe mixed 'em up for a spell. But they ain't no more dee-moralized than a cornered grizzly. They'll rally."

"Kit," Major McCleave said. "Let us at least hold this ground and this fort for now. We can observe the enemy tactics a while and then decide whether to attack or fall back to the Kiowa village. But to fall back right now would dishearten the men."

Kit considered the idea for a moment. "All right, Bill," he finally said. "We'll hold what we've got for a spell. But come sundown, I aim to have all the boys safe in camp."

Kit sent his subordinates to see after their own units then stepped outside of the walls to watch the cavalry horses graze, and to think. I could have hit him with a rock. I watched him for a while, reading the expression in his eyes. I could almost hear his thoughts intermingling with Vivaldi's third concerto. *Adagio molto.* He was actually considering taking the Comanche camp. He was thinking of his legacy. Kit was fifty-five years old and almost used up. A last great victory? He rubbed his left shoulder and winced. His breath came in short rasps.

Something came over me, and I felt my voice leave my body to cast itself against the adobes behind my old friend. "Kit."

He turned as if he would find me standing behind him. "Who's there?"

"It's me."

"Kid? Where the hell are you?" He wheeled about and looked for me.

"I am invisible."

Kit marched to the corner of the fort and looked around it, expecting to find me standing there. I was throwing my voice against the walls, as Burnt Belly had tried so many times to show me. Now, I was just doing it.

"Don't play games, Kid. Where the hell are you?"

"Go home, Kit. Save your boys. Don't go down the river."

"Where the hell *are* you?" He looked more afraid than I had ever seen him. Nothing much spooked Kit, unless it was something from the spirit world that he didn't understand. He had spent enough time with the Indians to know about dreams and visions and spirit voices.

"Come sundown, Kit. You'd best be gone come sundown."

"Kid, show yourself!"

"Come sundown."

The surgeon looked up from a badly wounded man. "You talking to me, Colonel?"

Kit wheeled and glanced all about the fort and prairie, expecting to find me. But I was transparent. "No, George. Just talkin' to myself."

※

Though rattled by my visit, Kit went back to his business of war, and I crawled back to the creek and walked to my horse. Returning the way I had come, I found Kills Something, One-Eyed Bear, Little Bluff, and some other chiefs in a heated council, surrounded by their most experienced warriors and by the elders and shamans. I left Buffalo Getter with Fears-the-Ground, who was listening from some distance away, still mounted. On foot, I pushed through the circle of warriors and forced my way to the center. Kills Something was trying to gain control of the excited men, but talk of the thunder guns had everyone alarmed.

"My brother!" I said to Kills Something.

The Indians fell silent at my arrival.

"Plenty Man. Speak."

"I have ridden to the enemy like a spirit stalker. They could not see me. I could hear their words and walk among them, and they did not know I passed there. I know what is in the hearts of our enemies."

Burnt Belly moaned in approval, and smiled, for he had schooled me in the ways of the spirit world and he admired this kind of talk, though he surely knew I was exaggerating my accomplishments.

Kills Something spoke: "Tell us what you have learned, my brother, so that we will know what to do."

"Little Chief is courageous. There is no fear in his heart. But he is careful. He is old and wise. He knows we number more than his bluecoats, but he does not know how many more. He thinks four to one. But he cannot see how far this village goes down the river. You know, my brothers, that we number ten warriors for every bluecoat.

"Now, the younger men under Little Chief want to fight. They want to attack this village with the thunder guns. If we do not make a great show of power now, they will convince Little Chief to do it. We must gather three thousand warriors and more. Mount your men on the best horses and make charge after charge."

"But the thunder guns!" said a warrior who had been fired on with the howitzer. "They shoot twice."

"Those guns are big, but they are heavy and slow. If we ride along the front line of the enemies, from north to south and from south to north at great speed on our ponies, the thunder guns cannot take aim on us. No one swats bees with a lodge pole."

Chief Little Bluff of the Kiowas laughed at the image.

"We must not surround them," I continued, for I still hoped to leave Kit a way out. "The ground behind them is no good. We must hold to the open ground between them and the village where we can ride with antelope speed. Those thunder guns must not roll one step closer to this village. If the bluecoats get those guns any closer, they will rip our lodges apart like a hailstorm tears the leaves from a tree. We must hold the ground before us and drive them back up the valley the way they have come. I will lead the first charge. Who will ride with me?"

A moment of silence passed, then my brother, Kills Something, raised his rifle. "I will ride with the slayer of the white buffalo."

"And I will!" shouted Fears-the-Ground, still mounted and holding Castchorn for me some distance away.

A dozen more warriors shouted their willingness to ride. Then a score, twoscore, and within seconds a hundred men were ready to brave the guns that shoot twice. By the time we reached the creek, two hundred had joined. I stopped outside of howitzer range and looked at the warriors around me. I was about to lead a charge on the soldiers of my own friend. But I had asked myself, as Kit had taught me, Is this *right*? And I knew it was. All the while, I knew he believed his own actions right, as well, and I wondered how two men, so alike in values and temperament, both true of heart, could end up pitted against each other in battle.

"If you stand still, you are a target for the thunder guns," I reminded the riders.

"Then why do we not *ride*?" insisted old Chief Little Bluff.

I smiled at him. "It is time." I loosed a war cry that had been building in me since Kit's soldiers killed All Horse and beat the hell out of me back in New Mexico. Buffalo Getter leapt sideways in excitement as the din of battle yells rose around me, then he led the charge across the creek. I held my mount back as we ran through the timber of Adobe Creek, then gave him his head as we reached the open prairie.

The view ahead of me was one of the finest sights I have ever seen. Painted and feathered Ute warriors on horses milled about in a line before the old fort. Three hundred soldiers in blue coats stood behind them ready to meet our charge, spaced several paces apart in a semicircle that embraced Adobe Walls and the artillery position on the knoll. The sun painted the old adobes a golden hue that complemented the tawny field of tall grass across which I galloped. To the right and a little beyond the fort, a cluster of bluecoats danced around the two howitzers perched on the rise.

I had forgotten how fast Castchorn could run. I felt amazed at the speed at which we flew over the prairie. Nothing but cold winter air stood between me and the enemy's guns. I thought about the gunners taking aim, and suddenly veered directly in toward the Utes, running for fifty yards before I dashed back away from the enemy's front, riding in irregular sawtooth jags to constantly vex the gunners. Angling back in toward the enemy, I dropped to the right of my mount, using his neck as my shield. I did not even draw a weapon, for it was my job to lead the charge at top speed, evading enemy gunfire. The warriors behind me would fling plenty of lead and arrow points.

The muzzle of a mountain howitzer sprouted a white cloud of smoke, the air whistled, and a second later the prairie soil behind me erupted. I glanced behind and saw two ponies down, but knew the men in the rear would pick up the riders, dead or alive. I dashed away from the enemy line, Castchorn finding new speed in escaping the gunfire. Bullets were cutting the grass all around me, and the shell from the second gun exploded to my left. Now I knew I had a few seconds while the gunners reloaded, and I veered toward the soldiers, screaming a war cry that tore at my throat like a storm wind.

"Shoot them!" I yelled to the closest warriors behind me, and the men began to rain their fire into the ranks of the enemy. The Utes were riding along with us, though they could not match our speed, and I saw one grab at a wounded arm, though he managed not to fall. A bluecoat rose from the grass and fired, only to catch an arrow in his leg, forcing a scream of pain and horror from his mouth. The bugler signaled for the soldiers to fall back. Probably, I thought, to keep them away from the cannon fire to come.

Now my pony danced under me in a feint to my right, then left, then right again as I evaded the rifle balls and the artillery shells I knew were coming next. I flew past Adobe Walls and recognized Kit at the corner, calmly shouting orders to his officers and men. Recklessly, I swerved directly toward the guns on the knoll, my intention being to get inside of the range the gunners had sighted. I knew my maneuver had worked when one shell, then another, whistled harmlessly overhead. The infantrymen around the gunners raised a severe defensive fire, and a bullet cut hair from Buffalo Getter's mane. I pulled myself upright on my pony and shook my fist at the soldiers as I led the riders behind me out of range toward the timber of Adobe Creek.

Reaching the cover of the trees, I turned to see how the Comanche and Kiowa defenders had fared. I saw several horses being ridden double, and one slain body being dragged toward me between two men. As they came closer, I recognized the dead warrior as young Battle Axe—the man I had myself rescued from a fallen pony once already today—and I knew he would not now be singing my praises in council.

"Throw him over my pony," I said. "I will take him back to the village."

In spite of Battle Axe's death, and several other men having earned bullet wounds, the scores of warriors who streamed into the protective trees glared with pride in their attack, and their morale remained fevered.

Back at the walls, the bugler blew the advance, signaling the soldiers to retake the ground they had given up during our charge.

"Keep moving!" I ordered. "The big guns can reach this timber."

The two warriors threw Battle Axe's body across my thighs, and we weaved our two hundred and more ponies through the brush and across the creek at a trot. A shell ripped into the branches at our rear and splintered a hackberry, killing the last pony in line with shrapnel and bloodying its rider with a flying tree limb that split his scalp.

From the prairie, I heard another huge charge of screaming Indians leaving the timber, and knew Kit's soldiers would finally be absorbing the dread of a true battle in hostile country right about now. Theirs was no longer a surprise attack at dawn, through an ill-prepared camp of waking Kiowas. They were aiming into the ranks of the greatest horseback warriors ever known to the world, and the most fearless fighters—men who believed that surviving to a ripe old age was an embarrassment, no matter how many battle scars they gathered or scalps they took. Attack these thousands of warriors with a mere three hundred soldiers? On their own ground? Outnumbered almost ten to one? Spraying bullets and cannon shell into the villages where their children played yesterday? Unless Kit proved to be one of the greatest military leaders of the Indian wars, his troops would fall like the autumn leaves fluttering down even now, blood-red, from the flame-leaf sumac thickets on the rocky slopes.

I heard Kit's bugler sounding the retreat again as I left the body of Battle Axe with his pregnant wife and his mother, both of whom began to wail piteously. I turned away before they could begin slashing their own arms and breasts with knife blades in the throes of their anguish. Their keening only stirred my desire to ride again before the gun sights of invading soldiers.

As I walked Buffalo Getter back toward the enemy, allowing him to cool slowly and rest for another charge, I came across Chief Little Bluff of the Kiowas, checking the wound of a bullet that had grazed the top of his war pony's rump.

"Uncle!" I shouted, riding to him as he remounted. "I know how to take the Utes out of this fight. Send some of your warriors around the soldiers and back to your village. Tell them to carry away everything of value that they can take from their lodges. When the Utes see this, they will not want to fight anymore, for they will want to go back and protect the things they thought they captured at dawn."

Little Bluff smiled. "You are wise, nephew. But slower than this old man." He tapped his chest, for the Indians believed that thoughts came from the heart rather than the head. "I sent the younger boys back to the village after the charge you led."

I nodded at the wisdom of the old Kiowa leader. "Then it is time to make another charge on the soldiers."

"Yes. This time, I will lead. Will you follow behind the great old warrior Dohasen?"

"It will be my honor to follow such a great leader."

FIFTY

Within the half hour, Little Bluff and I had recruited a hundred warriors for our charge, and we rode again under the fire of the rifles and thunder guns. On this charge, I noted that Kit's Ute scouts had fallen back behind the blue-coated skirmishers, and seemed more intent on watching their spoils evaporate from the Kiowa village than taking aim at the mounted Comanche and Kiowa defenders. I even saw the Ute scout Buckskin Charley conferring with Colonel Carson at Adobe Walls, no doubt begging Kit to fall back and secure the booty in the Kiowa camp.

Returning from this charge, my mount now covered with a lather of sweat, I noticed some of the young Kiowas lugging buffalo robes and other goods to the safety of Kills Something's camp. One of them, I noticed, had a bugle strapped across his shoulder.

"Boy!" I shouted. "Whose metal horn do you carry?"

"It is from the lodge of my grandfather, Dohasen."

"Do you know who I am?"

"Yes, you are Plenty Man."

"Your grandfather is an old friend. Will you give me his horn?"

"Yes, uncle." He pulled the leather strap over his head and handed it to me as I rode near.

"Now, you must do one other thing for me. Walk my war pony until he is rested. He has one more charge left in him today."

The boy grinned at the honor. "Yes, uncle." He tossed buffalo robes and blankets off his lap and took the reins of my war bridle.

I raised the bugle and blew a short note that tickled my lips. Walking now toward the timber, I made horse noises with my lips to prepare my mouth for the tingle of the bugle. I slipped far enough through the trees that I could see the action on the field. A Comanche charge had just galloped past Kit's front, north to south this time. The gunfire had ended, and the bugler played the advance. The soldiers rose from the places where they had hunkered in the grass and moved cautiously forward. I put my lips to my bugle and played the signal for "about-face." The soldiers stopped, confused by my bugle call. Some actually turned about and marched back a few steps. Gunfire ceased on both sides and several seconds passed as a grin formed on my face. Now Kit's bugler sounded "advance" again, and I answered with "retreat." From the walls: "advance." From the timber: "halt."

I could hear the laughter of the soldiers as they realized an enemy bugler was mocking their own. I made the notes blend somehow with the orchestra still playing Vivaldi's *Four Seasons* in my head. I played it *allegro,* like the third movement of *Der Herbst.* Vivaldi's "Autumn" was almost over. Winter was coming.

The soldiers were still laughing and taunting me, when I saw the howitzer fire. The flying shell whistled, and I dove between the limbs in the fork of a fallen hackberry. That Pettis was quite an artillery officer, for he had sighted in on me by sound alone and his shell erupted not forty yards to my right and sent shrapnel ripping through the timber all around me. The second shell landed even closer to my left. I peeked over my makeshift battlements. The prairie stood motionless and silent, except for the ringing in my ears.

I put the bugle to my lips and began to play an especially mournful rendition of taps. Laughter rose all along the ranks of bluecoats. Then, in the middle of the call, I sprang to my feet and began to blow reveille, as if resurrected from the dead. The laughter of the enemy roared and some cheered and applauded my interlude.

But now the warriors charged again, at least four hundred strong, the riders streaming from the wooded creek far to my right. The bluecoats quit laughing and took up their arms. The timing was good for the Comanches, for the cannon had just sighted on me and fired and would take precious seconds to reload and turn and aim. Kit's bugler sounded a retreat in the face of the onslaught, and I answered—out of pure orneriness—with the "charge." The bluecoats backed away, firing into the Indians, succeeding in dropping several ponies and unhorsing a few riders. The Indian casualties were increasing with the boldness of the assaults, and bloody men—dead and wounded—being dragged back to cover became a commonplace sight.

Pettis had reloaded before the last of the charge swept past him. His first shot exploded among the horsemen and knocked down three Indian mounts, but all three riders rose and ran toward rescuers who came to pick them up. The second howitzer round actually hit a horse in the shoulder, right in front of the rider's knee. The shell exploded inside the hapless steed, tearing the poor beast asunder and launching the warrior in an arch twenty feet above the prairie grasses. Two passing warriors reached low and grabbed the unconscious warrior, each by an arm, and dragged him to safety amid a hail of army bullets. I was shocked that the man had not been torn limb from limb, but it seemed the mass of the horse's musculature had protected him.

I ran to the place where the man was dragged into the timber, and found that the rider was my friend Fears-the-Ground. He was moaning in pain, but still unconscious. I followed to the safe area beyond howitzer range. There I checked Fears-the-Ground all over and found him bleeding from several flesh wounds. Miraculously, he had survived any mortal injuries. The sheer percussion of the shell had knocked his senses from him, however, and would leave him almost deaf the rest of his life.

"Take him back to his lodge on a pony drag," I told one of the rescuers. "His medicine forbids him to touch the ground, except in camp."

The man nodded his understanding and left with Fears-the-Ground.

"Nephew!" I shouted to the Kiowa boy who had been walking Castchorn. "My horse!"

The boy brought my war pony, and I formed up with the next big charge preparing to storm the army position at the walls. I happened to fall in beside young Quanah. Years later, Quanah would become a great Comanche leader, but I never heard any mention of his participation in this battle, though I know he was there. Quanah himself would never speak of it, simply because, I believe, he failed to accomplish anything worth bragging about in the fight. He was yet a young raider, only fifteen, still learning the violent ways of war.

Our charge was led by Kills Something himself, who had waited until now to lead what he intended to be the decisive assault on the invaders' position. With only three hundred soldiers in the field, most wielding single-shot rifles, and well over five hundred Indian riders streaming by with hawklike speed, firing multiple arrows, using our ponies as our shields, the odds of getting shot were lowered, and we pushed the soldiers back all the way to Adobe Walls, where they began to cluster for protection.

Some of the Indians grew so bold as to ride *between* the walls and the artillery position on the knoll, creating a cross fire that endangered the soldiers as much as the Indians. I was one who was so bold, and I remember feeling bullets tug both ways at the hair that streamed behind my head on this ride. Buffalo Getter had to leap the body of a dead soldier that appeared suddenly in the tall, brown grass as I broke through Kit's front. Those of us who had breached the bluecoat line rode a circle around the thunder guns on the knoll as the infantrymen protecting the artillery shrank back under a swarm of arrows. Lieutenant Pettis drew his revolver and railed at his scrambling men to reload the howitzers and stand their ground.

After galloping the symbolic conquering ring around the knoll, I peeled away from the rest of the riders behind Kit's lines. In all the confusion, I was able to ride unnoticed into the timber of Bent's Creek, where I had hidden before to spy on the enemy position. My pony was about done now anyway, so I walked him around in the woods a while to cool him down, then tied him to a tree. I was feeling reckless and bold after breaking through the lines and circling the big guns on the last charge. The spirit players echoed the *allegro non molto* in F minor, their music seeming to come up from the very earth. I was so exhausted, and my stomach so empty, and my nerves so wrought by excitement that I was nigh to having visions and hearing voices. I felt my powers of invisibility come over me again, and I began to walk through the woods toward the ruins of old Fort Adobe.

Coming out of the timber, I sneaked through the grass toward the walls. The dead grass was so luxuriant and tall here that a man as small as me could conceal himself in a crouch and approach the soldiers unseen. The soldiers had drawn closer together around the fort and around the artillery on the knoll. They all faced east, none thinking to look for an approach from the woods and bluffs at their rear. All the cavalry horses had been crowded back inside the fort ruins for protection, and it was toward this herd that I sneaked. I went quickly and fearlessly until I was close enough to hear the voices of the soldiers shouting to one another. Some of the voices rang with fear, but they were all about the business of surviving. Wounded men cried out in pain and others yelled for ammunition, water, bandages. Peeking over the tops of the blades of grass, I saw officers trotting toward the walls, and reasoned that another council of war was about to take place.

I ducked and walked in a crouch, coming as close to the fort as I could. Here, the grass had become trampled by men and beasts, giving the appearance of a dry moat around an ancient, embattled castle. Peering through the last upright stalks of grass, I looked at the backs of the soldiers and summoned my nerve. I decided to simply stand, and walk up to the west side of the wall. Should I crawl or crouch, I thought, my suspicious demeanor might attract attention from the corner of some soldier's eye. So I stood and relaxed, and strolled not so quickly up to the adobe walls. I remember being spotted by a soldier turning to spit with the wind. Apparently, he mistook me for one of his own Ute scouts, for he only glanced, and never raised an alarm.

I walked right up to the west wall and stepped through the gap in the crumbling adobes that had left the wall only three feet high here. Here, a hundred horses concealed me, and I moved through them calmly so as not to spook them. I could hear the officers conferring at the southeast corner of the walls, and I slipped among the horses to better understand their words. I moved slowly, reassuring each mount I came to with a gentle stroke and a grunt of Comanche horse talk. The cavalry ponies among which I passed were so crowded into the protection of the walls that it was a wonder one of them didn't step on my foot. When I could make out the conversation, I knelt among the shod hooves of the cavalry mounts and observed the blue-trousered legs of the officers as they reported to Kit.

". . . none killed; two wounded, sir," the shaky, boyish voice of some young officer was reporting.

"Pettis?" Kit said.

"One killed, six wounded, Colonel."

"Every man's accounted for, then?"

A general "Yes, sir" was the answer.

I saw Kit's squatty legs shift, his heel digging in the dirt. Beyond him, the surgeon knelt over a wounded man who was moaning, half-conscious. Grim-faced, the bloody medic turned and glanced at the officers, and would have seen me had he really looked. But, shadowed among the legs of the ponies, I was invisible, like a spotted ocelot peering out among cattails.

"What's your opinion, Bill?" Kit said to Major McCleave.

"We came here to punish the devils, and I recommend we follow our orders." The words said one thing, but the tone of McCleave's voice was nowhere near as sure as it had rung earlier in the day.

The rest of the men grunted in support. It was funny to watch the men's boots twist and shift. You can read a lot about a man's mind and heart by watching the way he stands. Though all the officers voiced agreement with McCleave, a couple of knees almost buckled.

"You mean attack the next village?" Kit asked.

"Exactly," McCleave said.

"Captain Witham?"

"Attack the devils," said a young voice, without hesitation.

"Fritz?"

There was a pause. "Attack. Of course, attack."

"Pettis?"

"Get my guns past Adobe Creek, Colonel, and I'll shell the daylights out of that camp. We've let them pin us down here long enough."

"Did we come here to shell women and children?" Kit growled.

"What would Captain Pfeiffer say if he was here?" Pettis asked. "He watched his wife, a servant girl, and two soldiers killed by Indians at the Hot Springs."

"Those were Mescaleros," Kit said, dismissing the argument. "Are we to punish these Comanche women and children for something some Mescaleros did hundreds of miles away? I don't think our orders say that."

At this moment, I saw a pair of moccasins and deerskin leggings step over the lowest part of the south adobe wall, and I cringed, for I knew those trappings belonged to Buckskin Charley, Kit's chief Ute scout. Worse yet, he squatted, Indian style, some distance away from the soldiers. I looked away from him, knowing he would feel my gaze should I stare at him.

"Colonel, if I may," said Major McCleave. I watched him take a step toward Kit. "These boys have come a long way. They will fight. A victory here would make history."

Kit chuckled. "History, huh, Bill?"

"It could turn the tide in the Indian wars."

Kit faced left to speak to Buckskin Charley in Ute, asking his opinion. To my relief, Charley stood to answer, saying that the Kiowas were steadily removing their things from the village already taken, depriving the Ute scouts of their well-earned plunder, for they had entered the village first. Kit acknowledged this and turned back to his officers. Buckskin Charley squatted again, and I closed my eyes so as to make myself invisible with my medicine. Vivaldi's warrior-fiddlers played a hushed *largo*.

"I admire your sand, boys," Kit began, "and it'll be noted in my report—*if* I survive to write one." He dug his heel in for his argument. I didn't see this, for my eyes were still closed, but I heard his spur rowel ring as he stamped. I stroked the foreleg of a cavalry mount so that the horse would let me become part of him, hiding me.

"Now, let's think this through," Kit continued. "Our orders said to punish the Kiowas and Comanches for raiding. We have taken a Kiowa camp and killed several of their men. By my count, we've killed about thirty Comanche warriors and wounded a good many more. Agreed?"

The men grumbled their "yes-sirs."

"But . . . We still have to burn the Kiowa camp. That chore's gotta be done, or capturing the camp means nothing."

"We can go back and destroy it," McCleave said, "*after* we rout the Comanches."

"Quiet, Major. You've had your say. Now, say we attack the Comanches. We're outnumbered five or six to one, boys. Maybe ten to one. Our mounts are jaded and some are hurt, while them Comanches have got more ponies than Mexico's got sticker patches. Our ammunition is low, and that camp is full of weapons and bullets, for sure, the way they've been firing on us. You want to shell the daylights out of women and children, Pettis; well, I don't have the stomach for that.

"And, for Christ's sake, have you forgotten about Colonel Abreu? Francisco's back there in our rear with only seventy-five men guardin' the supply train. When those Indians discover him—*and they will*—they will slaughter those boys and take our provisions. Where will that leave us, men? Two hundred miles from civilization without a bullet or a bean."

I could hear the collective sigh of the officers, some in relief, some in disappointment.

"Now, what is the right thing to do here? Don't answer, because I'm fixin' to tell you. We will form up and pull back to the Kiowa camp and burn it to the ground. Then we will commence to fight our way out of this bear trap. It won't be easy, boys, and you will realize how loco it would have been for us to attack that next village. You want history, Bill? Gettin' three hundred men massacred would sure enough make history. The enemy wears moccasins. We're the ones with boot heels, and they've sure got us on 'em. Come sundown we had better be back at our supply train, or we'll *be* history."

At this point, Kit started giving orders on how the men would proceed back to the Kiowa camp, and the first order was to remove the horses from the walls. "Form a column of fours, Bill—dismounted. Every fourth man will lead four mounts. Lieutenant Edmiston, deploy the infantry along both flanks and on our rear. Pettis, keep your guns in the rear, and keep them firing. We've got to save those howitzers at any cost, gentlemen."

The men dispersed to follow their orders, and I knew I had to get out of the adobe ruins before the soldiers came to get their horses. I slipped among the mounts, heading back to the hole in the west wall. Just before I stepped out through the hole, I got a wicked idea. Kit had ordered the horses led out in fours, so I took the reins of the four nearest to me and led them out, each pony stepping obediently over the low spot in the wall and following me onto the prairie. I led them casually toward the woods along Bent's Creek, hoping no one would make a complaint. In this, I was disappointed.

There was a ring on the cavalry saddle of the day where the reins of one mount could be tied to the saddle of the next, and that was how the horses were supposed to be moved—one tied to another. I, on the other hand, had simply grabbed four sets of reins in two hands and started walking. This unconventional way of moving the horses was what attracted Kit's attention.

"Hey!" came the shout. I pretended not to hear. "You, soldier! Tie them horses together the right way!" I walked on a few steps, and he shouted, louder, "Halt, there, soldier!"

I was halfway to the timber, so I sprang into the saddle of the mount nearest to me, and gave a Comanche war yell. "Come sundown, Kit!" I yelled, pointing up the valley. I screamed my war cry again and ran the ponies to the timber. I looked over my shoulder once and saw Kit standing with his hands on his hips. He was some distance away, and I was on a galloping horse, leading three others, but I will always believe that I saw a smile on his face.

"Let him go," Kit yelled, as I gained the timber and began picking my way through the trees and underbrush, back toward Castchorn.

FIFTY-ONE

My Comanche pony did not like being led along with the captured enemy horses at first, and he kicked and bit the one nearest to him. I admonished him in a stern voice, and he accepted his lot for the time being. I rode north, out of rifle range, and crossed the prairie in sight of Pettis's gunners with the stolen horses, screaming the "ye-ye-ye-ye!" of a successful Comanche horse thief. When I made my way back to the Comanche village, I found another party forming to make a charge on the soldiers, but I convinced them to wait until we had held a council of war so I could report what I had learned inside the walls.

Kills Something and the other chiefs gathered in the middle of a huge crowd of warriors and listened as I told them of my stealth and my invisibility among the horses. Burnt Belly was there, looking quite pleased with me for all that I had learned from him. I told what I had heard about the way the soldiers would retreat now, but I took my time in telling it, so that Kit would have time to form his column and get moving back toward the Kiowa village. I ended my tale by bragging about the four horses I had stolen right out from under the noses of the bluecoats. A great victory cheer rose to congratulate me, but when it died down, I again heard the wails of mourning women who had already lost husbands or sons in this battle.

"What does your heart tell you we must do now, my brother?" Kills Something asked me.

I glanced upward to the brilliant blue heavens. "Look where Father Sun now stands in the sky. He sees that we have won this fight. We have turned the bluecoats away from our families. But we must be careful. The war books of the bluecoats teach many dishonorable tricks. If we send all our warriors to destroy the soldiers, we will leave our villages unprotected.

There may be other soldiers coming from a different fort. Maybe many more. This is the way the bluecoats fight."

Kills Something frowned, but he nodded. "Plenty Man knows the ways of the white soldiers. I believe his heart is strong and his words are wise. He has stood among the enemy, invisible to them with his medicine, and he has listened to their plans. We should chase them out of our valley, but we must be careful. Many warriors must remain behind to guard this village in case other soldiers come, as Plenty Man has warned."

Now old Little Bluff, the Kiowa chief, dissented, holding his lance above his head. "They are going back to destroy the lodges of my people. We must kill them all!"

The Kiowas answered with a war cry, but Kills Something was not moved.

"Listen, uncle. Those soldiers are not worth killing. They are nothing to us now. We have shamed them into a retreat. They are beaten cowards. Killing them all would not amount to much. I would not even hang one of their scalps on my belt.

"Now, about your lodges. Were your people not warned in council one moon ago about camping so far away from the protection of the big village? You wanted the fresh water upstream, but the council warned you that this was a dangerous place to camp, and you did not listen. Your warriors fought well, but your village is lost now. How strong is your medicine? If it is strong, you should not care if everything you own is lost, for your medicine will bring you whatever you need to survive."

Little Bluff fumed. "Must I send my wife back to my village to cook a meal for them, and then lie on her back in my lodge and wait for them to use her like a slave-whore?"

"We will kill more bluecoats before this day has passed," Kills Something assured the Kiowas. "But we must not risk any more good warriors just to count coups on cowards. The thunder guns have already killed many good young men."

"What will we do, then?" Little Bluff demanded. "Will we attack, or talk?"

"Grandson!" said old Burnt Belly, raising his hand. "I have something to say."

"Yes, grandfather."

"I have dreamed about this fight," the old shaman said. "I know how we will protect our warriors from the thunder guns and still get close enough to shoot at the bluecoats. You have all wondered why I spoke against letting the horses graze in the valley this winter. Now you will see why. It is because of my vision. We have saved the winter grass here and it is brown and dry now." He held his hand up to feel the air. "The spirits have favored us with a good breeze from the north on this day. We must set fire to the grass behind the soldiers, and the smoke will hide us as we ride close to shoot at the cowards. I have seen this in dreams. Anyone who does not believe in my visions can stay back to protect the camp, as Plenty Man says we must do. That is all I have to say."

Kills Something smiled, as a glint of light sparked in his eye. "Burnt Belly has spoken. He is old and wise, and his visions have never failed us. Little Bluff, take your Kiowa warriors and set fire to the grass. The leaders of the brotherhoods will decide which warriors will attack through the smoke, and which will stay behind to protect the camp. I have spoken."

Kills Something raised his Henry rifle above his head and pushed a war cry from his lungs, up his throat. A deafening battle yell rose around him and spread outward like the percussion from a huge explosion. I knew that Kit's men could hear this yell from where they stood, and I knew it must have shaken them to the marrow, for it sounded like ten thousand spirit eagles singing at once.

When the trilling voices died down, we heard the bugle of the bluecoats sounding the retreat. I quickly groped for my own bugle, placed it against my lips, and answered with the charge as my stolen cavalry horses lunged against their reins with excitement. The laughter that spread around me filled every heart with courage and hope and, for a moment, drowned out the keening of the mourners among the lodges.

When the laughter died, the angry voice of Little Bluff began to shout. "I am a Kiowa chief! I do not wait for smoke to cover me when I charge! Any man brave enough to ride with me now to attack the bluecoats must have his bow strung!" He yelped once, and turned his war pony, charging through onlookers who scrambled out of his way as his leading warriors fell in behind him with war whoops. Comanche men anxious to make names for themselves also joined the hasty attack, as the party gained strength and thundered toward the timber that separated them from the retreating soldiers.

When the hoofbeats had died down, Kills Something said, "The first-year warriors of the Little Horse men will set fire to the grass. Go now, and get embers from the camp, and make much smoke."

I knew I had some time for all of this to take place, so I trailed Casthorn along with the cavalry ponies I had acquired. All these mounts were done in, and I needed a fresh horse with which to make my final charges of the day. What I might accomplish on these charges, other than getting myself killed or maimed, was beyond my ability to predict, but I was now so caught up in the machinations of the battle that I could not extricate myself from its bloody cogwheels. I stopped at the edge of camp to strip saddles and bridles from the army horses, then turned them into the herd.

As I threw down the last U.S. Army saddle, I heard the roar of the mountain howitzers, accompanied by a resounding volley of rifle fire and screams of suffering horses. I knew Little Bluff's followers had made a brave charge, but from the sounds of it, they had been drubbed soundly by the cool work of the veteran soldiery. I doubted anyone would attempt another charge without the cover of smoke.

Mounting Castchorn one last time, I walked among the large herd of Indian ponies and found my old reliable paint horse, Major. He had not been ridden in the course of the last moon, so he was sleek and ready, his feet sound. He was a bit aged for a frontier pony, but I had used him sparingly over the years, saving him for special work, like that at hand. He was smart and courageous and always trusted in me, sometimes to the point of foolhardiness. I had been riding Major that fateful day, four years ago, on the elk hunt, when Kit got tangled in his pony's reins and took a fall down the mountain. I knew Kit would remember this, and for some reason, I wanted him to know it was me charging through the smoke to brave the bullets of the soldiers. I wanted Kit to know that the beating his soldiers had given me after killing Tu Hud had not defeated me, and that I was as sure as ever that my course was right. Major was an eye-catching paint mount with plenty of white mottled by deep sorrel. If Kit caught a glimpse of him, he would know it was me, for the old voyageur had a good memory for quality horseflesh.

Major seemed glad to see me. He had the most expressive eyes of any horse I had ever owned, and he was asking me plain as day with those eyes what the hell all the commotion was about. "Come on, I'll show you," I said. I slipped my war bridle past his teeth and mounted bareback.

By the time I recrossed Adobe Creek, the grass was on fire in the prairie of Adobe Walls, the smoke flowing southward through the bend in the valley. The billowing gray cloud and the crackling blaze excited Major, which was good. It was easier to stick to a horse covered with a little sweat when riding bareback. As I trotted toward the grass fire, the Kiowa men began to appear in the smoke downwind of the flames, urging their ponies to brave the conflagration and get back to the fresh air upwind of the blaze. They came through in ones and twos, or in small groups, many of them dragging wounded or carrying corpses.

"They should have waited for the smoke," a familiar voice said to my left.

I turned and, to my surprise, I found Burnt Belly mounted and riding beside me, having slipped up on me in the chaos. "Grandfather," I said, almost scolding him with my tone. "Why are you here?"

He smiled and rubbed the lightning scar across his torso. "Do not talk to me as if I am too old to ride into battle. I have dreamed of this day. It is going to happen now."

"What?"

"That which is destined to happen. You will see. Come, and make this charge with me, Plenty Man."

He rarely called me by name to my face, and I took it as a compliment designed to win my approval. It worked, of course. Anyway, I knew that to argue with him was useless, for Burnt Belly had become accustomed to doing as he pleased. No one ever dared to make demands of him for fear of his powers.

"I will ride with you, grandfather, but I am not going to kill any white men. I only want to see the fight from the middle of it."

He nudged his mount up to a slow lope. "I have already seen it," he said. And we urged our skittish ponies toward a gap in the bright orange line of flames ahead.

Not any mount will carry a rider right into a prairie fire, but I asked Major to do just that, and he obeyed. We shot through a momentary pass in the flames and crossed the crooked orange line that crawled across the grassy plain. The smoke stung my eyes and lungs, and filled my nose with the pungent odor of burnt straw. The dense cloud soon thinned enough to see a few pony lengths ahead. Burnt Belly and I fell in with a general charge led by Kills Something. The smoke remained so thick that we were within pistol range before the uniforms began to appear through the choking cloud.

"Look, boys!" I heard a voice shout. "Fire!"

"No shit, Captain," said some soldier, his reply punctuated by a gunshot as I galloped by on Major, gaining speed.

"I mean fire your weapon, damn it!" The voice trailed off as Burnt Belly and I loosed our battle cries and charged along the left flank of the retreating column of fours protected by a line of infantry. The soldiers began to yell all manner of astonished oaths as we flew past them near enough to spit on them, yet neither Burnt Belly nor I drew a weapon. In the smoke, we appeared and vanished so quickly to most of the soldiers that they scarcely had time to see us, let alone take aim. Still, they began to take wild shots through the smoke and that made things hot.

I drew my revolver, not wanting to be found dead on the battlefield without a weapon in my hand. I made the charge of a lifetime, riding blindly past an enemy at near point-blank range, blinking away smoke-wrought tears, screaming at the top of my lungs. But the column of soldiers was long, and near the head, which was farthest away from the fire, the smoke began to twist away in tendrils, leaving bands of fresh air between, and the faces of the soldiers came clearer.

Glancing back, I looked for Burnt Belly, but he was no longer behind me. I pulled rein in the smoke to wait for him as other riders thundered madly by. Suddenly the smoke cleared, and I caught sight of a soldier just twenty paces from me, pulling his ramrod from his rifle. When he looked up, I recognized Luther Sheffield. The smoke veiled me again, and I heard him speak:

"Show yourself, damn it."

I reasoned that he had failed to recognize me, so I yelled, "Don't shoot, Luther!"

Another break in the cloud revealed his keen eye behind the irons of his rifle, and I knew he could have shot me through, but he hesitated long enough for the smoke to cover me again.

"Who the hell?"

I laughed and fired my pistol in the air just for fun, turning back now against the grain of the charge to find Burnt Belly. "Grandfather!" I yelled. "Where are you, old man?"

Suddenly a rider vaulted into view—some young Kiowa I did not know—and as he passed me he took a bullet that may well have been meant for me. It ripped through a jugular vein and his spinal column, killing him in a cruel instant of fate. Major leapt wildly away from the spray of blood and the falling body, but I managed to hang on as I found myself once again lost in the smoke cloud, thickening again as the fire pressed closer.

As I turned back toward the column of fours, I saw an image running like a specter through the smoke, an errant shaft of sunlight glinting on a knife blade held in the soldier's hand.

"No, Toribio!" I heard. "Get your Meskin ass back here, goddamn it!"

That was Blue Wiggin's voice, sure as I was alive. The cloud shifted, and I saw Toribio Trevino kneeling over the body of the dead Comanche warrior, his eyes gleaming vengeance as he groped madly at the hair and slashed savagely with the blade. More hooves thundered to my right, and I knew Toribio would be overtaken as he tried to collect his trophy, so I made Major spring in between the riders and Toribio. I screamed so that I would be heard, but almost too late, as three veteran Comanche horse warriors suddenly burst into view, smoke swirling around them like whirlpools in a muddy stream. They dodged three ways and we all slammed against one another, yet managed to stay horseback as they glared in anger at me, and rode away with the thickening smoke.

My eyes were stinging now, but I saw the scalped Comanche corpse on the ground, and caught sight of Toribio sprinting back to the column to the cheers of soldiers. I knew I had to get out of the way as the smoke began to choke Major and me, so I turned downwind and urged my mount to gallop. Finally, toward the very head of the column, the fresh prairie air began to find its way into my nostrils and lungs again and Major coughed as he ran, as if to clear the smoke and make way for pure wind. I heard a voice shouting and saw Kit on his horse.

"Fire the grass ahead, soldier! Burn it ahead of us! You, too, boy! Use your powder."

He came into view: the grizzled warrior, gaunt and gnarled on a walleyed horse; sitting there like part of the half-crazed beast between his knees. I could not help reining in to watch him for a spell, though bullets clipped the tall grass blades around me. He felt me watching, Indian-like. His pony sensed his alarm, and wheeled full around before he could check the animal. As if to answer, Major made a circle of his own, then Kit and I locked eyes and squinted at each other for a moment, dancing on our four-leggeds.

A billow of smoke. The hum of a musket ball. A death song. The smell of guts. A shout, a scream, a groan. The sting of cinders. An orchestra gone mad in mutiny, like the mind of a fiend; like a flock of thunderbirds low overhead; like a stampede of nightmares and terrors unleashed.

"Pettis! To the high ground! Right flank, Lieutenant Pettis. Get the guns up high, to . . ."

The voice trailed off as Kit rode one way and I rode the other.

I galloped to safety, running around the line of fire the soldiers had lit to burn the grass ahead of them—a simple stroke of commonsense genius on the part of Colonel Carson. Soon I thundered into the Kiowa camp. Here I found many Kiowa warriors and their women trying to carry their belongings away before the soldiers could return to destroy the village. They darted feverishly in and out of lodges and dragged all manner of property with them along a trail that circled back to the larger Comanche encampment downstream.

"Leave your things and get out!" I ordered. "The soldiers will be here soon. The big guns are going to fire into the village—the thunder guns that shoot twice!"

I shouted my warning again and again as I rode through the shambles, passing erstwhile belongings flung haphazardly about in the confusion. Not only did I see robes and blankets and weapons and Indian foods, but I also noticed things that were sure to anger the soldiers and make them think themselves justified in their dawn ambush of this gathering of families: a buggy and a spring wagon belonging to Little Bluff; white women's dresses and bonnets; white children's clothing; family photographs; books; soldiers' uniforms and weapons; and one particular scalp taken from a woman who had once combed long, beautiful blond hair.

I left the Kiowa camp and rode to higher ground to get a better view of the scene. Major used all of his muscle and the last of his wind to climb a bluff overlooking the Kiowa camp. He was really getting too old for this sort of exertion. From this vantage, I could see over the smoke from the grass fires. I spotted Lieutenant Pettis to my left, his men toiling to drag the two gun carriages up onto an elevation by hand, having unhitched them from their teams.

The top of this little elevation was barely large enough to accommodate the two mountain howitzers and all their accompanying equipage and soldiery; the elevation itself was just high enough to afford a view over the column of unhorsed soldiers. It was as if God himself had placed this little hillock here for Kit Carson's salvation. The column of soldiers was now strung out between the artillery and the Indians, protecting the gunners as they loaded their pieces.

The escaping column of soldiers had now stalled under fierce Comanche attacks concentrated along its left flank. The artillerymen positioned and loaded their pieces as if they themselves were on fire. I watched as they lobbed a deadly missile toward the charging Comanches, and when they did, the howitzer lurched backward and went tumbling down the back side of the little hill, the gunners chasing it. I laughed as the second cannon fired, with the same comical result. However, I knew that the men would soon have the guns back into position and would continue to shell the attacking Indians. Then they would unleash their deadly fire on the Kiowa village, clearing it of Indians so the soldiers could destroy it.

Entranced, I swept my gaze across the ground below. The first line of fire set by the Comanches had burned past half of the column of soldiers, and Indians were still charging the head of the column now where the smoke was thickest. The second line of fire, set by Kit's soldiers, had swept ahead and was now clouding the Kiowa camp. The soldiers I could see stood bravely upon their blackened ground, holding their positions, but there was great commotion I could only hear going on inside the cloud of smoke: gunshots, shouts, battle cries, screams of horses and men. Then, as my eyes searched this battle-torn valley, I spotted a white-haired rider slumped on his pony, far beyond the soldiers, heading back toward the Comanche camp.

"Burnt Belly," I said.

Major had caught his wind, and now plunged down off the bluff at my urging. I charged through the smoke ahead of the column of soldiers and rode hard across the prairie. As I overtook the old man on his pony, I slowed, so as not to excite his mount, and I heard his death song. Blood was streaming down his arm and onto the old fist that clenched the mane. I came around in front of him and saw the wound to his chest that gushed blood. A bullet had struck him right at the top of the old lightning scar that had burnt him so many winters ago.

He felt my presence there, and shifted his eyes to me. His death song ceased, and he smiled and reached to me. I saw him slipping from the pony and I quickly darted up to him to catch him. His strength was almost gone and he fell onto me, his weight pulling me down. I threw a leg over Major and jumped down, easing the old medicine man to the ground as gently as I could. I laid him in the grass so he could look up at the sky, and my panic began to consume me as I watched the blood well up from the hole in his chest. I put my hand over the wound, feeling the hot slickness of the old man's lifeblood as I tried in vain to stop the flow. Burnt Belly feebly pulled my hand away from his wound.

"It is as I have seen it in my visions," he said. "But even more beautiful."

"Grandfather," I said. "I must tell you."

He silenced me by raising a finger. "Quiet. I am listening to music." His eyes closed and he lay back and smiled.

"I love you, old man," I said in English. At least, I think it was English. My mind was quite cloudy.

His eyes opened, as if he had understood, and he looked right into my face. "You must remember the things I have taught you, Plenty Man. There is much yet to learn, but now you have only the spirits to teach you."

A cannon shot and a whistle of shell sang behind me, exploding among unlucky warriors. Burnt Belly seemed not to even hear the sound. His bloody hand groped until he found mine, and he gripped me like an eagle. "Grandson . . ." His breath was ragged, his eyes fluttering. "Make a smudge of fir needles when the Thunderbird comes. Do not let the beast catch you in his gaze . . ." His eyes closed and his body made a lurch. "The burden is too great for you to . . ."

The old man's chest fell and his grip went loose in my hand. His eyes opened and he stared at the sky, but he was not there.

I did not even feel like I was there anymore. My fatigue and my sorrow combined to sweep me into some peculiar state of half-consciousness. I remember seeing my tears fall into the blood on the old man's chest. I remember the reports of the cannon, and the shaking of the ground when the shells exploded. I remember mounting Major and standing guard over the corpse as I watched the battle, useless and detached from it all now, as if it had chewed me to ruin and spat me aside.

Lieutenant Pettis's howitzers scattered the Comanches and cleared the Kiowa camp. Kit's soldiers charged into the village to retake it. Come sundown, the lodges were afire, sending dots of orange embers aloft in the twilight. When darkness fell, the soldiers marched away up the valley, and the Indians let them go. I sat on my pony and stared stupidly. At some point, I lay forward across the withers of Major and went to sleep, my dreams intermingling with the events of the day.

I awoke on the ground, wrapped in a blanket, daylight coloring the sky. Someone must have found me, taken me from my horse, and covered me. Opening my eyes, I saw Major grazing not far away, having freed himself somehow of the war bridle. I got my body moving and looked to my left, where Burnt Belly had lain. But someone had carried his body away. From the Comanche camp, over a mile away, I heard the eerie music of mourners across the otherwise quiet valley.

Wearily, I pulled myself to my feet. The sun was about to rise over the eastern bluff. Major looked at me as he chewed his grass. I did not intend to catch him. I simply turned toward the camp and trudged that way. Major followed behind, pausing now and then to crop the tall grass, as if Burnt Belly had saved it just for him.

FIFTY-TWO

There. That is what you came to hear me tell. That is the way it happened. I was in the big, bloody middle of it. It happened on this very ground, sixty-three years ago. If you go snooping around these prairies and woods, you may still find rusty things dropped by dying men. It was among the most horrible and exhilarating days of my life. Yet, I admit that I would not have missed living it even now. I could do nothing to stop it. I could only suffer it along with everyone else.

They called it the Battle of Adobe Walls. It happened on November 25, 1864. Years later, it would become known as the "First" Battle of Adobe Walls, for a "second" battle was yet to come. I was here for that one, too, but that is a tale for another time. The first battle was a victory for the Indians, but it came at such a cost of lost men that little celebration followed. The Indians had driven the invaders out of the valley, but had killed only a few bluecoats and had taken no scalps. The official reports of the officers vary, for some men died of wounds after the actual battle, but the toll amounted to only a few dead and perhaps twenty wounded among the soldiers and their Ute scouts.

That Kit Carson got out of this valley with any men at all is a tribute to his leadership, coolness under fire, common sense, and almost total lack of desire for personal glory. Had he listened to his ambitious officers, and attacked the larger Comanche village, his command would have been slaughtered to the last man. He faced odds similar to those which, years later, General George Armstrong Custer would face at the Little Big Horn. Yet Carson kept his regiment together, refusing to divide his forces beyond the point of leaving his supply train behind under guard. He used his two pieces of artillery with brilliance, and it had been his own idea to trail the cannon along in the first place, cumbersome though they were. Kit knew he had been beaten at Adobe Walls, but he returned to Fort Bascom with light losses in the face of overwhelming opposition, and lived to tell the tale. Soon, he would be breveted general.

The Comanches and Kiowas lost almost one hundred killed, and twice that many wounded. Their victory was costly, and it fed their fear of and hatred for white men. Soldiers had now pierced the very heart of their country, delivered a telling blow, and gotten out. And the thunder guns. Oh, the dread of the gun that shoots twice. Those mountain howitzers so shook the warriors that forever after, when soldiers were sighted, the first question was always about the cannon: "The big guns? Did you see them? The guns on wheels? The guns that shoot twice?"

So it was that the victors of the First Battle of Adobe Walls suffered more than the vanquished invaders. For Little Bluff, Kills Something, and the other Indian leaders, it was a point of little pride. For Kit, who admitted that he had been whipped, it was nonetheless his greatest battle and one that he even boasted about in his reports to his superiors.

It was also Kit's last fight. After returning to Fort Bascom, most of his regiment was disbanded, his men mustered out. Kit was assigned to various duties on the plains and in the mountains. I would not see him during these years after Adobe Walls, for I suspected that his sense of duty might persuade him to have me arrested as a traitor.

Indeed, I had let events manipulate me into a precarious position. Once Kit's personal spy, I was now considered an enemy to the government. At least, I assumed that I was considered a turncoat. In reality, I would find out years later, few people thought about me as much as I thought about myself. It would appear that Kit himself was the only white man who knew that I had been with the Indians at Adobe Walls, and he would take that knowledge with him to the grave.

Yes, I would see Kit once more, but there were other matters to suffer first. Telling this grieves me to this day. I do not like to speak of it. I will not dwell upon it. But you should know what I have suffered, so that you may appreciate the strength of the human spirit, and the will of man to rise above the heaviest of all sorrows.

FIFTY-THREE

On the tenth day after the battle, a small, battered party of Arapahos dropped into the valley and shambled into camp. They ignored the wailing of the mourners and went straight to the biggest lodge in camp—that of Kills Something. I was summoned as a translator. There were four men and two women. One man had a bullet hole through his arm, and one woman had been shot through the thigh. The tale they told chilled my heart.

Up in Colorado, all Arapahos and Cheyennes who wanted to be considered friendly had been ordered to camp at the reservation on Sand Creek, so that the army would know that they desired peace. There, they would be protected. That was the promise of the soldier-chiefs.

Instead, the friendly Indians had been attacked. The slaughter had come at dawn. Soldiers charged the lodges and massacred men, women, and children, even mutilating bodies. It was said that Black Kettle, a Cheyenne chief, had raised an American flag, and waved a white banner of truce. White Antelope had run afoot to meet the soldiers, unarmed, begging them not to attack. He had been ridden down by the soldiers and shot, still wearing his peace medal given to him by President Lincoln in Washington, D.C. A bitter fight had lasted all day as a few survivors dug in to the creek bank and held off the soldiers. They had slipped away after dark, many of them wounded, all of them freezing and hungry.

The leader of the cowardly massacre had been the same man who had been ordering Indians to Sand Creek in the first place. Colonel John M. Chivington. The name made me shudder as I remembered how Chivington had tried to order Westerly and her sister, and William Bent's wife, Yellow Woman, to the camp at Sand Creek. What if he had come back for them? What if John Prowers and William Bent had been unable to keep their wives, and mine, from being sent to Sand Creek? My panic began to mount, and I wondered suddenly if Westerly was dead or alive; well or wounded and dying. A sickly dread fell upon me like an avalanche.

"Listen, my brothers," I asked the Arapahos after they had told their tale to the Comanche leaders. "Do you know Chief Lone Bear of the Cheyennes?"

"Yes," said the leader of the party, his visage locked in a stare of fatigue.

"Lone Bear has two daughters. One of them is my wife, Nomeme-ehne. Do you know her?"

The visiting Arapahos looked at one another, and then one spoke:

"I saw the daughters years ago. Beautiful girls."

"Yes. One daughter, Amache, is married to a white man—a good white man named John Prowers who lives at the town near the stockade of Owl Man. My wife lives there, also. I want to know that she is safe. My heart is heavy to think of this bad thing that has happened to you, but understand that I am worried about my wife. Was she at Sand Creek? Once before, the big bluecoat, Chivington, tried to send her there but Owl Man would not let it be."

The Arapahos stared at each other for a while, then the leader spoke. "This is a bad thing to talk about. I do not know what is true and what is not. There was much confusion, and no one knows all of those who were killed, for the people were scattered after the attack."

"Tell me what you know," I begged.

He sighed and looked at the floor of the lodge. "I know that the wife of Lone Bear was in the camp at Sand Creek. I know that a daughter came to visit her before the attack. But I do not know which daughter. I did not see her. I only heard about it. Also . . ."

"What?"

"I heard that Lone Bear's wife was killed. I do not know about the daughter. She may have left the camp before the attack. She may have escaped. I do not know. I should stop talking about it, because there is no truth in what I say, only guessing."

"Where have the survivors gone?"

"They are scattered, but we heard that the biggest camp is on the Smoky Hill River."

Overwhelmed with worry now, I got up and burst out of the lodge into the cold afternoon. For ten days I had been considering what I should do now that I had gone Indian and turned against the U.S. Army. I feared returning to Boggsville to collect my wife. I feared I would be arrested and tried for treason should I show my face in a white man's settlement. I had planned to have a secret letter delivered to Westerly, telling her where to meet me, so that we could stay among the Indians. Now, I did not even know if Westerly was still in Boggsville. I did not know if she was alive or dead.

I turned and ran to my lodge. By the time I got my herbs and medicines and other things together, the criers were spreading the distressing news about Sand Creek through the camp. I grabbed a bridle and some rope and went to catch horses.

"Plenty Man!"

I turned and saw young Quanah running toward me. "I have no time to talk, nephew."

"I heard about Sand Creek. I know you worry about your wife. I want to ride with you, uncle."

I simply nodded. "Hurry. I will not wait for you, and I will ride hard."

He smiled briefly and turned to sprint away.

By the time I caught two of my ponies with good bottom and a lot of wind, Quanah was also astride a horse and loping to catch up to me. We took the trail the Arapahos had ridden in on, and we went fast. I decided to go straight to the Sand Creek refugees. Boggsville was closer, but I reasoned that if Westerly was there she was safe. If, however, she had been at Sand Creek during the massacre, she might need my help right away. An agonizing thought nagged me. If she was slowly dying of some mortal wound, I might have just a few days to see her alive. I hated thinking of these things, but my mind would not stop considering every possibility. At the very best, assuming my wife was safe, she was nonetheless mourning the loss of her mother, who the Arapahos said had been killed in the massacre.

The ride was punishing. Not the riding itself, for a Comanche embraces physical hardship, especially astride a good mount. It was the not knowing; the constant hoping, fretting helplessness of it all. Quanah did not speak to me much on the trail, for he knew I was worried. He communicated with me only to discuss the trail and our progress. Thus we rode northwest without stopping or eating much for four days. We crossed the Arkansas thirty miles downstream of Boggsville and Bent's Stockade and angled due north, toward the headwaters of the Smoky Hill River, where we had heard most of the survivors of Sand Creek had fled. We scarcely saw a tree after leaving the Arkansas Valley. Here, the plains rolled away, hill after hill. The days were brisk; the nights bone-achingly cold.

Another day and a half of riding brought our fagged ponies to a blood-stained trail that led us to a wretched refugee camp of wailing mourners who shrieked their anguish as they slashed their own flesh with knives. A line of burial scaffolds stood on a hill overlooking the camp. My dread sank into my empty stomach like a hot coal. I spoke to the first woman I came to who was not mourning.

"I am looking for my wife."

She stared at me and Quanah for a few seconds. Then she began to laugh and I saw the sanity go right out of her eyes. Just as suddenly, she cut her own laughter off in her throat, and attacked Quanah's horse, pummeling the animal across the head before Quanah could rein away. Then the woman ran off, screaming through the camp.

"A crazy woman," Quanah said, obviously nervous about our greeting.

I nodded. "I hope not everyone in this camp has gone crazy."

"Look. Someone comes."

I followed Quanah's eyes and saw a middle-aged man limping toward me, using a stick as a crutch. His leg was badly swollen from a wound. "What do you want?" he said, a suspicious glare in his eyes.

"I am looking for my wife."

"Where have you come from?"

"Comanche land. I am Plenty Man. This is Quanah."

He looked south. "Did you see any soldiers?"

"No."

"Buffalo?"

"No. There is nothing out there. The plains are dead."

"Everything is dead," he replied. "Everything. Even the sky. The sun is not even warm anymore."

"I am looking for my wife. She may have been at Sand Creek. She is the daughter of Chief Lone Bear. Her name is Appears-with-the-West-Wind."

His mind seemed to roll back into the horror of that day on Sand Creek, and he looked afraid. "The wife of Lone Bear was at the camp on Sand Creek. She was killed."

"I have heard that. But her daughter?"

"A daughter was there, but I never heard her name."

"What happened to her?" I demanded.

"She came to this camp with the others." He spoke so quietly, I could barely hear.

"So, she is here?"

"She was here until . . . Until yesterday."

"Yesterday? Where has she gone?" My mind felt like a corkscrew, all twisted and cold.

"She has gone . . ." He shifted on his good leg, and winced at the pain of the wounded one. "She has gone . . ."

"Where? Tell me!"

His eyes began to creep laboriously across the camp, and his head turned so slowly that it seemed his neck must be in great pain. He twisted his whole body around to the right, his feet locked into place by the pain of his wounded leg. His eyes grew so sad and his face looked as if he would weep, but no tears came, and no sound escaped his mouth. His gaze crawled, as if he had to drag it like a dead thing. And I watched, a prisoner of my own terrors, as I saw where he would look, finally, when he willed his tortured eyes to show me where Westerly had gone. Now, before I even knew it, he was looking at the hill over the camp.

"She went there," he said. "The one farthest away."

The scaffolds stood like skeletal stalkers of life lurking over the camp, and I heard the winds of black death moaning among their poles. I screamed and kicked my pony, leaving Quanah and the wounded Arapaho man behind.

"I will join her soon!" he shouted at me as I ran my mount toward the burial scaffold.

Which daughter? Which one? Amache? Westerly? No, no, please, not Westerly. Please, oh, please . . . I felt the horrible guilt of wishing my sister-in-law dead.

I made the pony ride right up to the scaffold, though he didn't like the looks of it. I stood on his back and grabbed one of the four upright poles, almost totally mad with fear. I shimmied up the pole as I began to moan unintelligibly and uncontrollably. The scaffold was not made for someone to climb, and it swayed under my weight. I heard screams back at the camp, for what I was doing was ghoulishly unthinkable.

The body atop the platform was wrapped in a bloodstained blanket, tied up tightly with ropes and strips of rawhide, and lashed to the platform with more of the same. A great, bad buzzing sound filled my skull as I drew my knife to cut the ropes that ran across the shoulders and head of the corpse. Quanah had followed but stayed beyond the burial grounds. He scolded me from afar, but I could not even hear his words. I unfolded the top of the blanket as tears began to fill my eyes. I had to look. I had to see. I had to know.

I pulled the blanket back and saw the lifeless face of my beautiful wife, and I screamed in an inhuman voice that still wakes me sometimes in nightmares. I felt my fist clenching my knife so hard that it hurt, and some instinct I possessed for survival made me throw the weapon away for fear that I would plunge it into my own guts. I drew a breath that rushed into me like wind tearing a ragged battle flag, and forced the same air out, all black and boiling, in a scream of heartbroken anguish. Pieces of my soul came out in that scream, never to be reclaimed.

I felt myself falling. I hit the ground hard, and lay there stunned in every way a man can take a beating. Nothing was good inside me. My brain would not think, my heart would not beat, my blood flowed backward in my veins. My chest rose and fell in great sobs as I slipped into some sort of state of semiconsciousness that I embraced like a furlough from Hades.

A comforting sensation enveloped me. It was neither cold nor hot. I felt no pain. It wasn't dark, though neither was it bright. It was all very pleasant, though I still remembered the crippling pains of the real world— the world that I considered real. Then I heard the deep voice of a man laughing in such an easy, joyous way, that I did not at first recognize the voice until he spoke: "Plenty Man," he said in a chuckle. "Plenty, Plenty, Plenty . . . Man, Man, Man . . ."

It was Burnt Belly, speaking in a singsong voice I had never heard him use.

"You take too much care upon yourself. If only you knew. Your time there is but a blink. You are a shooting star—just a fleeting moment of bright-ness in a single night of all the nights of all the seasons of all of creation. You are the shadow of a soaring eagle that passes across the face of a sleeping man. You should go and find a tree that knows ten times the summers you have passed, and listen to that tree. Only then will you begin to know. You are one drop of rain, one breath from a newborn child. Yours is one small cloud that drifts across the moon. That is all. Nothing very bad ever lasts very long. You will see. I went ahead of you to tell you this. Westerly, too. We have not left you so very far behind. You will know in time, grandson."

He began to chuckle again, and I felt my pain returning. The envelope opened and poured me out like fetid water, back into my world of pain and sorrow. But just before I left the comfortable place behind, I heard Westerly's laughter traipse through the vacuum of the Great Beyond—easy and carefree—and it gave me a moment of respite from my grief. Then I fell into one of my deep, absorbing trances, leaving all feeling and consciousness behind.

I awoke shivering. Taking my usual time to look about and get moving, I found myself on the open plains, alone. The day was cloudy, the wind cold. I sat up and saw my horses staked down in a little draw. My personal belongings were on the ground beside me. I noticed the tracks of a pony drag trailing away, and reasoned that someone had transported me here on a travois. I got up and took care of my personal necessities. I had no motivation to do anything else but sit there. I admit that I cried some, but at least I no longer wailed like the madman who had fallen from Westerly's burial scaffold. All I could do to keep my sanity was to cling tenuously to the gossamer strains of Westerly's laughter that I had heard in my vision of the beyond.

After a while, though, my thoughts of grief hardened into anger. I thought of John Chivington and his soldiers attacking the very people to whom they had promised protection and peace. In my mind, Chivington himself had fired the bullet that mortally wounded my wife and made her last days on this earth a living hell. My mind rolled like a hoop on the plains that touched places of grief, then hope, then anger, then sorrow, then blood lust. I began to get the idea that the only way things would ever be right again with all of humanity was for me to find John Chivington and kill him dead.

At length, I saw Quanah returning to me over a hill, his pony still dragging the travois. It surprised me to see him coming, for I thought he had abandoned me as a madman. I pulled myself together and wiped the tears from my face. When Quanah came near, I saw a load of sticks and buffalo chips lashed down on the travois, as well as a young antelope carcass. He had bloodstains on his hands and face. My stomach growled, and I realized that I was still alive, and hungry.

Quanah looked at me fearfully. "Are you crazy?"

I shook my head. "No, nephew. I am not crazy. I know I acted that way for a while, but I am better now. I will not be going crazy like that again."

He looked as if he believed me. "That camp was full of bad spirits. I believe one of them got inside you."

I nodded. "Yes, but it is gone. I heard a vision, and that cured me."

"You *heard* a vision?"

"It is possible. When you hear a coyote far away in the dark, can you not see it in your heart?"

Quanah smirked and glanced across the bare hills. "That crazy woman at the camp wanted me to take something from her to give to you. I was afraid to touch it, so she put it in your parfleche bag."

"What is it?"

"I do not know. I was afraid of it. It is wrapped up in a piece of deerskin."

"I will look at it, then I will help you with that antelope."

He lifted his chin in approval, and jumped down from the horse to remove the travois. I went to my parfleche bag that carried my food and herbs and opened it carefully. I saw the deerskin, wrapped around the shape of a cylinder. Untying the thong around the deerskin, I found several sheets of paper, rolled up. They were pages torn from a Bible that had probably been given to some Arapaho or Cheyenne by a missionary. Aside from the printed words of the Gospel, these pages had handwriting on them, and my heart leapt when I realized that it sprang from Westerly's hand. Her lines of cursive ran counter to the printed lines in the Bible. The pen she had used seemed to have been a simple quill. The ink could only have been blood. I straightened the pages and turned them so that I could begin to read the difficult script. Before I even deciphered a letter, I could see that Westerly had been in pain, her hand trembling. She had written in Spanish, her favorite. *"Mi amor . . ."*

> *My love,*
>
> *I know everything you feel just now. Anger, sorrow, pain. Let the caress of every West Wind that touches you carry it all away from your heart. Shed those feelings like cottonwood leaves in the autumn, right down to the strong, graceful branches that we grew together. When the winter passes, as it always does, tender new buds will grow. There is a place for us in the Shadow Land, and you must do your duty until it is time for us to be together again. Do not think of revenge. That is not your duty. Do not let your heart grow black. Do as you have done all along. Help the People. Even when you despair, help them. And know that I have loved you from the moment I saw your face and heard your voice. Do not change*

the things I love. Do not let them change you. Everything you touch rings like the note of a songbird. You are the best thing that ever came to me, and without you my life would have meant nothing. Always remember that I think of you with every breath. Behind all my cares and joys, you are there, a beautiful warm comfort inside of me. Even now, my love. Even now. I smile, because of you. I leave you now, but only for a while. Mi alma will stay with you, and the spirits will bring us together again in time. Our love is too strong to die. Trust me. I love you.
Westerly.

In Spanish, the word *alma* can mean either "heart" or "soul." Or both. She had chosen her words well, even in her agony. I had to turn my face away to keep a tear from falling on the paper. During the reading of that letter my heart had swollen with a longing to hold her. It must have been so hard for her to pen those words with her own blood, yet she knew they would bring me relief and comfort and wisdom. I missed her even more now, and I knew I would for a long, long while.

Yes, her words had made me feel loved beyond my ability to convey the sensation to you. But do not think my difficulty would end there. I had many bitter days before me, and much hardship of the heart to suffer.

I looked up at Quanah. He was skinning the antelope. He glanced at me, a bit fearfully. I rolled the letter and, wrapping it again in the deerskin, I replaced it in my parfleche bag.

"I will make fire," I said. "Then I must burn some fir needles for smoke. The smoke will purify me, and protect me from the bad spirits of that crazy camp."

"Good," Quanah said. "I will pray with you, uncle. We should make a sweat lodge."

"We can do that later. There is no time now."

He looked at me, confused. "We have no hurry."

"Nephew, I must go back to that camp."

His eyes flared with fear. "Why would you go back there?"

"I do not want to go. But I must. I have medicine. I have powers that heal. That man with the bad leg—I can save him. And probably others, too. You do not have to go."

"Are you not afraid of that place? You went crazy there."

"My medicine is stronger now. I am not afraid. The bad spirits will run from me like rabbits. You do not have to follow me."

He carved at the meat for a while in silence. Finally, he said, "If I go back there with you, we must build a sweat lodge after we leave that place, so we can purify ourselves."

I nodded. "Yes, that is the way. That is good. We will help those people, then we will sweat."

FIFTY-FOUR

I did what I could to soothe the wounds of the people at the Bad Camp on the Smoky Hill River. The man with the wounded leg survived because of me and the things Burnt Belly had taught me. I saved a few others, but some were beyond my powers to help. Some of the wounds were horrible, and the suffering of the victims prolonged and severe. This served only to deepen my hatred for the leader of that massacre—John M. Chivington.

I said my prayers at Westerly's burial scaffold every morning and every evening, sometimes wailing right out loud like others at the camp. I knew my mourning had just begun. I missed my wife, the moments we shared, the love we made, the things we learned from each other. She was gone and I could not understand why it had to be so. She had brought no harm to anyone. It was the ultimate injustice that she had been taken from the world at all. That she had been taken from *me* was a crime against everything right and moral within the realm of men and gods. Someone should pay, I thought. What kind of man would let this go unpunished?

Quanah and I stayed for twenty-one days at the camp on the Smoky Hill. We heard many stories of Sand Creek, and began to piece together the story of the massacre. Westerly had gone there to visit her mother. When the attack came, Westerly's mother had been shot down instantly. Westerly escaped at first and ran up the creek but was shot in the back by a horseman. In my mind it had to have been John Chivington himself. She feigned death for a while until the attackers galloped past her, then she crawled into the creekbed where the survivors dug pits and mounted a desperate defense until nightfall. Unable to walk, Westerly had been carried away by rescuers after dark.

The survivors told heart-wrenching tales about that night. Bitterly cold wind whipped across the plains where the few people who remained unhurt attempted to save wounded men, women, and children by building fires of grass. Few people had had time to dress warmly before the dawn attack came, and almost everyone had lost robes and blankets fleeing for their lives. The adults covered poor, crying, naked, wounded children with mounds of grass in an attempt to keep them from freezing to death.

Westerly was one of these sufferers. My shame at not having been there to protect her at Sand Creek was almost enough in itself to kill me. I had been doing what I thought my heart dictated: saving the Comanches from a surprise attack by soldiers. And yet I had left my wife behind to fall victim to a far worse attack, unprotected by me.

Other details about the massacre began to take shape. Chivington began his attack by cutting the unsuspecting Indians off from their horse herd before dawn. At sunrise, he had loosed the staggering firepower of four howitzers upon the sleeping village, then charged seven hundred mounted soldiers into a camp of six hundred Cheyenne and Arapaho, two thirds of whom were women and children. Even children were shot down and scalped.

I also learned that the Bent brothers, Charles and George, had been present during the massacre. George had been wounded in the hip and had stayed at this very camp on the Smoky Hill for a few days before going to look for his brother. Some witnesses said that Charles, who had been living with the Indians, and fought as one of them during the battle, was captured by soldiers. Fearing that his younger brother had been executed, George had left the Smoky Hill to find out what had happened to Charles.

I pieced together what I could about Sand Creek, and did my best to heal the wounded at the Smoky Hill camp until one day a roving band of Cheyennes showed up with food and medicines to further care for the recovering wounded. As I had done all I could do for the people there, Quanah and I decided to leave. We had been there twenty-one days and it was time to move on. I cast a last gaze toward Westerly's funeral scaffold, and turned away. I knew she was no longer there.

Farther down the Smoky Hill River, we found some timber and, using bent willow boughs and buffalo robes, we made a sweat lodge just big enough for the two of us to crawl into. Quanah came out pure. I was not so sure about myself.

I had no one left to me but my Comanche family, yet I could not bring myself to go home to the Crossing and Adobe Walls for reasons I did not at first understand. At length, I realized that I wanted to linger in the country of my wife's people, the Cheyenne. I drifted aimlessly on the plains for a while, looking for trails to follow. It dawned on me that I was gravitating toward Boggsville, where Westerly's sister, Amache, lived with her husband, John Prowers. But I was not yet ready to risk showing my face there for fear of being arrested as a traitor. I was a fugitive again, destined to wander aimlessly in the wilderness. Quanah stayed with me. He did not even ask where we were going or what we were doing. He just rode with me and made himself useful.

One day we cut the trail of two Indian ponies in the snow, and followed the trail north. Finding the camp of the riders, we approached cautiously, and discovered the brothers George and Charles Bent huddled around a small cook fire, roasting a hare. They stood, and George greeted me in Cheyenne, saying, "Come, warm yourself, Plenty Man." His eyes looked troubled. Charles's eyes looked half-wild. He did not speak to me at all. They were dressed in full Cheyenne regalia, having shed all vestiges of the white man's clothing.

They shared their food with us and we all ate in silence. Finally, George wiped his fingers on his buckskin leggings and spoke:

"I must tell you something, Plenty Man." His eyes looked up from the ground between his feet.

I raised my hand to spare him the task. "I have come from the camp you left on the Smoky Hill River."

"Then you know?"

"Yes, my friend. I have been mourning since I found that wretched place."

"I would have stayed to help her, but she would not have it. She told me that she was beyond help, and that I should go look for my brother. She was a very brave woman. She told me that she was not afraid to die, but that she did not want to go without seeing her husband. Did you . . ."

I shook my head in sorrow and shame. "I got there a day too late. She wrote me a letter in her own blood."

We sat in silence for a long time, and Charles angrily threw some more sticks on the fire. Every move he made betrayed his ire with life.

"Tell me about Sand Creek," I said. "And whatever you know about what happened to Westerly."

George sighed. "Some Cheyennes were camped up the Purgatoire, near Boggsville, and your wife went to visit them. They said that they were going to Sand Creek, where they had been told by the soldiers that they would be treated as friendly Indians. Your wife heard from these Indians that her mother was in that camp, so she decided to go visit her mother. Your wife's other sister, Amache, almost went, too, but John Prowers would not let her go. Charles and I were in the camp at Sand Creek when your wife arrived."

"Did you speak to her then?"

"Just briefly, to welcome her to the camp. She got there just three days before the attack, and she spent all of her time with her mother. Now, back on the Arkansas, the day before the attack, Chivington showed up at my father's stockade and threw a guard around the place to keep my father or anybody else from riding out and warning the Cheyennes. Your brother-in-law, John Prowers, happened to be riding down to the stockade that morning to visit my father, and he saw what was going on. He tried to escape so he could ride to warn the Cheyennes, but the soldiers overtook him, and Chivington had him arrested and put under guard."

"Chivington arrested John? On what charge? By what authority?"

George could only shrug. "Whatever the charge was, it was dropped after the attack. John hates Chivington now. His wife lost a mother and a sister in the massacre. John is already talking about a court-martial, and he's not the only one."

"A court-martial is too good for that murdering bastard," I said. "A quick bullet through the brain would serve justice much quicker. Like you'd dispatch a coyote in a leg trap."

"You shouldn't talk like that," George said. "If somebody other than me and Charles heard you say that, and Chivington ended up dead . . . Well, if somebody is going to do it, they should just do it, and not talk about it . . ."

I nodded grimly. "Tell me about Sand Creek."

"Chivington left a small guard around the stockade and moved the rest of his troops to Fort Lyon. These were the sorriest white men you ever saw. They were not soldiers at all. They were miners and bullwhackers gathered for hundred-day enlistments. They were called 'the Hundred-Dazers.' Mostly, they were drunken Indian-haters. They had no uniforms and no training. Their officers were elected by vote, and knew nothing about military rules.

"Our brother, Robert, was at my father's stockade when they surrounded it, and Chivington ordered him to act as guide and take the troops to Sand Creek, even though he already had a guide."

"Who was that?"

"Old Jim Beckwourth."

"So what did Robert do?"

"He told Chivington to go to hell, but Chivington told Robert he would have him shot if he didn't guide the soldiers to Sand Creek. So our own brother had to scout for the bastards that were coming to kill us, but Robert didn't know that. He didn't know we were in the camp, and he didn't know that Chivington was going to massacre the whole camp. They went to Fort Lyon that day, and got more troops from Major Anthony. Old Jim Beckwourth collapsed at the fort—from the cold, he claimed. I think he knew what was coming and wanted out. I know Jim is old, but I never knew him to buckle under cold or anything else. So Robert was left as the only guide to lead Chivington's butchers that night to Sand Creek."

Charles spat in the fire at this recollection, and George went on to tell about the surprise attack at dawn, the battle that followed, and the horrendous ordeals of the survivors. When he had finished, I turned to young Charles. He happened to be sitting close to Quanah, to whom he had spoken not a single word or given a glance.

As I looked at them in the dim light of the flickering fire, I saw both similarities and contrasts between the two. They were about the same age—both around seventeen. Both were half-breeds. Charles was the son of a white trader and a Cheyenne mother. Quanah was the son of a Comanche chief and a captured white woman. Though Charles had seen many Indian camps as a child, he had been mostly raised and schooled among whites. Quanah, on the other hand, had grown up with Comanches. Charles had experienced warfare as a Confederate soldier and a Cheyenne brave. Quanah, as a Comanche raider. Charles was wild and bitter, his every expression and movement betraying his lust for killing and vengeance. Quanah, though fierce enough, seemed at peace with himself and his lot. I couldn't know it at the time, of course, for I could not yet foresee the future like Burnt Belly, but one of these half-breed boys would grow old and gray while the other would not see twenty-two.

"Do not look at me," Charles growled, though he had only felt my gaze, and had not looked up.

"I was just wondering," I said, "what happened with you at Sand Creek?"

"Something I will never allow to happen again. I was captured by the soldiers. Next time, I will fight to the death, and there will be some widows, orphans, and some new faces in hell before they rub me out."

"I understand," I said. "Kit's men captured me after beating my brains nearly out on the trail to Adobe Walls. I would rather die than suffer that humiliation again."

"We heard about that at Boggsville," George said. "Everything's gone crazy. Friend against friend. Brother against brother. These are dark times."

"The darkest," I agreed. "How did you get released if you were captured?" I asked Charles. He ignored me, so George answered for him:

"Along with Charles, they captured Blackfoot John's son, Jack Smith. Jack was just camping there, trading with the Indians. The soldiers executed him by firing squad."

"For what?" I said, remembering Jack Smith as a jolly young trader.

George shrugged. "I guess because he was a half-breed. They wanted to shoot Charles, too, but Charlie Autobee's boys were there, and they protested until Chivington agreed to turn Charles over to the old man."

Charles hissed at the mention of his father. "He's not *my* old man. I claim no white man as my father." He shot a quick glare up at me. "Or friend."

"I can't help being white, Charles."

"You can camp somewhere else."

"*Charles,*" George growled.

Charles dropped his taunting, and stared into the darkness. Quanah looked at me with some concern. The conversation had been in a mixture of Cheyenne and English, and Quanah had understood nothing but the tones of our voices. I signed my reassurance to him that everything was all right.

"Why are you camped out here?" I asked.

"None of your business," Charles responded.

George made a sign of caution toward his younger brother. "We are looking for soldiers—the ones from Sand Creek. Will you join us?"

I thought about this for a moment. This was a revenge mission. Westerly had warned me against this in her letter. "I want revenge on only one man—Chivington."

George shook his head. "You didn't see them. The men that followed Chivington were as bad as him. Worse, even. They scalped wounded children who were not yet dead. They hacked the bodies of women and warriors to pieces. Any soldier who rode with that devil should pay the price with his own life and his own blood."

I considered George's talk, and felt my lust for revenge swell. Yet I knew I had to find some limitations to my anger, lest I end up like Charles Bent—or even like John Chivington himself. "On this warpath, will you hold to the code of a Cheyenne warrior?"

"Of course," George said.

"Charles?"

The younger brother rose. "I *am* a Cheyenne warrior, goddamn you. You dare to question me, white man?"

George stood, grabbed Charles by the shoulder of his deerskin shirt, and shook him hard. "That's enough, Charles! Don't be a fool. Can't you tell a friend from an enemy anymore?"

Charles slapped George's hand away. "I won't answer to any white man. Or any goddamn Comanche, either. I am a Cheyenne warrior, and I answer to no one but my own spirits." Having said this, he stalked to a bedroll he had spread on the ground and, throwing himself down upon it, turned his back to us and covered himself with a buffalo robe.

George gave me an apologetic look and sat back down. We sat in silence for a long time as the tiny cook fire the brothers had built burned down to orange coals.

"Why this trail?" I asked George.

"Chivington's men went to Denver after the massacre. They displayed their scalps in a theater one night, to the cheers of the people there who treated them like war heroes. No one yet knows what cowards they were that day. I am going to try to have a talk with Governor Evans, to tell him what really happened. And if we happen to catch any of Chivington's men mustered out on the plains, we are going to kill them."

"How will you know them?"

"They will be riding Cheyenne ponies."

"Ponies get traded. You have to be sure. Now, if you found someone wearing one of those scalps from the People, then there would be little doubt."

George frowned and shrugged off my concerns. "We will know. Our hearts will tell us. If you had been there, you would understand." He stood and ambled over to his own bedroll and crawled into it. Though I didn't feel sleepy, my body was tired and I thought I should try to get some rest. I signed to Quanah that we should get our bedrolls down from our horses, and he agreed. Soon, everyone in camp was snoring softly but me. I lay in my robe and thought about Westerly—the days and nights we had spent together. I strained to see her smile and her sparkling eyes until I felt my head would burst. I thought about how she had died, and I felt my anger boil. I did not sleep that night.

FIFTY-FIVE

We rode north, up Black Squirrel Creek, until we came to the high divide where the creeks headed and the timber came spilling down from the mountains. On the other side of this wooded divide, new creeks began, these flowing northward. It was good country, owing to the timber that provided wood for fires and shelter for elk, deer, and smaller game. This peninsula of timber that swept out of the foothills and onto the plains along this high divide was known as "the Pinery" to white settlers. We rode through it watchfully, passing some places where men had cut down trees to use in building log cabins and barns. The big timbers had gouged the ground where teams of mules or oxen had dragged them away.

There are places along that divide where the timber ends abruptly, and a man can see for miles across treeless plains. We came to one of these places on the north side of the Pinery toward twilight. As we approached the edge of the timber, we rode cautiously, staying far enough back in the shadows so that we could reconnoiter the country without showing ourselves. In this way, we spotted a camp of hunters as we peered through the last line of trees. The plain smoke trail from their fire was the first sign that we saw of them, like a gray ribbon rising above the headwaters of Kiowa Creek. The party was less than five hundred yards from the timber, plainly visible down the slope below us. The hunters had two horses and three mules hobbled near their campfire. The two horses were fine-looking spotted ponies—Appaloosas from Nez Perce country. Two of the mules were bays, the other a sorrel. Two men and a boy stood around the fire. They seemed to be warming themselves as they roasted meat on a spit suspended over the fire. On the ground near them, I saw a dark mound that had to be the carcass of an elk.

The peculiar thing about this party was the way it *sounded*. One of the hunters was playing a harmonica, and the longer I watched, it became obvious that the boy was the one playing, for he held his hands to his face and danced next to the fire as he played. One of the men wore a big sombrero. The other man took his hat off for a second or two to scratch his head, and I recognized him as a black man. I knew who these men were. They did not know me, for I had never ridden up to their ranch to introduce myself, but I had seen them from afar for the past four years as I rode through this country. And I knew them by stories.

"That mule," Charles said. "The red one. That is Cut-Lip-Bear's mule. That mule was stolen from Sand Creek."

"Are you sure?" George asked. "That looks like the black man who works for Ab Holcomb over on the Monument."

"Yes, that's him," I agreed. "His name is Buster Thompson. The other man is Javier Maldonado, the vaquero that Holcomb brought back from Pigeon's Ranch. Those are not soldiers."

"That is Cut-Lip-Bear's mule," Charles insisted. "And now he is dead and someone should pay."

"Now, wait a minute," I argued. "That black man is called Buffalo Head by the Arapahos. He is a friend of Long Fingers, the Arapaho chief. That boy was a captive of the Comanches last winter. Buffalo Head went to get him back. Those are not enemies to the Cheyenne. They're not even white, except for the boy."

"The light is dying," Charles said, ignoring my every argument. "We don't have much time. We can ride east through the timber, and sneak up on them over that spur."

"They will have guns," George warned. "They've been hunting."

"You can't be serious about attacking *them*," I complained. "The black man's a farmer. The Mexican is just a hired ranch hand. And that boy. He's only ten years old. He and the black one play the violin. You kill them and you're just asking for trouble. They haven't harmed anyone."

"They have Cut-Lip-Bear's mule!" Charles insisted.

"Charles, there is no way you can tell from here which mule that is. There could be a hundred mules that look like that one from a quarter mile away."

"Enough talk. Daylight is slipping away. George and I are going to ride down there and kill them, and you can stay behind like a woman if you want to—you and this half-breed Comanche." He gestured toward Quanah with his tomahawk, reined his pony east.

"George, you're not going to let him . . ." I said.

George looked indecisive. "Somebody *should* pay," he said. "We'll have a closer look at that mule." He turned away to follow his brother.

"Charles has already made up his mind," I warned.

Quanah had not understood the conversation, but he could readily see the conflict. "Those are fine ponies," he said to me in Comanche, glancing down to the Appaloosas at the hunting camp. "This is a raid, yes?" He reined east to follow the Bent brothers.

I sat stupidly on my pony, uncertain what to do. Kit's advice rang in my head. *Is this right?* I knew it was not. These were the wrong men to punish for Sand Creek. By all accounts I had ever heard, the black man and the Mexican were just good, hardworking men. Yet I could not stop Charles from leading the others away. I could not stop him, but . . .

I drew my revolver and made a leap out of the timber and into the open. Angling the muzzle of the weapon slightly off to one side of the hunters, I jerked the trigger six times, shattering the good sounds of the distant mouth-harp music and the gentle hiss of the breeze through the pines. I holstered my pistol and released my best Comanche yell as I reached for my Henry rifle in its saddle scabbard. I smelled gun smoke as I watched the two men and the boy scramble for their mounts below. Now Charles was cursing me furiously as his pony's hooves beat the ridge toward me. I fired a rifle round from the Henry and slid the weapon back into the scabbard to deal with Charles.

Wheeling my mount, I found Charles charging me with his tomahawk over his head, his eyes blazing with anger at me for having spoiled his raid. I caught Charles's axe blade with my shield, which I had whipped around from my back just in time. The impact of his charge knocked me from my pony. He was falling over me and I grabbed him by the throat about the time I hit the ground on my back. Our ponies danced aside, and though the fall had fairly knocked my wind from me, I knew I'd better fight like hell because Charles seemed bent on killing me. I rolled, still holding his throat, and got on top of him. George was shouting at us both to stop. Charles made a wild swing with his tomahawk and it glanced off my skull, drawing blood. All I could think to do was to batter my forehead down onto the bridge of the young half-blood's nose, and the blow stunned him so that he dropped his weapon.

Quickly, I jumped to my feet and kicked the war axe aside. My lungs managed to suck in a little air, and I stumbled aside and fell to my knees to find George holding a gun on me. Behind him, Quanah had an arrow notched, prepared to send it through George's heart. Their eyes blazed with confusion and panic. I raised my hand to try to calm them, but just then, my pony trotted in front of me and something happened to him. He made a loud thudding sound and his head and neck just whipped toward me and sent him slamming to the ground, almost on top of Charles, where he lay groaning, half-conscious, on the ground. I looked down the slope and saw a white cloud of gun smoke streaming away from the black man called Buffalo Head. The boy who had been playing the harmonica was now holding the reins of two horses and a mule. Another smoke cloud appeared like a magician's bouquet and a blink later a rifle ball split bark from a tree behind me as it sang into the forest.

Those men may not have been very cautious about where they camped, but they were damn good shots, for they were coming much too close from a quarter mile off. I sucked in my first good breath of air since hitting the ground, glared at George, and pointed downhill. He swung his muzzle around and fired down at the camp as I grabbed Charles's wrist to drag him behind the first tree I came to. Quanah came to my aid, reaching low from his mount and using the power of his pony to haul Charles to safety. My pony had not fallen on my rifle, so I slipped it from the scabbard and stepped behind a tree. I used the lever to work a live round into the breech. George dismounted. He and I began returning fire from the cover of the trees, and the men below, enjoying no cover, decided to mount and flee rather than stand and fight. They left behind their elk carcass and the hobbled red mule that had caused all the confusion in the first place.

I had caught some wind in my lungs now, and I turned to George, angry over the loss of my pony and the painful axe wound to my scalp. "Now you can have a closer look at that damned red mule! If it is not the mule that belonged to Cut-Lip-Bear, then your brother should go home and stop looking for the wrong people to punish!"

George looked down at his brother, who was now regaining his senses and touching his broken nose. "He can't go home, Plenty Man. He doesn't know where it is. Maybe *you* are the one who should go home. Your heart is not in this fight we have taken on."

"You are right, George. My heart is not in it. I won't ride with you boys anymore and watch you destroy what your father has spent decades holding together. You could be helping him, but you're working against him, now. You're on a bad warpath. You should smoke and think and seek some wisdom over this before you destroy everything."

Just then, my pony, which I thought had been shot to death, began to lunge on the ground. We all turned to watch—even Charles, though still somewhat dazed. Quanah looked fearfully at the animal as he lifted his head and struggled to get his front hooves under him. Another effort, and the pony found his feet, wobbling a little as he rose. Blood ran from the off side of the mount's neck where a bullet had torn through the flesh above the spine. It was obvious to me that horse had simply been "creased" and rendered temporarily paralyzed, but George and Quanah looked at the beast as if it had risen from the dead. I was not above taking advantage of it.

"Now you see that my medicine is strong," I said in Spanish, so that both Quanah and the Bents could understand. "I was right to warn those men, and you all were wrong to wish them harm." I jutted my rifle triumphantly toward the sky and went to catch my wounded pony by the reins, hoping that he would not collapse under me, once I got mounted upon him.

FIFTY-SIX

Quanah and I rode home. We arrived at the Crossing in the middle of a blizzard to find that the entire village had moved on. We gathered some charred lodge poles from the Kiowa village Kit had destroyed, and with them and some pieces of buffalo-hide lodge covers that hadn't completely burned, we made a small shelter inside the old adobe walls where we could wait out the storm. We found no game stirring in the valley, so we had to kill and butcher our poorest mount. The pony was not likely to survive another freezing night anyway.

After the storm broke, Quanah drifted on to find his band of Wanderers, but I preferred to stay behind. The winter was a long one, and I remained alone in my despair. There were times when my wailing sobs echoed through the icy canyons like a demon's song. I ate only when my stomach twisted in knots of hunger, slept only when I dropped from sheer exhaustion, bathed only to torment myself with frigid waters cold enough to kill me. A couple of times I almost waited one second too long to drag myself through the hole I had chopped in the ice, sensing that beyond the aching agony of the cold there was comfort for the tortured heart and soul.

When spring came, I pulled myself together to some extent. I found Kills Something's band and rejoined them. The People looked at me differently, for I had grown gaunt and my eyes were hollow as caverns. Even my brother, Kills Something, avoided me, and I withdrew from the society of the village and traveled with it only for protection and convenience. I would wander all day and listen to trees and other plants that strained to talk to me. Sometimes I would shout at some bush or weed in frustration, making everyone in camp believe that I was quite touched. Yet they allowed me to remain, for I was learning spirit-secrets, and I could heal.

Always, always, I struggled with the same thoughts. Westerly, and how I missed her. My vision of Burnt Belly in the Shadow Land. My hatred of Chivington. I longed to seek the wisdom of my friends Owl Man and Little Chief—William and Kit. Dare I? Did a noose await me back in the towns of the white men? Did anyone remember me at all? Was I even alive? Did I ever even exist?

It went on like this for almost a year, and then something happened. A rattlesnake bit me on the buttocks as I went to sit on a fallen log. Got me right on the bare skin at the edge of my breechclout. I treated myself, as Burnt Belly had taught me, with an ointment of scraped coneflower root mixed with the grease of a bobcat, also chewing the sweet, tingly coneflower root. The cure worked, but the wound still swelled and hurt so badly for a couple of days that I realized that I was quite alive. I decided that I must make a change. My occasional cures with Kills Something's people did not warrant the spirits allowing me to exist on Mother Earth, and that was what the snake was sent to tell me when it bit me. I knew I had to make myself more useful.

I began remembering things other than my losses. Burnt Belly had taught me cures that I had never used. So I resolved to get serious about my career as a medicine man. I practiced the chants and incantations the old shaman had shared with me. I sought and collected healing herbs. The coneflower, in particular, became my favorite cure, for one day while I strolled alone on the prairie, a blooming coneflower spoke to me in a voice as clear as yours or mine—a feminine voice that listed her medicinal uses. I was stunned. The little purplish blossom could do much more than treat snake bite.

"My juice soothes and heals burns," Coneflower said. "My roots stop fits and stomach cramps. Dry my leaves and smoke them to cure headache. Chew my roots to soothe toothaches, swollen throat glands, and mouth sores."

Coneflower went on to tell me that she was particularly adept at purifying the blood and the entire system, increasing resistance to infection, speeding the healing of wounds, and boosting the body's natural immune system. Indeed, when so-called modern medicine finally discovers coneflower, it will become a household word, though I predict that our posturing physicians will probably refer to her by her scientific name derived from the Greek *echinos,* referring to the prickly stalks and leaves—*echinacea.*

During this time of self-recovery, I would also dream of captive children who wanted to go home—parents who missed them. Once, I had been a trader renowned for negotiating the release of captives and bringing them home. I knew it was high time I resumed my status as trader and ransom negotiator. I went to Kills Something one day, and told him that I was going away.

"Why do you leave?" he asked—the first words he had spoken to me in a dozen moons.

"My time for mourning has passed. I have work to do."

"Your work is here, healing the people."

"That is true, my brother. But I must also go between your people and the whites and save the Way of the *Noomah* as long as I can. The spirits call me to this task. I must make peace where I can, or war will destroy everything. Do you understand? Do you trust me to do this? I am no longer crazy, my brother. The demons have left my heart."

He looked me up and down. Finally, he smiled a little. "Yes, I see that you are back."

"I am sorry about the times I shouted at trees and upset the people. I had bad blood in my heart, but now I am pure again."

"What about the revenge you wish on the soldier chief from Sand Creek?"

I sighed and swept my eyes across the rolling plains of Texas. "I have given it over to the spirits. I will not seek him out, but if the spirits wish me to take my revenge on him, they will deliver him to me. It is no longer in my hands."

He nodded his approval. "Where will you go?"

"Back to Nuevo Mexico. I will come back with many good things to trade, like I did in the old days."

Kills Something smiled and sighed with no small measure of relief. "That would please me, and all of the people. But will the whites not kill you for fighting against the bluecoats?"

I smiled. "Do you remember how I became invisible at Adobe Walls when Little Chief and the bluecoats came?"

"*Aho.* The people still talk about it."

"Plenty Man will become invisible again. He will move among the whites and no one will ever see him."

Kills Something grinned, clearly gladdened to hear me boast again. "We will feast when you return, like we once did."

I offered my hand, and Chief Kills Something took it. "Until the Moon of Falling Leaves, my brother."

"May the spirits protect you."

〰〰〰

I decided to take on a new identity. I would call myself Geronimo Jones, and claim that I was half Mexican and half English—the bastard son of a British duke who, whilst philandering about northern Mexico on a lavish jaguar-hunting expedition, bedded my mother—a comely señorita from Agua Prieta—begetting me. Inventing a new past for myself entertained me as I rode westward to the settlements of New Mexico.

By the time I reached Santa Fe, I had cut my hair and started a beard. I quietly went about buying single articles of Mexican clothing at different stores so as not to draw attention to myself. I purchased high-top boots and huge spurs, a sombrero, riding britches with silver conchos, a red cotton shirt and a leather riding jacket. In this costume, I could walk right up to people I had known casually for years, and carry on a conversation with them without their ever knowing who I really was. It provided amusement that I dearly enjoyed and needed.

Sometimes, I would even start conversations about the exploits of the famous frontiersman Honoré Greenwood—*me*. It was great fun. I would get a conversation going by casually mentioning the name of Kid Greenwood, then I would listen to fanciful accounts of his duel with Snakehead Jackson, his infiltration of Sibley's brigade in San Antonio, his rescue of Captain Lord's men at Valverde, his slaying and scalping of the two Mescalero scouts with Paddy Graydon's outfit, the many children he had ransomed back from the wilderness tribes, and his service as trusted scout for the great Kit Carson.

There was even some talk of how Kit had forcibly detained me on the plains east of Fort Bascom, but oddly enough, no one in Santa Fe seemed to know that Honoré Greenwood had connived against Kit's regiment at Adobe Walls. I began to wonder how much of a fugitive I really was. But by now, I was having too much fun being Geronimo Jones. It was just such a relief not to have to be Honoré Greenwood for a while.

As Geronimo Jones, I became a new Comanchero. This did not float well with the established Comancheros of Santa Fe and Taos, who thought that I would horn in on their market. I had to back down more than one angry competitor wielding a gun or a knife, but eventually I convinced them all that I would not harm their trade, as I worked almost exclusively with one band of Indians far to the east—Kills Something's people.

And so passed the next three years of my life. Geronimo Jones became a celebrated figure in Santa Fe and Taos. More than one man claimed I was his cousin or nephew or uncle. The señoritas adored me, for I was the son of an English duke. A bastard son, perhaps, but blue-blooded nonetheless. I took to drinking tea, stating my intention to one day sail to England to have a cup with dear old dad.

I did not see Kit Carson during these years, for I spent much time out among the Comanches, venturing into New Mexico only twice a year, while the army relentlessly ordered Kit up and down every trail it had conquered between Washington, D.C., and Fort Sumner, New Mexico. He established Camp Nichols to protect the Santa Fe Trail; treated with the Indians, including Little Bluff, whose village he had burned at Adobe Walls; traveled east to visit kin in Missouri; reported to his superiors in Washington, D.C., where he was breveted general; served at Fort Union, Taos, Santa Fe, Maxwell's Ranch, and the Bosque Redondo; held a council with the Zuni Indians; and testified before a visiting Joint Special Committee from the U.S. Congress on Indian matters.

Finally, General Christopher Carson was granted command of Fort Garland, Colorado, where Josefa and his five children could join him. A sixth child, Stella, was born to General and Mrs. Carson at Fort Garland. Kit was fifty-seven. Josefa, thirty-nine.

Now, the only person to whom Geronimo Jones had revealed his true identity was Lucien Bonaparte Maxwell. Maxwell was a bigger rascal than I was, and I knew he would admire my guise. He delighted in encouraging me to tell lies about my nonexistent past to visitors at his hacienda, who were many in those days, as his ranch was a stage-coach stop. Maxwell stayed in constant contact with Kit, through messenger or mail, and kept me apprised of Kit's whereabouts and doings.

In the spring of 1868, I went to Maxwell's Ranch for an extended sojourn. I had arrived with a mule train of whiskey and all manner of other goods for the Comanchero trade, and Maxwell convinced me that I had better fatten those mules for a couple of weeks on oats before embarking on the long, dangerous trek into Comancheria. I gladly consented. Maxwell's Ranch was an oasis in the wilderness. Lucien himself had amassed great wealth during the Civil War and the Indian Wars, selling beef and other foodstuffs to the army and the Bosque Redondo Indian Reservation. One branch of the Santa Fe Trail ran past his place, and he could purchase goods from all over the world over the tailgate of a freight wagon.

So it was, one afternoon in April, that Lucien Maxwell and I happened to be sitting in the sunshine in front of his mansion, eating sardines and smoked oysters on English biscuits, and drinking Chinese tea, while we watched his servants and laborers go about their menial chores.

"What have you heard from Kit?" I asked, having held the question to myself long enough.

Maxwell frowned, then took a bite from a sort of sardine and oyster sandwich he had made between two crackers. "Not good," he said, crumbs spraying from his mouth. "Kit tried to resign his commission last summer because of his problem." Maxwell pointed to his left shoulder. "The goddamn army refused his resignation. Those bastards have used that man up, Kid. But he finally got them to muster him out last winter, and he moved to Boggsville. Josefa is pregnant again, of course. Those two breed like rabbits."

I chuckled, but the chuckle died quickly, and I suddenly missed old Kit very much. "Maybe I should go see him."

"Go see him," Lucien advised. "I've talked to Kit several times about that scrape at Adobe Walls, and he never mentions you taking sides with the Comanche. He doesn't even know that I know. We don't talk about it."

"I wasn't only taking the Comanche side," I argued. "I made damn sure the Indians didn't know about Kit's supply train. If they had found it, Kit's campaign would have ended in disaster."

"Yeah, yeah," Lucian said. "I know about that. But Kit don't know."

"I'd never tell him. He believes he himself got his boys out, and he did. I don't want him thinking otherwise. The point is that if I had really turned on Kit, I could have destroyed him, but my aim was not to beat him. My aim was to convince him to leave that valley with all practicable haste, and he did so, against the advice of his overzealous officers."

"Well, that's Kit. He's always done what he thought was right, and damn any man who didn't see it his way. You ought to go see him before it's too late."

"I didn't shoot any soldiers, you know," I said.

"What? At Adobe Walls?"

"Yeah. I fired a few shots in the air and screamed like a Comanche, but I never would have shot any of Kit's boys."

"I wondered about that. That's good to know. But you charged with the Indians more than once, right?"

"Oh, they tried their best to kill me, Lucien, but luck was with me that day." I sipped the last of my tea, which had gone cold. "I can't tell you how many times I've wished since then that I *had* caught a bullet that day. You know . . . Because of . . . Sand Creek. And Westerly."

I hadn't spoken of it to anyone until that moment, and I had to make a supreme effort to choke back my tears and not blubber like a fool in front of Lucien. I could already see that the subject made him uncomfortable. Lucien was a good man, but hardened by the frontier, and not given to showing much emotion. That's why I was so surprised to hear what he said next.

"I've been lucky. Kept Luz by my side all these years. Don't know what I'd do if I lost her. I can't imagine how you didn't just go plumb crazy, Kid, and I know you came close. That goddamn Chivington is just a dog, and that's all. And that rabble of his—they ought to all be *under* the jail. I can abide a hard case and a man who's quick to kill, but what they did warrants something worse than a firing squad for all of 'em. And ain't a one of 'em's been brought to trial. That Chivington resigned his commission just so's he couldn't be court-martialed. That's the act of a coward."

"I've pondered hunting him down," I admitted.

"Of course you have, and you're not the only one. It wouldn't do you no good though, Kid. Let him live with the shame of the blood of children on his hands. Serves him right."

"Still . . . I don't know what I'd do if I saw him across the street one day in some town. I don't know if I could stop myself from killing him."

"If I ever see him, I'll beat him to within a inch of his miserable life, I can promise you that. He better never show his sorry ass on *this* trail."

I let it go at that, and we began to talk about more pleasant matters. We sat there all afternoon, enjoying the sun's warm rays until it slipped behind the mountain. About the time we decided to pick up our chairs and carry them inside, we saw a rider coming at a trot from the Cimarron road to the north. A man who has watched horses and riders all his life can read a mount and a horseman at a glance. This rider had been on the trail for many a mile. The pony's head hung low. We waited, of course, for the newcomer to arrive before going inside.

"By God," I said.

Lucien squinted. "What? Who is it?"

"That's Blue Wiggins."

Lucien began to chuckle. "Wait till he meets Geronimo Jones. If you can pull this one off, Kid, you're a genius. Blue would know you in the dark."

So I fought back my grin, summoned up my gall, and waited for Blue to arrive.

"Howdy, Lucien," he said, riding up to the gate where we waited.

"Good God, Blue, you've ridden that pony near to death. "Garcia!" he shouted at one of his stable hands. *"Toca el caballo!"*

Blue got down and nodded at me, extending his hand. "Blue Wiggins," he said, handing his reins to the stable boy.

"Blue, this here is a *Comanchero amigo* of mine you might have heard of. Geronimo Jones, of Agua Prieta, Old Mexico."

Blue's eyebrows rose as he shook the kinks from his legs. "Yes, I have heard of you, Mr. Jones. I sure have. I've been wanting to meet you. I understand that you're an acquaintance of my friend Orn'ry Greenwood."

I feigned confusion. "Orn'ry?" I repeated.

"Plenty Man," Lucien explained, as if I needed the explanation.

I smiled and nodded, but kept my eyes shaded under my big sombrero. "Ah, Mucho Hombre. Sí, Mucho is a friend of mine." I leaned toward Blue and said in a stage whisper: "We are even closer than brothers."

I swear Blue looked at me with something akin to jealousy. "Same with *me* and Orn'ry. 'Mucho' as you call him. We were brothers, all right, but I haven't seen him in four years."

"Come on in the house, gentlemen, and take your hats off." Lucien could hardly contain himself. "Follow me."

We strolled up the stone walkway to the mansion, Lucien and I grabbing our chairs along the way.

"So you've seen Orn'ry? He's all right?"

"He's all right, *hermano.*" I paused and touched Blue on the sleeve. "A brother of Mucho's is a brother of mine. Yes, he is as well as you might expect. He's become a famous medicine man among the Comanches. He has five wives, thirteen children, and three thousand horses. He's like a rich *médico,* no?"

Lucien was chuckling under his breath, but Blue didn't seem to notice.

"I'll be damned," Blue said. "Can't say it surprises me much. When you reckon you'll see him again?"

"Oh, I see him all the time. I leave within the week for Comancheria. Shall I take him a message from you? A letter, even?"

"I wish you would. As soon as possible. Kit wants to see him." He looked at me to explain. "Kit Carson."

"Oh?" I said, slipping out of character.

"Yeah, the general's not well." He stopped in front of the door to the mansion and looked at Maxwell with the saddest of eyes. "I've got bad news, Lucien. Josefa died."

Now our trick on Blue didn't seem so funny, and I felt foolish for pushing it this far.

"Josefa?" Lucien said, the disbelief plain in his voice. "What? How?"

"She had the baby—Josefita, they named her. The baby's fine, but Josefa had problems. She died ten days later with the fever. I'm sorry, Lucien. You've got to help me tell Luz. I can face you, but not her."

"Oh, God," Lucien said, knowing how his wife, Luz, was going to grieve over the loss of her sister.

"Kit's heart is broken, and he's not long for the world. That problem in his chest has gotten worse." Blue turned to me. "Mr. Jones, I need you to get a message to Orn'ry. Kit wants to see him before he dies, and he doesn't have long."

Sheepishly, I dragged my sombrero from my head. "Blue," I said, in my own voice. "It's me. I'm sorry, Blue, we didn't know . . . It was supposed to be a joke."

Blue looked at me, and his jaw dropped. "But . . . You're . . ."

"It's me, Orn'ry. I took on another identity for my own protection. I'm sorry. I couldn't tell anyone but Lucien."

Blue bowed his head and fell against me in a mixture of fatigue, relief, and sorrow. I wrapped my arms around him in a big *abrazo* and even Lucien put his huge bear paws on us to comfort us.

"Where's Kit?" I asked.

"He's in the hospital at Fort Lyon. You'd better go soon, Orn'ry. You may already be too late."

Panic overwhelmed me, and I recalled the grief I felt arriving a day late at Westerly's side. I could not bear it again. I looked at Lucien. "I've got to go. Tell Luz I'm so sorry."

Lucien became very businesslike. "Take my fastest racehorse. I'll get you some food. We'll tell Luz—me and Blue. She'll understand that you had to go."

By the time I got Lucien's prize racehorse saddled, Blue was waiting for me at the gate with a sack of grub, a canteen, and my violin, which I had left at Lucien's for safekeeping. "Kit asked for the fiddle," Blue said. We tied my belongings to saddle strings, or stuffed them into saddle pockets.

"You've got a couple of hours of daylight left," Blue said.

"I know this trail in the dark."

"Be careful."

"I wouldn't count on that. Not for this ride."

"Well . . ."

I reached down to shake Blue's hand. "I've missed you, Blue. I'll see you soon, I promise."

He nodded and shook my hand, and it felt good to feel his friendship again. Luz screamed inside, and we both knew she had gotten the information out of Lucien. I pulled my brim down low, spurred the long-legged steed, and rode hell-bent for Raton Pass.

FIFTY-SEVEN

Four days later, I trotted into William Bent's Stockade. Lucien Maxwell's racehorse had all but given out, and I hoped to borrow a fast remount for the last five-mile leg to Fort Lyon. I found William watching over a Mexican laborer who was breaking ground for the stockade's garden, the Mexican driving a single mule before a turning plow. William was looking old and feeble now. The Sand Creek affair had torn his family apart and taken a lot out of him. Young Charles had joined the Dog Soldiers and become such a renegade that a bounty was now on his head. Charles had even threatened to kill his own father. William had disowned him. Anyway, William was fifty-eight years old, same as Kit, and had spent many a hard winter on the frontier.

When the old trader saw me, he looked me over and I could tell that he recognized Maxwell's horse, but not me. "What is it?" he asked, as if expecting more bad news.

"It's me, William. Honoré Greenwood."

He came closer to look, for his eyesight seemed to be failing him. "I thought you'd been killed for sure this time."

"I've come to see Kit. Is it too late?"

"You'd better hurry," William said, tilting his head and angling his eyes toward the corral. "I was with Kit at the fort yesterday, and I didn't think he'd last the night. I've already said my adios. We all have. Tom and Rumalda, John and Amache. Everyone. Doc Tilton told us to say good-bye and get the hell out. Said we were excitin' him too much. You better take George's buffalo horse. I hope you're not too late."

It seemed to take forever to switch my saddle from Maxwell's horse to George's. When I finally got mounted, William said, "Lope him the first mile, then open him up. He can run."

William was right. After I warmed the horse up a little, I touched him with my spurs and gave him his head. We struck the road to Fort Lyon, and the horse knew where we were going. George Bent had trained this mount to run buffalo, and kept him in shape for that job. He was sleek and lank and well muscled, and possessed a gallop smooth enough from which to draw a bead on a fleeing shaggy. I threw my sombrero off and left it beside the road because it just dragged too much wind. Now the spring air pulled at my locks. It felt good to finally be moving at full speed, but the worry nagged me. What if I was too late yet again?

Please, Kit, hold on. I want to say I'm sorry. I want to say good-bye.

That horse knew the crossing of the Arkansas and he plunged in almost without slowing down. He made lunges through the chest-deep water, not yet swollen from rains or snowmelt, much to my relief. Soon he was across and was gathering his great weight under his haunches for the last push into Fort Lyon.

I saw the rude buildings of the post, and slowed to a trot to explain myself to a sentry: "I'm a friend of Kit's. I want to see him before he dies."

The soldier shook his head once and started to say something, then changed his mind and waved me on. I rode to the hard-packed parade ground, and looked for officers' row—the next-to-last rock house, William had told me, the post surgeon's own quarters. I ignored a few soldiers going about their duties, and cantered right down the row of rude stone structures to find Aloys Scheurich—a relative of Kit's by marriage, and the godfather of his children—standing outside. He was looking at the ground with his hands in his pockets when he heard my approach and looked up to see me.

I jumped down from the saddle. "It's me, Aloys," I said. "It's Honoré Greenwood."

"*Gracias a Dios,*" he said, recognizing me. His Spanish was good, though saddled with a German accent. "I had heard you were . . . Well . . ."

"Is Kit . . . Is he . . . ?"

Scheurich shook his head. "He went to sleep, Mr. Greenwood."

"To *sleep?*"

Scheurich nodded. "I don't know if he'll wake up again. I don't know if he's got it in him."

I took three big steps to the door.

When I entered the dark room, I smelled tobacco smoke. I waited until my eyes adjusted. There, half sitting up on an Indian-style couch made of buffalo robes and blankets piled on the floor, an elderly man lay in repose. I took a moment figuring out that it was Kit. He had aged so that I almost didn't recognize him. I saw his old clay pipe on the floor of rough wooden planks, next to a coffee cup and a tin plate with a steak bone on it. He had eaten his last meal, it seemed, and smoked his last bowl. I just stood there staring down at all that was left of my old friend. He lay motionless, his eyes closed and sunken, his cheeks drawn, his hair long and thin, and his body wasted away under the blankets. I watched for what seemed like a whole minute, and he never took a breath.

My palms slammed against my temples in desperation, and I pulled at my own hair. I wheeled and looked out at nothing through the window and cried, "God, no!" I heard a snort and a cough. I turned, hopefully. Kit's eyes flew open, and he drew in a long, ragged breath that seemed just barely able to enter his lungs. Astonished, I lowered myself to one knee beside him.

"Who's there?" he whispered, squinting.

I leaned closer to him and saw a spark of life yet left in his eyes. "I thought you were dead," I said in relief.

He smiled a little, having recognized my voice. "I thought *you* were dead." The words came out with saw-blade edges.

I shook my head. "I've been staying scarce, that's all."

"What for? You didn't think I'd tell anybody about you at Adobe Walls, did you?"

"I wasn't sure. I turned against you, Kit. I'm sorry."

Slowly, he drew a gnarled arm out from under the army blanket. His hand shook a little as it reached for my shoulder and his breath tore in and out of his windpipe like a drill bit chiseling its way through hard rock. His grip felt almost as firm as ever as he grabbed my shoulder. "You did what you thought was right, Kid. You know I'd never cause you no trouble. Hell, nobody would believe me anyway, if I *did* tell 'em you was there."

I smiled, the relief of forgiveness flooding into me so that my eyes welled up with tears, and I had to wipe one away, right there in front of the great Kit Carson.

A door opened in a rickety partition wall, and a man walked in. "Who are you?" he demanded.

Kit calmed him with a feeble wave. "It's a friend, Doc. The best a man ever had. Kid, Doc Tilton."

I rose to shake the doctor's hand. He must have seen the questions in my eyes.

"He's in a bad way. We've talked it over, and I've told him frankly. The aneurysm that's been growing in his chest is now pressing against his trachea. There are two possibilities. It will rupture and he'll bleed to death internally, or it will swell until it blocks his windpipe and he'll suffocate."

"This is my last fight," Kit said. "I don't welcome the prospect of suffercatin'. The Comanches say if you die that way, your soul gets trapped in your body, and can't get to heaven."

I nodded grimly. "Your breath carries your prayers—and your soul—to the Great Beyond."

"I'm fightin' for a chance to bleed to death. Every breath is a little victory."

Doc Tilton scoffed. "You're going to heaven, General. Get that superstitious Indian claptrap out of your head. Don't get him excited, Mr. Greenwood. Let him relax." He looked at Kit with a kindly admiration. "I'll be in the next room if you need me, General."

Kit nodded, and the doctor left, leaving the door open this time.

When he was gone, Kit beckoned me closer with his hand, so I got down on my knees beside him.

"I always wondered . . ." He put his hand on my shoulder. "Was that you blowing the bugle?"

I chuckled at the memory. "Yes, that was me."

"I *knew* it. Had to be you to come up with that." He released his hold on my shoulder and laid his arm back down on the blanket. He looked vacantly toward the ceiling for a labored breath or two. "Kid . . . That time on the trail to Adobe Walls . . . Before the battle . . ."

"Yeah?" I knew what he was getting at.

"I'm sorry I let my boys go too far. I didn't mean for you to get your head caved half in."

"I brought it on myself. I was mad about that horse."

"I'm sorry about that horse, too. I wish none of that had ever happened."

"I do, too, Kit, but it doesn't matter now. You did what you thought was right. I never held it against you."

He lifted his hand for me to shake, and when I took it, he seemed so relieved that he grinned and closed his eyes for a few seconds as our hands stayed clasped, one within the other. "You were sure mad. Never knew you could git so orn'ry, Orn'ry." He clucked his tongue as he shook his head and smiled. "You put up one hell of a fight." Then the smile faded away and he lay there for a while, blinking. "Well, you know about my Chepita."

"Yes. I'm sorry. I wish I had seen her before . . ." I could not speak the words to finish the thought.

"You know how I feel, don't you?"

"Yes."

Our hands were still together, his eyes now closed. He squeezed my hand tighter, speaking more than words ever could have. I remember thinking that I had wasted my life. I should have become a surgeon. I possessed the intelligence and the dexterity. I wanted to cut Kit open and fix him right there—take out that thing that had been growing and swelling and cutting off his wind and lifeblood ever since that fall on our elk hunting trip, eight years ago.

"I should let you rest," I said, our hands finally slipping apart.

He shook his head feebly and reached for my sleeve. "Don't go yet. I'm fixin' to get *plenty* of rest. Since my Chepita died, I don't feel like I have much life left in me. But that ain't really it, Kid. You got through that, and I could, too. She wouldn't want me to just lay down and die, anyway. It ain't that."

"What is it, then?"

He raised his right hand and swung his arm across his body like the neck of a crane stalking a fish. His trigger finger uncoiled and he tapped his left shoulder where all the pain and swelling had choked the strength out of him. "It's *this*. I reckon I'd live to be a hunnerd if it wasn't for *this*."

The arm settled on his chest and the weight of it seemed too much for the old voyageur, so I gently lifted his arm and laid it back by his side. "What do you need me to do, Kit?"

He seemed to think about it very seriously for several seconds, as if he hadn't expected to see me here at all. "I've already made out my will. Tom's my administrator. He and Rumalda are gonna see that the children are taken care of somehow. I almost can't bear the thought of them bein' orphans. Help them, when you can, Kid. I know you're like me, and you can't root yourself, but when you pass through, teach the children things you know. Things out of them storybooks you read. School 'em for me, Kid. Lord knows I never could."

"I'd be proud to bring them a few books and read with them. Maybe teach them to play the violin, even."

His eyes flew open in a manner that surprised me. "Did you bring the fiddle?"

"Yes."

"Well, git it, Kid. Play for me one more time. I'd sure like that."

"Be glad to, Colonel." I got up, then realized my error. "I mean *General,* of course."

He lifted his fingers just enough to brush away the formalities. "Just call me Kit and be done with it. Go git that fiddle."

"Yes, sir." I rose, and turned to the door, bursting out into the sunshine.

"Is he . . . ?" Scheurich said.

"He wants me to play the violin for him," I said.

I untied the padded deerskin case that protected the old Stradivarius and began removing the instrument as I went back inside, followed by Aloys Scheurich. Kit's eyes were closed again, but I heard his breath carving its way into his lungs. When I plucked the strings, he opened his eyes slowly and looked about to see his friends.

I began to play the first concerto of Vivaldi's *Four Seasons,* for it was neither too morose nor too jolly. As the strains of that fine instrument began to fill the room, Doc Tilton came to the door, a sad and puzzled look clouding his face. Aloys Scheurich sat in a chair he had obviously occupied for quite some while before my arrival. I poured every bit of heart I had left into each note. Kit lay there, smiling.

"That's purdy," I heard the general say.

Oh, I've played some hard dirges and laments in my time, but that selection knocked holes in my heart. I continued my performance until Kit seemed almost asleep.

Then he lurched and coughed. He covered his mouth and hacked violently, this time spewing a spray of blood on his palm. My fingers died on the slender neck of the violin, and the bow fell from the strings. As Tilton and Scheurich rushed to either side, Kit stared at his bloody hand and smiled. He *smiled* with relief. He could feel the bleeding. He was not going to suffocate.

He looked up at me, his eyes piercing mine. "I'm *gone.*" His eyes looked one way—"Good-bye, Doctor"—then the other—"*Adiós, compadre.*" He looked again at me, at my fiddle, at my bow, and gestured for more music. He tried to speak to me, but a torrent of blood came out of his mouth instead, and gushed down his chin and onto his chest. He coughed through it and drew in a last labored breath.

I shut my eyes against a flood of tears, unable to watch him die. I set horsehair to catgut and played. The men returned Kit's parting words, but my tune was my farewell, as he had wished. I cried and played by heart, my tears running down my cheeks and onto the chinpiece of the violin. I vented my love and sorrow, the vibrations of the wood rattling my very teeth. And somewhere in the course of that rendering, General Christopher Carson set his spirit to yondering toward the Great Mystery on his final earthly breath.

In a voice that only I could understand, my violin sang a stanza from Kit's favorite poem, *The Lady of the Lake,* by Sir Walter Scott:

> *Soldier, rest! thy warfare o'er,*
> *Sleep the sleep that knows not breaking,*
> *Dream of battled fields no more,*
> *Days of danger, nights of waking.*

And the mountains took pause. The great birds of prey sprang from their perches and pressed their pinions against the chinooks. The lions roared and the grizzlies stood upright in reverence. And across some vestige of the trackless wilds, a thunderbolt struck a stony ridge and ushered the soul of a great man through the Pass of No Returning.

FIFTY-EIGHT

After we buried Kit, I stayed at Boggsville a while, helping with the spring chores, sharing memories about our departed hero. Tom Boggs and George Bent and I decided to finally break in that irrigation ditch we had surveyed several years before. Blue Wiggins came back up from Maxwell's Ranch and helped us carve the *acequia madre* with a hand-forged slip shovel pulled by a mule team. It was good, hard work, and every man and boy from Boggsville and William's stockade took a hand in it.

To divert the water from the river, we built a box of timbers down in the riverbed, which we slathered with tar to seal the cracks. This "tar box" as we called it, gave name to the channel we had dug, which was known as the "Tar Box Ditch." The day finally came when we closed the iron sluice gate to fill up the tar box, then watched the swelling waters pour into our meandering ditch. We all got a-horseback and chased the manmade rill down our ditch for seven miles, where it spilled back into the Purgatoire. We held quite a fiesta that night. As far as I know, the Tar Box Ditch still carries water from the Purgatoire, across a thousand acres of fields and pastures that surround what once was Boggsville.

It was time well spent, but I knew it had to end. I—as Geronimo Jones—still had trade goods waiting down at Maxwell's Ranch, and Kills Something's people would be wondering where Plenty Man had strayed off to right about now. So I packed my saddle pockets one morning and spent more than an hour saying farewell to my friends. I talked at length with William Bent, because I feared I would not see him alive again.

A regular crowd came out to send me off. Along with Tom and Rumalda were George Bent, John Prowers, and Amache. They had brought Kit's four oldest children—William, Teresina, Christopher, and Charlie—to bid me farewell. They ranged in age from fourteen to six. The younger children—Rebecca and Stella—and the infant, Josefita, were all napping. It saddened me to see the loss of their whole world in the eyes of the Carson orphans. But it was the sight of Amache that gripped my heart the hardest, for I saw some of Westerly in her features. I went to her and hugged her, but just briefly, for she was Cheyenne, and didn't go for much of that. I shook John's hand, and George's, and smiled sadly at the children, tousling Chistopher's hair.

When finally I slipped boot to stirrup and swung up, Blue Wiggins hailed me, saying, "Oh, Orn'ry, I almost forgot to tell you."

"What is it, Blue?"

"Down at Maxwell's I heard that Luther Sheffield has taken a job as deputy town marshal over at Trinidad. Thought you might ought to swing through and tell him howdy for the boys of Kit's First New Mexico Volunteer Cavalry."

"I'll sure do that very thing," I said.

And so I rode out on Maxwell's racehorse, now fattened and fleshed from weeks of rest and grain, and headed into the teeth of a spring rainstorm, bound for Trinidad. It wasn't hard to find the office of the town marshal and I only had to wait twenty-three minutes for Luther to finish his afternoon rounds and return. He was genuinely pleased to see me and, I could plainly see, very proud of his new office as deputy marshal. We didn't touch much upon the past, for therein lay our troubles. Instead, we talked about the town and the territory, and the prospects for the future. It had been a long time since I had felt compelled to speculate on things to come, but it felt good to do so.

Then, right in the middle of our pleasant conversation, a team of mules pulled a big Murphy freight wagon around the corner half a block from us. The vessel rattled down the street, away from us. Luther only glanced at it as he told me of a saloon fracas he had broken up the day before, but I had already looked the driver over and felt a heap of black malice drop from my heart and sink into the pit of my belly. The man driving the wagon was unmistakably John M. Chivington, the butcher of Sand Creek, and the murderer of my wife. I had heard that he had resigned his commission to avoid court-martial, and had turned from preaching to freighting. Luther was still talking, but I no longer heard his words.

Do you remember that match that I asked you to strike? That fiery symbol of my life? Well, it flared inside me like pitch pine in a firestorm.

The dormant seed of hatred burst into full bloom and I got so quickly to my feet that the chair I had been sitting on tipped back and fell on the planks of the porch. I heard Luther's story cease as I took two steps to my mount and drew a revolver from my saddlebag.

"Greenwood!" Luther said. "What in the hell?"

"Do you see who that was?" I pointed toward the wagon, which was lumbering slowly down the street, away from us.

"Who?"

"The driver on the seat of that wagon. That was Chivington. John Chivington."

A realization came over Luther as he glanced back and forth between the wagon and me. "Hold on, Greenwood. Now, you just settle down."

"Don't try to stop me, Luther. I'm gonna kill that son of a bitch."

"Don't *say* that." He looked both ways to make sure no one had heard me. "For God's sake, Greenwood, catch your breath. You can't go killing people."

"Just him. Just Chivington." I was checking my loads in the Navy Colt.

"No, no, no. Stop, damn it." He was moving toward me.

I went to mount, but he knocked my foot out of the stirrup and grabbed my rein, causing the horse to toss his head and swing his tail end against the hitching rail. Luther grabbed my left arm, and I cocked the pistol, still held muzzle down. Luther grew wide-eyed and put his hand on his sidearm. A moment passed when I did not know whether or not I would ruin my life forever in a fit of rage. I could have jammed my cocked revolver against Luther's chest and fired before he cleared his holster. I still cringe at the memory of almost having done that very deed. I still dream about it, but in my dream, I go ahead and do it, and pull the trigger, and wake up sweating and panting.

"Greenwood," Luther growled. "You can't kill him."

"I have to."

"No you don't. I can't let you."

"Why not?"

"It's my goddamn job. Don't be a fool!"

I shook my head. "I've got to kill him, Luther."

"You'll have to kill me first, Greenwood. Now, get ahold of yourself and talk sense. You can't just kill him."

"Let me do it, then arrest me. I have to kill him."

"Stop *saying* that!" His eyes widened with a new line of reasoning. "I once thought I had to kill you, but I was wrong. It's *wrong*. It's uncivilized. Remember what Kit always said: *Is this right?* He always asked that."

I glanced at the wagon and saw it blending in with the street traffic—the pedestrians and carriages and buckboards. "This is my chance for revenge, Luther. You've got to let me kill that bastard."

"I *can't* let you!"

"Why the hell not!" I shouted, my voice bouncing off the frame buildings of the new town.

Luther looked flustered as he searched for an answer. "Because if you kill *him*," he finally said, "then *I'll* be the sorriest son of a bitch in town!"

I trembled all over as I tried to hang on to the hatred. But I lost my grip on it and let out a gasp that was part sob and part guffaw. I looked down the street and found no sign of Chvington's wagon. I turned my eyes back to Luther, half laughing at his statement and half crying in confused obligation. I was not to kill John Chivington that day. The spirits had seen to it and they had used the most unlikely of vehicles to stop me—Luther Sheffield. I uncocked the revolver in my hand and bowed my head in some strange combination of relief and failure. Luther very slowly and gently eased the revolver from my grasp.

I never saw John M. Chivington again.

EPILOGUE

Ah, the sun now touches the western bluffs, and I have chores to do. My orchard needs tending. My ponies want grain. I had better get to work so that you good people may return to your homes. Well, perhaps a moment more, then. Yes, I should tell you that I never saw William Bent again, for he died shortly after Kit died. His son George lived until 1917, attempting, like his father, to ease the plight of the Cheyenne Indians in every way that he could. His younger brother Charles did not last nearly as long. Charles became a renegade Dog Soldier and at one point vowed to kill his own father, and might have someday, had not William died of natural causes. Charles died in agony not long after his father, of malaria in a Cheyenne camp.

Quanah is gone now, though I have much yet to tell you about him. Oh, yes, I have not even begun to talk about Quanah, but that will have to wait for another time.

Chivington? John M. Chivington suffered enough. While trying, unsuccessfully, to earn a living as a freighter, his wife and son drowned while crossing the North Platte in one of his wagons. There were those who said God made it happen to pay him back for all the wives and children he had taken from others at Sand Creek, but I could not embrace the notion of such a vengeful God. His freighting business failed and he moved from Nebraska to California to Ohio, and finally back to Denver, nowhere achieving the greatness he might have attained had his hatred for Indians not ruined his life. The stigma of Sand Creek hung over him as long as he lived, but he steadfastly stood behind his actions at that bloody place. He died of cancer in 1894.

Maxwell? As you know, Lucien Bonaparte Maxwell managed to get the United States Congress to grant him clear title to one million and seven hundred thousand acres, based on the old Mexican land grant he had purchased from its many shareholders. Can you just imagine such a domain? What did he do with it? Please, not now. I promise to tell you about it another time.

All the folks at Boggsville got along fine for a good while, even though the town itself died when the railroad reached Las Animas, just a few miles away. But Tom Boggs and John Prowers lived well and enjoyed their families. Amache took to wearing white women's clothing most of the time. She bought a bicycle, which she often rode to amuse the children.

But things were never the same after Sand Creek—after Kit and William passed away. It all changed rapidly then, and nothing of the old ways lasted long after that. I'll tell you about it next time we gather here. You will return, won't you? Oh, good. Do not be too long about it. I am ninety-nine years old, after all.

That reminds me. When Kit was on his deathbed, he asked the post surgeon, Dr. Tilton, "Doc, what am I to do now? I can't get along without a doctor."

"I will take care of you," Dr. Tilton said.

Kit smiled at him and said, "You must think I am not going to live very long."

So hurry back, if you wish to hear the rest. Go home and strike that match in the dark, as I have told you. Measure it against my ninety-nine years, and watch how quickly that last ember fades and vanishes. Do not stay away too long.

Next time? I will tell you about the slaughter of the buffalo. Oh, the buffalo . . . That is sad, but I have good things to recollect, as well. The bad comes with the good, and that is just all there is to it. I'll tell you about all of it in due time. About Kills Something and Quanah. Bat Masterson and Billy Dixon. The so-called Second Battle of Adobe Walls—nothing at all like the first. I will tell you about Isa-Tai, the Comanche shaman. Right now I will only say that he was no Burnt Belly. Never mind what I mean. You will know soon enough.

Now, run along. I want to be alone in my valley. I have heard my voice ramble all day, and I am weary of it. I long now to hear the spirit voices.

When the breeze moves this way—snakelike, as if deciding which way to blow—and twilight paints the bluffs, and the scents of blessed spring fill the air . . . That is when I hear the *other* voices—the spirit voices of the woods and the waters and the skies. The ghost voices of those who await beyond. Yes, I hear them—especially Burnt Belly. Sometimes Kit, and William. And others . . .

And sometimes . . . When the moon rises just so, half-full . . . And the breeze suddenly ceases for no reason at all . . . And all the creatures of the time between day and night hush their voices to alert me . . . Sometimes I can almost hear her laughter. Ah, sometimes I swear I *do* hear her. That beautiful strain, like a bubbling spring. That worry-free, singsong melody that consoles me. Yes, I hear Westerly beyond the shadows. She tells me time grows nigh. Maybe not today, or even tomorrow. But someday, her soul and mine shall forevermore cling together. Someday soon—come sundown.